Collected Stories of
JOHN O'HARA

Collected Stories of
JOHN O'HARA

Selected and with
an Introduction
by Frank MacShane

Random House New York

The following stories were first published in *The New Yorker*: "It Must Have Been Spring";
"Over the River and Through the Wood"; "Are We Leaving Tomorrow?"; "The Gentleman
in the Tan Suit"; "Olive"; "Pal Joey"; "Now We Know"; "Bread Alone"; "Graven Image";
"Drawing Room B"; "The Pretty Daughters"; "Imagine Kissing Pete"; "The Girl from
California"; "Winter Dance"; "The Flatted Saxophone"; "Fatimas and Kisses"; "Price's Al-
ways Open"; "The Moccasins"; "Good-by, Herman"; "Common Sense Should Tell You";
"Exactly Eight Thousand Dollars Exactly"; "Zero."

"Can I Stay Here?", "Our Friend the Sea"; and "The Hardware Man" were first published
in the *Saturday Evening Post*.

The stories originally appeared in book form in the following collections: *The Doctor's Son
and Other Stories*, Copyright 1935 by John O'Hara. Copyright renewed 1963 by John O'Hara.
Files on Parade, Copyright 1939 by Harcourt, Brace & Co. Inc. Copyright renewed 1967 by
John O'Hara. *Pipe Night*, Copyright 1945 by John O'Hara. Copyright renewed 1973 by
Katharine B. O'Hara and Wylie O'Hara Holahan. *Hellbox*, Copyright 1947 by John O'Hara.
Copyright renewed 1975 by Katharine B. O'Hara and Wylie O'Hara Doughty. *Sermons and
Soda Water*, Copyright © 1960 by John O'Hara. *Assembly*, Copyright © 1961 by John O'Hara.
The Cape Cod Lighter, Copyright © 1962 by John O'Hara. *The Hat on the Bed*, Copyright ©
1963 by John O'Hara. *The Horse Knows the Way*, Copyright © 1964 by John O'Hara. *Waiting
for Winter*, Copyright © 1966 by John O'Hara. *And Other Stories*, Copyright © 1968 by John
O'Hara.

Library of Congress Cataloging in Publication Data
O'Hara, John, 1905–1970.
Collected Stories of John O'Hara.
I. MacShane, Frank.   II. Title.
PS3529.H29A6   1985   813'.52   84-42661
ISBN 0-394-54083-2

Manufactured in the United States of America

Introduction
The Power of the Ear

To say that John O'Hara's stories stand up well, as they certainly do, is to use a physical term in an almost literal way. It means that they are as sturdy and fresh as they were when they were first created. This achievement—one of the most important in literature, since it earns the reader's trust—is due mainly to the way O'Hara used his ear to its best advantage. It was his greatest gift, and he relied on it from the start.

The ability of a writer to capture the speech of his character is often underestimated or even dismissed in favor of other qualities, but in fact it is far more important than subject matter or theme if the stories are to have life. Buffon said, "Le style est l'homme même," and it follows that the writer who has captured his character's voice has taken hold of the character himself, and the story starts from there.

The link between contemporary fiction and the oral tradition of epic and folk literature may seem remote, but in fact the two forms have much in common. When people gathered to hear the stories that were later attributed to Homer or collected in the Old Testament, they did so to find out what things were like in the past. They wanted to hear the voices of their ancestors; they wanted to know what people *said*. The bard or priest who told the stories was like Coleridge's Ancient Mariner, who took his listeners by the hand and recited his impassioned tale. He was memorable not for what he said but for how he said it; and for his special gifts, he sat at the right hand of the chieftain or king.

Then as now, authentic storytellers were those who had a good ear. They were able to report the very words that Achilles used when addressing his troops, or the actual lamentations of Job in the midst of his travails. Speech is not mere decoration. Its form and substance come from inner feelings and fundamental beliefs. It is the mark of human personality. Shaw's *Pygmalion* is a comedy about social distinctions, but it is also a commentary on the nature of truth. Professor Higgins and Liza use language in different ways not only because they were brought up in different places but because they have their individual ambitions and needs, and these are reflected in the way they talk.

Because of their intimacy and lack of sociological detail, short stories are especially dependent on the voice. Reading the dialogue of a short story is like eavesdropping on a good conversation. The enduring popularity of Dickens, Poe and Maupassant is based to a considerable degree on our ability to hear the voices of Ebenezer Scrooge, Roderick Usher and the habitués of the Maison Tellier.

From his beginnings as a young reporter in Pottsville, Pennsylvania, John O'Hara developed his powers of observation and imitation. He began at a time when newspaper columnists were far more influential than they are today. The most famous column was "The Conning Tower," edited by F. P. Adams for the New York *World*, but newspapers everywhere ran regular features by such writers as H. L Mencken, Ring Lardner, Robert Benchley and Alexander Woollcott. They were topical and generally relied on the rich resources of the American language for their flavor. O'Hara imitated his elders by writing satirical monologues and conversations, and he made his first national appearance in "The Conning Tower" in 1927 at the age of twenty-two. Within the year he moved to New York, where at the time nearly twenty daily newspapers were still being published. He got a job at the *Herald Tribune* and was soon part of the easy democracy of Bleeck's, Tony's, Jack and Charlie's 21 Club and other speakeasies. There he met all sorts of people—journalists, sports figures, politicians, actors, stockbrokers and playwrights—and he began to write sketches about them, several in the manner of Sinclair Lewis.

The New Yorker was then a young magazine, and soon O'Hara was writing for it. He extended his range and took his apprenticeship so seriously that he published forty-three stories in *The New Yorker* before he considered any of them worthy of inclusion in a book. O'Hara was not a satirist by nature; rather he had a fiction writer's interest in human character. For him, dialogue was a way of revealing human traits without spending much time on description and setting. He found that when he had a precinct cop pick up the telephone and say, "Wukkan I do fya?" he was able to depict the whole police station in those few words. When a teenage girl from Brearley or Chapin says, "Robert didn't come with she or I," she reveals in the grammatical error her breathless concern to appear grown-up.

"If people did not talk right, they were not real people," O'Hara observed when he was still a schoolboy, and it was as true of life as of art. "I do not believe," he later wrote, "that a writer who neglects or has not learned to write good dialog can be depended upon for accuracy in his understanding of character and his creation of characters."

Talk was, for O'Hara, the beginning of many of his stories. Often he would sit at his typewriter and start by thinking of a couple of faces he had seen. He would put the people together in a restaurant or on an airplane, and they would begin to talk. "I let them do small talk for a page or two," O'Hara explained, "and pretty soon they begin to come to life. They do so entirely through dialog. I start by knowing nothing about them except what I remember of their faces. But as they chatter away, one of them, and then the other, will say something that is so revealing that I recognize the signs of created characters. From then on it is a question of how deeply I want to interest myself in the characters."

Dialogue was not the only device O'Hara used to get into his stories, but in general he relied on actual things. He was interested in the telling detail, the phrase or name that had some resonance. A Brooks Brothers suit or a Swaine and Adeney's umbrella, the Racquet Club or Palmer Stadium, Romanoff's or the Twentieth-Century Limited, all carry much more than their surface identities. When O'Hara writes about a woman "pounding her Delman heels on the Penn Station floor," he creates a whole person in the phrase, just as he does with the woman who, getting into her car in the parking lot of a suburban railway station, "kicked off her shoes and put on a pair of loafers that lay on the floor."

By using such details, O'Hara invented almost single-handedly what came to be known as the *New Yorker* story. Arranging a brief encounter between two or more people speaking a language appropriate to the setting, O'Hara gives an impression of reality in a few phrases. Often the point is not immediately plain, for O'Hara believed that truth was allusive. But his themes were consistent, and they depended on having real people express themselves in real places.

If Napoleon was right in calling the Piazza San Marco in Venice "the best drawing room in Europe," O'Hara's stories as a whole provide the best conversation in America. Although he was for years associated with the upper-class world of New York, Philadelphia and Long Island, he had a remarkable range of subjects, more so than Faulkner or Fitzgerald or even Hemingway, whose work influenced him in many ways. The central characters of his stories are not only club men and business executives; they are country doctors, movie stars, beauticians, bartenders, schoolgirls, nightclub singers, gas station attendants, telephone operators and bus drivers. America in the twentieth century is what he knew, and in 1960 he said, "It is my business to write about it to the best of my ability, with sometimes the special knowledge that I have. I want to record the way people talked and thought and felt, and to do it with complete honesty and variety."

Behind the modesty of this statement lies O'Hara's vision of America and, by extension, of humanity everywhere. He saw society as a structure that rarely succeeded in covering up the disorders that lay beneath the surface of human intercourse. He saw decency and hope routinely destroyed by selfishness and cruelty, leaving individuals with little solace to face the essential solitude of life and death. Yet O'Hara's vision is not a cheerless one, for he also celebrated individual acts of kindness and imagination, and he does not pass judgment or apportion blame. His stories are peopled with such varied individuals—pretentious, gentle, deranged or simply pensive—that it seems clear that for all his doubts about humanity, O'Hara was in love with life itself. His testament as an artist is that his short stories, covering a period of over thirty-five years in the writing, are still extraordinarily alive.

This quality says a good deal about the short story in general and the reasons for O'Hara's pre-eminence in this form. It is sometimes fashionable to dismiss the short story and to attribute its apparent decline to the greater versatility of the novel and to the rise of nonfiction. But the trouble does not lie with the form but with its practitioners. A really good short-story writer will always find a popular audience. In recent times, J. D. Salinger, John Cheever and John Updike have been remarkably successful, and the reason is that they are all masters of the form. They all have a good ear and an eye for detail. These qualities give their work the same vitality that keeps collections of Chekhov and Poe on the paperback shelves in bookstores across the country.

John O'Hara belongs to this small company of great short-story writers simply because of the quality of his work. His aesthetic purposes were a direct extension of his attitude toward life itself. "Life goes on," he wrote as a young man, "and for the sake of verisimilitude and realism, you cannot positively give the impression of an ending: you must let something hang. A cheap interpretation of that would be to say that you must always leave a chance for a sequel. People die, love dies, but life does not die, and so long as people live, stories must have life at the end."

It is at their endings that O'Hara's stories give their greatest pleasure. Just when the story ends, or perhaps a few moments afterward, when all the pieces fall into place, the reader grasps what it is really all about. A sort of epiphany occurs. It can produce chill or warmth, depending on the story, but it is an organic part of the story itself. It is not a surprise ending like one in a Saki or Ambrose Bierce story, which loses its force once it is expressed. Rather it deepens the feelings that come from beneath the surface of the story. Emerging from the skillful mixture of fact and feeling in the story, it lingers on, like a phrase of music, in the memory. At the end of "We're Friends Again," one of the novellas in *Sermons and Soda-water*, the narrator speaks of a theme that is paramount in O'Hara's work. "What really can any of us know about any of us, and why must we make such a thing of loneliness when it is the final condition of us all?" Then he adds, "And where would love be without it?"

During his lifetime, O'Hara published eleven collections of short stories and three volumes of novellas, making a total of over four hundred pieces of short fiction. The present volume contains fewer than ten percent of these, but those reprinted here represent O'Hara's finest work. Although his first collection, *The Doctor's Son and Other Stories*, began with a novella as the title story, the stories O'Hara published from 1935 to 1949 were for the most part short, some of them containing as few as a thousand words. Then in 1948 O'Hara decided to turn his attention to longer fiction. Not having published any novels since *Hope of Heaven* in 1938, despite the earlier successes of *Appointment in Samarra* and *Butterfield 8*, he began a new and ambitious novel called *A Rage to Live*. Although it sold well and received some favorable notices, it was also subjected to a number of highly critical reviews. One that particularly annoyed O'Hara was written by Brendan Gill, who accused O'Hara of being prolix and declared that the book was a "catastrophe." What angered O'Hara most was that it was published in *The New Yorker*, for which he had a warm feeling and which he considered home, since, up to that time, it had published no fewer than 197 of his stories. For him, the review was a piece of treachery, and he complained about it to the editor, Harold Ross. Since he had also been squabbling for some time with Ross over methods of payment, O'Hara finally decided to break his connection with the magazine.

A decade passed without a single work by O'Hara appearing in *The New Yorker*. Then in 1960, after Ross's death, O'Hara was approached by William Maxwell, acting on behalf of the new editor, William Shawn, and *The New Yorker* bought the novella *Imagine Kissing Pete* for $10,000, a considerable sum at that time. In the final years of his life, O'Hara published frequently in *The New Yorker*, but now, living in isolation in Princeton, he became so prolific that no magazine could possibly keep up with his production. Between 1962 and 1968 he published five book-length collections of stories, in addition to four novels. Moreover, he was now writing much longer stories than he had formerly done, and many of them were too long for magazine publication. Reminiscential in tone, they were studies of characters and types he had known throughout his varied life in New York, Pennsylvania and especially in Hollywood, which was the setting of some of his most impressive later work. Writing in his Princeton study, surrounded by the memorabilia of a lifetime, he probed the nature of mortality and human character. These stories represent the best writing of his last years, more deeply felt and delicately told than his novels of the same period. Taken as a whole, his shorter work, starting from the sharp, incisive stories of his early years at *The New Yorker* and continuing into his more relaxed and expansive period in Princeton, represents the growth and maturity of one of the finest short-story writers of modern times.

Frank MacShane

Contents

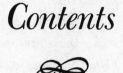

Collected Stories of
JOHN O'HARA

The Doctor's Son

My father came home at four o'clock one morning in the fall of 1918, and plumped down on a couch in the living room. He did not get awake until he heard the noise of us getting breakfast and getting ready to go to school, which had not yet closed down. When he got awake he went out front and shut off the engine of the car, which had been running while he slept, and then he went to bed and stayed, sleeping for nearly two days. Up to that morning he had been going for nearly three days with no more than two hours' sleep at a stretch.

There were two ways to get sleep. At first he would get it by going to his office, locking the rear office door, and stretching out on the floor or the operating table. He would put a revolver on the floor beside him or in the tray that was bracketed to the operating table. He had to have the revolver, because here and there among the people who would come to his office, there would be a wild man or woman, threatening him, shouting that they would not leave until he left with them, and that if their baby died they would come back and kill him. The revolver, lying on the desk, kept the more violent patients from becoming too violent, but it really did no good so far as my father's sleep was concerned; not even a doctor who had kept going for days on coffee and quinine would use a revolver on an Italian who had just come from a bedroom where the last of five children was being strangled by influenza. So my father, with a great deal of profanity, would make it plain to the Italian that he was not being intimidated, but would go, and go without sleep.

There was one other way of getting sleep. We owned the building in which he had his office, so my father made an arrangement with one of the tenants, a painter and paperhanger, so he could sleep in the room where the man stored rolls of wallpaper. This was a good arrangement, but by the time he had thought of it, my father's strength temporarily gave out and he had to come home and go to bed.

Meanwhile there was his practice, which normally was about forty patients a day, including office calls and operations, but which he had lost count of since the epidemic had become really bad. Ordinarily if he had been ill his practice would have been taken over by one of the young physicians; but now every young doctor was as busy as the older men. Italians who knew me would even ask me to prescribe for their children, simply because I was the son of Mister Doctor Malloy. Young general practitioners who would have had to depend upon friends of their families and fraternal orders and accidents and gonorrhea for their start, were seeing—hardly more than seeing—more patients in a day than in normal times they could have hoped to see in a month.

The mines closed down almost with the first whiff of influenza. Men who for years had been drilling rock and had chronic miner's asthma never had a chance against the mysterious new disease; and even younger men were keeling over, so the coal companies had to shut down the mines, leaving only maintenance men, such as pump men, in charge. Then the Commonwealth of Pennsylvania closed down the schools and churches, and forbade all congregating. If you wanted an ice cream soda you had to have it put in a cardboard container; you couldn't have it at the fountain in a glass. We were glad when school closed, because it meant a holiday, and the epidemic had touched very few of us. We lived in Gibbsville; it was in the tiny mining villages—"patches"—that the epidemic was felt immediately.

The State stepped in, and when a doctor got sick or exhausted so he literally couldn't hold his head up any longer, they would send a young man from the graduating class of one of the Philadelphia medical schools to take over the older man's practice. This was how Doctor Myers came to our town. I was looking at the pictures of the war in the *Review of Reviews*, my father's favorite magazine, when the doorbell rang and I answered it. The young man looked like the young men who came to our door during the summer selling magazines. He was wearing a short coat with a sheepskin collar, which I recognized as an S. A. T. C. issue coat.

"Is this Doctor Malloy's residence?" he said.

"Yes."

"Well, I'm Mr. Myers from the University."

"Oh," I said. "My father's expecting you." I told my father, and he said: "Well, why didn't you bring him right up?"

Doctor Myers went to my father's bedroom and they talked, and then the maid told me my father wanted to speak to me. When I went to the bedroom I could see my father and Doctor Myers were getting along nicely. That was natural: my father and Doctor Myers were University men, which meant the University of Pennsylvania; and University men shared a contempt for men who had studied at Hahnemann or Jefferson or Medico-Chi. Myers was not an M.D., but my father called him Doctor, and as I had been brought up to tip my hat to a doctor as I did to a priest, I called him Doctor too, although Doctor Myers made me feel like a lumberjack; I was so much bigger and obviously stronger than he. I was fifteen years old.

"Doctor Myers, this is my boy James," my father said, and without waiting for either of us to acknowledge the introduction, he went on: "Doctor Myers will be taking over my practice for the time being and you're to help him. Take him down to Hendricks' drug store and introduce him to Mr. Hendricks. Go over the names of our patients and help him arrange some kind of a schedule. Doctor Myers doesn't drive a car, you'll drive for him. Now your mother and I think the rest of the children ought to be on the farm, so you take them there in the big Buick and then bring it back and have it overhauled. Leave the little Buick where it is, and you use the Ford. You'll understand, Doctor, when you see our roads. If you want any money your mother'll give it to you. And no cigarettes, d'you understand?" Then he handed Doctor Myers a batch of prescription blanks, upon which were lists of patients to be seen, and said goodbye and lay back on his pillow for more sleep.

Doctor Myers was almost tiny, and that was the reason I could forgive him for not being in the Army. His hair was so light that you could hardly see his little moustache. In conversation between sentences his nostrils would twitch and like all doctors he had acquired a posed gesture which was becoming habitual. His was to stroke the skin in front of his right ear with his forefinger. He did that now downstairs in the hall. "Well . . . I'll just take a walk back to the hotel and wait till you get back from the farm. That suit you, James?" It did, and he left and I performed the various chores my father had ordered, and then I went to the hotel in the Ford and picked up Doctor Myers.

He was catlike and dignified when he jumped in the car. "Well, here's a list of names. Where do you think we ought to go first? Here's a couple of prescription blanks with only four names apiece. Let's clean them up first."

"Well, I don't know about that, Doctor. Each one of those names means at least twenty patients. For instance Kelly's. That's a saloon, and there'll be a lot of people waiting. They all meet there and wait for my father. Maybe we'd better go to some single calls first."

"O.K., James. Here's a list." He handed it to me. "Oh, your father said something about going to Collieryville to see a family named Evans."

I laughed. "Which Evans? There's seventy-five thousand Evanses in Collieryville. Evan Evans. William W. Evans. Davis W. Evans. Davis W. Evans, Junior. David Evans?"

"David Evans sounds like it. The way your father spoke they were particular friends of his."

"David Evans," I said. "Well—he didn't say who's sick there , did he?"

"No. I don't think anybody. He just suggested we drop in to see if they're all well."

I was relieved, because I was in love with Edith Evans. She was nearly two years older than I, but I liked girls a little older. I looked at his list and said: "I think the best idea is to go there first and then go around and see some of the single cases in Collieryville." He was ready to do anything I suggested. He was affable and trying to make me feel that we were pals, but I could tell he was nervous, and I had sense enough to know that he had better look at some flu before tackling one of those groups at the saloons.

We drove to Collieryville to the David Evans home. Mr. Evans was district superintendent of one of the largest mining corporations, and therefore Collieryville's third citizen. He would not be there all the time, because he was a good man and due for promotion to a bigger district, but so long as he was there he was ranked with the leading doctor and the leading lawyer. After him came the Irish priest, the cashier of the larger bank (of which the doctor or the lawyer or the superintendent of the mines is president), the brewer, and the leading merchant. David Evans had been born in Collieryville, the son of a superintendent, and was popular, a thirty-second degree Mason, a graduate of Lehigh, and a friend of my father's. They would see each other less than ten times a year, but they would go hunting rabbit and quail and pheasant together every autumn and always exchanged Christmas gifts. When my mother had large parties she would invite Mrs. Evans, but the two women were not close friends. Mrs. Evans was a Collieryville girl, half Polish, and my mother had gone to an expensive school and spoke French, and played bridge long before Mrs. Evans had learned to play "500." The Evanses had two children: Edith, my girl, and Rebecca, who was about five.

The Evans Cadillac, which was owned by the coal company, was standing in front of the Evans house, which also was owned by the coal company. I called to the driver, who was sitting behind the steering wheel, hunched up in a sheepskin coat and with a checkered cap pulled down over his eyes. "What's the matter, Pete?" I called. "Can't the company get rid of that old Caddy?"

"Go on wid you," said Pete. "What's the wrong wid the doctorin' business? I notice Mike Malloy ain't got nothin' better than Buicks."

"I'll have you fired, you round-headed son of a bitch," I said. "Where's the big lad?"

"Up Mike's. Where'd you t'ink he is?"

I parked the Ford and Doctor Myers and I went to the door and were let in by the pretty Polish maid. Mr. Evans came out of his den, wearing a raccoon coat and carrying his hat. I introduced Doctor Myers. "How do you do, sir," he said. "Doctor Malloy just asked me to stop in and see if everything was all right with your family."

"Oh, fine," said Mr. Evans. "Tell the dad that was very thoughtful, James, and thank you too, Doctor. We're all O.K. here, thank the Lord, but while you're here I'd like to have you meet Mrs. Evans. Adele!"

Mrs. Evans called from upstairs that she would be right down. While we waited in the den Mr. Evans offered Doctor Myers a cigar, which was declined. Doctor Myers, I could see, preferred to sit, because Mr. Evans was so large that he had to look up to him. While Mr. Evans questioned him about his knowledge of the anthracite region, Doctor Myers spoke with a barely discernible pleasant hostility which was lost on Mr. Evans, the simplest of men. Mrs. Evans appeared in a house dress. She looked at me shyly, as she always did. She always embarrassed me, because when I went in a room where she was sitting she would rise to shake hands, and I would feel like telling her to sit down. She was in her middle thirties and still pretty, with rosy cheeks and pale blue eyes and nothing "foreign" looking about her except her high cheek bones and the lines of her eyebrows, which looked as though they had been drawn with crayon. She shook hands with Doctor Myers and then clasped her hands in front of her and looked at Mr. Evans when he spoke, and then at Doctor Myers and then at me, smiling and hanging on Mr. Evans' words. He was used to that. He gave her a half smile without looking at her and suggested we come back for dinner, which in Collieryville was at noon. Doctor Myers asked me if we would be in Collieryville at that time, and I said we would, so we accepted his invitation. Mr. Evans said: "That's fine. Sorry I won't be here, but I have to go to Wilkes-Barre right away." He looked at his watch. "By George! By now I ought to be half way there." He grabbed his hat and kissed his wife and left.

When he had gone Mrs. Evans glanced at me and smiled and then said: "Edith will be glad to see you, James."

"Oh, I'll bet she will," I said. "Where's she been keeping herself anyway?"

"Oh, around the house. She's my eldest," she said to Doctor Myers. "Seventeen."

"Seventeen?" he repeated. "You have a daughter seventeen? I can hardly believe it, Mrs. Evans. Nobody would ever think you had a daughter seventeen." His voice was a polite protest, but there was nothing protesting in what he saw in Mrs. Evans. I looked at her myself now, thinking of her for the first time as someone besides Edith's mother. . . . No, I couldn't see her. We left to make some calls, promising to be back at twelve-thirty.

Our first call was on a family named Loughran, who lived in a neat two-story house near the Collieryville railroad station. Doctor Myers went in. He came out in less than two minutes, followed by Mr. Loughran. Loughran walked over to me. "You," he said. "Ain't we good enough for your dad no more? What for kind of a thing is this he does be sending us?"

"My father is sick in bed, just like everybody else, Mr. Loughran. This is the doctor that is taking all his calls till he gets better."

"It is, is it? So that's what we get, and doctorin' with Mike Malloy since he come from college, and always paid the day after payday. Well, young man, take this back to Mike Malloy. You tell him for me if my woman pulls through it'll be no thanks to him. And if she don't pull through, and dies, I'll come right down to your old man's office and kill him wid a rock. Now you and this one get the hell outa here before I lose me patience."

We drove away. The other calls we made were less difficult, although I noticed that when he was leaving one or two houses the people, who were accustomed to my father's quick, brusque calls, would stare at Doctor Myers' back. He stayed too long, and probably was too sympathetic. We returned to the Evans home.

Mrs. Evans had changed her dress to one that I thought was a little too dressy for the occasion. She asked us if we wanted "a little wine," which we didn't, and Doctor Myers was walking around with his hands in his trousers pockets, telling Mrs. Evans what a comfortable place this was, when Edith appeared. I loved Edith, but the only times I ever saw her were at dancing school, to which she would come every Saturday afternoon. She was quite small, but long since her legs had begun to take shape and she had breasts. It was her father, I guess, who would not let her put her hair up; she often told me he was very strict and I knew that he was making her stay in Collieryville High School a year longer than was necessary because he thought her too young to go away. Edith called me Jimmy—one of the few who did. When we danced together at dancing school she scarcely spoke at all. I suspected her of regarding me as very young. All the little kids at dancing school called me James, and the oldest girls called me sarcastic. "James Malloy," they would say, "you think you're sarcastic. You think you're clever, but you're not. I consider the source of that remark." The remark might be that I had heard that Wallace Reid was waiting for that girl to grow up—and so was I. But I never said things like that to Edith. I would say: "How's everything out in the metropolis of Collieryville?" and she would say they were all right. It was no use trying to be sarcastic or clever with Edith, and no use trying to be romantic. One time I offered her the carnation that we had to wear at dancing school, and she refused it because the pin might tear her dress. It was useless to try to be dirty with her; there was no novelty in it for a girl who had gone to Collieryville High. I told her one story, and she said her grandmother fell out of the cradle laughing at that one.

When Edith came in she took a quick look at Doctor Myers which made me slightly jealous. He turned and smiled at her, and his nostrils began to twitch. Mrs. Evans rubbed her hands together nervously, and it was plain to see that she was not sure how to introduce Doctor Myers. Before she had a chance to make any mistakes I shook hands with Edith and she said, "Oh, hello, Jimmy," in a very offhand way, and I said: "Edith, this is Doctor Myers."

"How do you do?" said Edith.

"How are you?" said the doctor.

"Oh, very well, thank you," Edith said, and realized that it wasn't quite the thing to say.

"Well," said Mrs. Evans. "I don't know if you gentlemen want to wash up. Jimmy, you know where the bathroom is." It was the first time she had called me Jimmy. I glanced at her curiously and then the doctor and I went to wash our hands. Upstairs he said: "That your girl, James?"

"Oh, no," I said. "We're good friends. She isn't that kind."

"What kind? I didn't mean anything." He was amused.

"Well, I didn't know what you meant."

"Edith certainly looks like her mother," he said.

"Oh, I don't think so," I said, not really giving it a thought, but I was annoyed by the idea of talking about Edith in the bathroom. We came downstairs.

Dinner was a typical meal of that part of the country: sauerkraut and pork and some stuff called nep, which was nothing but dough, and mashed potatoes and lima beans, coffee, tea, and two kinds of pie, and you were expected to take both kinds. It was a meal I liked, and I ate a lot. Mrs. Evans got some courage from somewhere and was now talkative, now quiet, addressing most of her remarks to Doctor Myers and then turning to me. Edith kept looking at her and then turning to the doctor. She paid no attention to me except when I had something to say. Rebecca, whose table manners were being neglected, had nothing to contribute except to stick out her plate and say: "More mash potatoes with butter on."

"Say please," said Edith, but Rebecca only looked at her with the scornful blankness of five.

After dinner we went to the den and Doctor Myers and I smoked. I noticed he did not sit down; he was actually a little taller than Edith, and just about the same height as her mother. He walked around the room, standing in front of enlarged snapshots of long-deceased setter dogs, one of which my father had given Mr. Evans. Edith watched him and her mother and said nothing, but just before we were getting ready to leave Mrs. Evans caught Edith staring at her and they exchanged mysterious glances. Edith looked defiant and Mrs. Evans seemed puzzled and somehow alarmed. I could not figure it out.

II

In the afternoon Doctor Myers decided he would like to go to one of the patches where the practice of medicine was wholesale, so I suggested

Kelly's. Kelly's was the only saloon in a patch of about one hundred families, mostly Irish, and all except one family were Catholics. In the spring they have processions in honor of the Blessed Virgin at Kelly's patch, and a priest carries the Blessed Sacrament the length of the patch, in the open air, to the public school grounds, where they hold Benediction. The houses are older and stauncher than in most patches, and they look like pictures of Ireland, except that there are no thatched roofs. Most patches were simply unbroken rows of company houses, made of slatty wood, but Kelly's had more ground between the houses and grass for the goats and cows to feed on, and the houses had plastered walls. Kelly's saloon was frequented by the whole patch because it was the postoffice substation, and it had a good reputation. For many years it had the only telephone in the patch.

Mr. Kelly was standing on the stoop in front of the saloon when I swung the Ford around. He took his pipe out of his mouth when he recognized the Ford, and then frowned slightly when he saw that my father was not with me. He came to my side of the car. "Where's the dad? Does he be down wid it now himself?"

"No," I said. "He's just all tired out and is getting some sleep. This is Doctor Myers that's taking his place till he gets better."

Mr. Kelly spat some tobacco juice on the ground and took a wad of tobacco out of his mouth. He was a white-haired, sickly man of middle age. "I'm glad to make your acquaintance," he said.

"How do you do, sir?" said Doctor Myers.

"I guess James here told you what to be expecting?"

"Well, more or less," said Doctor Myers. "Nice country out here. This is the nicest I've seen."

"Yes, all right I guess, but there does be a lot of sickness now. I guess you better wait a minute here till I have a few words with them inside there. I have to keep them orderly, y'understand."

He went in and we could hear his loud voice: ". . . young Malloy said his dad is seriously ill . . . great expense out of his own pocket secured a famous young specialist from Philadelphia so as to not have the people of the patch without a medical man . . . And any lug of a lunkhead that don't stay in line will have me to answer to . . ." Mr. Kelly then made the people line up and he came to the door and asked Doctor Myers to step in.

There were about thirty women in the saloon as Mr. Kelly guided Doctor Myers to an oilcloth-covered table. One Irishman took a contemptuous look at Doctor Myers and said: "Jesus, Mary and Joseph," and walked out, sneering at me before he closed the door. The others probably doubted that the doctor was a famous specialist, but they had not had a doctor in two or three days. Two others left quietly but the rest remained. "I guess we're ready, Mr. Kelly," said Doctor Myers.

Most of the people were Irish, but there were a few Hunkies in the patch, although not enough to warrant Mr. Kelly's learning any of their languages as the Irish had had to do in certain other patches. It was easy enough to deal with the Irish: a woman would come to the table and describe for Doctor Myers the symptoms of her sick man and kids in language that was painfully polite. My father had trained them to use terms like "bowel movement" instead of those that came more quickly to mind. After a few such encounters and wasting a lot of time, Doctor Myers more or less got the swing of prescribing for absent patients. I stood leaning against the bar, taking down the names of patients I didn't know by sight, and wishing I could have a cigarette, but that was out of the question because Mr. Kelly did not approve of cigarettes and might have told my father. I was standing there when the first of the Hunkie women had her turn. She was a worried-looking woman who even I could see was pregnant and had been many times before, judging by her breasts. She had on a white knitted cap and a black silk shirtwaist—nothing underneath—and a nondescript skirt. She was wearing a man's overcoat and a pair of Pacs, which are short rubber boots that men wear in the mines. When Doctor Myers spoke to her she became voluble in her own tongue. Mr. Kelly interrupted: "Wait a minute, wait a minute," he said. "You sick?"

"No, no. No me sick. Man sick." She lapsed again into her own language.

"She has a kid can speak English," said Mr. Kelly. "Hey, you. Leetle girl Mary, you daughter, her sick?" He made so-high with his hand. The woman caught on.

"Mary. Sick. Yah, Mary sick." She beamed.

Mr. Kelly looked at the line of patients and spoke to a woman. "Mame," he said. "You live near this lady. How many has she got sick?"

Mame said: "Well, there's the man for one. Dyin' from the way they was carryin' on yesterday and the day before. I ain't seen none of the kids. There's four little girls and they ain't been out of the house for a couple of days. And no wonder they're sick, runnin' around wild widout no—"

"Never mind about that, now," said Mr. Kelly. "I guess, Doctor, the only thing for you to do is go to this woman's house and take a look at them."

The woman Mame said: "To be sure, and ain't that nice? Dya hear that, everybody? Payin' a personal visit to the likes of that but the decent people take what they get. A fine how-do-ya-do."

"You'll take what you get in the shape of a puck in the nose," said Mr. Kelly. "A fine way you do be talkin' wid the poor dumb Hunkie not knowing how to talk good enough to say what's the matter wid her gang. So keep your two cents out of this, Mame Brannigan, and get back into line."

Mame made a noise with her mouth, but she got back into line. Doctor Myers got through the rest pretty well, except for another Hunkie who spoke some English but knew no euphemisms. Mr. Kelly finally told her to use monosyllables, which embarrassed Doctor Myers because there were some Irishwomen still in line. But "We can't be wasting no time on politeness," said Mr. Kelly. "This here's a doctor's office now." Finally all the patients except the Hunkie woman were seen to.

Mr. Kelly said: "Well, Doctor, bein's this is your first visit here you gotta take a little something on the house. Would you care for a brandy?"

"Why, yes, that'd be fine," said the doctor.

"James, what about you? A sass?"

"Yes, thank you," I said. A sass was a sarsaparilla.

Mr. Kelly opened a closet at the back of the bar and brought out a bottle. He set it on the bar and told the doctor to help himself. The doctor poured himself a drink and Mr. Kelly poured one and handed it to the Hunkie woman. "There y'are, Mary," he said. "Put hair on your chest." He winked at the doctor.

"Not joining us, Mr. Kelly?" said the doctor.

Mr. Kelly smiled. "Ask James there. No, I never drink a drop. Handle too much of it. Why, if I took a short beer every time I was asked to, I'd be drunk three quarters of the time. And another advantage is when this here Pro'bition goes into effect I won't miss it. Except financially. Well, I'll take a bottle of temperance just to be sociable." He opened a bottle of ginger ale and took half a glassful. The Hunkie woman raised her glass and said something that sounded more like a prayer than a toast, and put her whole mouth around the mouth of the glass and drank. She was happy and grateful. Doctor Myers wanted to buy another round, but Mr. Kelly said his money was no good there that day; if he wanted another drink he was to help himself. The doctor did not want another, but he said he would like to buy one for the Hunkie woman, and Mr. Kelly permitted him to pay for it, then we said goodbye to Mr. Kelly and departed, the Hunkie woman getting in the car timidly, but once in the car her bottom was so large that the doctor had to stand on the running board until we reached her house.

A herd of goats in various stages of parturition gave us the razz when we stopped at the house. The ground around the house had a goaty odor because the wire which was supposed to keep them out was torn in several places. The yard was full of old wash boilers and rubber boots, tin cans and the framework of an abandoned baby carriage. The house was a one and a half story building. We walked around to the back door, as the front door is reserved for the use of the priest when he comes on sick calls. The Hunkie woman seemed happier and encouraged, and prattled away as we followed her into the house, the doctor carefully picking his way through stuff in the yard.

The woman hung up her coat and hat on a couple of pegs on the kitchen wall, from which also hung a lunch can and a tin coffee bottle, the can suspended on a thick black strap, and the bottle on a braided black cord. A miner's cap with a safety lamp and a dozen buttons of the United Mine Workers of America was on another peg, and in a pile on the floor were dirty overalls and jumper and shirt. The woman sat down on a backless kitchen chair and hurriedly removed her boots, which left her barefoot. There was an awful stink of cabbage and dirty feet in the house, and I began to feel nauseated as I watched the woman flopping around, putting a kettle on the stove and starting the fire, which she indicated she wanted to do before going to look at the sick. Her breasts swung to and fro and her large hips jounced up and down, and the doctor smirked at these things, knowing that I was watching, but not knowing that I was trying to think of the skinniest girl I knew, and in the presence of so much woman I was sorry for all past thoughts or desires. Finally the woman led the way to the front of the house. In one of the two front rooms was an old-fashioned bed. The windows were curtained, but when our eyes became accustomed to the darkness we could see four children lying on the bed. The youngest and oldest were lying together. The oldest, a girl about five years old, was only half covered by the torn quilt that covered the others. The baby coughed as we came in. The other two were sound asleep. The half-covered little girl got awake, or opened her eyes and looked at the ceiling. She had a half-sneering look about her nose and mouth, and her eyes were expressionless. Doctor Myers leaned over her and so did her mother, speaking to the girl, but the girl apparently made no sense even in the Hunkie language. She sounded as though she were trying to clear her throat of phlegm. The doctor turned to me and said dramatically: "James, take this woman out and get her to boil some water, and go out to the car and get your father's instrument case." I grabbed the woman's arm and pulled her to the kitchen and made signs for her to boil some water, then I went out to the Ford and wrestled with the lid of the rear compartment, wondering what the hell Myers wanted with the instrument case, wondering whether he himself knew what he wanted with it. At last I yanked the lid open and was walking back with the leather case in my hands when I heard a loud scream. It sounded more deliberate than wild, it started so low and suddenly went so high. I hurried back to the bedroom and saw Doctor Myers trying to pull the heavy woman away from her daughter. He was not strong enough for her, but he kept pulling and there were tears in his eyes: "Come away, God damn it! Come away from her, you God damn fool!" He turned to me for help and said: "Oh, Jesus, James, this is awful. The little girl just died. Keep away from her. She had diphtheria!"

"I couldn't open the back of the car," I said.

"Oh, it wasn't your fault. Even a tracheotomy wouldn't have saved her, the poor little thing. But we've got to do something for these others. The baby has plenty of spots, and I haven't even looked at the other two." The other two had been awakened by their mother's screams and were sitting up and crying, not very loud. The woman had the dead girl in her arms. She did not need the English language to know that the child was dead. She was rocking her back and forth and kissing her and looking up at us with fat streams of tears running from her eyes. She would stop crying for a second, but would start again, crying with her mouth open and the tears, unheeded, sliding in over her upper lip.

Doctor Myers took some coins from his pocket and tried to make friends with the in-between kids, but they did not know what money was, so I left him to go in to see how the man was. I walked across the hall to the other bedroom and pulled up the curtains. The man was lying in his underwear; gaunt, bearded, and dead.

I knew he was dead, but I said: "Hyuh, John, hyuh." The sound of my voice made me feel silly, then sacrilegious, and then I had to vomit. I had seen men brought in from railroad wrecks and mine explosions and other violent-accident cases, but I had been prepared for them if only by the sound of the ambulance bell. This was different. Doctor Myers heard me being sick and came in. I was crying. He took a few seconds to see that the man was dead and then he took me by the arm and said: "That's all right, kid. Come out in the air." He led me outside into the cold afternoon and I felt better and hungry.

He let go of my arm. "Listen," he said. "As soon as you feel well enough, take the car and go to the hospital. The first thing you do there is get them to give you twenty thousand units of antitoxin, and while you're doing that tell them to send an ambulance out here right away. Don't go near anybody if you can help it except a doctor." He paused. "You'd better find out about an undertaker."

"You'll need more than twenty thousand units of antitoxin," I said. I had had that much in my own back when I was eight years old.

"Oh, no. You didn't understand me. The antitoxin's for you. You tell whoever's in charge at the hospital how many are sick out here, and they'll know what to send."

"What about you?"

"Oh, I'll stay here and go back in the ambulance. Don't worry about me. I want to stay here and do what I can for these kids." I suddenly had a lot of respect for him. I got into the Ford and drove away. Doctors' cars carried cardboard signs which said By Order State Department of Health, which gave them the right to break speed laws, and I broke them on my way to the hospital. I pulled in at the porte-cochère and met Doctor Kleiber, a friend of my father's and told him everything. He gave me antitoxin. He smiled when I mentioned getting an undertaker. "Lucky if they get a wooden rough box, even, James. These people aren't patients of Daddy's, are they, James?"

"No."

"Well then, I guess maybe we have to send an Army doctor. I'm full up so I haven't a minute except for Daddy's patients. Now go home and I'll take care of everything. You'll be stiff in the back and you want to rest. Goodbye now." So I drove home and went to bed.

III

I was stiff the next morning from the antitoxin, but it had not been so bad as the other time I had taken it, and I was able to pick up Doctor Myers at the hotel. "I feel pretty damn useless, not being able to drive a car," he said. "But I never had much chance to learn. My mother never had enough money to get one. You know that joke: we can't afford a Ford."

"Oh, well," I said, "in Philadelphia you don't need one. They're a nuisance in the city."

"All the same I'd like to have one. I guess I'll have to when I start practicing. Well, where to first?" We outlined a schedule, and for the next couple of days we were on the go almost continually. We hardly noticed how the character of the region was changed. There was little traffic in the streets, but the few cars tore madly. Most of them were Cadillacs: black, company-owned Cadillacs which were at the disposal of young men like Doctor Myers and the two drunken Gibbsville doctors who did not own cars; and gray Cadillacs from the USAAC base in Allentown, which took officers of the Army Medical Corps around to the emergency hospitals. At night the officers would use the cars for their fun, and there were a few scandals. One of my friends, a Boy Scout who was acting as errand boy—"courier," he called himself—at one of the hospitals, swore he witnessed an entire assignation between an Army major and a local girl who was a clerk in the hospital office. One officer was rumored to be homosexual and had to be sent elsewhere. Opinion among us boys was divided: some said he was taken away and shot, some said he was sent to Leavenworth, others said he was dishonorably discharged. The ambulances were being driven by members of the militia, who wore uniforms resembling those of the marine corps. The militia was made up of young men who were exempt from active service. They had to make one ambulance driver give up his job, because he would drive as fast as the ambulance would go even when he was only going to a drug store for a carton of soap. Another volunteer driver made so much noise with the ambulance bell that the sick persons inside would be worse off than if they had walked. The women of wealth who could drive their own cars drove them, fetching and carrying blankets and cots, towels and cotton, but their husbands made some of the women stop because of the dangers of influenza and Army medical officers. Mrs. Barlow, the leader of society, did not stop, and her husband knew better than to try to insist. She was charming and stylish and looked very English in her Red Cross canteen division uniform. She assumed charge of the emergency hospital in the armory and bossed the Catholic sisters and the graduate nurses around and made them like it. Her husband gave money and continued to ride a sorrel hunter about the countryside. The rector of the Second Presbyterian Church appeared before the Board of Health and demanded that the nuns be taken out of the hospitals on the ground that they were baptizing men and women who were about to die, without ascertaining whether they were Catholics or Protestants. The *Standard* had a story on the front page which accused unnamed undertakers of profiteering on "rough boxes," charging as much for pine board boxes as they had for mahogany caskets before the epidemic.

Doctor Myers at first wore a mask over his nose and mouth when making calls, and so did I, but the gauze stuck to my lips and I stopped wearing it and so did the doctor. It was too much of a nuisance to put them on and take them off every time we would go to a place like Kelly's, and also it was rather insulting to walk in on a group of people with a mask on your face when nobody in the group was wearing one. I was very healthy and was always glad to go in with the doctor because it gave me something to do. Of course I could have cleaned spark plugs or shot some air into the tires while waiting for the doctor, but I hated to monkey around the car almost as much as I liked to drive it.

In a few days Doctor Myers had begun to acquire some standing among the patients, and he became more confident. One time after coming from my father's bedroom he got in the car with some prescriptions in his hand and we started out. To himself he said, looking up from a prescription: "Digitalis . . . now I wonder?" I turned suddenly, because it was the first time in my life I had heard anyone criticize a prescription of my father's. "Oh, I'm sorry, Jimmy," he said.

"You better not ever let him hear you say anything about his prescriptions."

"Yes, I know. He doesn't want anyone to argue with him. He doesn't think I'm seeing as many people as I should."

"What does he expect?" I said.

"Oh, he isn't unreasonable, but he doesn't want his patients to think he's neglecting them. By the way, he wants us to stop in at the Evanses in Collieryville. The David Evanses. Mrs. Evans phoned and said their maid is sick."

"That's O.K. with me," I said.

"I thought it would be," he said.

Collieryville seemed strange with the streets so deserted as on some new kind of holiday. The mines did not work on holydays of obligation, and the miners would get dressed and stand around in front of poolrooms and saloons, but now they were not standing around, and there was none of the activity of a working day, when coal wagons and trucks rumble through the town, and ten-horse teams, guided by the shouted "gee" and "haw" of the driver, would pull loads of timber through the streets on the way to the mines. Collieryville, a town of about four thousand persons, was quiet as though the people were afraid to come out in the cold November gray.

We were driving along the main street when I saw Edith. She was coming out of the P. O. S. of A. Hall, which was a poolroom on the first floor and had lodge rooms on the two upper stories. It was being used as an emergency hospital. I pulled up at the curb and called to Edith. "Come on, I'll give you a ride home," I said.

"Can't. I have to get some things at the drug store," she said.

"Well, we're going to your house anyway. I'll see you there," I said.

We drove to the Evans house and I told the doctor I would wait outside until Edith came. She appeared in about five minutes and I told her to sit in the car and talk to me. She said she would.

"Well, I'm a nurse, Jimmy," she said.

"Yes, you are," I said scornfully. "That's probably how your maid got sick."

"What!"

"Why, you hanging around at the P. O. S. of A. Hall is probably the way your maid got sick. You probably brought home the flu—"

"Oh, my God!" she said. She was nervous and pale. She suddenly jumped out of the car and I followed her. She swung open the front door and ran towards the kitchen, and I was glad she did; for although I followed her to the kitchen, I caught a glimpse of Mrs. Evans and Doctor Myers in Mr. Evans' den. Through the half-closed doors I could see they were kissing.

I didn't stop, I know, although I felt I had slowed up. I followed Edith into the kitchen and saw she was half crying, shaking her hands up and down. I couldn't tell whether she had seen what I had seen, but something was wrong that she knew about. I blurted out, "Don't go in your father's den," and was immediately sorry I had said it; but then I saw that she had guessed. She looked weak and took hold of my arms; not looking at me, not even speaking to me, she said: "Oh, my God, now it's him. Oh, why didn't I come home with you? Sarah isn't sick at all. That was just an excuse to get that Myers to come here." She bit her lip and squeezed my arms. "Jimmy, you mustn't ever let on. Promise me."

"I give you my word of honor," I said. "God can strike me dead if I ever say anything."

Edith kissed me, then she called out: "Hey, where is everybody?" She whispered to me: "Pretend you're chasing me like as if I pulled your necktie."

"Let go!" I yelled, as loud as I could. Then we left the kitchen, and Edith would pull my necktie at every step.

Mrs. Evans came out of the den. "Here, what's going on here?"

"I'm after your daughter for pulling my tie," I said.

"Now, Edith, be a good girl and don't fight with James. I don't understand what's the matter with you two. You usedn't to ever fight, and now you fight like cats and dogs. You oughtn't to. It's not nice."

"Oh—" Edith said, and then she burst into tears and went upstairs.

I was genuinely surprised, and said: "I'm sorry, Mrs. Evans, we were only fooling."

"Oh, it's not your fault, James. She feels nervous anyhow and I guess the running was too much for her." She looked at the doctor as if to imply that it was something he would understand.

"I guess I'll go out and sit in the car," I said.

"I'll be right out," said the doctor.

I sat in the car and smoked, now and then looking at the second floor window where I knew Edith's room was, but Edith did not come to the window and in about twenty minutes the doctor came out.

"The maid wasn't sick after all," he said. "It was Mrs. Evans. She has a slight cold but she didn't want to worry your father. I guess she thought if she said she was sick, your father'd come out himself."

"Uh-huh," I said. "Where to now?"

"Oh, that Polish saloon out near the big coal banks."

"You mean Wisniewski's," I said.

IV

Doctor Myers must have known I suspected him, and he might even have suspected that I had *seen* him kissing Mrs. Evans. I was not very good at hiding my likes and dislikes, and I began to dislike him, but I tried not to show it. I didn't care, for he might have told my father I was unsatisfactory, and my father would have given me hell. Or if I had told my father what I'd seen, he'd have given Doctor Myers a terrible beating. My father never drank or smoked, and he was a good, savage amateur boxer, with no scruples against punching anyone smaller than himself. Less than a year before all this took place my father had been stopped by a traffic policeman while he was hurrying to an "OBS." The policeman knew my father's car, and could have guessed why he was in a hurry, but he stopped him. My father got out of the car, walked to the front of it, and in the middle of a fairly busy intersection he took a crack at the policeman and broke his jaw. Then he got back and drove around the unconscious policeman and on to the confinement case. It cost my father nearly a thousand dollars, and the policeman's friends and my father's enemies said: "God damn Mike Malloy, he ought to be put in jail." But my father was a staunch Republican and he got away with it.

I thought of this now and I thought of what my father would have done to Doctor Myers if he found out. Not only would he have beaten him up, but I am sure he would have used his influence at the University to keep Myers from getting his degree.

So I hid, as well as I could, my dislike for Doctor Myers, and the next day, when we stopped at my home, I was glad I did. My father had invented a signal system to save time. Whenever there was a white slip stuck in the window at home or at the office, that meant he was to stop and pick up a message. This day the message in the window read: "Mrs. David Evans, Collieryville."

Doctor Myers looked at it and showed it to me. "Well, on to Colliery-ville," he said.

"O.K., but would you mind waiting a second? I want to see my mother."

He was slightly suspicious. "You don't need any money, do you? I have some."

"No, I just wanted to see if she would get my father to let me have the car tonight." So I went in and telephoned to the Evanses. I got Edith on the phone and told her that her mother had sent for Doctor Myers.

"I know," she said. "I knew she would. She didn't get up this morning, and she's faking sick."

"Well, when we get there you go upstairs with the doctor, and if he wants you to leave the bedroom, you'll have to leave, but tell your mother you'll be right outside, see?"

"O.K.," said Edith.

I returned to the car. "How'd you make out?" said Doctor Myers.

"She thinks she can get him to let me have it," I said, meaning that my father would let me have the car.

When we arrived at the Evans house I had an inspiration. I didn't want him to suspect that we had any plan in regard to him, so I told him I was going in with him to apologize to Edith for our fight of the day before. There was the chance that Edith would fail to follow my advice and would come downstairs, but there was the equally good chance that she would stay upstairs.

The plan worked. In some respects Edith was dumb, but not in this. Doctor Myers stayed upstairs scarcely five minutes, but it was another five before Edith came down. Doctor Myers had gone out to wait in the Ford.

Edith appeared. "Oh, Jimmy, you're so nice to me, and I'm often mean to you. Why is that?"

"Because I love you." I kissed her and she kissed me.

"Listen, if my dad ever finds this out he'll kill her. It's funny, you and me. I mean if you ever told me a dirty story, like about *you* know—people—"

"I did once."

"Did you? I musn't have been listening. Anyhow it's funny to think of you and me, and I'm older than you, but we know something that fellows and girls our age, they only guess at.

"Oh, I've known about it a long time, ever since I went to sisters' school."

"And I guess from your father's doctor books. But this isn't the same when it's your own mother, and I bet this isn't the first time. My dad must have suspicions, because why didn't he send me away to boarding school this year? I graduated from high last year. I bet he wanted me to be here to keep an eye on her."

"Who was the other man?"

"Oh, I can't tell you. Nobody you know. Anyhow, I'm not sure, so I wouldn't tell you. Listen, Jimmy, promise to telephone me every time before he comes here. If I'm not here I'll be at the Bordelmans' or at the Haltensteins', or if not there, the Callaways'. I'll stay home as much as I can, though. How long is he going to be around here, that doctor?"

"Lord knows," I said.

"Oh, I hope he goes. Now give me a goodbye kiss, Jimmy, and then you have to go." I kissed her. "I'm worse than she is," she said.

"No, you're not," I said. "You're the most darling girl there is. Goodbye, Ede," I said.

Doctor Myers was rubbing the skin in front of his ear when I came out. "Well, did you kiss and make up?"

"Oh, we don't go in for that mushy stuff," I said.

"Well, you will," he said. "Well . . . on to Wizziski's."

"It's a good thing you're not going to be around here long," I said.

"Why? Why do you say that?"

"Because you couldn't be in business or practice medicine without learning Hunkie names. If you stayed around here you'd have to be able to pronounce them and spell them." I started the car. I was glad to talk. "But I tell you where you'd have trouble. That's in the patches where they're all Irish with twenty or thirty cousins living in the same patch and all with the same name."

"Oh, come on."

"Well, it isn't as bad as it used to be," I said. "But my father told me about one time he went to Mass at Forganville, about fifteen miles from here, where they used to be all Irish. Now it's half Polack. Anyhow my father said the priest read the list of those that gave to the monthly collection, and the list was like this: John J. Coyle, $5; Jack Coyle, $2; Johnny Coyle, $2; J. J. Coyle, $5; Big John Coyle, $5; Mrs. John Coyle the saloonkeeper's widow, $10; the Widow Coyle, $2. And then a lot of other Coyles."

He did not quite believe this, but he thought it was a good story, and we talked about college—my father had told me I could go to Oxford or Trinity College, Dublin, if I promised to study medicine—until we reached Wisniewski's.

This was a saloon in a newer patch than Kelly's. It was entirely surrounded by mine shafts and breakers and railroads and mule yards, a flat area broken only by culm banks until half a mile away there was a steep, partly wooded hill which was not safe to walk on because it was all undermined and cave-ins occurred so frequently that they did not bother to build fences around them. The houses were the same height as in Kelly's Patch, but they were built in blocks of four and six houses each. Technically Wisniewski's saloon was not in the Patch; that is, it was not on company ground, but at a crossroads at one end of the rows of houses. It was an old stone house which had been a tavern in the days of the King's Highway. Now it was a beery smelling place with a tall bar and no tables or chairs. It was crowded, but still it had a deserted appearance. The reason was that there was no one behind the bar, and no cigars or cartons of chewing tabacco on the back bar. The only decorations were a calendar from which the October leaf had not been torn, depicting a voluptuous woman stretched out on a divan, and an Old Overholt sign, hanging askew on the toilet door.

The men and women recognized Doctor Myers and me, and made a lane for us to pass through. Wisniewski himself was sick in bed, and everybody understood that the doctor would see him first, before prescribing for the mob in the barroom.

Doctor Myers and I went to Wisniewski's room, which was on the first floor. Wisniewski was an affable man, between forty and fifty, with a Teutonic haircut that never needed brushing. His body under the covers made big lumps. He was shaking hands with another Polack whose name was Stiney. He said to us: "Oh, hyuh, Cheem, hyuh, Cheem. Hyuh, Doc."

"Hyuh, Steve," I said. "Yoksheemosh?"

"Oh, fine dandy. How's yaself? How's Poppa? You tell Poppa what he needs is lay off this here booze." He roared at this joke. "Ya, you tell him I said so, lay off this booze." He looked around at the others in the room, and they all laughed, because my father used to pretend that he was going to have Steve's saloon closed by the County. "You wanna drink, Cheem?" he asked, and reached under the bed and pulled out a bottle. I reached for it, and he pulled the bottle away. "Na na na na na. Poppa close up my place wit' the County, I give you a drink. Ya know, miners drink here, but no minors under eighteen, hey?" He passed the bottle around, and all the other men in the room took swigs.

Doctor Myers was horrified. "You oughtn't to do that. You'll give the others the flu."

"Too late now, Doc," he said. "T'ree bottle now already."

"You'll lose all your customers, Steve," I said.

"How ya figure dat out?" said Steve. "Dis flu make me die, dis bottle make dem die. Fwit! Me and my customers all togeder in hell, so I open a place in hell. Fwit!"

"Well, anyhow, how are you feeling?" said the doctor. He placed a thermometer under Steve's arm. The others and Steve were silent until the temperature had been taken. "Hm," said Doctor Myers. He frowned at the thermometer.

" 'M gonna die, huh, Doc? said Steve.

"Well, maybe not, but you—" he stopped talking. The door opened and there was a blast of sweaty air from the barroom, and Mr. Evans stood in the doorway, his hand on the knob. I felt weak.

"Doctor Myers, I'd like to see you a minute please," said Mr. Evans.

"Hyuh, Meester Ivvins," called Steve. Evans is one name which is constantly pronounced the same by the Irish, Slavs, Germans, and even the Portuguese and Negroes in the anthracite.

"Hello, Steve, I see you're drunk," said Mr. Evans.

"Not yet, Meester Ivvins. Wanna drink?"

"No, thanks. Doctor, will you step outside with me?"

Doctor Myers stalled. "I haven't prescribed for this man, Mr. Evans. If you'll wait?"

"My God, man! I can't wait. It's about my wife. I want to know about her."

"What about her?" asked the doctor.

"For God's sake," cried Mr. Evans. "She's sick, isn't she? Aren't you attending her, or don't you remember your patients?"

I sighed, and Doctor Myers sighed louder. "Oh," he said. "You certainly—frightened me, Mr. Evans. I was afraid something had happened. Why, you have no need to worry, sir. She has hardly any temperature. A very slight cold, and she did just the sensible thing by going to bed. Probably be up in a day or two."

"Well, why didn't you say so?" Mr. Evans sat down. "Go ahead, then, finish with Steve. I'll wait till you get through. I'm sorry if I seemed rude, but I was worried. You see I just heard from my timber boss that he saw Doctor Malloy's car in front of my house, and I called up and found out that Mrs. Evans was sick in bed, and my daughter sounded so excited I thought it must be serious. I'll take a drink now, Steve."

"Better not drink out of that bottle, Mr. Evans," said the doctor, who was sitting on the edge of the bed, writing a prescription.

"Oh, hell, it won't hurt me. So anyhow, where was I? Oh, yes. Well, I went home and found Mrs. Evans in bed and she seemed very pale, so

I wanted to be sure it wasn't flu. I found out you were headed this way so I came right out to ask if you wouldn't come back and take another look. That's good liquor, Steve. I'll buy a case of that." He raised the bottle to his lips again.

"I'll give you a case, Meester Ivvins. Glad to give you a case any time," said Steve.

"All right, we'll call it a Christmas present," said Mr. Evans. "Thanks very much." He was sweating, and he opened his raccoon coat. He took another drink, then he handed the bottle to Stiney. "Well, James, I hear you and Edith were at it again."

"Oh, it was just in fun. You know. Pulling my tie," I said.

"Well, don't let her get fresh with you," he said. "You have to keep these women in their place." He punched me playfully. "Doctor, I wonder if you could come to the house now and make sure everything's all right."

"I would gladly, Mr. Evans, but there's all that crowd in the barroom, and frankly, Mrs. Evans isn't what you'd call a sick woman, so my duty as a—physician is right here. I'll be only too glad to come if you'd like to wait."

The Hunkies, hearing the Super talked to in this manner, probably expected Meester Ivvins to get up and belt the doctor across the face, but he only said: "Well, if you're sure an hour couldn't make any difference."

"Couldn't possibly, Mr. Evans," said Doctor Myers. He finished with Steve and told him to stop drinking and take his medicine, then he turned to leave. Steve reached under his pillow and drew out a bundle of money. He peeled off a fifty-dollar bill and handed it to the doctor.

"Oh, no, thanks," said Doctor Myers. "Doctor Malloy will send you a bill."

"Aw, don't worry about him, eh, Cheem? I always pay him firs' the mont', eh, Cheem? Naw, Doc, dis for you. Go have a good time. Get twenty-five woman, maybe get drunk wit' boilo." I could imagine Doctor Myers drinking boilo, which is hot moonshine. I nudged him, and he took the money and we went to the barroom.

I carried the chair and table and set them in place, and the Hunkies lined up docilely. Mr. Evans waited in Steve's room, taking a swig out of the bottle now and then until Doctor Myers had finished with the crowd. It was the same as usual. It was impractical to get detailed descriptions from each patient, so the flu doctor would ask each person three or four questions and then pretend to prescribe for each case individually. Actually they gave the same prescription to almost all of the patients, not only to save time, but because drug supplies in the village and city pharmacies were inadequate, and it was physically impossible for druggists to meet the demand. They would make up large batches of each doctor's standard prescription and dole out boxes and bottles as the patrons presented the prescriptions.

It took about two hours to dispose of the crowd at Steve's. Mr. Evans told Doctor Myers to come in the Cadillac because it was faster than the Ford—which I denied. I followed in the Ford and got to the Evans house about three minutes after the Cadillac. Edith met me at the door. "Oh, what a scare!" she said.

"If you think you were scared, what about me?" I said. I told her how I had felt when her father appeared at Steve's.

"Your father phoned and wants you to take that Myers home," she said, when I had finished.

"Did he say why?" I asked.

"No, he just said you weren't to make any more calls this afternoon."

"I wonder why."

"I hope it hasn't got anything to do with him and my mother," she said.

"How could it? Only four people know about it. He couldn't guess it, and nobody would tell him. Maybe he's got up and wants me to drive for him."

"Maybe . . . I can't think. I'm afraid of them up there. Oh, I hope he goes away." I kissed her, and she pushed me away. "You're a bad actor, James Malloy. You're bad enough now, but wait till you grow up."

"What do you mean grow up? I'm almost six feet."

"But you're only a kid. I'm seventeen, and you're only fifteen."

"I'll be in my seventeenth year soon." We heard footsteps on the stairs, and Doctor Myers' voice: ". . . absolutely nothing to worry about. I'll come in again tomorrow. Goodbye, Mr. Evans. Goodbye, Edith. Ready, Jim?"

I gave him my father's message and we drove home fast. When we got there one of the Buicks was in front of the house, and we went in the living-room.

"Well, Doctor Myers," my father said. "Back in harness again. Fit as a fiddle, and I want to thank you for the splendid attention you've given my practice. I don't know what my patients would have done without you."

"Oh, it's been a privilege, Doctor. I'd like to be able to tell you how much I've appreciated working for you. I wouldn't have missed it for the world. I think I'd like to serve my internship in a place like this."

"Well, I'm glad to hear it. I'm chief of staff at our hospital, and I'm sorry I can't offer you anything here, but you ought to try some place like Scranton General. Get the benefit of these mining cases. God damn interesting fractures, by the way. I trephined a man, forty-eight years old—all right, James, I'll call you when I need you." I left the room and they talked for half an hour, and then my father called me. "Doctor Myers wants to say goodbye."

"I couldn't leave without saying goodbye to my partner," said the doctor. "And by the way, Doctor Malloy, I think I ought to give part of this cheque to James. He did half the work."

"If he did I'll see that he gets his share. James knows that. He wants one of these God damn raccoon coats. When I was a boy the only people that wore them drove hearses. Well—" My father indicated that it was time for the doctor and me to shake hands.

"Quite a grip James has," said the doctor.

"Perfect hands for a surgeon. Wasted though," my father said. "Probably send him to some God damn agricultural school and make a farmer out of him. I want him to go to Dublin, then Vienna. That's where the surgeons are. Dublin and Vienna. Well, if you ever meet Doctor Deaver tell him I won't be able to come down for the Wednesday clinics till this damn thing is over. Good luck, Doctor."

"Thank you, many thanks, Doctor Malloy."

"James will drive you to the hotel."

I took him to the hotel and we shook hands. "If you ever want a place to stay in Philadelphia you're always welcome at my house." He gave me the address of a fraternity house. "Say goodbye to the Evanses for me, will you, Jim?"

"Sure," I said, and left.

My father was standing on the porch, waiting impatiently. "We'll use the Buick," he said. "That Ford probably isn't worth the powder to blow it to hell after you've been using it. Do you really want one of those livery stable coats?"

"Sure I do."

"All right. Now, ah, drive to Kelly's." We drove to Kelly's, where there was an ovation, not too loud, because there were one or two in the crowd on whom my father was liable to turn and say: "You, ya son of a bitch, you haven't paid me a cent since last February. What are you cheering for?" We paid a few personal visits in the Patch. At one of them my father slapped a pretty Irish girl's bottom; at another he gave a little boy a dollar and told him to stop picking his nose; at another he sent me for the priest, and when I came back he had gone on foot to two other houses, and was waiting for me at the second. "What the hell kept you? Go to Terry Loughran's, unless the skunk got another doctor."

"He probably did," I said jovially. "He probably got Lucas."

"*Doctor* Lucas. Doctor Lucashinsky. Ivan the Terrible. Well, if he got Lucas it serves him right. Go to Hartenstein's."

We drove until one o'clock the next morning, taking coffee now and then, and once we stopped for a fried egg sandwich. Twice I very nearly fell asleep while driving. The second time I awoke to hear my father saying: ". . . And my God! To think that a son of mine would rather rot in a dirty stinking newspaper office than to do this. Why, I do more good and make more money in twenty minutes in the operating room than you'll be able to make the first three years you're out of college. If you *go* to college. Don't drive so fast!"

It was like that for the next two days. I slept when he allowed me to. We were out late at night and out again early in the morning. We drove fast, and a couple of times I bounded along corduroy roads with tanks of oxygen (my father was one of the first, if not the first, to use oxygen in pneumonia) ready to blow me to hell. I developed a fine cigarette cough, but my father kept quiet about it, because I was not taking quinine, and he was. We got on each other's nerves and had one terrible scene. He became angered by my driving and punched me on the shoulder. I stopped the car and took a tire iron from the floor of the car.

"Now just try that again," I said.

He did not move from the back seat. "Get back in this car." And I got back. But that night we got home fairly early and the next morning, when we had to go out at four o'clock, he drove the car himself and let me sleep. I was beginning to miss Doctor Myers. It was about eight o'clock when I came down for breakfast, and I saw my father sitting in the living-room, looking very tired, staring straight ahead, his arms lying on the arms of the chair. I said hello, but he did not answer.

My mother brought me my breakfast. "Did you speak to your father?"

"Oh, I said hello, but he's in a stupor or something. I'm getting sick of all this."

"Hold your tongue. Your father has good reason to be unhappy this morning. He just lost one of the dearest friends he had in the world. Mr. Evans."

"Mr. Evans!" I said. "When'd he die?"

"At about four o'clock this morning. They called your father but he died before he got there. Poor Mrs. Evans—"

"What he die of? The flu?"

"Yes." I thought of the bottle that he had shared with Steve and the other Hunkies, and Mrs. Evans' illness, and Doctor Myers. It was all mixed up in my mind. "Now you be careful how you behave with your father today," my mother said.

I called up Edith, but she would not come to the phone. I wrote her a note, and drove to Collieryville with some flowers, but she would not see me.

Even after the epidemic died down and the schools were reopened she would not see me. Then she went away to school and did not come home for the Easter holidays, and in May or June I fell in love with another girl and was surprised, but only surprised, when Edith eloped. Now I never can remember her married name.

1935

It Must Have Been Spring

It must have been one of the very first days of spring. I was wearing my boots and my new corduroy habit, and carrying my spurs in my pocket. I always carried my spurs on the way to the stable, because it was eight squares from home to the stable, and I usually had to pass a group of newsboys on the way, and when I wore the spurs they would yell at me, even my friends among them. The spurs seemed to make a difference. The newsboys were used to seeing me in riding breeches and boots or leather puttees, but when I wore the spurs they always seemed to notice it, and they would yell "Cowboy-crazy!", and once I got in a fight about it and got a tooth knocked out. It was not only because I hated what they called me. I hated their ignorance; I could not stop and explain to them that I was not cowboy-crazy, that I rode an English saddle and posted to the trot. I could not explain to a bunch of newsboys that Julia was a five-gaited mare, a full sister to Golden Firefly, and that she herself could have been shown if she hadn't had a blanket scald.

This day that I remember, which must have been one of the very first days of spring, becomes clearer in my memory. I remember the sounds: the woop-woop of my new breeches each time I took a step, and the clop sound of the draught horses' hooves in the thawed ground of the streets. The draught horses were pulling wagon-loads of coal from the near-by mines up the hill, and when they got halfway up the driver would give them a rest; there would be a ratchety noise as he pulled on the brake, and then the sound of the breast chains and trace chains loosening up while the horses rested. Then presently the loud slap of the brake handle against the iron guard, and the driver yelling "Gee opp!", and then the clop sound again as the horses' hooves sank into the sloppy roadway.

My father's office was on the way to the stable, and we must have been at peace that day. Oh, I know we were, because I remember it was the first time I wore the new breeches and jacket. They had come from

Philadelphia that day. At school, which was across the street from our house, I had looked out the window and there was Wanamaker's truck in front of our house, and I knew that The Things had come. Probably crates and burlap rolls containing furniture and rugs and other things that did not concern me; but also a box in which I knew would be my breeches and jacket. I went home for dinner, at noon, but there was no time for me to try on the new things until after school. Then I did hurry home and changed, because I thought I might find my father in his office if I hurried, although it would be after office hours, and I wanted him to see me in the new things.

Now, I guess my mother had telephoned him to wait, but then I only knew that when I got within two squares of the office, he came out and stood on the porch. He was standing with his legs spread apart, with his hands dug deep in his hip pockets and the skirt of his tweed coat stuck out behind like a sparrow's tail. He was wearing a gray soft hat with a black ribbon and with white piping around the edge of the brim. He was talking across the street to Mr. George McRoberts, the lawyer, and his teeth gleamed under his black mustache. He glanced in my direction and saw me and nodded, and put one foot up on the porch seat and went on talking until I got there.

I moved toward him, as always, with my eyes cast down, and I felt my riding crop getting sticky in my hand and I changed my grip on it and held the bone handle. I never could tell anything by my father's nod, whether he was pleased with me or otherwise. As I approached him, I had no way of telling whether he was pleased with me for something or annoyed because someone might have told him they had seen me smoking. I had a package of Melachrinos in my pocket, and I wanted to throw them in the Johnstons' garden, but it was too late now; I was in plain sight. He would wait until I got there, even though he might only nod again when I did, as he sometimes did.

I stood at the foot of the porch. "Hello," I said.

He did not answer me for a few seconds. Then he said, "Come up here till I have a look at you."

I went up on the porch. He looked at my boots. "Well," he said. "Did you polish them?"

"No. I had Mike do it. I charged it. It was a quarter, but you said—"

"I know. Well, you look all right. How are the breeches? You don't want to get them too tight across the knee or they'll hurt you."

I raised my knees to show him that the breeches felt all right.

"Mm-hmm," he said. And then, "Good Lord!" He took off his hat and laid it on the porch seat, and then began to tie my stock over again. I never did learn to tie it the way he wanted it, the way it should have been. Now I was terribly afraid, because he could always smell smoke—he didn't smoke himself—and I remembered I had had a cigarette at recess.

But he finished tying the stock and then drew away and commenced to smile.

He called across the street to Mr. McRoberts. "Well, George. How does he look?"

"Like a million, Doctor. Regular English country squire, eh?"

"English, hell!"

"Going horseback riding?" said Mr. McRoberts to me.

"Yes," I said.

"Wonderful exercise. How about you, Doctor? You ought to be going, too."

"Me? I'm a working man. I'm going to trephine a man at four-thirty. No, this is the horseman in my family. Best horseman in Eastern Pennsylvania," said my father. He turned to me. "Where to this afternoon? See that the mare's hooves are clean and see if that nigger is bedding her the way I told him. Give her a good five-mile exercise out to Indian Run and then back the Old Road. All right."

I started to go. I went down the porch steps and we both said goodbye, and then, when I was a few steps away, he called to me to wait.

"You look fine," he said. "You really look like something. Here." He gave me a five-dollar bill. "Save it. Give it to your mother to put in the bank for you."

"Thank you," I said, and turned away, because suddenly I was crying. I went up the street to the stable with my head bent down, because I could let the tears roll right out of my eyes and down to the ground without putting my hand up to my face. I knew he was still looking.

1934

Over the River and Through the Wood

Mr. Winfield's hat and coat and bag were in the hall of his flat, and when the man downstairs phoned to tell him the car was waiting, he was all ready. He went downstairs and said hello to Robert, the giant Negro chauffeur, and handed Robert the bag, and followed him out to the car. For the first time he knew that he and his granddaughter were not to make the trip alone, for there were two girls with Sheila, and she introduced them: "Grandfather, I'd like to have you meet my friends. This is Helen Wales, and this is Kay Farnsworth. My grandfather, Mr. Winfield." The names meant nothing to Mr. Winfield. What did mean something was that he was going to have to sit on the strapontin, or else sit outside with Robert, which was no good. Not that Robert wasn't all right, as chauffeurs go, but Robert was wearing a raccoon coat, and Mr. Winfield had no raccoon coat. So it was sit outside and freeze or sit on the little seat inside.

Apparently it made no difference to Sheila. He got inside, and when he closed the door behind him, she said, "I wonder what's keeping Robert?"

"He's strapping my bag on that thing in the back," said Mr. Winfield. Sheila obviously was not pleased by the delay, but in a minute or two they got under way, and Mr. Winfield rather admired the way Sheila carried on her conversation with her two friends and at the same time routed and rerouted Robert so that they were out of the city in no time. To Mr. Winfield it was pleasant and a little like old times to have the direction and the driving done for you. Not that he ever drove himself anymore, but when he hired a car, he always had to tell the driver just where to turn and where to go straight. Sheila knew.

The girls were of an age, and the people they talked about were referred to by first names only. Ted, Bob, Gwen, Jean, Mary, Liz. Listening with some care, Mr. Winfield discovered that school acquaintances and boys whom they knew slightly were mentioned by their last names.

Sitting where he was, he could not watch the girls' faces, but he formed his opinions of the Misses Wales and Farnsworth. Miss Wales supplied every other word when Sheila was talking. She was the smallest of the three girls, and the peppy kind. Miss Farnsworth looked out of the window most of the time, and said hardly anything. Mr. Winfield could see more of her face, and he found himself asking, "I wonder if that child really likes anybody." Well, that was one way to be. Make the world show *you*. You could get away with it, too, if you were as attractive as Miss Farnsworth. The miles streamed by and the weather got colder, and Mr. Winfield listened and soon understood that he was not expected to contribute to the conversation.

"We stop here," said Sheila. It was Danbury, and they came to a halt in front of the old hotel. "Wouldn't you like to stop here, Grandfather?" He understood then that his daughter had told Sheila to stop here; obediently and with no dignity he got out. When he returned to the car, the three girls were finishing their cigarettes, and as he climbed back in the car, he noticed how Miss Farnsworth had been looking at him and continued to look at him, almost as though she were making a point of not helping him—although he wanted no help. He wasn't really an *old* man, an *old man*. Sixty-five.

The interior of the car was filled with cigarette smoke, and Miss Farnsworth asked Mr. Winfield if he'd mind opening a window. He opened it. Then Sheila said one window didn't make any difference; open both windows, just long enough to let the smoke get out. "My! That air feels good," said Miss Wales. Then: "But what about you, Mr. Winfield? You're in a terrible draught there." He replied, for the first use of his voice thus far, that he did not mind. And at that moment the girls thought they saw a car belonging to a boy they knew, and they were in Sheffield, just over the Massachusetts line, before Miss Farnsworth realized that the windows were open and creating a terrible draught. She realized it when the robe slipped off her leg, and she asked Mr. Winfield if he would mind closing the window. But he was unable to get the crank started; his hands were so cold there was no strength in them. "We'll be there soon," said Sheila. Nevertheless, she closed the windows, not even acknowledging Mr. Winfield's shamed apologies.

He had to be first out of the car when they arrived at the house in Lenox, and it was then that he regretted having chosen the strapontin. He started to get out of the car, but when his feet touched the ground, the hardpacked frozen cinders of the driveway flew up at him. His knees had no strength in them, and he stayed there on the ground for a second or two, trying to smile it off. Helpful Robert—almost too helpful; Mr. Winfield wasn't that old—jumped out of the car and put his hands in Mr. Winfield's armpits. The girls were frightened, but it seemed to Mr. Winfield that they kept looking toward the library window, as though they were afraid Sheila's mother would be there and blaming them for his fall. If they only knew . . .

"You go on in, Grandfather, if you're sure you're all right," said Sheila. "I have to tell Robert about the bags."

"I'm all right," said Mr. Winfield. He went in, and hung up his coat and hat in the clothes closet under the stairs. A telephone was there, and in front of the telephone a yellow card of numbers frequently called. Mr. Winfield recognized only a few of the names, but he guessed there was an altogether different crowd of people coming up here these days. Fifteen years make a difference, even in a place like Lenox. Yes, it was fifteen years since he had been up here in the summertime. These trips, these annual trips for Thanksgiving, you couldn't tell anything about the character of the place from these trips. You never saw anybody but your own family and, like today, their guests.

He went out to the darkened hall and Ula, the maid, jumped in fright. "Ugh. Oh. It's you, Mr. Winfield. You like to scare me."

"Hello, Ula. Glad to see you're still holding the fort. Where's Mrs. Day?"

"Upstairs, I think . . . Here she is now," said Ula.

His daughter came down the steps; her hand on the banister was all he could see at first. "Is that you, Father? I thought I heard the car."

"Hello, Mary," he said. At the foot of the stairs they went through the travesty of a kiss that both knew so well. He leaned forward so that his head was above her shouder. To Ula, a good Catholic, it must have looked like the kiss of peace. *Pax tibi,* Mr. Winfield felt like saying, but he said, "Where have you—"

"Father! You're freezing!" Mrs. Day tried very hard to keep the vexation out of her tone.

"It was a cold ride," he said. "This time of year. We had snow flurries between Danbury and Sheffield, but the girls enjoyed it."

"You go right upstairs and have a bath, and I'll send up—what would you like? Tea? Chocolate? Coffee?"

He was amused. The obvious thing would be to offer him a drink, and it was so apparent that she was talking fast to avoid that. "I think cocoa would be fine, but you'd better have a real drink for Sheila and her friends."

"Now, why do you take that tone, Father? You could have a drink if you wanted it, but you're on the wagon, aren't you?"

"Still on it. Up there with the driver."

"Well, and besides, liquor doesn't warm you up the same way something hot does. I'll send up some chocolate. I've put you in your old room, of course. You'll have to share the bathroom with one of Sheila's friends, but that's the best I could do. Sheila wasn't even sure she was coming till the very last minute."

"I'll be all right. It sounds like—I didn't bring evening clothes."

"We're not dressing."

He went upstairs. His room, the room itself, was just about the same; but the furniture was rearranged, his favorite chair not where he liked it best, but it was a good house; you could tell it was being lived in, *this year*, today, tomorrow. Little touches, ashtrays, flowers. It seemed young and white, cool with a warm breath, comfortable—and absolutely strange to him and, more especially, he to it. Whatever of the past this house had held, it was gone now. He sat in the chair and lit a cigarette. In a wave, in a lump, in a gust, the old thoughts came to him. Most of the year they were in the back of his mind, but up here Mr. Winfield held a sort of annual review of far-off, but never-out-of-sight regrets. This house, it used to be his until Mary's husband bought it. A good price, and in 1921 he certainly needed the money. He needed everything, and today he had an income from the money he got for this house, and that was about all. He remembered the day Mary's husband came to him and said, "Mr. Winfield, I hate to have to be the one to do this, but Mary—Mary doesn't— well, she thinks you weren't very nice to Mrs. Winfield. I don't know anything about it myself, of course, but that's what Mary thinks. I expected, naturally, I thought you'd come and live with us now that Mrs. Winfield has died, but—well, the point is, I know you've lost a lot of money, and also I happen to know about Mrs. Winfield's will. So I'm prepared to make you a pretty good offer, strictly legitimate based on current values, for the house in Lenox. I'll pay the delinquent taxes myself and give you a hundred and fifty thousand dollars for the house and grounds. That ought to be enough to pay off your debts and give you a fairly decent income. And, uh, I happen to have a friend who knows Mr. Harding quite well. Fact, he sees the President informally one night a week, and I know he'd be only too glad, if you were interested . . ."

He remembered how that had tempted him. Harding might have fixed it so he could go to London, where Enid Walter was. But even then it was too late. Enid had gone back to London because he didn't have the guts to divorce his wife, and the reason he wouldn't divorce his wife was that he wanted to "protect" Mary, and Mary's standing, and Mary's husband's standing, and Mary's little daughter's standing; and now he was "protecting" them all over again, by selling his house so that he would not become a family charge—protecting the very same people from the embarrassment of a poor relation. "You can have the house," he told Day. "It's worth that much, but no more, and I'm grateful to you for not offering me more. About a political job, I think I might like to go to California this winter. I have some friends out there I haven't seen in years." He had known that that was exactly what Mary and her husband wanted, so he'd gone.

There was a knock on the door. It was Ula with a tray. "Why two cups, Ula?" he said.

"Oh. Di put two cups? So I did. I'm just so used to putting two cups." She had left the door open behind her, and as she arranged the things on the marble-topped table he saw Sheila and the two other girls, standing and moving in the hall.

"This is your room, Farnie," said Sheila. "You're down this way, Helen. Remember what I told you, Farnie. Come on, Helen."

"Thank you, Ula," he said. She went out and closed the door, and he stood for a moment, contemplating the chocolate, then poured out a cup and drank it. It made him a little thirsty, but it was good and warming, and Mary was right; it was better than a drink. He poured out another cup and nibbled on a biscuit. He had an idea: Miss Farnsworth might like some. He admired that girl. She had spunk. He bet she knew what she wanted, or seemed to, and no matter how unimportant were the things she wanted, they were the things she wanted, and not someone else. She could damn well thank the Lord, too, that she was young enough to have a whack at whatever she wanted, and not have to wait the way he had. That girl would make up her mind about a man or a fortune or a career, and by God she would attain whatever it was. If she found, as she surely would find, that nothing ever was enough, she'd at least find it out in time; and early disillusionment carried a compensatory philosophical attitude, which in a hard girl like this one would take nothing from her charm. Mr. Winfield felt her charm, and began regarding her as the most interesting person he had met in many dull years. It would be fun to talk to her, to sound her out and see how far she had progressed toward, say, ambition or disillusionment. It would be fun to do, and it would be just plain nice of him, as former master of this house, to invite her to have a cup of cocoa with him. Good cocoa.

He made his choice between going out in the hall and knocking on her door, and knocking on her door to the bathroom. He decided on the second procedure because he didn't want anyone to see him knocking on her door. So he entered the bathroom and tapped on the door that led to her room. "In a minute," he thought he heard her say. But then he knew he must have been wrong. It sounded more like "Come in." He hated people who knocked on doors and had to be told two or three times to come in, and it would make a bad impression if he started the friendship that way.

He opened the door, and immediately he saw how right he had been in thinking she had said "In a minute." For Miss Farnsworth was standing in the middle of the room, standing there all but nude. Mr. Winfield instantly knew that this was the end of any worthwhile life he had left.

There was cold murder in the girl's eyes, and loathing and contempt and the promise of the thought his name forever would evoke. She spoke to him: "Get out of here, you dirty old man."

He returned to his room and his chair. Slowly he took a cigarette out of his case, and did not light it. He did everything slowly. There was all the time in the world, too much of it, for him. He knew it would be hours before he would begin to hate himself. For a while he would just sit there and plan his own terror.

1934

Price's Always Open

The place where everybody would end up before going home was Price's. This was the second summer for Price's. Before that it had been a diner and an eyesore. The last man to run the diner had blown town owing everybody, and somehow or other that had put a curse on the place. No one, not even the creditors, wanted to open up again, and time and the weather got at the diner and for two years it had stood there, the windows all smashed by passing schoolboys, the paint gone, and the diner itself sagging in the middle like an old work horse. Then last summer Mr. Price got his bonus and he went into the all-night-restaurant business.

The first thing he did was to get permission to tear down the diner and put up his own place. It was a corner plot, and he built his place twice as wide as the diner had been. The Village Fathers were only too glad to have Mr. Price build. In other times they never would have let the place go the way the diner had. The neatness of the village was always commented upon by new summer people and bragged about by those who had been coming there for generations. But things being the way they were . . . So Mr. Price built a sort of rustic place, which, while not in keeping with the rest of the village architecture, was clean and attractive in its way. All the signboards were simulated shingles, and the lettering has been described as quaint. Mr. Price frankly admitted he got his idea from a chain of places in New York. There was one neon sign that stayed on all night, and it said, simply, "PRICE'S." Nothing about what Price's was; everyone knew.

Mr. Price had one leg, having left the other somewhere in a dressing station back of Château-Thierry. He was not a cook but a house painter, and he had had to employ a couple of short-order cooks from New York and Boston. But Mr. Price was always there. Not that anyone ever wondered about it, but it might have been interesting to find out just when he slept. He was at his position near the cash register all night, and he certainly was there at noon when the chauffeurs and a few summer-hotel clerks and people like that would come in for lunch. As a matter of fact, he did not need much sleep. No day passed without his leg bothering him, and seeing people took his mind off his leg. Best of all, he liked late at night.

Saturday night there was always a dance at the yacht club. That was a very late crowd. The dances were supposed to stop at one, but if the stricter older members had gone home, the young people would keep the orchestra for another hour or two, and even after that they would hang around while one of the boys played the piano. The boy who played the piano was Jackie Girard.

They were a nice bunch of kids, practically all of them, and Mr. Price had known their fathers and mothers for years, or many of them. Sometimes the wife's family had been coming to this island for years and years; then she married the husband, a stranger, and the husband and wife would start coming here and keep coming. Sometimes it was the husband who was old summer people. Most of the present younger crowd had been coming here every summer for fifteen, twenty years. One or two of them had been born here. But Jackie Girard was Mr. Price's favorite. He was born here, and unlike the others, he lived here all year round.

Jackie had a strange life with the summer people, and it probably was that that made Mr. Price feel closer to him than to the others. The others were nice and respectful, and they always said *Mister* Price, just as Jackie did. But they were summer people, and the winters were long. Not that Jackie was here in the winter any more, but at least he came home several times in the winter. Jackie was at college at Holy Cross, and naturally his holidays were spent here.

The strange life that Jackie had apparently did not seem strange to him. He was not a member of the yacht club, naturally. Jackie's father was a carpenter, the best in the village; the best out of three, it's true, but head and shoulders above the other two. Henry Girard was a French Canuck and had been in the Twenty-sixth Division with Mr. Price, but never an intimate of Mr. Price's. Jackie had three sisters; one older, two younger. Jackie's mother played the organ in the Catholic church. The older sister was married and lived in Worcester, and the younger ones were in high school. Anyway, Jackie was not a member of the yacht club, but he was almost always sure of being invited to one of the dinners before the regular Saturday-night dance. He was one of the clerks at the hotel, and that, plus an occasional five or ten from his sister in Worcester, gave him just enough money to pay for gas and his incidental expenses. He could hold his end up. The only trouble was, except for Saturday and Sunday, he did not have much end to hold up.

There were gatherings, if not parties, practically every night of the week. Every Thursday, for instance, the large group of young people would split up into smaller groups, sometimes three, four, five, and after dinner they would go to the boxing matches. Jackie was not invited to these small dinner parties. He had been invited two or three times, but his mother had told him he had better not go. For herself, she wished he could have gone, but his father would not have approved. After Jackie had regretted the few invitations he got, the summer people figured it out that all he cared about was the yacht-club dances. He was the only town boy who was invited to yacht-club dances, and they figured that that was all he wanted. It did not take them long to decide that this was as it should be all around. They decided that Jackie would feel embarrassed at the smaller parties, but that he did not need to feel embarrassed at the club dances, because in a sense he was earning his way by playing such perfectly marvelous piano. But this was not the way Mr. Price saw it.

Almost every night but Saturday Jackie would drop in. Two nights a week he had been to the movies, which changed twice a week, but Mr. Price at first wondered what Jackie would do to kill time the other nights. Jackie would show up around eleven-thirty and sit at the counter until some of the summer crowd began to arrive. They would yell at him, "Hi, Jackie! Hi, keed! How's it, Jackie?" And Jackie would swing around on his stool, and they would yell at him to come on over and sit at a table with them. And he would sit at the table with whichever group arrived first. In the early part of the summer that did not mean any special group, because when the other groups would arrive, they would put all the tables together and form one party. Then there would be some bickering about the bill, and more than once Mr. Price saw Jackie grab the check for the whole party. It was not exactly a big check; you could not eat much more than forty cents' worth at Mr. Price's without making a pig of yourself, and the usual order was a cereal, half-milk-half-cream, and a cup of coffee; total, twenty cents. But you take fourteen of those orders and you have a day's pay for Jackie.

As the summer passed, however, the large group did break into well-defined smaller groups; one of six, several of four. By August there would be the same foursomes every night, and of these one included the Leech girl.

The Leeches were not old people in the sense that some of them were. The Leeches belonged to the newcomers who first summered in this place in 1930 and 1931. They had come from one of the more famous resorts. Louise Leech was about twelve when her family first began to come to this place. But now she was eighteen or nineteen. She had a Buick convertible coupé. She was a New York girl, whereas most of the other boys and girls were not New Yorkers; they all went to the same schools and colleges, but they did not come from the same home towns. Some came from as far west as Denver, as Mr. Price knew from cashing their checks. And even what few New York girls did come to this place were not New

York friends of the Leeches. Mr. Leech was here only on week-ends and his wife was away most of the time, visiting friends who had not had to give up Narragansett. Louise herself was away a good deal of time.

It was easy to see, the first summer Louise was grown up, that she was discontented. She did not quite fit in with the rest of the crowd, and she not only knew it but she was content not to make the best of it. Mr. Price could hear the others, the first summer he was in business, making remarks about Louise and her thinking she was too good for this place. And they had been saying something like it the early part of this summer, too. But after the Fourth of July, somewhere around there, they began to say better things about her. Mostly they said she really wasn't so bad when you got to know her. To which a few of the girls said, "Who wants to?" And others said, "She doesn't like us any better. We're still not good enough for her. But Sandy is." Which did explain a lot.

Sandy—Sandy Hall—was from Chicago, but what with prep school and college and this place and vacation trips, he probably had not spent a hundred days in Chicago in the last seven years. In a bathing suit he was almost skinny, except for his shoulders; he looked cold, he was so thin. But Mr. Price had seen him in action one night when one of the Portuguese fishermen came in drunk and got profane in a different way from the way the summer people did. Sandy had got up and let the Portuguese have two fast hard punches in the face, and the fisherman went down and stayed down. Sandy looked at the man on the floor—it was hard to tell how long he looked at him—and suddenly he kicked him. The man was already out, and so there was no need to kick him, but the kick had several results. One was that Mr. Price brought a blackjack to work the next night. The other result was something Mr. Price noticed on Louise's face.

He had not had much time to take it all in, as he had had to leave the cash register to help the night counterman drag the fisherman out of the place. But he remembered the expression on the girl's face. It began to appear when the fisherman went down from the punches, and when Sandy kicked the man, it was all there. Mr. Price, standing where he did, was the only one who caught it. He thought of it later as the way a girl would look the first time she saw Babe Ruth hit a home run, provided she cared about home runs. Or the way she would look if someone gave her a bucketful of diamonds. And other ways, that would come with experiences that Mr. Price was sure Louise never had had.

Sandy had not come with Louise that night, but Mr. Price noticed she went home with him. And after that night they were always together. They were part of a foursome of whom the other two were the dullest young people in the crowd. It took Mr. Price some time to determine why this was, but eventually he did figure it. The foursome would come into Price's, and Louise and Sandy would watch the others while they ordered; then Sandy would say he and Louise wanted the same, and from then on neither Sandy nor Louise would pay any attention to the other two. Stooges.

Another thing that Mr. Price noticed was that Jackie could not keep his eyes off Louise.

Along about the latter part of August, it was so obvious that one night Mr. Price kidded Jackie about it. It was one of the nights Jackie dropped in by himself, and Mr. Price said, "Well, she isn't here yet."

"Who isn't here?"

"The Leech girl."

"Oh," said Jackie. "Why, did anybody say anything to you? Is that how you knew I liked her?"

"No. Figured it out for myself. I have eyes."

"You're a regular Walter Winchell. But don't say anything, Mr. Price."

"What the hell would I say, and who to?"

"I'll be back," said Jackie. He was gone for more than an hour, and when he returned the crowd was there. They all yelled as usual, but this time one of the girls added, "Jackie's tight." He was, rather. He had a somewhat silly grin on his face, and his nice teeth made a line from ear to ear. Several tables wanted him to join them and they were friendly about it. But he went to the table where sat Louise and Sandy and the others.

"Do you mind if I sit down?" he said.

"Do you mind?" said Sandy.

"No," said Louise.

"Thank you. Thank you," said Jackie. "Go fights?"

"Mm-hmm," said Sandy.

"Any good? Who won?"

"The nigger from New Bedford beat the townie," said Sandy. "Kicked the Jesus out of him."

"Oh, uh townie. You mean Bobbie Lawless. He's nice guy. Za friend of mine. I used to go to high school—"

"He's yellow," said Sandy.

"Certainly was," said Louise.

"Nope. Not yellow. Not Bobbie. I used to go to high school with Bobbie. Plain same football team."

"Where do you go to school now?" said Sandy.

"Holy Cross. We're gonna beat you this year."

"What is Holy Cross?" said Louise.

Sandy laughed. Jackie looked at her with tired eyes.

"No, really, what is it?"

" 'Tsa college. It's where I go to college. Dint you ever hear of Holy Cross? Give another hoya and a choo-choo rah rah—"

"O.K.," said Sandy.

"I'll sing if I wanta. I'll sing one of your songs. Oh, hit the line for Harvard, for Harvard wins today—"

"Oh, go away," said Sandy.

"Yes, for God's *sake*," said Louise.

"Oh, very well, Miss Leech. Very well." Jackie put his hands on the table to steady himself as he got to his feet, but he stared down into her eyes and for two seconds he was sober.

"Come on, Jackie, you're stewed." Mr. Price had come around from the cash register and had taken Jackie by the right arm. At that moment Sandy lashed out with a right-hand punch, and Jackie fell down. But he had hardly reached the floor before Mr. Price snapped his blackjack from his pocket and slapped it down on the front of Sandy's head. Sandy went down and there was blood.

"Anybody else?" said Mr. Price. By this time the night counterman had swung himself over the counter, and in his hand was a baseball bat, all nicked where it had been used for tamping down ice around milk cans. None of the summer crowd made a move; then Mr. Price spoke to two of the young men. "Get your friend outa here, and get out, the whole goddam bunch of you." He stood where he was, he and the counterman, and watched the girls picking up their wraps.

"Aren't you going to do anything?" Louise screamed. "Chuck! Ted! All of you!"

"You get out or I'll throw you out," said Mr. Price. She left.

There were murmurs as well as the sounds of the cars starting. Thinking it over, Mr. Price agreed with himself that those would be the last sounds he ever expected to hear from the summer crowd.

1937

Are We Leaving Tomorrow?

It was cool, quite cool, the way the weather is likely to be at an in-between resort when the Florida season is over but the Northern summer season has not yet begun. Every morning the tall young man and his young wife would come down the steps of the porch and go for their walk. They would go to the mounting block where the riders would start for the trails. The tall young man and his wife would stand not too close to the block, not speaking to anyone; just watching. But there might have been a little in his attitude, in his manner, of a man who felt that he was starting the riders, as though his presence there made their start official. He would stand there, hatless and tan, chin down almost to his chest, his hands dug deep in the pockets of his handsome tweed topcoat. His wife would stand beside him with her arm in his, and when she would speak to him she would put her face in front of him and look up. Almost always his answer would be a smile and a nod, or perhaps a single word that expressed all he wanted to put into words. They would watch the riders for a while, and then they would stroll over to the first tee of the men's golf course to watch the golfers start off. There it would be the same: not much talk, and the slightly superior manner or attitude. After they had watched their quota of golfers they would go back to the porch and she would go up to their rooms and a Negro bellboy would bring him his papers, the *Montreal Star* and the *New York Times*. He would sit there lazily looking at the papers, never so interested in a news item that he would not look up at every person who came in or went out of the hotel, or passed his chair on the porch. He watched every car come up the short winding drive, watched the people get in and out, watched the car drive away; then when there was no human activity he would return to his paper, holding it rather far away, and on his face and in his eyes behind the gold-rimmed spectacles there was always the same suspicion of a smile.

He would go to his room before lunch, and they would come down together. After lunch, like most everyone else, they would retire, apparently for a nap, not to appear until the cocktail hour. They would be the first, usually, in the small, cheery bar, and until it was time to change for dinner he would have a highball glass, constantly refilled, in his hand. He drank slowly, sipping teaspoonfuls at a time. In that time she might drink two light highballs while he was drinking eight. She always seemed to have one of the magazines of large format in her lap, but at these times it was she who would look up, while he hardly turned his head.

Not long after they came she began to speak to people; to bow and pass the time of day. She was a pleasant, friendly little woman, not yet thirty. Her eyes were too pretty for the rest of her face; in sleep she must have been very plain indeed, and her skin was sensitive to the sun. She had good bones—lovely hands and feet—and when she was in sweater and skirt her figure always got a second look from the golfers and riders.

Their name was Campbell—Douglas Campbell, and Sheila. They were the youngest people over fifteen in the hotel. There were a few children, but most of the guests were forty or thereabouts. One afternoon the Campbells were in the bar and a woman came in and after hesitating at the entrance she said, "Good afternoon, Mrs. Campbell. You didn't happen to see my husband?"

"No, I didn't," said Mrs. Campbell.

The woman came closer slowly and put her hand on the back of a chair near them. "I was afraid I'd missed him," she said to no one; then suddenly she said, "Do you mind if I sit with you while he comes?"

"No, not at all," said Mrs. Campbell.

"Please do," said Campbell. He got to his feet and stood very erect. He set his glass on the little table and put his hands behind his back.

"I'm sorry I don't remember your name," said Mrs. Campbell.

"Mrs. Loomis."

Mrs. Campbell introduced her husband, who said, "Wouldn't you like a cocktail meanwhile?"

Mrs. Loomis thought a moment and said she would—a dry Daiquiri. Then Campbell sat down, picking up his drink and beginning to sip.

"I think we were the first here, as usual," said Mrs. Campbell, "so we couldn't have missed Mr. Loomis."

"Oh, it's all right. One of us is always late, but it isn't important. That's why I like it here. The general air of informality." She smiled. "I've never seen you here before. Is this your first year?"

"Our first year," said Mrs. Campbell.

"From New York?"

"Montreal," said Mrs. Campbell.

"Oh, Canadians. I met some awfully nice Canadians in Palm Beach this winter," said Mrs. Loomis. She named them off, and Mrs. Campbell said they knew them, and he smiled and nodded. Then Mrs. Loomis tried to remember the names of some other people she knew in Montreal (they turned out to have been Toronto people), and Mr. Loomis arrived.

A white-haired man, a trifle heavy and about fifty, Mr. Loomis wore young men's clothes. He was brown and heavy lidded. He had good manners. It was he who corrected his wife about the people from Montreal who actually were from Toronto. That was the first time the Loomises and the Campbells had done more than speak in passing, and Mrs. Campbell was almost gay that afternoon.

The Campbells did not come down to dinner that evening, but they were out for their stroll the next morning. Mr. Loomis waved to them at the first tee, and they waved—*she* waved, Campbell nodded. They did not appear for cocktails that afternoon. For the next few days they took their stroll, but they had their meals in their room. The next time they came to the cocktail lounge they took a small table at the side of the bar, where there was room only for the table and two chairs. No one spoke to them, but that night was one of the nights when the hotel showed movies in the ballroom, and after the movie the Loomises fell in with them and insisted on buying them a drink, just a nightcap. That was the way it was.

Mr. Loomis brought out his cigar case and offered Mr. Campbell a cigar, which was declined, and gave the orders for drinks, "Scotch, Scotch, Scotch, and a Cuba Libre." Mrs. Loomis was having the Cuba Libre. As the waiter took the order Mr. Campbell said, "And bring the bottle."

There was a fraction of a second's incredulity in Mr. Loomis's face; incredulity, or more likely doubt that he had heard his own ears. But he said, "Yes, bring the bottle." Then they talked about the picture. It had been a terrible picture, they all agreed. The Loomises said it was too bad, too, because they had crossed with the star two years ago and she had seemed awfully nice, not at all what you'd expect a movie star to be like. They all agreed that the Mickey Mouse was good, although Mr. Loomis said he was getting a little tired of Mickey Mouse. Their drinks came, and Mrs. Loomis was somewhat apologetic about her drink, but ever since she had been in Cuba she'd developed a taste for rum, always rum. "And before that gin," said Mr. Loomis. Mr. Campbell's glass was empty and he called the waiter to bring some more ice and another Cuba Libre, and he replenished the highball glasses from the bottle of Scotch on the table.

"Now this was my idea," said Mr. Loomis.

"Only the first one," said Mr. Campbell. They let it go at that, and the ladies returned to the subject of the star of the picture, and soon Mr. Loomis joined in. They got all mixed up in the star's matrimonial record, which inevitably brought up the names of other movie stars and *their* matrimonial records. Mr. and Mrs. Loomis provided the statistics, and Mrs. Campbell would say yes or no as the statement or opinion required. Mr. Campbell sipped his drink wordlessly until the Loomises, who had been married a long time, became simultaneously aware of Mr. Campbell's silence, and they began directing their remarks at him. The Loomises were not satisfied with Mr. Campbell's ready assents. They would address the first few words of a remark to the young wife, because she had been such a polite listener, but then they would turn to Mr. Campbell and most of what they had to say was said to him.

For a while he would smile and murmur "Mmhmm," more or less into his glass. Then it seemed after a few minutes that he could hardly wait for them to end an item or an anecdote. He began to nod before it was time to nod, and he would keep nodding, and he would say, "Yes, yes, yes," very rapidly. Presently, in the middle of an anecdote, his eyes, which had been growing brighter, became very bright. He put down his drink and leaned forward, one hand clasping and unclasping the other. "And—yes—and—yes," he kept saying, until Mrs. Loomis had finished her story. Then he leaned farther forward and stared at Mrs. Loomis, with that bright smile and with his breathing become short and fast.

"Can I tell you a story?" he said.

Mrs. Loomis beamed. "Why, of course."

Then Campbell told a story. It had in it a priest, female anatomy, improbable situations, a cuckold, unprintable words, and no point.

Long before Campbell finished his story Loomis was frowning, glancing at his wife and at Campbell's wife, seeming to listen to Campbell but always glancing at the two women. Mrs. Loomis could not look away; Campbell was telling her story, and he looked at no one else. While Mrs. Campbell, the moment the story was begun, picked up her drink, took a sip, and put the glass on the table and kept her eyes on it until Campbell signaled by his chuckling that the story was at an end.

He kept chuckling and looking at Mrs. Loomis after he had finished, and then he smiled at Loomis. "Huh," came from Loomis, and on his face a muscular smile. "Well, dear," he said. "Think it's about time—"

"Yes," said Mrs. Loomis. "Thank you so much. Good night, Mrs. Campbell, and good night." Campbell stood up, erect, bowing.

When they were entirely out of the room he sat down and crossed his legs. He lit a cigarette and resumed his drinking and stared at the opposite wall. She watched him. His eyes did not even move when he raised his glass to his mouth.

"Oh," she said suddenly. "I wonder if the man is still there at the travel desk. I forgot all about the tickets for tomorrow."

"Tomorrow? Are we leaving tomorrow?"

"Yes."

He stood up and pulled the table out of her way, and when she had left he sat down to wait for her.

1938

Pal Joey

Dear Pal Ted:

Well at last I am getting around to knocking off a line or two to let you know how much I appprisiate it you sending me that wire on opening nite. Dont think because I didnt answer before I didnt apprisiate it because that is far from the case. But I guess you know that because if you knew when I was opening you surely must be aware how busy Ive been ever since opening nite. I figure you read in *Variety* what date I was opening in which case I figure you have seen the write ups since then telling how busy Ive been and believe me its no exagerton.

Well maybe it seems a long time since opening nite and in a way it does to me too. It will only be five weeks this coming Friday but it seems longer considering all that has happened to your old pal Joey. Its hard to believe that under two months ago Joey was strictly from hunger as they say but I was. The last time I saw you (August) remember the panic was on. I figured things would begin to break a little better around August but no. A couple spots where I figured I would fit in didnt open at all on acct of bankroll trouble and that was why I left town and came out this way. I figured you live in a small town in Michigan and you can stay away from the hot spots because there arent any and that way you save money. I was correct but I sure didnt figure the panic would stay on as long as it did. I finely sold the jalloppy and hocked my diamond ring the minute I heard there would be a chance down this way. I never was in Ohio before but maybe I will never be any place else. At least I like it enough to remain here the remainder of my life but of course if NBC is listening in Im only kidding.

Well I heard about this spot through a little mouse I got to know up in Michigan. She told me about this spot as it is her home town altho spending her vacation every year in Michigan. I was to a party one nite (private) and they finely got me to sing a few numbers for them and the mouse couldn't take her eyes off me. She sat over in one corner of the room not paying any attenton to the dope she was with until finely it got so even he noticed it and began making cracks but loud. I burned but went on singing and playing but he got too loud and I had to stop in the middle of a number and I said right at him if he didnt like it why didnt he try himself. Perhaps he could do better. The others at the party got sore at him and told him to pipe down but that only made him madder and the others told me to go ahead and not pay any attenton to him. So I did. Then when I got finished with a few more numbers I looked around and the heel wasnt there but the mouse was. She didnt give me a hand but I could tell she was more impress than some that were beating their paws off. So I went over to her and told her I was sorry if it embarrassed her me calling attention to her dope boy friend but she said he wasnt a boy friend. I said well I figured that. I said she looked as if she could do better than him and she said, "you for instance" and I said well yes. We laughed and got along fine and I took her home. She was staying with her grandmother and grandfather, two respectible old married people that lived there all their life. They were too damn respectible for me. They watched her like a hawk and one oclock was the latest she could be out. That to me is the dumbest way to treat that kind of a mouse. If its going to happen it can happen before nine oclock and if it isnt going to happen it isnt going to no matter if you stay out till nine oclock the next morning. But whats the use of being old if you cant be dumb? So anyway Nan told me about this spot down here and knew the asst mgr of the hotel where the spot is and she said she would give me a send in and if I didnt hold them up for too much of the ready she was sure I could get the job. I sing and play every afternoon in the cocktail bar and at night I relieve the band in the ballroom. Anyway I figured I would have to freshen up the old wardrobe so I had to get rid of the jalloppy and hock my diamond ring. I made the trip to Ohio with Nan in her own jalloppy which isnt exactly a jalloppy I might add. Its a 37 Plymouth conv coop. It took us three days to go from Mich. to Ohio but Ill thank you not to ask any questions about my private life.

This asst mgr auditioned me when we finely arrived and I knew right away I was in because he asked me for a couple of old numbers like Everybody Step and Swanee and a Jerry Kern medley and he was a Carmichael fan. Everything he asked me for I gave him and of course I put up a nice appearance being sunburned and a white coat from the proseeds of selling the jalloppy and hocking the ring. I rehearsed with the band altho Collins the leader hates my guts and finely I talked this asst mgr into letting me do a single irregardless of the band and he did.

Well you might say I ran the opening nite. I m.c'd and they had a couple kids from a local dancing school doing tap, one of them not bad altho no serious competiton for Ginger Rogers. They were only on for the first week. They also had another mouse who was with the band, living with the drummer. She tried to be like Maxine. Well she wasnt even colored, thats how much like Maxine she was. The local 400 turned out for the opening nite and inside a week I was besieged with offers to entertain at private parties which I do nearly every Sunday as the bar and ballroom are not open Sunday or at least I do not work. In additon to the job at the hotel and the private parties you probably have read about the radio job. I went on sustaining the first week and by the end of the second week I got myself a nice little commercial. I am on just before the local station hooks up with NBC Blue Network five nites a week but I dont think you can catch me in New York. Not yet! My sponsor is the Acme Credit Jewellery Company but I only have eight more weeks to go with them then I am free to negosiate with a better sponsor. Still Im not complaining. Your old pal Joey is doing all right for himself. I get a due bill at the hotel and what they pay me in additon aint hay. I also have the radio spot and the private parties. I went for a second hand Lasalle coop and I am thinking of joining the country club. I go there all the time with some of the local 400 so I figure I might as well join but will wait till I make sure I am going to stay here. I get my picture in the paper and write ups so much that I dont even bother to put them in my scrap book any more.

The crowd at the club are always ribbing me about it and accuse me of having the reporters on my payroll but I just tell them no, not the reporters, the editors. I am a little sore at one of the papers because the local Winchell links my name constantly with the name of a very sweet kid that I go to the club and play golf with. Not that it isnt true. We see each other all the time and she comes to the hotel practically every nite with a party and when Im through for the nite we usely take a ride out to a late spot out in the country. Her father is president of the second largest bank. It is the oldest. The biggest bank was formally two banks but they merged. Her name is Jean Spencer and a sweeter kid never lived. I really go for her. But this local Winchell took a personal dislike to me and made a couple cracks about us. One was "That personality boy at a downtown hotel has aired the femme that got him the job and is now trying to move into society." Me trying to move in to society! Society moved in on me is more like it. Jean was burned because she was afraid her father might see the item and when I meet her father I dont want him to have the wrong impression. I think the colyumist got the item from my ex-friend Nan. I didnt see much of her when I was rehearsing and the afternoon of opening nite she called up and said she wanted to come but what the hell could I do? Ask for a big table when they were getting $5 a head cover charge? I was glad enough to get the job without asking too many favors. Then a week or so later she called up and asked me could I let her have $50. I asked her what for and she hung up. Well if she didnt even want to do me the curtesy to tell me what for I wasnt going to follow her around begging her to take it. But I gave it a few days thought and decided to let her have it but when I phoned her they said she quit her job and left town. I understand from Schall the asst mgr that she sold her Plymouth and went to N.Y. Her name is Nan Hennessey so if you run into her anywhere youll know her. She could be worse, that is worse on the eye, a little dumb tho.

Well pally, they will be billing me for stealing all their writing paper if I dont quit this. Just to show you I dont forget I inclose $30. Ill let you have the rest as soon as possible. Any time I can help you out the same way just let me know and you can count on me. I guess you kissed that fifty goodbye but that isnt the way I do things. But I guess you know that, hey pal?

All the best from
Pal Joey
1938

The Gentleman in the Tan Suit

Robert, she supposed, was well dressed. Well dressed for San Francisco. He was not well dressed according to the standards Mary had had to adopt as Mr. Monkton's secretary. In the years that she had been Mr. Monkton's secretary Mary had had to learn about Charvet and Peal and those people. She knew how much it cost to have a pair of shoes sent back to Peal for rebuilding. She knew it cost two or three dollars more than the shoes Robert was wearing would cost new. Mr. Monkton was one of the best-dressed men downtown, and one thing she had noticed about Mr. Monkton's clothes was that no matter what he wore in the country (and she knew little enough about that), his city clothes were not the kind that would have to be pressed after a single wearing. That was the way Robert's clothes impressed her in the first few seconds. The suit was too light a tan, so light that she did not see how he could keep it clean after one ride in a taxi, and already it had wrinkles at the side of the knee and in the elbows that would not disappear into the cloth. She noticed that his shirt was only half a shade away from the tan of the suit; the tie was tan with white figures, the socks were silk, tan silk. The shoes were tan. The hat was tan, with only the beginning of finger marks where it was dented in the crown. Kay probably thought he dressed wonderfully. Mary thought it was awful.

Mary had come home and found him here. Not to her surprise; she knew they were coming, Kay and Robert. She had wondered a little about the young man's curiosity, what kind of curiosity would make him want to meet his wife's sister after he had been married a year, and make him want it so much that he would be willing to spend so much money. Mary had written in answer to Kay's letter, telling her that unless it was New York they wanted to see, why not save the money and she would come out to San Francisco when Mr. Monkton went abroad in October. But Kay had replied that all their plans had been made—Robert had made them. His pay cut had been restored, his father had given them money for a new car, which they did not need, and—this was something Mary supplied without any information from her younger sister—apparently they had not done any planning towards having a baby. The money was there, so Mary told them to come on.

Robert was alone in the apartment when Mary arrived there. He was sitting on the davenport, with one arm along the arm of the davenport, and the other arm along the back. It looked like a position that had just been assumed, but when Mary saw how many cigarettes had been smoked and noticed that there was no impression in any of the chairs or elsewhere in the davenport, she thought she had an idea what kind of young man her sister had married. She had seen many, many young men waiting for Mr. Monkton, sitting in that same position, not insulted when Mr. Monkton would go out with his hat on, ignoring them. They would wait in the reception-room for Mary and ask for another appointment, and another, if necessary, until Mr. Monkton would keep an appointment, or talk to them in the elevator or somewhere. Young men who sat that way almost always got to see Mr. Monkton. Usually that was as much as they did get, but Mary knew that they felt they had made a contact. And so Mary knew her sister had married a young man who knew how to wait. What they said about the men who made them wait was another matter; she had heard them more than once at Schrafft's and places like that, sometimes identifying Mr. Monkton by name: "Why, I waited for that bastard Monkton. . . ." Mary, when she wasn't too tired, delighted in passing close to young men whom she thus overheard, knowing they would recognize her and get the lump because they could not be sure she had not overheard them.

Robert turned his head when she let herself in the apartment. He did not stand until he had a look at her. He laughed and showed his teeth. Mary knew him for the kind of young man who would go to his dentist regularly just to be able to say (truthfully) that dentists would starve if everybody had teeth like his. His teeth were so good and so obviously good all the way back that there was no suspense to watching them. She wondered if he ever bit Kay.

"You're Mary, I'll bet," he said.

"Yes," she said. "And Robert. How are you, Robert? I'm so glad to see you." She struck the same note on glad and see, which took the curse off the sentence.

"I'm glad to see you, too, Mary," he said.

She wondered whether there was any special reason, the way he said it. They shook hands a long time, and his not kissing her right away was something in his favor. "Do I kiss my sister-in-law?" he said.

"Mm-hmm." She extended her cheek.

He was a little embarrassed after kissing her. "That's the first girl outside of Kay I've kissed since God knows when. Anyway two years is a conservative estimate."

What did he want? Did he want her to relay that to Kay, or was he lying, or was he trying to boast about his fidelity? "Well, that's pretty good for these times," she said.

"Good, hell, it's perfect," he said. "Kay will be here any minute. She's supposed to be here now, but I guess she had to stop and buy something, is my guess."

"How about a cocktail?"

"Not for me, thanks," he said. "If you want one."

"We'll wait till Kay gets here, then," she said.

"I only drink beer except on state occasions. Not that this—"

"Well, I should think!"

"Well, you know, like football games or sumpn. Kay likes a cocktail, though. You bet. She makes about the only decent cocktail I ever drank. She's going to be awfully glad to see you. Gee, five years. I guess she was only eighteen when you saw her last time."

"You understand about my not going home for the wedding, don't you, Robert?"

"Sure. I said to Kay, I said, 'Listen, a job's a job these days. You can't expect your sister to just up and—' "

"Oh. Did you have to explain? I mean apologize for me?"

"Well, frankly, you know. It's a year ago now, so it's all over and done with, but, yes, in a way. I didn't have to—you wouldn't call it apologize, but Kay couldn't get it through her head that you couldn't just up and go, right in the middle of winter. I said to her, 'Listen,' I said, 'this Mr. Monkton'—your boss—'I happen to know he's a big shot, and secretary to him probably means a twenty-four-hour-a-day job.' She got it finally. "Hell, your aunt and uncle, they were swell." He stopped abruptly and sat down. He looked up at Mary. "You know what?"

"What?"

"You know what suddenly occurred to me—oh, after we were married. I don't know how to put this."

"You can say anything to me."

"Well, I didn't realize till after we were married why she wanted you to be there." He shook his head. "You know, Kay didn't know a goddamn thing. You know?"

"Oh." She sat beside him. "I thought girls today—I suppose I've been living in New York such a long time."

"Not Kay. And your aunt never told her anything."

"But twenty-two years old."

"That's what I thought."

"Oh, I should have gone home. How about now?"

He smiled. "Okay now. Yes, she's all right now. We've been married a year, you know." He stood up. "Well, I guess this is a hell of a way to talk the first ten minutes I meet my wife's sister. But that was the only thing—I admit I sort of held it against you myself, but I don't any more."

"I *couldn't* be so thoughtless."

"*It's* all right," he said. "Honestly, there's nothing to worry about any more. See, it's all *right* now, so I thought Kay and I—it'd be a good idea for her to come East and see you, now that everything's all right."

Mary looked at him and burst into tears.

1935

Good-by, Herman

Miller was putting his key in the lock. He had two afternoon papers folded under one arm, and a package—two dress shirts which he had picked up at the laundry because he was going out that night. Just when the ridges of the key were fitting properly, the door was swung open and it was his wife. She was frowning. "Hello," he said.

She held up her finger. "Come in the bedroom," she said. She was distressed about something. Throwing his hat on a chair in the foyer, he followed her to the bedroom. She turned and faced him as he put down his bundle and began taking off his coat.

"What's up?" he said.

"There's a man in there. He came to see you. He's been here for an hour and he's driving me crazy."

"Who is he? What's it all about?"

"He's from Lancaster, and he said he was a friend of your father's."

"Well, has he been causing any trouble?"

"His name is Wasserfogel, or something like that."

"Oh, hell. I know. Herman Wasservogel. He was my father's barber. I knew he was coming. I just forgot to tell you."

"Oh, you did. Well, thanks for a lovely hour. Hereafter, when you're expecting somebody, I wish you'd let me know beforehand. I tried to reach you at the office. Where were you? I tried everywhere I could think of. You don't know what it is to suddenly have a perfectly strange man—"

"I'm sorry, darling. I just forgot. I'll go in."

He went to the living-room, and there sat a little old man. In his lap was a small package, round which he had wrapped his hands. He was looking down at the package, and there was a faint smile on his face, which Miller knew to be the man's customary expression. His feet, in high, black shoes, were flat on the floor and parallel with each other, and

Miller guessed that this was the way the little old man had been sitting ever since he first arrived.

"Herman, how are you? I'm sorry I'm late."

"Oh, that's all right. How are you, Paul?"

"Fine. You're looking fine, Herman. I got your letter and I forgot to tell Elsie. I guess you know each other by now," he said as Elsie came into the room and sat down. "My wife, Elsie, this is Herman Wasservogel, an old friend of mine."

"Pleased to meet you," said Herman.

Elsie lit a cigarette.

"How about a drink, Herman? A little schnapps? Glass of beer?"

"No, thank you, Paul. I just came; I wanted to bring this here. I just thought maybe you would want it."

"I was sorry I didn't see you when I was home for the funeral, but you know how it is. It's such a big family, I never got around to the shop."

"Henry was in. I shaved him three times."

"Yes, Henry was there longer than I was. I was only there overnight. I had to come right back to New York after the funeral. Sure you won't have a beer?"

"No, I just wanted to bring this in to give to you." Herman stood up and handed the little package to Paul.

"Gee, thanks a lot, Herman."

"What's that? Mr. Wasserfogel wouldn't show it to me. It's all very mysterious." Elsie spoke without looking at Herman, not even when she mentioned his name.

"Oh, he probably thought I'd told you."

Herman stood while Paul undid the package, revealing a shaving mug. "This was my father's. Herman shaved him every day of his life, I guess."

"Well, not every day. The Daddy didn't start shaving till he was I guess eighteen years old, and he used to go away a lot. But I guess I shaved him more than all the other barbers put together."

"Damn right you did. Dad always swore by you, Herman."

"Yes, I guess that's right," said Herman.

"See, Elsie?" said Paul, holding up the mug. He read the gold lettering: " 'J. D. Miller, M.D.' "

"Mm. Why do you get it? You're not the oldest boy. Henry's older than you," said Elsie.

Herman looked at her and then at Paul. He frowned a little. "Paul, will you give me a favor? I don't want Henry to know it that I give you this mug. After the Daddy died, I said, 'Which one will I give the mug to?' Henry was entitled to it, being the oldest and all. In a way he should have got it. But not saying anything against Henry—well, I don't know."

"Mr. Wasserfogel liked you better than he did Henry, isn't that it, Mr. Wasserfogel?" said Elsie.

"Oh, well," said Herman.

"Don't you worry, Herman, I'll keep quiet about it. I never see Henry anyway," said Paul.

"The brush I didn't bring. Doc needed a new one this long time, and I used to say to him, 'Doc, are you so poor yet you won't even buy a new shaving brush?' 'I am,' he'd say to me. 'Well,' I said, 'I'll give you one out of my own pocket for a gift.' 'You do,' he'd say, 'and I'll stop coming here. I'll go to the hotel.' Only joking, we were, Mrs. Miller. The Doc was always saying he'd stop coming and go to the hotel, but I knew better. He was always making out like my razors needed sharpening, or I ought to get new lights for my shop, or I was shaving him too close. Complain, complain, complain. Then around the first of last year I noticed how he'd come in, and all he'd say was, 'Hello, Herman. Once over, not too close,' and that's all he'd say. I knew he was a sick man. He knew it, too."

"Yes, you're right," said Paul. "When'd you get in, Herman?"

"Just today. I came by bus."

"When are you going back? I'd like to see some more of you before you go away. Elsie and I, we're going out tonight, but tomorrow night—"

"Not tomorrow night. Tomorrow night is Hazel's," said Elsie.

"Oh, I don't have to go to that," said Paul. "Where are you stopping, Herman?"

"Well, to tell you the truth, I ain't stopping. I'm going back to Lancaster this evening."

"Why, no! You can't. You just got here. You ought to stick around, see the sights. Come down to my office and I'll show you Wall Street."

"I guess I know enough about Wall Street; all I want to know. If it wasn't for Wall Street, I wouldn't be barbering at my age. No. Thanks very much, Paul, but I got to get back. Got to open the shop in the morning. I only have this relief man for one day. Young Joe Meyers. He's a barber now."

"Well, what the hell? Keep him on for another day or two. I'll pay him. You've got to stick around. How long is it since you've been to New York?"

"Nineteen years last March I was here, when young Hermie went to France with the Army."

"Herman had a son. He was killed in the war."

"He'd be forty years old, a grown man," said Herman. "No. Thank you, Paul, but I think I better be going. I wanted to take a walk down to where the bus leaves from. I didn't get my walk in today yet, and that will give me the chance to see New York City."

"Oh, come on, Herman."

"Don't be so insistent, Paul. You can see Mr. Wasserfogel wants to go back to Lancaster. I'll leave you alone for a few minutes. I've got to start dressing. But not too long, Paul. We've got to go all the way down to Ninth Street. Good-by, Mr. Wasserfogel. I hope we'll see you again sometime. And thank you for bringing Paul the cup. It was very sweet of you."

"Oh, that's all right, Mrs. Miller."

"Well, I really must go," said Elsie.

"I'll be in in a minute," said Paul. "Herman, you sure you won't change your mind?"

"No, Paul. Thank you, but I have the shop to think of. And you better go in and wash up, or you'll catch the dickens."

Paul tried a laugh. "Oh, Elsie isn't always like that. She's just fidgety today. You know how women get."

"Oh, sure, Paul. She's a nice girl. Very pretty-looking. Well."

"If you change your mind—"

"Nope."

"We're in the phone book."

"Nope."

"Well, just remember, if you *do* change your mind; and I really don't know how to thank you, Herman. You know I mean it, how much I appreciate this."

"Well, your Dad was always good to me. So were you, Paul. Only don't tell Henry."

"That's a promise, Herman. Good-by, Herman. Good luck, and I hope I'll see you soon. I may get down to Lancaster this fall, and I'll surely look you up this time."

"Mm. Well, *auf Wiedersehen*, Paul."

"*Auf Wiedersehen*, Herman."

Paul watched Herman going the short distance to the elevator. He pushed the button, waited a few seconds until the elevator got there, and then he got in without looking back. "Good-by, Herman," Paul called, but he was sure Herman did not hear him.

1937

Olive

Miss Bishop had been the hotel's guest six months without having put in or received a call worth listening in on. Within a month of Miss Bishop's checking in, Olive, the day operator, knew all the regulars, outgoing and incoming: the hairdresser in East Forty-seventh Street, the bank downtown, the drycleaner, the drugstore, and the Jersey City number. The Jersey City number Olive came to know as Miss Bishop's aunt; a stingy old woman, Olive thought. When Miss Bishop put in a call for the Jersey City number, the call would last ten minutes and sometimes more, but when the aunt's voice asked for Miss Bishop the call stayed within three minutes.

It was always the same. The call would come in at nine or thereabouts, just after Miss Bishop had asked for a waiter to take away the breakfast things: "Olive, will you send someone up please for the breakfast dishes?" An hour later Miss Bishop would appear at the desk and cash a small check, usually ten dollars. Then she would sit and wait for her aunt, who might arrive five minutes later, or might keep Miss Bishop waiting a couple of hours. When the old woman arrived Miss Bishop would go out with her and be gone until three in the afternoon, returning with a few small packages. She would stop at the news-stand and Charlie would hand her the *Sun*, and she would sit reading it in the chair she preferred, in a corner of the small lobby. She would be reading five or ten minutes and Colonel Browder would join her.

Colonel Browder was easily thirty years older than Miss Bishop, but they got along very well together. Miss Bishop never smoked unless Colonel Browder was with her—at least not in the lobby or any of the public part of the hotel. As far as Olive knew, Miss Bishop may have smoked her head off in her room. She must have done something in her room, she spent so much time there.

The Colonel and Miss Bishop were the only guests in the hotel to take tea, and it was understood that the tea and cinnamon toast were to be put on the Colonel's monthly bill without its being presented to him each afternoon.

It was easy to see that the Colonel welcomed the arrival of Miss Bishop at the hotel. When she first came he had been a widower three months and everyone had got used to not having Mrs. Browder around. Her absence made a difference: there was no one to go around complaining of dusty chairs and frequently non-existent cockroaches in the corner nearest the dining-room. For a while the hotel staff missed Mrs. Browder because it was so pleasant without her belly-aching around; and then when the staff had become accustomed to her not being there the Colonel began to miss her. He went around, as Semple, the day clerk, said, like a chicken with its head cut off. When Mrs. Browder died everyone said it was a good thing for the Colonel, and he seemed to think so at first, but that was because he had things to do the first few weeks after her death. When those things had been attended to was when he began to go around like a chicken with its head cut off. Then Miss Bishop arrived and Mr. McLoughlin, the manager, introduced the Colonel to her and they became friends.

The Colonel had given up his parlor-bedroom-bath when Mrs. Browder passed on, and at the time of the change Olive thought to herself that it didn't make much difference in her young life; the only time the Colonel ever used his phone was to ask for the correct time by her clock, and not by the Meridian number. The Colonel sometimes told Olive the telephone was a waste as far as he was concerned. Too much telephoning. People ought to walk more and use their legs. He said it was just as easy to walk a block or two for whatever you wanted as to telephone. Olive did not reply that she thought he was crazy, which was her first thought, or that she knew he used the nickel coin-box in the rear of the dining-room. With these old babies that lived in the hotel you had to keep a civil tongue in your head.

But after Miss Bishop and the Colonel had pretty well established their tea-time as one of the customs of the hotel Olive began to notice that the Colonel was using his phone, and for outside calls. The little matters that took him either on short walks or to the nickel coin-box, he was beginning to take care of from his room, with calls which cost him a dime apiece. Olive thought about this a long time before she saw what it meant—that the Colonel liked to stay around the hotel as much as possible, or rather to leave it as little as possible; and the reason he did not use the five-cent pay station was that he did not want Miss Bishop to see him chiseling. This, and the standing order for tea, which was fifteen dollars a month extra on his bill, convinced Olive that the old boy was going for Bishop.

And she was at least thirty years his junior. Bishop was around thirty-six, giving her a break, and the Colonel was what you might call a well-preserved seventy.

When Olive noticed the Colonel taking an interest in Miss Bishop she began to watch for something big to happen, and then when nothing big happened she kept her eye open for little things. The Colonel always gave Olive five dollars for Christmas—five for her, and five apiece for the other operators, which was the biggest present the operators got. But this did not make Olive warm up to the Colonel. Without doing anything to show it, the Colonel managed to give the impression that he thought talking to telephone operators was beneath him. You could see it in other things: he would talk to Henry, the head waiter, by the hour, or to Tommy Bond, the night clerk. But he would not waste much time with Mc-Loughlin and he hardly ever said a word to any of the bellboys. In other words, a snob. Tommy Bond had gone to a school named Andover and a year to Yale College before the depression got him; Henry (who was not so snobbish that he would not reach for Olive whenever he got a chance), he would listen while the Colonel talked about the wines which he seldom bought. Olive knew McLoughlin noticed it, too. "As long as they pay their bills that's all I'm innarested in. I don't care if they think I'm the dirt under their feet as long as they get it up the first of the month," McLoughlin would say. Olive did not feel the same way about it. Other people thought she was plenty all right. Tommy Bond thought so. Tommy Bond would be getting ready to leave when Olive came to work in the morning, and he always had a few words to say of a kidding nature, not too personal, but Olive knew by the way a man looked at you how he felt about you. She knew Tommy preferred her to Bishop, for instance.

But even that was not satisfactory to Olive. She wondered why it had not occurred to her before, but thinking about how Tommy liked her, she resented it. She resented being liked by the men around the place and not by the women—Miss Bishop now, and Mrs. Browder before. Sex got into it when it was a case of a kid like Tommy Bond liking you. A kid like Tommy liked you irregardless. Telephone operator or society déb-utante, when a kid like Tommy liked you he didn't care who you were, because what made the difference was sex. Whereas with the Colonel, sex did not enter into the consideration. With Miss Bishop the same. She was a woman, so there was no sex to confuse the issue. Therefore, when Bishop and the Colonel did not like her, that meant it was because they were snobbish about her. What the hell right did they have to be snobbish about her? She was as good as they were any day. She earned her own living and she had good morals.

In regard to her likes and dislikes, Olive never did anything about them until something happened that made her express approval or disapproval, hatred or love. If she liked someone she did not do anything about it until the name of the party came up in a way that led to Olive's coming right out and saying she liked So-and-so; and if underneath she hated someone, it stayed underneath until the occasion when she would get on record as hating them. The occasion when she expressed her feelings about the Colonel and Miss Bishop came fairly soon after she had made up her mind about them.

Melba, the relief operator, came on one afternoon as Olive was quitting for the day, and she made some crack about the Colonel and Miss Bishop. The crack was something unimportant, like: "Mm. The love birds are having their tea." It was unusual because Melba seldom said anything about the guests, but this day she must have got out of the wrong side of the bed or something.

Olive looked over to the corner of the lobby where the two were conversing. "Yeah," said Olive. "What is that, anyway? That Bishop. And him. It's enough to make you sick to your stomach, watching them."

"Why, what do they do?" said Melba, who was a little surprised that a casual remark had such effect on Olive.

"What do they do?" said Olive. "Any minute I expect him to give her the business."

"Why, he's too *old*. Isn't he?"

"Too old? He isn't too old to look right through a person worse than any of the bellhops. Didn't you ever notice it?"

"In a way I did," said Melba, who had noticed no such thing, but was not going to tell Olive so.

"Just because he has one foot in the grave don't mean *any*thing," said Olive.

Having thus committed herself, Olive never let up on Miss Bishop and the Colonel. Every time she had a chance she said something against them, always against them as a unit. "Those two," it was. It began to tell in her attitude towards them, and she was curt to Miss Bishop one day over the phone, so much so that Miss Bishop said, "Look here, Olive, don't you talk to me that way."

"If you have any complaints to make you complain to Mr. McLoughlin," said Olive.

"Well, if you're not careful I will," said Miss Bishop.

"Go ahead and see if I care," said Olive. "You or Colonel Browder."

"What about Colonel Browder? What are you talking about?"

"I guess you know," said Olive, and pulled out the cord, disconnecting Miss Bishop. Miss Bishop signaled her to come back, but she made her wait. When she plugged in again and connected Miss Bishop the latter said, "Is this Olive?"

"Yes. Who do you think?"

"Either you apologize or I'll report you to Mr. McLoughlin. I won't have your nasty little insinuations. You're impertinent."

"Go ahead and report me. I don't care."

Miss Bishop did not report Olive, but the next day Olive learned that when the month was up Miss Bishop was leaving the hotel. The day after that she learned, by listening to a conversation, that Miss Bishop was going to live with her aunt in Jersey City temporarily until she found another place. "If you come over here you might as well stay," said the aunt. "I don't see why I should go on paying rent for two places."

In what was left of the month Olive was a little afraid Bishop might go to McLoughlin and snitch on her, but not really afraid. People like Bishop did not get you fired; they were the ones that were afraid, afraid you would get even with them for having you fired.

After Bishop left, Olive looked for some difference on the part of the Colonel. She thought he might be rude to her. But no; his attitude towards her did not change. He didn't notice her. She did hear him tell Semple that for the time being he would go on having tea served, as he expected Miss Bishop to drop in now and then. But she never did.

1935

Do You Like It Here?

The door was open. The door had to be kept open during study period, so there was no knock, and Roberts was startled when a voice he knew and hated said, "Hey, Roberts. Wanted in Van Ness's office." The voice was Hughes'.

"What for?" said Roberts.

"Why don't you go and find out what for, Dopey?" said Hughes.

"Phooey on you," said Roberts.

"Phooey on *you*," said Hughes, and left.

Roberts got up from the desk. He took off his eyeshade and put on a tie and coat. He left the light burning.

Van Ness's office, which was *en suite* with his bedroom, was on the ground floor of the dormitory, and on the way down Roberts wondered what he had done. It got so after a while, after going to so many schools, that you recognized the difference between being "wanted in Somebody's office" and "Somebody wants to see you." If a master wanted to see you on some minor matter, it didn't always mean that you had to go to his office; but if it was serious, they always said, "You're wanted in Somebody's office." That meant Somebody would be in his office, waiting for you, waiting specially for you. Roberts didn't know why this difference existed, but it did, all right. Well, all he could think of was that he had been smoking in the shower room, but Van Ness never paid much attention to that. Everybody smoked in the shower room, and Van Ness never did anything about it unless he just happened to catch you.

For minor offenses Van Ness would speak to you when he made his rounds of the rooms during study period. He would walk slowly down the corridor, looking in at each room to see that the proper occupant, and no one else, was there; and when he had something to bawl you out about, something unimportant, he would consult a list he carried, and he would stop in and bawl you out about it and tell you what punishment went with it. That was another detail that made the summons to the office a little scary.

Roberts knocked on Van Ness's half-open door and a voice said, "Come in."

Van Ness was sitting at his typewriter, which was on a small desk beside the large desk. He was in a swivel chair and when he saw Roberts he swung around, putting himself behind the larger desk, like a damn judge.

He had his pipe in his mouth and he seemed to look over the steel rims of his spectacles. The light caught his Phi Beta Kappa key, which momentarily gleamed as though it had diamonds in it.

"Hughes said you wanted me to report here," said Roberts.

"I did," said Van Ness. He took his pipe out of his mouth and began slowly to knock the bowl empty as he repeated, "I did." He finished emptying his pipe before he began to smoke. He took a long time about it, and Roberts, from his years of experience, recognized that as torture tactics. They always made you wait to scare you. It was sort of like the third degree. The horrible damn thing was that it always did scare you a little, even when you were used to it.

Van Ness leaned back in his chair and stared through his glasses at Roberts. He cleared his throat. "You can sit down," he said.

"Yes, sir," said Roberts. He sat down and again Van Ness made him wait.

"Roberts, you've been here now how long—five weeks?"

"A little over. About six."

"About six weeks," said Van Ness. "Since the seventh of January. Six weeks. Strange. Strange. Six weeks, and I really don't know a thing about you. Not much, at any rate. Roberts, tell me a little about yourself."

"How do you mean, Mister?"

"How do I mean? Well—about your life, before you decided to honor us with your presence. Where you came from, what you did, why you went to so many schools, so on."

"Well, I don't know."

"Oh, now. Now, Roberts. Don't let your natural modesty overcome the autobiographical urge. Shut the door."

Roberts got up and closed the door.

"Good," said Van Ness. "Now, proceed with this—uh—dossier. Give me the—huh—huh—*lowdown* on Roberts, Humphrey, Second Form, McAllister Memorial Hall, et cetera."

Roberts, Humphrey, sat down and felt the knot of his tie. "Well, I don't know. I was born at West Point, New York. My father was a first lieutenant then and he's a major now. My father and mother and I lived in a lot of places because he was in the Army and they transferred him. Is that the kind of stuff you want, Mister?"

"Proceed, proceed. I'll tell you when I want you to—uh—halt." Van Ness seemed to think that was funny, that "halt."

"Well, I didn't go to a regular school till I was ten. My mother got a divorce from my father and I went to school in San Francisco. I only stayed there a year because my mother got married again and we moved to Chicago, Illinois."

"Chicago, Illinois! Well, a little geography thrown in, eh, Roberts? Gratuitously. Thank you. Proceed."

"Well, so then we stayed there about two years and then we moved back East, and my stepfather is a certified public accountant and we moved around a lot."

"Peripatetic, eh, Roberts?"

"I guess so. I don't exactly know what that means." Roberts paused.

"Go on, go on."

"Well, so I just went to a lot of schools, some day and some boarding. All that's written down on my application blank here. I had to put it all down on account of my credits."

"Correct. A very imposing list it is, too, Roberts, a very imposing list. Ah, to travel as you have. Switzerland. How I've regretted not having gone to school in Switzerland. Did you like it there?"

"I was only there about three months. I liked it all right, I guess."

"And do you like it here, Roberts?"

"Sure."

"You do? You're sure of that? You wouldn't want to change anything?"

"Oh, I wouldn't say that, not about any school."

"Indeed," said Van Ness. "With your vast experience, naturally you would be quite an authority on matters educational. I suppose you have many theories as to the strength and weaknesses inherent in the modern educational systems."

"I don't know. I just—I don't know. Some schools are better than others. At least I like some better than others."

"Of course. Of course." Van Ness seemed to be thinking about something. He leaned back in his swivel chair and gazed at the ceiling. He put his hands in his pants pockets and then suddenly he leaned forward. The chair came down and Van Ness's belly was hard against the desk and his arm was stretched out on the desk, full length, fist closed.

"Roberts! Did you ever see this before? Answer me!" Van Ness's voice was hard. He opened his fist, and in it was a wristwatch.

Roberts looked down at the watch. "No, I don't think so," he said. He was glad to be able to say it truthfully.

Van Ness continued to hold out his hand, with the wristwatch lying in the palm. He held out his hand a long time, fifteen seconds at least, without saying anything. Then he turned his hand over and allowed the watch to slip onto the desk. He resumed his normal position in the chair.

He picked up his pipe, slowly filled it, and lit it. He shook the match back and forth long after the flame had gone. He swung around a little in his chair and looked at the wall, away from Roberts. "As a boy I spent six years at this school. My brothers, my two brothers, went to this school. My *father* went to this school. I have a deep and abiding and lasting affection for this school. I have been a member of the faculty of this school for more than a decade. I like to think that I am part of this school, that in some small measure I have assisted in its progress. I like to think of it as more than a mere steppingstone to higher education. At this very moment there are in this school the sons of men who were my classmates. I have not been without my opportunities to take a post at this and that college or university, but I choose to remain here. Why? Why? Because I love this place. I love this place, Roberts. I cherish its traditions. I cherish its good name." He paused, and turned to Roberts. "Roberts, there is no room here for a thief!"

Roberts did not speak.

"There is no room here for a thief, I said!"

"Yes, sir."

Van Ness picked up the watch without looking at it. He held it a few inches above the desk. "This miserable watch was stolen last Friday afternoon, more than likely during the basketball game. As soon as the theft was reported to me I immediately instituted a search for it. My search was unsuccessful. Sometime Monday afternoon the watch was put here, here in my rooms. When I returned here after classes Monday afternoon, this watch was lying on my desk. Why? Because the comtemptible rat who stole it knew that I had instituted the search, and like the rat he is, he turned yellow and returned the watch to me. Whoever it is, he kept an entire dormitory under a loathsome suspicion. I say to you, I do not know who stole this watch or who returned it to my rooms. But by God, Roberts, I'm going to find out, if it's the last thing I do. If it's the last thing I do. That's all, Roberts. You may go." Van Ness sat back, almost breathless.

Roberts stood up. "I give you my word of honor, I—"

"I said you may go!" said Van Ness.

Roberts was not sure whether to leave the door open or to close it, but he did not ask. He left it open.

He went up the stairs to his room. He went in and took off his coat and tie, and sat on the bed. Over and over, first violently, then weakly, he said it, "The bastard, the dirty bastard."

1939

Now We Know

Where Mary Spellacy worked, in the office of a fairly big theatrical manager, the office rules were elastic. Nobody ever got there before Mary, and Mary never got there before ten-thirty. The boss, of course, had a key, and if he wanted to go to work before Mary opened up, there was nothing to stop him. The permanent staff was small: the boss, the press agent, the bookkeeper, the boss's secretary, and Mary, who called herself a receptionist, as indeed she was, along with her other duties of typing, running the tiny switchboard, and anything else she felt like doing. There were a lot of things she liked about her job: the pay was good and there were generous, unexpected bonuses when the boss had a hit or was drunk; Mary saw a lot of celebrities and knew precisely their relationships with the boss; she went to all of the boss's first nights and, through an understanding with other girls similarly placed in other offices, she got to quite a few first nights of other producers. The boss never bothered her and the press agent had not made a pass in three years. But the best, or certainly not the least attractive, feature of the job was the starting time in the morning. She had been hired to start at ten, but in three and a half years she had inched the starting time closer to eleven, with only a few ineffectual cracks from the bookkeeper, who gave up after she saw that Mary was in solid with the boss.

It wasn't that Mary was a lazy girl. But she liked a good time, and when you live a four-dollar taxi haul from Times Square you are likely to miss out on your sleep if you have dates in town. Mary liked her eight hours.

Because she lived in the far reaches of Queens, at the end of the bus line, Mary frequently was the first passenger on the bus which took her to the subway. Over a period of years she had known by sight, or to say hello to, dozens of bus-drivers, but Herbert was the only one with whom she got on more intimate terms.

One day Herbert was sitting in the bus waiting for time to start a new trip. Mary had been a passenger of his often enough so that they would nod and smile and say good morning, but this morning something seemed to have got into Herbert. Ordinarily he was a rather sad-eyed Jew with what Mary called a little muzzy that made him look somewhat like an ugly Ronald Colman. He had a beautiful smile, with that lingering sadness in it. But he was full of the devil this particular morning, and when Mary arrived at the bus he pretended not to have seen her. She tapped lightly on the glass door, and instead of touching the pneumatic door-opener, he looked down at his fingernails and pretended to polish them on his trousers and held up his hands as though he were seriously contemplating the effect of the polishing. Mary tapped again, but this time Herbert looked at his watch, frowned, then put the bus in gear and raced the engine, but he didn't release the clutch. Mary banged harder on the door, and now, pretending to notice her for the first time, Herbert slipped the bus out of gear and pulled the door-opener.

"You!" said Mary, studying him.

He smiled and said, "*Good* morning."

He spoke so affably, so politely, that Mary could not be sure of her suspicions. But Herbert did the same thing the next morning and Mary said, "Some people are blind in one eye and can't see out of the other. I wonder how they get jobs driving a bus."

"Do you mean me, for instance?"

"If the shoe fits, and also some people must be so hard of hearing they ought to wear a hearing device."

"I don't possibly see what you mean."

The third morning Mary simply walked to the door of the bus and did not tap on the door. This time Herbert made her wait a minute or so, then, looking to his left and up in the sky at an imaginary airplane, he distracted Mary's attention so that she too looked up to the sky, and at that moment Herbert touched the door-opener. He turned and burst out laughing.

"J-o-x—jokes," said Mary, dropping her money in the box. The next morning Mary decided to fool *him*. Instead of going to the door of the bus, she walked straight to a spot just in front of the windshield and leaned against the bus, reading her paper. He let her read undisturbed for a full two minutes, then blasted away on the horn, and she jumped.

"Damn you!" she yelled. She wanted to get inside and crown him, but he sat there laughing and wouldn't open the door. When her anger subsided, she made up her mind not to ride with Herbert that day. She sat down on the wooden bench at the bus stop and resumed the appearance of reading her paper. Herbert opened the door, but Mary did not take her eyes off the paper. Herbert began to worry; not only was she really angry and obviously determined not to ride with him but he was a minute over his starting time. He got out.

"I apologize," he said.

"I refuse to accept your apology. I'll take the next bus, and I have a good notion to report you. The nerve."

"You wouldn't do that, would you? You know it was only kidding."

"Yes, and you take advantage of that. Just because you know I'm sap enough that I wouldn't report you."

"If I thought you were the kind that would turn me in, I never would have started the gag in the first place. I mean it was a compliment."

"It wasn't any compliment blowing that horn. That terrorized me."

"I'm sincerely sorry and offer my humble apologies. Please get in."

She hesitated, then said, "Oh, all right, but cut the comedy. I have a job the same as you have."

They got in. She fished in her bag for the money.

"No, the ride's on me this morning. *Every* morning, I'd *like* it to be."

"A nickel won't break me," said Mary. "And anyway, I don't *know* you."

"I know. What's your name? I don't even know your name."

"Why do you want to know my name?"

"My name is Lewis. Herbert Lewis. If you wanted to turn me in any time, that's my name."

"Are you inferring that you're gonna pull the same kind of tricks again, because my patience is just about exhausted."

"A-a-a-h, it was just to relieve the monotony and I thought you looked like a good sport that could take it. Maybe I *was* fresh."

"*May*be!" She paid her fare and chose a seat toward the back of the bus to discourage any further conversation. She could tell by the fact he did not greet the other passengers that he was pretty darn miserable. At the subway station, instead of taking the center door, which would have been more convenient, she walked to the front of the bus, and just as she was leaving she turned to him and gave him her best smile and said "Goo'bye." As she crossed the street and went into the station, she felt his eyes on her all the way, and she knew how he was looking.

For the next few days there were no more tricks, but warm smiles passed between them, and Mary guessed that he was beginning to look forward to their morning encounters just as much as she was, which was a lot. She got so now she sat near the front, near him. In that way they eventually found out the facts about each other: that he was married, two kids, 3-A, lived in Jackson Heights, had a Chevvie. He also told her that he had wanted to study medicine, took piano lessons for two years when he was a kid, gave up smoking for six months but put on so much weight his clothes would hardly fit him, had a brother in the Coast Guard, thought the movies were a waste of time, and had not seen a Broadway show since "Meet the People," to which he had gone with his wife's sister and her husband. Mary supplied such information as the fact that she had been to Cuba on a cruise, put ammonia in a Coke for a hangover, had more friends Jews than she did Irish, had taken piano lessons for two years when she was a kid, liked steak well done on the outside but rare on the inside, had wanted to become a nun when she was twelve, and lived with her mother and three sisters in the fourth house in that row of houses that you could see from the end of the bus line. In a few weeks they knew all they had to know about each other to fall in love, and after the period of unconscious caution it became a case of who would make the first move.

One morning Mary said to him, "I can get you two tickets for a show Tuesday night if you want to go."

"You mean passes?"

"Yes. My boss, we have a new show opening Friday and the way we do it, they like to show it to an audience before the critics see it, so Tuesday the employees of the Brooklyn Edison, I think it is, or maybe it's Bond Bread, anyway this kind of an employees' club gets tickets for nothing. It's the same cast and everything as the opening night but of course no critics are allowed in. We just want to get the audience reaction. Sort of a dress rehearsal with people out front so they can tell where the laughs are and what to cut, et cetera. Would you like to go and take your wife?"

"Listen, Mary, I hate my wife."

"Oh. Well, I just thought, you know."

"Don't think I don't appreciate your offer, because I do. Sincerely. But you go to a show, you're suppose to go to have a good time, take somebody you're fond of that you can have an enjoyable evening. My wife just don't fit in that category. I'm not saying anything behind her back. Everybody knows it, and it was her idea in the first place. I mean she took to disliking me before I took to disliking her. It's only the kids—a-a-a-h! You make a kind gesture and what do I do, I shoot off my mouth, but I might as well, Mary, because I love *you*, Mary. I'm gettin' changed over to another run. I might as well tell you that while I'm blabber-mouthing. You don't have to take any responsibility or get the idea because I love you you have any—responsibility. But it's doing me no good torturing myself and now getting drunk, so I asked them to change me to another run."

"You did? When do you change?"

"Monday night I change with a fellow over at Forest Hills—he lives nearer, where it'll be more convenient for him. That's a week from Monday night. Christ, I think of you all day. She's all right, my wife, but a lot of people in this world—phooey. You're not saying anything. Well, I guess I know what you're thinking."

"Not by the way you say that you don't. I have to think."

"No you don't. I told you you didn't have any responsibility. I only told you for my own satisfaction."

"You're wrong there, Herbert. I have the responsibility that I let you be the first to say anything. If you hadn't said anything, I would have said something. Or showed it somehow, and prob'ly did. Well, at least we got it out in the open."

"Yes, I guess so. Anyway, now we know."

1943

Free

Mrs. Ford tipped the bellboy and the porter, and thanked the assistant manager who had accompanied her to her room. They left, and she took off her hat and sailed it across the room, the first impulsive gesture she had allowed herself that morning. On the train, coming across the Jersey meadows, there had been a visible sparkle in the air, and in the station she had wanted to send her bags on with the redcaps so that she could go outside and walk to the hotel. There was always something about that first whiff of New York air, and it had looked especially good this morning. But that was an irregularity, and for a year there had been no such irregularities in her life, not even such a slight one. Then when she arrived at the hotel that slight irregularity had been followed by a major one: just as she was approaching the desk she had had an almost overwhelming impulse to register under a phony name. A name had come to her: Mrs. James J. Jameson. It may have been a name that had been somewhere buried in her morning paper. It was a name that meant not a thing in the world to her, but for a second or two it had been a very real name—her own. But of course she had registered under her real name. There were so many reasons for that—in the first place, the simple one was that she had had reservations under her own name; the second, that the manager of the hotel knew her; the third—there didn't have to be a third, or a second, or a first. Not those kinds. The big thing was that overnight, almost literally overnight (three nights, actually) she had not been able to get away from the uninterrupted conventionality of a year.

Yet she was glad these impulses had been there. They showed that something inside her was ready for this freedom that was hers once a year at this time. She sat down and kicked off her shoes and lit a cigarette. She put her feet up on the small, uncomfortable-looking desk chair, and she leaned back, her right hand over her left breast. It was an attitude in which she often found herself when she was lost in thought, but now she was not lost in thought. She was just thinking that for three days she had not had to worry about how anyone else was sleeping or not sleeping. For more than three days she had not spoken to anyone she had not wanted to speak to, nor read anything she had not wanted to read. When mealtime came she had had to think only of her own wishes, and not the needs of her children and the tastes of her husband. There had been a telegram waiting for her downstairs, the same kind of telegram that had been sent two or three times to the train. She knew, to be sure, that her husband's secretary had sent the telegrams—maybe he hadn't, but it didn't really make much difference. The point was that he was all right and the boys were all right. Another point was that they all probably were enjoying her visit to New York as much as she was, albeit for different reasons.

She undressed and let herself into a warm tub, knowing that when she got out she would be cool again. The room was quite warm, but not so warm if you were naked. She lay naked and glowing on the bed, staring at the ceiling, and now she was quite cool. It was, indeed, a fact that her feet were definitely cold. It was a fact that did not disturb her much. She was thirty-three, and it was no news to her that her feet did get cold.

She began to plan her day. To begin with, she was going to spend a lot of money for things to clothe and adorn this now naked body, these cold feet, this head and hands. At the train in Pasadena Joe had suddenly been more generous than she had expected. He had given her all his cash (and he always carried a large sum), and besides what he had given her she had some of her own. This year she would buy one thing for evening that, if she wanted to, she could wear just one night in New York; something that would knock someone's eye out. It would be something that she would not dare wear in Pasadena. She would buy *that* dress *today*. The other things that could be sent home—they could be spread out over several days' shopping. She would have lunch alone and she would walk a lot, and stop here and there to buy things that cost five dollars, two dollars, a dollar. They might make Christmas presents (after all, that was what she was really here for), but they wouldn't have to. Somewhere on Madison Avenue she would be on her way from one shop to another, and she would be feeling just fine, what with the air, a good lunch and two cognacs afterward, and the whole feeling of being in New York again. At the corner of—oh, say, Forty-ninth, traffic would halt her at the curb. She would be standing there with a dozen other people, poor unconscious people who were *always* in New York. They wouldn't know how good she was feeling, so good that she would let it show in her eyes. And then, on the other side of the stream of shiny black cars, would be a man.

She would see him, but he would have seen her first. She would know that someone was staring at her, and he would have an honestly amused smile on his face, because he had caught what was in her eyes. He would know. This man would know.

She would look him straight in the eye, for just a second, and then look away. But she would not be able to do anything about what he saw in her eyes, and she would be flustered. (What a word!) The cars would keep them apart, then the cop's whistle would blow and the Madison Avenue bus would snort and be off, and half way across the street she would come close enough to touch the man and they would get as close to each other as they could without touching. Not looking at each other until they were so close. Then a quick look, and this time he would not smile.

She would walk on, knowing that he had turned around in the hope that she too would turn around. And would she? She never had.

1945

Too Young

It was the time of year when once again Bud was made to feel very young. It had happened last year, and it had happened the year before; it seemed as though it had been happening a great many more years than that. It *always* seemed that the Tuesday after Labor Day was around again; Father would be staying at the apartment in town, planning to come out for two or three weekends but not making it. The fathers of the other kids the same way. It just seemed that there were no older men at the beach club, giving you black looks or even coming right out and telling you if you did not get the heck off the tennis courts when they wanted to play their stiff and creaky mixed doubles. Through the summer, being with your own bunch, you did not think much about being young or old or anything. But when the fathers started to go back to town, and the young married people, only the mothers and the young boys and girls were left, and it made you remember that you were young.

Much too young to be in love with Kathy Mallet.

This had been the first summer Bud had come right out and called her Kathy. "Hyuh, Kathy," he often would say.

"Hello, Bud," she would say. "When are we going to have that match?"

"Any time you say," he would say.

She had started it. Watching him play one day in June, she had sat there and had seen him just *cream* Ned Work. He *creamed* him: 6–4, 6–2. It had been exciting knowing that Kathy was taking the trouble to wait and watch him before she went on to play. It was the best compliment he ever had from anybody. Then she had said, "Will you play me some-time, Bud?" And he had told her any time. They were always talking about it, but all summer they never got around to it, and now Bud was a little glad, because he could have beaten Kathy. He didn't want to do that, and yet he couldn't have played her and insulted her by easing up on her.

In ten years he would be twenty-five and Kathy would be twenty-nine. That wasn't so bad. Both in their late twenties. And by that time she no longer would be a little tall for him. He had heard a thousand times that on his mother's side they were all six-footers and all got their height in their teens, just sprouted up suddenly.

In no time he would be back at school, and naturally Kathy, back in college, would be going to New Haven and Princeton and New York all the time, because they had an awful lot of liberty where Kathy went to college and were in New York half the time. He would be very lucky to see her before next June. He wished he could do something or give her something that would make her just think of him once in a while during the school year. Well, there was one thing: he could beat her at tennis. That would make her remember him. He could make it up to her years from now. Someday in the future he would say to her, offhand, "Darling, I remember when I was just a kid—oh, back in thirty-nine—and I decided the only way to make you remember me that year was to beat you straight sets. Remember that time I practically forced you to play me?"

The hall clock said twenty after three, and he remembered that there was a touch-football game at three, so there wouldn't be many guys on the tennis courts and most of the girls of his own crowd would be watching the silly game. It seemed like an ideal day to challenge Kathy, if she happened to show up at the club, which she usually did every afternoon anyway. He put on white flannels and went out and took his mother's car and drove to the club. He noticed that Kathy's tan Ford convertible sedan was parked at the Mallet's porte-cochère. That meant she was home. Good. On his way to the club he had a bad moment when he saw Martin standing beside his motorcycle. Martin was tough. Watkins, the other cop, wasn't so bad, but some of the guys said that Martin never gave anybody a break. If you didn't have a license, that was just too bad. Some of the guys said Martin actually carried a list of the kids that had licenses, and Bud had no license. But today Martin did not even notice Bud. Bud looked in the mirror to make sure, but Martin was already looking in the opposite direction.

At the club, Bud parked the car just inside the parking space, behind the high hedge, but on second thought he decided not to get out. He would stretch out and seem casual, and then when Kathy arrived he would sit up and say, "Oh, you wouldn't like a little tennis, would you, Kathy? We haven't much time left before college opens." No, it would be better to say when *school* opens; some people said school when they meant college, whereas if he said college, she would think he was being silly to talk about college when everybody knew he had three more years before he would get to college.

He stretched out, sure that he was looking casual enough. He stayed there quite a while and one or two cars came and went, and the casual attitude was becoming uncomfortable when he heard a car coming pretty fast, and then, faster, a motorcycle.

The motorcycle caught up to the car only a few yards away from the club entrance. Without looking, he knew who was on the motorcycle: Martin. He raised his head and sure enough, the car was Kathy's tan Ford.

Bud sank down in the seat, so that Martin would not see him, and he heard Martin start out the regular cop's line: "Well, baby, you *were* in a hurry."

He could not hear what Kathy said, but he hoped she said something that would put Martin in his place for calling her baby. The next thing Bud heard was unexpected. Martin said, "*You* can't duck *me* this way. Why weren't you there yesterday? I waited till seven o'clock."

"I told you I wouldn't be there," said Kathy.

"Oh, I *know* you *told* me. But *I* told *you* to *be* there, and you weren't. What is this, the brusheroo?"

"I told you I was never going there again. And I'm not," said Kathy.

"What's the matter with you? Why don't you stop this? All summer— you're the one, half the time you were the one that wanted to meet *me*."

"I know, I know. But it's over."

"No, get that out of your head. It isn't over."

"I'm not going to meet you again. I don't *want* to meet you again."

"Yes, but I want to meet you. You'll meet me. You be there at six o'clock."

"No, I won't, so don't wait for me," said Kathy.

"Listen, you little bitch, you *be* there," said Martin.

"No," said Kathy.

There was a moment's silence, then, "Are you gonna be there?"

"No," said Kathy. Then, "All right."

"O.K. I didn't hurt your arm. I'll be there at six o'clock," said Martin. The motorcycle spat a couple of times and went away.

Bud heard Kathy's Ford come into the parking space and heard her slam the door and the sound of her steps on the gravel. He waited until he heard the door of the bar slam to, then he got out of the car. No one must see him; he could tell his mother he had forgotten about her car. Right now he wanted to walk alone and to think thoughts that he hated and that would forever ruin his life. And the god-damn awful part was that there was nothing, nothing, nothing to do but what he was doing now. "Let me alone!" he said, to no one.

1945

Bread Alone

It was the eighth inning, and the Yankees had what the sportswriters call a comfortable lead. It was comfortable for them, all right. Unless a miracle happened, they had the ball game locked up and put away. They would not be coming to bat again, and Mr. Hart didn't like that any more than he was liking his thoughts, the thoughts he had been thinking ever since the fifth inning, when the Yanks had made their five runs. From the fifth inning on, Mr. Hart had been troubled with his conscience.

Mr. Hart was a car-washer, and what colored help at the Elbee Garage got paid was not much. It had to house, feed, and clothe all the Harts, which meant Mr. Hart himself; his wife, Lolly Hart; his son, Booker Hart; and his three daughters, Carrie, Linda, and the infant, Brenda Hart. The day before, Mr. Ginsburg, the bookkeeper who ran the shop pool, had come to him and said, "Well, Willie, you win the sawbuck."

"Yes sir, Mr. Ginsburg, I sure do. I was watchin' them newspapers all week," said Mr. Hart. He dried his hands with the chamois and extended the right.

"One, two, three, four, five, six, seven, eight, nine, anduh tenner. Ten bucks, Willie," said Mr. Ginsburg. "Well, what are you gonna do with all that dough? I'll bet you don't tell your wife about it."

"Well, I don't know, Mr. Ginsburg. She don't follow the scores, so she don't know I win. I don't know what to do," said Mr. Hart. "But say, ain't I suppose to give you your cut? I understand it right, I oughta buy you a drink or a cigar or something."

"That's the custom, Willie, but thinking it over, you weren't winners all year."

"No sir, that's right," said Mr. Hart.

"So I tell you, if you win another pool, you buy me *two* drinks or *two* cigars. Are you going in this week's pool?"

"Sure am. It don't seem fair, though. Ain't much of the season left and maybe I won't win again. Sure you don't want a drink or a cigar or something?"

"That's all right, Willie," said Mr. Ginsburg.

On the way home, Mr. Hart was a troubled man. That money belonged in the sugar bowl. A lot could come out of that money: steak, stockings, a lot of stuff. But a man was entitled to a little pleasure in this life, the only life he ever had. Mr. Hart had not been to a ball game since about fifteen or twenty years ago, and the dime with which he bought his ticket in the pool every week was his own money, carfare money. He made it up by getting rides home, or pretty near home, when a truck-driver or private chauffeur friend was going Harlem-ward; and if he got a free ride, or two free rides, to somewhere near home every week, then he certainly was entitled to use the dime for the pool. And this was the first time he had won. Then there was the other matter of who won it for him: the Yankees. He had had the Yankees and the Browns in the pool, the first time all season he had picked the Yanks, and it was they who made the runs that had made him the winner of the ten dollars. If it wasn't for those Yankees, he wouldn't have won. He owed it to them to go and buy tickets and show his gratitude. By the time he got home his mind was made up. He had the next afternoon off, and, by God, he was going to see the Yankees play.

There was, of course, only one person to take; that was Booker, the strange boy of thirteen who was Mr. Hart's only son. Booker was a quiet boy, good in school, and took after his mother, who was quite a little lighter complected than Mr. Hart. And so that night after supper he announced, "Tomorrow me and Booker's going over to see the New York Yankees play. A friend of mine happened to give me a choice pair of seats, so me and Booker's taking in the game." There had been a lot of talk, and naturally Booker was the most surprised of all—so surprised that Mr. Hart was not sure his son was even pleased. Booker was a very hard one to understand. Fortunately, Lolly believed right away that someone had really given Mr. Hart the tickets to the game; he had handed over his pay as usual, nothing missing, and that made her believe his story.

But that did not keep Mr. Hart from having an increasingly bad time from the fifth inning on. And Booker didn't help him to forget. Booker leaned forward and he followed the game all right but never said anything much. He seemed to know the game and to recognize the players, but never *talked*. He got up and yelled in the fifth inning when the Yanks were making their runs, but so did everybody else. Mr. Hart wished the game was over.

DiMaggio came to bat. Ball one. Strike one, called. Ball two. Mr. Hart wasn't watching with his heart in it. He had his eyes on DiMaggio, but it was the crack of the bat that made Mr. Hart realize that DiMaggio had taken a poke at one, and the ball was in the air, high in the air. Everybody around Mr. Hart stood up and tried to watch the ball. Mr. Hart stood up too. Booker sort of got up off the seat, watching the ball but not standing up. The ball hung in the air and then began to drop. Mr. Hart was judging it and could tell it was going to hit about four rows behind him. Then it did hit, falling the last few yards as though it had been thrown down from the sky, and smacko! it hit the seats four rows behind the Harts, bounced high but sort of crooked, and dropped again to the row directly behind Mr. Hart and Booker.

There was a scramble of men and kids, men hitting kids and kids darting and shoving men out of the way, trying to get the ball. Mr. Hart drew away, not wanting any trouble, and then he remembered Booker. He turned to look at Booker, and Booker was sitting hunched up, holding his arms so's to protect his head and face.

"Where the hell's the ball? Where's the ball?" Men and kids were yelling and cursing, pushing and kicking each other, but nobody could find the ball. Two boys began to fight because one accused the other of pushing him when he almost had his hand on the ball. The fuss lasted until the end of the inning. Mr. Hart was nervous. He didn't want any trouble, so he concentrated on the game again. Booker had the right idea. He was concentrating on the game. They both concentrated like hell. All they could hear was a mystified murmur among the men and kids. "Well, somebody must of got the god-damn thing." In two minutes the Yanks retired the side and the ball game was over.

"Let's wait till the crowd gets started going, Pop," said Booker.

"O.K.," said Mr. Hart. He was in no hurry to get home, with the things he had on his mind and how sore Lolly would be. He'd give her what was left of the ten bucks, but she'd be sore anyhow. He lit a cigarette and let it hang on his lip. He didn't feel so good sitting there with his elbow on his knee, his chin on his fist.

"Hey, Pop," said Booker.

"Huh?"

"Here," said Booker.

"What?" said Mr. Hart. He looked at his son. His son reached inside his shirt, looked back of him, and then from the inside of the shirt he brought out the ball. "Present for you," said Booker.

Mr. Hart looked down at it. "Lemme see that!" he said. He did not reach for it. Booker handed it to him.

"Go ahead, take it. It's a present for you," said Booker.

Suddenly Mr. Hart threw back his head and laughed. "I'll be a god-damn holy son of a bitch. You got it? The ball?"

"Sure. It's for you," said Booker.

Mr. Hart threw back his head again and slapped his knees. "I'll be damn—boy, some Booker!" He put his arm around his son's shoulders and hugged him. "Boy, some Booker, huh? You givin' it to me? Some Booker!"

1939

Graven Image

The car turned in at the brief, crescent-shaped drive and waited until the two cabs ahead had pulled away. The car pulled up, the doorman opened the rear door, a little man got out. The little man nodded pleasantly enough to the doorman and said "Wait" to the chauffeur. "Will the Under Secretary be here long?" asked the doorman.

"Why?" said the little man.

"Because if you were going to be here, sir, only a short while, I'd let your man leave the car here, at the head of the rank."

"Leave it there *anyway*," said the Under Secretary.

"Very good, sir," said the doorman. He saluted and frowned only a little as he watched the Under Secretary enter the hotel. "Well," the doorman said to himself, "it was a long time coming. It took him longer than most, but sooner or later all of them—" He opened the door of the next car, addressed a colonel and a major by their titles, and never did anything about the Under Secretary's car, which pulled ahead and parked in the drive.

The Under Secretary was spoken to many times in his progress to the main dining room. One man said, "What's your hurry, Joe?" to which the Under Secretary smiled and nodded. He was called Mr. Secretary most often, in some cases easily, by the old Washington hands, but more frequently with that embarrassment which Americans feel in using titles. As he passed through the lobby, the Under Secretary himself addressed by their White House nicknames two gentlemen whom he had to acknowledge to be closer to The Boss. And, bustling all the while, he made his way to the dining room, which was already packed. At the entrance he stopped short and frowned. The man he was to meet, Charles Browning, was chatting, in French, very amiably with the maître d'hôtel. Browning and the Under Secretary had been at Harvard at the same time.

The Under Secretary went up to him. "Sorry if I'm a little late," he said, and held out his hand, at the same time looking at his pocket watch. "Not so very, though. How are you, Charles? Fred, you got my message?"

"Yes, sir," said the maître d'hôtel. "I put you at a nice table all the way back to the right." He meanwhile had wigwagged a captain, who stood by to lead the Under Secretary and his guest to Table 12. "Nice to have seen you again, Mr. Browning. Hope you come see us again while you are in Washington. Always a pleasure, sir."

"Always a pleasure, Fred," said Browning. He turned to the Under Secretary. "Well, shall we?"

"Yeah, let's sit down," said the Under Secretary.

The captain led the way, followed by the Under Secretary, walking slightly sideways. Browning, making one step to two of the Under Secretary's, brought up the rear. When they were seated, the Under Secretary took the menu out of the captain's hands. "Let's order right away so I don't have to look up and talk to those two son of a bitches. I guess you know which two I mean." Browning looked from right to left, as anyone does on just sitting down in a restaurant. He nodded and said, "Yes, I think I know. You mean the senators."

"That's right," said the Under Secretary. "I'm not gonna have a cocktail, but you can. . . . You want a cocktail?"

"I don't think so. I'll take whatever you're having."

"O.K., waiter?" said the Under Secretary.

"Yes, sir," said the captain, and went away.

"Well, Charles, I was pretty surprised to hear from you."

"Yes," Browning said, "I should imagine so, and by the way, I want to thank you for answering my letter so promptly. I know how rushed you fellows must be, and I thought, as I said in my letter, at your convenience."

"Mm. Well, frankly, there wasn't any use in putting you off. I mean till next week or two weeks from now or anything like that. I could just as easily see you today as a month from now. Maybe easier. I don't know where I'll be likely to be a month from now. In more ways than one. I may be taking the Clipper to London, and then of course I may be out on my can! Coming to New York and asking *you* for a job. I take it that's what you wanted to see me about."

"Yes, and with hat in hand."

"Oh, no. I can't see you waiting with hat in hand, not for anybody. Not even for The Boss."

Browning laughed.

"What are you laughing at?" asked the Under Secretary.

"Well, you know how I feel about him, so I'd say least of all The Boss."

"Well, you've got plenty of company in this goddam town. But why'd you come to me, then? Why didn't you go to one of your Union League or Junior League or whatever-the-hell-it-is pals? There, that big jerk over there with the blue suit and the striped tie, for instance?"

Browning looked over at the big jerk with the blue suit and striped tie, and at that moment their eyes met and the two men nodded.

"You *know* him?" said the Under Secretary.

"Sure, I know him, but that doesn't say I *approve* of him."

"Well, at least that's something. And I notice he knows you."

"I've been to his house. I think he's been to our house when my father was alive and naturally I've seen him around New York all my life."

"Naturally. Naturally. Then why didn't you go to *him*?"

"That's easy. I wouldn't like to ask him for anything. I don't approve of the man, at least as a politician, so I couldn't go to him and ask him a favor."

"But, on the other hand, you're not one of our team, but yet you'd ask me a favor. I don't get it."

"Oh, yes you do, Joe. You didn't get where you are by not being able to understand a simple thing like that."

Reluctantly—and quite obviously it was reluctantly—the Under Secretary grinned. "All right. I was baiting you."

"I know you were, but I expected it. I have it coming to me. I've always been against you fellows. I wasn't even for you in 1932, that's a hell of an admission, but it's the truth. But that's water under the bridge—or isn't it?" The waiter interrupted with the food, and they did not speak until he had gone away.

"You were asking me if it isn't water under the bridge. Why should it be?"

"The obvious reason," said Browning.

" 'My country, 'tis of thee'?"

"Exactly. Isn't that enough?"

"It isn't for your Racquet Club pal over there."

"You keep track of things like that?"

"Certainly," said the Under Secretary. "I know every goddam club in this country, beginning back about twenty-three years ago. I had ample time to study them all then, you recall, objectively, from the outside. By the way, I notice you wear a wristwatch. What happens to the little animal?"

Browning put his hand in his pocket and brought out a small bunch of keys. He held the chain so that the Under Secretary could see, suspended from it, a small golden pig. "I still carry it," he said.

"They tell me a lot of you fellows put them back in your pockets about five years ago, when one of the illustrious brethren closed his downtown office and moved up to Ossining."

"Oh, probably," Browning said, "but quite a few fellows, I believe, that hadn't been wearing them took to wearing them again out of simple loyalty. Listen, Joe, are we talking like grown men? Are you sore at the Pork? Do you think you'd have enjoyed being a member of it? If being sore at it was even partly responsible for getting you where you are, then I think you ought to be a little grateful to it. You'd show the bastards. O.K. You showed them. Us. If you hadn't been so sore at the Porcellian so-and-so's, you might have turned into just another lawyer."

"My wife gives me that sometimes."

"There, do you see?" Browning said. "Now then, how about the job?"

The Under Secretary smiled. "There's no getting away from it, you guys have got something. O.K., what are you interested in? Of course, I make no promises, and I don't even know if what you're interested in is something I can help you with."

"That's a chance I'll take. That's why I came to Washington, on just that chance, but it's my guess you can help me." Browning went on to tell the Under Secretary about the job he wanted. He told him why he thought he was qualified for it, and the Under Secretary nodded. Browning told him everything he knew about the job, and the Under Secretary continued to nod silently. By the end of Browning's recital the Under Secretary had become thoughtful. He told Browning that he thought there might be some little trouble with a certain character but that that character could be handled, because the real say-so, the green light, was controlled by a man who was a friend of the Under Secretary's, and the Under Secretary could almost say at this moment that the matter could be arranged.

At this, Browning grinned. "By God, Joe, we've got to have a drink on this. This is the best news since—" He summoned the waiter. The Under Secretary yielded and ordered a cordial. Browning ordered a Scotch. The drinks were brought. Browning said, "About the job. I'm not going to say another word but just keep my fingers crossed. But as to you, Joe, you're the best. I drink to you." The two men drank, the Under Secretary sipping at his, Browning taking half of his. Browning looked at the drink in his hand. "You know, I was a little afraid. That other stuff, the club stuff."

"Yes," said the Under Secretary.

"I don't know why fellows like you—you never would have made it in a thousand years, but"—then, without looking up, he knew everything had collapsed—"but I've said exactly the wrong thing, haven't I?"

"That's right, Browning," said the Under Secretary. "You've said exactly the wrong thing. I've got to be going." He stood up and turned and went out, all dignity.

1943

Common Sense
Should Tell You

There were five in the party, and when they had been seated, the proprietor came over to their table. He nodded to the two girls and to two of the men, none of whose names he knew, although the girls spoke to him by name. Then he said to the third man, "Glad to see you in Chicago, Mr. Spring. Gonna be with us a while, I hope."

"Hello, Mike," said Mr. Spring. He shook hands without standing up. "No, I'm on my way back to the Coast. Just staying overnight."

"Whenner you gonna stay over a couple days again? Like to throw a little party for you again. Remember that one six or seven years ago? In nineteen-and-thirty-nine, I think it was."

"Indeed I do remember it. I'll never forget it. But those days are gone forever, I'm afraid."

"Not for you, Mr. Spring," said Mike. He leaned over and whispered in Spring's ear. "If you see anything in the show you like I'll be glad to fix it up for you."

"Thanks, Mike. I'll let you know. Uh, you know all these people? This is Harry Field, charge of publicity on the Coast, and this is Jake Coombs, my trainer, and I forget the young ladies' names."

"Betty Donaldson," said Betty Donaldson. "Hello, Mike."

"Audrey French," said Audrey French. "Hello, Mike."

"Oh, I've known Mike for years," said Harry Field. "I very seldom pass through Chicago without dropping in."

"That's right," said Mike. "Well, enjoy yourselves, Mr. Spring." He left them, stopping to speak to the maître-dee and at two or three tables, obviously explaining to the people at the tables that Mr. Spring was Mr. Spring, the famous Hollywood producer, an old friend, on his way back to the Coast with his press agent and trainer. The pretty girls were Chicago girls.

The floor show had not started and the relief band was at work. "You people dance if you feel like it," said Mr. Spring.

"Don't you want to, Mr. Spring?" said Field.

"Not right away," said Mr. Spring. His four companions got up and Mr. Spring was alone, practically the first time he had been alone in the two days since he had left Johns Hopkins. He took out a cigar from a case which had been given him by an ex-President of the United States. He replaced the case in the coat of a suit which he had bought from Eddie Schmidt. He snipped off the end of the cigar with a gold cigar cutter which an English actor had bought for him at Asprey's, and lit the cigar with a gold lighter-and-watch which he could not with any certainty ever have identified, since he possessed at least twenty exactly like it. He got a good light and then remembered the orders of the men at Johns Hopkins. "You'd better limit yourself to two a day, Mr. Spring," one man had said. "None at all, if you can do without them. No brandy. No golf. I don't want you to drive a car or gamble or run upstairs, and try to keep your temper and don't get in quarrels with people. No more making speeches."

"You don't leave me much. What about women?"

The doctor had smiled. "From my information, Mr. Spring, you're going to go right on doing as you please about women, but common sense should tell you . . ."

"What if I ignored everything you tell me?"

"Then one of these days you'll feel as if somebody had given you a good swift kick all over the whole left side of your body."

"How long'll that last?"

"I don't know. You might lose your eyesight, too."

"How long'll I last if I *take* your advice?" Mr. Spring had asked.

The doctor had hesitated. "As a rule, I give an evasive answer to that one, but with you I don't think I have to. Take care of yourself, and you have between five and ten years more."

"It hardly seems worth it, does it?"

The doctor had been slightly shocked and annoyed. "I don't know why not. A lot of people that come here would be glad of your chance."

"You're a Catholic, aren't you, Doctor? I never been able to understand how a Catholic can be a good doctor or a good doctor can be a Catholic. Notwithstanding a lot of them are."

"Well, we haven't got time to go into that now, Mr. Spring. I have other patients waiting."

"I beg pardon, Doctor." It was not often that Mr. Spring was put in his place.

He let the cigar go out, resting the lighted end in the ashtray. He watched the dancers with no interest and hummed with the music. When his companions returned he put his right hand on the back of the chair to his right, then put his left hand on the back of the chair to his left. This served as a substitute for standing up for the young ladies. Betty and Audrey looked at him, waiting for him to say something.

"Enjoy your dance?" he said.

They said they had, and he nodded with solemn approval, putting across the further idea that he didn't feel like talking, whereupon Harry and Jake reopened their conversations with the girls. Almost immediately the floor show started.

It was awful. It hadn't been good to begin with, but tonight everyone played with the knowledge that Mr. Spring was at Table 12. In case anyone didn't know the location of Table 12, it was the table behind which stood a captain and two waiters, and if people to the rear could not see through the captain and waiters, that was too bad.

The chorus came out, bumping into each other and generally lousing up the routine in their eagerness to smile for Mr. Spring. The master of ceremonies trotted out to the microphone and tried hard not to look in Mr. Spring's direction, but before he was halfway through his song he was looking nowhere else. Zita and Leonardo, the society dancers, kept to Mr. Spring's side of the floor, and Leonardo almost dropped Zita during a spin. The chorus and the show-girls came out again and got in each other's way; Patsy Whitney, who did imitations, became confused at finding herself started on a rather mean imitation of one of Mr. Spring's stars after Mike had distinctly told her to leave it out tonight; Bobby Renwick, the harmonica player, came right over and stood at the edge of the floor and played Gershwin, Grieg, Arlen, Brahms, and Ravel for a table two removed from Mr. Spring's, an error attributable to Bobby's nearsightedness. It all came to some kind of climax during the finale, when one chorus girl was sent into such a bad fall that the other girls had to dance around her while she was getting to her feet. The other girls grinned, but the one little girl cried, got out of the line, and ran off.

"Harry," said Mr. Spring.

"Yes, Mr. Spring." Harry, Jake, Audrey, and Betty turned to Mr. Spring, and the captain and waiters behind him leaned forward.

"Just Harry," said Mr. Spring to his companions. He whispered in Harry's ear. "Tell Mike I want to see him."

Harry got up from the table, and when he came back Mike was with him. "Here he is," said Harry.

"Yes, I know," said Mr. Spring. "Mike, who's the little girl took the spill?"

Mike leaned down and put a hand on Mr. Spring's shoulder. "Her name is Zita. Zita and Leonardo. I got them out of a hotel in Detroit."

"I don't mean her," said Mr. Spring. "She's all right, but a dime a dozen, Mike. *You* know that. I mean the chorus kid. The number they just finished."

"Oh. She's—I think her name is—" Mike halted and whispered to the captain of waiters, who whispered back. Mike nodded and continued. "Goes by the name of Hilary Kingston. You like her?"

"I might," said Mr. Spring. His companions drank their champagne and tried to pick up their talk where they had left off and to keep talking until the arrival of Hilary Kingston. In a few moments she was there. With a flat-palm gesture, like someone testing a mattress, Mr. Spring bade Harry and Jake and the girls to remain seated. He rose. He put out his hand. "Are you all right, Hilary?" he said. "Sit here next to me." She sat on the chair only just vacated by Audrey, who remained standing while a waiter brought another chair.

"Thanks," said Hilary Kingston. She folded her hands in her lap.

"Did you get hurt? I mean when you fell that time?" asked Mr. Spring.

"No, sir. Not when I fell. I think one of the kids kicked me here, but I can take it," said Hilary. She was wearing a flannel suit and she indicated a slit in the coat where a pocket might have been.

Mr. Spring sternly did not lower his eyes to the place indicated. He smiled. "I was worried for you. It reminded me of when a jockey's thrown in a horse race and I can't look at anything else only him till I see the other horses are safely past him, Hilary. Even when I have a horse running in that particular race. I always shut my eyes to everything else. That can be awful, you know."

"Yes, I know," she said.

"Do you like horse racing, Hilary?"

"Like them? Love them is more the word. This Jake. Is he your trainer?"

Mr. Spring smiled. "If you mean does he train my horses, no. He trains *me*. I have a workout with him every day, boxing, road work, massaging. No, you're thinking of Jock, not Jake. Jock Doyle. He trains my horses, Hilary. But I'm glad to see you have an interest in horse racing. That means two things we have in common. You said you can take it, and so can I. And you like horse racing."

"If I could be a boy, that's what I'd be," said Hilary.

"What?" asked Mr. Spring.

"A jockey."

"Well, just let me say I prefer you the way you are." Mr. Spring smiled.

"Thanks."

Mr. Spring smiled directly at Hilary, straight in the eye and then at the place in her coat where she had thought she might have been kicked. "Did you ever know Harry before?"

"Harry who?"

"Well, if you don't know Harry who, then you didn't. Mr. Field, the handsome gentleman in the blue suit."

"Oh, I don't think he's so handsome," said Hilary.

"You don't? He's considered a very good-looking man, I've always heard."

"Oh, I have nothing against him."

"Very nice fellow to be with and a very good host," said Mr. Spring.

"I thought he worked for you."

"He works for the same company, but when we're out like this, it isn't any question of working for me. All I can say is I'm glad he brought me here. You can see I'm not *with* anybody, Hilary. At least not till you so kindly joined us. Harry's having a party a little later. Would you like to go with me? I'm sure it'll be all right with Mike. I've known Mike since probably before you were born."

"I was born in 1927."

"Oh, is that so?" said Mr. Spring. He leaned forward and spoke to Harry. "Harry, I have a new recruit for your party back at the suite."

"What's that, Mr. Spring?" said Harry.

"I said I persuaded Miss Kingston to join your little party back at the suite," said Mr. Spring. He turned back to Hilary. "If you think there'll be any trouble about you doing another show, I can speak to Mike."

"That's all right, Mr. Spring. That was the last show. We don't do any more."

"Well, that's fine. Then we can go to Harry's party. Harry, whenever you're ready, we are."

"Right," said Harry, signalling to the captain.

Mr. Spring was smiling. He leaned toward Hilary. "We don't have to all go in the same car if you prefer," he said.

"I don't care," said Hilary.

Mr. Spring raised his head. "Harry, Miss Kingston and I will go in the black car and meet you there, if that's all right."

"Right," said Harry.

Mr. Spring smiled, took out a special Upmann cigar from the ex-President's case, snipped off the end with the English actor's Asprey cutter, and put the cigar in his mouth. Then the smiling corners of his mouth turned down for the lighting of the cigar, and he remembered who had given him the cigar case and the cigar cutter and, more clearly, he remembered the words of the doctor in Baltimore. He snapped the lighter shut and turned to Hilary.

"Maybe you don't want to go on this party," he said. He hoped she would say no, but he knew she would say yes.

1946

Drawing Room B

Nobody big had taken Leda Pentleigh to the train, and the young man from the publicity department who had taken her was not authorized to hire the Rolls or Packard that used to be provided for her New York visits. Nor had they taken their brief ride from the Waldorf to Grand Central. This time, she was riding west on the Broadway and not the Century, had come to the station in an ordinary taxicab, from a good but unspectacular hotel north of Sixtieth Street. Mr. Egan, it is true, was dead, but his successor at Penn Station, if any, did not personally escort Leda to the train. She just went along with the pleasant young hundred-and-fifty-a-week man from the publicity department, her eyes cast down in the manner which, after eighteen years, was second nature to her in railroad stations and hotel lobbies, at tennis matches and football games. Nobody stopped her for her autograph, or to swipe the corsage which the publicity young man's boss had sent instead of attending her himself. Pounding her Delman heels on the Penn Station floor, she recalled a remark which she was almost sure she had originated, something about the autograph hounds not bothering her: it was when they didn't bother you that they bothered you. Of course, it was Will Rogers or John Boles or Bill Powell or somebody who first uttered the thought, but Leda preferred her way of putting it. The thought, after all, had been thought by thousands of people, but she noticed it was the way *she* expressed it that was popular among the recent johnny-come-latelies when they were interviewed by the fan magazines. Well, whoever had said it first could have it; she wouldn't quarrel over it. At the moment of marching across Penn Station, there seemed to be mighty few travellers who would take sides for or against her in a controversy over the origin of one of her routine wisecracks; far from saying, "There goes Leda Pentleigh, who first said . . ." the travellers were not even saying, "There goes Leda Pentleigh—period." The few times she permitted her gaze to rise to the height of her fellow-man were unsatisfactory; one of the older porters raised his hat and smiled and bowed; two or three nice-appearing men recognized her—but they probably were Philadelphians in their thirties or forties, who would go home and tell their wives that they had seen Leda Pentleigh in Penn Station, and their wives would say, "Oh, yes. I remember her," or "Oh, yes. She was in Katie Hepburn's picture. She played the society bitch, and I'll bet she's qualified." Katie Hepburn, indeed! It wasn't as if Katie Hepburn hadn't been in pictures fifteen years. But no use getting sore at Katie Hepburn because Katie was a few years younger and still a star. At this thought, Leda permitted herself a glance at a Philadelphia-type man, a man who had that look of just about getting into or out of riding togs, as Leda called them. He frowned a little, then raised his hat, and because he was so obviously baffled, she gave him almost the complete Pentleigh smile. Even then he was baffled, had not the faintest idea who she was. A real huntin'-shootin' dope, and she knew what he was thinking— that here was a woman either from Philadelphia or going to Philadelphia and therefore someone he must know. The gate was opened, and Leda and Publicity went down to her car. Publicity saw that she was, as he said, all squared away, and she thanked him and he left, assuring her that "somebody" from the Chicago office would meet her at Chicago, in case she needed anything. Her car was one of the through cars, which meant she did not have to change trains at Chicago, but just in case she needed anything. (Like what, she said to herself. Like getting up at seven-thirty in the morning to be ready to pose for photographs in the station? Oh, yes? And let every son of a bitch in the Pump Room know that Leda Pentleigh no longer rated the star treatment?)

In her drawing room, Leda decided to leave the door open. There might, after all, be a Coast friend on the train. If she wanted to play gin with him—or her—she could do it, or if she wanted to give her—or him—the brush, she knew how to do that, too. Her window was on the wrong side of the car to watch people on the platform, and she sat in a corner where she could get a good look at the passengers going by her door. She opened a high-class book and watched the public (no longer so completely hers) going by. They all had that beaten look of people trying to find their space; bent over—surely not from the weight of their jewelry boxes and briefcases—and then peering up at the initial on her drawing room, although they could plainly see that the room was occupied by a striking, stunning, chic, glamorous, sophisticated woman, who had spent most of the past week in New York City, wishing she were dead.

She drove that little thought out of her mind. It would do no good now to dwell on that visit, ending now as the train began to pull out—her first visit to New York in four years, and the unhappiest in all her life. What the hell was the use of thinking back to the young punk from one of the dailies who had got her confused with Renée Adorée? What difference the wrong tables in restaurants and the inconveniently timed appointments at hairdressers and the night of sitting alone in her hotel room while a forty-dollar pair of theatre tickets went to waste? The benefit in Union City, New Jersey. The standup by Ken Englander, the aging architect, who had been glad enough in other days to get once around the floor with her at the Mayfair dances. The being made to wait on the telephone by the New York office of her agent, her own agent. The ruined Sophie dress and the lost earring at that South American's apartment. Why think of those things? Why not think of the pleasanter details of her visit?

Think, for instance, of the nice things that had been said about her on that morning radio program. Her appearance had been for free, but the publicity was said to be valuable, covering the entire metropolitan area and sometimes heard in Pennsylvania. Then there was the swell chat with Ike Bord, publicity man for a company she had once been under contract to. "*Whenner you coming back to us, Leda?* . . . Anything I can do for you while you're in town, only too glad, you know. I didn't even know you were here. Those bums where you are now, they never get anything in the papers." And it was comforting to know she could still charge things at Hattie's, where she had not bought anything in four years. And the amusing taxidriver: "Lady, I made you right away. I siss, 'Lydia Penley. Gay me an autograft fa Harry.' Harry's my kid was killed in the U.S. Marines. Guadalcanal. *Sure, I remember you.*" And, of course, her brother, who had come down all the way from Bridgeport with his wife, bringing Leda *a pair of nylons and a bona-fide cash offer* in case she had a clean car she wasn't using. The telephone service at her hotel had been something extra special because one of the operators formerly had been president of Leda's Brooklyn fan club. Through it all was the knowledge that her train fare and hotel bill were paid for by the company because she obligingly posed for fashion stills for the young-matron departments of the women's magazines, so the whole trip was not costing her more than eight or nine hundred dollars, including the visit to Hattie's. There were some nice things to remember, and she remembered them.

The train rolled through Lancaster County, and it was new country to Leda. It reminded her of the English countryside and of American primitives.

She got up and closed her door once, before washing her hands, but reopened it when she was comfortable. Traffic in the passageway had become light. The train conductor and the Pullman conductor came to collect her tickets and asked for her last name. "Leda Pentleigh," she said. This signified nothing to the representative of the Pennsylvania Railroad, but the Pullman conductor said, "Oh, yes, Miss Pentleigh. Hope you have an enjoyable trip," and Leda thanked him and said she was sure she would, lying in her beautiful teeth. She was thinking about sending the porter for a menu when the huntin'-shootin' type stood himself in her doorway and knocked.

"Yes?" she said.

"Could a member of Actors' Equity speak to you for a moment, Miss Pentleigh?" he said. He didn't so much say the line as read it. She knew that much—that rehearsal was behind the words and the way he spoke them.

"To be sure," she said. "Sit down, won't you?"

"Let me introduce myself. My name is Kenyon Littlejohn, which of course doesn't mean anything to you, unless you've *seen* me?"

"I confess I did see you in the station, Mr. Littlejohn. In fact, I almost spoke to you. I thought I recognized you."

He smiled, showing teeth that were a challenge to her own. He took a long gold case out of his inside coat pocket and she took a cigarette. "That can mean two things," he said. " Either you've seen me—I've been around a rather long time, never any terribly good parts. I've usually got the sort of part where I come on and say, 'Hullo, thuh, what's for tea? Oh, crompits! How jolly!' " She laughed and he laughed. "Or else you know my almost-double. Man called Crosby? Very Back Bay-Louisburg Square chap from Boston. Whenever I've played Boston, people are always coming up to me and saying, 'Hello, Francis.' "

"Oh, I've met Francis Crosby. He used to come to Santa Barbara and Midwick for the polo."

"That's the chap," said Kenyon Littlejohn, in his gray flannel Brooks suit, Brooks shirt, Peal shoes, Players Club tie, and signet ring. "No wonder you thought you knew me, although I'm a bit disappointed it was Crosby you knew and not me."

"Perhaps I did know you, though. Let me see—"

"No. Please don't. On second thought, the things I've been in—well, the things I've been in have been all right, mostly, but as I said before, the parts I've had weren't anything I particularly care to remember. Please let me start our acquaintance from scratch."

"All right," she said.

He took a long drag of his cigarette before going on. "I hope you don't think I'm pushy or anything of that sort, Miss Pentleigh, but the fact is I came to ask your advice."

"You mean about acting?" She spoke coldly, so that this insipid hambo wouldn't think he was pulling any age stuff on her.

"Well, hardly that," he said. He spoke as coldly as he dared. "I've very seldom been without work and I've lived quite nicely. My simple needs and wants. No, you see, I've just signed my first picture contract—or, rather, it's almost signed. I'm going out to California to make tests for the older-brother part in 'Strange Virgin.' "

"Oh, yes. David's doing that, isn't he?"

"Uh—yes. They're paying my expenses and a flat sum to make the test, and, if they like me, a contract. I was wondering, do you think I ought to have an agent out there? I've never had one, you know. Gilbert and Vinton and Brock and the other managers, they usually engage me themselves, a season ahead of time, and I've never *needed* an agent, but everybody tells me out there I ought to have one. Do you agree that that's true?"

"Well, of course, to some extent that depends on how good you are at reading contracts."

"I had a year at law school, Miss Pentleigh. That part doesn't bother me. It's the haggling over money that goes on out there, and I understand none of the important people deal directly with the producers."

"Oh, you're planning on staying?"

"Well . . ."

"New York actors come out just for one picture, or, at least, that's what they say. Of course, they have to protect themselves in case they're floperoos in Hollywood. Then they can always say they never planned to stay out there, and come back to New York and pan pictures till the next offer comes along, if it ever does."

"Yes, that's true," said Mr. Littlejohn.

" '*That* place,' they say. 'They put caps on your teeth and some fat Czechoslovakian that can't speak English tries to tell you how to act in a horse opera,' forgetting that the fat Czechoslovakian knows more about acting in his little finger than half the hamboes in New York. Nothing *personal*, of course, Mr. Little."

"Thank you," said Mr. Littlejohn.

"But I've got a bellyful of two-hundred-dollar-a-week Warfields coming out and trying to high-hat us, trying to steal scenes and finding themselves on the cutting-room floor because they don't know the first thing about picture technique, and it serves them right when they find themselves out on their duffs and on the way back to their Algonquins and their truck-garden patches in Jackson Heights or wherever they live. God damn it to hell, making pictures is work!"

"I realize—"

"Don't give me any of that I-realize. Wait'll you've got up at five and sweated out a scene all day and gone to the desert on location and had to chase rattlesnakes before you could go to bed. Find out what it's like and then go back and tell the boys at the Lambs Club. Do that for twenty or fifteen years." She stopped, partly for breath and partly because she didn't know what was making her go on like this.

"But we're not all like that, Miss Pentleigh," said Littlejohn when she did not go on.

His talking reminded her that she had been talking to a human being and not merely voicing her hatred of New York. His being there to hear it all (and to repeat it later, first chance he got) made her angry at him in particular. "I happen to think you are, eef you don't mind. I don't care if you're Lunt and Fontanne or Helen Hayes or Joe Blow from Kokomo—if you don't click in Hollywood, it's because you're not good enough. And, oh, boy, don't those managers come out begging for us people that can't act to do a part in their new show. When they want a name, they want a movie name. Why, in less than a week, I had chances to do a half a dozen plays, including a piece of the shows. What good can New York do me, I ask you."

"The satisfaction of a live audience," he said, answering what was not a question. "Playing before a—"

"A live audience! On a big set you play to as many people as some of the turkeys on Broadway. Live audience! Go to a première at Graumann's Chinese or the Cathay Circle and you have people, thousands, waiting there since two o'clock in the afternoon just to get a look at you and hear you say a few words into the microphone. In New York, they think if they have three hundred people and two cops on horses, they have a crowd. On the Coast, we have better than that at a preview. A *sneak* preview! But of course you wouldn't know what that is."

"Really, Miss Pentleigh, I'm very glad to be going to Hollywood. I didn't have to go if I didn't want to."

"That wasn't your attitude. You sat down here as if you were patronizing me, *me*! And started in talking about agents and producers as if Hollywood people were pinheads from Mars. Take a good gander at some of the swishes and chisellers on Broadway."

"Oh, I know a lot about them."

"Well, then, what are you asking me for advice for?"

"I'm terribly sorry," he said, and got up and left.

"Yes, and I think you're a bit of a swish yourself," said Leda to the closed door. She got a bottle of Bourbon out of her bag and poured herself a few drinks into doubled paper cups and rang for the porter.

Presently, a waiter brought a menu, and by that time Leda was feeling fine, with New York a couple of hundred miles and a week and a lifetime behind her. Dinner was served, and she ate everything put before her. She had a few more shots and agreed with her conscience that perhaps she had been a little rough on the actor, but she had to take it out on somebody. He wasn't really too bad, and she forgave him and decided to go out of her way to be nice to him the next time she saw him. She thereupon rang for the porter.

"Yes, Ma'am?" said the porter.

"There's a Mr. Entwhistle—no, that's not his name. Littlefield. That's it. Littlefield. Mr. Littlefield is on the train. He's going to California. Do you think you could find 'im and ask 'im that I'd tell 'im I'd like to speak to him, please?"

"The gentleman just in here before you had your dinner, Ma'am?"

"Yes, that's the one."

"Mr. Littlejohn. He's in this same car, PA29. I'll give him your message, Ma'am."

"Do that," she said, handing the waiter a ten-dollar bill.

She straightened her hair, which needed just a little straightening, and assumed her position—languor with dignity—on the Pullman seat, gazed with something between approval and enchantment at the darkening Pennsylvania countryside, and looked forward to home, California, and the friends she loved. She could be a help to Mr. Littlejohn (*that* name would have to be changed). She *would* be a help to Mr. Littlejohn. "That I will, that I will," she said.

1947

The Pretty Daughters

The Major climbed in the company car and gave the driver the address. He put the attaché case beside him, stretched out his legs at an angle, and lit a cigar. At the exit gate the plant guard picked up the Major's pass and gave him a snappy non-reg salute, and the Major was on his way.

The night before and that morning there had been a heavy fall of snow. It had stopped now, but there had not been time to clear the streets, and the car's progress toward the city's residential district was slow. The Major was enjoying his cigar, the fact that soon he would be out of the Army, and the ride. It took him back to Christmas holidays twenty years ago when he would visit his classmates in cities like Hartford and Buffalo and Harrisburg. Once you got out of the built-up districts and into the sections where the houses were larger and had more ground around them, each anonymous house would hold a promise of fun. White house. Redbrick house. French type. Georgian type. Dutch Colonial type. Old Manse type. You didn't know who lived in any of them, but maybe in one of them, as you went from the station to the home of the people you were visiting, there would be a girl, a pretty daughter. Maybe at the very moment you passed her house she was out skiing or tobogganing, or maybe she was right there, taking a nap so she would look her best for the dance that night, the dances that occurred every night of your visit to these towns—Columbus, Reading, Binghamton. You never got to know much about the towns. If you did happen to drive a borrowed car, you were told where to go and how to get there, and "there" meant someone's house or the country club or the city club or the big hotel. You never stayed long enough to find your way about the town, and anyhow most of the driving was done at night, in a Packard or a Jordan or a Marmon or a Ford, with the side curtains flopping and the tire chains banging.

In the daytime if you went anywhere it usually was to someone's house three or four doors away, and you walked. You wore your coonskin coat and no hat and galoshes. You would time your arrival so that you would get there after the athletic ones who had been sliding down some hill. Everybody would drink a lot of tea and eat a great many watercress sandwiches. The girls would kick off their ski boots, which they wore whether they had been skiing or sitting around the country-club fireplace. The mother of the hostess of the moment would look in and there would be introductions and then she would depart, and presently the father would come home and beam on everyone, kissing most of the girls and making a joke about taking the boys to see the moose head in his den. The daughter of the house would pretend to be irritated. "Lord and *Tay*lor, Daddy! You'll have everybody fried before the Baldwins'." The boys would go to Daddy's den and have straight whiskey or ginger-ale highballs, and Daddy would shake up Orange Blossoms and take the shaker back to the girls. He would return to the den and politely inquire about the out-of-town boy's school and family origins and then he would turn the job of barkeep over to his son, if any, or to a neighbor's son who had the run of the house, and excuse himself to get into his tux or full dress . . .

"Was that twenty-three thirty-eight, sir?" said the driver.

"I think so. Wait till I look." The Major opened his trench coat and unbuttoned the top left pocket of his blouse. He read from a slip of paper. "Twenty-three forty-eight," he said.

The driver slowed down until the car was barely moving. "I think this must be it. I don't see no number, but that last was twenty-three thirty-eight."

"I think you're probably right," said the Major. "I'll get out here."

"I'll go up and ask if it's the right house," said the driver.

"Will you? Fine. Thanks."

The driver went up to the porte-cochère, following car tracks that obviously had been made hours before and in which there were a few footprints. In a few minutes he was back. "Yes, sir, this is it. They're expecting you. Major Robb, the lady said."

"That's me," said the Major. He got out and gave the driver two dollars. "I'll get a taxi from here. You needn't wait."

He followed the driver's path and was knocking the snow off his feet when the door opened, before he had rung.

"Come in, Major Robb. I'm Jean Reeves. Mother's around the corner at a meeting and she told me to entertain you till she got here."

"That's very nice of you," he said. He put his gear on a chair in the dark hall and followed the girl into a small, panelled room, in which there was a fire. The girl was quite tall and she wore a slipover and a cardigan, a tweed skirt, moccasins, a pearl necklace. He placed her age at twenty, but knew he must be wrong—she should be younger—and he was confused by her total lack of resemblance to Nancy, who beside this girl would be short and probably, by this time, sturdy. This girl had a superb, pared-down figure.

"I'd never know you were Nancy's daughter."

"I'm not. I'm her stepdaughter. She inherited me when she married Daddy."

"Oh, that explains it. I'm sorry your father's not here. I'd like to have met him."

"He had to go to Chicago this morning. I suppose Mother told you. We'll have tea when she gets here. Meanwhile, would you like something else? We have just about everything."

"I'd love a, uh, Bourbon with a piece of ice in it," he said. "No fruit, no bitters, no sugar. Can you swing that?"

"That can be arranged and it's what I want, too." She opened a panelled door to a bar. He stood by the fire until she handed him his drink, and they sat down, facing each other, in front of the fireplace.

"Well, this is mighty pleasant. I was afraid your mother wouldn't remember me when I phoned."

"Well, frankly, she was quite surprised. But pleased, I can tell you that." She smiled. For the first time he noticed she was wearing a miniature Navy cap device.

"I see the Navy has moved in," he said.

"In a manner of speaking," she said.

"In a manner of speaking? Not married."

"Not married, but spoken for, in a manner of speaking."

"The Navy has good taste," said Robb.

"Thank you. And I'm glad to hear you say it, not only because of me, but don't you get tired of hearing the Army pan the Navy and vice versa? It's pretty silly."

"It is if you're fighting the kind of war I'm fighting. It doesn't make a hell of a lot of difference what color suit I wear. You can see by the absence of any ribbons that I haven't been using up much plasma."

"Well, you're a major, though."

"Even that's fairly recent, and I'm getting out pretty soon. I'm doing just about what I've always done, except I'm doing it for slightly less money. In civil life I'm a lawyer. I read contracts. In the Army I'm a lawyer, reading contracts. What about you, Jean? What did you do before the war? Paint, for instance?"

"Why did you happen to pick on that?"

"I used to know a girl in New York that looked a little like you. She was an artists' model and she painted."

"Oh, that's a relief. The kind of painting I've done wouldn't justify my looking artistic."

"Don't let it worry you. Even if I hadn't known the other girl painted, I would have guessed that you'd done some posing."

"I have a little, for Mother."

"Does she paint, too? I didn't know that. Of course. I haven't seen her in fifteen years or more, so in that time she could have turned into a—a rodeo rider."

"That sounds a little disrespectful, but I'll let it pass."

"It isn't a bit disrespectful. I once knew a damned attractive rodeo rider. Very pretty, very intelligent, went to the University of Wyoming."

The girl nodded. "Mother did say you—you got around a lot."

"What did she *actually* say?" He smiled.

She hesitated. "Well, she said that if the term had been used in her day, you'd probably have been called a wolf."

"*Dear* Nancy. That's quite a build-up, isn't it?" He was annoyed.

"I think she's wrong about wolf."

"Why?"

She considered a moment. "Because wolf means predatory. I don't think Mother knows that. Wolf's a new word since her day. I think she thinks anybody that goes around with a lot of girls is a wolf. That isn't what wolf means, necessarily. A wolf—a wolf is out to make a score, just for the sake of the score. I don't think you're that."

"Thank you," he said. "You're not entirely right about me, but thank you."

"Why? Were you a wolf? Or *are* you?"

He studied his glass. "I've—I've done some howling on occasion. Put it that way. The fact is, I suppose your mother is justified. Shall I wait outside till your mother gets here?"

She did not answer, but got up and took his glass and filled it again, and her own with it.

"How old are you, Jean?"

"Twenty-three. Why?"

"I don't know," he said. He was suddenly unaccountably depressed.

She waited for him to go on, and when he did not, she addressed him rather too heartily. "What's come over you? Don't sit there making a long face."

"And don't you give me orders. Remember I'm old enough to be your father."

"And don't you pull rank on me, or age either."

"I can certainly pull age on you."

"Oh, no," she said. She put her hand over the Navy pin. "Do you think this stands for some twenty-three-year-old j.g.? How old are *you*?"

"Thirty-nine."

She laughed condescendingly. "A boy. This character is forty and a lieutenant commander."

"Maybe he's a *young* forty. I'm an old thirty-nine."

"You're both the same."

He realized that the time had passed for making jokes. "What did you mean when you said you were spoken for? I assume the gentleman is married."

"Very much married. Very *happily* married, probably, although he'd never admit it to me. Spoken for? I don't know what I did mean. I don't know why I said that, any more than I know why I wear this pin." She looked down at it and then very deliberately took it off. "I hope that will do some good."

"Maybe it will," he said, "if you want it to enough."

"Good God! If I want it to! He won't answer my phone calls. He's in San Francisco, but I know he's been East twice without looking me up or letting me know so I could go and see him. He's one of you New Yorkers. You probably know him. Nobody *here* knows him. Oh, he is *really* a bastard."

Her fury was exciting, but Robb did not know what to do next, or say. "We all are," he said.

"Yes," she said. She looked at him intently. "Why did you look up Mother after all these years?"

"In the neighborhood. Thought it'd be nice to see her again."

"No," she said.

"No?"

"No. You thought to yourself, 'Nancy lives in this town. Might be a good idea to look her up. She might not be too bad and it might be a very nice thing. A very nice thing.' That's what you thought."

He laughed. "You're exactly right. That's exactly what I did think."

"Of course it was. Well, Major Robb, you'd be disappointed, if I know you. She's completely domesticated, doing good works and not taking care of her figure. Oh, I can see your face when you get your first look at Mother. In fact, you're beginning to look that way now."

"I'll try not to any more," he said. He showed his teeth in a burlesque smile. "Is that better?"

"You have nice teeth," she said.

"Thanks. Listen, kid, do you want me to go?" When she did not answer, he went on. "You do, don't you?"

"No," she said.

"I ought to wait and say hello to your mother."

"I don't want you to go." She stood up and then seemed not to know why she stood up. She looked at him helplessly and he got up and put his arms around her. She shut her eyes and kissed him, but there was nothing to it.

"I'm sorry, Jean," he said.

"I wanted you to kiss me."

"That isn't what I'm sorry about," he said. She looked down and away from him.

"You're sorry for me?"

"Yes."

"I'll say goodbye now," she said.

"All right," he said. She went out of the room and he heard her go upstairs, heard her moving around on the floor above, and again came that feeling of depression, but now, with it, the feeling that he was beginning to serve a sentence.

1945

The Moccasins

About twenty people were sitting in the half darkness of the living room and the even darker screened-in porch, but the people were in twos and fours, conversing quietly or not at all, so it did not seem like a party. The gathering lacked the unity of noise that often goes with a much smaller group. It did have something else, which could have been an air of unified expectancy, or simple languorousness, or the two combined. Mary thought she sensed both, as though the people were just sitting around, lying around, waiting for something, but nothing in particular, to happen. It was late at night. The people were all—except for one woman—deeply tanned, and half of them could have got their tan from sports, which would account for their being tired. None of the men got up when Mary and her brother followed the Negro houseman into the living room. A portly man in an unbuttoned Hawaiian printed shirt was playing drums, using the wire brushes softly and expertly to the recorded music of the Dorsey brothers on the radio-phonograph. He was one of the brownest of all, down his chest to the khaki shorts and then again down his legs to his short socks. He flashed a smile and waved a wire brush in greeting, but went on playing without interruption, more interested in the tune, "Blue Lou," than in the arrival of Mary and her brother.

A stout, golden-haired woman, the only person not burned by the sun, came up to greet Mary and Jack. Her smile was quick and polite and no more, implying that that would be all until the visitors identified themselves—and that if the identification were not satisfactory, the newcomers would be thrown right out.

"Mrs. Fothergill, I'm Jack Tracy, and this is my sister Mary."

The smile immediately warmed. "Oh, yes. Why, yes! I'm very *pleased*. Carl *Shepherd*."

"That's right," said Jack. He looked around, but in the dim light he could not recognize anyone. "He here?"

"No, he isn't. He isn't here *yet*, but he phoned from Hobe Sound. He's coming all right, and we're expecting you—my husband and I. Doc!" she called to the man at the drums.

He nodded in time with the music and spoke on the beat: "Com-eeng, Moth-thurr." The record ended and he joined the three. He moved quickly and with power that would not be good to run up against, but his gait was feminine. He waddled. Then immediately there was another contradiction—his hands were large and his grip was strong. He probably had been a capable guard in the late Hugo Bezdek or early Rockne era. His thin gray hair was parted in the middle and he looked as though he ought to be wearing a fraternity pin. His wife introduced the Tracys, and he put one hand on Jack's shoulder and the other on Mary's, which was bare.

"Carl'll be scooting in here any minute, but what's to keep us from a little libation? You name it, and we have it," he said. "There's a little thing of mine own called a Crusher." He grinned.

"Now, Doc," said Mrs. Fothergill.

"What's a Crusher?" Mary asked.

"You wouldn't want to try it and see, would you?"

"Maybe I'd just better have a Scotch," said Mary.

"Aw, no clients?" said Doc.

"Well . . ." said Mary.

"That's more like it," said Doc. "How about you, Mr. Tracy?"

"I think I'd better stick to bourbon-and-soda, sir," said Jack.

"Maybe you're right, if you've been drinking bourbon," said Doc. He chuckled. "I thought you were starting from scratch."

"*I* am," said Mary.

"Then, you come right along with Dr. Fothergill and learn how to make a Crusher. Mr. Tracy, you go along with *Mother*gill and give the ladies a treat." He put his arm around Mary and took her to a bar, which was on the porch.

"Fothergill and Mothergill, that's cute," said Mary.

He laughed. "I don't know who thought that up—at least, not in this generation. It's an old family joke, of course, back in West Virginia, where I come from, but they started calling us that, when we got married, in New York, too. Cannes. California. Down here. Whenever we meet a new crowd, sooner or later somebody'll get the idea of calling us Fothergill and Mothergill. Shanghai. India. Nairobi."

"You've lived everywhere," said Mary.

"Pretty near. Just about approximately everywhere—everywhere they'll have us," he said. He automatically but precisely mixed the drink during his chatter.

"This is a darling house," said Mary.

"It is that, all right. Frank and Hazel *really* know how to live."

"Who?"

"Oh, don't you know Frank and Hazel—the Blaylocks? You don't suppose this house belongs to us! No, child. We happen to know these friends of ours, and Hazel Blaylock broke her leg skiing up in the Laurentians, so they asked Mothergill and I to come down and open it for them, hold the fort till—now a little dash of Pernod. There. Yes, we keep it open for them till Hazel's leg heals, and, of course, much as we adore Hazel and much as I admire a pretty leg—well, we hope she takes good care of that leg for another month. Up north. That'll bring us right up to when we want to go to Palm Springs. There, take a sip of that and hold on to the top of your head."

Mary tasted the drink, putting a hand on her head. She smiled. "No effect so far."

"Of course not. I exaggerate a little, but it does have a wallop. Now your brother's, and one for Dr. Fothergill, and then you come over and sit with me." He made two highballs. As he was about finished, a man and a woman who had been talking earnestly in a far corner of the porch started for the door, which opened, Mary now could see, out onto a boat landing. A speedboat was tied up there.

"Hey, Buzz, don't go out there without a flashlight," Doc said.

"We know our way around," said the woman.

"Around each other," said Doc. "No, seriously—take a flashlight.

"Why?" said Buzz.

"Moccasins," said Doc. He reached under the bar.

The man looked at the woman and frowned. She shrugged, whereupon the man took the torch from Doc and they went out to the speedboat.

"If she feels that way about it, it must be love," said Doc. "Come on."

"Love could never get me to go out there," said Mary.

"Not at your age," said Doc.

Doc paused to give one of the highballs to Jack, who was sitting with Mrs. Fothergill and a couple—a young girl whom Mary had seen in New York and a second-rate movie actor, whom she had not noticed before. Then she and Doc went on inside to chairs near the drums.

"If you want to play, go ahead," said Mary.

"I will later. Just now I'd rather fan the breeze with you."

"All right," said Mary. "What did you mean about not at my age?"

They lit cigarettes before he answered. "At your age, love comes to *you*, and plenty of it, I imagine. You don't have to walk through moccasins for it."

"No?"

He studied her, then shook his head. "No." He waited a moment and then decided not to say what he might have been going to say. He swallowed half his highball before going on, and when he did, he returned to the chit-chat form. "Where do you usually go for the winter?"

"I've usually been in school."

"Good Lord, I knew you were young, but not that young. You probably came out this year."

"Last summer," she said.

"Last summer. Are you from Long Island?"

"Yes," she said.

"I smell money," he said. "Oh, sure. Your father is probably Herman Tracy."

"Yes," she said.

"Well, you've got nothing to worry about, except taxes, your head on a pikestaff, and stuff. Where does Carl Shepherd fit in? If I'm asking too many questions, it's because I always do. You're not related to Carl?"

"No," she said.

"That answers a *lot* of questions," he said.

"Does it? That's good," she said.

He smiled. "Don't be haughty with old Doc Fothergill. If I have your age right, I knew Carl before you were born, and if I haven't got it right, I'm only wrong by a year or so."

"Really?"

"Really," he said. "Now, I don't figure where your brother comes in." He looked out to the porch. "Well, now, maybe I do. In just this short space of time, he seems to be moving in on little Emily. Got that hambo from Hollywood talking to himself. I hope your brother can handle a sneak punch."

"How do you mean?"

"Well, our actor friend was doing all right with Emily before your brother got here," he said. "That's what I meant by a sneak punch. Mr. Hollywood's a bad actor, and I can say that again."

"Jack's a good fighter."

"Then that's settled. Maybe he belongs here," said Doc.

"Well, I should hope so."

"No, you shouldn't hope so," said Doc. The houseman took Doc's empty glass and Mary shook her head. Somebody got up and turned on the phonograph, which filled in the silence between Mary and Doc. She turned and saw that he was watching her. He smiled.

"Just beautiful, that's all."

"Thank you," she said.

"Not quite all. There's a lot of other things I'd like to know about you."

"Ask," she said.

"No. The things I want to know, you don't ask. You find out, but you don't ask. And it wouldn't do me any good to know anyway."

"No?"

The houseman handed Doc his drink. "No," said Doc. He drank deeply again, and looked slowly around the room and out to the porch. Two couples were dancing, the partners holding close to each other, and the conversations in the two rooms remained as subdued as when Mary had arrived at the party. Doc leaned forward and turned his head so that he faced Mary.

"Well?" she said.

"I'd give a year of my life to kiss you. Not a future year, mind you. One of the good ones."

"Would you?" she said.

"However, that's out of the question, for sixteen thousand reasons, so will you do me another favor?"

"I won't kiss you," she said.

"I have another favor. Will you please go home? Will you do me a favor and do yourself a favor and get out of here?"

"All right," she said, and started to rise. He reached out and touched her hand, but she pulled it away and went out to her brother. It took a minute to persuade him to leave, and Doc could not hear what words she used in doing it. When they came to the living room, Doc got up.

"I'll show you the way," he said.

"Thanks, we can find it," Mary said.

He walked with them to their car. "Tracy, I'd like to say one thing to your sister."

"My guess is you've said too much already. I probably ought to punch you in the nose, if I knew what this was all about."

"You don't, and anyway don't try it," said Doc. He spoke to Mary. "Just remember one thing. You don't have to walk through moccasins for it."

"What's he talking about?" said Jack.

"Oh, who cares?" said Mary.

1947

Imagine Kissing Pete

To those who knew the bride and groom, the marriage of Bobbie Hammersmith and Pete McCrea was the surprise of the year. As late as April of '29 Bobbie was still engaged to a fellow who lived in Greenwich, Connecticut, and she had told friends that the wedding would take place in September. But the engagement was broken and in a matter of weeks the invitations went out for her June wedding to Pete. One of the most frequently uttered comments was that Bobbie was not giving herself much opportunity to change her mind again. The comment was doubly cruel, since it carried the implication that if she gave herself time to think, Pete McCrea would not be her ideal choice. It was not only that she was marrying Pete on the rebound; she seemed to be going out of her way to find someone who was so unlike her other beaus that the contrast was unavoidable. And it was.

I was working in New York and Pete wrote to ask me to be an usher. Pete and I had grown up together, played together as children, and gone to dancing school and to the same parties. But we had never been close friends and when Pete and I went away to our separate prep schools and, later, Pete to Princeton and I to work, we drifted into that relationship of young men who had known each other all their lives without creating anything that was enduring or warm. As a matter of fact, I had never in my life received a written communication from Pete McCrea, and his handwriting on the envelope was new to me, as mine in my reply was to him. He mentioned who the best man and the other ushers would be— all Gibbsville boys—and this somewhat pathetic commentary on his four years in prep school and four years in college made an appeal to home town and boyhood loyalty that I could not reject. I had some extra days coming to me at the office, and so I told Pete I would be honored to be one of his ushers. My next step was to talk to a Gibbsville girl who lived in New York, a friend of Bobbie Hammersmith's. I took her to dinner at an Italian speakeasy where my credit was good, and she gave me what information she had. She was to be a bridesmaid.

"Bobbie isn't saying a word," said Kitty Clark. "That is, nothing about the inner turmoil. Nothing *intime*. Whatever happened happened the last time she was in New York, four or five weeks ago. All she'd tell me was that Johnny White was impossible. Impossible. Well, he'd been very possible all last summer and fall."

"What kind of a guy was he?" I asked.

"Oh—*attractive*," she said. "Sort of wild, I guess, but not a roué. Maybe he is a roué, but I'd say more just wild. I honestly don't know a thing about it, but it wouldn't surprise me if Bobbie was ready to settle down, and he wasn't. She was probably more in love with him than he was with her."

"I doubt that. She wouldn't turn around and marry Pete if she were still in love with this White guy."

"Oh, *wouldn't* she? Oh, are you ever wrong there. If she wanted to thumb her nose at Johnny, I can't think of a better way. Poor Pete. You know *Pete*. Ichabod McCrea. Remember when Mrs. McCrea made us stop calling him Ichabod? Lord and Taylor! She went to see my mother and I guess all the other mothers and said it just had to stop. Bad enough calling her little Angus by such a common nickname as Pete. But calling a boy Ichabod. I don't suppose Pete ever knew his mother went around like that."

"Yes he did. It embarrassed him. It always embarrassed him when Mrs. McCrea did those things."

"Yes, she was uncanny. I can remember when I was going to have a party, practically before I'd made out the list Mrs. McCrea would call Mother to be sure Pete wasn't left out. Not that I ever would have left him out. We all always had the same kids to our parties. But Mrs. McCrea wasn't leaving anything to chance. I'm dying to hear what she has to say about this marriage. I'll bet she doesn't like it, but I'll bet she's in fear and trembling in case Bobbie changes her mind again. Ichabod McCrea and Bobbie Hammersmith. Beauty and the beast. And actually he's not even a beast. It would be better if he were. She's the third of our old bunch to get married, but much as I hate to say it, I'll bet she'll be the first to get a divorce. Imagine *kissing* Pete, let alone any of the rest of it."

The wedding was on a Saturday afternoon; four o'clock in Trinity Church, and the reception at the country club. It had been two years since I last saw Bobbie Hammersmith and she was now twenty-two, but she could have passed for much more than that. She was the only girl in her crowd who had not bobbed her hair, which was jet-black and which she always wore with plaited buns over the ears. Except in the summer her skin was like Chinese white and it was always easy to pick her out first in group photographs; her eyes large dark dots, quite far apart, and her lips small but prominent in the whiteness of her face beneath the two small dots of her nose. In summer, with a tan, she reminded many non-operagoers of Carmen. She was a striking beauty, although it took two years' absence from her for me to realize it. In the theatre they have an expression, "walked through the part," which means that an actress played a role without giving it much of herself. Bobbie walked through the part of bride-to-be. A great deal of social activity was concentrated in the three days—Thursday, Friday, and Saturday—up to and including the wedding reception; but Bobbie walked through the part. Today, thirty years later, it would be assumed that she had been taking tranquilizers, but this was 1929.

Barbara Hammersmith had never been anything but a pretty child; if she had ever been homely it must have been when she was a small baby, when I was not bothering to look at her. We—Pete McCrea and the other boys—were two, three, four years older than Bobbie, but when she was fifteen or sixteen she began to pass among us, from boy to boy, trying one and then another, causing several fist fights, and half promising but never delivering anything more than the "soul kisses" that were all we really expected. By the time she was eighteen she had been in and out of love with all of us with the solitary exception of Pete McCrea. When she broke off with a boy, she would also make up with the girl he had temporarily deserted for Bobbie, and all the girls came to understand that every boy in the crowd had to go through a love affair with her. Consequently Bobbie was popular; the boys remembered her kisses, the girls forgave her because the boys had been returned virtually intact. We used the word hectic a lot in those days; Kitty Clark explained the short duration of Bobbie's love affairs by observing that being in love with Bobbie was too hectic for most boys. It was also true that it was not hectic enough. The boys agreed that Bobbie was a hot little number, but none of us could claim that she was not a virgin. At eighteen Bobbie entered a personal middle age, and for the big social occasions her beaus came from out-of-town. She was also busy at the college proms and football games, as far west as Ann Arbor, as far north as Brunswick, Maine. I was working on the Gibbsville paper during some of those years, the only boy in our crowd who was not away at college, and I remember Ann Arbor because Bobbie went there wearing a Delta Tau Delta pin and came back wearing the somewhat larger Psi U. "Now don't you say anything in front of Mother," she said. "She thinks they're both the same."

We played auction bridge, the social occupation in towns like ours, and Bobbie and I were assimilated into an older crowd: the younger married set and the youngest of the couples who were in their thirties. We played for prizes—flasks, cigarette lighters, vanity cases, cartons of cigarettes— and there was a party at someone's house every week. The hostess of the evening usually asked me to stop for Bobbie, and I saw her often. Her father and mother would be reading the evening paper and sewing when I arrived to pick up Bobbie. Philip Hammersmith was not a native of Gibbsville, but he had lived there long enough to have gone to the Mexican Border in 1916 with the Gibbsville company of mounted engineers, and he had gone to France with them, returning as a first lieutenant and with the Croix de Guerre with palm. He was one of the best golfers in the club, and everyone said he was making money hand-over-fist as an independent coal operator. He wore steel-rim glasses and he had almost completely gray hair, cut short. He inspired trust and confidence. He was slow-moving, taller than six feet, and always thought before speaking. His wife, a Gibbsville girl, was related, as she said, to half the town; a lively little woman who took her husband's arm even if they were walking only two doors away. I always used to feel that whatever he may have wanted out of life, yet unattained or unattainable, she had just what she wanted: a good husband, a nice home, and a pretty daughter who would not long remain unmarried. At home in the evening, and whenever I saw him on the street, Mr. Hammersmith was wearing a dark-gray worsted suit, cut loose and with a soft roll to the lapel; black knit four-in-hand necktie; white shirt; heavy gray woolen socks, and thick-soled brogues. This costume, completely unadorned—he wore a wrist watch—was what he always wore except for formal occasions, and the year-to-year sameness of his attire constituted his only known eccentricity. He was on the board of the second most conservative bank, the trustees of Gibbsville Hospital, the armory board, the Y.M.C.A., and the Gibbsville and Lantenengo country clubs. Nevertheless I sensed that that was not all there was to Philip Hammersmith, that the care he put into the creation of the general picture of himself—hard work, quiet clothes, thoughtful manner, conventional associations—was done with a purpose that was not necessarily sinister but was extraordinarily private. It delighted me to discover, one night while waiting for Bobbie, that he knew more about what was going on than most of us suspected he would know. "Jimmy, you know Ed Charney, of course," he said.

I knew Ed Charney, the principal bootlegger in the area. "Yes, I know him pretty well," I said.

"Then do you happen to know if there's any truth to what I heard? I heard that his wife is threatening to divorce him."

"I doubt it. They're Catholics."

"Do you know her?"

"Yes. I went to Sisters' school with her."

"Oh, then maybe you can tell me something else. I've heard that she's the real brains of those two."

"She quit school after eighth grade, so I don't know about that. I don't remember her being particularly bright. She's about my age but she was two grades behind me."

"I see. And you think their religion will keep them from getting a divorce?"

"Yes, I do. I don't often see Ed at Mass, but I know he carries rosary beads. And she's at the eleven o'clock Mass every Sunday, all dolled up."

This conversation was explained when Repeal came and with it public knowledge that Ed Charney had been quietly buying bank stock, one of several moves he had made in the direction of respectability. But the chief interest to me at the time Mr. Hammersmith and I talked was in the fact that he knew anything at all about the Charneys. It was so unlike him even to mention Ed Charney's name.

To get back to the weekend of Bobbie Hammersmith's wedding: it was throughout that weekend that I first saw Bobbie have what we called that faraway look, that another generation called Cloud 90. If you happened to catch her at the right moment, you would see her smiling up at Pete in a way that must have been reassuring to Mrs. McCrea and to Mrs. Hammersmith, but I also caught her at several wrong moments and I saw something I had never seen before: a resemblance to her father that was a subtler thing than the mere duplication of such features as mouth, nose, and set of the eyes. It was almost the same thing I have mentioned in describing Philip Hammersmith; the wish yet unattained or unattainable. However, the pre-nuptial parties and the wedding and reception went off without a hitch, or so I believed until the day after the wedding.

Kitty Clark and I were on the same train going back to New York and I made some comment about the exceptional sobriety of the ushers and how everything had gone according to plan. "Amazing, considering," said Kitty.

"Considering what?"

"That there was almost no wedding at all," she said. "You must promise word of honor, Jimmy, or I won't tell you."

"I promise. Word of honor."

"Well, after Mrs. McCrea's very-dull-I-must-say luncheon, when we all left to go to Bobbie's? A little after two o'clock?"

"Yes."

"Bobbie asked me if I'd go across the street to our house and put in a long distance call to Johnny White. I said I couldn't do that, and what on earth was she thinking of. And Bobbie said, 'You're my oldest and best friend. The least you can do is make this one last effort, to keep me from ruining my life.' So I gave in and I dashed over to our house and called Johnny. He was out and they didn't know where he could be reached or what time he was coming home. So I left my name. *My* name, not Bobbie's. Six o'clock, at the reception, I was dancing with—I was dancing with *you*."

"When the waiter said you were wanted on the phone."

"It was Johnny. He'd been sailing and just got in. I made up some story about why I'd called him, but he didn't swallow it. '*You* didn't call me,' he said. '*Bobbie* did.' Well of course I wouldn't admit that. By that time she was married, and if her life was already ruined it would be a darned sight more ruined if I let him talk to her. Which he wanted to do. Then he tried to pump me. Where were they going on their wedding trip? I said nobody knew, which was a barefaced lie. I knew they were going to Bermuda. Known it since Thursday. But I wouldn't tell Johnny . . . I don't like him a bit after yesterday. I'd thought he was attractive, and he *is*, but he's got a mean streak that I never knew before. Feature this, if you will. When he realized I wasn't going to get Bobbie to come to the phone, or give him any information, he said, 'Well, no use wasting a long-distance call. What are you doing next weekend? How about coming out here?' 'I'm not that hard up,' I said, and banged down the receiver. I hope I shattered his eardrum."

I saw Pete and Bobbie McCrea when I went home the following Christmas. They were living in a small house on Twin Oaks Road, a recent real-estate development that had been instantly successful with the sons and daughters of the big two- and three-servant mansions. They were not going to any of the holiday dances; Bobbie was expecting a baby in April or early May.

"You're not losing any time," I said.

"I don't want to lose any time," said Bobbie. "I want to have a lot of children. Pete's an only child and so am I, and we don't think it's fair, if you can afford to have more."

"If we can afford it. The way that stock market is going, we'll be lucky to pay for this one," said Pete.

"Oh, don't start on that, Pete. That's all Father talks about," said Bobbie. "My father *was* hit pretty hard, but I wish he didn't have to keep talking about it all the time. Everybody's in the same boat."

"No, they're not. *We're* on a *raft*."

"I asked you, please, Pete. Jimmy didn't come here to listen to our financial woes. Do you see much of Kitty? I've owed her a letter for ages."

"No, I haven't seen her since last summer, we went out a few times," I said.

"Kitty went to New York to try to rope in a millionaire. She isn't going to waste her time on Jim."

"That's not what she went to New York for at all. And as far as wasting her time on Jim, Jim may not want to waste his time on her." She smiled. "Have you got a girl, Jim?"

"Not really."

"Wise. Very wise," said Pete McCrea.

"I don't know how wise. It's just that I have a hell of a hard time supporting myself, without trying to support a wife, too," I said.

"Why I understood you were selling articles to magazines, and going around with all the big shots."

"I've had four jobs in two years, and the jobs didn't last very long. If things get any tougher I may have to come back here. At least I'll have a place to sleep and something to eat."

"But I see your name in magazines," said Pete. "I don't always read your articles, but they must pay you well."

"They don't. At least I can't live on the magazine pieces without a steady job. Excuse me, Bobbie. Now you're getting *my* financial woes."

"She'll listen to yours. It's mine she doesn't want to hear about."

"That's because I know about ours. I'm never allowed to forget them," said Bobbie. "Are you going to all the parties?"

"Yes, stag. I have to bum rides. I haven't got a car."

"We resigned from the club," said Pete.

"Well we didn't *have* to do that," said Bobbie. "Father was going to give it to us for a Christmas present. And you have your job."

"We'll see how much longer I have it. Is that the last of the gin?"

"Yes."

Pete rose. "I'll be back."

"Don't buy any more for me," I said.

"You flatter yourself," he said. "I wasn't only getting it for you." He put on his hat and coat. "No funny business while I'm gone. I remember you two."

He kept a silly grin on his face while saying the ugly things, but the grin was not genuine and the ugly things were.

"I don't know what's the matter with him," said Bobbie. "Oh, I do, but why talk about it?"

"He's only kidding."

"You know better than that. He says worse things, much worse, and I'm only hoping they don't get back to Father. Father has enough on his mind. I thought if I had this baby right away it would—you know—give Pete confidence. But it's had just the opposite effect. He says it isn't his child. *Isn't his child!* Oh, I married him out of spite. I'm sure Kitty must have told you that. But it *is* his child, I swear it, Jim. It couldn't be anybody else's."

"I guess it's the old inferiority complex," I said.

"The first month we were married—Pete was a virgin—and I admit it, I wasn't. I stayed with two boys before I was married. But I was certainly not pregnant when I married Pete, and the first few weeks he was loving and sweet, and grateful. But then something happened to him, and he made a pass at I-won't-say-who. It was more than a pass. It was quite a serious thing. I might as well tell you. It was Phyllis. We were all at a picnic at the Dam and several people got pretty tight, Pete among them.

And there's no other word for it, he tried to rape Phyllis. Tore her bathing suit and slapped her and did other things. She got away from him and ran back to the cottage without anyone seeing her. Luckily Joe didn't see her or I'm sure he'd have killed Pete. You know, Joe's strong as an ox and terribly jealous. I found out about it from Phyllis herself. She came here the next day and told me. She said she wasn't going to say anything to Joe, but that we mustn't invite her to our house and she wasn't going to invite us to hers."

"I'm certainly glad Joe didn't hear about it. He would do something drastic," I said. "But didn't he notice that you two weren't going to his house, and they to yours? It's a pretty small group."

She looked at me steadily. "We haven't been going anywhere. My excuse is that I'm pregnant, but the truth is, we're not being asked. It didn't end with Phyllis, Jim. One night at a dinner party Mary Lander just slapped his face, in front of everybody. Everybody laughed and thought Pete must have said something, but it wasn't something he'd said. He'd taken her hand and put it—you know. This is *Pete! Ichabod!* Did you ever know any of this about him?"

"You mean have I heard any of this? No."

"No, I didn't mean that. I meant, did he go around making passes and I never happened to hear about it?"

"No. When we'd talk dirty he'd say, 'Why don't you fellows get your minds above your belts?' "

"I wish your father were still alive. I'd go see him and try to get some advice. I wouldn't think of going to Dr. English."

"Well, you're not the one that needs a doctor. Could you get Pete to go to one? He's a patient of Dr. English's, isn't he?"

"Yes, but so is Mrs. McCrea, and Pete would never confide in Dr. English."

"Or anyone else at this stage, I guess," I said. "I'm not much help, am I?"

"Oh, I didn't expect you to have a solution. You know, Jim, I wish you would come back to Gibbsville. Other girls in our crowd have often said it was nice to have you to talk to. Of course you were a very bad boy, too, but a lot of us miss you."

"That's nice to hear, Bobbie. Thank you. I may be back, if I don't soon make a go of it in New York. I won't have any choice."

During that Christmas visit I heard other stories about Pete McCrea. In general they were told as plain gossip, but two or three times there was a hint of a lack of sympathy for Bobbie. "She knew what she was doing . . . she made her bed . . ." And while there was no lack of righteous indignation over Pete's behavior, he had changed in six months from a semi-comic figure to an unpleasant man, but a man nevertheless. In half a year he had lost most of his old friends; they all said, "You've never seen such a change come over anybody in all your life," but when they remembered to call him Ichabod it was only to emphasize the change.

Bobbie's baby was born in April, but lived only a few weeks. "She was determined to have that baby," Kitty Clark told me. "She had to prove to Pete that it was anyway *conceived* after she married him. But it must have taken all her strength to hold on to it that long. All her strength *and* the baby's. Now would be a good time for her to divorce him. She can't go on like that."

But there was no divorce, and Bobbie was pregnant again when I saw her at Christmas, 1930. They no longer lived in the Twin Oaks Road house, and her father and mother had given up their house on Lantenengo Street. The Hammersmiths were living in an apartment on Market Street, and Bobbie and Pete were living with Mrs. McCrea. "Temporarily, till Pete decides whether to take this job in Tulsa, Oklahoma," said Bobbie.

"Who do you think you're kidding?" said Pete. "It isn't a question of me deciding. It's a cousin of mine deciding if he'll take me on. And why the hell should he?"

"Well, you've had several years' banking experience," she said.

"Yes. And if I was so good, why did the bank let me go? Jim knows all this. What else have you heard about us, Jim? Did you hear Bobbie was divorcing me?"

"It doesn't look that way from here," I said.

"You mean because she's pregnant? That's elementary biology, and God knows you're acquainted with the facts of life. But if you want to be polite, all right. Pretend you didn't hear she was getting a divorce. You might as well pretend Mr. and Mrs. Hammersmith are still living on Lantenengo Street. If they were, Bobbie'd have got her divorce."

"Everybody tells me what I *was* going to do or *am* going to do," said Bobbie. "Nobody ever consults me."

"I suppose that's a crack at my mother."

"Oh, for Christ's sake, Pete, lay off, at least while I'm here," I said.

"Why? You like to think of yourself as an old friend of the family, so you might as well get a true picture. When you get married, if you ever do, I'll come and see you, and maybe your wife will cry on my shoulder." He got up and left the house.

"Well, it's just like a year ago," said Bobbie. "When you came to call on us last Christmas?"

"Where will he go now?"

"Oh, there are several places where he can charge drinks. They all think Mrs. McCrea has plenty of money, but they're due for a rude awakening. She's living on capital, but she's not going to sell any bonds to pay his liquor bills."

"Then maybe *he's* due for a rude awakening."

"Any awakening would be better than the last three months, since the bank fired him. He sits here all day long, then after Mrs. McCrea goes to bed he goes to one of his speakeasies." She sat up straighter. "He has a lady friend. Or have you heard?"

"No."

"Yes. He graduated from making passes at all my friends. He had to. We were never invited anywhere. Yes, he has a girl friend. Do you remember Muriel Nierhaus?"

"The chiropractor's wife. Sure. Big fat Muriel Minzer till she married Nierhaus, then we used to say he gave her some adjustments. Where is Nierhaus?"

"Oh, he's opened several offices. Very prosperous. He divorced her but she gets alimony. She's Pete's girl friend. Muriel Minzer is *Angus McCrea's* girl friend."

"You don't seem too displeased," I said.

"Would you be, if you were in my position?"

"I guess I know what you mean. But—well, nothing."

"But why don't I get a divorce?" She shook her head. "A spite marriage is a terrible thing to do to anybody. If I hadn't deliberately selected Pete out of all the boys I knew, he'd have gone on till Mrs. McCrea picked out somebody for him, and it would almost have had to be the female counterpart of Pete. A girl like—oh—Florence. Florence Temple."

"Florence Temple, with her cello. Exactly right."

"But I did that awful thing to Pete, and the first few weeks of marriage were just too much for him. He went haywire. I'd slept with two boys before I was married, so it wasn't as much of a shock to me. But Pete almost wore me out. And such adoration, I can't tell you. Then when we came back from Bermuda he began to see all the other girls he'd known all his life, and he'd ask me about them. It was as though he'd never seen them before, in a way. In other ways, it was as though he'd just been waiting all his life to start ripping their clothes off. He was dangerous, Jim. He really was. I could almost tell who would be next by the questions he'd ask. Before we'd go to a party, he'd say 'Who's going to be there tonight?' And I'd say I thought the usual crowd. Then he'd rattle off the list of names of our friends, and leave out one name. That was supposed to fool me, but it didn't for long. The name he left out, that girl was almost sure to be in for a bad time."

"And now it's all concentrated on Muriel Minzer?"

"As far as I know."

"Well, that's a break for you, *and* the other girls. Did you ever talk to him about the passes he made at the others?"

"Oh, how could we avoid it? Whoever it was, she was always 'that little whore.' "

"Did he ever get anywhere with any of them?"

She nodded. "One, but I won't tell you who. There was one girl that didn't stop him, and when that happened he wanted me to sleep with her husband."

"Swap, eh?"

"Yes. But I said I wasn't interested. Pete wanted to know why not? Why wouldn't I? And I almost told him. The boy was one of the two boys I'd stayed with before I was married—oh, when I was seventeen. And he never told anybody and neither have I, or ever will."

"You mean one of our old crowd actually did get somewhere with you, Bobbie?"

"One did. But don't try to guess. It won't do you any good to guess, because I'd never, never tell."

"Well, whichever one it was, he's the best liar I ever knew. And I guess the nicest guy in our whole crowd. You know, Bobbie, the whole damn bunch are going to get credit now for being as honorable as one guy."

"You were all nice, even if you all did talk too much. If it had been you, you would have lied, too."

"No, I don't think I would have."

"You lied about Kitty. Ha ha ha. You didn't know I knew about you and Kitty. I knew it the next day. The very next day. If you don't believe me, I'll tell you where it happened and how it happened, and all about it. That was the great bond we had in common. You and Kitty, and I and this other boy."

"Then Kitty's a gentleman, because she never told me a word about you."

"I kissed every boy in our crowd except Pete, and I necked, heavy-necked two, as you well know, and stayed with one."

"The question is, did you stay with the other one that you heavy-necked with?"

"You'll never know, Jim, and please don't try to find out."

"I won't, but I won't be able to stop theorizing," I said.

We knew everything, everything there was to know. We were so far removed from the technical innocence of eighteen, sixteen, nineteen. I was a man of the world, and Bobbie was indeed a woman, who had borne a child and lived with a husband who had come the most recently to the knowledge we had acquired, but was already the most intricately involved in the complications of sex. We—Bobbie and I—could discuss him and still remain outside the problems of Pete McCrea. We could almost remain outside our own problems. We knew so much, and since what we knew seemed to be all there was to know, we were shockproof. We had come to our maturity and our knowledgeability during the long decade of cynicism that was usually dismissed as "a cynical disregard of the law of the land," but that was something else, something deeper. The law had been passed with a "noble" but nevertheless cynical disregard of men's right to drink. It was a law that had been imposed on some who took pleasure in drinking by some who did not. And when the law was an instant failure, it was not admitted to be a failure by those who had imposed it. They fought to retain the law in spite of its immediate failure and its proliferating corruption, and they fought as hard as they would have for a law that had been an immediate success. They gained no recruits to their own way; they had only deserters, who were not brave deserters but furtive ones; there was no honest mutiny but only grumbling and small disobe- diences. And we grew up listening to the grumbling, watching the small disobediences; laughing along when the grumbling was intentionally funny, imitating the small disobediences in other ways besides the customs of drinking. It was not only a cynical disregard for a law of the land; the law was eventually changed. Prohibition, the zealots' attempt to force total abstinence on a temperate nation, made liars of a hundred million men and cheats of their children; the West Point cadets who cheated in ex- aminations, the basketball players who connived with gamblers, the thou- sands of uncaught cheats in the high schools and colleges. We had grown up and away from our earlier esteem of God and country and valor, and had matured at a moment when riches were vanishing for reasons that we could not understand. We were the losing, not the lost, generation. We could not blame Pete McCrea's troubles—and Bobbie's—on the South- ern Baptists and the Northern Methodists. Since we knew everything, we knew that Pete's sudden release from twenty years of frustrations had turned him loose in a world filled with women. But Bobbie and I sat there in her mother-in-law's house, breaking several laws of possession, pur- chase, transportation and consumption of liquor, and with great calmness discussing the destruction of two lives—one of them hers—and the loss of her father's fortune, the depletion of her mother-in-law's, the allure of a chiropractor's divorcée, and our own promiscuity. We knew everything, but we were incapable of recognizing the meaning of our complacency.

I was wearing my dinner jacket, and someone was going to pick me up and take me to a dinner dance at the club. "Who's stopping for you?" said Bobbie.

"It depends. Either Joe or Frank. Depends on whether they go in Joe's car or in Frank's. I'm to be ready when they blow their horn."

"Do me a favor, Jim. Make them come in. Pretend you don't hear the horn."

"If it's Joe, he's liable to drive off without me. You know Joe if he's had a few too many."

In a few minutes there was a blast of a two-tone horn, repeated. "That's Joe's car," said Bobbie. "You'd better go." She went to the hall with me and I kissed her cheek. The front door swung open and it was Joe Whipple.

"Hello, Bobbie," he said.

"Hello, Joe. Won't you all come in? Haven't you got time for one drink?" She was trying not to sound suppliant, but Joe was not deceived.

"Just you and Jim here?" he said.

"Yes. Pete went out a little while ago."

"I'll see what the others say," said Joe. He left to speak to the three in the sedan, and obviously he was not immediately persuasive, but they came in with him. They would not let Bobbie take their coats, but they were nice to her and with the first sips of our drinks we were all six almost back in the days when Bobbie Hammersmith's house was where so many of our parties started from. Then we heard the front door thumping shut and Pete McCrea looked in.

There were sounds of hello, but he stared at us over his horn-rims and said to Bobbie: "You didn't have to invite me, but you could have told me." He turned and again the front door thumped.

"Get dressed and come with us," said Joe Whipple.

"I can't do that," said Bobbie.

"She can't, Joe," said Phyllis Whipple. "That would only make more trouble."

"What trouble? She's going to have to sit here alone till he comes home. She might as well be with us," said Joe.

"Anyway, I haven't got a dress that fits," said Bobbie. "But thanks for asking me."

"I won't have you sitting here—"

"Now don't make matters worse, Joe, for heaven's sake," said his wife.

"I could lend you a dress, Bobbie, but I think Phyllis is right," said Mary Lander. "Whatever *you* want to do."

"*Want* to do! That's not the question," said Bobbie. "Go on before I change my mind. Thanks, everybody. Frank, you haven't said a word."

"Nothing much for me to say," said Frank Lander. But as far as I was concerned he, and Bobbie herself, had said more than anyone else. I caught her looking at me quickly.

"Well, all right, then," said Joe. "I'm outnumbered. Or outpersuaded or something."

I was the last to say goodbye, and I whispered to Bobbie: "Frank, eh?"

"You're only guessing," she said. "Goodnight, Jim." Whatever they would be after we left, her eyes were brighter than they had been in years. She had very nearly gone to a party, and for a minute or two she had been part of it.

I sat in the back seat with Phyllis Whipple and Frank Lander. "If you'd had any sense you'd know there'd be a letdown," said Phyllis.

"Oh, drop it," said Joe.

"It might have been worth it, though, Phyllis," said Mary Lander. "How long is it since she's seen anybody but that old battle-ax, Mrs. McCrea? God, I hate to think what it must be like, living in that house with Mrs. McCrea."

"I'm sure it would have been a *lot* easier if Bobbie'd come with us," said Phyllis. "That would have fixed things just right with Mrs. McCrea. She's just the type that wants Bobbie to go out and have a good time. Especially without Pete. You forget how the old lady used to call up all the mothers as soon as she heard there was a party planned. What Joe did was cruel because it was so downright stupid. Thoughtless. Like getting her all excited and then leaving her hung up."

"You've had too much to drink," said Joe.

"*I* have?"

"Yes, you don't say things like that in front of a bachelor," said Joe.

"Who's—oh, Jim? It is to laugh. Did I shock you, Jim?"

"Not a bit. I didn't know what you meant. Did you say something risqué?"

"My husband thinks I did."

"Went right over my head," I said. "I'm innocent about such things."

"So's your old man," said Joe.

"Do you think she should have come with us, Frank?" I said.

"Why ask me? No. I'm with Phyllis. What's the percentage for Bobbie? You saw that son of a bitch in the doorway, and you know damn well when he gets home from Muriel Nierhaus's, he's going to raise hell with Bobbie."

"Then Bobbie had nothing to lose," said Joe. "If Pete's going to raise hell with her, anyway, she might as well have come with us."

"How does he raise hell with her?" I said.

No one said anything.

"Do you know, Phyllis?" I said.

"What?" said Phyllis.

"Oh, come on. You heard me," I said. "Mary?"

"I'm sure I don't know."

"Oh, nuts," I said.

"Go ahead, tell him," said Frank Lander.

"Nobody ever knew for sure," said Phyllis, quietly.

"That's not true. Caroline English, for one. She knew for sure."

Phyllis spoke: "A few weeks before Bobbie had her baby she rang Caroline's doorbell in the middle of the night and asked Caroline if she could stay there. Naturally Caroline said yes, and she saw that Bobbie had nothing but a coat over her nightgown and had bruises all over her arms and shoulders. Julian was away, a lucky break because he'd have gone over and had a fight with Pete. As it was, Caroline made Bobbie have Dr. English come out and have a look at her, and nothing more was said. I mean, it was kept secret from everybody, especially Mr. Hammersmith. But the story got out somehow. Not widespread, but we all heard about it."

"We don't want it to get back to Mr. Hammersmith," said Mary Lander.

"He knows," said Frank Lander.

"You keep saying that, but I don't believe he does," said Mary.

"I don't either," said Joe Whipple. "Pete wouldn't be alive today if Phil Hammersmith knew."

"That's where I think you're wrong," said Phyllis. "Mr. Hammersmith might want to kill Pete, but killing him is another matter. And what earthly good would it do? The Hammersmiths have lost every penny, so I'm told, and at least with Pete still alive, Mrs. McCrea supports Bobbie. Barely. But they have food and a roof over their heads."

"Phil Hammersmith knows the whole damn story, you can bet anything on that. And it's why he's an old man all of a sudden. Have you seen him this trip, Jim?" said Frank Lander.

"I haven't seen him since the wedding."

"Oh, well—" said Mary.

"You won't—" said Joe.

"You won't recognize him," said Frank Lander. "He's bent over—"

"They say he's had a stroke," said Phyllis Whipple.

"And on top of everything else he got a lot of people sore at him by selling his bank stock to Ed Charney," said Joe. "Well, not a lot of people, but some that could have helped him. My old man, to name one. And I don't think that was so hot. Phil Hammersmith was a carpetbagger himself, and damn lucky to be in the bank. Then to sell his stock to a lousy stinking bootlegger . . . You should hear Harry Reilly on the subject."

"I don't want to hear Harry Reilly on any subject," said Frank Lander. "Cheap Irish Mick."

"I don't like him any better than you do, Frank, but call him something else," I said.

"I'm sorry, Jim. I didn't mean that," said Frank Lander.

"No. It just slipped out," I said.

"I apologize," said Frank Lander.

"Oh, all right."

"Don't be sensitive, Jim," said Mary.

"Stay out of it, Mary," said Frank Lander.

"*Everybody* calm down," said Joe. "Everybody knows that Harry Reilly is a cheap Irish Mick, and nobody knows it better than Jim, an Irish Mick but not a cheap one. So shut the hell up, everybody."

"Another country heard from," said Phyllis.

"Now *you*, for Christ's sake," said Joe. "Who has the quart?"

"I have my quart," said Frank Lander.

"I have mine," I said.

"I asked who has mine. Phyllis?"

"When we get to the club, time enough," said Phyllis.

"Hand it over," said Joe.

"Three quarts of whiskey between five people. I'd like to know how we're going to get home tonight," said Mary Lander.

"Drunk as a monkey, if you really want to know," said Joe. "Tight as a nun's."

"Well, at least we're off the subject of Bobbie and Pete," said Phyllis.

"I'm not. I was coming back to it. Phyllis. The quart," said Joe.

"No," said Phyllis.

"Here," I said. "And remember where it came from." I handed him my bottle.

Joe took a swig in the corner of his mouth, swerving the car only slightly. "Thanks," he said, and returned the bottle. "Now, Mary, if you'll light me a cigarette like a dear little second cousin."

"Once removed," said Mary Lander.

"Once removed, and therefore related to Bobbie through her mother."

"No, *you* are but I'm not," said Mary Lander.

"Well, you're in it some way, through me. Now for the benefit of those who are not related to Bobbie or Mrs. Hammersmith, or Mary or me. Permit me to give you a little family history that will enlighten you on several points."

"Is this going to be about Mr. Hammersmith?" said Phyllis. "I don't think you'd better tell that."

"You're related only by marriage, so kindly keep your trap shut. If I want to tell it, I can."

"Everybody remember that I asked him not to," said Phyllis.

"Don't tell it, Joe, whatever it is," said Mary Lander.

"Yeah, what's the percentage?" said Frank Lander. "They have enough trouble without digging up past history."

"Oh, you're so noble, Lander," said Joe. "You fool nobody."

"If you're going to tell the story, go ahead, but stop insulting Frank," said Mary Lander.

"We'll be at the club before he gets started," said Phyllis.

"Then we'll sit there till I finish. Anyway, it doesn't take that long. So, to begin at the beginning. Phil Hammersmith. Phil Hammersmith came here before the war, just out of Lehigh."

"You're not even telling it right," said Phyllis.

"Phyllis is right. I'm screwing up my own story. Well, I'll begin again. Phil Hammersmith graduated from Lehigh, then a few years *later* he came to Gibbsville."

"That's better," said Phyllis.

"The local Lehigh contingent all knew him. He'd played lacrosse and he was a Sigma Nu around the time Mr. Chew was there. So he already had friends in Gibbsville."

"Now you're on the right track," said Phyllis.

"Thank you, love," said Joe.

"Where was he from originally?" I asked.

"Don't ask questions, Jim. It only throws me. He was from some place in New Jersey. So anyway he arrived in Gibbsville and got a job with the Coal & Iron Company. He was a civil engineer, and he had the job when he arrived. That is, he didn't come here looking for a job. He was hired before he got here."

"You've made that plain," said Phyllis.

"Well, it's important," said Joe.

"Yes, but you don't have to say the same thing over and over again," said Phyllis.

"Yes I do. Anyway, apparently the Coal & Iron people hired him on the strength of his record at Lehigh, plus asking a few questions of the local Lehigh contingent, that knew him, *plus* a very good recommendation he'd had from some firm in Bethlehem. Where he'd worked after getting out of college. But after he'd been here a while, and was getting along all right at the Coal & Iron, one day a construction engineer from New York arrived to talk business at the C. & I. Building. They took him down-cellar to the drafting-room and who should he see but Phil Hammersmith. But apparently Phil didn't see him. Well, the New York guy was a real wet smack, because he tattled on Phil.

"Old Mr. Duncan was general superintendent then and he sent for Phil. Was it true that Phil had once worked in South America, and if so, why hadn't he mentioned it when he applied for a job? Phil gave him the obvious answer. 'Because if I had, you wouldn't have hired me.' 'Not necessarily,' said Mr. Duncan. 'We might have accepted your explanation.' 'You say that now, but I tried telling the truth and I couldn't get a job.' 'Well, tell me the truth now,' said Mr. Duncan. 'All right,' said Phil. So he told Mr. Duncan what had happened.

"He was working in South America. Peru, I think. Or maybe Bolivia. In the jungle. And the one thing they didn't want the natives, the Indians, to get hold of was firearms. But one night he caught a native carrying an armful of rifles from the shanty, and when Phil yelled at him, the native ran, and Phil shot him. Killed him. The next day one of the other engineers was found with his throat cut. And the day after that the native chief came and called on the head man of the construction outfit. Either the Indians thought they'd killed the man that had killed their boy, or they didn't much care. But the chief told the white boss that the next time an Indian was killed, two white men would be killed. And not just killed. Tortured. Well, there were four or maybe five engineers, including Phil and the boss. The only white men in an area as big as Pennsylvania, and I guess they weighed their chances and being mathematicians, the odds didn't look so hot. So they quit. No hero stuff. They just quit. Except Phil. He was fired. The boss blamed Phil for everything and in his report to the New York office he put in a lot of stuff that just about fixed Phil for good. The boss, of course, was the same man that spotted Phil at the C. & I. drafting-room."

"You told it very well," said Phyllis.

"So any time you think of Phil Hammersmith killing Pete McCrea, it wouldn't be the first time," said Joe.

"And the war," I said. "He probably killed a few Germans."

"On the other hand, he never got over blaming himself for the other engineer's getting his throat cut," said Joe. "This is all the straight dope. Mr. Duncan to my old man."

We were used to engineers, their travels and adventures in far-off places, but engineers came and went and only a few became fixtures in our life. Phil Hammersmith's story was all new to Mary and Frank and me, and in the cold moonlight, as we sat in a heated automobile in a snow-covered parking area of a Pennsylvania country club, Joe Whipple had taken us to a dark South American jungle, given us a touch of fear, and in a few minutes covered Phil Hammersmith in mystery and then removed the mystery.

"Tell us more about Mr. Hammersmith," said Mary Lander.

Mary Lander. I had not had time to realize the inference that must accompany my guess that Frank Lander was the one boy in our crowd who had stayed with Bobbie. Mary Lander was the only girl who had not fought off Pete McCrea. She was the last girl I would have suspected of staying with Pete, and yet the one that surprised me the least. She had always been the girl our mothers liked us to take out, a kind of mothers' ideal for their sons, and possibly even for themselves. Mary Morgan Lander was the third generation of a family that had always been in the grocery business, the only store in the county that sold caviar and English biscuits and Sportsmen's Bracer chocolate, as well as the most expensive domestic items of fruit, vegetables, and tinned goods. Her brother Llewellyn Morgan still scooped out dried prunes and operated the rotary ham slicer, but no one seriously believed that all the Morgan money came from the store. Lew Morgan taught Sunday School in the Methodist Episcopal Church and played basketball at the Y.M.C.A., but he had been to Blair Academy and Princeton, and his father had owned one of the first Pierce-Arrows in Gibbsville. Mary had been unfairly judged a teaser, in previous years. She was not a teaser, but a girl who would kiss a boy and allow him to wander all over her body so long as he did not touch bare skin. Nothing surprised me about Mary. It was in character for her to have slapped Pete McCrea at a dinner party, and then to have let him stay with her and to have discussed with him a swap of husbands and wives. No casual dirty remark ever passed unnoticed by Mary; when someone made a slip we would all turn to see how Mary was taking it, and without fail she had heard it, understood it, and taken a pious attitude. But in our crowd she was the one person most conscious of sex and scatology. She was the only one of whom I would say she had a dirty mind, but I kept that observation to myself along with my theory that she hated Frank

Lander. My theory, based on no information whatever, was that marriage and Frank Lander had not been enough for her and that Pete McCrea had become attractive to her because he was so awful.

"There's no more to tell," said Joe Whipple. We got out of the car and Mary took Joe's arm, and her evening was predictable: fathers and uncles and older brothers would cut in on her, and older women would comment as they always did that Mary Lander was *such* a sensible girl, *so* considerate of her elders, a *wonderful* wife to Frank. And we of her own age would dance with her because under cover of the dancing crowd Mary would wrap both legs around our right legs with a promise that had fooled us for years. Quiet little Mary Lander, climbing up a boy's leg but never forgetting to smile her Dr. Lyons smile at old Mrs. Ginyan and old Mr. Heff. And yet through some mental process that I did not take time to scrutinize, I was less annoyed with Mary than I had been since we were children. I was determined not to dance with her, and I did not, but my special knowledge about her and Pete McCrea reduced her power to allure. Bobbie had married Pete McCrea and she was still attractive in spite of it; but Mary's seductiveness vanished with the revelation that she had picked Pete as her lover, if only for once, twice, or how many times. I had never laughed at Mary before, but now she was the fool, not we, not I.

I got quite plastered at the dance, and so did a lot of other people. On the way home we sang a little—"Body and Soul" was the song, but Phyllis was the only one who could sing the middle part truly—and Frank Lander tried to tell about an incident in the smoking-room, where Julian English apparently had thrown a drink in Harry Reilly's face. It did not seem worth making a fuss about, and Frank never finished his story. Mary Lander attacked me: "You never danced with me, not once," she said.

"I didn't?"

"No, you didn't, and you know you didn't," she said. "And you always do."

"Well, this time I guess I didn't."

"Well, *why* didn't you?"

"Because he didn't want to," said Frank Lander. "You're making a fool of yourself. I should think you'd have more pride."

"Yeah, why don't you have more pride, Mary?" said Joe Whipple. "You'd think it was an honor to dance with this Malloy guy."

"It is," I said.

"That's it. You're getting so conceited," said Mary. "Well, I'm sure I didn't have to sit any out."

"Then why all the fuss?" said Frank Lander.

"Such popularity must be deserved," I said, quoting an advertising slogan.

"Whose? Mary's or yours?" said Phyllis.

"Well, I was thinking of Mary's, but now that you mention it . . ." I said.

"How many times did he dance with *you*, Phyllis?" said Joe.

"Three or four," said Phyllis.

"In that case, Frank, Jim has insulted your wife. I don't see any other way out of it. You have to at least slap his face. Shall I stop the car?"

"My little trouble-maker," said Phyllis.

"Come on, let's have a fight," said Joe. "Go ahead, Frank. Give him a punch in the nose."

"Yeah, like you did at the Dam, Frank," I said.

"Oh, God. I remember that awful night," said Phyllis. "What did you fight over?"

"Bobbie," I said.

"Bobbie was the cause of *more* fights," said Mary Lander.

"Well, we don't need her to fight over now. We have you," said Joe. "Your honor's been attacked and your husband wants to defend it. The same as I would if Malloy hadn't danced with *my* wife. It's a good thing you danced with Phyllis, Malloy, or you and I'd get out of this car and start slugging."

"Why did you fight over Bobbie? I don't remember that," said Mary.

"Because she came to the picnic with Jim and then went off necking with Frank," said Phyllis. "I remember the whole thing."

"Stop *talking* about fighting and let's *fight*," said Joe.

"All right, stop the car," I said.

"Now you're talking," said Joe.

"Don't be ridiculous," said Phyllis.

"Oh, shut up," said Joe. He pulled up on the side of the road. "I'll referee." He got out of the car, and so did Frank and I and Phyllis. "All right, put up your dukes." We did so, moved around a bit in the snow and slush. "Go on, mix it," said Joe, whereupon Frank rushed me and hit me on the left cheek. All blows were directed at the head, since all three of us were armored in coonskin coats. "That was a good one, Frank. Now go get him, Jim." I swung my right hand and caught Frank's left eye, and at that moment we were all splashed by slush, taken completely by surprise as Phyllis, whom we had forgotten, drove the car away.

"That bitch!" said Joe. He ran to the car and got hold of a door handle but she increased her speed and he fell in the snow. "God damn that bitch, I should have known she was up to something. Now what? Let's try to bum a ride." The fight, such as it was, was over, and we tried to flag down cars on their way home from the dance. We recognized many of them, but not one would stop.

"Well, thanks to you, we've got a nice three-mile walk to Swedish Haven," said Frank Lander.

"Oh, she'll be back," said Joe.

"I'll bet you five bucks she's not," I said.

"Well, I won't bet, but I'll be damned if I'm going to walk three miles. I'm just going to wait till we can bum a ride."

"If you don't keep moving you'll freeze," said Frank.

"We're nearer the club than we are Swedish Haven. Let's go back there," I said.

"And have my old man see me?" said Joe.

"Your old man went home hours ago," I said.

"Well, somebody'll see me," said Joe.

"Listen, half the club's seen you already, and they wouldn't even stop," I said.

"Who has a cigarette?" said Joe.

"Don't give him one," said Frank.

"I have no intention of giving him one," I said. "Let's go back to the club. My feet are soaking wet."

"So are mine," said Frank. We were wearing pumps, and our feet had been wet since we got out of the car.

"That damn Phyllis, she knows I just got over a cold," said Joe.

"Maybe that's why she did it," I said. "It'd serve you right if you got pneumonia."

We began to walk in the middle of the road, in the direction of the clubhouse, which we could see, warm and comfortable on top of a distant plateau. "That old place never looked so good," said Joe. "Let's spend the night there."

"The rooms are all taken. The orchestra's staying there," I said.

We walked about a mile, our feet getting sorer at every step, and the combination of exhaustion and the amount we had had to drink made even grumbling an effort. Then a Dodge touring car, becurtained, stopped about fifty yards from us and a spotlight was turned on each of our faces. A man in a short overcoat and fur-lined cap came toward us. He was a State Highway patrolman. "What happened to you fellows?" he said. "You have a wreck?"

"I married one," said Joe.

"Oh, a weisscrackah," said the patrolman, a Pennsylvania Dutchman. "Where's your car?"

"We got out to take a leak and my wife drove off with it," said Joe.

"You from the dance at the gulf club?"

"Yes," said Joe. "How about giving us a lift?"

"Let me see you' driwah's license," said the cop.

Joe took out his billfold and handed over the license. "So? From Lantenengo street yet? All right, get in. Whereabouts you want to go to?"

"The country club," said Joe.

"The hell with that," said Frank. "Let's go on to Gibbsville."

"This aint no taxi service," said the cop. "And I aint taking you to no

Gippsfille. I'm on my way to my substation. Swedish Haven. You can phone there for a taxi. Privileged characters, you think you are. A bunch of drunks, you ask me."

I had to go back to New York on the morning train and the events of the next few days, so far as they concerned Joe and Phyllis Whipple and Frank and Mary Lander, were obscured by the suicide, a day or two later, of Julian English, the man who had thrown a drink at Harry Reilly. The domestic crisis of the Whipples and the Landers and even the McCreas seemed very unimportant. And yet when I heard about English, who had not been getting along with his wife, I wondered about my own friends, people my own age but not so very much younger than Julian and Caroline English. English had danced with Phyllis and Mary that night, and now he was dead. I knew very little about the causes of the difficulties between him and Caroline, but they could have been no worse than the problems that existed in Bobbie's marriage and that threatened the marriage of Frank and Mary Lander. I was shocked and saddened by the English suicide; he was an attractive man whose shortcomings seemed out of proportion to the magnitude of killing himself. He had not been a friend of mine, only an acquaintance with whom I had had many drinks and played some golf; but friends of mine, my closest friends in the world, boys-now-men like myself, were at the beginning of the same kind of life and doing the same kind of thing that for Julian English ended in a sealed-up garage with a motor running. I hated what I thought those next few days and weeks. There is nothing young about killing oneself, no matter when it happens, and I hated this being deprived of the sweetness of youth. And that was what it was, that was what was happening to us. I, and I think the others, had looked upon our squabbles as unpleasant incidents but belonging to our youth. Now they were plainly recognizable as symptoms of life without youth, without youth's excuses or youth's recoverability. I wanted to love someone, and during the next year or two I confused the desperate need for love with love itself. I had put a hopeless love out of my life; but that is not part of this story, except to state it and thus to show that I knew what I was looking for.

2.

When you have grown up with someone it is much easier to fill in gaps of five years, ten years, in which you do not see him, than to supply those early years in the life of a friend you meet in maturity. I do not know why this is so, unless it is a mere matter of insufficient time. With the friends of later life you may exchange boyhood stories that seem worth telling, but boyhood is not all stories. It is mostly not stories, but day-to-day, unepisodic living. And most of us are too polite to burden our later-life friends with unexciting anecdotes about people they will never meet. (Likewise we hope they will not burden us.) But it is easy to bring old friends up to date in your mental dossiers by the addition of a few vital facts. Have they stayed married? Have they had many more children? Have they made money or lost it? Usually the basic facts will do, and then you tell yourself that Joe Whipple is still Joe Whipple, plus two sons, a new house, a hundred thousand dollars, forty pounds, bifocals, fat in the neck, and a new concern for the state of the nation.

Such additions I made to my friends' dossiers as I heard about them from time to time; by letters from them, conversations with my mother, an occasional newspaper clipping. I received these facts with joy for the happy news, sorrow for the sad, and immediately went about my business, which was far removed from any business of theirs. I seldom went back to Gibbsville during the Thirties—mine and the century's—and when I did I stayed only long enough to stand at a grave, to toast a bride, to spend a few minutes beside a sickbed. In my brief encounters with my old friends I got no information about Bobbie and Pete McCrea, and only after I had returned to New York or California would I remember that I had intended to inquire about them.

There is, of course, some significance in the fact that no one volunteered information about Bobbie and Pete. It was that they had disappeared. They continued to live in Gibbsville, but in parts of the town that were out of the way for their old friends. There is no town so small that that cannot happen, and Gibbsville, a third-class city, was large enough to have all the grades of poverty and wealth and the many half grades in between, in which $10 a month in the husband's income could make a difference in the kind and location of the house in which he lived. No one had volunteered any information about Bobbie and Pete, and I had not remembered to inquire. In five years I had had no new facts about them, none whatever, and their disappearance from my ken might have continued but for a broken shoelace.

I was in Gibbsville for a funeral, and the year was 1938. I had broken a shoelace, it was evening and the stores were closed, and I was about to drive back to New York. The only place open that might have shoelaces was a poolroom that in my youth had had a two-chair bootblack stand. The poolroom was in a shabby section near the railroad stations and a couple of cheap hotels, four or five saloons, an automobile tire agency, a barber shop, and a quick-lunch counter. I opened the poolroom door, saw that the bootblack's chairs were still there, and said to the man behind the cigar counter: "Have you got any shoelaces?"

"Sorry I can't help you, Jim," said the man. He was wearing an eyeshade, but as soon as he spoke I recognized Pete McCrea.

"Pete, for God's sake," I said. We shook hands.

"I thought you might be in town for the funeral," he said. "I should have gone, too, I guess, but I decided I wouldn't. It was nice of you to make the trip."

"Well, you know. He was a friend of my father's. Do you own this place?"

"I run it. I have a silent partner, Bill Charney. You remember Ed Charney? His younger brother. I don't know where to send you to get a shoelace."

"The hell with the shoelace. How's Bobbie?"

"Oh, Bobbie's fine. *You* know. A lot of changes, but this is better than nothing. Why don't you call her up? She'd love to hear from you. We're living out on Mill Street, but we have a phone. Call her up and say hello. The number is 3385-J. If you have time maybe you could go see her. I have to stay here till I close up at one o'clock, but she's home."

"What number on Mill Street? You call her up and tell her I'm coming? Is that all right?"

"Hell, yes."

Someone thumped the butt of a cue on the floor and called out: "Rack 'em up, Pete?"

"I have to be here. You go on out and I'll call her up," he said. "Keep your shirt on," he said to the pool player, then, to me: "It's 402 Mill Street, across from the open hearth, second house from the corner. I guess I won't see you again, but I'm glad we had a minute. You're looking very well." I could not force a comment on his appearance. His nose was red and larger, his eyes watery, the dewlaps sagging, and he was wearing a blue denim work shirt with a dirty leather bow tie.

"Think I could get in the Ivy Club if I went back to Princeton?" he said. "I didn't make it the first time around, but now I'm a big shot. So long, Jim. Nice to've seen you."

The open hearth had long since gone the way of all the mill equipment; the mill itself had been inactive for years, and as a residential area the mill section was only about a grade and a half above the poorest Negro slums. But in front of most of the houses in the McCreas' row there were cared-for plots; there always had been, even when the mill was running and the air was full of smoke and acid. It was an Irish and Polish neighborhood, but knowledge of that fact did not keep me from locking all the doors of my car. The residents of the neighborhood would not have touched my father's car, but this was not his car and I was not he.

The door of Number 402 opened as soon as I closed my car door. Bobbie waited for me to lock up and when I got to the porch, she said: "*Jim.* Jim, Jim, Jim. How nice. I'm so glad to see you." She quickly closed the door behind me and then kissed me. "Give me a real kiss and a real hug. I didn't dare while the door was open." I kissed her and held her for a moment and then she said: "Hey, I guess we'd better cut this out."

"Yes," I said. "It's nice, though."

"Haven't done that since we were—God!" She stood away and looked at me. "You could lose some weight, but you're not so bad. How about a bottle of beer? Or would you rather have some cheap whiskey?"

"What are you drinking?"

"Cheap whiskey, but I'm used to it," she said.

"Let's both have some cheap whiskey," I said.

"Straight? With water? Or how?"

"Oh, a small slug of whiskey and a large slug of water in it. I'm driving back to New York tonight."

She went to the kitchen and prepared the drinks. I recognized some of the furniture from the Hammersmith and McCrea houses. "Brought together by a shoestring," she said. "Here's to it. How do I look?"

"If you want my frank and candid opinion, good enough to go right upstairs and make up for the time we lost. Pete won't be home till one o'clock."

"If then," she said. "Don't think I wouldn't, but it's too soon after my baby. Didn't Pete tell you I finally produced a healthy son?"

"No."

"You'll hear him in a little while. We have a daughter, two years old, and now a son. Angus McCrea, Junior. Seven pounds two ounces at birth."

"Good for you," I said.

"Not so damn good for me, but it's over, and he's healthy."

"And what about your mother and father?" I said.

"Oh, poor Jim. You didn't know? Obviously you didn't, and you're going to be so sorry you asked. Daddy committed suicide two years ago. He shot himself. And Mother's in Swedish Haven." Swedish Haven was local lore for the insane asylum. "I'm sorry I had to tell you."

"God, why won't they lay off you?" I said.

"Who is they? Oh, you mean just—life?"

"Yes."

"I don't know, Jim," she said. "I've had about as much as I can stand, or so I keep telling myself. But I must be awfully tough, because there's always something else, and I go right on. Will you let me complain for just a minute, and then I'll stop? The only one of the old crowd I ever see is Phyllis. She comes out and never forgets to bring a bottle, so we get tight together. But some things we don't discuss, Phyllis and I. Pete is a closed subject."

"What's he up to?"

"Oh, he has his women. I don't even know who they are any more, and couldn't care less. Just as long as he doesn't catch a disease. I told him that, so he's been careful about it." She sat up straight. "I haven't been the soul of purity, either, but it's Pete's son. Both children are Pete's. But I haven't been withering on the vine."

"Why should you?"

"That's what *I* said. Why should I have nothing? Nothing? The children are mine, and I love them, but I need more than that, Jim. Children don't love you back. All they do is depend on you to feed them and wash them and all the rest of it. But after they're in bed for the night—I never know whether Pete will be home at two o'clock or not at all. So I've had two tawdry romances, I guess you'd call them. Not you, but Mrs. McCrea would."

"Where is dear Mrs. McCrea?"

"She's living in Jenkintown, with an old maid sister. Thank heaven they can't afford carfare, so I'm spared that."

"Who are your gentlemen friends?"

"Well, the first was when we were living on the East Side. A gentleman by the name of Bill Charney. Yes, Ed's brother and Pete's partner. I was crazy about him. Not for one single minute in love with him, but I never even thought about love with him. He wanted to marry me, too, but I was a nasty little snob. I *couldn't* marry Bill Charney, Jim. I just couldn't. So he married a nice little Irish girl and they're living on Lantenengo Street in the house that used to belong to old Mr. Duncan. And I'm holding court on Mill Street, thirty dollars a month rent."

"Do you want some money?"

"Will you give me two hundred dollars?"

"More than that, if you want it."

"No, I'd just like to have two hundred dollars to hide, to keep in case of emergency."

"In case of emergency, you can always send me a telegram in care of my publisher." I gave her $200.

"Thank you. Now I have some money. For the last five or six years I haven't had any money of my own. You don't care how I spend this, do you?"

"As long as you spend it on yourself."

"I've gotten so stingy I probably won't spend any of it. But this is wonderful. Now I can read the ads and say to myself I could have some expensive lingerie. I think I will get a permanent, next month."

"Is that when you'll be back in circulation again?"

"Good guess. Yes, about a month," she said. "But not the same man. I didn't tell you about the second one. You don't know him. He came here after you left Gibbsville. His name is McCormick and he went to Princeton with Pete. They sat next to each other in a lot of classes, McC, McC, and he was sent here to do some kind of an advertising survey and ran into Pete. They'd never been exactly what you'd call pals, but they *knew* each other and Mac took one look and sized up the situation and— well, I thought, why not? He wasn't as exciting as Mr. Charney, but at

one time I would have married him. *If* he'd asked me. He doesn't live
here any more."

"But you've got the next one picked out?"

"No, but I know there will be a next one. Why lie to myself? And why
lie to you? I don't think I ever have."

"Do you ever see Frank?"

"Frank? Frank Lander? What made you think of him?"

"Bobbie," I said.

"Oh, of course. That was a guess of yours, a long time ago," she said.
"No, I never see Frank." She was smoking a cigarette, and sitting erect
with her elbow on the arm of her chair, holding the cigarette high and
with style. If her next words had been "Jeeves, have the black Rolls
brought round at four o'clock" she would not have been more naturally
grand. But her next words were: "I haven't even thought about Frank.
There was another boy, Johnny White, the one I was engaged to. *Engaged
to.* That close to spending the rest of my life with him—or at least part
of it. But because he wanted me to go away with him before we were
married, I broke the engagement and married Pete."

"Is that all it was? That he wanted you to go away with him?"

"That's really all it was. I got huffy and said he couldn't really love me
if he wanted to take that risk. Not that we hadn't been taking risks, but
a pre-marital trip, that was something else again. My five men, Jim. Frank.
Johnny. Bill and Mac. And Pete."

"Why didn't you and Frank ever get engaged?"

"I wonder. I *have* thought about *that*, so I was wrong when I said I
never think of Frank. But Frank in the old days, not Frank now. What
may have happened was that Frank was the only boy I'd gone all the way
with, and then I got scared because I didn't want to give up the fun,
popularity, good times. Jim, I have a confession to make. About you."

"Oh?"

"I told Frank I'd stayed with you. He wouldn't believe he was my first
and he kept harping on it, so I really got rid of Frank by telling him you
were the first."

"Why me?"

"Because the first time I ever stayed with Frank, or anybody, it was at
a picnic at the Dam, and I'd gone to the picnic with you. So you were
the logical one."

"Did you tell him that night?"

"No. Later. Days later. But you had a fight with him that night, and
the fight made it all the more convincing."

"Well, thanks, little pal," I said.

"Oh, you don't care, do you?"

"No, not really."

"You had Kitty, after all," she said. "Do you ever see Kitty?"

"No. Kitty lives in Cedarhurst and they keep to themselves, Cedarhurst people."

"What was your wife like?"

"She was nice. Pretty. Wanted to be an actress. I still see her once in a while. I like her, and always will, but if ever there were two people that shouldn't have got married . . ."

"I can name two others," said Bobbie.

"You and Pete. But you've stuck to him."

"Don't be polite. I'm stuck with him. Can you imagine what Pete would be like if I left him?"

"Well, to be brutally frank, what's he like anyway? You don't have to go on paying for a dirty trick the rest of your life."

"It wasn't just a dirty trick. It would have been a dirty trick if I'd walked out on him the day we were getting married. But I went through with it, and that made it more than a dirty trick. I *should have* walked out on him, the day we got married. I even tried. And he'd have recovered— then. Don't forget, Pete McCrea was used to dirty tricks being played on him, and he might have got over it if I'd left him at the church. But once I'd married him, he became a different person, took himself much more seriously, and so did everyone else. They began to dislike him, but that was better than being laughed at." She sipped her drink.

"Well, who did it? I did. Your little pal," she said. "How about some more cheap whiskey?"

"No thanks, but you go ahead," I said.

"The first time I ever knew there *was* a Mill Street was the day we rented this house," she said, as she poured herself a drink. "I'd never been out this way before."

"You couldn't have lived here when the mill was operating. The noise and the smoke."

"I can live anywhere," she said. "So can anyone else. And don't be too surprised if you find us back on Lantenengo. Do you know the big thing nowadays? Slot machines and the numbers racket. Pete wants to get into The Numbers, but he hasn't decided how to go about it. Bill Charney is the kingpin in the county, although not the real head. It's run by a syndicate in Jersey City."

"Don't let him do it, Bobbie," I said. "Really don't."

"Why not? He's practically in it already. He has slot machines in the poolroom, and that's where people call up to find out what number won today. He might as well be in it."

"No."

"It's the only way Pete will ever have any money, and if he ever gets his hands on some money, maybe he'll divorce me. Then I could take the children and go away somewhere. California."

"That's a different story. If you're planning it that way. But stay out of The Numbers if you ever have any idea of remaining respectable. You can't just go in for a few years and then quit."

"Respectable? Do you think my son's going to be able to get into Princeton? His father is the proprietor of a poolroom, and they're going to know that when Angus gets older. Pete will never be anything else. He's found his niche. But if I took the children to California they might have a chance. And *I* might have a chance, before it's too late. It's our only hope, Jim. Phyllis agrees with me."

I realized that I would be arguing against a hope and a dream, and if she had that much left, and only that much, I had no right to argue. She very nearly followed my thinking. "It's what I live on, Jim," she said. "That—and this." She held up her glass. "And a little admiration. A little—admiration. Phyllis wants to give me a trip to New York. Would you take us to '21' and those places?"

"Sure."

"Could you get someone for Phyllis?"

"I think so. Sure. Joe wouldn't go on this trip?"

"And give up a chance to be with Mary Lander?"

"So now it's Joe and Mary?"

"Oh, that's old hat in Gibbsville. They don't even pretend otherwise."

"And Frank? What about him?"

"Frank is the forgotten man. If there were any justice he ought to pair off with Phyllis, but they don't like each other. Phyllis calls Frank a wishy-washy namby-pamby, and Frank calls Phyllis a drunken trouble-maker. We've all grown up, Jim. Oh, haven't we just? Joe doesn't like Phyllis to visit me because Mary says all we do is gossip. Although how she'd know *what* we do . . ."

"They were all at the funeral, and I thought what a dull, stuffy little group they've become," I said.

"But that's what they are," said Bobbie. "Very stuffy and very dull. What else is there for them to do? If I were still back there with them I'd be just as bad. Maybe worse. In a way, you know, Pete McCrea has turned out to be the most interesting man in our crowd, present company excepted. Joe was a very handsome young man and so was Frank, and their families had lots of money and all the rest of it. But you saw Joe and Frank today. I haven't seen them lately, but Joe looks like a professional wrestler and I remember how hairy he was, all over his chest and back and his arms and legs. And Frank just the opposite, skin like a girl's and slender, but now we could almost call *him* Ichabod. He looks like a cranky schoolteacher, and his glasses make him look like an owl. Mary, of course, beautifully dressed I'm sure, and not looking a day older."

"Several days older, but damn good-looking," I said.

A baby cried and Bobbie made no move. "That's my daughter. Teething. Now she'll wake up my son and you're in for a lot of howling." The son began to cry, and Bobbie excused herself. She came back in a few minutes with the infant in her arms. "It's against my rules to pick them up, but I wanted to show him to you. Isn't he an ugly little creature? The answer is yes." She took him away and returned with the daughter. "She's begun to have a face."

"Yes, I can see that. Your face, for which she can be thankful."

"Yes, I wouldn't want a girl to look like Pete. It doesn't matter so much with a boy." She took the girl away and when she rejoined me she refilled her glass.

"Are you sorry you didn't have children?" she said.

"Not the way it turned out, I'm not," I said.

"These two haven't had much of a start in life, the poor little things. They haven't even been christened. Do you know why? There was nobody we could ask to be their godfathers." Her eyes filled with tears. "That was when I really saw what we'd come to."

"Bobbie, I've got a four-hour drive ahead of me, so I think I'd better get started."

"Four hours to New York? In that car?"

"I'm going to stop and have a sandwich halfway."

"I could give you a sandwich and make some coffee."

"I don't want it now, thanks."

We looked at each other. "I'd like to show how much I appreciate your coming out to see me," she said. "But it's probably just as well I can't. But I'll be all right in New York, Jim. That is, if I ever get there. I won't believe that, either, till I'm on the train."

If she came to New York I did not know about it, and during the war years Bobbie and her problems receded from my interest. I heard that Pete was working in a defense plant, from which I inferred that he had not made the grade in the numbers racket. Frank Lander was in the Navy, Joe Whipple in the War Production Board, and by the time the war was over I discovered that so many other people and things had taken the place of Gibbsville in my thoughts that I had almost no active curiosity about the friends of my youth. I had even had a turnover in my New York friendships. I had married again, I was working hard, and most of my social life originated with my wife's friends. I was making, for me, quite a lot of money, and I was a middle-aged man whose physician had made some honest, unequivocal remarks about my life expectancy. It took a little time and one illness to make me realize that if I wanted to see my child grow to maturity, I had to retire from night life. It was not nearly so difficult as I had always anticipated it would be.

After I became reconciled to middle age and the quieter life I made another discovery: that the sweetness of my early youth was a persistent and enduring thing, so long as I kept it at the distance of years. Moments would come back to me, of love and excitement and music and laughter that filled my breast as they had thirty years earlier. It was not nostalgia, which only means homesickness, nor was it a wish to be living that excitement again. It was a splendid contentment with the knowledge that once I had felt those things so deeply and well that the throbbing urging of George Gershwin's "Do It Again" could evoke the original sensation and the pictures that went with it: a tea dance at the club and a girl in a long black satin dress and my furious jealousy of a fellow who wore a yellow foulard tie. I wanted none of it ever again, but all I had I wanted to keep. I could remember precisely the tone in which her brother had said to her: "Are you coming or aren't you?" and the sounds of his galoshes after she said: "I'm going home with Mr. Malloy." They were the things I knew before we knew everything, and, I suppose, before we began to learn. There was always a girl, and nearly always there was music; if the Gershwin tune belonged to that girl, a Romberg tune belonged to another and "When Hearts Are Young" became a personal anthem, enduringly sweet and safe from all harm, among the protected memories. In middle age I was proud to have lived according to my emotions at the right time, and content to live that way vicariously and at a distance. I had missed almost nothing, escaped very little, and at fifty I had begun to devote my energy and time to the last, simple but big task of putting it all down as well as I knew how.

In the midst of putting it all down, as novels and short stories and plays, I would sometimes think of Bobbie McCrea and the dinginess of her history. But as the reader will presently learn, the "they"—life—that had once made me cry out in anger, were not through with her yet. (Of course "they" are never through with anyone while he still lives, and we are not concerned here with the laws of compensation that seem to test us, giving us just enough strength to carry us in another trial.) I like to think that Bobbie got enough pleasure out of a pair of nylons, a permanent wave, a bottle of Phyllis Whipple's whiskey, to recharge the brightness in her. As we again take up her story I promise the reader a happy ending, if only because I want it that way. It happens also to be the true ending. . . .

Pete McCrea did not lose his job at the end of the war. His Princeton degree helped there. He had gone into the plant, which specialized in aluminum extrusion, as a manual laborer, but his IBM card revealed that he had taken psychology courses in college, and he was transferred to Personnel. It seemed an odd choice, but it is not hard to imagine that Pete was better fitted by his experience as a poolroom proprietor than as a two-year student of psychology. At least he spoke both languages, he liked the work, and in 1945 he was not bumped by a returning veteran.

Fair Grounds, the town in which the plant was situated, was only three miles from Gibbsville. For nearly a hundred years it had been the trading center for the Pennsylvania Dutch farmers in the area, and its attractions had been Becker's general store, the Fair Grounds Bank, the freight office of the Reading Railway, the Fair Grounds Hotel, and five Protestant churches. Clerks at Becker's and at the bank and the Reading, and bartenders at the hotel and the pastors of the churches, all had to speak Pennsylvania Dutch. English was desirable but not a requirement. The town was kept scrubbed, dusted and painted, and until the erection of the aluminum plant, jobs and trades were kept in the same families. An engineman's son worked as waterboy until he was old enough to take the examinations for brakeman; a master mechanic would give his boy calipers for Christmas. There were men and women in Fair Grounds who visited Gibbsville only to serve on juries or to undergo surgery at the Gibbsville Hospital. There were some men and women who had never been to Gibbsville at all and regarded Gibbsville as some Gibbsville citizens regarded Paris, France. That was the pre-aluminum Fair Grounds.

To this town in 1941 went Pete and Bobbie McCrea. They rented a house no larger than the house on Mill Street but cleaner and in better repair. Their landlord and his wife went to live with his mother-in-law, and collected the $50 legally frozen monthly rent and $50 side payment for the use of the radio and the gas stove. But in spite of under-the-table and black-market prices Peter and Bobbie McCrea were financially better off than they had been since their marriage, and nylons at black-market prices were preferable to the no nylons she had on Mill Street. The job, and the fact that he continued to hold it, restored some respectability to Pete, and they discussed rejoining the club. "Don't try it, I warn you," said Phyllis Whipple. "The club isn't run by your friends any more. Now it's been taken over by people that couldn't have got in ten years ago."

"Well, we'd have needed all our old friends to go to bat for us, and I guess some would think twice about it," said Pete. "So we'll do our drinking at the Tavern."

The Dan Patch Tavern, which was a new name for the renovated Fair Grounds Hotel bar, was busy all day and all night, and it was one of the places where Pete could take pleasure in his revived respectability. It was also one of the places where Bobbie could count on getting that little admiration that she needed to live on. On the day of Pearl Harbor she was only thirty-four years old and at the time of the Japanese surrender she was only thirty-eight. She was accorded admiration in abundance. Some afternoons just before the shift changed she would walk the three blocks to the Tavern and wait for Pete. The bartender on duty would say "Hi, Bobbie," and bring her currently favorite drink to her booth. Sometimes there would be four men sitting with her when Pete arrived from the plant; she was never alone for long. If one man tried to persuade her to leave, and became annoyingly insistent, the bartenders came to her rescue. The bartenders and the proprietor knew that in her way Bobbie was as profitable as the juke box. She was an attraction. She was a good-looking broad who was not a whore or a falling-down lush, and all her drinks were paid for. She was the Tavern's favorite customer, male or female, and if she had given the matter any thought she could have been declared in. All she wanted in return was a steady supply of Camels and protection from being mauled. The owner of the Tavern, Rudy Schau, was the only one who was aware that Bobbie and Pete had once lived on Lantenengo Street in Gibbsville, but far from being impressed by their background, he had a German opinion of aristocrats who had lost standing. He was actively suspicious of Bobbie in the beginning, but in time he came to accept her as a wife whose independence he could not condone and a good-looking woman whose morals he had not been able to condemn. And she was good for business. Beer business was good, but at Bobbie's table nobody drank beer, and the real profit was in the hard stuff.

In the Fair Grounds of the pre-aluminum days Bobbie would have had few women friends. No decent woman would have gone to a saloon every day—or any day. She most likely would have received warnings from the Ku Klux Klan, which was concerned with personal conduct in a town that had only a dozen Catholic families, no Negroes and no Jews. But when the aluminum plant (which was called simply The Aluminum or The Loomy) went into war production the population of Fair Grounds immediately doubled and the solid Protestant character of the town was changed in a month. Eight hundred new people came to town and they lived in apartments in a town where there were no apartments: in rooms in private houses, in garages and old stables, in rented rooms and haylofts out in the farming area. The newcomers wasted no time with complaints of double-rent, inadequate heating, holes in the roof, insufficient sanitation. The town was no longer scrubbed, dusted or painted, and thousands of man-hours were lost while a new shift waited for the old to vacate parking space in the streets of the town. Bobbie and Pete were among the lucky early ones: they had a house. That fact of itself gave Bobbie some distinction. The house had two rooms and kitchen on the first floor, three rooms and bath on the second, and it had a cellar and an attic. In the identical houses on both sides there were a total of four families and six roomers. As a member of Personnel it was one of Pete's duties to find housing for workers, but Bobbie would have no roomers. "The money wouldn't do us much good, so let's live like human beings," she said.

"You mean there's nothing to buy with the money," said Pete. "But we could save it."

"If we had it, we'd spend it. You've never saved a cent in your life and neither have I. If you're thinking of the children's education, buy some more war bonds and have it taken out of your pay. But I'm not going to share my bathroom with a lot of dirty men. I'd have to do all the extra work, not you."

"You could make a lot of money doing their laundry. Fifty cents a shirt."

"Are you serious?"

"No."

"It's a good thing you're not, because I could tell you how else I could make a lot more money."

"Yes, a lot more," said Pete.

"Well, then, keep your ideas to yourself. I won't have boarders and I won't do laundry for fifty cents a shirt. That's final."

And so Bobbie had her house, she got the admiration she needed, and she achieved a moderate popularity among the women of her neighborhood by little friendly acts that came spontaneously out of her friendly nature. There was a dinginess to the new phase: the house was not much, the men who admired her and the women who welcomed her help were the ill-advantaged, the cheap, the vulgar, and sometimes the evil. But the next step down from Mill Street would have been hopeless degradation, and the next step up, Fair Grounds, was at least up. She was envied for her dingy house, and when Pete called her the Queen of the Klondike she was not altogether displeased. There was envy in the epithet, and in the envy was the first sign of respect he had shown her in ten years. He had never suspected her of an affair with Mac McCormick, and if he had suspected her during her infatuation with Bill Charney he had been afraid to make an accusation; afraid to anticipate his own feelings in the event that Charney would give him a job in The Numbers. When Charney brought in a Pole from Detroit for the job Pete had wanted, Pete accepted $1,000 for his share of the poolroom and felt only grateful relief. Charney did not always buy out his partners, and Pete refused to wonder if the money and the easy dissolution of the partnership had been paid for by Bobbie. It was not a question he wanted to raise, and when the war in Europe created jobs at Fair Grounds he believed that his luck had begun to change.

Whatever the state of Pete's luck, the pace of his marriage had begun to change. The pace of his marriage—and not his alone—was set by the time he spent at home and what he did during that time. For ten years he had spent little more time at home than was necessary for sleeping and eating. He could not sit still in the same room with Bobbie, and even after the children were born he did not like to have her present during the times he would play with them. He would arrive in a hurry to have his supper, and in a short time he would get out of the house, to be with a girl, to go back to work at the poolroom. He was most conscious of time when he was near Bobbie; everywhere else he moved slowly, spoke deliberately, answered hesitantly. But after the move to Fair Grounds he spent more time in the house, with the children, with Bobbie. He would sit in the front room, doing paper work from the plant, while Bobbie sewed. At the Tavern he would say to Bobbie: "It's time we were getting home." He no longer darted in and out of the house and ate his meals rapidly and in silence.

He had a new girl. Martha—"Martie"—Klinger was a typist at the plant, a Fair Grounds woman whose husband was in the Coast Guard at Lewes, Delaware. She was Bobbie's age and likewise had two children. She retained a young prettiness in the now round face and her figure had not quite reached the stage of plumpness. Sometimes when she moved an arm the flesh of her breast seemed to go all the way up to her neckline, and she had been one of the inspirations for a plant memo to women employees, suggesting that tight sweaters and tight slacks were out of place in wartime industry. Pete brought her to the Tavern one day after work, and she never took her eyes off Bobbie. She looked up and down, up and down, with her mouth half open as though she were listening to Bobbie through her lips. She showed no animosity of a defensive nature and was not openly possessive of Pete, but Bobbie knew on sight that she was Pete's new girl. After several sessions at the Tavern Bobbie could tell which of the men had already slept with Martie and which of them were likely to again. It was impossible to be jealous of Martie, but it was just as impossible not to feel superior to her. Pete, the somewhat changed Pete, kept up the absurd pretense that Martie was just a girl from the plant whom he happened to bring along for a drink, and there was no unpleasantness until one evening Martie said: "Jesus, I gotta go or I won't get any supper."

"Come on back to our house and have supper with us," said Pete. "That's okay by you, isn't it, Bobbie?"

"No, it isn't," said Bobbie.

"Rudy'll give us a steak and we can cook it at home," said Pete.

"I said no," said Bobbie, and offered no explanation.

"I'll see you all tomorrow," said Martie. "Goodnight, people."

"Why wouldn't you let her come home with us? I could have got a steak from Rudy. And Martie's a hell of a good cook."

"When we can afford a cook I may hire her," said Bobbie.

"Oh, that's what it is. The old snob department."

"That's exactly what it is."

"We're not in any position—"

"*You're* not."

"*We're* not. If I can't have my friends to my house," he said, but did not know how to finish.

"It's funny that she's the first one you ever asked. Don't forget what I told you about having boarders, and fifty cents a shirt. You keep your damn Marties out of my house. If you don't, I'll get a job and you'll be just another boarder yourself."

"Oh, why are you making such a stink about Martie?"

"Come *off* it, Pete, for heaven's *sake*."

The next statement, he knew, would have to be a stupidly transparent lie or an admission, so he made no statement. If there had to be a show-down he preferred to avert it until the woman in question was someone more entertaining than Martie Klinger. And he liked the status quo.

They both liked the status quo. They had hated each other, their house, the dinginess of their existence on Mill Street. When the fire whistle blew it was within the hearing of Mill Street and of Lantenengo Street; rain from the same shower fell on Mill Street and Lantenengo Street; Mill Street and Lantenengo Street read the same Gibbsville newspaper at the same time every evening. And the items of their proximity only made the nearness worse, the remoteness of Mill Street from Lantenengo more vexatious. But Fair Grounds was a new town, where they had gone knowing literally nobody. They had spending money, a desirable house, the respectability of a white-collar job, and the restored confidence in a superiority to their neighbors that they had not allowed themselves to feel on Mill Street. In the Dan Patch Tavern they would let things slip out that would have been meaningless on Mill Street, where their neighbors' daily concern was a loaf of bread and a bottle of milk. "Pete, did you know Jimmy Stewart, the movie actor?" "No, he was several classes behind me, but he was in my club." "Bobbie, what's it like on one of them yachts?" "I've only been on one, but it was fun while it lasted." They could talk now about past pleasures and luxuries without being contradicted by their surroundings, and their new friends at the Tavern had no knowledge of the decade of dinginess that lay between that past and this present. If their new friends also guessed that Pete McCrea was carrying on with Martie Klinger, that very fact made Bobbie more credibly and genuinely the woman who had once cruised in a yacht. They would have approved Bobbie's reason for not wanting Martie Klinger as a guest at supper, as they would have fiercely resented Pete's reference to Bobbie as the Queen of the Klondike. Unintentionally they were creating a symbol of order that they wanted in their lives as much as Bobbie needed ad-miration, and if the symbol and the admiration were slightly ersatz, what, in war years, was not?

There was no one among the Tavern friends whom Bobbie desired to make love with. "I'd give a week's pay to get in bed with you, Bobbie," said one of them.

"Fifty-two weeks' pay, did you say?" said Bobbie.

"No dame is worth fifty-two weeks' pay," said the man, a foreman named Dick Hartenstein.

"Oh, I don't know. In fifty-two weeks you make what?"

"A little over nine thousand. Nine gees, about."

"A lot of women can get that, Dick. I've heard of women getting a diamond necklace for just one night, and they cost a lot more than nine thousand dollars."

"Well, I tell you, Bobbie, if I ever hit the crap game for nine gees I'd seriously consider it, but not a year's pay that I worked for."

"You're not romantic enough for me. Sorry."

"Supposing I did hit the crap game and put nine gees on the table in front of you? Would you and me go to bed?"

"No."

"No, I guess not. If I asked you a question would you give me a truthful answer? No. You wouldn't."

"Why should I?"

"Yeah, why should you? I was gonna ask you, what does it take to get you in bed with a guy?"

"I'm a married woman."

"I skipped all that part, Bobbie. You'd go, if it was the right guy."

"You could get to be an awful nuisance, Dick. You're not far from it right this minute."

"I apologize."

"In fact, why don't you take your drink and stand at the bar?"

"What are you sore at? You get propositioned all the time."

"Yes, but you're too persistent, and you're a bore. The others don't keep asking questions when I tell them no. Go on, now, or I'll tell Rudy to keep you out of here."

"You know what you are?"

"Rudy! Will you come here, please?" she called. "All right, Dick. What am I? Say it in front of Rudy."

Rudy Schau made his way around from the bar. "What can I do for you, Bobbie?"

"I think Dick is getting ready to call me a nasty name."

"He won't," said Rudy Schau. He had the build of a man who had handled beer kegs all his life and he was now ready to squeeze the wind out of Hartenstein. "Apolochise to Bobbie and get the hell outa my place. And don't forget you got a forty-dollar tab here. You won't get a drink nowheres else in tahn."

"I'll pay my God damn tab," said Hartenstein.

"That you owe me. Bobbie you owe an apolochy."

"I apologize," said Hartenstein. He was immediately clipped behind the ear, and sunk to the floor.

"I never like that son of a bitch," said Rudy Schau. He looked down at the unconscious Hartenstein and very deliberately kicked him in the ribs.

"Oh, *don't*, Rudy," said Bobbie. "*Please* don't."

Others in the bar, which was now half filled, stood waiting for Rudy's next kick, and some of them looked at each other and then at Rudy, and they were already to rush him. Bobbie stood up quickly. "Don't, Rudy," she said.

"All right. I learned him. Joe, throw the son of a bitch out," said Rudy. Then suddenly he wheeled and grabbed a man by the belt and lifted him off the floor, holding him tight against his body with one hand and making a hammer of his other hand. "You, you son of a bitch, you was gonna go after me, you was, yeah? Well, go ahead. Let's see you, you son of a bitch. You son of a bitch, I break you in pieces." He let go and the man retreated out of range of Rudy's fist. "Pay your bill and don't come back. Don't ever show your face in my place again. And any other son of a bitch was gonna gang me. You gonna gang Rudy, hey? I kill any two of you." Two of the men picked Hartenstein off the floor before the bartender got to him. "Them two, they paid up, Joe?"

"In the clear, Rudy," said the bartender.

"You two. Don't come back," said Rudy.

"Don't worry. We won't," they said.

Rudy stood at Bobbie's table. "Okay if I sit down with you, Bobbie?"

"Of course," said Bobbie.

"Joe, a beer, please, hey? Bobbie, you ready?"

"Not yet, thanks," she said.

Rudy mopped his forehead with a handkerchief. "You don't have to take it from these bums," said Rudy. "Any time any of them get fresh, you tell me. You're what keeps this place decent, Bobbie. I know. As soon as you go home it's a pigpen. I get sick of hearing them, some of the women as bad as the men. Draft-dotchers. Essengial industry! Draft-dotchers. A bunch of 4-F draft-dotchers. I like to hear what your Daddy would say about them."

"Did you know him, my father?"

"Know him? I was in his platoon. Second platoon, C Company. I went over with him and come back with him. Phil Hammersmith."

"I never knew that."

Rudy chuckled. "Sure. Some of these 4-F draft-dotchers from outa town, they think I'm a Nazi because I never learn to speak good English, but my Daddy didn't speak no English at all and he was born out in the Walley. My old woman says put my dischartch papers up over the back-bar. I say what for? So's to make the good impression on a bunch of draft-dotchers? Corporal Rudolph W. Schau. Your Daddy was a good man and a good soldier."

"Why didn't you ever tell me you knew him?"

"Oh, I don't know, Bobbie. I wasn't gonna tell you now, but I did. It don't pay to be a talker in my business. A listener, not a talker."

"You didn't approve of me, did you?"

"I'm a saloonkeeper. A person comes to my—"

"You didn't approve of me. Don't dodge the issue."

"Well, your Daddy wouldn't of liked you coming to a saloon that often. But times change, and you're better off here than the other joints."

"I hope you don't *mind* my coming here."

"Listen, you come here as much as you want."

"Try and stop me," she said, smiling.

Pete joined them. "What happened to Dick Hartenstein?" he said.

"The same as will happen to anybody gets fresh with your wife," said Rudy, and got up and left them.

"There could be a hell of a stink about this. Rudy could lose his license if the Company wanted to press the point."

"Well, you just see that he doesn't," said Bobbie.

"Maybe it isn't such a good idea, your coming here so often."

"Maybe. On the other hand, maybe it's a wonderful idea. I happen to think it's a wonderful idea, so I'm going to keep on coming. If *you* want to go to one of the other places, that's all right. But I like Rudy's. I like it better than ever, now."

No action was taken against Rudy Schau, and Bobbie visited the Tavern as frequently as ever. Hartenstein was an unpopular foreman and the women said he got what had been coming to him for a long time. Bobbie's friends were pleased that their new symbol had such a forthright defender. It was even said that Bobbie had saved Hartenstein from a worse beating, a rumor that added to the respect she was given by the men and the women.

The McCrea children were not being brought up according to Lantenengo Street standards. On the three or four afternoons a week that Bobbie went to the Tavern she would take her son and daughter to a neighbor's yard. On the other afternoons the neighbors' children would play in her yard. During bad weather and the worst of the winter the McCreas' house was in more frequent service as a nursery, since some of the neighbors were living in one- or two-room apartments. But none of the children, the McCreas' or the neighbors', had individual supervision. Children who had learned to walk were separated from those who were still crawling, on the proven theory that the crawling children were still defenseless against the whimsical cruelties of the older ones. Otherwise there was no distinction, and all the children were toughened early in life, as most of their parents had been. "I guess it's all right," Pete once said to Bobbie. "But I hate to think what they'll be like when they get older. Little gangsters."

"Well, that was never your trouble, God knows," said Bobbie. "And I'm no shining example of having a nannie take care of me. Do you remember my nannie?"

"Vaguely."

" 'Let's go and see the horsies,' she'd say. And we'd go to Mr. Duncan's stable and I'd come home covered with scratches from the stable cat. And I guess Patrick was covered with scratches from my nannie. Affectionate scratches, of course. Do you remember Mr. Duncan's Patrick?"

"Sure."

"He must have been quite a man. Phyllis used to go there with her nannie, too. But the cat liked Phyllis."

"I'm not suggesting that we have a nannie."

"No. You're suggesting that I stay away from the Tavern."

"In the afternoon."

"The afternoon is the only time the mothers will watch each other's children, except in rare cases. Our kids are all right. I'm with them all day most of the time, and we're home every evening, seven nights a week."

"What else is there to do?"

"Well, for instance once a month we could go to a movie."

"Where? Gibbsville?"

"Yes. Two gallons of gas at the most."

"Are you getting the itch to move back to Gibbsville?"

"Not at all. Are you?"

"Hell, no."

"We could get some high school kid to watch the children. I'd just like to have a change once in a while."

"All right. The next time there's something good at the Globe."

Their first trip to the Globe was their last. They saw no one they knew in the theatre or in the bar of the John Gibb Hotel, and when they came home the high school kid was naked in bed with a man Pete recognized from the plant. "Get out of here," said Pete.

"Is she your kid, McCrea?"

"No, she's not my kid. But did you ever hear of statutory rape?"

"Rape? This kid? I had to wait downstairs, for God's sake. She took on three other guys tonight. Ten bucks a crack."

The girl put on her clothes in sullen silence. She never spoke except to say to the man: "Do you have a room some place?"

"Well," said Pete, when they had gone. "Where did you get her from? The Junior League?"

"If you'd stared at her any more you'd have had to pay ten dollars too."

"For sixteen she had quite a shape."

"She won't have it much longer."

"You got an eyeful, too, don't pretend you didn't."

"Well, at least she won't get pregnant that way. And she *will* get *rich*," said Bobbie.

Pete laughed. "It was really quite funny. Where *did* you get her?"

"If you want her name and telephone number, I have it downstairs. I got her through one of the neighbors. She certainly got the word around quickly enough, where she'd be. There's the doorbell. Another customer?"

Pete went downstairs and informed the stranger at the door that he had the wrong address.

"Another customer, and I think he had two guys with him in the car. Seventy dollars she was going to make tonight. I guess I'm supposed to report this at the plant. We have a sort of a V-D file of known prostitutes. We sic the law on them before they infect the whole outfit, and I'll bet this little character—"

"Good heavens, yes. I must burn everything. Bed linen. Towels. Why the little bitch. Now I'm getting sore." She collected the linen and took it downstairs and to the trash burner in the yard. When she returned Pete was in bed, staring at the ceiling. "I'm going to sleep in the other room," she said.

"What's the matter?"

"I didn't like that tonight. I don't want to sleep with you."

"Oh, all right then, go to hell," said Pete.

She made up one of the beds in the adjoining room. He came and sat on the edge of her bed in the dark. "Go away, Pete," she said.

"Why?"

"Oh, all right, I'll *tell* you why. Tonight made me think of the time you wanted to exchange with Mary and Frank. That's all I've been able to think of."

"That's all passed, Bobbie. I'm not like that any more."

"You would have got in bed with that girl. I saw you."

"Then I'll tell you something. You would have got in bed with that man. I saw you, too. You were excited."

"How could I help being excited, to suddenly come upon something like that. But I was disgusted, too. And still am. Please go away and let me try to get some sleep."

She did not sleep until first light, and when the alarm clock sounded she prepared his and the children's breakfasts. She was tired and nervous throughout the day. She could not go to the Tavern because it was her turn to watch neighbors' children, and Pete telephoned and said bluntly that he would not be home for supper, offering no excuse. He got home after eleven that night, slightly drunk and with lipstick on his neck.

"Who was it? Martie?" said Bobbie.

"What difference does it make who it was? I've been trying to give up other women, but you're no help."

"I have no patience with that kind of excuse. It's easy enough to blame me. Remember, Pete, I can pick up a man as easily as you can make a date with Martie."

"I know you can, and you probably will."

It was the last year of the war, and she had remained faithful to Pete throughout the life of their son Angus. A week later she resumed her affair with Bill Charney. "You never forgot me," he said. "I never forgot you, either, Bobbie. I heard about you and Pete living in Fair Grounds. You know a couple times I took my car and dro' past your house to see which one it was. I didn't know, maybe you'd be sitting out on the front porch and if you saw me, you know. Maybe we just say hello and pass the time of day. But I didn't think no such thing, to tell you the God's honest truth. I got nothing against my wife, only she makes me weary. The house and the kids, she got me going to Mass every Sunday, all like that. But I ain't built that way, Bobbie. I'm the next thing to a hood, and you got that side of you, too. I'll make you any price you say, the other jerks you slept with, they never saw that side of you. You know, you hear a lot about love, Bobbie, but I guess I came closer to it with you than any other woman I ever knew. I never forgot you any more than you ever forgot me. It's what they call a mutual attraction. Like you know one person has it for another person."

"I know."

"I don't see how we stood it as long as we did. Be honest, now, didn't you often wish it was me instead of some other guy?"

"Yes."

"All right, I'll be honest with you. Many's the time in bed with my wife I used to say to myself, 'Peggy, you oughta take lessons from Bobbie McCrea.' But who can give lessons, huh? If you don't have the mutual attraction, you're nothin'. How do you think I look?" He slapped his belly. "You know I weigh the same as I used to weigh? You look good. You put on a little. What? Maybe six pounds?"

"Seven or eight."

"But you got it distributed. In another year Peggy's gonna weigh a hundred and fifty pounds, and I told her, I said either she took some of that off or I'd get another girl. Her heighth, you know. She can't get away with that much weight. I eat everything, but I do a lot of walking and standing. I guess I use up a lot of excess energy. Feel them muscles. Punch me in the belly. I got no fat on me anywhere, Bobbie. For my age I'm a perfect physical specimen. I could get any amount of insurance if I got out of The Numbers. But nobody's gonna knock me off so why do I want insurance? I may even give up The Numbers one of these days. I got a couple of things lined up, strictly, strictly legitimate, and when my kids are ready to go away to school, I may just give up The Numbers. For a price, naturally."

"That brings up a point."

"You need money? How much do you want? It's yours. I *mean* like ten, fifteen gees."

"No, no money. But everybody knows you now. Where can we meet?"

"What's the matter with here? I told you, I own this hotel."

"But I can't just come and go. People know me, too. I have an idea, though."

"What?"

"Buy a motel."

"Buy a motel. You know, that thought crossed me a year ago, but you know what I found out? They don't make money. You'd think they would, but those that come out ahead, you be surprised how little they make."

"There's one near Swedish Haven. It's only about a mile from my house."

"We want a big bed, not them twin beds. I tell you what I could do. I could rent one of the units by the month and move my own furniture in. How would that suit you?"

"I'd like it better if you owned the place."

"Blackmail? Is that what you're thinking about? Who'd blackmail me, Bobbie? Or my girl? I'm still a hood in the eyes of some people."

There was no set arrangement for their meetings. Bill Charney postponed the purchase of the motel until she understood he had no intention of buying it or of making any other arrangement that implied permanence. At first she resented his procrastination, but she discovered that she preferred his way; he would telephone her, she would telephone him whenever desire became urgent, and sometimes they would be together within an hour of the telephone call. They spaced out their meetings so that each one produced novelty and excitement, and a year passed and another and Bobbie passed the afternoon of her fortieth birthday with him.

It was characteristic of their relationship that she did not tell him it was her birthday. He always spoke of his wife and children and his business enterprises, but he did not notice that she never spoke of her home life. He was a completely egocentric man, equally admiring of his star sapphire ring on his strong short-fingered hand and of her slender waist, which in his egocentricity became his possession. Inevitably, because of the nature of his businesses, he had a reputation for being close-mouthed, but alone with Bobbie he talked freely. "You know, Bobbie, I laid a friend of yours?"

"Was it fun?"

"Aren't you gonna ask me who?"

"You'll tell me."

"At least I guess she's a friend of yours. Mary Lander."

"She used to be a friend of mine. I haven't seen her in years."

"Yeah. While her husband was in the service. Frank."

"You're so busy, with all your women."

"There's seven days in the week, honey, and it don't take up too much of your time. This didn't last very long, anyway. Five, maybe six times I slept with her. I took her to New York twice, that is I met her there. The other times in her house. You know, she's a neighbor of mine."

"And very neighborly."

"Yeah, that's how it started. She come to my house to collect for something, some war drive, and Peggy said I took care of all them things so when I got home I made out a cheque and took it over to the Landers' and inside of fifteen minutes—less than that—we were necking all over the parlor. Hell, I knew the minute she opened the door—"

"One of those mutual attractions?"

"Yeah, sure. I gave her the cheque and she said, 'I don't know how to thank you,' and I said if she had a couple minutes I'd show her how. 'Oh, Mr. Charney,' but she didn't even tell me to get out, so I knew I was in."

"What ever broke up this romance?"

"Her. She had some guy in Washington, D.C., she was thinking of marrying, and when I finally got it out of her who the guy was, I powdered out. Joe Whipple. I gotta do business with Joe. We got a home-loan proposition that we're ready to go with any day, and this was three years ago when Joe and I were just talking about it, what they call the talking stage."

"So you're the one that broke it off, not Mary."

"If a guy's looking at you across a desk and thinking you're laying his girl, you stand to get a screwing from that guy. Not that I don't trust Joe, because I do."

"Do you trust Mary?"

"I wondered about that, if she'd blab to Joe. A dame like Mary Lander, is she gonna tell the guy she's thinking of marrying that she's been laying a hood like me? No. By the way, she's queer. She told me she'd go for a girl."

"I'm surprised she hasn't already."

"Maybe she has. I couldn't find out. I always try to find out."

"You never asked me."

"I knew you wouldn't. But a dame like Mary, as soon as she opened the door I knew I was in, but then the next thing is you find out what else she'll go for. In her case, the works, as long as it isn't gonna get around. I guess I always figured her right. I have to figure all angles, men *and* women. That's where my brother Ed was stupid. I used to say to him, find out what kind of a broad a guy goes for before you declare him in. Ed used to say all he had to do was play a game of cards with a guy. But according to my theory, everybody goes into a card game prepared. Both eyes open. But not a guy going after a broad. You find out more from broads, like take for instance Mary. Now I know Frank is married to a dame that is screwing his best friend, laid a hood like me, and will go for a girl. You think I'd ever depend on Frank Lander? No. And Joe Whipple. Married to a lush, and sleeping with his best friend's wife, Mary."

"Then you wouldn't depend on Joe, either?"

"Yes, I would. Women don't bother him. He don't care if his wife is a lush, he'll get his nooky from his best friend's wife, he *isn't* going to marry her because that was three-four years ago, and he's tough about everybody. His wife, his dame, his best friend, *and* the United States government. Because I tell you something, if we ever get going on the home-loan proposition, don't think Joe didn't use his job in Washington every chance he got. The partnership is gonna be me and Joe Whipple, because he's just as tough as I am. And one fine day he'll fall over dead from not taking care of himself, and I'll be the main guy. You know the only thing I don't like about you, Bobbie, is the booze. If you'd lay off the sauce for a year I'd get rid of Peggy, and you and I could get married. But booze is women's weakness like women are men's weakness."

"Men are women's weakness."

"No, you're wrong. Men don't make women talk, men don't make women lose their looks, and women can give up men for a hell of a long time, but a female lush is the worst kind of lush."

"Am I a lush?"

"You have a couple drinks every day, don't you?"

"Yes."

"Then you're on the way. Maybe you only take three-four drinks a day now, but five years from now three or four drinks will get you stewed, so you'll be stewed every day. That's a lush. Peggy eats like a God damn pig, but if she ever started drinking, I'd kick her out. Fortunately her old man died with the D.T.'s, so she's afraid of it."

"Would you mind getting me a nice double Scotch with a little water?"

"Why should I mind?" He grinned from back molar to back molar. "When you got a little load on, you forget home and mother." He got her the drink, she took it in her right hand and slowly poured it down his furry chest. He jumped when the icy drink touched him.

"Thank you so much," she said. "Been a very pleasant afternoon, but the party's over."

"You sore at me?"

"Yes, I am. I don't like being called a lush, and I certainly don't like you to think I'd make a good substitute for Peggy."

"You *are* sore."

"Yes."

The children did not know it was her birthday, but when Pete came home he handed her two parcels. "For me?" she said.

"Not very much imagination, but I didn't have a chance to go to Gibbs-ville," he said.

One package contained half a dozen nylons, the other a bottle of Chanel Number 5. "Thank you. Just what I wanted. I really did."

He suddenly began to cry, and rushed out of the room.

"Why is Daddy crying?" said their daughter.

"Because it's my birthday and he did a very sweet thing."

"Why should he cry?" said their son. He was nine years old, the daughter eleven.

"Because he's sentimental," said the daughter.

"And it's a very nice thing to be," said Bobbie.

"Aren't you going to go to him?"

"Not quite yet. In a minute. Angus, will you go down to the drug store and get a quart of ice cream? Here's a dollar, and you and your sister may keep the change, divided."

"What flavor?" said the boy.

"Vanilla and strawberry, or whatever else they have."

Pete returned. "Kids gone to bed?"

"I sent them for some ice cream."

"Did they see me bawling?"

"Yes, and I think it did them good. Marjorie understood it. Angus was a little mystified. But it was good for both of them."

"Marjorie understood it? Did you?"

"She said it was because you were sentimental."

He shook his head. "I don't know if you'd call it sentimental. I just couldn't help thinking you were forty years old. Forty. You forty. Bobbie Hammersmith. And all we've been through, and what I've done to you. I know why you married me, Bobbie, but why did you stick it out?"

"Because I married you."

"Yes. Because you married Ichabod. You know, I wasn't in love with you when we were first married. You thought I was, but I wasn't. It was wonderful, being in bed with you and watching you walking around without any clothes on. Taking a bath. But it was too much for me and that's what started me making passes at everybody. And underneath it all I knew damn well why you married me and I hated you. You were making a fool of me and I kept waiting for you to say this farce was over. If you had, I'd have killed you."

"And I guess rightly."

"And all the later stuff. Running a poolroom and living on Mill Street. I blamed all of that on you. But things are better now since we moved here. Aren't they?"

"Yes, much better, as far as the way we live—"

"That's all I meant. If we didn't have Lantenengo Street and Princeton and those things to look back on, this wouldn't be a bad life for two ordinary people."

"It's not bad," she said.

"It's still pretty bad, but that's because we once had it better. Here's what I want to say. Any time you want to walk out on me, I won't make any fuss. You can have the children, and I won't fight about it. That's my birthday present to you, before it's too late. And I have no plans for myself. I'm not trying to get out of this marriage, but you're forty now and you're entitled to whatever is left."

"Thank you, Pete. I have nobody that wants to marry me."

"Well, maybe not. But you may have, sometime. I love you now, Bobbie, and I never used to. I guess you can't love anybody else while you have no self-respect. When the war was over I was sure I'd get the bounce at the plant, but they like me there, they've kept me on, and that one promotion. We'll never be back on Lantenengo Street, but I think I can count on a job here maybe the rest of my life. In a couple of years we can move to a nicer house."

"I'd rather buy this and fix it up a little. It's a better-built house than the ones they're putting up over on Fair Grounds Heights."

"Well, I'm glad you like it too," he said. "The other thing, that we hardly ever talk about. In fact never talk about. Only fight about sometimes. I'll try, Bobbie. I've been trying."

"I know you have."

"Well—how about you trying, too?"

"I did."

"But not lately. I'm not going to ask you who or when or any of that, but why is it you're faithful to me while I'm chasing after other women, and then when I'm faithful to you, you have somebody else? You're forty now and I'm forty-four. Let's see how long we can go without cheating?"

"You don't mean put a time limit on it, or put up a trophy, like an endurance contest? That's the way it sounds. We both have bad habits, Pete."

"Yes, and I'm the worst. But break it off, Bobbie, whoever it is. Will you please? If it's somebody you're not going to marry, and that's what you said, I've—well, it's a long time since I've cheated, and I like it much better this way. Will you stop seeing this other guy?"

"All right. As a matter of fact I *have* stopped, but don't ask me how long ago."

"I won't ask you anything. And if you fall in love with somebody and want to marry him—"

"And he wants to marry me."

"And he wants to marry you, I'll bow out." He leaned down and kissed her cheek. "I know you better than you think I do, Bobbie."

"That's an irritating statement to make to any woman."

"I guess it is, but not the way I meant it."

Now that is as far as I need go in the story of Pete and Bobbie McCrea. I promised a happy ending, which I shall come to in a moment. We have left Pete and Bobbie in 1947, on Bobbie's fortieth birthday. During the next thirteen years I saw them twice. On one occasion my wife and I spent the night with them in their house in Fair Grounds, which was painted, scrubbed and dusted like the Fair Grounds houses of old. My wife went to bed early, and Pete and Bobbie and I talked until past midnight, and then Pete retired and Bobbie and I continued our conversation until three in the morning. Twice she emptied our ash trays of cigarette butts, and we drank a drip-flask of coffee. It seemed to me that she was so thorough in her description of their life because she felt that the dinginess would vanish if she once succeeded in exposing it. But as we were leaving in the morning I was not so sure that it had vanished. My wife said to me: "Did she get it all out of her system?"

"Get what out of her system?"

"I don't know, but I don't think she did, entirely."

"That would be asking too much," I said. "But I guess she's happy."

"Content, but not happy," said my wife. "But the children are what interested me. The girl is going to be attractive in a few more years, but that boy! You didn't talk to him, but do you know about him? He's fourteen, and he's already passed his senior mathematics. He's *finished* the work that the high school seniors are supposed to be taking. The principal is trying to arrange correspondence courses for him. He's the brightest student they ever had in Fair Grounds High School, ever, and all the scientific men at the aluminum plant know about him. And he's a good-looking boy, too."

"Bobbie didn't tell me any of this."

"And I'll bet I know why. He's their future. With you she wanted to get rid of the past. She adores this boy, adores him. That part's almost terrifying."

"Not to me," I said. "It's the best thing that could have happened to her, and to Pete. The only thing that's terrifying is that they could have ruined it. And believe me, they could have."

In 1960, then, I saw Pete and Bobbie again. They invited me, of all their old friends, to go with them to the Princeton commencement. Angus McCrea, Junior, led his class, was awarded the mathematics prize, the physics prize, the Eubank Prize for scholarship, and some other honors that I am sure are listed in the program. I could not read the program because I was crying most of the time. Pete would lean forward in his chair, listening to the things that were being said about his son, but in an attitude that would have been more suitable to a man who was listening to a pronouncement of sentence. Bobbie sat erect and smiling, but every once in a while I could hear her whisper, "Oh, God. Oh, God."

There, I guess, is our happy ending.

1960

The Girl from California

The limousine stopped and the driver paid the toll and waited for his change. The attendant in the toll booth looked at the couple in the back of the car and smiled. "Hyuh, Vince. Hello, Barbara," he said.

"Hyuh, fella," said Vincent Merino.

"Hello," said Barbara Wade Merino.

"Going to Trenton, Vince?" said the attendant.

"That's right."

"I knew you was from Trenton. Good luck, Vince. So long, Barbara," said the attendant.

"Thanks, fella," said Vince Merino. The car moved along. "He knew I was from Trenton."

"Jesus, I'm glad to get out of that tunnel," said his wife. "I get the worst claustrophobia in a tunnel."

"Well, with me it's the opposite. I hate to ride in an airplane."

"I know," said Barbara. "Jack Spratt could eat no fat, his wife could eat no lean."

"We're gonna both of us eat plenty of fat where we're headed for. Today you forget about the calories. *And don't be nervous.* Take it easy. My fathernmother are no more different than your fathernmother. My mother aint even Italian."

"I know. You told me."

He tried to distract her. "You see them broken-down shacks and all? That used to be a pig farm, and you know something? The guy that owned it ran for President of the United States."

"Who cares?"

"Well, your mothernfather are always talking about America, the land of opportunity. Now you can tell them you seen a pig farm on the Jersey meadows, and the owner run for President the United States. I never heard of that in California."

"Thanks for trying to take my mind off it, but I wish today was over. What else will we do besides eat?"

"I don't know. Maybe the old man will make the load. If he's as nervous as you are, he could easily make the load. He could be starting right now. I hope not, though. He starts hitting the grappa, by the time we get there he could be passed out."

"How long does it take for us to get there?"

"About an hour and a half, I guess."

"Maybe I could go to sleep."

"You mean now?"

"Yes. You got any objections?"

"No, no objections if it'll calm you down."

"You sound disappointed."

"Not exactly, but if you go to sleep you're not gonna see New Jersey. I just thought, I know a hell of a lot about California, but you never saw New Jersey except from ten thousand feet up."

"On the train from Washington last year, when I was making those personal appearances."

"Yeah. The only reason why you took the train was because the whole East was fogged in. A hell of a lot you saw that time. All right, go to sleep if it'll relax you."

She put her hand on his cheek. "You can show me New Jersey on the way back."

"Sure. That's when *I'll* want to sleep."

"I wish we were both in bed right now," she said.

"Cut that out, Barbara. You're taking an unfair advantage."

"Oh, go to hell," she said, and turned her back and pulled the robe over her shoulder.

In a little while she fell asleep. She was always able to fall asleep. On the set, when she was making a picture, she could finish a take and go to her portable dressing-room and sack right out. Or if they were home and had had a fight, she would slam the bedroom door and in five minutes' time she would be sound asleep. "With Bobbie it's a form of escape," her sister said. "She's very fortunate in that respect."

"I'm built like a cow, so it's only natural," Barbara would say.

"Don't knock the build," Vincent had said. "It gets you two hundred gees a picture. And me. It got you me. You'd of been one of them boy types I wouldn't of looked at you. I wouldn't of *looked* at you."

The smell of a cigarette or the sound of the radio would wake her up, so he postponed a smoke and sat in silence as the car sped along the Turnpike . . . Then he realized that he had been asleep, too. He looked out on both sides but failed to recognize his surroundings. From his watch he made a quick calculation; they were ten, fifteen—more or less—minutes from the Trenton exit. He put his hand on his wife's hip and shook gently.

"Bobbie. Barbara. Get with it, kid."

"Huh? Huh? What? Where are we? Oh. Hello. Are we there yet?"

"I figured we're not far from it."

"Ask him. The driver," she said.

Vincent pressed the switch that lowered the division. "How much longer we got, driver?"

"We'll be in Trenton in five minutes, Mr. Merino. Then it's up to you."

"Thanks," said Vincent. "How about a little coffee?"

"All right," she said. "I'll do it." She poured coffee from a vacuum bottle. She put a lump of sugar in his cup and drank hers black and unsweetened. He gave her a lighted cigarette.

"Well, we're almost there," he said.

"Is the fellow from *Life* going to be there?"

"I don't know for sure. I doubt it. As soon as I told them it wasn't gonna be every Italian in Mercer County they lost interest."

She looked at herself in her vanity mirror. "Thank God for that, at least. Anyway they make a habit of sending a photographer and bossing everybody around, and that's the last you ever hear of it."

"I know. I don't even know for sure if my brother's coming from Hazleton. Both of my sisters will be there, that's for sure. But I bet their husbands have to work. My other brother Pat, him and another fella from Villanova. You couldn't *keep* them away."

"I hope I get them all straight."

"Pat's the college boy and he looks something like me. My eldest sister is France. Frances. My younger sister is Kitty. She's about the same age as you."

"Frances is the older one and Kitty's the younger one. And Pat's the college boy, and resembles you. What about your brothers-in-law? What are their names?"

"Take my advice and don't find out their names. That way my sisters won't get jealous, if you don't know their husbands' names. Anyway, I bet they won't be there."

"Who else?"

"The priest. Father Burke. And maybe Walter Appolino and his wife. He's a senator. State senator. If he wants us to pose for a picture, why, we better."

"What's the priest gonna be there for?"

"Well, maybe he won't come, being's we got married by a justice of the peace."

"Are they all going to make a stink about that? Because if they do, I'm going to turn right around and go back to New York. I don't have to take anything from them."

"You won't have to. Kitty's husband aint a Catholic and her kids aren't being raised Catholic. I aint worried about that, so don't you be. The only trouble I predict is if my old man makes the load, and Pat starts trying to make a pass at you. I'll give the son of a bitch a punch in the mouth if he does."

"Listen to who's talking."

"Right. Exactly. Listen to who's talking is right. He patterns himself after me because just because he happens to be Vince Merino's brother. Well, hands off Vince Merino's wife, Pasquale Merino, if you don't want to go back to Villanova minus a couple teeth. And don't you encourage him. Don't stand too close to him. He don't need any encouragement in that direction."

"Is there any of your old girl friends going to be there?"

"Not unless my brother Ed comes from Hazleton. I used to date her before Ed did."

"Did you score with her? I don't have to ask, I guess."

"Well, if you don't have to ask, why ask? What's the use of asking a question that you know the answer beforehand? Sure I scored, but not after she started dating Ed. Only Ed don't believe that. I don't think Ed'll be there."

"She probably throws it up to him that she could have married you."

"Hey, you're pretty smart. That's what she does do. And is she ever wrong? I wouldn't of married her even if I'd of kept on living in Trenton."

"Why not?"

"Because she thought she owned me, and she didn't."

"*I* own you, don't I?"

"Well, I guess so, but that was my own free will. I wanted to own you, so I let you own me. But I never wanted to own her. What the hell? I did own her and I never even wanted to. She was all right for then, but I never intended to be stuck in Trenton all my life. I hope they don't come. I hope there's only my two parents, and my sisters without their stupid husbands, and my kid brother if he behaves himself. Oh, Walter Appolino. Walter is more used to meeting celebrities, like he goes to New York all the time and every time he goes to the Stork Club. Walter was the first guy I ever knew that went to the Stork Club, when I was sixteen or seventeen years of age."

"Large deal."

"Come off it, Bobbie. When you were sixteen who did *you* know that went to the Stork Club?"

"When I was sixteen—well, *seventeen*—I was going there myself."

"Yeah, I guess so." Vincent now gave his full attention to the task of directing the driver through the streets of Trenton. In time they stopped at a detached white frame house which had a front porch, a front and back yard, and a one-car garage in the rear. "This is it," he said. "Is it worse or better than you expected?"

"Frankly, better."

He smiled. "My old man's a bricklayer at Roebling's. I bet he makes better than your old man."

"I didn't say he didn't. That's your mother in the doorway?"

"Yeah, that's Mom. Hey, Mom, wuddia say?" He got out of the car and embraced his mother. Barbara followed him. "Three guesses who this is."

"How do you do, Mrs. Merino?" said Barbara.

"I'm pleased to meet you, Barbara." Mrs. Merino shook hands with her daughter-in-law. "Come on in and be introduced to the others."

"Who all's here, Mom?" said Vincent. "Did Pop make his load?"

"What kind of talk is that? No, he didn't make any load. Is that the way you talk about your father?"

"Forget it. Who else is inside?"

"The Appolinos. Walter and Gertrude Appolino. He's the state senator. Senator Appolino, but a great friend of ours. And his wife. And my two daughters. Vince's two sisters, Frances and Catherine. Both married. Barbara, do you want to go upstairs and freshen up first, or will I introduce you to the others?"

There was no need to reply; all the others came out on the porch and Mrs. Merino made the introductions. As soon as all the names were mentioned there was a sudden, blank silence.

"All right, everybody stand here like a bunch of dummies," said Vincent. "Let's go inside or we'll have the whole neighborhood standing around." Two girls and a boy in their early teens came forward with autograph books and held them out to Barbara and Vincent.

"Put 'To my old friend Johnny DiScalso,' " said the boy.

"The hell I will," said Vincent. "Who are you? Pete DiScalso's kid?"

"Yeah."

"Your old man arrested me for driving without a license. You're lucky I sign my name for you. Who are you, girl?"

"Mary Murphy."

"Which Murphy? Your old man sell washing machines?"

"He used to but not any more."

"Is this your sister?"

"Yeah, I'm her sister. Monica Murphy. Our father used to sell washing machines but now he don't any more."

"Leo Murphy, Vince," said Senator Appolino. "I got him fixed up as an attendant over in the State House. Very good man, Vince, you know what I mean."

"Oh, sure. Leo's all right. Give my regards to your father, girls."

"Thanks, Vince," said the senator. "All right, girls, run along now. And, Vince?"

"What?"

"Forgive and forget. Put 'To my old friend Johnny DiScalso.' I'd appreciate it, you know?"

"Votes?" said Vincent.

"Sixteen guaranteed, sometimes more," said the senator. "And, Barbara, you, if you don't mind? Just something personal for Johnny? 'To my friend,' or something like that? Appreciate it. Appreciate it very much, Barbara."

"All right," said Barbara.

"Fine. Fine," said the senator. "Vince, I'm sorry Gert and I have to go to a colored funeral, but we'll be back later and your parents said it'd be all right if I brought a few friends back with us. Okay?"

"I don't know how long we'll *be* here, Walt."

"Yeah, but I'd appreciate it very *much*, Vince. I kind of promised these people, you know what I mean?"

"How many, Walt?"

"Under forty or fifty. They just want to say hello and like shake hands with you and Barbara. Ten minutes of your time, that's all, and a couple pictures for the papers. Ten minutes, fifteen minutes."

"If we're still here, Walt," said Vincent.

"Yeah. Well, I'd appreciate it, Vince. I really would. I more or less promised them, and I sure would hate to disappoint them. It'd look funny, you know, you coming back to the old home town and didn't see anybody. You know what some people would say, and I wouldn't want them saying that about Vince Merino and his lovely bride Barbara. I'm not gonna say goodbye, folks. We'll be back before you know it."

The senator and his wife departed, and the group on the front porch went inside to the parlor. "Pop, wud you tell Walt?" said Vincent after the women went upstairs.

"Huh. I didn't tell him, he told me. Right away he seen it in the paper you and Barbara was in New York, would you be coming to Trenton? Your mother told him yes. Here he is."

"You need him?"

"Well, I don't *need* him. Maybe he needs me as much as I need him, but you got that crazy brother Pat, you never know what he's gonna do, so it's no use antagonizing Walt."

"Yeah. Where is Pat?"

"He'll be here, him and his roommate with his second-hand, third-hand Jag. The roommate keeps the car in Philly. They'll end up with a broken neck, the two of them. Well, it won't be long till the army gets him. He won't be staying at Villanova much longer."

"Why don't you knock a little sense into him?"

"Wait'll you see him and you'll know why. You didn't see him since he filled out. He could take you or me or maybe the two of us."

"Huh. How's Ed?"

"Ed? Oh, him and Karen are like cats and dogs. She was here in Trenton a couple of weeks ago but she never came near us. She was here for two weeks last summer and never came around. They're all washed up. Ed was here in March or April, sometime, and he stayed drunk for two days. Your mother and I couldn't get anything out of him, but you can put two and two together."

"Well, give me some *good* news. Are France and Kitty all right?"

"Oh, I guess they're all right. Kitty was fooling around with some married man till your mother and France, and Father Burke got into it. Harry was responsible for that, but that don't give Kitty grounds to fool around with a married man."

"But France is all right?"

"Yeah. Well, you'd never know it now that France was a pretty girl when she was around sixteen."

"No."

"You got a good-looking girl for a wife. She even looks better in real life. You gonna have kids?"

"Well, not for a while."

"Yeah, I see what you mean. She put on weight you might have a hard time getting it off again. I don't blame you. Save your money and then have the kids. What is she? Twenty-three or four?"

"She's twenty-four."

"Well, maybe she could have one the year after next and then wait a while."

"How are *you*, Pop?"

"Oh, hell, I'm all right, I guess. Why? Do I look as if I wasn't?"

"You look all right. How old are you now?"

"I'm a day older than I was this time yesterday. How old do you think I am?"

"I don't know. Around fifty?"

"Well, close. I'm forty-eight. I was bothered with this hernia last year, you remember when I was operated? I was made foreman, so I don't have as much heavy work."

"You still like your booze?"

"Huh. You wouldn't of had the nerve to ask me that five years ago. I don't drink no more. A little beer and a little wine, but no hard stuff. I cut out the hard stuff. Monday mornings I used to start getting dizzy up on the scaffolding, so I quit everything but a little wine and beer. But Ed's making up for it, and so's Pat. They'll scrape him up off the road one of these days. He's a wise guy, you can't tell him anything that he don't know all the answers. Is that your Chrysler outside?"

"Hired."

"What are you driving now?"

"I got an Austin-Healey, but I had it for two years and I'm thinking of getting something else. I only put about fourteen thousand miles on it, being away so much making pictures overseas."

"What happens with Barbara when you go away like that?"

"Well, the only time since we were married, she was in the same picture."

"Yeah, but I see where you're going to Portugal and she won't be there. What do you do then?"

"I don't know. It never happened since we were married."

Vince's father pointed a finger at him. "Start a baby. Take my advice and start a baby right away. Maybe it'll keep you straight. I don't know her, but I know you. The only thing that'll keep you straight is maybe if you have a baby started. Maybe. Forget the money, Vince. Forget it."

"Pop?"

"What?"

"How are you and Mom getting along?"

"What kind of a question is that to ask me? Who the hell do you think you are?"

"Oh-ho-ho. I touched a sore spot. Accidentally I touched a sore spot. Are you fooling around with somebody, Pop?"

"Did she say something to you?"

"When would she have a chance to say something to me?"

"Over the phone she could have."

"No, she didn't say nothing. But you took it so big, as soon as I asked you how you were getting along. I knew if it wasn't the booze it's either a woman or money. And you were never stingy. I'll give you that."

Andrew Merino's blue Tyrolean eyes showed trouble. He put his hand on his son's knee. "You're a man now, Vince, but some things you're still not old enough. I don't want to talk about it."

"Who is she? She older, younger? Married?"

"When I tell you this, it's the God's honest truth. I was never in bed with her."

"Oh, Pop. Come off it. You're a pretty good-looking guy."

"Oh, hell, I was as bad as you or Pat back in my twenties."

"Does Mom know the woman?"

"Don't say it that way, Vince. That sounds as if there was something, and there aint. I have a cup of coffee with her."

"At her house?"

"I never been inside her house."

"Does she feel for you?"

Andrew Merino hesitated, then nodded. "But she won't see me after work. She's in the office."

"Then what's Mom's beef?"

"Huh. Wait till you're married that long. We were twenty years of age when we got married. You'll find out."

"I come here to show my wife a typical Italian family, my folks. My Italian father and my Irish mother by the name of Merino. Mr. and Mrs. Andrew Merino, Trenton, New Jersey. And you wanta know something? The old lady give me a look when I got out of the car, and right away, *right away* I got the whole picture. You hung back and didn't hardly say anything. Then I thought to myself, Pop had this operation a year ago."

"No, it aint the operation, Vince."

"Oh, you don't have to tell me now, but that's what I thought. Five years ago you wouldn't of let Walt Appolino be the take-charge guy, not in your house. You sure you don't have a guilty conscience, Pop?"

"I got a guilty conscience for my thoughts. But what do you want, Vince? Do you want me to tell my own son that I don't love his mother? That's my guilty conscience, but I don't have to tell that in confession."

"You go to confession."

"No."

"You don't, hey?"

"No, and that's why your mother thinks there's something going on. I been two years without making my Easter duty. She says to me, next Sunday's the last chance to make your Easter duty. I tell her to mind her own business. Then she's positive I'm going to bed with Violet Constantino."

"Oh, Violet Constantino. Johnny's wife. That's who it is? She used to be a good-looking woman."

"She didn't only used to be. But Violet don't have to make her Easter duty. She's a Methodist, so your mother can't keep tabs on her that way."

"Pop, you gotta get this thing straightened out."

"I know. I know, Vince. To tell you the truth, I was hoping I could talk to you about it. I can't talk to nobody else."

"What does Johnny Constantino think of the whole thing?"

"Johnny Constantino," said Andrew Merino. He shook his head. "Him and I go bowling every Wednesday night."

"That don't answer my question, Pop."

"It wasn't suppose to. I was just thinking, him and I go bowling every Wednesday night, plus I give him a ride home from lodge meeting once a month. And I wonder. We been friends all our life, from boyhood, then I reach the age of forty-six and all of a sudden I fall in love with Violet, his wife for twenty years. I don't get anywhere with her, a cup of coffee in the morning, and 'How are you?' "

"Wuddia mean you never been inside her house?"

"I never been inside of their house. The two women don't get along. When do you remember me or your mother being inside the Constantinos'? Never."

"Well, they always lived the other side of town somewhere."

"If they lived over there next door it would be the same."

"Why don't Mom like her?"

"Well, the last couple years you can figure it out why. But before that your mother didn't like any woman that had a job. Violet had a diploma from commercial school and she could always get a job in an office. The best your mother could ever get was waitress or extra saleslady at Christmas. It wasn't her fault. She didn't have the education. But she used to say Violet was high-hatting her. But if it wasn't that she'd of found some other excuse. She don't like Johnny, either. Your mother don't like many people outside of her own family. The Appolinos and Father Burke. But she don't like ordinary people. I'm surprised those Murphy kids and Johnny DiScalso had the nerve to come here today. She chases any kids that run across our lawn."

"Not when I was a kid."

"Oh, not when you was a kid. You know why. She wanted all the kids playing in our yard. That way she'd know where you were. And France. And Kitty. And Ed. But the minute they all grew up, no more kids playing on the front lawn. No more kids in the back yard. It's a wonder France or Kitty ever got a husband. 'Go down and tell them it's time to go home,' she used to say, when one of the girls had a boy friend. Eleven o'clock! Those girls were brought up strict. They might as well of had Father Burke living in the house. You didn't see any of that, but I saw plenty. And what could I do? Give her any opposition and she'd say, all right, if I wanted to be responsible. You remember young Audrey Detmer?"

"On Bergen Street?"

"Got knocked up when she was fifteen and they had five boys that she didn't know which one was the father. 'You want another Audrey Detmer in your own family?' she used to say. Your mother. Well, we almost did, with Kitty. Kitty's first was six months after she married."

"Listen, Pop, I could of told you a few things about Kitty."

"I wouldn't of been surprised. Well, here they come down. You want a shot of something, or a cocktail? What kind of a cocktail does Barbara drink?"

"She can't handle it. She'll drink a little vino, and that's all I want."

Andrew Merino grinned. "You still got the weak stomach?"

"For liquor."

"Well, you can get drunk on wine, but you don't get Irish-drunk like Ed and Pat."

"Yeah? What about you and your grappa?"

"I never drank it because I liked it, Vince. I only drank it for the effect."

"To forget about Mom, huh?"

"Now, now, you don't have to say that," said Andrew Merino.

"What don't he have to say?" said his wife.

"I was talking to *him*, Kate. I wasn't talking to you," said Andrew Merino.

"All right, have your secrets," said Kate Merino. "I guess we're gonna have to start eating without Pat and his friend. Barbara, you sit anywhere you want to."

"She's suppose to sit next to me," said Andrew Merino.

"Well, she don't have to if she don't want to."

"The place of honor is on my right."

"I was gonna have her sit next to Walt, but he had to go to some funeral," said Kate Merino.

"Yeah. I wish it was his," said Andrew Merino. "Sit here, Barbara. You like Italian food?"

"I love it."

"You got any real Italian restaurants out in Hollywood?"

"Oh, sure. Lots of them."

"Well, my wife is Irish but she knows how to cook Italian food, so dig in. You know what that is, don't you? Thatsa leetla beeta Eyetalian prawn? You like da prawn?"

"Oh, cut the dialect, Pop," said Kitty.

"I no talka the dialect. Me speaka da perfect English, yes-no, Barbara?"

"Sure. Perfect."

"Lay off, Pop," said Vince.

The meal proceeded, and since they were all good eaters, the conversation was incidental to the enjoyment of the food. "I want to help you with the dishes, Mrs. Merino," said Barbara.

"No, we'll leave them till later, but thanks for making the offer," said Kate Merino.

"Would you smoke a cigar, Vince? I got some cigars," said Andrew Merino.

"No thanks, Pop. Maybe Barbara would like one."

"Don't give them that kind of an impression," said Barbara. "But I'll have a cigarette if you'll give me one."

"I ate so much I don't want to get up from the table. I don't want to move," said Vince, lighting his wife's cigarette. He passed his case along to the others, and they lit their own.

"Boy, solid gold," said France. "Can I read what it says inside?"

"From the studio. I know it by heart. 'To Vincent Merino for the Oscar he earned and will some day get. 1958.' That's when everybody said I was gonna get the Oscar."

"It shows what the studio thought of you, and that's what counts," said his mother.

"You're so *right* it's what counts," said Vince.

"We all sat here that night watching the TV," said France. "We were just as nervous as you were, if not more so. They put the TV camera on you, and you sure were nervous."

"Who did you go to that with, sweetie?" said Barbara.

"Renee Remy, who else? Who did you?"

"I don't remember."

"Brad Hicks," said France. "The TV director."

"Figures," said Vince.

"Well, I didn't know you then."

"Was that the front door?" said Kate Merino. "That'll be Pat, just when we're all finished eating."

Kitty Merino got up and went to the hall door. They all watched her, and she held her hand to her mouth and whispered to them: "It's *Karen*."

"Oh, Christ," said Andrew Merino.

"Anybody home?" Karen's voice called out.

"We're all back here, Karen," said Kitty. "Come on back."

"Is that you, Karen?" called Kate Merino. "We're in the dining-room." Then, to the others: "Now don't anybody say anything, then maybe she won't stay. Just be polite."

Karen appeared in the hall doorway. "Hello, everybody. A regular family gathering, eh? Hello, Mrs. Merino. Pop. Kitty. France. Oh, hello, Vince."

"Hello, Karen," said Vince. "Ed with you?"

"No, he had to work but he sends everybody regards."

"Introduce you to my wife. Barbara, this is Karen, my brother Ed's wife."

"Hello, Karen," said Barbara, extending a hand.

"Well, naturally I recognize you, but I'm pleased to meet you personally."

"Did you have your lunch, Karen?" said Kate Merino. "We're keeping stuff warm for Pat and a friend of his, but the way it looks I don't think they're gonna be here."

"Oh, I ate over an hour ago, thanks. At my family's."

"How's your mother?" said Kate Merino.

"She seems better."

"Karen's mother had a serious operation for cancer," said Kate.

"They think they got it all," said Karen.

"We called up when she was in the hospital," said France.

"She told me, yes. She appreciated it."

"How's Ed?" said Vince.

"Oh, just the same."

"I wish he would of come with you. I didn't see Ed since you moved to Hazleton."

"Is it that long? Well, you'd still recognize him."

"Will you have a drink of something, Karen?" said Andrew Merino.

"No thanks. Ed takes care of that department," said Karen.

"Is Ed lushing it up?" said Vince.

"Now, Vincent!" said his mother.

"Yes, speak to him, even if he is the big movie star," said Karen. "Ed's your own brother."

"I just asked a simple question."

"Yeah. Simple," said Karen. "You ever been to Trenton before, Barbara?"

"No, only passed through it on the train."

"Yeah, that's what they say about Trenton," said Karen. "What part of the country did you originate?"

"Well, I was born in Montana, but my parents moved to L.A. when I was two years old."

"I had an uncle worked in Montana. Did you ever hear of Missoula, Montana? It sounds like you ought to use it cooking, but there is such a place."

"I heard of it, but I left there when I was two years old."

"Azusa. You got some funny names in California, too. Is there such a place as Azusa, or did they just make that up for a gag?"

"It's real," said Barbara.

"They got just as funny names around Hazleton, where I live. Did you ever hear of Wilkes-Barre? And they used to have a place called Maw Chunk. M, a, u, c, h, c, h, u, n, k. I don't pronounce it right but then they changed it to Jim Thorpe. From Maw Chunk to Jim Thorpe."

"Let's go sit in the front parlor," said Kate Merino. "It's nicer in there."

"What's wrong with here? I like sitting around the table," said Vince.

"The dirty dishes. Come on, everybody. Andy, bring two chairs for the Appolinos."

"Oh, is Walt coming?" said Karen.

"Walt and Gert. They were here early and then they had to go to a funeral," said Andrew Merino.

"What did you think of Walt, Barbara? Quite the big shot around here, so he thinks."

"He seemed all right."

"Who else was here? Father Burke?" said Karen. "He's usually here, too."

"Is that suppose to be some kind of a crack, Karen?" said Vince.

"You haven't changed."

"No, neither have you," said Vince. "You always came in this house with a chip on your shoulder."

"Take it easy, everybody," said Andrew Merino.

"Goodbye, everybody," said Karen.

"Goodbye? You just got here," said Kate Merino.

"I know where I'm not wanted," said Karen. She looked at everyone in the room, individually, except Vince, then went back in the hall and out the front door.

"Huh," said Vince.

"I wonder when she came down from Hazleton," said Kitty. "I bet she's been here a week or more."

"What possessed her to come over here today, if that's as long as she was going to stay," said Kate Merino. "To see Vince and Barbara, I know, but common politeness she should have stayed longer."

"Well, common politeness or whatever you want to call it, Bobbie and I gotta be going," said Vince.

"So soon?" said Kate Merino.

"Mom, I didn't give any time how long we'd stay. I got an interview at five o'clock at the hotel, and Bobbie has to do a TV tape."

"Well, this wasn't much of a visit, but I guess it's better than none. I don't know what we'll tell Walt," said Kate Merino.

"Vince didn't make Walt any promises," said Andrew Merino.

"I didn't make anybody any promises. I wasn't sure we could get here at all," said Vince.

"I wish I would of thought to bring my camera," said Kitty.

The chauffeur was asleep in the car, and a dozen women and children were standing quietly on the sidewalk when Vincent and Barbara left the house. As though by some tacit agreement the family all stood on the porch to wave farewell.

"Back to New York, Mr. Merino?" said the chauffeur.

"But fast," said Vince. "Go to the end of this street and turn right, then the first left and that'll put us on U.S. 1. After that you look for Turnpike signs." He pressed the button that raised the division.

"If you got anything to say, save it till later," said Vince. "I don't want to talk about them."

"Well, now you know something."

"What?"

"You used to say to me, why didn't we go visit my folks. It was only thirty miles."

"You knew it was gonna be like this?"

"It could have been a lot worse," said Barbara. "You showed good sense leaving. They hate us, they all hate us. Either way, they hate us. If we're nice, they hate us just as much as if we treat them like dirt."

"All but Pop."

"Yeah, I guess he was all right, but he didn't fit in with the rest of them."

"Pop didn't? How didn't he fit in?"

"Don't ask me how. I just felt sorry for him," said Barbara. She took his hand. "What are you smiling at?"

"That Pat. Wait till he gets there and we're halfway to New York."

"Families," she said. "They're just like everybody else. They don't like us. Well, I didn't use to like Ava Gardner before I was in pictures. Or Lana Turner. Who did they think they are?"

"And now they're you, huh?"

"Sure."

"You want to go to sleep?"

"Wait till we get out of the built-up section. They're liable to think I'm drunk."

"I'd like to see the look on Walt's face, with his fifty politicians."

"Erase them from your mind, honey. It's the best way," she said.

1961

In the Silence

The two friends were having coffee together after one of their Saturday lunches. As happens in friendships, they could be silent without awkwardness, and during one such silence Charles Ellis casually picked up a small book that was lying on the coffee table. It was a club roster, bound in two colors and with the club insigne stamped on the front cover, and below the symbol a slip of paper was glued on, which in typescript read: "Not to be removed from Lounge." Ellis leafed through the book and was about to put it down when a name caught his eye. "Know anybody named Holderman?"

"No, I don't think so," said James Malloy.

"Joseph W. Holderman 2d, Eagle Summit, P-A. Joined here in 1916. I've seen that name for years and I was always going to ask you about it. If anybody'd know that name, you would."

"I do know it."

"Thought you said you didn't," said Ellis.

"Holderman alone didn't mean anything, but when you gave it the full treatment, I not only know the name. I know the man. Not only know the man, I've been to his house at Eagle Summit. What would you like to know about him?"

"Well, the only reason I'm curious about him is I've seen his name in this book all these years, and I wondered about him. I've never seen him, I've never heard anyone speak of him, and why does a man that lives in a place called Eagle Summit, Pennsylvania, keep up his membership in this club? He's been a member for forty-five years, so he isn't any chicken. Nowadays you hear men like that say they're over-clubbed. Oh, wait a second, he's a life member. Doesn't have to pay dues any more."

"I think Holderman would pay dues anyway."

"What for? So that he can wear the club tie?"

"You may think you're kidding, but that's one of the reasons."

"Sounds pretty stuffy to me," said Ellis.

"He's anything but," said Malloy. "He's no chicken, as you say. He must be in his middle seventies, but I'd like to see him again before he dies. Or *I* do. Have I aroused any more curiosity about Joseph W. Holderman 2d, of Eagle Summit, Pennsylvania?"

"Some. Give."

"I'd love to," said Malloy. . . .

First I must tell you a little about Eagle Summit (said Malloy), where it is and what kind of country it's in. There's almost no such place as Eagle Summit, it's so small. It is, or was, a post office, which was also the general store. A Protestant church, very likely Presbyterian in that part of the country. A garage that was once a blacksmith shop. Mind you, I'm talking about the way it was when I saw it in 1927. There were some private houses, a doctor lived in one and had his office there. There was a little building that was a sort of township hall, with a couple of cells in the back. The village wasn't big enough to have a bank or a movie theater. It wasn't even on the railroad, not even a branch or a spur. It was in the mountains in North Central Pennsylvania, and the nearest town of any considerable size was Williamsport. Eagle Summit was hardly more than a clearing in the woods, and the people that lived there dreaded a forest fire more than anything else in the world. The village could have been completely wiped out without anyone outside's knowing the difference, at least for a week or so. There were only three telephones in the village itself. The town hall's, the general store's, and the doctor's, and one other about two miles away, at the Holdermans' house, but I don't want to get ahead of myself. I want to give you some more geography, et cetera.

The state highway didn't run through Eagle Summit. The village was on a county road, which was originally, I imagine, scratched out by prison labor, if they could get that many prisoners, or more likely the road was built by the loggers. Timber was the only industry in that part of the State. Thousands and thousands of acres of virgin timber, but so hard to get to it and to move it away that a great deal of it was left unspoiled. It was wild country. Two hundred yards away from Eagle Summit and you were a thousand years in the past, back before Columbus discovered the country. It's doubtful if there were even Indians until the Seventeenth Century, and in two minutes by car you could be transported to a time when there was only bear and elk and deer, panther, eagles, wildcats. And I assure you that if you had to spend the night on the road, if your car broke down, you'd know they were still there. If you stopped to take a leak and turned off your motor the thing that struck you most forcibly was the silence, the enormous silence. If there was no wind—that is, if you were between Eagle Summit and the actual top of the mountain— the silence would be so absolute, such a new experience, that it became spooky, and it would be actually reassuring to hear some animal cry, some bird. And then your reassurance would vanish, because almost immediately you'd get the feeling that you were being watched. And no doubt you were. I'm told that that happens when you're in the jungle. It happened to me during the war, in the Admiralties, but then there was a reason because we'd been told that there were Japs hiding out, sniping at the Seabees. At Eagle Summit it was different. It was a civilized man, me, in a place where I didn't belong. A trespasser. And I knew I was a trespasser and felt guilty about it. This place belonged to the animals and they were sending me thought waves, warnings to get the hell out of there or take the consequences. Boy, the back of my neck was awfully cold. Anyway, I guess that's enough geography. Now for the human element.

As you know, I didn't go to Groton. I went to a school in Niagara Falls that was older than Groton but considerably less fashionable. I probably never would have heard of the school if my father hadn't gone there. It's no longer in existence. But I went there for a year. It was an all-day train ride, or a sleeper jump, and I preferred the day train because I was young and fascinated by any travel. I got a kick out of taking the train to Reading, thirty-five miles away, and any trip longer than that was sheer delight, not to be wasted in sleep. In those days I never took a nap on a train. Too much to see. Well, in 1924, I was on my way back to school after Easter vacation. I was rich, must have had twenty or thirty dollars in my kick, either from bridge or a crap game, and when I changed trains and got on the Buffalo Day Express, as it was called, I brought a Pullman chair. Two of my classmates from Baltimore were on the train, but riding day coach. The hell with them, I said. I'll ride the plush. Splurge. I can see my classmates any time.

So I sat in the Pullman, really luxurious they were then, too. Beautiful woodwork. Mother-of-pearl in the paneling. Big chairs. A brass spitoon. A polite porter who knew his job and had plenty of self-respect, instead of these characters that hate their jobs and hate you. Comfort and ease, and always the *people* that got on and off along the way. Some of them knew each other, some of them didn't.

At a place called Carter City, a station beyond Williamsport, I looked out the car window to see who was getting on, and I noticed three people. Obviously a man and his wife saying goodbye to a third man. I'll come back to the third man in a minute, but first the man and his wife. This man was about six feet tall. He was in his middle thirties, and wearing a Norfolk suit with knickerbockers, thick-soled shoes with fringed tongues, and a cap made of the same material as the suit. A few years earlier it was collegiate to wear a Norfolk suit, but this wasn't a collegiate-type suit. This was English Country. It had four buttons, like ours, but the top button was left unbuttoned, which we never did. His wife was wearing a tweed suit, too, and a brown felt hat. She was quite short, and she and her husband were laughing very heartily at something their friend was saying. I naturally couldn't hear them through the double windows of the Pullman. Then the conductor spoke to them—they obviously knew him and he them—and the third man kissed the woman and shook hands with the man, picked up his bag, which was a beautifully banged-up but saddle-soaped kit bag, and another piece of luggage that I thought contained fishing tackle. He got on the Pullman-car platform as the train started to move, and I heard him calling out a final remark in French. I couldn't understand what he said, but there was no mistaking it for anything but French. He was holding the door open, and I heard the woman call out something in French, and then she and her husband turned and headed for their car. The car was a grey Pierce-Arrow, a Series 30, or about a 1921 or '22 model. It was a chummy roadster. That is, it seated four, with divided front seats. Also called a clover-leaf, if you recall. But it was a hell of an automobile. It had no trouble going eighty or eighty-five, and this particular job had Westinghouse shock absorbers. That model was a favorite with people who wanted a sports car but wanted the weight and size of the Pierce. There were two of them in my home town, and oddly enough one of them was painted grey, too.

The whole picture fascinated me, of course. The people, the car, and the *place*. You wouldn't have given them a second look on Long Island or the Philadelphia Main Line, but this was in the woods of North Central Pennsylvania. There were plenty of rich people in Williamsport, but this wasn't Williamsport. This was Carter City. Well, as it happened, not entirely by accident, I had lunch with the third man. He was a really big fellow. Six-four, two-thirty, and he had a beard. Also he needed a haircut, and I noticed paint stains on his back hair. I'll tell you about him some other time, but he turned out to be Rollo Fenner, the painter. The name struck a vague gong, not that I knew anything about painters, but as we made conversation in the dining-car he got on the subject of football and then I remembered. He'd been All-American at Harvard. Was with the Morgan-Harjes Unit during the war, and lived in Paris. I just didn't have the nerve to ask him what he was doing in Pennsylvania. We got along fine and he gave me his card, told me to look him up in Paris, and he was such delightful company that he really made my trip.

We now perforce skip a year or two. Or three. I got out of school and went to work on a newspaper, working my tail off, loving it, and practically unaware that I was doing grown men's work for twelve dollars a week. The cheap son of a bitch that I worked for—oh, well. Anyway, I had a car, a little four-cylinder Buick roadster, and because of it I got some assignments that you could only cover if you had a car, and on a staff of two women and five men, I was the only one that could drive. So one day the editor called me to his private office, which of course he called a sanctum sanctorum, without knowing a God damn word of Latin, and he said, "James, I have a strange hunch. Read this." He showed me a piece of U.P. copy that had come in over the Morse wire. A flyer had tried to make an emergency landing on a country road near a place called Eagle Summit. Plane caught fire, and the pilot was burned to death, before he'd had a chance to get out of the plane. "Do you know who that might be? It might be Lindbergh! The Lone Eagle!" I thought he was crazy, but he'd convinced himself that Lindbergh, who *was* flying all over the country, getting receptions, was the man who was killed. I think Lindbergh was overdue some place, too. "How long would it take you to drive up there in your car?" Well, four or five hours, I told him. So he gave me some money, swore me to secrecy, and off I went, in quest of the biggest story of the century. Naturally I was to go have a look at the dead pilot, then telephone back if I thought it was Lucky Lindy, and Gibbsville would scoop the world. Or Bob Hooker would have a scoop, not I.

But I was young, so off I went. I knew the roads for the first hundred and fifty miles, and I was convinced that all I had to do was keep the throttle on the floor-board and I'd have a Pulitzer prize. But after I got off the state highways I began to run into trouble, and the closer I got to Eagle Summit, the more trouble I had. The Buick was developing a tappet knock, or what I hoped was a tappet knock. I much preferred a tappet knock to what I really knew it was—a loose connecting rod. I knew it would be getting dark soon, and I'd seen enough of the territory to know I didn't want to spend the night on the road. Not that road.

But the little Buick made it to Eagle Summit and I went to the town hall and introduced myself to a man there, the township supervisor. I said I was from one of the Williamsport papers and asked him if I could have a look at the pilot. "What's left of him," he said. "I got him back there in a cell." So he took me back and one look convinced me that I wasn't going to win the Pulitzer prize. Whoever he was, the poor guy, he wasn't Slim Lindbergh or Slim Anybody. His face was all burnt away, but the legs and torso belonged to a short stout man. Incidentally, the town supervisor was sore as hell at the dead man. Apparently they all hated airplanes and pilots. "He could of started a fire that would destroy this town," he said. Well, I didn't argue with him. I thanked him and got in my car, but it wouldn't start. I pushed it to the garage and asked the proprietor what he thought. He had a look and confirmed my suspicions. Connecting rod. Could he fix it? He'd have to call up and see where he could get one. It wasn't loose. It was broken. So he called up a Buick dealer in Williamsport and they had a spare, but he couldn't leave right away. I asked him where I could spend the night, and he said I could drive to Williamsport with him and go to a hotel, or I could ask the supervisor to let me sleep in a cell. There were no hotel accommodations in Eagle Summit, obviously, and obviously he didn't give a damn where I slept. While I was thinking it over I heard a Klaxon outside, and I looked and saw a grey Pierce-Arrow, pulled up at the gas tank. At first it was just another grey Pierce, but then the driver got out and it was the man I'd seen at the Carter City station three years earlier. He was even wearing the same Norfolk jacket, but instead of knickers, slacks. He came in and said hello to the garage man, and nodded to me. "Fill it up, will you please, Ed? And fix the puncture in the rear wheel spare." Ed said he wouldn't be able to fix the puncture because he had to drive to Williamsport. And so forth and so on. Leave the spare, he'd fix it the next day. Joe. He called the man Joe.

Well, I was a fresh kid. Twenty-two, and the whole scene at the railroad station came back to me, so I said to Joe, "How is Rollo Fenner?" And of course that baffled him. He tried to pretend that he really recognized me, but all the time racking his brains. Where had he met this kid? Finally it was too much for him and he said so. "I'm sorry," he said, "but I can't remember where I met you." So then I told him the whole story, and he was fascinated that I'd remember. Then I told him why I was in Eagle Summit, and he talked about the newspaper business, about which he knew absolutely nothing, and then about my car. And I told him the truth, by the way. That I was from Gibbsville, not Williamsport. The only reason I'd lied to the supervisor was that I'd learned from experience that if there's anything people dislike more than a newspaper reporter, it's a newspaper reporter from some far-off place. So Mr. Joe Holderman asked me if I knew some friends of his in Gibbsville, and I did, and gave him some details that proved that I knew them pretty well. This conversation took place while Ed was filling Holderman's gas tank, and taking off the spare tire from the carrier in the rear. He didn't have side mounts on that car, unlike most Pierces of that vintage. Anyway, he said it was ridiculous for me to go to a hotel in Williamsport or sleep in the lock-up when he had plenty of room at his house, and after a polite but not very firm protest I accepted his kind invitation. I could tell that Ed, the garage man, thought Holderman was out of his mind. But I could also see that what Ed thought made not the slightest bit of difference to Holderman, and off we went.

He lived about two miles away, in the woods, and the roads were frightful, but when you got there—what a house! It was a sort of super-shooting lodge, is the only way I can describe it. It was in a clearing, but not so much of a clearing that it wasn't protected by the trees when the wind was strong, or in a blizzard. It was a log cabin, luxury style. Two stories and a garage in the cellar, and a porch that went around three sides, and after we put the car away he showed me the view from the porch. From one side of the porch you could see, oh, probably twenty miles that looked like solid timber-land. And from all three sides you saw nothing but acres of forest. It took my breath away, literally, because I just stood and looked without saying a word. It was still daylight, and a wisp of smoke in the distance he said was Williamsport, about twenty miles away as the crow flies, but longer by road. He had a big telescope on the porch, and he gave me a look through it and I could see the fire wardens' towers on the tops of the other mountains. "I'm a sort of honorary fire warden," he said. "Let me show you something." He went to an instrument on a tripod that turned out to be a heliograph. He began working it. "My wife and I have learned the Morse Code. She's faster than I am. I'm signaling to that tower down there to the southeast. He hasn't seen me yet. There! Now he's answering. I'm telling him I just got home. I always tell him when I leave, just so that he can keep an eye on our house. It gives him something to do to break the monotony. He has field glasses but they're not as powerful as my telescope. When I get a new one I'm going to give him this one."

"Have you got a telephone here?"

"Yes, we have, and so has he. But there are times when you can't depend on it. We get some pretty terrific electrical storms in the mountains, and in the winter—you can imagine the snow."

"And at night, I suppose you can communicate with a flashlight?" I said.

"Correct. I have a little flashlight in the shape of a 25-automatic, and that's all I need. Pull the trigger for dots and dashes."

"He can see that that far away?"

"Oh, my yes. When there's no moon I can see him light his pipe. Just the light from his match. He's only about five-and-a-half miles away. Of course I can't always get him right away. He doesn't sit in the dark all night. He'd go out of his mind. And unfortunately for us, he's only there during the fire season. I mean unfortunately because he varies our routine, too. We like to talk to him."

"Do you know him?"

"Yes, we've had him here for dinner several times. Him and his wife. But frankly he's better company at this distance, and so is she. He talks better by heliograph. In fact, when he's been here he's been very economical with his words, and she's not a very stimulating conversationalist."

"Who, me?"

We turned, and there was Holderman's wife, pretty and short as I remembered her, although not quite so short, with no gigantic Rollo Fenner to make a contrast. Holderman introduced me and explained that I was spending the night and so forth, and she volunteered to show me around the house.

It was what you might imagine. Three rooms and kitchen on the first floor. The middle room was two stories high, with exposed rafters and an open stairway. A magnificent big open fireplace, and on the floor were bear rugs with heads and teeth. All around on the walls were mounted elk and deer and wildcat heads and some stuffed trout and pike. The

trophies you'd expect from that part of the world, and a tiger head and a water buffalo and some others from I guess India and Africa. Big tables. Navajo rugs. Big chairs and sofas. In a room on one side of the center room Holderman had a desk and filing case and typewriter and small adding machine, obviously his office. Then on the *other* side of the big room, suddenly you're in an elegant drawing-room. Gilt furniture, light blue carpet. Small paintings, including two by Rollo Fenner. In other words, a completely feminine room. Jade ash trays, for instance. A Chippendale closet filled with bits of china. You couldn't imagine a quicker or more complete escape from the rustic, masculine atmosphere of the center room. But you didn't have to imagine it, because on the second floor, one of the bedrooms was just as feminine, with a canopied bed and a chaise-longue. I almost had to laugh, but I'm glad I didn't. There were three other bedrooms, and they were the rustic type that you'd expect, heavy furniture, sporting prints, trophies. The feminine bedroom was next door to a bedroom that you could easily tell was where they slept most of the time, but there was no connecting door between those two rooms. In her room there was one bed, not quite a double bed. In the other room, twin beds. On the other side of the second story, connected by a balcony, or a gallery, were two guest rooms, and I was given one of those. Between those two rooms there was a connecting bath, but the bathroom on the other side of the house was in the rear. It seemed like an odd arrangement to me. Her personal bedroom had the best view, south and east. It was in the front of the house, whereas their joint bedroom had only a one-elevation view. Her room was an escape from an escape, but there again I'm getting ahead of myself.

All in all, it seemed to me to be the most comfortable house I'd ever been in. Comfort, informality, and easy luxury. Because the luxury was there, too, don't think it wasn't. The center room downstairs, for instance. Polished hardwood floor. You wouldn't walk across *it* in hob-nailed boots. And the furniture didn't come from the army-and-navy store. When I said super-hunting lodge, that's what I meant, and I'm telling you so much about the house because I spent two nights there and nearly two days, and all I learned about the Holdermans was during that time.

They had a couple. I have to invent names for the couple, because I don't remember their right names. Let's say Jack and Carolyn. They had their own cabin, back of the main house and in a different clearing. They were older than the Holdermans. Jack was about fifty. Carolyn, probably in her late forties. Natives, but Joe Holderman and his wife, Violet, had taught them the little niceties. Jack was a woodsman, but he functioned as a butler, at least in some things. He wore a lumberjack shirt and no coat, but for instance he unpacked my small bag and put my things away, and he mixed and served the cocktails before dinner. But he didn't serve dinner. His wife did the cooking—or maybe he did. I don't know. But she waited on the table. Not in maid's uniform, but she knew how to serve. I have to jump around a little bit. For instance, Jack ran my tub before dinner, and while I was taking my bath he pressed my suit, brushed my shoes. And later in the evening, my bed was turned down and one of Holderman's bathrobes was lying on the bed and a pair of bedroom slippers. All done by Jack and Carolyn. Dinner, by the way, was served in the big center room. There was no dining-room as such.

I was pooped. I called up my boss and told him there was no story and that I had engine trouble and wouldn't be back till late the next day. All he said was that I'd have to make it up by working some Sunday. Hell, I worked nearly every Sunday anyway. So after dinner—oh, about nine-thirty or so—Holderman suggested that I go to bed. Had a hard time keeping my eyes open. The long trip, the mountain air, cocktails and a big meal. So I went to bed and slept like an innocent child for about four hours. Then I awoke completely refreshed, turned on the light, and looked around for something to read. I could hear a big grandfather's clock strike the half hours, and I decided to go downstairs and get a magazine. They had everything. *Vanity Fair, The New Yorker, Collier's, Life, Scribner's, Spur, The Field, Country Life, Punch.* And the latest issues, at that. So I put on Holderman's bathrobe and slippers and had no trouble finding my way, because there was a light burning in the big room. Then I noticed that a light was coming from Holderman's office, although the door was closed, and on the way downstairs I heard his typewriter. I felt rather sneaky, so when I'd chosen a magazine I knocked on his door, the office door. He opened it. He was wearing pajamas and a bathrobe, and he had a pipe in his hand. I said I didn't want him to think he was imagining things, and showed him the magazine. "Oh, I heard every sound you made," he said. "Come in and have a chat, if you like." He had a Thermos of coffee and a couple of sandwiches wrapped in wax paper. He offered me coffee, but I didn't want to get too wide awake, but I sat down and had a cigarette. "This is when I do my writing," he said. "I'm writing a history of the Holderman family, because I'm the last of my line and when I die, we disappear. We weren't very distinguished," he said, "but we did open up a lot of the country around here. I've been at it ever since my wife and I were told we couldn't have children." Naturally he didn't dwell on that, and in fact I was a little surprised that he even mentioned their inability to produce. But he gave me a few more facts, family stuff that I don't remember, but I remember what he told me about himself. He'd gone to school at Andover and that was where he'd met Rollo Fenner, and on a visit to Fenner's house in Maine he'd met Violet Fenner, Rollo's sister. He went to Cornell, but quit college to join the Morgan-Harjes Unit when Fenner did. Then he joined the American army, came home after the war, and married Violet Fenner.

Well, I began to wonder why he was lying to me, and such stupid, insane lying. He was then at least forty years old. And if he'd quit college in 1916, say at the age of twenty, he'd still only be thirty-one. But he was every bit of forty and possibly a year or two older. And yet he was telling me all this with a straight face, to no purpose as far as I could see except that he was off his rocker. And yet he seemed normal, rational, certainly well behaved. He was a polite and considerate host, and at dinner he and his wife had been conventional to the point of dullness. The only out-of-the-ordinary thing I'd noticed at all was her extra-feminine drawing-room and bedroom. And that wasn't too extraordinary. An attractive woman like that, buried in the Northern Pennsylvania woods, it would have been more remarkable if she hadn't wanted some feminine touches, some refuge from this shooting-lodge atmosphere. But I began to wonder what I'd got myself into, and frankly wished that I could get the hell out. But I was stuck, at least till morning, till I could get a ride to Williamsport.

Now this was no wild man. Everything he said was told in the belief that it would be accepted as unquestioned fact. No striving to convince me. And after about a half an hour he very politely suggested that I go back to bed and apologized for boring me with reminiscence, et cetera. And he never had the least suspicion that I was questioning any of his statements. Nevertheless he had told me some absolutely incredible lies, and to tell you the truth, when I went up to my room, I locked the door.

Naturally I didn't go to sleep for several hours. I put out my light, and then I could look out the window and see that the light was still on in his office, and it stayed on for a couple of hours. I guess I got back to sleep sometime between four and five o'clock, and once I thought I heard people talking, but I couldn't be sure. I slept till about seven-thirty and was awakened by the grey Pierce leaving the property, with Holderman at the wheel. No more sleep for me, so I went downstairs and Carolyn was around, dusting furniture or whatever, and I ordered my breakfast. Then Mrs. Holderman, Violet, showed up. Asked me how I'd slept and so on, and said she was afraid she had bad news for me, although not for her and her husband. She said Ed had called, the garage owner, and he hadn't been able to go pick up the spare part for my car, but would do so that morning. He guessed my car might be ready late that day. So I was stuck with the Holdermans, one of them at least a congenital liar, and the other, Violet, I wasn't sure what. She had a cup of coffee and a cigarette with me, and in the most offhand way she said, "Did you and Joe have a nice chat last night?"

"Yes," I said. "He told me about the family history he's working on."

"Yes, he's been at that a long time," she said. "Sometimes I wish he wouldn't work so hard on it. But he wants to get it all down on paper. When he was in the war he saw so many men die that he developed a fatalistic attitude. The impermanence, you know. Impermanence of life. Don't count on any tomorrow."

"I guess that affected a lot of men's thinking," I said.

"Yes, and especially those that were wounded. My husband was very badly wounded at Belleau Wood," she said.

"In the Marine Corps?" I said.

"Yes. His being alive at all is a miracle, and he's had two operations since the war and is facing another. For two years after the war he was stone deaf," she said. "He hears perfectly well," she said, "but they want to operate again to correct a constant ringing noise. He has a hard time sleeping."

I said, "I hadn't realized he was in the Marines."

"Yes," she said. "He was so pleased to get in. My brother, Rollo, was quite a well-known football player at Harvard, and then he went to live in Paris to study painting, and when the war came Rollo joined the ambulance corps. Came through the war unscathed. Joe had tried out for football at Cornell, but was too light or anyway didn't do very well, and Rollo used to tease him about it. So Joe had something to crow about when he got the Distinguished Service Cross—but at what a price! I don't mean to imply that there's any hostility between them," she said. "If they were real brothers they couldn't be closer than they are." She said her brother visited them whenever he came back to the States, and the two boys, she called them, practically ignored her when Rollo was here. They'd roomed together all through Andover and had gone on a big-game hunting expedition in India the year before she married Joe. She pointed to a tiger head and skin and said that Rollo had shot it. Given it to them as a wedding present, and then gave up hunting. Joe hadn't done any hunting either, since the war. She said I might have noticed something missing in a house like theirs, and I said I couldn't think of a thing that was missing, and she said, "Well, wouldn't you expect to see a gun closet?" And it was true, there were no firearms of any kind visible. "Joe won't have them around," she said. Jack had a rifle and shotguns, but he kept them back in his own cabin.

I relaxed a bit after my conversation with Violet and I got curious about how they spent their days. Also, to be completely honest about it, although she was about forty, which was a very advanced age for me at the time, she looked very inviting in a sweater and skirt and a little pearl necklace. And as the kids say nowadays, she was sending me a message, or so I believed. Let's say the air was heavy with sex, and I wasn't sure whether she knew it or not. I would have been embarrassed to admit to any of my contemporaries that a woman of forty could make me horny, but she did. But the fact that she *was* forty kept me from making a pass at her, although I had several opportunities during the day. I had just enough doubt about what I was feeling, or suspecting, so that I was still a little afraid that if I did make an actual pass, she'd be horrified—or amused. So for the rest of the day I was in a very confused state, hoping for an opportunity to be alone with her, and then when I was alone with her, several times, I couldn't quite carry out my evil intentions. The first move had to come from her.

Well, Holderman came back from Eagle Summit, with the mail and some parcel post, and a report on my car. As to the car, he'd simply *ordered* the garage man to close up and drive to Williamsport. And he could *do* that. He didn't say so, but I inferred that he had money in the garage. But the stuff he brought back from the Eagle Summit post office was interesting. I didn't get to see any of the letters, of course, but he and Violet opened the packages in my presence. For her, some special kind of expensive soap that I forget the name of but I'd heard my aunt speak of it. It was made in France. In his package, two pipes. He'd sent them away to have new bits put in the bowls. I could see that Holderman and his wife got real pleasure out of their parcel post. Like kids. And he explained it. He said, "We live up here in the backwoods, but we don't lose touch with the world. We get all the latest magazines, and we're always sending away for things, little things." And he told me that he kept up his membership in a New York club—this one, without a doubt—although he hadn't been inside the place more than twice since the war, and didn't know when he'd use it again. And every four or five years he'd order a new suit, give an old one to Jack, although the old one hadn't been worn very much, and Jack would give the suit to his son, who was in college somewhere, probably the only boy in the school wearing a hundred-and-fifty-dollar suit. Holderman was getting very close to raising the question why he or they chose to live in the woods, and she was quick enough to anticipate it and she changed the subject. I should mention the fact that nothing he said or did would have aroused the least suspicion as to his being a healthy, normal middle-aged man. Having been alerted to it by her, I could see that he let his hair grow in a strange way around his ear, to cover a bald spot that I assumed was where he'd been operated on. But as far as his conversation and behavior were concerned, he was perfectly all right.

They had two people coming for lunch, a state senator and his wife, who arrived in a big Cunningham phaeton driven by a chauffeur. The wife was related to Holderman, and the senator was just a dull politician who didn't contribute anything and didn't try to hide the fact that he considered the visit a waste of his valuable time. He knew my boss. All those guys knew each other, the subsidized newspaper editors and the politicians that were stooging for big industries in the legislature. They were all grafters in one form or another. They'd all sold out years ago, and they all had big cars and houses in the country or Atlantic City, and I never knew a one of them that didn't overestimate his influence. As long as they voted right they were in, but without the money from the big industries they couldn't have run for dogcatcher. Holderman was rich, but I don't believe he was the big stockholder in any single company of any size. When the senator and his wife left, Holderman was rather apologetic to me. He said his cousin was good company, but she always insisted on bringing her husband. Actually the senator's wife was a rather ordinary woman but at least she'd prattled away during lunch, and she seemed to amuse Violet Holderman. Violet said, "We do our entertaining, such as it is, between Easter and Thanksgiving. After that we can always expect snow, and people are afraid of being marooned up here." So once or twice a week they'd have friends for lunch, but very seldom for dinner.

In the afternoon, after the statesman and wife departed, Holderman and I went for a hike up to the top of the mountain. I was in pretty good shape from tennis and golf, and I lived in a hilly town, but I couldn't keep up with him. On the very top of the mountain he'd put up a sort of shelter. It was open on all four sides, but offered protection from the rain if the rain came straight down. He explained that it was actually a shelter from the rain and the sun. I hadn't thought of the sun. There were no chairs. Only benches, and I sat down to get my breath, and he was quite pleased that a young squirt half his age was winded and he was not. "You see, I'm used to the altitude and you're not," he said. "We're almost three thousand feet above sea level here." Not a great height, but enough to make a difference if you weren't used to it, he said. The view there was of course better than from his house, and he entertained me with a geographical and historical lecture. It was mostly all new to me, and he told it well.

We went back to the house and Violet was waiting for us. That is, she had tea for us and she liked breaking out the best stuff. Holderman commented on it. He said I ought to be complimented, and I was, although I had no way of knowing that she didn't use the silver tea service every afternoon. It would have been in character for her, or them, to use the silver set regardless of guests or no guests. There was a great deal of elegance to the way they lived, notwithstanding the tweeds and lumberjack shirts and the atmosphere of roughing it in the woods. They *weren't* roughing it in the woods. I caught on to the fact that what they were doing was living like the rich on the North Shore, or maybe more like Aiken, although I've never been to Aiken. But with the difference that they didn't belong to any colony, like Aiken people or Westbury people. Then I realized, of course, that the big difference was really the isolation from people. They had people in for meals, but they didn't say anything about going out. No mention was made of going to other people's houses. And then I began to see, with what I'd already found out, that they lived the way they wanted to live because it was the way they *had* to live.

I wasn't finding out much about how they spent their days, what they did with their time, and then within two or three minutes I got some enlightenment on that subject. Holderman finished his tea and said he thought he'd have a nap, and he left us. She said to me, "I'm so glad when he does that. Sleep is *so* important." Then she told, just as though I'd asked her a direct question, that they never planned anything far ahead, and never had people in more than twice a week. In that way, with such an open schedule, he could go take a nap whenever he felt like it. So that was how they spent their days, waiting for sleep to overtake him. I asked her, "What do you do, Mrs. Holderman?" "What do I do?" she said. "Well, I sew. I do needlepoint." She was teaching Carolyn needlepoint. She'd tried painting, but had given it up because she'd felt that all the talent in that direction had gone to her brother. Very discouraging to look at some of the things her brother had dashed off when he visited them, and she had to work so hard to no avail. She took me to the drawing-room and had me take another look at her brother's paintings, and I dutifully admired them, although actually I was more interested in nature's handiwork—her figure. And ready for the first sign of an invitation from her. But no sign was given. However, the cosmic urge, as we used to call it, was somewhere in her thoughts, in the back of her mind. We went back to the big room and she asked me all about my marital status or engagement status. Did I have a girl? Did I have a lot of girls? Were the girls as wild as older people said they were, or was that exaggerated? Girls had so much more freedom these days, et cetera. The people who'd been there for lunch that day had a daughter that was causing them all sorts of trouble. Sent home from Wellesley, et cetera. Violet said she was glad she didn't have to bring up a daughter in 1927, and that, of course, brought us right back to the house in the woods.

A young newspaper reporter sees so much in the first few years that he begins to think he's seen it all. That makes for a very unattractive wise-guy attitude, what I call unearned cynicism. After you've lived a good many years I don't see how you can be anything but cynical, since all any of us have a right to expect is an even break, and not many get that. But I thought I knew it all, and I didn't. It took me many more years to realize that a reporter covering general news lives an abnormal life, in that he sees people every day at the highest or lowest point of their lives. Day after day after day, people in trouble with the law, having accidents, losing control of themselves—or experiencing great successes. In one month's time a district man would see enough crime and horror and selfishness to last most people the rest of their lives. I can remember a young reporter telling me, when I first went to New York, that when you've seen one electrocution you've seen them all. Well, at that stage of my career I probably would have said the same thing, if I'd thought of it and had seen any electrocutions. God knows I'd seen plenty of nasty things. But I was much too young and comparatively inexperienced to be so omniscient about the Holdermans. At about five-thirty that afternoon, after Violet and I had had our little chat, I was ready to be on my way, quite convinced that I had them ticketed. They'd been interesting enough. Unusual. A war casualty and his reasonably attractive wife, holed up in the woods in an atmosphere of quiet luxury. But they'd become what they call in the newspaper business a one-day story, and I was ready to move on.

From this distance I can be perfectly honest and admit that I was still a little bit hoping she'd make a play for me. I'd never necked or laid a woman quite as old as forty, but there was one in her thirties that used to call me up when her husband was out of town. I don't know why she counted on my keeping my mouth shut. Twenty-two-year-old boys do a lot of boasting. But anyway, Violet was *there*, and *I* was there, and we had a whole evening ahead of us, possibly just the two of us. And she was radiating sex.

Well, she went and had a bath before dinner and so did I, and when I came downstairs she said Holderman was still asleep and we'd eat without him. We did, and after dinner we listened to the radio. They had a special high-powered set, marvelous reception up there in the mountains, and I asked her if she wanted to dance. I'll never forget how she looked at me. She smiled and shook her head, and for the first time I realized that she'd been reading my mind. She didn't say a word. Just smiled and shook her head. She was nice enough not to put it into words. You know—she could have said we didn't dare. Worse yet, she could have danced with me and *then* made a big thing about loyalty to her husband. In any event, I knew right away that she was never going to make a play for me, and that I'd better not make one for her. And with that out of the way, definitely, I relaxed and had a better time. I turned off the radio and we talked. About books and authors. All along the balcony above us the walls were lined with books, and she'd read them. I read a lot then, much more than I do now, and we'd both read a lot of the same things. It wasn't often that I got a chance to pour out what I felt about writing, especially to an attractive woman, and pour it out I did. Then along about nine-thirty Holderman appeared, very apologetic about missing dinner and yet not very refreshed from his long nap. He was in a fog.

She got him something to eat but she wouldn't let him drink any coffee. She wanted him to go back to bed, but he argued with her and as a matter of fact got a little nasty. Nasty for him, that is. "I don't really need you to decide when I should sleep," he said.

"Not deciding anything, just suggesting," she said.

Well, I hung around for a little while, then I said goodnight to them and went to my room. I went to sleep and I don't know how long I slept. Past midnight. And I was awakened by a sound that I thought was some animal. A roaring sound. Not so much noisy as deep, as though the animal were saying the word roar over and over again. Roar, roar, roar, roar. I got fully awake and got up, and by this time I realized that it was not an animal but Holderman, having a nightmare in his office. I was going to go downstairs and actually had my door open, and then I saw her. She was in her nightgown, hurrying across the big room to Holderman's office, and in a minute or so they came out of the office. They had their arms around each other's waists and she was talking to him. I couldn't tell what she was saying because he was talking too. Then they went up the stairs to her room, the fancy bedroom, and she closed the door, and I closed mine.

Try and go back to sleep under those circumstances, but I did, eventually. In the morning I went down to breakfast and Holderman was there, I remember he was wearing the same old Norfolk jacket and smoking a pipe. "Your car is ready," he said. "I'll take you down to Eagle Summit as soon as you've had breakfast." He was rested and relaxed, and affable. Violet waited on me herself, and she was happy too. I was finishing breakfast and Holderman said he'd go down and get the Pierce started and I could come down when I was ready, no hurry. Soon as I finished my packing.

She lit my cigarette while I was having my second cup of coffee. "Now you understand us a little better," she said.

"A little," I said.

"Oh, you will a lot when you think about us," she said. "I saw your door open last night."

"Oh," I said, which was all I could think of to say.

Then she said, "You're going to be a nice man, you have feelings."

And I said, "Well, you're a nice woman. You have feelings."

"People aren't nice without them. *He* has them." Then she said, "Do you see anything here you'd like to take home with you? As a memento?" I looked around and God knows there were a lot of things, an embarrassment of riches, so to speak, and she obviously wanted me to take something, so I picked up an old-fashioned silver match-safe. "How about this?" I said. "It's yours," she said. "And this," and she kissed me. "Just a token," she said. And she knew what I was thinking—wondering why all the generosity. "Why?" she said. "Because I've watched your young eyes taking in everything, and your curiosity's been very complimentary," she said. "Give me your address, where I can write to you. I think you'll want to know how he comes out of this next operation, and I'd like to be able to tell you. I hardly need tell you that it won't be on his ear," she said.

Well, she never did write to me, never a line. And while I'm on the subject, I haven't the faintest idea what happened to the match box. It was very good-looking. On one side was a picture of a pack of hounds baiting a bear. I think the other side was blank.

1961

Exactly Eight Thousand
Dollars Exactly

What had once been a pleasant country club, its members consisting largely of young couples on the way up, was now an "industrial park"; and on the old site of the tennis courts was a long, low, windowless building, a laboratory for research in synthetics. The clubhouse was still recognizable beneath the renovations that had converted it into executive offices, but the first and eighteenth fairways were leveled off and covered with blacktop, a parking area for the plant employees. At approximately the location of the second tee there was a roped-off space, with a sign that warned against getting too close to the helicopter which transported plant officials to the municipal airport. One reminder of the former character of the place remained: a golf cart carried officials from the helicopters to the executive offices. A ten-foot-high fence surrounded the entire property and above the fence was strung barbed wire. The fence proper was painted white, but there is no way to make barbed wire look like anything but barbed wire.

The man in the small Renault stopped his car at the gate, and a man in uniform, with a badge that said "Security Officer" and a revolver holster, bent over to speak to the driver of the car. "Good afternoon, sir. May I help you?" The *may* sounded false and sissy, as though it seemed false and sissy to the officer himself.

"Yes, thanks. I'm here to see Mr. D'Avlon."

"Yes sir. Name please?"

"Mr. Charles D'Avlon," said the driver of the car.

"Oh, right. You're expected, Mr. D'Avlon." The guard could not refrain from a surprised look at the small car. "Will you just pin this badge on your lapel and return it to the officer on duty on your way out?" Charles D'Avlon accepted a plastic square which had a safety pin attached to the reverse side; on the obverse side was printed "VISITOR—D'Avlon Industries—355—This badge must be worn at all times while visitor is on Company property. Please return to Security Officer, Main Gate, on completion of visit."

"Where do I park?"

"A space reserved for you, Number 355, executive parking. That'll be that third row. One, two, three. Please leave your key in the car."

"Oh? Why?"

"That's regulations, sir. All cars."

"My brother's, too?"

"Yes sir. Mr. Henry D'Avlon leaves his key in the car just the same as I do."

"A somewhat different car from mine, though, I imagine."

"Well, you see that black and gray Rolls? That's your brother's. But the key's in it just the same. That's in case we have to move the cars in a hurry."

"In an emergency?"

"Correct."

"Such as an explosion?"

"Any emergency that comes up," said the guard. He did not like the word explosion or the slightly frivolous tone of D'Avlon's remark. "By the time you got your car parked the escort will be there to escort you to Executives' Reception." The guard went back into his glass sentry box and picked up a telephone. D'Avlon drove to the parking space.

The escort was a younger man in a uniform similar to the guard's but without the revolver. "Your first visit, I understand," said the escort.

"My first visit to the plant. I've been here before, but when it was a golf club."

"Oh, yes. That was quite some time ago."

"I would think before you were born."

"I guess *so*," said the young man.

"Are we waiting for someone else?"

"Just waiting for you to pin your badge on."

"Even if I'm with you?"

"Everybody has to wear his badge. You wouldn't get ten feet without it."

"What would happen to me?"

"Be detained. If you didn't have a satisfactory explanation you'd be arrested for trespassing. You saw all those signs on the fence. This is a pretty efficient operation."

"Is that since the explosion?"

"We've always taken security precautions here," said the young man, evasively.

"Why don't *you* carry a gun?"

"What makes you think I don't?" The young man reached in his pocket and brought out a .25 automatic. "It's no .38, but a lot of women have got rid of a lot of husbands with one of these. They aren't bulky, slip into your pants pocket, and some visitors don't feel right walking with a man with a holster. But if you hit a man in the throat with one of these slugs, he wouldn't be much use."

"Can you hit a man in the throat?"

"In the eye, with a little time and the right distance. Some cops call it a jealousy gun. And we practice firing it. The women don't even practice, and look what they do with it. It's a mean little fellow. This way, sir."

The handsome young woman in Executives' Reception bowed and smiled at Charles D'Avlon and apparently pushed a button that released the lock on the door into a corridor. At any rate she did not speak to D'Avlon or to the young security officer. "This way, sir," said the young man. They rode one flight up in an automatic elevator, then proceeded to the end of the second-story corridor, to a door marked President. The young man held that door open for Charles D'Avlon, and a man rose to greet the stranger.

"Okay, Mr. Lester?" said the security officer.

"Okay, Van," said the man addressed. He was about forty-five, wore half-shell glasses and a blue four-in-hand that was embroidered with what appeared to be a long exclamation point. His dark blue suit had narrow lapels and his pocket handkerchief, neatly folded, showed enough to reveal, in the very center, the initials D.W.L. "Have a seat, Mr. D'Avlon. Your brother will be right with you. You have a nice trip out?"

"Out from town, or out from Connecticut?"

"Well—from Connecticut."

"Oh, it was all right. Gave me a chance to see a lot of the country."

"Didn't you use to live here?"

"Oh, sure. We were born here, but it's all changed. I used to play golf here when I was a young man. Do you know where you're sitting?"

"How do you mean?"

"You're sitting in the ladies' can. That's what this was. The ladies' locker-room."

"I wasn't with the company then."

"There wasn't any company then."

"No, I guess not," said Mr. Lester. He sat with his hands folded on his desk.

"Go ahead with your work, if you want to. Don't let me hold you up," said Charles D'Avlon.

"I'm waiting for—there he is," said Mr. Lester. He rose as the door at his right was opened.

"Hello, Chiz," said the man in the doorway. "Come on in."

"Hello, Henry," said Charles D'Avlon. The brothers shook hands and Charles entered the president's office.

It was a corner room with a magnificent view of the rolling countryside and a distant mountain. "I was just telling your man Lester, his office is in the ladies' can."

"Well, that proves one thing," said Henry. "You haven't changed much. You always liked to throw people a little off balance."

"Don't be disagreeable, Henry. It's tough enough to be here under the circumstances. Don't make it tougher."

"Chiz, you're the one that always makes things tougher for yourself."

"I didn't say you made things tougher. I just said they were tough enough. I swore I'd never ask you for a nickel, but here I am."

"Yes," said Henry. "Well, we got right to the point. How much do you want?"

"A lot."

"Oh, I guessed that. If it was a little you wouldn't feel you had to make such a long trip. How much, Chiz?"

"Eight thousand dollars."

"All right. But why eight? Why not five, or why not ten? I'm curious to know how you arrived at the figure eight thousand."

"I thought it would sound businesslike."

"As though you'd figured it out very carefully. Okay, it does," said Henry. He spoke into the inter-com on his desk. "Dale, will you make out a cheque, my personal account, eight thousand dollars, payable to Charles W. D'Avlon, and bring it in for my signature as soon as it's made out? Thank you."

"Aren't you interested in what I want it for?" said Charles.

"Not very much. You have some story, and it comes to eight thousand dollars. You probably need five, but you thought you might as well get three extra."

"That's right," said Charles. "But I hate to waste the story. I had a good one."

"Write it and sell it to a magazine."

"I can't write. If I could write I'd have plenty of material, but first you said you were interested in why I said eight thousand, and in the next breath you don't want to hear my story."

"I wanted to see if you'd admit it was a story. If you hadn't admitted it I'd have had the cheque made out for four thousand. But you were frank, and that's as close as you ever come to being honest. So you get your eight thousand."

"If I'd known it was going to be this easy—"

"No. You might have got ten, but no more."

"Then give me ten."

"Not a chance," said Henry. There were two light taps on the door, Lester came in and laid the cheque on Henry's desk and departed. Henry signed and pushed the cheque toward his brother.

"Cheque protector and everything. Exactly eight thousand exactly," said Charles. "Now I'm interested to know why you gave me any money at all. You didn't have to. Does it give you a sense of power? Does it go with that Rolls-Royce you have down there, and all this high-powered security stuff?"

"To a certain extent I guess it does. But there's more to it than that, Chiz."

"Of course."

"You see, I've always wondered when you'd finally put the touch on me. Not that I lay awake nights, but I knew you would some day. And now you have, for eight thousand dollars. I'm getting off light. Because you must know damn well that this is all you'll ever get from me."

"That occurred to me."

"When we were boys and you used to knock me around I used to feel sort of sorry for you. You'd beat the hell out of me and walk away with something of mine. A fielder's glove, or a necktie. But what you didn't know was that I was dying to *give* you the God damn glove or tie. Anything you asked for of mine, you could have had. But you preferred violence and theft, and naturally I could take only so much and then I began to hate you."

"And still do."

"Does that surprise you? Yes. Because as you grew older that was the way you were with everybody, all through your life. If you look out that window you'll see a research laboratory where the tennis courts used to be. One night after a dance I was getting in that little Oakland I had, that Grandmother gave me for my twenty-first birthday. You ought to remember it, you smashed it up, you son of a bitch. Anyway, I didn't have a date and I was by myself and I heard a girl crying. It was Mary Radley, sitting on the bench between the first and second courts. She was ashamed to go back to the clubhouse with her dress all torn. You. You didn't have to be brutal with Mary Radley. Nobody did, but especially you. But that was your way, and that was when I first realized that it wasn't just a question of being a bully to your kid brother. You were a bully, net."

"Okay," said Charles. "Well, it's your turn to be the bully. Thanks for the money."

"Wait a minute. I haven't finished. I want you to hear a few things, and you'll damn well listen or I'll stop payment on that cheque."

"Captive audience. All right," said Charles.

"You've never changed. Both your wives took all they could stand, your children don't want to be anywhere near you. Have you ever wondered why?"

"Not very much. The children were brought up by their mothers, and their mothers saw to it that I didn't get any of the best of it. I wrote them off very early."

"Not your daughter. You showed up at her graduation and made her leave her mother and stepfather to go on some excursion with you. Whimsical cruelty, that was. Because you then sent her back to her mother and never did any more about her. Not a thing, financially or otherwise."

"Her mother has plenty of glue. One thing I did for my children was make sure they had rich mothers."

"Yes. Who also could afford *you* before there were any children, and after."

"The fact of the matter is that both my wives proposed to me, Henry."

"I have no doubt of it. You were very skillful. I understand your first wife forced you to accept a wedding present of two hundred thousand dollars."

"Two-fifty. A quarter of a million. All long since gone, I regret to say."

"But your second wife—"

"An iron-bound trust. I couldn't get my hooks on any of that. Where did you find out so much about my affairs?"

"When I was around trying to raise the money to get this business started, I encountered a certain amount of resistance because of the name. Even when they found out I wasn't you, people were still very dubious, especially New York and Philadelphia people. Don't ever go back to Philadelphia, Chiz. They really don't like you there."

"I'm desolated."

"You're not, but you ought to be."

"I really am. There are a couple of rich widows in Philadelphia that could make me entirely independent of people like you. But the Girard Trust Company and that other one, they probably take a dim view of me. It's too bad, too, because both of these women, or I should say either one of them could make me comfortable in my old age. I'm crowding sixty, you know."

"Oh, I know."

"The next fifteen years, I don't look forward to them the way things are at present. You may have to take me on as a night watchman."

"Fat chance. And that brings me to another point I was going to make. Or my earlier point about your being a bully. Do you realize that before you came in this room I already knew that you'd been shooting off your mouth about the explosion we had here three years ago? Our Security people couldn't believe their ears. The first man you talked to lost a brother in that explosion. The second man, the young fellow, was very badly burned and had to have skin-grafting operations that took over a year. But your feeble jokes, aside from any question of taste, were your way of bullying people, the way you used to be to caddies and waiters when this was the club. Five men were killed in that explosion, and it's no joke around here. It's no joke anywhere. For your information, both Security officers were convinced that you were an impostor, that you weren't my brother at all. For your additional information, Chiz, I wish they'd been right."

Charles D'Avlon rose. "Well, that sounds pretty final," he said. He went over to the window and looked out at the laboratory. "Mary Radley," he said. "She was certainly a little tramp."

1960

Winter Dance

When the big Packard Twin-Six came rumbling into view it was an exciting sight to the boy. The radiator and hood had a leather cover that was streaked with ice. Strapped to the spare tires at the rear of the car was a long-handled shovel, crusted with snow. Icicles hung from the fenders, and the running-boards carried an extra thickness of frozen slush. All the side curtains were securely in place. The windshield was solid ice except for an arc, directly in front of the chauffeur, which the manually operated wiper had kept partially clear. The heavy car moved slowly as the tire chains bit into the snow. You could not see the spokes of the artillery wheels; they were hidden by a disc of ice and snow. But the big car had made it, as it nearly always made it in spite of the winter in the mountains. Now, moving slowly along South Main Street, the car made the boy think of those trains in the far West that were drawn by two and three locomotives up and through the mountain passes. There was something triumphant and majestic now in the way the big Packard eased its way along South Main. Here it was safe and sound, the dignified winner over fifteen miles of narrow, winding mountain roads and the hazards that winter could put in its way.

The boy watched the Packard until it came to a stop ten feet from the curb but as close as it could get to Winkleman, the furrier's.

"There goes your girl, Ted."

"Aw, shut up," said the boy.

"She's stopping at Winkleman's. Why don't you go in and price his coonskins? He has a coonskin in the window."

"And a card on it saying three hundred dollars," said the boy.

"Well, ask him if he's got any for less."

"In front of her?" said the boy.

"Okay. I was only trying to be helpful."

"We could take a walk down and have a *look* at the coat," said the boy.

"And wait till she comes out? She may be all day. Go on in and try it on."

"Winkleman knows I'm not in the market for a coonskin," said the boy.

"Listen, for Christ's sake, Ted. This is your best chance to talk to her. You know where she's probably going from there."

"I know."

"You want to talk to her, don't you?"

"Sure," said the boy.

"And not with the older crowd."

"Yes," said the boy.

"Well, you won't be able to get her away from the older crowd. Even if you cut in on her, they won't let you get two steps with her."

"Shall we take a walk down to Winkleman's?" said the boy.

"Give her a few seconds to get out of the car and inside of the store."

"That's a good idea. We'll wait till she gets inside," said the boy. "But then I don't know what to say."

"Just strike up a conversation."

"That's easier said than done," said the boy. "Think of something."

"Well, just casually sidle up to her and say, 'Oh, hello, Natalie. Going to the tea dance?' And she'll say, 'Yes, are you?'"

"End of conversation," said the boy.

"Not necessarily. Ask her where she's staying tonight."

"I know where she's staying, and anyway, she'll think it's kind of fresh. It's none of my business where she's staying," said the boy.

"Well, have you got some money with you?"

"Dollar and forty, forty-five cents."

"That's enough. Ask her if she wants a hot chocolate. She just had a cold ride, and I'll bet she'd welcome a hot chocolate."

"*I've* never asked her to have a hot chocolate."

"What if you haven't? You have to start sometime, you dumb bastard. I'll bet she'd give anything for a hot chocolate. That's a cold ride, believe you me. And even if she says no, at least she'll give you credit for being considerate. My sister Kit, I've heard her say a hundred times, next to a good dancer, if a boy's considerate."

"She's liable to think I'm too young to buy her a hot chocolate. She's at least twenty."

"You have a dollar and forty cents. A hot chocolate will set you back fifteen cents. She knows fifteen cents won't break you. Maybe she won't even think of that, if she *wants* a hot chocolate. She's probably half frozen."

"No. They have one of those charcoal heaters, and sixty-five robes. It's as warm in her car as Mrs. Hofman's limousine."

"How do you know?"

"Because last year she gave us all a ride home from tobogganing."

"Natalie?"

"Well, not Mrs. *Hofman*. Huh. Fancy that, Mrs. Hofman giving us a ride in her limousine. I'd like to see *that*."

"Well, she's inside. Now's your chance."

"I wish it was some other store," said the boy. "I don't like to go barging in Winkleman's. That's a woman's store."

"He has a man's raccoon coat in the window. And who else is going to buy a raccoon if we don't? Not my *father*. Not *your* father. Maybe Winkleman will think you're getting one for a Christmas present. *I* am, but not this year."

"Oh, I'm getting one, next year or the year after," said the boy.

"Well, then you have a good excuse."

"The only trouble is, Winkleman will start waiting on us, and then how do I get to strike up a conversation with *her*? 'What can I do for you, boys?' And then I barge over and ask her if she wants a hot chocolate. Boy, will she see through that. She'll know we followed her in, and she'll be sore as hell."

"She'll be so busy she won't pay any attention till you speak to her. Didn't you ever go shopping with a woman?"

"Oh, you know so much about everything, you make me sick."

"You're the one that makes me sick. What's the worst she can do? Chop off your head and put it on a pikestaff? The positively worst she can do is say, 'No thank you, Ted. I do not wish a hot chocolate.'"

"If I thought for sure she wanted a hot chocolate," said the boy. "Maybe she's not going to stay in there very long. By the time we get there maybe she'll be just leaving. Nobody gets to the tea dance before six. She's spending the night at Margery Hill's. If they all left at half past five, they'll be at the club around six. If she has to change her dress, that'll take her at least a half an hour. Five o'clock. I'm trying to dope out whether she's going to be in Winkleman's long enough. And anyway, maybe she's going some place else besides Winkleman's. I don't think Winkleman's is such a good idea. I'll bet she has other places to go. No, she wouldn't have time for a hot chocolate."

"Well, you're right. She's leaving Winkleman's. Let's see where she goes."

The girl in her six-buckle arctics came out of the fur shop, stepped into the snowbank and got in her car. The boy and his friend watched the big Packard moving slowly southward and turning west into Lantenengo Street. They did not speak until the car was out of sight.

"Well, you're fifteen cents ahead. Buy *me* a hot chocolate."

"You just had one," said the boy.

"I could polish off another."

"Oh, all right. Then what? Shall we start for the club?"

"Christ, it's only twenty after four."

"I have to pick up the kid sister. The old man wouldn't let me have the car unless I dragged her. *They* want to get there *early*. They *always* want to get there early."

"Yeah, they don't want to miss anything. What's there to miss before six o'clock? But what do *you* want to get there early for?"

"Because my damn kid sister wants to, and my old man said I had to," said the boy. "And I have to dance the first dance with her, and if she's left in the lurch I have to dance with her, and when she's ready to go home *we* have to go home. God damn it I wish I had my own car."

"I'm getting one when I graduate. I don't know whether I want a Ford or a Dodge."

"New or second-hand?"

"Brand-new."

"The Dodge costs more, but around here you need a Ford for the hills," said the boy.

"Yeah, but I wouldn't use it much around here. I'd use it mostly in the summer, and the Vineyard's practically all flat."

"I never thought of that," said the boy. "Well, I guess we ought to get started."

"Where's your car?"

"Henderson's Garage. The old man left it there to get new chains put on. Finish your hot chocolate. You'll get plenty at the club, free."

"It'll have skin on it. Christ, I hate skin on hot chocolate. It makes me puke."

"You're so delicate," said the boy.

"Well, do you like it?"

"No," said the boy. "But I have sense enough to drink tea."

The orchestra was playing "Rose of the Rio Grande," a fine fox trot with a melody that could just as easily have had a lyric about China, and the next tune *was* about Chinese—"Limehouse Blues." The band was just getting started, and trying to fill the dance floor.

"Stop trying to lead," said the boy.

"Oh, you stop being so bossy," said his sister. "Why are you so grouchy? Because your girl isn't here? Well, here she comes."

"Where?"

"In the vestibule. All the older crowd. Margery Hill has a new hat. Oh, isn't that becoming?"

" 'Oh, isn't that becoming?' You sound like Mother."

"And you sound like the Terrible-Tempered Mr. Bangs. Oh, hello, Ralph. Are you cutting in on my adorable brother? Teddy, dear, will you relinquish me?"

"Thanks for the dance," said the boy. He joined the stag line and lit a cigarette.

"Got a butt?"

"Hello, Jonesy. Sure," said the boy, offering a pack.

"Your girl's here. Just got here a minute ago."

"Oh, crack wise," said the boy, and turned away. Presently the fellows from the older crowd gathered in the vestibule, waiting for the girls to come downstairs from the ladies' dressing-room.

"Hello, Teddy," said Ross Dreiber.

"Hello, Ross," said the boy.

"Why aren't you out there tripping the light fantastic? Looking them over?"

"Just looking them over."

"Any new talent? I see your sister. She fourteen?"

"Fifteen."

"Fifteen. Well, I'll be out of college by the time she's allowed to go to proms. But she certainly has sprung up since last summer."

"Sure has."

"What have you got? Two more years?"

"One more after this," said the boy.

"Then where?"

"Lafayette, I guess. Maybe Princeton."

"Well, when you get ready to go, if you decide on Lafayette, I'd be glad to write a letter to our chapter there. You know you can't go wrong with Deke, anywhere. What was your father?"

"Theta Delt."

"Well, I have nothing to say against Theta Delt. They're a keen organization. But take a look at Deke before you shake hands. And think twice about Princeton, boy. I know a lot of good eggs were awfully disappointed they went to Princeton. Take my word for it. But of course it all depends on the man."

"Yeah. Sure."

"Have you got another butt on you? . . . Omars! My brand! Deke for you, boy. You even smoke the right cigarettes."

The boy held a match to Dreiber's cigarette.

"*Hello, Teddy.*"

He turned. "Hello, Nat," he said.

"Finish your cigarette, Ross. I'll dance with Teddy. Or are you waiting for somebody?"

"No, I'm not waiting for anybody. But do you mean it?"

"Of course I do. Come on," she said.

"Probably get about two steps," said the boy.

"Well, then let's walk down to the other end of the room and start from there. Shall we?"

"Fine," said the boy.

She took his arm and they marched to the far end of the room. She greeted friends along the way, but said nothing to the boy. Then she held up her arms and said, "All right?" and they began to dance. He was good, and he had self-confidence because he was good. She was good, and she liked dancing with him. There was no need to talk, and at this end of the room people got out of their way. They got all through two choruses of "Stumbling" before the music stopped. "Oh, that was grand," she said. She applauded with him.

"Shall we sit down?" said the boy.

"Well, I think I'd better find our crowd."

"Don't do that, Nat. Please?" said the boy.

"No, Teddy. I must, really," she said. "Cut in later."

"Couldn't we just sit down a minute?"

She shook her head. "You know they'll only kid you."

"Oh, you know that?"

"Uh-huh. They kid me too, don't forget."

"They do? Who does?"

"Oh, my crowd. Same as your crowd kids you."

"You're not sore at me because they kid you?"

"Of course not. And don't you be embarrassed, either."

"You know it's all my fault, Nat," said the boy.

She hesitated. "You mean on account of the postcard?"

"I showed it to everybody. I shouldn't have."

"Well, if I felt like sending a friend of mine a postcard," she said.

"But I went around bragging about it, and showing it to everybody."

"Well, if you wanted to. I don't even remember what I said on the card."

" 'You would love it here. Lots of good trout fishing. Have gone on two pack trips. See you at Christmas. Natalie.' And a picture of the ranch."

"I remember," she said. "Not very incriminating, was it? Will you take me over to their table now, Teddy?"

"And your word of honor you're not annoyed with me."

"Only if you let them embarrass you," she said.

"Nat?"

"What?"

"I don't have to say it, do I? You know, don't you? You do know?"

She nodded. "Give me your arm," she said.

1962

The Flatted Saxophone

Something happens to the tone of a tenor saxophone when it is played out-of-doors; they always sound flat, especially at wedding receptions, when the guests are queued up for the exchange of mutterings with the bridal party. The dancing has not begun, and the orchestra seems neglected and lonely and the tenor saxophone is expressing the musicians' self-pity. Later, when the bride and groom have done their turn (to a two-tune medley of "I Love You Truly" and "Get Me to the Church on Time"), and general dancing is under way, the flatness of the tenor sax is not so noticeable. It gets lost in the babble of human voices, especially the women's voices, and the musicians have stopped feeling sorry for themselves, the tenor sax therefore has nothing to express, the orchestra plays "From This Moment On" at the cadence of the Society Bounce, and if the tenor sax is flat, so too may be the champagne, but it does not matter much.

"The way I look at it," said George Cushman, "if I want good champagne, I've got some at home. And if I want to hear good saxophone, I'll find out where Bud Freeman's working."

"I didn't hear a word you said," said Marjorie Cushman.

"That's perfectly all right," said her husband. "I'll repeat it, word for word, but if I do you're going to say it wasn't worth repeating—and you'll be right."

"Oh, we're in *that* mood," said Marjorie Cushman. A man came to their table and asked her to dance. "Now don't let anyone grab my chair."

"I'll put my feet up on it," said George Cushman.

"You don't have to do *that*," she said. "Just keep an eye on it."

"I'll keep an eye on you, too," he said, but she did not hear him.

He was now alone at a table for six, and a man and a woman separately asked if all the chairs were taken. "Sorry, all spoken for," he said. A third person, a young man in a cutaway, simply put his hands on the backs of two chairs and started to walk away with them.

"Hold on, sonny boy," said George Cushman. "Bring them back. Just put them right back where you found them."

"Sorry," said the young man, and replaced the chairs.

"And try asking, next time," said George Cushman.

"Why should I?" said the young man, and went away.

"Yeah, why should you, you little jerk," said George Cushman. "With your soft collar and your A. T. Harris cutaway."

A woman seated herself in the chair next to him. "You look lonesome all by yourself, Georgie," she said.

"Oh, hello, Becky," he said. "Yeah, I'm just sitting here eating my heart out, thinking of my lost youth."

"Our lost youth," said Becky Addison.

"No, I wasn't thinking about your lost youth. Just mine. If you want to think about yours, okay. Do you miss it?"

"Not terribly," she said.

"You know, neither do I. Mine, I mean. Not yours. How many weddings have you and I been at? The same weddings, I mean."

"You and I? Oh, dear," she said. "Well, we started going to the same weddings over forty years ago."

"Right."

"And those first years, there were a lot of weddings," she said.

"A powerful lot. Everybody got married, everybody."

"Just about," she said.

"Excuse me, Becky," he said. "Waiter, you wouldn't want to do us a special favor and bring us four Scotches and water, would you?"

"Hello, Mr. Cushman. Yes, sure. I'll bring you a whole tray full. You don't remember me, but I worked at your daughter's wedding."

"Good for you, glad to see you again," said George Cushman. The waiter interrupted his passing of champagne to go to the bar.

"You must have done very well by the waiters at Sue's wedding," said Becky Addison. "Most of them, if you ask them to get you a Scotch, they'll say yes and that's the last you ever see of them."

"It's funny, I don't remember this fellow at all. They were paid by the caterer, but then I gave each of them a five-dollar tip. So now we can have Scotch. That's called bread cast on the waters, Becky. I know you never read the Bible, so I'm explaining it to you. Where is the great man?"

"Charles? My lord and master?"

"Well, who else?"

"He's in Mexico City," she said. "I see Marjorie. Looks lovely."

"She *is* lovely, and she's my wife, and I am devoted to her, and I am not good enough for her, and nobody knows what she sees in me."

"You don't have to lay it on that thick, not with me," said Becky Addison.

"No, I guess not," said George Cushman. "Have a cigarette?"

"I've quit," she said.

"No special reason, I hope," he said.

"No, not really. That is, I haven't been forbidden to smoke. Combination of hysteria from reading all those things in the magazines, *and* I *was* smoking too *much*. Sixty cigarettes a day. So I quit, and I've gained ten unnecessary pounds."

"In how long?"

"Nine weeks tomorrow," she said.

"Nine weeks. Speaking of which, we never did finish guessing how many weddings we'd been to."

"No. Well, the weddings we went to and were in, including our own. Those years there were a lot of big weddings. And lately, the last few years, our children's weddings and our friends' children. An average of five a year, do you think?"

"Times forty. Two hundred. It somehow seems more than that," he said.

"But I don't think you and I have been to two hundred of the same weddings, have we? Maybe we have," she said.

"Pretty close to it," he said. "And the funny thing is, we nearly always sit together, at least for a little while. Did you come alone?"

"Yes," she said. "I didn't go to the church. Did you? I suppose you did."

"Try and keep Marjorie from missing any part of it. Yes, we were there. Marjorie burning up because we didn't have any special pew to go to. To *think* that Ann Bartholomew, her own second cousin, didn't have us sitting with family. Well, maybe Marjorie has a point. There were plenty of people there I never saw before."

"*Weren't* there? I mean, *aren't* there? Looking around here I don't know half the people our age," she said.

"Why don't you and I get married, Becky? Would you like to toy with that idea?"

"I did once," she said.

"Oh, that was when we were in love. Christ, that was that greasy kid stuff."

"Mm-hmm."

"It doesn't take any real imagination to think about getting married when you're twenty years old."

"Eighteen and twenty-one, I think we were," she said.

"At that age, and especially you and I, we didn't know what you did next except get married. God, how long would we have lasted? Two years, do you think?"

"Two or three," she said. "Or as soon as we found out we didn't love each other. Thank God we found it out without getting married."

"I know, and that makes it so much better now," he said. "Would you leave Charley now?"

"No, I don't think so," she said.

"Well, you don't have to ask me if I'd leave Marjorie. Like a shot, would be the answer."

"Then why haven't you?" she said.

"I don't know. I could give you plenty of reasons. *She* gave me plenty of reasons."

"But they were never good enough reasons, were they? You wanted to stay married to her, so you did."

"Yes, that's true," he said. "But I'd leave her now, like a shot. To marry you, that is."

"Georgie, I know what's behind this," she said.

"You do? What?"

"It's a very romantic notion," she said. "It's not young romantic. It isn't that. But it's as desperate as young love."

"It's more so," he said.

"Yes," she said. "The feeling that we'd be happy together with what time we have left."

"You guessed it," he said. "And we would be, Becky."

"We might be. We probably could be," she said. "If we could get up right now and walk out together, if that's all there was to it. But two old crows like us, Georgie. All that time we'd have to spend with lawyers. Your lawyers, my lawyers. Marjorie's. Charles's. Who gets what? Charles would want the Andrew Wyeth, but I'd want it too. By the time we got through all that we'd both be exhausted, you and I. And we'd start asking ourselves, what the hell *for*?"

"Jesus, you're practical," he said.

"I am now. You would be later," she said. "Neither one of us is strong enough to go through all that. Or what we feel isn't strong enough, this loving each other dearly. And that's what it is, Georgie. Loving each other dearly. The dear, wonderful love of two old friends."

He nodded. "You're right," he said.

She put her hand on his. "Come on, dance with me," she said.

"Good," he said, and got to his feet. Then, "Let's wait. I promised Marjorie I'd guard these chairs."

"All right," she said. "Oh, look. Our friend, with there-must-be-sixteen Scotches. I've never *seen* so many Scotches."

"I told you, bread cast on the waters," said George Cushman.

"One, two, three, four, five, six, seven, eight, nine, ten, eleven, twelve, thirteen, fourteen, fifteen, *sixteen*, seventeen, eighteen, nineteen. Nineteen Scotches," she said. "You didn't really want to dance, did you, Georgie?"

1963

The Friends of Miss Julia

The old lady stood waiting at the receptionist's desk. It was a circular room, with niches in the wall and in each niche, under a pin-spot, was displayed one or another of Madame Olga's beauty preparations. Two or three women were seated, not together, on the curved banquette against the wall. High above and behind the receptionist's desk were the hands of a hidden clock, imbedded in the wall, with the Roman numerals signifying 12, 3, 6, and 9, with brass studs substituting for 1, 2, 4, 5, 7, 8, 10, and 11. According to the hands of the clock the time was five minutes to ten.

The old lady looked at the vacant desk, and turned to the other women, but they volunteered nothing. Then a curved door opened and a chic young woman appeared. "Oh, it's Mrs. Davis," said the young woman. "And you have Miss Julia, don't you?"

"Yes, at ten o'clock," said Mrs. Davis.

The young woman looked down at a large white leather appointment book, which lay open on the desk. "Just a set, wasn't it?"

"Yes, that's all," said Mrs. Davis.

"Well—I don't know what to say," said the young woman.

"Did you give my appointment to someone else?"

"No, it isn't that," said the young woman. "We're having quite a mixup here." She lowered her voice. "The trouble is—Miss Julia was taken suddenly ill."

"Oh, I'm sorry. I hope it's nothing serious."

"Well—I'm afraid it is. I'm going to have to cancel all her appointments. But I could take care of your set if you don't mind waiting. I mean I could squeeze you in, since you're already here. It just happened about fifteen or twenty minutes ago. We got a doctor from next door, he's in there now."

"Oh, it does sound serious. Is it the heart?"

"It must be," said the young woman. "They sent for the ambulance. Taking her out the back way. Miss Judith is in a real flap, worrying about Miss Julia and the customers and all."

"Well, never mind about me," said Mrs. Davis.

"Oh, I'll fit you in, but you may have to wait a little while. Have a seat, Mrs. Davis, and I don't think you'll have to wait *very* long. But don't say anything to the other ladies, please. They don't know what's going on back there, and Miss Judith gave us orders. But I know Miss Julia was always a friend of yours."

"Was?"

"They're not very hopeful," said the young woman. A light flashed on the young woman's desk and she picked up the telephone. "Yes?" she said. She listened, replaced the telephone, and now addressed the customers. "Ladies, I'm terribly sorry, but that was Miss Judith, our manager. We're going to have to cancel all appointments for today."

"Oh, come *on*," said one of the customers. "I drove all the way in from Malibu this morning. You can't do this to me."

"What's the big idea?" said a second customer. "I've had this appointment for over a week, and I have seventy *people* coming for dinner tonight. What are you going to say about that? Damn whimsical, if you ask me."

"I'm sorry, Mrs. Polk, but *all* appointments are cancelled," said the young woman.

"Well, give us a reason, for heaven's sake," said the first woman.

"The reason is—all right, I'll give you a reason. Our Miss Julia dropped dead, if that's enough reason for you. Do you want to go in and take a look yourself?"

"You don't have to be rude," said the first woman. "Are you closing for the day?"

"Yes, we're closing for the day," said the young woman.

"Well, when you open up again I hope there'll be some changes around here," said the first woman.

"Oh, go to hell," said the young woman. By mutual instinct she went to and was embraced by Mrs. Davis, and the other women left. The young woman was weeping, and Mrs. Davis guided her to the banquette. "She was so nice, such fun, Miss Julia."

"Always very jolly," said Mrs. Davis. "Always some little jokes to tell."

"It was so *quick*," said the young woman. "I was talking to her only five minutes before."

"That's a mercy, when it's quick," said Mrs. Davis.

"I was going to have lunch with her today," said the young woman. "We always had lunch together every Wednesday. Every Wednesday since I worked here, we always went over to the Waikiki. That's a Hawaiian place over on South Beverly?"

"Yes," said Mrs. Davis. She rested a hand on the younger woman's shoulder.

"Every Wednesday, without fail. We always sat at the same booth, and she and Harry Kanoa, the bartender, they used to carry on a conversation in Hawaiian. She could speak it a little. Did you ever know she was a hairdresser on the *Lurline?*"

"The boat?" said Mrs. Davis.

"I forget how many trips she told me she made," said the young woman. "But a lot. She always wanted to go back to the Islands. She was going next October. She had me almost talked into going with her. I've never been to the Islands."

"No, neither have I."

"I'm all right now, Mrs. Davis. I just suddenly couldn't hold it in any longer."

"That's all right, dear. Do you good."

The young woman smiled. "You called me dear. You don't even know my name, do you, Mrs. Davis?"

"I guess I don't, no."

"It's Page. Page Wetterling. I always have a hard time convincing people, but it's my real name. My mother always liked the name Page. Some of the customers thought Miss Judith gave me the name because I had to page people, but that wasn't it. I have it on my birth certificate."

"It's a pretty name," said Mrs. Davis.

"Listen, I'll ask one of the other operators if they'll give you a set."

"Oh, don't do that, Page, I only have it done to occupy the time. It's something to do."

"But you have pretty hair. Let me speak to Miss Frances. Did you ever have her?"

"No, I never had anyone but Miss Julia."

"Miss Frances is really the best. She's the one all the other operators go to to do their hair, but she doesn't have the personality."

"Yes, I know which one she is," said Mrs. Davis. "But I'd just as soon go without it today."

"Well, do you want me to put you down for your usual time next Wednesday?"

"Yes, you might as well," said Mrs. Davis.

"Does it make any difference who?" said Page Wetterling.

"None. They gave me Miss Julia the first time, two years ago, and I stayed with her ever since. It's only something to do."

"I'll let you try Miss Frances."

"You better ask her first. Maybe she won't want to be bothered with an old lady."

"Oh, listen. Don't you think they all know what you gave Miss Julia for Christmas? I could tell you some big movie stars that are nowhere near as generous. She'll take you."

"All right," said Mrs. Davis.

"None of them are going to be working today, but they'd gladly give you a set before they go home. We're closing up. I'm going to type out a little notice to put on the front door."

"Then do you get the day off?"

"No. I have to be here to answer the phone, change appointments. I get my lunch hour is all. I'd rather anyway, something to do, like you say."

"I guess I didn't mean it the same way."

"Oh, I know what you meant, Mrs. Davis. A lot of the ladies only come here for something to do. Do you want me to try and get you an appointment somewhere else? I know the girl at the Lady Daphne's. Or if you wanted to try George Palermo's, but he's down there near Bullock's Wilshire."

"My hair can go without," said Mrs. Davis. "But thank you, Page. Here."

"What's this? Five dollars? You don't have to give me anything, Mrs. Davis. I wouldn't take it. Absolutely. Listen, if it wasn't for you I'd of really blown my lid. Not that I worry about my job. I have other offers any time I want to leave Madame Olga's."

"Then let me take you to lunch. Would you like to have lunch at Romanoff's?"

"I'd love to, but you don't have to do anything for me, Mrs. Davis."

"It'd be my pleasure. I guess we ought to reserve a table. Can you make an outside call on that phone? Tell them it's Mrs. Davis, Walter Becker's mother-in-law. Or Mrs. Walter Becker's mother."

"Is that so? I didn't know you were related to Walter Becker. That's the television producer Walter Becker?"

"Yes, he married my daughter. He's always trying to get me to go to Romanoff's, but I never do unless I'm with him or my daughter. I guess they know me there, but mention his name to make sure."

Page Wetterling made the telephone call and hung up. "A very nice table for two, they said," she said. "I'll meet you there at ha' past twelve. Okay?"

The old lady was tired when at last she could present herself at the restaurant. She was taken to her table—a good location, but not one of the very best—and she ordered a glass of port wine. She knew she should have ordered sherry, but she was past caring about such things. The proprietor came to her table. "*Nice* to see you, Mrs. Davis. Hope you enjoy your lunch," he said, bowed, and passed on. If he noticed her preference for port over sherry he gave no sign. He was less impassive, as were the other men at the very best tables, when Page Wetterling entered the room. She was a handsome girl in the marketplace of pretty women, but she was unknown to the men in the restaurant; a new face, no handsomer or prettier than the others, but new and unidentified.

"You want to know something? I've never been here before," said Page Wetterling. "I'll have a—oh—a Dubonnet." The waiter left to get her drink, and she did a quick survey of the room. "Some of these women are trying to place me. They can't remember where they know me from."

"I thought a girl like you would be here every day," said Mrs. Davis.

"Never was here in my life before," said Page Wetterling. "My husband could never afford it, when I was married, and since then whenever I dated a man that had the money, we always went some place else. My first visit to the famous Romanoff's and I was *born* in Southern California. Whittier. Do you know where Whittier is?"

"I've heard of it, but I've only been here a little over two years. All I know is Beverly Hills and Holmby Hills and Westwood. And Hollywood. I was there a few times to watch them televise."

"What did you do after you left the salon? Did you find something to kill the time?"

"It wasn't easy. I went to the jewelry store, but I didn't have any intention of buying. Then to the toy store and I spent some money there, on my grandchildren. Then I stopped in at the drug store and had a Coke. Mostly to sit down, though. Then I went and sat on a bench at one of the bus stops, till it was time to come here. What did you do? Were you kept busy?"

"Oh, was I? The elevens and the eleven-thirties and the twelves started coming in, piling up on top of the other. I could have made easily a hundred dollars on tips if I could have sneaked in a few customers. But Miss Judith sent all the operators home. Nobody paid the least attention to the sign on the door. Some of them didn't stop to read it, but others came in and tried to bribe me to sneak them in. One woman offered me fifty dollars. I wonder what *she's* doing tonight. You don't spend that kind of money for a little family party at home. They all went away mad except a few of them. Miss Julia's regulars. But even one of them acted like a perfect bitch. Pardon me for saying that, but that's what she was. You'd of thought Miss Julia was some kind of a machine, that broke down just to louse up this woman's schedule. If I didn't get away from women once in a while I'd begin to hate them all. And you know, they more or less *have* to be nice to me. I make all the appointments, and for instance if two women want to have a permanent for the same time, I can tell one of them that she can't have that time. Or I can call up and tell a woman she has to change her time, and there's nothing she can do about it. Miss Judith can't be bothered with those small details. Oh, that one that threatened to have me fired this morning. Wait till she wants a favor. Do you like women, Mrs. Davis?"

"The majority. Not all."

"Well, if you had my job you'd learn to appreciate the nice ones. But believe me, they're not in the majority. You saw two of the worst examples today. And *I* saw one of the nicest ones. *You.*"

"Thank you," said Mrs. Davis. "I guess most of them wish they looked like you, Page."

"But those that can't, why don't they try to develop a nice disposition?"

"Why aren't you a model, with your looks and all?"

"I was, but that's for the birds. I like to eat, not starve myself to death. I eat as much as most men. I eat a steak three or four nights a week, and wait till you see what I put away for lunch. That's why most of the models I know have such lousy dispositions. They don't get enough to eat. And my doctor told me when I was still married, he said standing around like that all day and undernourished, if you *got* pregnant, if you *could*, you were undernourishing yourself and undernourishing the baby. Well, I didn't get pregnant, thank goodness, but I quit modeling."

"Wish to order luncheon, ladies?" said the captain.

"I know what I want, Mrs. Davis," said Page Wetterling. "I want the chicken pot pie, with noodles. I was never here before, but I heard it was good here."

"I'll have that, too," said Mrs. Davis.

The girl was stimulated, and all through the meal she was entertaining. She made no pretense of a blasé indifference to the movie and television stars, and she consumed even the crust of the chicken pot pie.

"A fruit compote?" said the captain.

"I'll have that," said Page Wetterling. "You have some, too, Mrs. Davis. You didn't eat half your chicken."

"All right," said Mrs. Davis. "You'd think *I* was trying to be a model, but I never eat much."

The girl smiled at the old lady's little joke. "You know, you have a wonderful sense of humor. If more women had a sense of humor, but the women that come into the salon, and places like this, if they had a sense of humor they wouldn't be so cranky all the time. Oh-oh, we're getting a visitor. I think it's your son-in-law, from his picture."

"Hello, Mom." The speaker was a heavy-set man in a blue suit with only a hint of lapels, a very narrow blue four-in-hand, a white-on-white shirt with a tab collar. He leaned down with the heels of his hands on their table.

"Oh, hello, Walter. This is my friend Miss Wetterling, and this is my son-in-law, Mr. Becker."

"I see you finally got here under your own steam," said Walter Becker. "Or did the young lady bring you?"

"No, it was her idea," said Page Wetterling.

"Where did you two know one another, if that's a valid question?"

"I work at the beauty salon where Mrs. Davis goes."

"I see. Then you're *not* in pictures or like that? I thought I didn't recognize you. I was just saying to Rod Proskauer. Well, Mom, I just came over to say hello and pick up the tab. Nice to see you, Miss?"

"Wetterling. Page Wetterling."

"Uh-huh. Mom, I see you this evening, right?" Walter Becker returned to his table—one of the very good ones.

"He calls you Mom," said Page.

"Yes."

"What's your daughter like? She never comes in our salon."

"No. She used to, but her hairdresser opened up her own place. I went there when I moved to California, but it was twenty dollars for practically nothing. Madame Olga's isn't cheap, but I dont want to spend twenty dollars every time. Ten is bad enough, for a person my age. It's sheer waste of money. Most of my life I didn't have money to spend in a beauty parlor. I gave myself a shampoo maybe once a week, maybe not that often. With soap, too. No Madame Olga special preparations. But out here I got into the habit, and Miss Julia was nice."

"Yes. We'll all miss her. She used to come in some mornings and just hearing her describe her hangover—maybe it was hell for her, but she kept us all laughing."

"I know," said the old lady. "Well, I guess you have to get back and answer the phone. I'll take you there in a taxi, it isn't much out of my way."

"I certainly do appreciate this, Mrs. Davis. How about you being my guest next Wednesday? I'll put you down for an eleven-thirty, how would that be? Then you won't have all that time in between."

"Well, I'd like it, but are you sure you would?"

"Of course I would. I'll take you to the Waikiki. They have American food, if you don't go for Polynesian."

"Oh, I don't much care what I eat," said Mrs. Davis.

As the next Wednesday got nearer, Mrs. Davis was tempted to cancel her hair appointment, and thus to relieve the girl of the obligation of taking her to lunch. What pleasure would one so young and pretty get out of taking an old woman to lunch? But Page Wetterling was a warm and friendly girl, and if *she* wanted to get out of the engagement, there were ways of doing so, right up to the very last minute.

"When you're through with Miss Frances, I have my car. We can ride over to the Waikiki together," said Page, after greeting the old lady. "That is, if we still have our date?"

"Oh, that'll be nice," said Mrs. Davis.

The Waikiki consisted of many small rooms rather than a single large one. Bamboo was used everywhere in the furniture and the decorative scheme, and the lighting was dim. From a loudspeaker came the tune "South Sea Island Magic," insistently but quietly, and the patrons and staff all seemed to know each other—or to be about to. "Hi, Page," said the bartender.

"Aloha, Harry," said the girl. "Oooma-ooma nooka-nooka ah-poo ah ah."

The bartender laughed. "That's right. You're getting there. A little at a time. Hey, Charlie. Table Four for Page and her guest."

"Table Four? You mean Table Two," said the waiter Charlie.

"No, I mean Table Four," said Harry.

"Page sits at Table Two," said Charlie. "You're losing your grip, Mr. Harry Kanoa. Where were you last night?"

"Table Four, Table Four," said the bartender.

"I do want Table Four, Charlie," said Page.

"All right, sweetheart, Table Four you want, you can have it. Anything your heart's desire. You bring your mama today?"

"No, this is a friend of mine. Mrs. Davis. This is Charlie Baldwin."

"Of the Baldwin Locomotive Baldwins, no relation to any other Baldwins," said Charlie.

"I don't know what he means by that, but he always says it," said Page.

"Go to the Islands, sweetheart. You'll soon find out," said Charlie. "Care for native dishes or American today? Mainland, I should say. We have statehood. Goodie, goodie. Drinks, ladies? We don't make money on our food, only on drinks. Ha ha ha ha. Page? A double frozen Daiquiri? Or have a Statehood Special. It's almost the same as a Zombie. No more than two to a customer."

"I'm a working girl."

"No profit today, huh? Mama, you want to try a Statehood Special?"

"No thank you," said Mrs. Davis.

"No sale. Well, then, what do you want to eat? Have the Charlie Baldwin Special. I recommend it. I made it up. It's roast pork with baked pineapple and an avocado with Russian dressing. You like it, Page, so why don't the both of you have it?"

"All right, Mrs. Davis?"

"Not the pork, thank you. Maybe an avocado salad?" said Mrs. Davis. "And some iced tea, please."

The old lady liked the Waikiki. The atmosphere of gay informality was just fine—so long as she could sit back and enjoy it without having to take part in it. Nearly everyone who came in knew Page Wetterling; a few stopped to express their regret at the passing of Julia. Mrs. Davis wanted to come back again, but in order to do so she would have to invite her new young friend to Romanoff's.

"Would you like to go to Romanoff's next Wednesday?" said the old lady.

"Listen, I'd like to go there any time."

It was understood that they would have lunch together every Wednesday, alternating the restaurants, and the arrangement was satisfactory to both women. In a few weeks the old lady had heard a great deal of Page's past and current history; it took a little longer for Mrs. Davis to tell much about herself. "I gabble, gabble, prattle," said Page. "I tell you more than I ever told my own mother, and that's for sure."

"I like to listen," said Mrs. Davis.

"Where does your daughter go for lunch?" said Page. "I keep thinking we'll run into her at Romanoff's."

"I guess she goes to Perino's. There, and a French place on Sunset Boulevard. She doesn't care for Romanoff's. She says the men get all the attention there. She likes to get all dressed up when she goes out."

"But a lot of women go to Romanoff's."

"I don't know. She has some reason," said Mrs. Davis.

"You give me the impression that you don't like it very much in California."

"I guess I'm still new here," said the old lady.

"Did your daughter make you move here?"

"My son-in-law. Walter Becker. He was the one. He was for years making a nice living with the radio, the TV. But then like it happened overnight he suddenly owned or part-owned three TV shows, and he sold them for a big profit and now he's in business for himself. Walter is a rich man. A Rolls-Royce car. A home in Beverly Hills on the other side of Sunset back of the hotel. Contributes to charities. It's impossible for him to go broke again. He gets a certain amount for life as a consultant with the CBS. I give him credit, he worked hard for it. But I don't know. He didn't have to make me move out here."

"Why did he, then?"

"He didn't want to have Walter Becker's mother-in-law living in a little apartment in New York City. I loved that apartment. I had a sittingroom for if I wanted to have some ladies in to play cards. A nice bedroom to sleep in. I never had to complain about the heat. They kept it warm no matter what the temperature was outside. It wasn't big, but to me it was big enough. I had two radios. One in my bedroom that I could listen to taking a bath, and one in the kitchen. And a 21-inch TV in the sittingroom. If I didn't feel like going out I could send around to the delicatessen. They delivered. Sometimes I didn't go out for two or three days. Old people are supposed to get lonely, but I wasn't. My whole life I grew up in an apartment that wasn't big enough for our family. I and my two sisters slept in the same room, my three brothers in their room. I got married and I slept in the same bed with my husband over thirty years and my two daughters they had the same bed in their room. That was supposed to be the diningroom. Then my husband passed on and my both daughters got married and I moved to a smaller apartment. Such a pleasure, a genuine luxury I had. Within easy walking distance of 149th Street, if I wanted to shop or go to a show. I was the envy of the other ladies."

"It sounds perfect," said Page.

"Uh-huh. But Walter wanted me out here. My daughter, too, but more Walter. He wanted a grandmother for his children. His mother died young, so it was me."

"You were still their grandmother, whether you lived here or back East."

The old lady shook her head. "With Walter it has to be seen. He has to show people every room in the house and everything in all the closets. 'My wife has sixty-four pairs of shoes,' he says to them, and he opens the closet door to prove it. The same way with a grandmother. A grandmother in New York isn't the same thing as a grandmother in the house!"

"But it must be nice living with your grandchildren," said Page.

"They're getting used to me," said the old lady. "They never saw me till two years ago I came here. My own daughter had to get used to me." She nodded in agreement with herself. "And *I* had to get used to *them*."

"Did you make any new friends here?"

"Here is not so easy to make new friends," said Mrs. Davis. "At my age it's too late to learn to drive a car. I have to take a taxi everywhere. The other ladies are in the same situation. My daughter would take me in her car if I asked her, but I don't like to ask her."

"You were really happier in your little apartment," said Page.

"I admit it, but I don't want to say anything to them. They think they're doing the right thing. My son-in-law took me to the TV studios, introduced me to Red Skelton and Lucille Ball and many more. Walter said I would have something to write about when I wrote to my friends. But then he asked me to show him the letter and I couldn't hurt his feelings. I wrote a letter to my friend Mrs. Kornblum, a neighbor of mine in the same building, but I couldn't show it to Walter. It was a homesick letter. I said Lucille Ball was nice, but I'll bet not as good a stuss-player as another friend of ours, Mrs. Kamm. Stuss is a game of cards we used to play. Walter asked me did I tell my friends about him owning a Rolls-Royce. I would never do that, brag about my son-in-law. One of our friends made herself obnoxious bragging so much about her son getting elected state senator. The Senator, she called him. You would of thought he was Jacob Javits instead of just a senator in Albany."

"Wouldn't it be easier if you got yourself a little apartment here?"

"I don't want a little apartment here. I just want to go home to my own apartment, East A Hundred and Fifty-third Street, The Bronx, New York. Or one just like it."

"Then go," said Page Wetterling.

"What?"

"Just go, Mrs. Davis. Just tell your daughter and your son-in-law that you're leaving next Tuesday."

"How many times I thought of that, Page. How many times."

"But did you ever say anything to them?"

"No. I wouldn't know how. They think they're doing everything for me. It would be like a slap in the face to them."

"Well, didn't you ever slap your daughter when she was little?"

"Many times. A good slap was what she needed, and I gave it to her. And her sister. And their father, too."

"You never slapped Walter Becker, though."

"No. Sometimes I felt like it, but I never did."

"But you're not afraid of him?" said Page.

"Of *him?*"

"Then slap him. I don't mean with your hand across his face. But tell him you're going back to New York. And don't let him give you a con. Don't let him argue with you. Buy your ticket on the plane and write to Mrs. Kornblum that you're coming."

"Not Mrs. Kornblum, but Mrs. Kamm would have room for me. Page, you're putting ideas in my head."

"Not me. It's all your idea. I'm just giving you a little push. Do you have the cash?"

"Plenty. They give me a hundred dollars a week spending money. Why, were you going to offer me the loan?"

"Yes."

"You're a true friend, and for such a young girl to know so much," said Mrs. Davis.

"I can't take all the credit, Mrs. Davis. Miss Julia knew you were miserable."

"That's why she was always trying to cheer me up."

"She had a big heart," said Page Wetterling.

The old lady smiled. "Don't you give *her* all the credit, either, Miss Page Wetterling."

"Why, I don't have any idea what you're talking about, Mrs. Davis."

"I'll put it in a letter," said Mrs. Davis.

1963

How Can I Tell You?

A T-Bird and two Galaxies was very good for one day, especially as the T-Bird did not involve a trade-in. The woman who bought it, Mrs. Preston, had come in and asked for Mark McGranville and shown him a magazine ad. "Do you have one of these in stock, in red?" she said.

"Not on the floor, Mrs. Preston," he said. "But I can have one for you inside of two hours."

"You can? Brand-new?"

"Brand-new," he said.

"Red, like this?"

"The exact same color, the same body job, white walls, radio and heater. I could have it in front of your house inside of two hours. And if you were thinking of getting rid of your ranch wagon, I can allow you—well, let's see what the book says."

"Did I say I wanted to trade in my ranch wagon? I love it. I wouldn't think of getting rid of it. I want the Thunderbird for Buddy. He just passed all his exams and he's coming home for the weekend."

"Well, you know exactly what he wants, Mrs. Preston. Because he's been in here a couple times, looking at T-Birds. He's a very lucky boy."

"He's a good boy, Mark. Not a lucky boy."

"Yes, he's one of the best," said Mark McGranville.

"And you say you can have a car just like this in two hours? Where do you have to go for it?"

"Oh, all I have to do is pick up the phone, call the factory distributor, and tell him what I want."

"But how do you know he has what *I* want?"

"Because we dealers get a list of what was shipped to the factory distributor. I guarantee you I have just what you want. I'll bring it to your door this afternoon, personally, and be glad to take care of the registration, insurance, all the details. Would you want us to finance it for you?"

"I would not. You bring the car around and I'll give you a cheque for the whole thing, license and everything. I don't suppose you could have his initials put on today?"

"If you let me have the car overnight I can have his initials put on and bring it back to you before noon tomorrow. R. W. P.?"

"R. W. P. That's right. In yellow. Yellow would be better on red."

"About three quarters of an inch high? Or smaller? Maybe a half an inch. A half an inch in yellow shows up well. If he wants bigger initials later, that's easy to fix."

"I'll leave that to you, Mark. And you'll take care of everything? He gets home tomorrow afternoon."

"He couldn't have a nicer surprise. It is a surprise, isn't it?"

"It certainly is. It's a surprise to *me*. I wasn't going to buy him a car till he graduates. But he's been so good, and why not let him have the fun out of it?"

"You're right, Mrs. Preston."

"How's Jean? And the children?"

"They're fine, thank you. Very fine."

"You get credit for this sale, don't you?"

"You bet I do," he said. "Appreciate your asking for me."

"Well, you've always been a good boy, too, Mark. I'm sure your mother's very pleased with you."

"Thank you."

"Your mother's a fine woman, Mark. Any time she's thinking of going back to work again, I hope she lets me know first."

"She would, that's for sure. But I guess she likes keeping house for my sister. They have that little ranch-type out at Putnam Park, the two of them. Mary has her job at the Trust Company, and my mother has enough to keep her occupied."

"Very nice for both of them. Well, I mustn't keep you any longer. You have some telephoning to do."

"Thank you very much, Mrs. Preston," he said. He accompanied her to her ranch wagon, held the door open for her, and waited in the parking lot until she turned the corner.

The other transactions of the day were more typical, not sales that were dropped in his lap by a Mrs. Preston. But all three sales should have made him feel better than he felt on the way home, and he did not know why he should find himself wanting a drink and, what's more, heading for Ernie's to get it.

He locked his car and entered the taproom, hung his hat and coat on a clothestree, and took a seat in a booth. Ernie came to wait on him.

"Well, hi, stranger," said Ernie.

"Hello, Ernie," said Mark McGranville. "Quiet."

"Well, a little early. Never much action before six. The lunch trade till ha' past two, then maybe a few strays during the afternoon. How's it with you?"

"Not bad. Pretty good."

"Ed and Paul were in last night, them and their wives for dinner. Paul made a pretty good load. What's her name, his wife?"

"Charlotte."

"She snuck over and asked me to cut his drinks, but I couldn't do that. I said to her, what'd she want to do? Get me in trouble? You know Paul, he caught me watering his drinks and he'd have it all over town in no time. He's no bargain anyway, Paul."

"No, he's a noisy son of a bitch when he makes the load."

"But he's a friend of yours, though, isn't he?"

"I guess so," said Mark. "Let me have a bourbon and soda, will you, Ernie?"

"Why sure. Is there anything the matter, Mark?"

"No. Why?"

"I don't know. You want any particular bourbon?"

"I wouldn't be able to tell the difference. You know that."

"*Okay, okay,*" said Ernie. He pantomimed getting a kick in the behind and went to the bar to get Mark's drink. He returned with a small round tray on which were a highball glass, a shot glass with the bourbon, a small bottle of club soda. "There you are. That's Old Gutburner, the bar bourbon."

"Old what?"

"Gutburner. Old Gutburner. That's what Paul calls the bar bourbon. It ain't all that bad. You want some music?"

"Christ, no."

"You just want to sit here and nobody bother you. Okay," said Ernie. He walked away, spinning the inverted tray on his forefinger, and Mark had a couple of sips of his drink. He waited for some pleasant effect, and when none came, he finished the drink in a gulp. "Ernie? Bring me another shot, will you?"

"Right," said Ernie. He served a second shot glass of the bourbon. "You got enough soda there? Yeah, you got enough soda."

"I don't want any soda. I'm drinking this straight."

"Yeah, bourbon ought to be drunk straight. Bourbon has a flavor that if you ask me, you oughtn't to dilute it. That is, if you happen to like the taste of bourbon in the first place. Personally, I don't. I'll take a drink of bourbon, like if I'm at a football game to see the New York Giants. Or you take if I'm out in the woods, looking for deer, I usely take a pint of rye with me, or sometimes bourbon. It'll ward off the cold and the taste lasts longer. But for all-day drinking, I stick to scatch. You don't get tired of the taste of scatch. Your rye and your bourbon, they're too sweet if you're gonna drink all day. You know a funny thing about scatch, it's getting to be the most popular drink in France and Japan. That was in an article I read, this magazine I get. You know, in this business we get these magazines. I guess you have them in the car business. Trade publications, they're known as."

"Even the undertakers."

"Huh?"

"The undertakers have trade publications."

"They do, ah? Well, wuddia know. I guess every business has them."

"Every business is the same, when you come right down to it," said Mark McGranville.

"Well that's a new one on me. We're all in it for the money, but what's the same about selling cars and pushing Old Gutburner?"

"What you just said," said Mark McGranville. "We're all in it for the money. You. Me. Undertakers."

"You're talking like an I-don't-know-what," said Ernie.

"I know I am. What do I owe you?"

"Be—nothing," said Ernie.

"On the house?"

"Come in again when you'll get some enjoyment out of it. I don't want to take your money under these conditions."

"You, Ernie?"

"Yeah, me. You got sumpn eatin' you, boy, whatever it is."

"I know I have," said Mark McGranville. "Maybe it's the weather. I don't know."

"Well, my booze won't do it any good, Mark. I get days like this myself, once in a great while. The women get them all the time, but that's different. Take in a show tonight. You know this English fellow, with the big gap in his teeth. Terry?"

"Terry-Thomas."

"He's at the Carteret. He's always good for a laugh. You're not a booze man, Mark. Some are, but not you. You were taking it like medicine, for God's sake. Castor oil or something."

"Yeah. Well, thanks, Ernie. See you," said Mark McGranville.

He could not understand why he went through dinner and the entire evening without telling Jean about the T-Bird and the two Galaxies in one day. He knew that it was because he did not want to give her any good news; that much he understood. She would respond to the good news as she always did, enthusiastically and proudly, and he was in no mood to share her enthusiasm or accept the compliment of her pride in him. All that he understood, but he could not understand why he preferred to remain in this mood. She would cheer him up, and he did not want to be cheered up. He was perfunctory when the kids kissed him goodnight, and after the eleven o'clock news on the TV he rose, snapped the power dial, and went to the bedroom. He was in bed when Jean kissed him goodnight and turned out the light.

"Mark?" she said, from her bed.

"What?"

"Is there something the matter?"

"Nope."

"Goodnight," she said.

"Goodnight," said Mark McGranville.

Five, ten dark minutes passed.

"If you don't want to tell me," she said.

"How the hell can I tell you when I don't know myself?" he said.

"Oh," she said. "Shall I come over?"

"I just as soon you wouldn't," he said. "I don't know what it is."

"If I come over you'll sleep better," she said.

"Jean, please. It isn't that. Christ, I sold two Galaxies and a T-Bird today—"

"You *did?*"

"That ought to make me feel good, but I don't know what's the matter with me. I had a couple drinks at Ernie's, but nothing."

"I knew you had something to drink. It didn't show, but I could smell it."

"Oh, I'm not hiding anything."

"You hid it about the Galaxies and the T-Bird."

"I know I did. I'd have told you in the morning."

"All right. Goodnight."

"Goodnight," he said.

He thought his mind was busy, busy, busy, and that he had been unable to get to sleep, but at five minutes past two he looked at the radium hands of the alarm clock and realized that he must have slept for at least an hour, that some of the activity of his mind was actually dreams. They were not frightening dreams or lascivious ones; they were not much of anything but mental activity that had taken place while he thought he was awake but must have been asleep. Jean was asleep, breathing regularly. She made two musical notes in deep sleep, the first two notes of "Yes Sir That's My Baby"; the *yes* note as she exhaled, the *sir* as she drew breath. And yet he could tell, in spite of the dark, that she would be slightly frowning, dreaming or thinking, one or the other or both. He had so often watched her asleep, physically asleep, and making the musical notes of her regular breathing, but the slight frown revealing that her mind was at work, that her intelligence was functioning in ways that would always be kept secret from him, possibly even from herself. It was not that her sleeping face was a mask; far from it. The mask was her wakeful face, telling only her responses to things that happened and were said, the obvious responses to pleasant and unpleasant things in life. But in the frowning placidity of sleep her mind was naked. It did not matter that he could not read her thoughts; they were there, far more so than when she was awake.

He got out of bed and went to the warm living room and turned on one bulb in a table lamp. He lit a cigarette and took the first drag, but he let it go out. He was thirty years old, a good father, a good husband, and so well thought of that Mrs. Preston would make sure that he got credit for a sale. His sister had a good job, and his mother was taken care of. On the sales blackboard at the garage his name was always first or second, in two years had not been down to third. Nevertheless he went to the hall closet and got out his 20-gauge and broke it and inserted a shell.

He returned to his chair and re-lit the cigarette that had gone out, and this time he smoked rapidly. The shotgun rested with the butt on the floor, the barrel lying against his thigh, and he held the barrel loosely with the fingers of his left hand as he smoked. The cigarette was now down to an inch in length, and he crushed it carefully.

Her voice came softly. "Mark," she said.

He looked at the carpet. "What?" he said.

"Don't. Please?"

"I won't," he said.

1963

Ninety Minutes Away

It was a very cold night in February. More snow was expected, but apparently it was waiting for the temperature to go up a little. In the streets the going was rough; snow piled high in the gutters, ruts in the roadway frozen solid, and the sidewalks were hazardous with patches of ice. Not many people were to be seen on the streets of South Taqua, although it was the night before Washington's Birthday and the mines would be idle the next day. The people who had gone in to Taqua to see a movie were already home. The store window lights were out. The only illumination was from overhead arc-lights at three intersections, and from the Athens, the all-night restaurant. A few cars were parked near the Athens, as near as they could get.

Harvey Hunt paid his check at the Athens, folded his muffler over his chest, turned up his overcoat collar, put on his hat and went out. He took a few steps on the sidewalk, and someone called to him from the doorway of the Athens. "Hey, Harve, you forgot your arctics."

"I'll be back for them later," said Harvey Hunt. "But thanks."

He resumed his walk to the borough hall, a block away, sliding where there was enough ice, walking flatfooted where the ice was patchy. Half-way to borough hall he covered his nose with the muffler; the wind was strong and cold and made breathing difficult.

He entered the borough hall through the side door marked Police. The room he entered was warm, small, and crowded with desks, chairs, filing-cases, fire extinguishers, assorted traffic signs and stanchions, a gun closet, a small telephone switchboard, a couple of rubber tires, an oxygen tank, new and old first-aid kits, clothestrees, several pairs of hip boots. There was only one human being in the room, sitting at the desk near the switchboard. He was a rather handsome man who was getting thick through the middle. He wore a dark woollen shirt with sergeant's chevrons and a silver-plated shield. In one hip pocket was a .38 revolver, encased in a pocket holster. In his shirt pockets were three or four fountain pens and pencils. "Shut the door, shut the door," he said.

"Let me get inside first," said Harvey Hunt. "What's doing, Ken?"

"You'll find out soon enough," said the sergeant.

Harvey Hunt took off his overcoat and hat and hung them on a clothes-tree. "All right, what's doing?"

"Nothing, yet, but there will be," said Ken. "Just keep your shirt on. I wouldn't get you here on a false alarm."

"What kind of a story is it?"

The policeman looked up at the wall clock. "It's a raid."

"A Prohibition raid?"

"I wouldn't get you down here on a Prohibition raid," said Ken.

"I noticed you looking at the clock. Is the raid going on now?"

"Yes. I wouldn't of told you that much if it wasn't."

"Are you afraid I'd have tipped off somebody?"

"Not intentionally. But by accident you could have."

"The raid was supposed to start at eleven o'clock?"

"Five after eleven. Eleven-five," said Ken. "They'll be coming in pretty soon."

"Then tell me what it's all about."

"All right, I guess it's all right now," said Ken. "You know Buddy Spangler's place, out there by the freight yards."

"Sure. I know every saloon in the county. I haven't been to Spangler's much, but I know the place. It's back off the main road."

The cop nodded. "That's where the raid is."

"Who's raiding it? Not just your fellows."

"All our fellows are in it, but the raid was partly our fellows, partly the state cops. The orders came from the county attorney's office. They didn't tell us anything about it till around nine o'clock. They didn't want any leak. There isn't any of our fellows would spill the beans, but the county attorney wanted to make sure."

"Now maybe you're ready to tell me what *kind* of a raid it is."

"It's a dirty show. Spangler imported in some women from Allentown and Bethlehem, and they're putting on a dirty show. Spangler didn't invite any of the local men, or anyway only two or three. He's charging five dollars a head admission. Men from Gibbsville and Reading, Hazleton. Business men. Sports. Somebody tipped off the county attorney, and he notified the state cops. They got here around nine o'clock and told us about it so we wouldn't look bad. McCumber, Jefferson, O'Dwyer, and Snyder. Those are our men. The state cops are some in uniform and some in plain clothes."

"Who will they arrest? Spangler and the women. But those business men, they won't arrest them."

"No, they won't arrest them. But the county attorney, Millner, he's there and he'll recognize them, most of them, anyway."

"How nice for Millner. He's going to run for judge this year."

"You don't have to look at it that way. Millner's doing his job. And he could of left us out in the cold. We get just as much credit as anybody else. Millner's all right."

"Well, this won't do him any harm. Raiding a dirty show, and getting something on all those business men. They'll shell out when he starts running for judge."

"Why shouldn't they? You always take the opposite side. You don't believe any cop is honest. Or politician."

"As far as I know, *you're* honest, Ken."

"I'm pretty honest. And I don't like dirty shows in this town. Mc-Cumber don't either. This is a pretty clean town, considering. We got a lot of church people here."

"You don't have to tell me," said Harvey Hunt. "Are they bringing them in here, the prisoners?"

"Bringing them here, then we gotta wake up Squire Palsgrove if he's home asleep. They'll get a hearing, and I guess most likely keep them here overnight. Take them to the county jail tomorrow. It depends on if they get somebody to go their bail tonight."

"Depends on how high the bail is."

"It'll be as high as Squire Palsgrove can make it. That you can be sure of."

"You say the women came from Allentown?"

"Allentown and Bethlehem, according to what I heard. Three of them and their pimp. They're supposed to come from Allentown, but who knows where they come from originally? Allentown is what they say, Allentown and Bethlehem. But they might as well come from New York City."

"Or South Taqua," said Harvey.

"There you go again, always taking the opposite side."

"I was just kidding you, Ken."

"I don't say we don't have some immoral women in South Taqua. That wouldn't be true. You'll come across immoral women everywhere you go, I guess. That's been my experience. But we never had a whorehouse in South Taqua since McCumber was chief of police. McCumber won't tolerate it, and I won't either. The people don't want a whorehouse in this town."

"It would save some of the men a trip to Taqua."

"Taqua and South Taqua are a very different thing. They got three times our population in Taqua. Maybe we get a black eye for having this raid in South Taqua, but it'll be worth it to get rid of Buddy Spangler. He don't care anything about the reputation of this town, or else he wouldn't let them put on a dirty show in his place."

"What kind of a dirty show is it?"

"How should I know what kind? They're all the same, aren't they?"

"Did you ever see one?" said Harvey.

Ken paused. "Yes, I saw one."

"Not here in town, though."

"No, not here in town. Wilkes-Barre, when I was a young fellow. Before I was a police officer. Some little town outside of Wilkes-Barre. There was things went on you wouldn't believe if you didn't see them with your own eyes. You'd wonder how a woman could stoop so low. I was around nineteen or twenty at the time, and I never forgot it."

"What were *you* doing there?"

"What was I doing? You mean why did I go? Well, in those days I wasn't married, and just like all the young fellows my age I was after all I could get. We all went after as much as we could get. I had a friend of mine had an auto. It was a big old second-hand Chandler. We used to drive around every Sunday afternoon, him and I. Half of those girls never had a ride in an automobile, and all we had to do was open the door and they'd get in. I used to raise a lot of hell in those days."

"And you were a good-looking fellow before you began to put on that weight."

"I sowed my wild oats. But as soon as I got married I settled down. With some fellows it's just the opposite. They get married, and they're no sooner married than they start chasing after other women. I don't believe in that. You marry a woman, you ought to settle down. Unless *she* won't settle down. But that don't often happen . . . Car outside. I guess that's them."

The office door opened and the newcomers streamed in. There were three women, each carrying a small overnight bag and keeping close to each other; there were five men. It was easy to tell which man was Spangler, and which was Millner, the county attorney. Spangler was wearing a suede windbreaker and a hunting cap. He was dissolute-looking and harassed, and except for Millner the other men pushed him around. Millner was very much in charge, better dressed than the others, who were police officers in plain clothes.

"Here they are, Sergeant," said Millner. "Will you call up Squire Palsgrove? I'd like to get them committed as soon as possible."

"Snyder, you call the squire. I want to book these people. Your name?" said Ken.

"You know my name."

"Come on, Spangler. Answer my questions. I don't know your first name."

"Marvin J. Spangler."

"Age?"

"Thirty-seven."

"Occupation?"

"Hotelkeeper."

"You don't have a license to run a hotel."

"Then put down—restaurant proprietor."

"Rest. Prop.," Ken wrote in the book. "Address?"

"You know that. Washington Street."

"You ever been arrested before?"

"Plenty."

"What's the charge, Mr. Millner?" said Ken.

"Chief, do you want to make the charges?" said Millner.

"Conspiring to give an indecent performance," said McCumber. "Disorderly conduct. Resisting arrest. Illegal possession of firearms. Selling intoxicating liquor without a license. Lewd and immoral conduct. Running a bawdyhouse. We got him on about ten counts. Lock him up, Snyder."

Snyder, one of the plainclothes policemen, took Spangler's arm and led him out of the office to a cell.

"All right, young woman," said Ken. "Your name."

"Gloria Swanson."

"Don't get fresh here. I said your name."

"Mary Smith."

"Mary Smith, huh," said Ken. "Age?"

"Twenty," said Mary Smith. The others laughed.

"You must of had a hard life," said Ken. "Occupation?"

"Manicurist," said Mary Smith.

"She really is, too," said one of the other women.

"I didn't ask you," said Ken. "Address?"

"Bellyvue Stratford Hotel, Philadelphia. Bellyvue. Get it?" The men and women laughed.

"Ever been arrested before?" said Ken.

"Never," said Mary Smith, and the women laughed.

"How many times you been arrested before, Mary Smith?" said Ken.

"I don't know. I didn't keep a diary."

"What's the charge, Chief?" said Ken.

"Against all three of these women, indecent performance, indecent exposure, soliciting, illegal possession of narcotics. No, strike that out. We only found narcotics on this one. Jefferson, take her back and put her in Cell Two."

"You're not gonna put me in a cell with that Spangler gorilla," said Mary Smith.

"You'll be with the other women," said McCumber. He nodded to Jefferson, who led her out.

A second woman now stood before Ken. "My name is Jane Doe, age twenty, address Seventh and Hamilton, Allentown, PA. Occupation, artist's model. No previous arrests. And did anybody ever tell you you look like Bryant Washburn, because you do?"

"Seventh and Hamilton?" said Ken. "That's where the monument is."

"I know. I live up there on top of the monument."

"Cut the comedy," said Ken. "Snyder, put her in with the other one, Cell Two."

"Do I get anything to eat here? I'm hungry. If I pay for it myself can I send out for something to eat?" said Jane Doe.

"What do you want?" said Ken.

"Steak tartare with a raw egg on top. Here's a buck, that oughta take care of it. And tea with lemon and sugar."

"We'll see. Go on, beat it," said Ken. "Chief, I understood they had a pimp with them."

"He got away," said McCumber. "We don't know how he got away, but he got away all right. He won't get far, the state police'll pick him up."

"All right, you, young woman," said Ken. "Your name."

"Jean Latour."

"How do you spell that?" said Ken.

"J, e, a, n, capital L, a, t, o, u, r."

"Age what?"

"Seventeen."

Ken looks at her. "I almost believe you. How old *are* you?"

"I'll be eighteen on my next birthday."

"You're starting early," said Ken.

"Huh. I started before this."

"How many arrests?"

"None. I was never arrested before."

"Where do you live? On top of the monument with that Smith woman?"

"That was Jane, that lived on top of the monument. Mary lives at the Bellyvue. Bellyvue. Funny." She giggled.

"We book this one on the same charges, Chief?" said Ken.

"This one was the worst," said McCumber.

"The best, you mean. I get the most pay," said Jean.

"You'll need it," said Ken. "What occupation?"

"Dancer and actress. And *singer*," said Jean.

"Put down prostitute for this one," said McCumber.

"All right, put down prostitute. I don't give a damn. Put down whore if you want to."

"The youngest, and the worst," said McCumber.

"Give me a cigarette, somebody," said Jean.

Harvey offered her his pack, as the others remained still. "You don't look like a cop. What are you, a lawyer?"

"I'm a reporter."

"Oh, are you gonna take my picture?"

"No."

"Then give me a good writeup, if you're not gonna take my picture. What paper is it gonna be in?"

"The Taqua *Chronicle*."

"The what?"

"The Taqua *Chronicle*."

"I never heard of it," she said. "Is that just local?"

"That's all," said Harvey.

"Oh, *well*. The hell with *that*. I thought maybe you were on some big paper, from Philly. But you're just a hick reporter, like these hick cops." She spat the smoke out of her lungs. "I have a proposition. You're the chief, huh?"

"I'm the chief," said McCumber.

"But he's higher than you," said Jean, pointing the cigarette at Millner. "Who do I have to talk to to get out of this?"

"Save your breath," said Millner.

"I don't want to spend the night with those other girls. I never saw them before tonight. How about if you get me a room in the hotel? I don't care which one of you. I'll give you a good time."

McCumber and Millner were silent, but she did not give up.

"All right. I tell you what I'll do. Get me a room in the hotel, and whatever I make I'll split with you, fifty-fifty."

Millner and McCumber were still silent.

"Then how about this? You can have all I make over ten dollars."

The silence continued.

"What's the *matter* with you? Don't you have any manhood? You? Reporter? Will you help me out?"

"I don't have the say," said Harvey.

"Take her back and put her in a cell," said Ken.

The telephone rang, and Ken answered it. "Police headquarters, Sergeant Dunlop. Yeah. Yeah. Oh. All right, Mrs. Palsgrove." He hung up. "That was Mrs. Palsgrove. Squire couldn't get his car started, and she don't want him out in this cold. He won't be here tonight. Now what do we do, Chief?"

"Up to Mr. Millner," said McCumber.

"Nothing we can do. Leave these people here tonight and give them a preliminary hearing in the morning. We can hold the women for a medical examination anyway, that's the law. We'll take all four of them to Gibbsville tomorrow and put them in the county jail."

"You're not gonna put me in any jail," said Jean. "I want a lawyer."

"You can get one tomorrow, but you're still going to jail. You admit you're a prostitute," said Millner.

"You can't prove it. I was never arrested before in my whole life, you dirty son of a bitch," said Jean. "You. Reporter. You put it in the paper that I asked for a lawyer, and they wouldn't let me have one. You didn't arrest any of those johns. Who was that hot-pants funnyman that got up on the stage, that respectable business man? He was as much in the act as anybody. But I don't see *him* here. You let him put his clothes on and get away, but he was as much in it as we were."

"Who was it, Millner?" said Harvey, grinning.

"Never you mind, Hunt," said Millner. "Don't you start poking your nose in where it doesn't belong."

"That's what I do for a living, Millner," said Hunt. "If this broad finds out who the business man was, she could subpoena him when she goes to trial."

"Who's going to help her find out? You?" said Millner.

"Well, I could," said Harvey.

"Yes, I suppose you could," said Millner.

"And you don't want that, do you?" said Harvey. "If this kid gets herself a smart lawyer, somebody like Bob Dockstader, Dockstader could subpoena your business man and maybe he could even subpoena some of the other sports, the ones you didn't arrest."

"Say, Hunt, are you a reporter or what are you?" said Millner. He turned to McCumber. "What about this fellow, Chief? Is he in some kind of a racket?"

"Not that I know of, but he's very contrary," said McCumber.

"He's against everything," said Ken. "If you're *for* something, he'll be against it. He's an againster."

"Oh, one of those," said Millner. "Well, Hunt, what is it you want? Not that I couldn't get you fired in one phone call. Your boss is a man I know better than you do."

"You could get me fired, all right. But if you did, then believe me I'd go right to Bob Dockstader, and the two of us would have a lot of fun with you when you get into court. You just threatened me, Millner, so now I'm not on your side at all. Maybe I was before, but I'm not now."

"I didn't threaten you. I said I *could* get you fired, but I never said I was going to," said Millner.

"Nuts. I know what you're thinking, Millner. You're thinking this kid and Spangler and the others will plead guilty and there won't be any trial. That's the way it always works in these cases. But you respectable lawyers don't think much of Dockstader, and he doesn't like you either. Dockstader would plead them all not guilty just for the fun of it."

"Everybody knows what Dockstader is," said Millner. "These are the kind of people he has for clients. What I want to know is, what do you want? Speak up. You want something."

"Let this kid off," said Hunt.

"Let her off? You're crazy. She was the worst of all four of them," said Millner.

"That's right, there were four. The pimp you let get away. All these South Taqua cops and the state police, but the pimp eluded your grasp. The pimp and your business man were the only ones that got away. Can you imagine Dockstader when he gets you all in court. I can just see it. The courtroom'll be crowded. Probably Number Three Courtroom. And Dockstader starts asking a lot of embarrassing questions. The whole thing will be embarrassing anyway. Millner, you taking charge of the raid personally, and Dockstader will want to know why. Chief, you letting the pimp get away. And all these prominent guys under subpoena."

"What are you trying to do, Hunt?" said Millner.

"I don't know. But I never like it when some politician says he'll get me fired. Oh, I know I'll be out of a job tomorrow, but I've been out of work before."

"Just out of curiosity, why do you want me to go easy on this Latour woman?" said Millner.

"I didn't say I wanted you to go easy on her. I said let her go."

"Why? What's she to you?" said Millner.

"Yeah, I don't understand it myself," said Jean Latour. "I never saw him before I came in here."

"Because she's pretty, and I like pretty dames," said Harvey.

"That's not your reason," said Millner.

"Then you tell me what my reason is. I don't know. She said she was never arrested before, and I believe her. Maybe that's the reason."

"Maybe she was never arrested before, although I doubt that. But if you could have seen her an hour ago you wouldn't worry so much about whether she was arrested or not. Ask any of these police officers. This young woman has absolutely no morals. In all my—"

"That's a speech you can save till you take her to court," said Harvey.

"You didn't even pay your way in, did you, Mister?" said Jean. "What are you squawking about? The johns that were there all paid to get in. And it was private."

"Hunt, even you can see that this young woman has no morals. The only thing that counts with her is money. No guilty feelings, no regrets. Only money."

"You know, Millner, you put your finger on it. I've been trying to dope out why I'm on her side, and you found the reason for me. She has no morals."

"Then what are you defending her for?" said Millner.

"Because I never saw anybody like her before. She isn't like those other dames. She doesn't even look like them. She's a very unusual dame. But if you throw her in the clink, she'll be just like all the others."

"I told you," said Ken to Millner. "He likes to be different. Always different. He comes in here every day and there's hardly a day he don't come out with some new idea. Wants to be different. I think he's a Socialist, into the bargain."

"The hell I am," said Harvey. "But different, yes. Come to think of it, I voted for you, Millner. Because it didn't look like you had a chance."

"Appreciate that, I'm sure," said Millner.

"That's all right. I won't vote for you for judge."

"Hunt, we've had enough talk from you. You're only a reporter, and you wouldn't be here if you didn't work for the *Chronicle*. So shut up. You have your story, so shut up and get out." The speaker was Mc-Cumber, the police chief.

"Okay," said Harvey. "But Millner knows where I'm going tomorrow morning, first thing. I know I won't have a job tomorrow, but I'm sure as hell going to call on the Honorable Mr. Dockstader. Then we'll watch the fur fly."

Millner was frowning, deep in thought and trying to make a decision. "Chief," he said to McCumber. "We have Spangler and those women in there. I'll let them plead guilty and go to prison. But if this fellow and Dockstader get together, there'll be a court trial and a lot of pretty well-known men will have to appear. You know what Dockstader is like when he gets somebody on the stand, and a lot of reputations will be ruined. If this goes to trial there'll be no stopping Dockstader, you know that."

"That shyster lawyer," said McCumber. "He ought to be disbarred."

"And some day maybe he will be. I'd like to help bring that about," said Millner.

"And I'll tell him you said that in front of five police officers, Millner," said Harvey. "I just want to remind you, Millner. Dockstader has never been up on charges before the Bar Association, but you and the chief have been making statements about him, *in front of witnesses*, that he could sue you for. These cops are officers of the law, and they won't all perjure themselves to protect you and McCumber."

Millner realized he had made a mistake. "I'd be glad to take my chances if Dockstader wanted to sue."

"You're bluffing. These are good cops, and they won't lie on the stand to save your neck. Also, Millner, you're from Gibbsville, not South Taqua. Here they don't like Gibbsville people very much. But you were saying something to the chief, and I don't want to interrupt that."

"I'd like to give you a punch in the nose, but I'll deny myself that luxury," said Millner. "Chief, if you have no serious objection, I'm willing to let this Latour woman go. Provided that she leaves here tonight, right away, and this fellow Hunt goes with her."

"Hey, Reporter! You got me off," said Jean Latour. "Do you have a car?"

"Not so fast," said Harvey.

"Now what do you want?" said Millner.

"Two weeks' pay, at thirty-five dollars a week. That's what the paper would give me if they fired me. I've been with them three years."

Millner took a roll of bills from his pants pocket. "Here's your seventy dollars. On your way."

"And don't come back," said McCumber. "You or the woman. Snyder, you go with them and see that they leave town."

"I want to go to the boarding-house and get my other suit."

"See that he packs his suitcase and is out of town in a half an hour," said McCumber. "Go on, get them all out of here." McCumber was displeased with Millner's deal. He hardly looked at Millner.

"You gotta give me more than a half an hour, McCumber," said Hunt. "I have to stop and get my arctics at the Athens, and I don't know how long it'll take me to get my car started."

"Go on, get out. Just get out," said McCumber.

"Well, Miss Latour," said Harvey. "Fate has thrown us together."

"Yeah," she said. "Well, goodbye, boys, no hard feelings."

"Goodbye, you guys," said Harvey.

The cops did not respond, vocally or otherwise.

"Come on, little one," said Harvey.

"One thing," said Jean to the men. "I still never been in jail."

Snyder gave Jean and Harvey a couple of hard nudges, and all three left the room. "Wow, is it always as cold as this?" said Jean.

"I have to stop and get my arctics," said Harvey.

"I oughta brought along a pair of arctics," said Jean. "What kind of a car do you have? I hope it's a closed car."

"It's a Ford coop."

"Does it have a heater in it? Where we going?"

"Where do you want to go?"

"I got a friend of mine I can stay with her, in Allentown."

"Where do *you* live? Where is home base for you?" said Harvey.

"You mean where do I keep my wardrobe?" she said. "I got most of it in my room, in Philly. I got a room in a hotel there. I didn't bring much tonight. You don't need much on this kind of a job."

"No, I guess not." They were outside the Athens. "Here's where I left my arctics. Do you want a cup of coffee? Snyder, how about you? You want a cup of coffee?"

"My orders are to—"

"Aw, come off it, Snyder. Have a cup of coffee with us," said Harvey.

"Listen, you," said Snyder. "Quit stalling around. Get your arctics and then we go to your boarding-house, and you get the hell out of town."

"What are *you* so sore about all of a sudden?" said Harvey.

"This here little tramp ought to be run out of town on a rail, and you're no better. I should of known all along what you were. A lousy pimp."

"I'll be right out," said Harvey. He entered the Athens, put on his arctics, and returned to the sidewalk, where the girl and the policeman were staring at each other.

The cold wind discouraged conversation during the three-block walk to Harvey's boarding-house. "If you're in such a hurry, Snyder, you can see if you can get my car started. The key's in it. Kid, you can sit in the car with him while he warms up the engine."

"She don't sit in any car with me," said Snyder. "She can wait inside with you. And you be out in ten minutes or I'll come and get you."

In about fifteen minutes Jean and Harvey were ready to drive away. "Well, Snyder, South Taqua is safe once more. No more sin in South Taqua."

"Birds of a feather flock together," said Snyder.

"Goodbye, copper. Keep your knees together," said Jean.

"Get outa here, you little bum."

"We're off!" said Harvey. "Off in a cloud of dust."

"Where to?" said the girl.

"Well, we'll try Allentown first. Maybe if the roads aren't too bad we can make Philly tonight."

"Let's try to get to Philly," she said.

It was about thirty-five miles to Allentown and the road was sometimes blown clean by the valley winds, sometimes they had to proceed in low gear through snow and ice. The girl fell asleep ten minutes out of South Taqua and stayed asleep until Harvey found a garage in Allentown that was still open. Drowsy, the girl said she wanted to continue to Philadelphia, and almost immediately fell asleep again.

On North Broad Street, when they were getting closer to City Hall, Harvey shook her knee until she came awake. This time she was fully awake. "Why look where we are. Old Willie Penn. Boy, I'm glad I'm not sitting up there with him, like Jane. What's on top of the monument in Allentown?"

"Do you want to go back and look?" said Harvey. "Where is this hotel you stay at?"

"You go around City Hall and then on Market Street I'll show you," said Jean Latour. "They'll be surprised to see *me*."

"They may be surprised to see me, too," said Harvey.

"Not as much," she said.

It was not a hotel of faded elegance; it was an establishment that had never had any grandeur, built and furnished for the brief accommodation of transients. The atmosphere, and the night clerk, proclaimed the motto: No questions asked.

"Hello, Jean," said the night clerk. "Back already?"

"I couldn't stay away from you," she said. "You know that, Albert. Any messages for me?"

"Not since I came on. I'll look in your box. No. Nothing there. Do you have your key?"

"I got my key."

"The elevator's out of order again. You'll have to walk up," said Albert. "Your friend gonna register?"

"No, he's with me," said Jean.

"That'll be one dollar," said Albert.

"If you don't register you have to give Albert a dollar," said Jean.

"Either that or I have to charge her the double rate," said Albert.

"But this goes into your pocket," said Harvey.

"Yeah, I get a dollar. The other way, she has to pay the double rate, or else I have to register you and charge you for a single."

"Oh, I don't mind paying the buck. I just didn't understand the racket, but now I do," said Harvey.

"Where's Henry?" said Jean. "He ought to be here to carry our baggage upstairs. I give him enough tips."

"I sent him home early. He was coughing, coughing, coughing, and I didn't want to catch his God damn cold."

"All right, we'll carry our own."

Her room was three flights up but they were not long flights. Above the main floor the rooms were low-ceilinged. In Jean's room there was a double brass bed. Harvey looked at the bed and said, "What's this going to cost me?"

"Well, I know you only have around seventy dollars on you," she said.

"Not only *on* me, but that's my entire bankroll. I have to get a job quick, and probably sell my car."

"What would you say to five dollars? I usually get more. Twenty-five I been getting. I only take a few regulars."

"Five is all right," he said. "Maybe if I get a job in Philly I'll get to be one of your regulars."

"Maybe, who knows?" she said.

"At least it's warm here," he said. "This is where you make your headquarters?"

"It's one of the places. Why, because you don't see my wardrobe?"

"Not only that. It doesn't look as if you spent much time here."

"You're very observing," she said. "All right, I'll tell you. I got a keeper, an old guy around fifty years of age. He has an apartment. That is, I have, and he pays for it. That's where I live mostly."

"Where is he now?"

"In Florida. Palm Beach, Florida. But I couldn't bring you to the apartment. I don't trust the elevator man. He spies on me."

"How can you take a chance on lousing up that arrangement?"

"You mean like working for Spengler, or Spangler, or whatever his name is? Well, I'll tell you. I got a hundred dollars from Spengler-Spangler, and if it wasn't for those cops I would have picked up easily another hundred. Easily. There was one guy there tonight, I think he was a bootlegger. I could of got a hundred from just him. He was flashing money around there like it was going out of style. He gave Mary ten dollars just to sit on one guy's lap. He wanted to see what the guy would do if he got a naked girl on his lap."

"What did he do?"

"Oh—he started to wrestle around with her. This bootlegger wanted me to go back to Griggsville with him."

"Gibbsville."

"Yeah. He had some scheme. I don't know what."

"But you were taking a big chance, going up to South Taqua. As it was, you got pinched."

"I know. But *you* sit around doing nothing, going to the movies, and the elevator man spying on you. See how long before *you* went crazy. I heard about this chance to make a few dollars and have a little fun, and Spangler guaranteed me there wouldn't be any trouble. That Spangler, I shoulda known he was a small-time smallie. I hope they give him ten years. Do you know what he got those other girls for? Twenty-five apiece. And what will they get out of it? What kind of a rap will they get, do you know?"

"Oh—six months, maybe. They'll plead guilty and get off pretty light."

"Six months! You call that light?"

"They could get more, if Millner wanted to get tough with them. But he's only after two things. He wants to put Spangler away, and he wants to have this hanging over some of those men that were there. He's going to run for county judge, and that costs money in Lantenengo County. Every little bit helps."

"I didn't trust him either. All that time he was calling me names, if there was nobody else there I could tell by the way he was looking at me."

"I'm not so sure. Millner's supposed to be a family man. In politics he's a double-crosser and everything else. But I never heard about him and the women."

"You make me laugh," she said. "You stood up for me, but I know why and so do you. There's only the two kinds of men. The real queers, that get sick if a woman touches them. They can't help it, they were born that way, and I'm afraid of some of *them*. But the others, I don't care if they're a family man or a priest or what, if they can like one woman they can like them all. And if they don't like me, believe me, I know what they are. All those cops tonight, I could of got a week's pay out of all of them. Even the old chief, he was afraid to look at me."

"What about the fellow behind the desk? The sergeant?"

"Him? Oh boy. He was kind of handsome-looking, too. I bet I could have got him to let me go before the night was over."

"Where did you get all this information? When did you start finding out so much about men?"

She laughed. "They always want to know that. Simple. When I was a kid, one of the towns where I lived there was a man there that if I put my hand in his pocket he let me keep what I found. The son of a bitch, he used to put five or ten pennies there ahead of time, never anything like a big quarter. Cheap thrill for him, but I didn't care. I used to pester him to let me put my hand in his pocket. It's a wonder I have any teeth left, I used to eat so much candy."

"Did you know what he was doing?"

"What he was doing, or what I was doing? Sure. How could I help it? The penny game. I knew what was there besides those pennies. It wasn't his *coat* pocket, for God's sake. I probably would have got him up to a dollar bill, most likely, but we had to move to another town. Otherwise I probably wouldn't have a tooth left in my head. I used to eat those penny creams, and do you remember those peanut-butter bolsters, all covered with chocolate? Every day after school. One day I ate ten of those penny creams and I got sick, and that took away my taste for creams. But carmels I liked. I guess they were good for my teeth, you had to chew carmels. Look. See my teeth? I have these two fillings and that's all."

"And what did you do in the next town?"

"The next town? You mean when we moved from Pittsburgh?"

"Wherever the guy was that you played the penny game with."

"That was Pittsburgh. Then we moved to Buffalo, New York, but we didn't stay there very long. My old man worked on the railroad and he got his leg cut off."

"Did he lose his job?"

"His job? He got killed."

"How old were you?"

"When my old man got killed? Search me. Ten? Eleven? I don't remember."

"Who took the place of the guy that gave you the candy money?"

"Where did I get money from? Why do you want to know that for?"

"Don't tell me if you don't feel like it," said Harvey.

"Oh, well, I might as well tell you. You couldn't report me to the police for that. I used to steal. Some boy I knew, the two of us used to go around and steal stuff. We used to steal things out of cars, and off the clotheslines. The five-and-dime. The most we ever got was five dollars, a fur neckpiece we swiped off a clothesline. The other kid used to take the stuff to some hockshop near where the boats came in. We never got what the stuff was worth. I'll bet you that fur neckpiece was worth a hundred dollars. Maybe more. But we only got five for it. Or that was what he said, the other kid. Maybe he was holding out on me. But we didn't stay there very long. My mother divided us up. I and my two older sisters went to live with my aunt and uncle. Paterson, New Jersey. And the three youngest to another aunt and uncle in Cleveland, Ohio."

"Where did your mother go?"

"Oh, she got sick. Consumption. She died, too. That was after I ran away. They wouldn't give us any money, and my two older sisters went to work in the mills. But I knew where he hid his money, my uncle, and I took a hundred and fifteen dollars and went to New York. He kept his money in a cigar box under the bathtub. I had a hard time finding it, but I knew it was somewhere in that house, so I used to search every room when they were out. They used to go to the eight o'clock Mass every Sunday, and I went to the nine. The children's Mass. So while they were out I gave that house a good going-over till I found out where he kept the money. There was over three hundred dollars in the box, but I only took a hundred and fifteen."

"Why a hundred and fifteen?"

"It was five twenties and three fives. Eight bills. In case he got back early from Mass I didn't want him to notice that some of it was gone. You know, if he took a quick look, he wouldn't notice only eight bills were gone. Unless he counted. If he counted, I was licked. But he came home from Mass, and I started out for the nine, only I never went to the church. I rode on a couple of trolleys and got to Newark and took the Tube to New York and went to the movies. The Rivoli. I sat in the back till my eyes got used to the dark and I could see better. Then I waited a while till I picked out some john that was there alone, and I got up and sat next to him."

"And then you were on your way," said Harvey.

"Not with the first one. He got up and changed his seat. But the next one I didn't have to do anything. He started on me, the second one. He sure did. He was a john, all right." She laughed. "He took me to some hotel, a dump like this, and around ten o'clock that night I cried and said I was afraid to go home. My father would kill me. Kill him, too. I said I was gonna give myself up to the police. Well, we argued back and forth till finally he gave me all he had on him, sixty or seventy dollars, and said I was to stay there till Tuesday and he'd come and take me away. To Florida. I knew he was never coming back, the son of a bitch, and I didn't care. I had about a hundred and eighty dollars, and I wasn't worried."

"Then what happened?"

"Well, the fellow that ran the hotel came to the room the next day. He said I had to get out, and I said the john was coming to get me the next day. The manager knew damn well he wasn't, but he said he'd give me till the next day. Well, about a half an hour later this woman came in my room. She pretended to feel sorry for me and all, but she was just sizing me up. Finally she said to me, she said she knew I was a little hooker and if I wanted to do business I had to do business with her. I swore up and down I didn't know what she was talking about, and I didn't know very much, to tell the truth. I could tell she wasn't sure whether I was telling the truth or not. She just couldn't figure me out. Then I said to her, I wasn't what she thought I was, but I ran away from home and the police would be looking for me. I said I had to stay there for a while and I had thirty dollars that the john gave me. I said I was a virgin, but if there was no other way to make money, I'd work for her. She fell for it. She said I didn't exactly have to work for her, but some johns liked it if a young girl was there to watch. And that was how I really got started."

"How long did you work there?"

"A week. She paid me fifty dollars for the week and my room rent, and at the end of the week I went down to Florida with her boy friend. He and I got married down there. He ran a clip-joint in Miami, and that was where I started singing."

"Oh, you sing?"

"You heard me tell those cops I was a singer. I sing as good as anybody around. I ought to be getting a thousand dollars a week. I can sing rings around Ruth Etting, *or* Helen Morgan. I traveled all over the country with a couple bands. Teddy Bryer. You ever hear of Teddy Bryer?"

"Yes, I heard of him."

"He came in the joint one night and heard me sing. Came back every night for a week, and when the band was going north I went with them."

"What about your husband?"

"Him. I walked out on him. He wanted Teddy to buy up my contract, a thousand dollars. Teddy hit him so hard I thought he killed him. Teddy knew I didn't have any contract. You don't know Teddy, I can see that. He punches first and argues after. He gets in trouble with everybody. The union. The dance-hall managers. He'll go right down in the crowd, come down off the bandstand, and punch some stranger and you won't ever know what Teddy had against him. That's what finally broke up the band, his bad temper. He beat up the piano player for making a play for me, and they took it up with the union. Teddy was fined and he refused to pay the fine."

"So that's what happened to Teddy Bryer. He used to play at the parks, near the place where you were tonight."

"Then I went with Bobby Beach and the Beach Boys. I made two records with them. I did the vocal on one and the other was a duet with Bobby. I did the vocal on 'Sunny Side of the Street.' The trouble with that was we made it for one of the small companies, and it was a lousy arrangement. Bobby wouldn't spend money for an arranger. He'd take the stock arrangements and fool around with them himself, to save a dollar. If I could have stayed with Teddy six more months he was just beginning to get in good with Victor again. He had some fight with them, too. He fought with everybody."

"Well, you're a girl of many talents," said Harvey.

"You think you're sarcastic, but I do have one talent, and that's singing. I know what you had reference to, but some day you can forget all about that. You and everybody else. Because I'll tell you something, boy. The way those cops looked at me tonight, and you saw them. That's the way the people look at me when I sing, even with a lousy band like Bobby Beach behind me. You ask the musicians. What girl singer is the best? They'll name off Ruth Etting, Helen Morgan, Lee Wiley, half a dozen others. But the musicians that heard me, they'll tell you. And they know."

"Well, you're still young."

"You bet I am. Some day you'll be bragging that you laid Jean Latour. And people won't believe you."

"Well, so far I don't believe it myself. And you know what, kid? I'm dead tired."

"You mean you just want to sleep?"

"You had a nap in the car."

"Yes, I'm ready to go. I can stay up the rest of the night."

"How about if I grab about an hour? What will you do?"

"I'll take a bath," she said.

"Just give me about an hour," he said. The long day, the cold drive, the warmth of the room made sleep, just a little sleep, more desirable than the girl. There was, in fact, and considering the girl's build, a strange absence of urgency in his desire for her. He had not yet touched her body, although he had every intention of doing so. He was not going to leave this room unsatisfied, and his willingness to postpone his pleasure with her now, in favor of sleep, was so that when he awoke he would be strong and virile.

"I'm gonna turn on the water in the bathtub," she said. "Will it keep you awake."

"Nothing'll keep me awake, now," he said. He got out of his suit and shirt and lay on the bed in his B.V.D.'s. He heard the water plunging into the tub, and in two minutes he was dead asleep.

When his sleep was over, that first heavy sleep, the room was dark, but he was a man who had slept in many places and at odd times of day and night, and he awoke knowing exactly where he was. He looked at his wristwatch, glowing in the dark, and guessed that he had been unconscious about two hours. His next conscious thought was the irritating observation that he was alone in the bed. He would have liked to wake up with her beside him and to give her a good lay, perhaps even before she was fully awake. He fumbled around for a match or a light switch. He could find neither, and he got out of bed and by following the length of the bed went straight to the hall door, and now he found the light switch in the wall. He went to the window and pulled the shade aside. First light had come. Now he had a look in the bathroom and saw that there were still a couple of inches of water in the tub and it did not appear to be water that anyone had used for a bath. No human body had been in that water, and the soap in the dish was dry and hard, the rubber sponge was brittle.

Little by little he began to realize that when she left the room she had taken away everything that belonged to her. There were some cigarette butts in the ash trays, and in the bathroom a small bottle containing a couple of powdery aspirins. But everything else was gone, and he remembered now that there never had been much of hers in the room. Immediately he made a couple of quick steps to his suit, which lay on an easy chair. As he knew it would be, his wallet was empty of money; in his pants pockets she had left a five-dollar bill and eighty-four cents in coins.

"Not even rolled," he said aloud. He laughed angrily at himself. "Not even rolled, not even laid, not even got a hangover." He took the receiver off the hook and waited for the switchboard to respond. He waited and waited before he got a response.

"Hello?"

"Hello, Albert. Did I interrupt your sleep?"

"No, I had the buzzer off. I didn't take notice to the light flashing," said Albert.

"Did our young lady leave any message for me?"

"No, she didn't say anything. I got her a taxi and she left here about an hour ago, I guess it was."

"Do you know where she went? Not that you'd tell me."

"Well, I don't know for sure *where* she went."

"But you have a pretty good idea," said Harvey.

"I guess that's right."

"But you wouldn't tell *me*," said Harvey.

"No."

"Why did she take all her stuff with her? I understood she had this room on a permanent basis."

"All her stuff? She didn't have much stuff. She paid up for the last couple of days and checked out. You can stay there till tonight if you want to. The room's paid for till six o'clock tonight."

"She walked off with my bankroll, but you don't know anything about that, do you?"

"No, but what the hell? You weren't born yesterday. You didn't look to me like some college kid. You been around, I could see that."

"I'd like to get that money back, or some of it. I'll give you ten bucks for her address and phone number."

"You don't *have* ten bucks, you just said. No, I don't know her phone number, so I couldn't give you that if I wanted to. And I wouldn't give you her address. Not for ten bucks, anyway."

"Did you ever lay her, Albert?"

"Why?"

"I just wondered whether it was because you liked her personally, or the little tips you get."

"Oh, well I guess it's both. I laid her one time."

"Only once? Wouldn't you like to again?"

"Well, she's pretty. She sure is built. But I could get fired if I let her stay here free."

"She's too expensive for you," said Harvey. "When do you guess she'll be back here again?"

"I wouldn't want to make a guess on that. She comes and goes. Like maybe I won't see her for weeks at a time, then she'll have the room for a whole week. She had some piano player here for over a week one time. He was a piano player in some orchestra down on South Broad Street. A baldheaded fellow. He'd roll in here drunk every night, and she'd be here all day, till it was time for him to go to work. I'd come on about usual time, eight o'clock, and they'd just be leaving."

"I understand she's a pretty good singer," said Harvey.

"That's the first I ever heard of it, but that wouldn't prove anything. I only knew her from coming in here. She has some rich guy, but she sure is the little two-timer."

"And yet I like her, don't you?"

"Well, yes, I guess so, and she's only a kid. But when it comes to money—oh, boy. They ought to have her over at the Bourse."

"Well, I guess you're not going to help me out with her address," said Harvey.

"No. You gotta find that out for yourself, but this is a big city. If I was you, buddy, the best thing is to forget about it. You got taken. Too bad. But look at me. I got asthma. I think I get it from the soap they use here, scrubbing the floors."

"If I get my money back I'll buy you a bottle of cologne," said Harvey. "It's all right for me to leave my suitcase here?"

"Till six o'clock tonight. If you want a cheaper room, I got one for a dollar and a half a night. It's an inside room, quiet. And the weekly rate is nine dollars, the same as if you were getting one night free. You share a toilet and a shower with another guy, but he's away a good deal of the time. He's a salesman, an elderly bachelor or maybe a widower, I don't know which. That's as good as you'll find anywhere in town."

"And I may run into Jean if she comes back here. I'll let you know tonight," said Harvey.

As a reporter he was pleased with the information he had extracted from Albert, and reasonably confident that in one or two further conversations he would be successful in his attempt to learn Jean Latour's address. He went back to bed and slept until ten o'clock. He shaved and dressed and went out and had a good breakfast; fried eggs, French fries, toast and coffee. He was going to need all his strength.

He went to the garage where he had left his car, and asked for the boss. "How much will you give me for the Ford coop?" said Harvey.

"I wouldn't give you five dollars for it," said the manager. "I can't use it."

"I paid six hundred for it a year ago, and it's in pretty good condition. Give me four hundred for it."

"No sale."

"Look at the rubber. Those are all new, all four."

"I can see that, but I'm not buying."

"Give me two hundred for it," said Harvey. "You can make yourself a quick hundred and a half on that. You know you can. I think you could probably get five hundred dollars for this car."

"Then you get it."

"Make me an offer. I need money quick. Or how much would you *lend* me on it?"

"I wouldn't lend you a nickel on a Lincoln phaeton," said the manager. "I'll give you seventy-five dollars for the car."

"Make it an even hundred."

"You got the papers on it?"

"I have the bill of sale, the registration, and my driver's license. I'm a newspaper reporter, and I just lost my job. Will you give me a hundred?"

"All right, I'll give you a hundred dollars," said the manager. The papers were signed, the money handed over.

"I'll be interested to see what price you put on it," said Harvey.

"I'll show you," said the manager. He took a piece of soap and wrote on the windshield: "For Quick Sale—$495."

"Nice going," said Harvey.

"What the hell, you would of taken seventy-five," said the manager. "You got no kick coming."

"Only one thing more. Will you kiss me? I like to be kissed when I'm getting screwed," said Harvey.

"So long, buddy, I'm a busy man," said the manager.

Harvey returned to the hotel and paid a week's rent on the $1.50 room, commencing that night after six. He then went to Jean's room and made half a dozen telephone calls to newspaper offices. He had some luck. A day rewrite man on the *Public Ledger* agreed to meet him for a drink late in the afternoon; a copyreader on the *Inquirer* said he would nose around and see if there might be a job for him; a sportswriter on the *Evening Ledger* invited him to go to the fights that night and have drinks later with a fight promoter who was a soft touch for newspaper men. All at once Philadelphia was a warm and friendly town. At least it was a town of *brotherly* love, he told himself.

In a few days he had a job as a rewrite man on the morning *Ledger*. It paid forty dollars a week. It was not exactly what he wanted; he preferred to be a leg man, but he did not know Philadelphia too well; his personal acquaintance with the geography of the city was only less limited than his contacts with the police and other such news sources. But rewrite was a job he could hold down, and live on, while he was getting better acquainted in the city. Accidentally Jean Latour had done him a couple of favors by getting him out of South Taqua and by stealing his money, but they were not favors he would have to return.

In the succeeding weeks he could find no one among his newspaper acquaintances who had ever heard of the girl, and he guessed that Albert had tipped her off that he was living at the Royal, which was the uninspired name of the hotel. Another guess that concerned Albert was a wrong one; Albert kept the secret of Jean's address, and with the occupational suspiciousness of a night clerk he refused to be drawn into conversation about the girl. Often at night Harvey would stop for a chat with Albert before going upstairs to bed. The Royal had no kitchen, and Albert brought his own lunch, to be eaten at midnight. Henry was always sent out to get hot coffee, and Harvey would sometimes order a container for himself. He had begun to like the Royal; it was certainly a more inviting place than the rooming-house in South Taqua, a cheerless room in a cheerless house, that he had gone to only for sleep. The Royal had the smell that went with the unending war against vermin, but it had the fascinatingly unwholesome human traffic of its lobby and elevator and halls. The majority of the male guests were horse-players, including two men who worked in bookmaking establishments. The women were anybody's women, trying not to think of the day when nobody would want them. It was an orderly place; the police had their instructions from the landowners' representatives at district headquarters. Out in Chestnut Hill the real owners of the Royal were pleased with any property that paid its own way and showed a little profit; over on the Main Line it might not have pleased Mr. Gaston Pennington to learn that indirectly he was a minor contributor to the income of his cousins who owned the Royal. Gaston Pennington was the gentleman who supported Jean Latour.

For Harvey Hunt this was a period of contentment. The three years in South Taqua had been easy and not unpleasant, and should have provided contentment but had actually been a period of unrest. In South Taqua he did his work, the pay was not bad; he was given passes to the movie theater in Taqua and small discounts at the store where he bought his clothes. The business department helped him to buy a car. He was rewarded for small favors with the small graft that was a perquisite of small-town newspaper reporting. He gave the name and address of Levy's store when writing that Levy's daughter had won a mathematics prize at State, and Levy would pay for the puff with a free pair of shoes, Bostonians worth ten dollars a pair, retail. Harvey got a complimentary weekly five-dollar meal ticket at the Exchange Hotel for remembering to mention the hotel in his accounts of Rotary luncheons. He was not much of a drinker, but he would run up a bill for pints of whiskey at Mac McDonald's Pharmacy, and McDonald would forgive the debt in appreciation of an occasional news item that tied in with a paid advertisement of a shipment of exotic French perfumes and Eastman Kodaks.

Literary brilliance would have been wasted in the columns of the *Chronicle*, and Harvey Hunt was not the man who could supply it. He had not gone into the game as a trainee in belles-lettres. Until senior year in high school he had more or less wanted to try for an appointment to West Point or Annapolis, but his Congressman lived in the next county, and neither Harvey nor his father or mother knew exactly how to go about getting the appointment. It had not been a burning desire in any case. Harvey's father was station agent for the New York Central at Elk City in one of the sparsely populated northern counties of Pennsylvania, and he had wanted Harvey to learn a trade, but Harvey's mother had insisted on the boy's finishing high school.

The Hunts lived in an apartment on the second story of the Elk City railway station, and Mrs. Hunt earned three dollars a week on the local paper by reporting the comings and goings of her fellow citizens. It had not occurred to her that there might be a future in journalism for her son, but when Harvey wrote an account of an accident to a circus train a couple of miles down the track, she brought the article with her to the newspaper office. It was printed in its entirety, and the publisher of the paper said that Harvey had a real knack. Harvey received no payment for the article, but he was given his first byline, and his fate was sealed. At the end of high school he became a reporter at double his mother's salary.

The paper died three years later. It was not a paper that was much better or much worse than many others. It had been publishing for forty years, into the second generation of the family that founded it. It had never known any extensive prosperity. It had served the community reasonably well, but only as a convenience. There had rarely been any reason for a citizen to read the paper unless he were personally involved in the content, and between such personal involvements the citizen would lose interest in the paper. It made no difference to him whether the paper came out or not, and when finally publication was suspended no one asked, "What will we ever do without the *Constitution*?" The *Constitution* would be missed, they said, but there was no sense of emergency, no dramatic effort to revive the paper while there was still a chance. The publisher wept privately, settled with his creditors for fifteen cents on the dollar, and took a job in the county office of the Sealer of Weights and Measures. Only then did he realize that for fifteen years he had neglected to send away copies of his paper to be bound.

Paper by paper Harvey Hunt made his way southward through the Commonwealth, making friends with other newspaper men, but acquiring no other assets. On one paper he received pay for one week out of five; on another he was fired for using the publisher's office for a rendezvous with a young woman; on another paper he quit because he was not given a single day off during a twenty-one-day stretch. In Reading he was fired for lying about his salary on his previous job; in Allentown he was offered a five-dollar raise by the publisher of the Taqua *Chronicle*, who liked a story he wrote about a South Taqua mining disaster. There had never been any complaints about his work as such, and during his time in South Taqua he was given good reason to believe that he could stay there forever, eventually to take over as the publisher retired.

The publisher was a man who had other and more profitable interests than the *Chronicle*: a stone quarry, the gas company, half a block of business properties, and, through his wife's inheritance, a nice income from electric power and light. John Barringer was the *owner* of the *Chronicle*, and he made it pay. His interest in the paper was in making it pay, just as he made his stone quarry and his real estate pay, and if he was only vaguely aware of the existence of Munsey and Ochs, Pulitzer and Northcliffe, he was even less aware of the Kents and Chapins and Wattersons and Whites. He was an owner-publisher and not an editor-publisher. Nevertheless he ran a successful paper, because he published the kind of paper he liked to read and his preferences reflected the tastes of most of the solvent readers of his paper. To that extent he was a good editor by accident. When by accident something got into the *Chronicle* that he did not like, he nearly always learned next day that his readers had not liked it either. The *Chronicle* seldom carried a story longer than one column, and almost never was there a story that was given a two-column headline.

For Harvey Hunt that meant a lot of work; many news stories rather than one or two big ones. It was the best sort of training. Because he was under restrictions of space, he was prevented from acquiring bad stylistic habits. Because he was expected to bring in quantities of items, he learned not to waste time in useless questions. John Barringer, who literally could not have named the capital of Maryland and had never heard of Bonar Law, described Harvey Hunt as the best reporter he had ever known, and from time to time he would drop a clumsy hint that Harvey ought to settle down with a nice local girl and get ready to take over the managing of the *Chronicle*. Barringer was a man of his word, and Harvey Hunt knew that if he stayed on in South Taqua, Barringer would make it easy for him to buy the *Chronicle*. But Harvey grew restive under the gentle pressure of John Barringer. Without knowing what it was, without trying very hard to understand it, there was something about the life he led in South Taqua that was worse than being broke and jobless, and he never experienced the slightest regret either for leaving South Taqua or for the manner of his leaving. John Barringer would not have fired him for quarreling with Millner, but John Barringer would not have been able to help him understand why he wanted to come to the defense of a girl like Jean Latour. An older man ought to be able to understand such things, but John Barringer only understood that it was time to settle down with a nice local girl as a step toward taking over the *Chronicle*.

In Philadelphia, sitting behind the switchboard with Albert and listening to the horse-players' lies, Harvey Hunt was more truly at home than he had ever been. The Market Street trolleys did not have to make so much of a clangor, but at least they made it all the time, all through the night, so that you needed nothing to tell you that South Taqua was past and gone. You could wake up in the dark of four A.M. and some angry motorman would stomp his bell for you, and you would go back to sleep. In a big city like Philadelphia there was always enough news to fill the paper. You did not have to worry about the news supply, as you did on a small-town paper. Harvey Hunt was appalled at the waste of news by the big city papers. In Philadelphia they had a Chinatown that should have provided hundreds of fascinating news items but was practically ignored; the city was a seaport, with ships arriving and sailing for places all over the world but nobody ever did a story on the seaport. There was surely one good news story a day in each of the big department stores; stories in the theaters, among the highbrow musicians, in the fancy hotels. You simply could not have two million persons living together without creating the frictions that result in news items. To a man who had worked in the small towns of eastern Pennsylvania the city was inexhaustibly rich with unwritten columns of wonderful, exciting stuff. To Harvey Hunt, blasé was a word that went with long cigarette holders and the magazine *Vanity Fair*, and in the excitement of his first year in a big city he felt the need to live forever.

He saw a tall man in a brown broadcloth greatcoat with a fur collar, brown spats, brown Homburg, waxed moustache, and monocle. He saw the man again, and noticed that in the band of the Homburg, the man wore a tiny feather. He had never seen any such man in Allentown, but he saw him half a dozen times, and as the weather improved the man was in different costume but always had the glass in his eye or dangling from a thin cord. There was an elderly lady who rode around in a baby Renault towncar, which had a chauffeur and footman. There was no such turnout in Reading or Bethlehem. In the dead of winter he saw young men carrying oddly shaped tennis racquets, escorting young women carrying similar racquets. He had never seen any such racquets in Scranton or Wilkes-Barre. He had never seen a Negro policeman, or a Boy Scout wearing bare-kneed shorts, a subway or an "L" train, a fire-fighting water tower, an eight-oar shell or a single sculler, four Japanese couples in evening dress at a theater together, a department store with its own bugle corps, a house of prostitution where men went to meet other men, a butler in knee breeches (perhaps the father of one of those Boy Scouts?). He had never seen so many rich people, so many poor people, so many people, and he wanted to know all about all of them.

He began with the obvious ones, the men and women who worked on the paper with him. He had heard of them because of their bylines—the general news reporters, the political reporters, and the sports writers. They never looked the way he expected them to. Walter J. Bright, who covered major crimes of violence, should not have looked like a policeman but he might at least have looked like a private detective. Instead he was a short stout man who wore a slouch hat in and out of the office and believed that every man and woman was guilty as charged, should be sent to the electric chair, and would be so if it were not for the bungling and venality of the prosecutors. He was married and had a homely daughter who worked in the classified-ad department.

Theodore N. Kruger, the top political writer, was thin to the point of emaciation, and owed at least part of his success to his ability to sit up all night, drinking whiskey with the politicians and remembering what they told him when they, but not he, got drunk. He had a modest fortune, acquired by being let in on state and municipal real-estate deals. He would buy a piece of property, sell it to the city, and divide his profits with the proper officials, whose names were kept out of the original transactions. He was a Swarthmore graduate and eventually the one to enlighten Harvey Hunt on the oddly shaped tennis racquets.

Martha Swanson came as a surprise to Harvey Hunt. The stories he read under her byline were so completely unadorned with feminine touches—they were, in fact, stories that would not ordinarily have been assigned to a woman—that during his first weeks in the office he had her confused with Miss Pitney, a secretary in the financial department who affected Eton collars and Windsor ties, and wore rimless pince-nezs. Martha Swanson, although she usually wore tailored suits, was abundantly feminine. She wore single-pearl earrings and a seed-pearl necklace, and whether she had on one of her cashmere pullovers or a shirtwaist, her bosom was distracting. Between assignments she would sit at her desk, bent over a Modern Library volume, chain-smoking, not taking off her hat, always at the ready, so to speak. She was a trifle overweight, completely at home in her surroundings, and Harvey Hunt guessed that all romantic notions between her and the men on the staff were a thing of the past. They referred to her as Swanson behind her back, and she was always good for a five- or ten-dollar touch. She appeared to be lazy, but when she went out on a story she worked hard and efficiently. In time Harvey Hunt learned that she was the daughter and only child of O. C. Swanson, a San Francisco newspaper man and magazine writer who was a friend of Herbert Hoover's *and* Woodrow Wilson's. She was divorced from Don Bushmiller, the one-time Stanford football and track star, and when Harvey Hunt asked her to have dinner with him she smiled and said, "I don't see why not."

They went to a more or less open speakeasy in an alley, where the steaks and chops were reasonably priced and the liquor was safe. She knew the waiters by name, and they knew her tastes in food and drink. "You come here often?" he said.

"Force of habit," she said. "It was the first place I went to when I started working in Philly."

They had visitors from other tables, and the bill came to fourteen dollars. "Have you got enough?" she said. "I have some money, and there's no reason why you should buy drinks for my friends."

"I can swing it," he said.

"Well, if you're sure. The next time we'll go Dutch. I make more money than you do, and it isn't fair to have you pay for those extra drinks. I mean it. Here, why don't we start now? I'll pay half."

"All right, if you insist."

"You have to watch out for that Morton fellow. He'll sit all night and never pay for a drink. He's that kind."

They walked to her flat—in another alley—and he was overwhelmed by the presence of her books. From floor to ceiling three walls were covered with filled shelves. "They're not all mine," she said. "Some of them were my father's. I got rid of a lot when I left San Francisco, but they're beginning to pile up again. I hate to part with a single one of them, but I have no room for my pictures." In her bedroom the wall space was taken by a profusion of Japanese prints and American moderns. "All from San Francisco. The prints are good. They were my father's and he knew what he was doing. The others are mine, and it's too soon to say whether they'll stand the test of time. I'm beginning to get tired of some of them. The ones I liked the most when I bought them, I bought them for their colors, but they're going to be the first to go the next time I move. Do you care anything about pictures?"

"Not very much," he said.

"If you want to use the bathroom, there it is. Would you like a drink?

I have some gin and some rye. I'm going to have a rye and ginger ale. You?"

"Okay," he said.

While he was in the bathroom she stood behind a screen and changed into a pajama suit. "Your drink is on the brass tray. I'll be with you in a minute."

She rejoined him presently and sat with her legs folded under her on a studio couch.

"Do you mind if I ask, is that a picture of you in the bathroom?"

"The nude, you mean? Yes, that's me. As I was six years ago. Seven."

"Who painted it?"

"People always ask that. It was painted by a man that didn't like women, obviously, but I think it's pretty good."

"Why would you pose for a man that didn't like women?"

"Oh, he wasn't the only one I posed for. Wouldn't you pose if someone asked you to?"

"I'd never pose for a woman that didn't like men," he said.

"Very few women artists that don't like men. That is, women artists that would ask a man to pose in the nude."

"I never thought of that, he said.

"There's always sex in it when a woman asks a man to pose, at least I think there is. No matter what they say. But men *and* women can have a woman pose without sex entering into it."

"Do you think so?" he said.

"I know so. I used to pose for just about anybody and everybody that asked me to."

"I'll never be an artist," he said. "I couldn't keep my hand steady if I had a naked girl in the same room with me."

"Well, then, don't be an artist."

"I couldn't be anyway," he said. "I have no talent for it."

"Are you writing a novel?"

"Hell, no. I have no talent for that either. I'd never have the patience to write fiction. Are you writing one?"

"Oh, I've written two. Neither one published. One I wouldn't even show to anyone. Some day, when I have enough money, I'm going to take a year off and write one good novel. Just one. I'll publish it under an assumed name and then go back to the newspaper business. I couldn't publish it under my own name because I'd never have any peace. I could never cover another story without having all the other reporters saying I was the one that wrote that novel. But I know I can write one good novel. Just one."

"About your own life?"

"Well, mostly."

"Then wouldn't people recognize it anyway, even if you used a phony byline?"

"Some people would recognize themselves, but they'd keep quiet about it. They wouldn't brag about being in it. What I wouldn't like would be every reporter and rewrite man trying to go on the make for me because I wrote the book. That would get to be a bore, and I like this business. I expect to stay in it all my life."

"You don't intend to get married again?"

"Later on, maybe. When I'm thirty-five or forty I might marry a newspaper man and the two of us can settle down with a small paper somewhere."

"Where have I heard *that* before?" he said.

"You probably heard yourself say it."

"Not me. No more small-town papers for me," he said. "From here I go to New York, get a job on the *News*. The big money."

"And then what?"

"Oh, I don't know. By the time I'm forty I'll be ready to take over as managing editor. I'll either stay with Patterson, or Hearst will make me an offer."

"How can you be so sure of yourself?"

"I never was till I came to Philly, but I'm a city man. I wasn't here two days before I knew that. I was a different person. It was as different as day and night, working upstate and working in the city. You wouldn't understand that, coming from San Francisco, and your father a big shot."

"Oh, it isn't hard to understand," she said. "I'm not over-awed by Philly, but it's the East, and I guess I was a little nervous about that. In San Francisco everybody knew who my father was, even people he'd never met. But here the only people that knew of him were a few newspaper men and some of the big politicians. So his reputation didn't help me much here. San Francisco is a real newspaper town. Philly isn't."

"Why?"

"Well just tell me one newspaper man in Philly that has the same standing my father had. Don't waste your time. There isn't any. What have they got here that corresponds to the Bohemian Club? Certainly not the Union League, and certainly not The Rabbit or the Fish House. Or the Philadelphia Club. My father belonged to the Pacific Union, which corresponds to the Philadelphia Club, but what newspaper man could ever get in the Philadelphia Club?"

"I'm not much for clubs. I've never belonged to one and never wanted to."

"You'll change you mind about that when you start making big money."

"I doubt it."

"What's the most you ever earned?"

"What I'm getting now. Fifty."

"Then you haven't started making real money. And incidentally, you're getting forty, not fifty. They don't pay fifty for your job, and you won't get fifty till you've been on the paper five years. If then. You're wise to think ahead. New York. You could probably start at seventy-five on the *News*, but wait a while and start at a hundred. I could get a hundred on the *News*, but I'd hate the kind of assignments they'd give me. I don't want to cover those love-nest stories, but that's what I'd get on the *News*. One of the reasons why I stay here is because they let me do general assignments."

"You're trying to be your father all over again."

"Not a chance. But at least I'm covering stories they don't usually give to women. I showed them I could in San Francisco, and when they took me on here they knew I could."

"Yes, you're good," said Harvey Hunt. "You're as good as any of the men."

"I'm better than most of them. I'd had several offers from magazines. *Collier's. Cosmo.* But they offer me two or three hundred for pieces they'd pay a man five hundred or a thousand. And I told them so. When they pay me men's prices, I'll write for them, but not before."

"It's nice to be able to afford your independence."

"Yes, my father took care of that. Insurance, and some stocks and bonds. I could have got alimony, too. Don's family have money. But, I'm against alimony for women that have no children."

"Why did you break up?"

"None of your business."

"The only way to find out is to ask questions."

"You're not on a story now," she said.

"Not for the *Ledger*, but for my own curiosity. I never knew anybody like you before."

"What's so different about me?"

"Damn near everything. The way you think. Your independence."

"I think it's time for you to go home now, Hunt."

"I was thinking just the opposite."

"I know you were. That's why I'm sending you home."

He got up and sat beside her, but she would not put down her highball. "You're going to spill my drink," she said.

"Then let me put it somewhere out of the way."

"Why? I'm not going to go to bed with you."

"Why not? Because you make sixty-five a week and I make forty?"

"Partly that, I guess."

"Put the God damn drink away and give it a chance," he said.

She smiled, then placed the drink on the floor. "All right," she said. "Now show me how irresistible you can be."

"No I won't," he said. "If you don't want it, I don't want it either. You're so God damn independent, you ought to know that much."

"Well, you're not as sure of yourself as I thought you were."

"I'm sure of myself, but now I'm not so damn sure of you. You like wearing pants because it comes natural to you. Goodnight, Swanson old boy."

"Goodnight," she said. She was angry. She remained immobile until he had closed the door behind him.

He did not see her during the next three days. She was in Atlantic City on a bankers' convention, a "must" story that even she could not make readable. On the third day she returned to Philadelphia on an early afternoon train. He saw her come in the office, have a few minutes' chat with the city desk, collect her mail, go to her desk, toss her hat on the desk and run her fingers through her hair to fluff it up. She lit a cigarette and examined her mail, half of which she dropped into the wastebasket unopened. So far she had not looked in his direction. She read her letters, and apparently answered one immediately, or so he judged by the fact that she put some notepaper in her typewriter, tapped out a few lines, and copied the address before signing and sealing the letter. Now she looked around the room, and he averted his gaze just a fraction of a second before her eyes fixed on him. He could see her slowly get up and slowly make her way to his desk.

"Hello," she said.

"Oh, hello. When did you get back from the shore?"

"Just now. I'm going to cash an expense-account cheque. Do you want to have dinner?"

"I can't leave here before nine, nine-thirty."

"That's all right. I have a lot of little things to do. Will you stop for me when you can get away, or would you rather meet me at Kessler's."

"Kessler's, a little after half-past nine."

"I brought you some salt-water taffy."

"You did?"

"Of course not. I've had the most boring three days—but I won't inflict that on you. Nine-thirty, then?"

She was at the restaurant when he arrived. She was wearing a light blue bouclé dress, as simple in design as all her clothes, but made more feminine by the color and the material. "Well, sorehead, what have you been doing for excitement?" she said.

"Reading those stories of yours from the convention."

"Never mind," she said. "It's a front-office must, and the first time they ever let a woman cover it."

"How did the bankers feel about *that*?"

"One or two of them thought it was a great idea."

"Those were the ones that didn't bring their wives."

"None of them brought their wives, not while the convention was on. Some of the wives began showing up this morning."

"A good time for you to get out of town," he said.

"Aren't you going to say you missed me? Try to say something nice, can't you? After all, I invited you to dinner. I have my expense-account cheque—and this."

"What's that?"

"A twenty-five dollar bonus, from upstairs."

"You don't deserve it."

"You don't think so, but the convention chairman did. He called the paper to say so, hence the bonus."

"Then you'll be getting a lot of bankers' conventions from now on."

"Not if I can help it," she said. "Let's order. Anything but seafood in any form. Let's have something like Wiener schnitzel. Or spaghetti. Just so it doesn't come out of the ocean."

They arrived at steaks and beer, and when she finished her tenderloin she said, "As a matter of fact I had a steak yesterday, but no matter what I ate in Atlantic City it all seemed like lobster Newburg."

"I went there for a week when I was a kid. My old man was a station agent and we used to get passes. We went to quite a few places that way, but we never had enough dough to stay very long. We stayed at a hotel on South Carolina Avenue, all three of us in the same room. We didn't have as much privacy as we did at home, and I always liked my privacy, even when I was little."

"So did I," she said. "I still do. Don never understood that. My husband. He wanted to do everything together, and I *mean* everything. He wanted our house to be like a locker room, and it was."

"Is that why you broke up?"

"No. Although that may have been at the base of it. We had a good-sized house down on the Peninsula, and it wasn't a question of being in cramped quarters."

"I spent eleven years in a sort of an apartment on the second story of a railroad station, but I always had my own room."

"How could you sleep, with those trains going by at all hours?"

"I never heard them. That is—I knew when they were late, so I heard that much. But the noise didn't bother me. It's a funny thing. I like my privacy, but I don't mind noises. Where I live now is about as noisy as any place in the city—except maybe the Baldwin Locomotive Works. But noises mean people, and I like to be near people. With my privacy, but knowing that people are somewhere around. I'd go crazy on a farm. I never wanted to be a cowboy, not after I found out how much time they spend miles away from anybody."

"I'm the same way, I guess. I don't mix much with people, but I like being in the midst of them, where things are going on. Then I like to go home to my flat and be alone. But not really alone. I just want to be able to shut people out when I feel like it. I suppose everybody is more or less the same way, really. Although I'm not so sure about that. My father wasn't. He was really gregarious, always on the go, loved his clubs. He would even have had a good time at that convention. And they would have loved him. He would have come away from there with a hundred new friends."

"Did you?"

"Me? I have no friends."

"I don't have so many myself."

"Everybody has a best friend, some people have two or three best friends, but not me. I was a terrible pain to the girls in my sorority. They were to me, too. But they used to give me lectures on the subject of cooperation, and friendship and loyalty. I had nothing against loyalty, but cooperation meant practically nothing to me. And as for friendship— I was bid to four sororities, and I know exactly why. They were the best. The richest and the most social. But I was bid because everybody knew who my father was. Friend of Mr. Hoover's and Woodrow Wilson's. Pictures in the paper with Lloyd George and Clemenceau. I didn't have to be rich. The rich people cultivated my father. It was a mark of being somebody to say you were a friend of O. C. Swanson. Not only on the Coast, either. He went to New York and Washington two or three times a year and to Europe on assignments, and when he came home he'd have all sorts of offers to move back East. But he had California all to himself, and if he'd gone back East he would have lost some of his individuality. So when O. C. Swanson's daughter went to Stanford the parents and the alumni saw to it that I was rushed."

"Did you know that was why it was?"

"Of course. I'd known it all my life, practically. It wasn't only because my father was a famous reporter. Even before he won the Pulitzer prize or was given the Legion of Honor, my father attracted people by sheer force of personality. When we were still living at a small hotel we always had famous visitors, every Sunday night. Opera singers. Politicians. Writers. Stage people. When I was about eight years old I played a duet with Paderewski. He was there on a concert tour, and I had no idea who he was. Madame Schumann-Heink always had supper at our apartment, whenever she was in San Francisco. They all could have gone anywhere they liked, but they came to our apartment in the Belvedere."

"Was your mother artistic or anything like that?"

"My mother? No, not a bit. She was educated, the University of Minnesota. Her father was a dairy farmer, Swedish. But she stayed in the background. Nothing to contribute. Well—*contribute*? They used to quarrel about money, how much those parties used to cost, and all he had was his reporter's pay till the paper began to realize that Mr. Hearst had his eye on him. That was when Daddy's boss, Mr. Stewart, invited Margaret Anglin to his house for supper and Anglin said she was having supper with us. Made it a rule whenever she came to San Francisco. A *rule*. They gave my father a raise and something extra for the parties. But I'll say this for my father. He never invited Mr. and Mrs. Stewart to our parties, and he never went to the Stewarts'. When Daddy was put up for the Bohemian Club he never even asked Mr. Stewart for a letter. Got in without him. If you want to know where I got my so-called independence, it was from him. Then that wonderful day when Daddy went to see Mr. Stewart about a raise, and Mr. Stewart said he thought Daddy was entitled to more money and offered him two hundred a week. 'I thought that was about as high as you'd go,' Daddy said, and walked out without another word. That same day he signed his first big contract with *Collier's*. When Mr. Stewart heard about it he was wild. Came to see my father and accused him of all sorts of ingratitude and so forth. 'You'll see how far you get without the paper,' said Mr. Stewart. And Daddy said, 'So will you, Charlie, you tight-fisted bastard.' Mr. Stewart tried to keep Daddy out of the Pacific Union, but he didn't get very far with that. The men that put my father up were much more important than Mr. Stewart ever was and he just didn't have the nerve to go against them. And Daddy *looked* more like a Pacific Union member than Mr. Stewart. He was six-foot-one and never an ounce of fat. Spent a lot of money on clothes. You should have seen him all dressed up for some big banquet. Full dress, of course, and he had a medal that hung around his neck and the Legion of Honor badge. It was no wonder the women fell for him."

"I was going to ask you about that."

"Well, he couldn't help it. My mother should have made more of an effort, but she was really a farm girl. If she'd had her way—I can remember her trying to persuade him. 'Olaf, let's go back to Minney-*saw*-ta!' Minney-*saw*-ta. My grandfather wanted Daddy to take over the farms. My mother's father, that is. My paternal grandfather was a carpenter, nicely fixed but nowhere near as much money as my mother's family. When they had those spats over how much the Sunday night suppers were costing, my mother would threaten to leave him. She complained that she was paying for the parties, which I guess was true, but all she ever did was threaten him. And she didn't really like it when he began making more money. She didn't have that hold over him anymore."

"He liked the ladies," said Harvey.

"The *ladies* liked *him*. Even when I was a little girl I could see that, and that was behind my mother's bickering about money. He'd go on those long trips, especially when *Collier's* used to send him abroad, and when he got home you'd think she'd be glad to see him but instead of that they hardly spoke for several days. I know why, now. She was accusing him of having other women, and I suppose he didn't deny it. But she didn't make any effort to live up to what *he* was. She was pretty, and she spoke three languages. English, French, and Swedish. She played the piano and the organ. She could have been more of a help to him, and I'm sure *Collier's* would have been glad if they'd moved to New York and did a lot of entertaining. But Daddy didn't really want to live in New York, and Mama didn't even want to live in San Francisco."

"Well, if your old man was running around with other women, he was smart to keep your mother in San Francisco."

"That isn't why he wanted to stay there. I told you before, he had California all to himself."

"Sure. But he was away on trips a good deal of the time."

"You've got it all wrong. If she'd made the effort to keep up with him— but she wouldn't."

"Didn't she ever try to get a divorce?" said Harvey.

"What?"

"Why didn't she divorce him? All those women, she could have taken him for plenty, and she certainly would have got custody of you."

"Don't you know? I thought you knew."

"Knew what? She *did* divorce him?"

"She committed suicide," said Martha Swanson.

The casualness of her statement made it no less abrupt. "No, I didn't know that. How would I have known it?"

"I guess I thought everybody knew it. I've always thought everybody knew everything about my father."

"He was a big name to me, but I never knew much about his personal life," he said. "O. C. Swanson, on the cover of *Collier's*, and you always see his name with Richard Harding Davis, Frank Ward O'Malley, Irvin S. Cobb. And I've seen pictures of him. But I never knew anything about his family life. Now I think of it, I sort of had the idea he was a bachelor."

"He was no bachelor. He was a wonderful father," she said. "He came home that day, late in the afternoon, and the maid said my mother left word she didn't want to be disturbed, not even for lunch. She was going to stay in bed all day. She did that sometimes, and the maid knew why. So did my father. So did I."

"Hitting the booze?"

"Yes," said Martha Swanson. "She'd do it for two or three days at a time, pretending to have a sick headache but actually just locking herself up with a bottle. She'd been doing that for a couple of years, every few weeks. Their friends didn't know it, but Daddy did, and I did, and the maid was a Swedish woman that they got from one of my grandfather's farms. Practically a member of the family. So my father went to their room and he found her there, hanging from the big four-poster. She'd been dead six or seven hours, maybe a little longer."

"Any letters or anything like that?"

"No," said Martha Swanson. "So my father cut her down and phoned the police, and said he wouldn't be there when they got there. They ordered him to stay, but he said he'd be back around eight o'clock. They asked him where he was going but he wouldn't tell them, and hung up on them. He went out and got in his car and drove as fast as he could to Stanford. I was a junior. He wanted to get there and tell me before anyone else did."

"How far was it?"

"Oh, under thirty miles. I'd just finished supper and was listening to some records. He came in and beckoned to me. The other girls started making a fuss over him, the way they always did, but he told them they'd have to excuse him. I don't know *what* he told them, but they knew something was up and they behaved I will say very sensibly. He took me to the car and we drove away, and then he stopped the car and told me what'd happened. He said there were only the two of us now, and that whenever I got over the shock he'd let me do whatever I liked. Stay in school, or quit, or go abroad. But I wasn't shocked. My first reaction, to tell you the truth, was anger."

"Angry with him, or with your mother?" he said.

"With her. It was like publicly blaming him for all her own deficiencies. That's really what it was, too. Have you covered many suicides?"

"A few," he said.

"Isn't that what most of them are? Blaming the world, or some individual? Getting even with somebody?"

"I guess some of them are," he said.

"Most of them," she said. "And the way she did it. Taking all her clothes off and hanging herself to the bed. She knew that's how he'd find her, and she made sure Minnie wouldn't be the one to find her."

"Strange she didn't leave a note," he said.

"That was part of it. People could make up their own stories, and you can be damn sure they did. Horrible stories. And you can imagine Stewart had a field day. Don't think he'd miss a chance like that. 'The nude body of Mrs. O. C. Swanson,' up in the lead. The other papers were bad enough, but Stewart was awful. You know how they can tell you to play up a story, play down certain angles and so forth. Stewart must have stood over the rewrite man and made sure my father got all the worst of it. A lot of people stopped speaking to Stewart, but of course there were some jealous ones that relished every minute of it."

"What happened to you? Did you stay in school?"

"I never went back. I didn't even go back to get my clothes. I had another girl bring them to my house. If my mother'd lived I'd have stayed to graduate, but only because I didn't want to be at home with her. I'd had a few dates with Don before my mother committed suicide, and he came to see me during the notoriety. He graduated that year, and he was so nice and easygoing that I married him. Worse luck for both of us."

"Why?"

"He was a wild bull. Do you remember the Wild Bull of the Pampas?"

"Luis Angel Firpo," said Harvey Hunt. "The Argentine boxer."

"Yes," she said. "Don was known as the Wild Bull of the Campus, but he'd never been that way when I went out with him. Quite the opposite, in fact. Maybe because I wouldn't neck with him, not at all. Other girls would come back from dates with him and tell these awful stories, but I'd go out with him and there'd be nothing like that. It wasn't only that I wasn't a necker. It was Don himself, and he worshiped my father. He was always disappointed if my father wasn't home when he came to our house. Don was a famous athlete, but he wanted people to think he had brains, and most of all he wanted Daddy to think he wasn't just a big football hero. 'What did your father say about me?' he used to ask. He'd read Daddy's pieces in *Collier's* and bore the hell out of Daddy, trying to discuss inflation in Germany and things like the trouble between Peru and Chile. Way over his head. But Daddy treated him as though he were the Secretary of State. Nobody ever knew it when they bored Daddy. He used to say to me, 'You'll never know when some dull bastard's going to turn out to be very useful.' "

"And so you married the dull bastard."

"Well, he was better than that. For one thing, he was a beautiful specimen of manhood, whether he was in a track suit or a Tux. He was almost as striking-looking as Daddy, although in a different way, and girls made fools of themselves over him. And he knew it. He knew he had that power over women. Animal magnetism."

"But not over you."

"Yes he had. But I'd met a lot of famous people for a girl of my age, and a Stanford athlete didn't turn my head the way it did some girls. I never have been one to show what's going on inside of me. Also, I knew my father expected a great deal of me. When I asked him for permission to marry Don he said he considered Don a fine boy, good family, well off financially, popular. The only thing he wanted to be sure of was that I'd seen enough of the world to be sure I was ready to settle down to being Don's wife. What a wonderful man! He was trying to tell me that he understood me better than I understood myself, but at the same time he didn't want to frighten me off marriage. So we were married, quietly, because of my mother. And on my wedding night I wanted to run away."

"You were a virgin?"

"Of course. Not a dumb virgin. I knew what it was all about. But I'd married a man that had had dozens of affairs, if not hundreds, and he expected me to be as sophisticated as he was. Well, I just wasn't. In the first place, his uncle had lent us his yacht for our wedding trip. Well, even if it was a big yacht, I was the only female aboard and there was a crew of four or maybe five. It was like being in a hospital for an operation, with all those men knowing we were just married and staring at me. The yacht would slow down for meals, so's not to spill things, I guess, but I wanted to stop completely so I could go for a swim. I just felt that if I could put on a bathing suit and dive into the ocean I'd feel better. But Don said we'd have plenty of time for swimming when we got to Honolulu. That was one small thing, and I couldn't explain it to him without sounding ridiculous, so I went without my swim. And felt dirty all the way to the Islands. In Honolulu I insisted on staying at a hotel. Anything to get away from that boat. If there had only been one other woman aboard, a maid, they'd have had someone else to stare at. I tried to persuade Don to come back on a steamship, and he thought I was crazy. I should have pretended I got seasick, but I couldn't have got away with it. If anything I was a better sailor than Don, having sailed small boats most of my life. So we didn't exactly get off to a good start. And then before we had our first wedding anniversary I had a stupid affair with an artist and Don found out about it. That gave him all the excuse he needed, and that was the story of our marriage. *Well!* Did you ask me the story of my marriage? You got it anyway."

"And what ever happened to Don?"

"Why, he's happy as a clam. He has two five-handicaps, one at golf and one at polo. Trying to raise the one and lower the other, and he will, make sure of that. And he has a five-year-old son."

"Five seems to be his lucky number."

"Exactly. No doubt he has five girl friends, too. He married a dumb little girl from Santa Barbara, with all the money in the world, and he doesn't have to pretend any more that his brains are going to waste. I hear from him now and then."

"Do you ever see him?"

"What you really want to know—yes. After we were divorced, and I'd had one or two affairs of my own. That was what finally made me quit my job in San Francisco. I wasn't very proud of myself, listening to him tell me how much he loved me when I knew his dumb little wife was having a baby. He was telling the same thing to the other women, and really believing it."

"But *you* didn't love *him*."

"Of course not. But I never refused to see him, and as long as I stayed in San Francisco that's the way it was going to be. When my father died the only person I could bear to talk to was Don. The only living human being I wanted to be with. The night of the funeral I went away with Don. We drove to Elko, Nevada, and stayed two days. If we could have stayed in Elko, who knows? I might have been there yet. No, that's silly. But I was happier those two days with Don than I've ever been with anyone. I'm a Swede. We like a little misery with our pleasure."

"I guess I do too, and I'm Scotch-Irish," he said.

"There was a fascinating little tramp in Atlantic City. I couldn't figure out who she was with, because I never saw her with any of the bankers. They all wore badges with their names on them. She was there with one of them, I'm sure of that, but she never appeared in public with him. Whenever I saw her she was alone, riding on the Boardwalk in a wheel chair, and I saw her several times in the elevator. She must have been staying at the Marlborough, where I was."

"Why was she so fascinating?"

"Because I think she just this minute came in with that big fellow. Do you know Gaspar Pennington? Does that name mean anything to you? It isn't Gaspar, it's Gaston. Gaston Pennington."

"Yes, I've seen the name and I've written it in some connection or other," said Harvey Hunt.

"Old Philadelphia, Main Line."

"Oh—the fellow with the monocle? Standing at the bar between us and the girl?"

"Yes, you can't see her till he gets out of the way."

"I've seen him around, and wondered who he was," said Harvey.

"Gaston Pennington. One of the few loafers in Philadelphia. Most of them have jobs, but Pennington keeps busy doing nothing. He knew my father *and* my ex-husband."

"Have you ever been out with him?"

"No, he steers clear of the press. You can be sure he didn't come here because he wanted to. The girl must have brought him."

"How did you meet him?"

"I never have met him, actually. He called me up one day at the office, four or five years ago. Said he'd been to San Francisco and someone had told him to look me up. He'd been there a lot, to play polo at Burlingame, and had met my father and Don. He was leaving for Florida the next day, but he'd like to take me to lunch when he got back. That was the last I ever heard from him. That's a great custom in Philadelphia, in case you haven't run into it yourself. They invite you, but they don't say when, and they feel they've done their duty. So Pennington hasn't the least idea what I look like."

"You're right about the dame. She's a tramp," said Harvey Hunt. "Her name is Jean Latour."

"She could have been more imaginative than that. You know her?"

"Yes."

"You've had business dealings with her?"

He laughed. "Wasn't for her I wouldn't be sitting here tonight."

The room was dark enough for anyone who wanted to pretend not to see anyone else to pretend to blame it on the dim lighting. Jean Latour now did just that. She recognized Harvey Hunt, but gave no sign.

"Did you see that?" said Martha Swanson. "Either she's very nearsighted or she doesn't want to have any more dealings with you. Tell me about her. I gave you *my* life history."

"Let's watch and see what she does," he said.

Pennington, standing behind Jean Latour, leaned down to hear what she was saying. Obviously he was protesting, then he shrugged his shoulders in controlled exasperation, dropped some money on the bar, and followed the girl to the door. Kessler, the proprietor, hurried to them, concerned by their sudden decision to leave.

"Kessler doesn't often get a Gaston Pennington in his place," said Martha Swanson.

Kessler, giving up, went back to the bar and questioned the bartender, who was very busy and impatient with Kessler's agitated interrogation.

"Kessler doesn't know who to blame," said Martha Swanson. "If he knew it was you, you'd most likely get a Mickey Finn. *After* he found out what you had to do with it. On second thought, maybe he *wouldn't* give you a Mickey. He'd wonder what you knew that could upset Pennington, or the girl, and no matter what you told him, he wouldn't believe you. He'd always think you were holding out on him. *I'm* pretty curious *myself.*"

"You sure have made a study of Kessler," said Harvey Hunt.

"He's one of the biggest phonies I've ever known. He doesn't give a damn about us. It's the people we bring in that count with him. The sports writers bring the prizefighters and baseball players, the rest of us bring the politicians. It was the same in San Francisco. The newspaper people find a place they like and can afford, and pretty soon the place is popular and the prices go up, and the newspaper crowd can't go there any more."

"We're here now."

"We're not here every night, not any more," she said. "Get back to your friend with the phony French name. She looks to me like a Polish girl from the coal regions. Is that where you knew her? She's awfully young, but then most of them are, and anyway you wouldn't mind that, would you?"

"She claims to be seventeen."

"I don't think she *is* much more," said Martha Swanson. "But why are you stalling me off? Where do you fit in?"

"I never did fit in, if you know what I mean," he said.

"I'd have to be stupid *not* to know what you mean," said Martha Swanson. "*At all*? Why did she look at you that way?"

"It's a long story," said Harvey Hunt.

"Well, tell it, for heaven's sake. Kessler stays open till four."

He told his story of Jean Latour as fully as it came to him, and Martha Swanson was so quiet that he needed her interruptions—to reorder a drink, to light a cigarette—to reassure him of her attention. Her interruptions were never in the form of questions, and when he finished the story she remained silent. Her silence made him uneasy.

"Are you still awake?" he said.

"Yes, I'm awake," she said.

"I thought maybe you'd fallen asleep."

"No, I didn't fall asleep," she said.

"You sure seemed it," he said.

"Well, that was because right at the beginning I wanted to ask you a question, but I didn't like to interrupt."

"What was the question?" he said.

"The question was, why did you want to play a sort of Galahad for this girl? Why did you want to go to bat for her?"

"I honestly don't know. I've had almost a year to figure that out, and I still don't know."

"Just obeyed an impulse," she said.

"She wasn't an ordinary, banged-up whore," he said. "And she wasn't the usual run of sixteen-seventeen-year-old tarts. I've seen plenty of them, plenty. You do, in the places where I've worked. The coal towns, where the girls quit school at thirteen or fourteen and get work in the stocking factories. And places like Reading and Allentown, they get jobs in the silk mills and so forth, and they have to bring home all their pay. If they hold out a buck or two they get hell beaten out of them, and they soon find out that there're other ways of making a little money on the side. Some of them run away, some of them are sent to the Catholic Protectory. This kid didn't happen to come from the anthracite region, but the background was the same. But *she* wasn't the same. She was worse—but she was better."

"You didn't know all that when the police brought her in."

"No. But if she wanted to stay out of jail, I wanted to help *keep* her out. I don't *know* why. Maybe just because it was what she wanted."

"In other words, you fell for her," said Martha Swanson.

"That's just it. I don't think I did. But maybe I did."

"Well, you did a nice thing—"

"And I got what I deserved," said Harvey Hunt.

"She's sorry, though. She has it on her conscience. I saw her look at you."

"I'd hate to bet on that."

"But you wish it were so," said Martha Swanson. "Let's ask Kessler what he knows about her."

Kessler when questioned, became suspicious. "Why do you want to know about *her*?"

"Now, Kessler, you know better than that," said Martha. "If you have nothing to say, all right."

"Oh, I got no objections," said Kessler. He plainly could not bear to be left out of things, even to be left out by his own doing. "Martha, you can always wheedle me around your little finger. Lemme sit down a minute here. Now, you want to know who she is and all? Too much I can't tell you because there's a lot I don't know. She showed up around town a couple years ago, not in my place so much but I seen her around. First with guys from dance orchesters. Then lo and behold she stard once in a while I seen her with Gaston Pennington. Pretty big stuff for her. Then the next I heard he was paying the rent. A lotta little girls would give their eyeteeth to have Gaston Pennington pay the rent, but there's one thing with Gat. That's what they call him. Gat. A girl that he pays the rent, she gotta be there, at his beck and call. He's not an every-night guy, but they gotta be there. He don't come in here much because he don't like the newspaper reporters, so she come in here with other guys, and I said to myself I bet her days are numbered because she's two-timing Gat, and one of these nights she won't be there when he wants her. But I guess she was lucky so far. He's always going away some place, but she don't know when he'll be back. Gat's a very close-lipped guy. What I call very close-lipped."

"Why did they suddenly leave here tonight?" said Martha.

"Oh, you know. Gat's the kind of a guy, he's changeable. Very changeable. I seen him order a whole meal and send it all back because he decide he wanted something else. He'll pay for it. No trouble about paying. But very, very changeable. Very changeable. You take now tonight, maybe he decide he didn't want to eat with her. And I gotta yumor him or he could raise my rent. He owns all the way to Spruce Street."

"Does he own the building where she lives?" said Harvey Hunt.

"That I'd have to guess, because I don't know where she lives. I asked her, but she clammed up on me."

"You could follow her home," said Harvey.

"Yes, I could. And I could not only get my rent raised, but he could refuse to renew my lease. And it ain't like I could move next door or across the street. She's a nice little dish, but first I gotta think of my business. No broad is worth that much to me, not with what I got coming in here from all the shows. Not to mention I'm a married man and Miss Latour looks at all the angles. All the angles, that kid." He looked to the right, to the left, and behind him, leaned forward and lowered his voice. "I could ask where was she yesterday and the day before and I *know* where she was and who with. But I don't want her sore at me. Not her. You know, some day she's liable to turn up with somebody I don't want to tangle with. I don't mean like Gat Pennington. I mean—well, shall be nameless."

"You mean one of the big boys in the racket?" said Martha Swanson.

"Draw your own conclusions," said Kessler.

"Oh, don't be so mysterious," said Martha Swanson. "If you mean Choo-Choo Klein why don't you say so? Is that who she was with in Atlantic City?"

"Wuddia wanta know all this for, Martha? You starting a big exposé?"

"You hit it," she said. "We just discovered that the Wanamaker Bugle Corps are taking over South Philly. It's going to mean a new gang war."

Kessler looked at her without changing his frozen half smile. He tapped the table with his fingertips. "Martha, where you from originally?"

"San Francisco," she said. "Why?"

"Oh, yeah. They got a big Chinese population out there. Bigger than here."

"Yes, why?"

"Did you ever cover a story where a man got his head cut off? Did you ever *see* a man with his head cut off?"

"No."

"Well, I did. Don't kid around about gang wars, Martha. Just don't kid around."

"Or I'm liable to get hurt?" she said.

"If it was you I wouldn't give a damn," said Kessler. "I don't care what happens to you. But I care what happens to me. Just don't kid around about gang wars, and keep your nose out of where it don't belong. You're liable to say the wrong thing and it wouldn't be *you* that got hurt."

"I'm sorry, Kessler," she said. "But you're not going to get hurt over anything I say."

"As usual, you don't know a God damn thing. Even the cops know more than you newspaper reporters. I had one of the owners of a paper in here one night and he stard shooting off his mouth about Choo-Choo Klein. And all the time you know who was sitting at the next table? Choo-Choo Klein. Choo-Choo knew who *he* was, but the newspaper fellow didn't know Klein when he saw him. Would you know Choo-Choo?"

"Of course."

"How about you, Hunt? Would you reccanize him?"

"I met him the second night I was in Philly. Sure I'd know him. That's not saying he'd know me."

"Would you know his brother? Either one of you?" said Kessler.

"I didn't know he had a brother," said Martha Swanson.

"Well, he has a brother. He has a brother is a respectable business man. But the brother that's a respectable business man, *he* has Choo-Choo Klein for his brother, if you follow me." Kessler was in a conflict between the urge to shut up and the compulsion to talk. "Martha, you was down't the shore? Then did you happen to see a fellow there looked like Choo-Choo only heavier set and darker complected?"

"I didn't happen to notice. But that was Choo-Choo's brother?"

"Draw your own conclusions. I din tell you nothing. Have a drink on the house." He stood up and left them.

"I've found him very unreliable. He never knows as much as he likes you to think he knows, but in this case he produced a few facts. Very interesting, your little tramp two-timing Gaston Pennington with the gangster's brother. When I go home tonight I'm going to go through the handouts from the convention, see if I can find Choo-Choo Klein's respectable brother."

"It must be pretty well known that he has a brother."

"Yes, but I didn't know it, and neither did you. Shall we wait for the free drink or would you like to go home and listen to some records?"

They went to her apartment. "I have all of Art Hickman and the early Whiteman records. Whenever I get homesick for San Francisco I play them. Well, not all of them, that'd take all night. But they were both friends of Daddy's. I'll see if I can find the dope on Klein. Meanwhile, help yourself to a drink, and fix me a rye and soda, please?"

He prepared the drinks and she found a publicity sheet from the convention. "Uh-huh," she said. "M. A. Klein, president, Barnegat Bank and Trust Company, Hamilton Bays, New Jersey. That must be near Atlantic City, Barnegat."

"Say any more about him?"

"No, this is just a list of the men attending the convention, and where they were staying. But M. A. Klein doesn't give a hotel address."

"Why are we so interested in M. A. Klein?"

"I thought you'd be," said Martha Swanson.

"Do you know what I think? I think you're interested in Gaston Pennington."

"And why do you say that?" she said.

"A hunch."

She took a long, deep breath. "That's twice tonight you surprised me. First when you told me about your reaction on seeing that girl in the police station. And now, Gaston Pennington. If you surprise me one more time I'm going to have to change my impression of you."

"What's your impression of me?"

"That you were just another newspaper man on the make."

"Maybe that's all I am, but what's wrong with that? I don't pretend to be an O. C. Swanson. I'm a fast, accurate rewrite man, without any flowers, or I'm a damn good reporter. If I can get off rewrite I'll show this town what a good reporter I am. In fact, I'd like to go out on a story against you, Martha. I'd come back with stuff you never thought of."

"Maybe you would. I don't feel like arguing. Play 'Rose Room,' and imagine yourself in San Francisco."

"It makes me think of Joe Nesbitt at Harveys Lake."

"All right. I'll think of San Francisco, you think of Harveys Lake, whatever that is. But don't let's argue."

When the record was finished she asked to play it over again, and the second time it was finished he looked at her, implying the question, did she want it again? She shook her head. He sat beside her and took her in his arms and kissed her, and she was acquiescent. With their faces close together she looked at him. "I don't know," she said.

"What don't you know?" he said.

"Why I like you. But I do. Will it be all over the city room tomorrow?"

"No."

"I'd hate that. They've all tried, and got nowhere. A year from now you can talk, but don't for a while, will you please?"

"I won't."

"You've been pretty lonely, too. God knows *I* have. God *knows* I have."

There were three weeks, nearly four, of their well-kept secret, achieved by their meeting only in her apartment and staying apart when they were in the office. When they made love they spoke of love, but they avoided the committal declarations and plans. There was a continuing passion that carried them from day to day and that enabled them to postpone the calmer declarations and long-range plans. His hours were later than hers, and he would go to the flat and eat her dinner and stay until she had left in the morning. At the Royal the change in his routine had been noticed by a vaguely resentful Albert. "Don't see as much of you these last couple of nights," said Albert.

"Well, as long as I pay my rent," said Harvey Hunt.

"Oh, I wasn't thinking about the rent," said Albert. "Y'aren't the only one keeps their room and don't sleep in it, much."

"I know. I remember. She been in lately?"

"Yesterday. And asked about you," said Albert.

"Asked about me? She didn't leave an envelope with seventy bucks in it, did she?"

"Not with me. And there's nothing in your box that I can see, so I guess she didn't. I thought maybe you run across her somewhere."

"No."

"That's what I thought, though. Something she said made me almost positive, like as if she was expecting to see you. Maybe she was just looking for you."

"She wouldn't be looking for me, Albert. And I'm not looking for her. Only the seventy bucks she swiped, that's all I ever want from Miss Latour."

"Yesterday was the first time she was here since you checked in. Well, maybe not the first. But not more than twice or three times since you checked in. Other times she didn't want to run into you, but yesterday she particularly asked for you. Maybe she had the seventy on her and wanted to pay you back, I don't know."

"As much chance of that as a celluloid cat in hell," said Harvey. "Just tell her to leave the money in an envelope, and I'll give you ten of it."

"Ten dollars, or ten percent?"

"Dollars, Albert."

"Didn't you run across her anywhere, hey?"

"And don't want to," said Harvey. "I'll have some laundry I want done."

"You can leave it here on your way out and it'll be taken care of."

"Thanks, Albert," said Harvey Hunt.

He did not always see Albert when he went to the Royal to change his linen. On some mornings he slept past Albert's time to leave. On one such morning it was close to ten o'clock before he got to the room at the Royal, and when he let himself in, she was there.

"Kind of late," she said.

"Well, so are you. Damn near a year. Have you got seventy dollars that belongs to me?"

"Right there it is, on the dresser. Seven tens. Count them to make sure."

"Thank you. Anything else you want?"

"You don't have a cigarette on you? I smoked all mine, waiting for you to show up."

"If you want a Fatima."

"Yeah, for a change. Beggars can't be choosers. And a light, please?"

"Take the pack and the matches."

"Trying to get rid of me?"

"I want to change my clothes and go to work."

"You don't have to be bashful with me. I've seen everything you have."

"So you have. All the same, I'd just as soon you let me have some privacy."

"Don't be such an old maid," she said. "I'll go as soon as I finish my cigarette. For seventy bucks I'm entitled to that."

"All right, if you put it that way."

"Why didn't you give me a tumble at Kessler's that night?"

"It seemed to me, you got the hell out of there fast when you saw me."

"I tried to say hello to you."

"No you didn't."

"I did so, but you were sneaking a feel with that dame, I guess. Is that who you're getting it from that you're so bashful? I didn't think much of her. Big tits, that's all. Probably hangers, too. Takes off her brazeer and *blump*, down they go. Is that what you like?"

"Smoke your cigarette."

"Don't hurry me. I don't like to be hurried. I like to take it slow—and easy. Slow—and easy."

He laughed. "I was just thinking of you and your dude with the monocle. That must be a funny sight."

"That dude could buy and sell you *and* your paper. You know Kessler's? He owns all that land. He happens to be one of the richest men in Philly."

"I know all about him. And M. A. Klein, too, for that matter."

She was startled. "Who did you say?"

"You heard me, you're not handcuffed. I said M. A. Klein, the president of the Barnegat Trust Company. Whose brother—"

"Where did you get all that? From Kessler? That son of a bitch Kessler. He talks too much." She was confused by fear. "You got it from Kessler, didn't you? Listen, please tell me. I gotta know, for certain reasons I gotta know. I'll do anything you want, but only tell me, was it Kessler?"

"I won't tell you anything. You're a two-timing, triple-timing little bitch, and—"

"I know, but this is different. Harvey, I'll get in that bed and give you the biggest thrill you ever got from any woman. You want a thrill, and you like me. I know you do, the minute you saw me. You gave up your job for me. And I like you, too, even if I did steal a few dollars from you. Honey, let me show you how I can give you a thrill. Will you let me show you?"

"No."

"You're sore at me, that's it." She looked about her from place to place, then rushed to him and pulled his belt out of the loops and handed it to him. "Beat me. You want to beat me. Look, I'll take everything off and you can hit me with your belt. I'll like it if you do, Harvey."

"Stop! Cut it out!"

She sat wearily on the edge of the bed. "A fellow wanted to give me a thousand dollars if I let him, and I wouldn't. A thousand dollars. I don't know what else I can offer you, Harvey. If I give you this ring will you tell me?"

"Why do you want to know that so much? What difference does it make who told me?"

"Oh, if you only knew," she said. "Please tell me if it was Kessler."

"First you tell me why it's so important to know where I found out."

"I can't, I can't, I can't. I can't tell you anything. Don't you see I'm scared?"

"Look, you're not going to get anything out of me. And I have to go to work, so beat it. What the hell did you come here for?"

"I don't even remember that," she said. "Oh, I remember all right. I came here to pay you back the money, and then we could be friends again."

"We never were friends," he said.

"Yes, you liked me. There was something going, don't deny that."

"Well, it didn't last very long."

"No. I always louse things up. But that's all I came here for, I swear to God."

"You're a natural-born liar."

"I know," she said. Behind the conversation it was apparent that she was thinking of something else. "But this is one time I'm going to tell you the truth. This part will be the truth. Will you believe me?"

"I doubt it, but go ahead and try."

She waited, and in her manner and appearance there was so much defeat, so complete a lack of her young arrogance—the kind that had made her so defiant in the South Taqua police station—that she was half convincing even before she began to speak. "You know how I got started and all that, way back. You know all about me, or a hell of a lot. And I never claimed to be a Sodality girl. And you know I got this Pennington fellow keeping me, and I cheat on him. I admit all that, and why shouldn't I? Who do I have anything to hide from? Even Pennington isn't that much of a chump that he thinks I sit home all the time, waiting for him to get horny. We have a kind of an understanding, where he don't ask me questions because he knows I'll just fill him full of lies. Oh, he's all right, Pennington."

"Gat," said Harvey Hunt.

"That's what they call him," she said. "Then I don't know, several months ago I met a fellow and I didn't know very much about him except he had money and he lived out of town. How I happened to meet him was Pennington took me to New York and then he went to Boston and I was on the train back to Philly and I saw this fellow. He rode with me as far as Broad Street Station and I gave him my phone number. He said his name was Mr. Little. The *L* didn't go with the initials on his suitcase, but I didn't think I was ever gonna see him again, but I did. A week or so and he called me up and I went out with him in his car. We had dinner out near Paoli, out in that direction, and I liked him and we went to some apartment of a friend of his. That's the way it was for a couple months. Then one day I was home and the doorbell rang and this stranger came in and asked me if I knew him. I said I didn't. I didn't know him, and why should I? He said he was Max Klein's brother and I said I didn't know any Max Klein and to get the hell out or I'd call the cops. He laughed at that. Well, he called me a lot of names till I finally convinced him I didn't know any Max Klein, but from the description I figured out he was talking about my friend Little. This took about half an hour, I guess, and it finally dawned on me who this fellow was. 'Are you *Choo-Choo* Klein?' And he said he was. Well, *then* I knew who he was all right. I said I was pleased to meet him and he got friendlier. No pass, but flattered me a little. He said he could easily understand how his brother could go for me and all that. Then came the payoff, why he was there. The brother was legitimate, ran a bank down at the shore, and had a wife and kids and all. I was to give him up. Give him up? Outside of a few meals and maybe two or three hundred dollars for presents I didn't have anything to give up. Little was nothing in my young life. Two or three hundred bucks and a couple bottles of per-*fume*. Choo-Choo peeled off four hundred-dollar bills. 'For your trouble,' he said. The next time the brother called I was to brush him off and make it stick. Then Choo-Choo got a little nasty again, just a little but enough so I remembered who I was talking to. He said if I did see his brother again a lot of things could go wrong for me. Like I could get in a taxi some night and it'd be a long time before I got home again. He wanted that brother respectable, he wanted that bank respectable. He didn't want his brother playing around and getting talked about. On the other hand, if I was a nice kid and did what he said, I'd get a little bonus at Christmas when he handed around his other bonuses. I said I didn't want a bonus, but maybe he could fix it so I could sing in a club. I was fed up with hanging around with nothing to occupy my time. He said that could be arranged."

"You always land on both feet, don't you?" said Harvey Hunt.

"The next time Little phoned I said I was all sewed up. I couldn't give him any more time. He knew about Pennington and he said he'd top what Pennington was giving me, but I said it wasn't only the money. I made up a story that Pennington wanted to marry me, and Little said he'd match that offer too. He'd marry me. I said Pennington's both offers were better than his, and all bets were off. I hung up, but a couple days later he was on the phone again and I almost told him to go talk to his brother, but I didn't. I hung up on him that time and the next, but then I realized he was hanging around Philly getting drunk, and what good was that doing me? So I said I'd see him once more, and I did. That was when I told him about Choo-Choo coming to see me, and believe me, that scared him. He told me Choo-Choo didn't give a damn about him, but he wanted him respectable to please their mother. Choo-Choo worshiped the old lady, even if she treated him like dirt. She called Choo-Choo a gunsel and some other Jewish name, but Max was a good boy. So I said I didn't want to get my little ass in a sling because of some old lady I never even heard of. Well, he didn't want any trouble with Choo-Choo either. He went home the next day and I thought that would be the last of him, but no.

"I had guys stuck on me before, carrying the torch. But Max Klein was different. Why different? Well in some ways they're all different and in some ways they're all the same, only Max was more different than any-body. He'd sit and look at me and say did I realize what we were? According to him we were a tragedy. A tragedy? I didn't want to be any tragedy. He said we were doomed, and I didn't want to be doomed. This guy ran a little bank down at the shore and he had a brother the top guy in the mob. I didn't get it, this tragedy, this doomed. I was just a girl trying to get along, and I didn't want any of this Shakespeare. He said we were invented by Shakespeare, and I'm lucky I even heard of Shakespeare. But he must of appealed to me, because otherwise why would I take all those chances? I always said I wouldn't see him again, but he could always talk me into it. And God knows there was nothing in it for me. A fifty-dollar bill once in a while. And as far as being the great lover, this guy was on a par with—well—"

"Albert, at the Royal?"

"All right, Albert. To tell you the truth, Albert was better. At least with Albert he didn't kid around. I wouldn't have him again, but he can satisfy a woman, and that's more than you can say for most of them. Albert told you, hey?"

"Sure."

"Well, all right, if he wants to brag about it. If I said he was a liar nobody'd believe him, so I don't worry about Albert ruining my reputation."

"Go on about Klein," said Harvey Hunt.

"Nobody caught on, because I made him go on the wagon and pay attention to his bank. He had to do that or I'd get in trouble with Choo-Choo, and so would he, and if he didn't I wouldn't meet him. We never went to the same place twice, in case Choo-Choo was suspicious. We went to Trenton, Baltimore, Wilmington, Reading. A different hotel every time, and only for one night. It was costing him money, but it was costing me almost as much. Why did I want to take all these chances with a guy that was a lousy lay. He was, he was a lousy lay. And all he could talk about was the sword of democracy hanging over us. Jesus! I don't know. Did I get a kick out of taking the chances? I must of. I don't know what else. What the hell was in it for me, I'll never know. Oh, maybe I got a kick out of outsmarting Choo-Choo. I guess there was that. I guess so. I don't like to take orders from anybody, whether he's a big-shot racket guy or a wealthy millionaire, I don't like to take orders. And Choo-Choo never got wise. Every so often I'd be out with Pennington and I'd see Choo-Choo and he'd just give me a little tumble, just enough to get it across to me that I was doing great. Then like a stupid dumbbell I said I'd meet Max at that convention down at the shore. There was three or four hundred guys there and I could of been with any one of them, the way Max figured it, and that made it safe, according to him. But safe? You know about it, that broad knows about it, and who else? If Choo-Choo Klein finds out, me there with his brother and all those bankers, in one of the big Boardwalk hotels—I'm finished. I'd be afraid to take a taxi, I'd be afraid to walk on Walnut Street in broad daylight. And if you found out from Kessler, that's as good as Choo-Choo finding out, because Kessler made a play for me and I said I'd rather get in bed with his busboy." She had come to the end of her speech, and she was now in an attitude of waiting.

"It was Kessler," said Harvey Hunt.

"Yes, I guess I knew it all along," she said. "If it was anything else I could go to Pennington. He very seldom turns me down when I ask him something. But I can't ask him to get me out of this."

"Probably not," said Harvey Hunt.

"Ten o'clock in the morning and I'm afraid to go out on the street," she said. "All of a sudden I don't have any place to go."

"Do you think it's as bad as all that?"

"Yes. The minute Kessler opens his mouth, and maybe he opened it last night."

"How do you think Kessler found out?"

"What's the difference, how? Maybe it was something that broad said that was with you. Maybe he saw us in Baltimore a month ago and we didn't see him. Kessler's like an old-maid gossip. He hears plenty, and he has to be in on everything. What he don't know he makes guesses at."

"Well, what do you do next? I mean today?"

She opened her purse, turned it upside down to dump the contents in her lap. "A hundred and forty-two dollars, and some cents," she said.

"Plus seventy."

"No, you keep that. It won't do me much good. This ring. My pin. The earrings. I got about six hundred dollars in the bank. Will you do me a favor?"

"If I can," he said.

"Will you put me on the train? Go all the way with me to the seat in the coach, and stay with me till the train leaves?"

"I never went all the way with you, and I never stayed with you," he said. "All right."

"I owe you that, don't I? Well, I made you a good offer and you turned me down."

"What happens when you get to New York?"

"New York? Don't you remember me telling how I started out in New York? New York's easy, and don't forget I learned a few things since the first time I went there."

"Well, be sure and let me know how you make out."

"Let you know? Read the papers. Or *I* know. I got a better idea. You come with me."

"Sure. Great," he said.

"Listen, I'm gonna need a press agent. Don't get stuck here all your life. You're still young."

"A minute ago you were shaking."

"I know I was, but all of a sudden I can hardly wait to hit the big town again. Harvey, this is a chance for you, too. We just pull out of here and get a whole new start. Will you do it? Harvey, I know I'm right. I go by feelings, and I got a feeling. This is the exact minute for both of us."

"For you, not for me. Or maybe for me, too, but I don't have the same feeling."

"Oh, I see. You know what's gonna happen to you, don't you? You'll end up marrying that dame and living out in West Philly, and five years from now I'll come here with some big show and you'll wish you went with me today."

"It's a possibility," he said.

1963

Our Friend the Sea

On the second day out Donald Fisher finished his work, the daily task he had assigned himself, by eleven o'clock. It could hardly be called work, since it consisted largely of reading more or less confidential biographical sketches of the men and women he would be associated with in the London branch. The sketches were easy to read, having been prepared by some anonymous individual in Personnel who had a lighter touch than the Bank usually permitted itself, and the confidential nature of the write-ups gave the author some leeway. "McPherson," according to one sketch, "has made himself agreeable to our English friends with his fund of slightly risqué stories. He is in great demand as an after-dinner speaker." Donald Fisher was not sure he would like McPherson. On the other hand he looked forward to meeting Rathbun, whom he knew only through office correspondence. Rathbun, according to his sketch, had stayed in England after the war. He was Harvard '16 and had gone up to Oxford for a year, taking advantage of the opportunity offered to American officers, and had joined the Bank in 1920. Rathbun was a member of Sunningdale and played golf in the high seventies. Married. Four sons. Somewhat of an expert in *arbitrage*, which Donald Fisher already knew. Rathbun sounded like his kind of man.

"Don't try to read these all at once," the Boss had said. "Two a day should be enough, and then you won't get them all mixed up in your mind. And there *are* only ten men you'll have to know about, to start with. They're the ones you'll be seeing the most of." It was interesting to find that on his first day's reading he had formed a favorable impression of one man and an unfavorable impression of another. It would be even more interesting a year from now to find out how these first impressions held up. He wished he knew what *really* made the Bank decide to send him to London. He had never been abroad, anywhere, and as far as he knew he had no living relatives in the British Isles. Nevertheless the Bank had chosen him over two other men, and the Bank usually knew what it was doing. "We would like you to stay at a hotel for two or three weeks, and *then* send for your wife," the Boss had said. "Get acquainted with the men at the Bank, the different routines, and learn a little bit about London. The time will pass very quickly, you'll find, and we've learned that it's better all around if a man doesn't try to do too much all at once. First few weeks in a new town. And especially since neither you nor Mrs. Fisher knows London."

That was perfectly all right; although he had not informed the Bank, his wife was four months pregnant, and he *wanted* to spare her at least some of the chore of looking for an apartment, which he must remember to call a flat. Moreover, at this particular stage of her pregnancy—it was her first—Madeleine, to put it mildly, did not need him around. She was peevish and bilious, and spent a great deal of time apologizing for her physical and mental state. This would pass, she assured him, and by the time he was ready for her to come to London, she would be more like her real self; her mother said so, and all her married friends had said so. It was just that at this particular time she felt unattractive and could not bear to have him touch her, or even to be sympathetic. "*Don't* keep saying you understand," she said, the night before he sailed. "How could you possibly understand? I feel awful and I look awful. I've never had a hickey in my life before, and now look at my chin. *Two* hickeys and another one coming."

"I should have told the Bank," he had said. "They *might* have postponed my transfer."

"I don't want them to. I want you to go to London and be away from me for that long, and then we'll be glad to see each other again and I'll be out of this slough of despond. And I want the baby to be born in London."

"Why?"

"Oh, it's silly, but a girl I went to school with was born in Mexico City. She was an American, but it always seemed rather chic to be able to say you were born in some foreign country."

"And you won't miss Dr. Lane?"

"I love Dr. Lane, but truthfully I'd rather have a total stranger there at the final moment. Dr. Lane would be like having my uncle there."

"Well, I'm sure there are lots of good doctors on Harley Street."

"London is the largest city in the world, so I guess they must know how to deliver a baby. *I'm* going to be all right, Don. Stop fussing over me."

Her sourness at least had had an effect that a more pleasant leavetaking might not have achieved. She not only didn't mind his going away; she desired it. Consequently he was able to enjoy his first voyage in a big ocean liner, unharassed by twinges of conscience. He had had breakfast in his stateroom, and in a little while he would take his place at the purser's table for his first official meal. So far he had not seen anyone he had ever met before, and he now set forth on a brisk walk around the promenade deck.

On someone's advice he booked a deck chair on the starboard side, but for the present he was more interested in having a look around the ship, and after three or four turns about the prom deck, he ascended to the boat deck, port side. There he found a place between lifeboats that he liked, and he stood at the rail and watched the sea flowing past.

He was there he knew not how long before he had a thought of himself, and when the thought came it was that he was alone and at peace, that there was nothing between him and the North Pole but all that restless water. Just below him the water streamed by, and lulled him to a wakeful sleep; and if he looked out beyond the racing stream, he saw the beginning of the vastness that lay between him and the top of the world. Behind him was the superstructure of the ship, and inside the ship were two thousand men and women; but he could not see them or hear them, and for as long as he gazed out on the sea, they did not exist. No one existed. He could not remember another time when he had such a sense of being alone on the planet and feeling neither sorrow nor joy. Beyond the ship-made stream of the ocean the sea was quiet and not watery; more like a purple-black mass of sticky stuff for a Peter to walk on. And it was all there was between him and the top of the world—where there was no one either.

He felt a drowsiness that was unrelated to the pull of sleep, and he moved away from the rail and sat on a large box marked Life Preservers. He lit a cigarette and tried to get free of the desire to return to the rail and renew the experience of aloneness. It was wrong, against everything he felt and believed, to want nothing but emptiness when his life had been so full. It was wrong and dangerous now, when he had started a new life that was no longer his after it passed from his body into the body of the woman he loved, and yet was his because it had once been his. It was wrong and ungrateful to want that aloneness when he had been honored with the confidence of good men. He dropped his cigarette on the planking and rubbed it with the sole of his shoe until it was no longer recognizable as anything but a few shreds of tobacco and a tiny scrap of paper. The wind came and blew it all away.

And now he turned his head because something had happened far to the right of him that immediately and completely banished his aloneness. What had happened was that nothing had happened, but far to the right, toward the bow of the ship, a woman's white skirt had been fluttered by the breeze, and the white movement had caught his eye.

She was leaning against the rail, as he had been, but she was standing with her head back on her shoulders, accepting the breeze and the noonday sun, and he knew without confirmation that her eyes would be closed and that she was sure she was alone. She had not been there when he came up to the boat deck, and he was certain she had not passed behind him on her way to the spot where she now stood. She was wearing one of those little French hats they called a beret, a blue jacket, the white skirt, black silk stockings, and black-and-white saddle shoes. And now he saw that there was a book under her arm. She slowly raised her right hand and slowly slipped the beret back and off her head, and the wind took hold of her hair but she did not move. Her hair was blond and short, and she was young.

He watched her with an odd sense of deity, as God might watch her, and as though she were playing with the wind and the sun as her personal playmates. He had not yet seen her face, but she had grace. Then suddenly the wrath of God came down on him and on her—or so it seemed for one full second: the ship's whistle blasted forth. The girl—or woman—was startled and jumped back from the rail. Amidst the shock of the whistle blast a ship's bell had begun to strike, pairs of sounds that Donald Fisher took to be eight bells. Noon. He looked at his watch, and he saw that at the same moment the girl was looking at hers. Her game with the wind and sun was over. She bent over, smoothed back her hair and put on her beret, turned, and now she was coming toward him and inevitably would have to pass him.

He was awkward, embarrassed, and trapped, as though he had been apprehended in the act of peeping at her through a bathroom window. She was halfway toward him before she saw him, and he knew that for her it was like having been the victim of the peeper through the bathroom window. He could see her drawing her teeth back over her lower lip, and then abruptly she turned around and walked toward the bow, unwilling or unable to come any closer to him. He had violated her solitude.

Her name was Miss Constance Shelber, a simple deduction arrived at by reading the names of the passengers at Table 4. She was certainly not Mr. or Mrs. Jack Rappaport, Sir John or Lady Castlemund, Dr. or Mrs. John J. O'Keefe, Prof. or Mrs. Otto H. Von Riegenbusch. Or J. B. L. Hantlee, the medical officer. Miss Constance Shelber, of Rochester, N.Y., she had to be, and was. She came down to lunch in a different costume from the blue and white she had worn on the boat deck. She threaded her way among the tables until she reached Table 4. The men all rose, the ship's doctor introduced her to the other passengers, and she took the last vacant seat. It was then that Donald Fisher was able to guess her identity.

"Very attractive young lady," said Mrs. Harris, on his right. "Oh, I saw you perk up and look, Mr. Fisher. Well, I can tell you who she is, if you haven't guessed. Her name is Constance Shelber, and she comes from Syracuse. *Not* Syracuse. *Rochester.* Upstate New York."

"Oh, you know her?" he said.

"She sat with us last evening at dinner, before the seatings were announced. Maybe a handsome young man like yourself could draw her out. We couldn't. She told us her name, but that's all she volunteered. Mr. Harris had to ask a separate question for everything else. Where she came from, where she's going. I asked her what she was going to do abroad—not curiosity, just polite conversation. And she said one word. 'Hide.' Well, ordinarily the next question would be what was she going to hide from, but she looked at me as much as to say she dared me to ask it, probably so she could give me some impertinent answer. But I fooled her. I didn't ask her, and what's more I didn't pay any attention to her for the rest of the meal. But she's attractive. Or maybe *unusual*. Unusual would be the better word for her. She doesn't do anything to attract, so I won't call her attractive. And yet she does attract, so maybe attractive is the right word after all, but not in the usual sense." Mrs. Harris paused. "She certainly does attract *you*, Mr. Fisher. You haven't taken your eyes off her."

"I was listening," he said.

No matter how hard he tried, he could not look at anyone at his own table without then turning to look at Constance Shelber. It was a kind of trade: a look at Mr. Harris or the purser and convention, in exchange for a look at a girl who had already begun to crowd his wife and his job out of his life. And he barely knew her name.

She finished her meal and left the table, and on her way out she nodded to Mrs. Harris, and during that momentary delay of her exit she saw, merely saw, Donald Fisher. He was ready to nod at her, but her eyes traveled past him. "Miss Shelber! Miss Shell-berr," said Mrs. Harris.

The girl halted.

"Would you care to join us for coffee? In the smoke room? This is Mr. Fisher, Miss Shelber."

"Oh, thank you, but I have to write some letters," said the girl. "But thank you." She resumed her exit, not once having looked at Donald Fisher, even to acknowledge the single introduction.

"Well, I did my little bit," said Mrs. Harris. "Now you've been formally introduced."

"Thanks, but she doesn't think so. Anyway, Mrs. Harris, I'm a married man."

"Shipboard," said Mrs. Harris. "And you two are bound to get together as sure as God made little green apples."

"Well, you know what little green apples can do to you," said Donald Fisher.

"Oh—now that's a pretty wise statement for a young man your age," said Mrs. Harris. "If you're as wise as that then I didn't do any harm introducing you."

He declined Mrs. Harris's invitation to coffee in the smoke room. "I have a lot of letters to write, and I really have," he said. He also knew now where the Harrises would be and where Constance Shelber would not be—the smoke room. He went everywhere else he thought she might be that was available to him, and he had abandoned his search when he saw her stretched out on a deck chair, with a writing tablet lying on her rug. Inadvertently he had passed in front of her twice without seeing her. Now he sat on the chair next to hers and faced her.

"That wasn't my doing, that introduction," he said.

"Wasn't it? I was almost sure it was," she said.

"Well, it wasn't," he said.

"Then what are you doing here now?"

"Do you want me to go away?"

She shrugged her shoulders. "You're sitting in someone else's chair."

"Goldilocks. Me, not you," he said. "I'm sitting in someone else's chair."

"I got the point," she said.

"Let's be friends, Miss Shelber. I'm not a tea-fighter, a lounge lizard. A snake."

"Anyone can see that," she said. "You're an up-and-coming young business man. Probably a member of Skull and Bones."

"Not even the right college. I went to Hamilton, and I know you heard of it because you're from Rochester."

"Not only heard of it, I've *been* there."

"Did you like it?"

"What are you trying to do, prolong this conversation? I suppose Mrs. Harris told you I wanted to hide. Well, that's what I told her. Do you expect me to tell you anything different?"

"No. I discovered this morning that I like to be alone, too. And I guess that's hiding."

"Then you ought to understand it in someone else."

"All right, I give up. But I'm not going to give up the boat deck, Miss Shelber. I was there first."

"I was there first, I was there first. You really sound like a ten-year-old boy. All right, I'll stay on the other side, if I disturb you. And you stay on your side."

"And you sound like a disagreeable little girl. It's a shame, too, because you and I are the logical ones on this boat to be friends."

"Why?"

"Well, for the same reason that the ship's doctor had you put at his table. But that's only one of the obvious reasons. The others I don't care to talk about."And so, suiting the action to the word, he went to his side of the boat deck. Nice to've seen you, Miss Shelber."

There were some clouds now, between him and the North Pole, and although it was only a few minutes past three o'clock, the evening had begun. The daylight was there, but daytime had gone. All that vastness was getting ready for the night—if night made any difference to the vastness. And why should it, apart from the sun sucking water out of the sea, the moon doing its mysterious things to the tides? The clouds would break and the water would be returned to the sea; the moon would go away—hide?—and the sea would rest. Donald Fisher was back where he wanted to be, untroubled now by thoughts of wrong or right, of his spent seed in the womb of his wife, of the trust of good men. All the way to the North Pole, if he did not look too far to right or left, he was alone in the world, had always been alone and would always be. Nothing had ever happened to him, nothing ever would. *Cogito, ergo sum?* Well, he had begun to doubt even that.

Because he felt rather sad for the ocean, getting ready for the night, he knew that he existed and that the ocean existed. *Cogito, ergo sum.* This vastness, millions of square miles, was his friend.

Then she was there beside him, standing so close to him that her arm was pressed against his. "Is there room for me, too?" she said.

"Yes," he said.

"Do you love it as much as I do?" she said.

"I don't know. I was just thinking it's my friend."

"Oh, I never thought of it that way."

"I've never really seen it till today," he said.

The space at the rail was small, between two stacks of lifeboats and the stanchions that held the lifeboats. He put his arm around her shoulders, and he knew that she understood he was merely making room for her. They looked out at the sea for a while, and then she turned her face to his and he kissed her once on the mouth. There was only the one kiss and she turned away and looked out at the sea again.

"You ought to have a coat," she said.

"I'm all right," he said.

"If you want to go down and get a coat, I'll wait for you," she said.

"I wouldn't think of leaving you, not now."

"That's good," she said. She turned her face again to him to be kissed, and he kissed her. "Are you happy?"

"You know I am," he said.

"Mm-hmm." Her assenting murmur was gentle and old, like the echo of some grandmother, and unlike anything he had noticed about her.

"How old are you?" he said.

"Twenty-two," she said. "How old are you?"

"Twenty-seven," he said.

"Why isn't your wife with you?"

"How do you know I have a wife?"

"I don't, but you are married, aren't you?"

"Yes. Married two years. I'm going to London on a new job. Same firm, but a new job. She's coming over later. You guessed that I was married, I guess that you're not."

"No, I'm not," she said.

"You're Miss on the passenger list, but I would have guessed it anyway. I think you're getting away from some man. Is that what you meant by hiding?"

"Yes. Partly. But the man is dead," she said. "I'm not a very nice girl."

"Who said so?"

"I say so. He was married, and he killed himself."

"On account of you?"

"Yes, I'll take the blame. His wife wouldn't give him a divorce, but I'm the guilty party. So it seems, at least."

"Was he a lot older?"

"Twelve years. He was thirty-four."

"Were you in love with him?"

"At first. Very much so."

"And then what?"

"And then I wasn't in love with him, but that didn't seem to make much difference. To him, or to anybody. He wouldn't let *me* go. His wife wouldn't let *him* go. I would have had to marry him if she had, and that would have been almost as bad as this. *This*, meaning that I'll never be able to live in Rochester again. *Not* you and me. So I'm not a nice girl, Donald Fisher."

"He couldn't have been much of a fellow," he said.

"He wasn't. He really wasn't. But I wasn't any judge of that. I was nineteen years old, and going to house-parties at Hamilton and Cornell. All of a sudden I was a dangerous woman, carrying on an affair with a married man. I wish I loved him. It wouldn't have been so bad if I'd gone on loving him, especially now. But he's going to be with me the rest of my life, and I don't love him. I don't even feel very sorry for him. The only one I feel sorry for is his daughter, nine years old. She was crazy about her father, and every year, little by little, she's going to hate me more and more. That's a terrible way for a child to grow up."

"What are you going to do?"

She smiled. "You mean hide? Not really, just stay out of the way of Rochester people. My father and mother are coming over this summer and we're motoring through France, Germany, Switzerland. They're going back in August, and I'll stay on somewhere. Paris, most likely. I have friends there, quite a few, actually. Eventually I suppose I'll marry some foreigner."

"Why a foreigner?"

"Oh, because an American would like to go home, and I just couldn't go through all that hell, when his family and friends find out about my Rochester past. And they would. No matter where I went in the United

States, it'd all come out again. In Europe I don't think it would matter so much. I'll have quite a lot of money some day, and European men take that into consideration."

"Won't you miss Rochester? Your friends there?"

"Oh, sure. Not that I have so many friends there at the moment. But I like it there. I ride, and sail, and if you like music, Rochester is getting to be quite a place to be. It was my *home*."

. . . A man had chosen death to life without her, and Donald Fisher could understand that. That other man had no doubt kissed her one day for just a kiss, and you could not kiss this girl and let it go at that. You could not look at her and let it go at that. Donald Fisher reminded himself that he had fallen in love with her before even seeing her face. Was it her grace? Yes, but not that entirely. Her figure? Her figure was no better than Madeleine's . . .

"I'll be getting off at Cherbourg," she said. "You go on to Southampton."

"Yes, it seems strange to stop at France first and then come back to England."

"Not if you look at the map," she said.

"I confess I haven't looked at the map."

"I feel robbed already," she said. "They're sending me away from you before the trip is over."

"Well, we have four more days," he said.

"Have you any friends aboard?"

"Not a soul I ever saw before."

"Neither have I," she said. "The sweetest thing is the way we take so much for granted. We haven't had to say much, either. I told you about me, and I can guess about you."

"There isn't much to tell about me," he said.

"I didn't mean your background, who your wife was, where you live. I meant a man who could think of the ocean as his friend. I understand that much better than if you explained it. It's why I went looking for you."

"But you didn't know that when you went looking for me."

"Yes I did. Not that one thing, but I knew there'd be something like it. I knew you were that kind of man."

"*I* didn't," he said.

"Then maybe you never were until today. Or maybe you just don't know much about yourself."

"That's the truth. I don't know much about myself. I never thought there was very much to know."

"That's *good*," she said. "You see, I know all about *my*self. Past, present, and future. And God! what a future. A selfish man shot himself, and because of that I can see my whole life, every day of it. A nine-year-old girl growing up to hate me, hate me, hate me. A nasty Rumanian marrying me for my money. And me going off on little trips with other nasty Rumanians. And two trips to Rochester, one when my father dies and the other when my mother dies. But I'll remember you, Donald Fisher, because you're the only nice thing that's happened to me in two years. And maybe the last nice thing that ever will happen to me."

"I love you," he said.

"Stop there," she said. "Don't say any more. I know you love me, and I love you. But let's not say any more. I've been through all the rest of it. I know every word of it, and I don't want to hear the same words from you. Will you come up here every day?"

"I'm planning to. Aren't you?"

She turned and looked up at him with a smile. "I *had* planned to," she said.

"Good," he said.

"Now I am going down and write some letters," she said.

"Will you have a cocktail with me before dinner? How about seven-thirty in that Terrace Room, whatever they call it."

She kissed him lightly on the cheek, and left him.

That much had happened and been said, and how right she was to let him say no more. He was experiencing automatic love, a different thing from love at first sight. He wished he could tell his new friend, the sea, why it was different; instead he could tell himself that he had not had to wait for first sight, a look at her face. The moment his eye caught the flicker of her white skirt, even before he saw the rest of her, her welcome to the wind and the sun, her hair—a sound that was neither a bell nor a pistol shot announced to him that she had arrived and love had begun. None of the things that matter to people who have just discovered each other had mattered to him—or to her. She snubbed him, repulsed him, and then she had gone looking for him. And when she found him he was not surprised. It was easy to believe that he had been expecting her all his life, and he believed it.

He would have a cocktail with her, he would meet her after dinner, he would get a small table where they could talk while the other passengers danced. He would begin to tell her that her life was not going to be a succession of Rumanians and flights from Rochester, of an embittered nine-year-old girl's growing hatred and of the untold miseries she was foreseeing. She would not have to remember him; he would be there. Tonight he would go slowly, because the things he would begin to tell her would have to be in the same words that she had heard before. But haste was not on their side anyway; it would be a year before he could leave Madeleine. And there was the Bank. As he thought of the Bank he recalled a remark of the Boss's that gave a clue to the choice of him over the other two candidates for the London job. It was six months ago, but they must have been already deciding on the man. "Don, we like the way you make up your mind and stick to it," the Boss had said. Well, the Bank would find that his mind was made up about Constance.

Constance. The first time he had thought of her by name. It was a strange name on his tongue, and as a name it was not yet in his heart. But to her he was Donald-Fisher, the full name. Everything was new, and haste was not on their side. So much was it not on their side that he had not noticed the passing time or the darkling of the vastness. But the vastness was not the same as it had been. The sea was still his friend, but he was no longer alone. He thanked the sea for having been his friend, but he would never really need that friendship again.

He went to his stateroom and was pleased to see that the steward had laid out his evening clothes. It reminded him of the weekend at the Boss's country place, when he knew he was being looked over for the London job. This was the second time in his life that clothes had been laid out for him. Oh, there would be a lot of new things from now on. He went to the bathroom to run a tub, and found that it had already been run for him. Razor, shaving brush, shaving stick on the lavatory, all ready for him, but he could do without a second shave. He took off his clothes and got into the tub, and the water was just warm enough. He lathered himself with the English soap, and when he had rinsed off the foam he lay back in a state of relaxation that was better than sleep.

In that state he did not immediately notice that the water in the tub had become completely still, as though he were in a tub on *terra firma*. He followed this discovery with the realization that all was quiet, that what was missing was the vibrant drone of the engines. And then he knew that the ship had stopped.

He got out of the tub and rang for the steward. Now that he was out of the bathroom he could hear people in the passageway outside the stateroom. They were all talking, but he could not make out what they said as they hurried past his room. He rang again for the steward, and in a minute or two there was a knock on his door and the stewardess entered. "No cause for alarm, sir," she said.

"But the engines are stopped," he said.

"Yes sir. They're lowering a boat, sir," she said.

"Lowering a boat? What is it, some kind of a drill?"

"No, sir. I'm sorry to say, sir, a passenger seems to have jumped overboard. That's all I can tell you, sir. I wouldn't give much for his chances in the dark. I mean to say, there's no moon, is there?"

"His chances? It was a man?"

"Well, now you ask, I don't know as it is, sir. I really don't know very much about it. Just what I was told, sir. *Is* there anything else, sir?"

"No, that's all, thanks," he said.

Some poor son of a bitch, he thought, and went on dressing. He was torn between going to the Terrace Bar and going to watch the rescue operations. The Terrace Bar won out; she would need him now, with her own experience of suicide.

The Bar was completely deserted of passengers. "A bit of excitement, sir. Not every day in the week they stop this 'ere ship. May I serve you, sir?"

"A dry Martini, I think I'll have," he said.

"Dry Martini. Very good, sir. The gentleman wouldn't by any chance be Mr. Donald Fisher, sir?"

"Yes, that's me."

"Oh, well now I've been asked to deliver this note to the gentleman. One of the stewards left it here about an hour ago, sir. To be handed to Mr. Donald Fisher, sir."

"Thank you. I'll have my drink at the table," he said.

He sat down and lit a cigarette, and waited for the steward to serve his cocktail before opening her letter.

It was not a letter. It was a piece of the ship's notepaper, and all that was written on it was the bare sentence: "The sea is a friend of mine, too."

He returned the notepaper to the envelope and put it in his pocket. He took a sip of his cocktail.

"Oh, there's Mr. Fisher!" It was the voice of Mrs. Harris. "You're a very clever young man, Mr. Fisher. Why do you suppose she did it?"

"I have no idea, unless she meant what she said to you."

"Said to me? What did she say to me?" said Mrs. Harris.

"That she wanted to hide."

"Of course! Of *course!*" Mrs. Harris said more, but her words were overwhelmed by the wrathful blast of the ship's whistle.

"Means we're getting under way," said the steward. "Giving up the search."

"Well, you couldn't see anything out there anyway," said Mrs. Harris. "She came from Rochester, New York. I must try to think of who I know there."

"Oh, why bother, Mrs. Harris?" said Donald Fisher.

"Perhaps you're right," she said. "You know, you impress me, Mr. Fisher. What's the *name* of that bank you work for?"

1963

Can I Stay Here?

The famous actress went to the window and gazed down at the snow-covered Park. The morning radio had said there would be snow, and there it was, an inch of it settled on trees and ground, and making her warm apartment so comfortable and secure. She would not have to go out all day. John Blackwell's twenty-one-year-old daughter was coming for lunch, and would probably stay an hour and a half; then there would be nothing to do until Alfredo Pastorelli's cocktail party, and the weather had provided an excuse for ducking that. As for dinner at Maude Long's, any minute now there would be a telephone call from Maude. Any minute—and this was the minute.

"Mrs. Long on the phone, ma'am," said the maid.

"I'll take it in here, Irene."

"Yes ma'am," said the maid.

"Hello, Maudie. I'll bet I know what you're calling about."

"Oh, Terry, have you taken a look outside? I just don't think it's fair to ask George and Marian to go out in weather like this. I could send my car for them, but that'd mean O'Brien wouldn't get home till after midnight. And he's been so good lately."

"So you've called off the party. Don't fret about it, Maudie," said Theresa Livingston.

"You sure you don't mind? I mean, if you'd like to come to me for dinner, just the two of us. We could play canasta. Or gin."

"Maudie, wouldn't you just rather have a nice warm bath and dinner on a tray? That's what I plan to do, unless you're dying for company."

"Well, if you're sure you don't mind," said Maude Long.

"Not one single bit. This is the kind of day that makes me appreciate a nice warm apartment. Oh, the times I'd wake up on days like this and wish I could stay indoors. But would have to get up and play a matinee at the Nixon. That's in Pittsburgh, or was."

"Yes, it's nice to just putter, isn't it?" said Maude Long. "What are you going to wear?"

"Today?"

"Yes. I always like to know what you're wearing. What do *you* wear when you're just staying home doing nothing?"

"Well, today I'll be wearing my black net. That sounds dressy, but I'm having a guest for lunch. A young girl that I've never met, but her father was an old beau of mine and she's coming to see me."

"That could be amusing. Could be a bore, too."

"I can get rid of her, and don't think I won't if she turns out to be a bore."

"Trust you, Terry. Well, let's one of us call the other in a day or so, and I'm sorry about dinner."

Having committed herself to her black net, Terry Livingston reconsidered. In fairness to John Blackwell she could not give his daughter the impression that his actress girl friend had turned into a frump. Not that the black net was frumpish, but it *was* black net, and something brighter would be more considerate of John, and especially on a day like this. "I'm not going to keep this on, Irene. What have I got that's brighter?"

"Your blue silk knit, ma'am. With that you can start breaking in those blue pumps."

"I wonder what jewelry. This young lady that's coming for lunch, I've never seen her, but her father was one of my biggest admirers, back in the Spanish-American War days."

"Aw, now ma'am."

"Well, it wasn't World War Two, I can tell you," said Theresa Livingston. "And not too long after World War One."

"Try her with one good piece," said Irene. "I always like your diamond pin with the squiggly gold around it."

"With the blue silk knit, do you think?"

"If you wear it over to the one side, casual."

"All right. You've solved the problem. And I suppose I ought to start breaking in those pumps."

"They've been just sitting there ever since you bought them, and the old ones are pretty scuffed," said Irene. "Will you be offering her a cocktail, the young lady?"

"Oh, she's old enough for that. Yes. Let's put out some gin and vodka. They drink a lot of vodka, the young people."

"And I'll send down for a waiter at one o'clock."

"A little earlier. Have him here to take our order at one sharp."

"I won't promise he'll be here. That's their busiest time, but I'll try. In case you may want to get rid of her, what?"

"The usual signal," said Theresa Livingston. "At two-fifteen I'll ask you if you've seen my cigarette holder. You pretend to look for it. You find it and bring it in and remind me that I have to change for my appointment."

"Where is the appointment supposed to be?"

"Three o'clock, downtown in my lawyer's office."

"Just so I make sure," said Irene. "I made a botch of it the last time Mrs. Long was here."

"Oh, well, with Mrs. Long it didn't matter. I wonder if I ought to have some little present for Miss Blackwell. Her father was very generous to me. Some little spur-of-the-moment gift that I won't miss."

"You have any number of cigarette lighters that you don't hardly ever use."

"Have I got any silver ones? A gold one would be a little too much, but a silver one might be nice."

"You've one or two silver, and a couple in snakeskin."

"The snakeskin. Fill one of the snakeskins and put a flint in it if it needs it. I'll have it in my hand. A spontaneous gesture that I'm sure she'll appreciate, just before she's leaving. 'I want you to take this. A little memento of our first meeting.' "

"I'll pick out a nice one. Snakeskin or lizard, either one."

"And you'll see about the drinks? Tomato juice, in case she asks for a Bloody Mary. Now what else? We'll have the table in the center of the room. I'll take the chair with my back to the light. At this hour of the day it doesn't make a great deal of difference, but she's young and she might as well get the glare. You listen to what I order and be sure the waiter puts my melon or whatever on that side of the table."

"Yes ma'am."

"When she gets here I'll be in my bedroom. They'll announce her from downstairs and I'll wait in my bedroom. You let her in. She'll naturally turn right, I imagine, and you tell her I'll be right with her. I don't like that picture of President Eisenhower where it is. Let's take it off the piano and put it more where she can see it. I don't suppose she'd recognize Moss Hart, so we'll leave that there. Dwight Wiman? No, she wouldn't know who he was. She might recognize Noel Coward's picture, so we won't disturb that. That's a wonderful picture of Gary Cooper and I. I must remember to have that enlarged. Gary. Dolores Del Rio. A writer, his name I forget. Fay Wray. That's Cedric Gibbons. He was married to Dolores Del Rio. Frances Goldwyn. Mrs. Samuel. Dear Bill Powell and Carole Lombard. There we all are, my first year in Hollywood. My second, actually, but I have no pictures of the first time. That was a Sunday luncheon party at Malibu. Look at Gary, isn't he darling? He wasn't a bit interested in me, actually. That was when he and the little Mexican girl, Lupe Velez, they were quite a thing at that time. You know, I haven't really looked at that picture in ages. Certainly dates me, doesn't it? And this one. Do you know who that is? I must have told you."

"I never remember his name."

"That's H. G. *Wells*. One of our *great* writers. Not one of ours in the American sense. But British. I think he was out there visiting Charlie Chaplin or somebody. They all went to Hollywood sometime or other. Never mind. I made a lot of money in pictures, and people heard of me that never would have if I'd confined myself to the theater. Well, this isn't getting into my blue knit."

"You have over a half an hour," said the maid.

They went to the bedroom. Irene laid out the blue dress, and produced three cigarette lighters. "You don't want to give her the one with the watch in it," said Irene. "I took notice, the watch is from Cartier's."

"No, I'll take this little thing. I think it must be lizard. Quite gay, don't you think? And doesn't go at all badly with my dress. I haven't the faintest idea who gave me this one."

"Just so it wasn't the young lady's father."

"Oh, no. Not John Blackwell. Downstairs, in the safe, that's where I keep his presents. Or at least I've had most of them reset, but he never gave me any cigarette lighters. He's president of the United States Casuality and Indemnity Company, and his father was, before him. One of those firms that you don't hear much about, but I wish I had their money. Baltimore. Did you ever hear of a horse called One No Trump? A *famous* horse. I'm not sure he didn't win the Kentucky Derby. This girl's father owned him. I'll tell you another little secret to add to your collection. For when you write your memoirs. Mr. Blackwell, John, always wanted to name a horse after me, but of course he was married and I was too, at the time, and we were both being *very* discreet. I just wonder how much this girl today knows about me. Anyway, John knew he couldn't actually call a horse by my name, but he had a very promising filly that he thought would win the Kentucky Derby. Only one filly ever won the Derby, you know. A horse with the unfortunate name of Regret. So John wanted to name this filly after me, but instead of giving it my name, he gave it my initials. He called it Till Later. T.L. That was our secret. *One* of them, I might add. Oh, dear, I think of all the little lies we told to protect other people. Including this girl that's coming today. *There.* How do I look?"

"Let me just smooth the skirt down over the hips," said Irene.

"It has a tendency to crawl up. I wonder if I ought to put on another slip?"

"You'll be sitting down most of the time. It's not very noticeable. Here's your pin," said Irene.

"Right about here, do you think?"

"Yes. Maybe about an inch lower."

"Here?" said Theresa Livingston.

"Just right."

"There. Now we're ready for Miss Evelyn Blackwell."

"She ought to be here in another five minutes."

"I hope she's prompt."

"She will be, if she knows what's good for her," said Irene.

"Well, if she's anything like her father. He had the best manners of any man I ever knew." Theresa Livingston lit a cigarette, had a couple of looks at herself in the full-length triplicate mirrors. She was alone now; Irene was in the kitchen. Being alone was not bad. Ever since she had rated her own dressing-room—and that was a good many years—Theresa had always insisted upon being alone for the last five minutes before going on for a performance. It gave her time to compose herself, to gather her strength, to be sick if she had to be, to slosh her mouth out with a sip of champagne which she did not swallow, to get ready for the stage manager's summons, to go out there and kill the sons of bitches with her charm and beauty and talent. Perceptive of Irene to have realized that this was just such a time, if only for an audience of one young girl. Too perceptive. All that prattle had deceived Theresa herself without for one minute deceiving Irene.

She wanted to remain standing so as not to give the blue silk knit a chance to crawl up, but after ten minutes she was weary. The buzzer sounded, and Theresa heard Irene going to the hall door. It was the waiter with the menus. Loyally Irene was annoyed by the young girl's lateness. "Why don't you just order for the both of you?" said Irene. "Or do you want me to?"

"I'm not terribly hungry," said Theresa. "You order, Irene."

"Yes. Well, the eggs Florentine. Start with the melon. The eggs Florentine. You won't want a salad, so we won't give *her* one. And finish up with the lemon sherbet. Light, but enough. And you'll want your Sanka. Coffee for her. How does that sound to you?"

"Perfect. And it'll take a half an hour before it gets here. She certainly ought to be here by then."

"If she isn't, I'm not going to let her come up."

"Oh, well, traffic. She'll have *some* good reason."

"What's wrong with the telephone? She could of let us know," said Irene. "I'll give him the order and then *you're* gonna have a glass of champagne."

"All right," said Theresa.

"We'll give her till ha' past one on the dot," said Irene.

It was ten minutes short of one-thirty when the girl arrived. "She's here," said Irene. "But you'll have to judge for yourself the condition she's in."

"You mean she's tight?" said Theresa.

"She's something, I don't know what."

"What is she like? Is she attractive?"

"Well, you don't see much of the face. You know, the hair hides the most of it."

"What makes you think she's tight?"

" 'Hi,' she said. 'Hi. Is Miss Livingston at home? I'm expected. Expected.' I said yes, she was expected. Didn't they call up from downstairs? 'Oh, that's right,' she said. 'Oh, there's Ike,' she said. 'Isn't he cute?' Ike. Cute."

"Oh, dear. Well, let's get it over with," said Theresa. "Tell her I'll be right out."

"I'll tell her you're on the long distance," said Irene.

"It might be a good idea to stay with her. Keep an eye on her so she doesn't start helping herself to the vodka. Is she that type?"

"I wouldn't put it past her," said Irene. "I wouldn't put anything past this one. And remember, you're supposed to be going downtown and see your lawyer."

"Yes, we won't need the cigarette holder bit."

Theresa Livingston allowed a few minutes to pass, then made her brisk entrance, and saw immediately that Irene had not exaggerated. The girl stood up and behind her lazy grin was all manner of trouble. Theresa Livingston gave her the society dowager bit. "How do you do, my dear. Have you told Irene what you'd like to drink?"

"She didn't ask me, but I'll have a vodka martini. I might as well stick with it."

"Irene, will you, please?" said Theresa Livingston. "Nothing for me. I've ordered lunch for both of us. Save time that way, you know. The food is good here, but the service can be a little slow."

"I know."

"Oh, you've stopped here?"

"No, we always stay at the Vanderbilt, but I was with some friends in the What-You-Call-It-Room, downstairs."

"I see," said Theresa.

"I guess I was a little late, but I got here as soon as I could."

"Well, let's not talk about that," said Theresa. "Why don't you sit there and I'll sit here. I was so pleased to hear from your father. I hadn't realized he had a daughter your age. Did you come out, and all the rest of those things?"

"Oh, two years ago. The whole bit."

"And from your father's note I gather you've given up school. Are you serious about wanting to be an actress?"

Irene served the cocktail, and the girl drank some of it. "I don't know. I guess I am. I want to do something, and as soon as I mentioned the theater, Daddy said he knew you. I guess if you were a friend of Daddy's you know how he operates. If I said I wanted to be in the Peace Corps he'd fix it with President Johnson, or at least try."

"Well, I don't know about that, but your father was a very good friend of mine when we were younger. Not that I've seen him in—oh, dear, before you were born."

"Oh, I know that. It's been Mrs. Castleton ever since I can remember."

"What's been Mrs. Castleton?"

"Daddy's girl friend."

"But your father and mother are still married, aren't they?"

"Of course. Mummy's not giving up all that loot, and why should she? Could I have another one of these? I'll get it, don't you bother."

"Well, yes. You may have to finish it at the table."

"Do you want to bet?" The girl took her glass to the portable bar. "First Mummy said they'd stay married till after I came out, although why that's important even in Baltimore. But then I came out, and nothing more was heard about a divorce. If Aunt Dorothy wanted him to get a divorce he'd get it, but being Dorothy Castleton is still a little bit better socially than being Dorothy Blackwell. And they're all old."

"Yes, we are."

"I didn't mean that personally, Miss Livingston."

"I don't know how else you could mean it, considering that I'm the same age as your father and mother. I don't know about Mrs. Castleton, of course."

"Same age. All in their late fifties or early sixties, I guess. Anyway, not exactly the *jeunesse dorée*."

"No. Well, Baltimore doesn't seem to be very different from any place else, does it? And meanwhile, your father asked me to have a talk with you about the theater. Which I'm very glad to do. But *you*. *You* don't seem to have any burning, overwhelming desire to become an actress."

"I couldn't care less, frankly. It's Daddy that as soon as I mention the theater—"

"How did you happen to mention it, though?"

"How did I happen to mention it? Well, I guess I said I wanted to do *something*, but when it came down to what I could do, we exhausted all the possibilities except riding in horse shows and modeling."

"So naturally you thought of going on the stage."

"No, I didn't. That was Daddy's idea. This whole thing was his idea. I think he just wanted to name-drop that he knew you. I have no delusions about being an actress, for Christ's sake."

Irene went to the door to admit the waiter with the rolling table.

"You would have lost your bet," said the girl. "I won't have to finish my drink at the table."

"Well, then, it isn't a question of my using my influence to get you into the American Academy or anything like that," said Theresa. "I must say I'm relieved. I certainly wouldn't want to deprive a girl of a chance that really cared about the theater."

"Forget it. I'm sorry I wasted your time, but it wasn't all my fault.

Daddy's a powerhouse, and when he gets an idea he keeps after you till you give in."

"Shall we sit down? Why don't you sit there, and I'll sit here," said Theresa.

They took their places at the table, but the girl obviously had no intention of touching her melon. "Would you rather have something else?" said Theresa. "Tomato juice, or something like that? We wouldn't have to send downstairs for it."

"No thanks."

"We're having eggs Benedict," said Theresa.

"Eggs Florentine, ma'am," said Irene.

"Don't worry about me," said the girl.

"Have you had any breakfast, other than a vodka martini?" said Theresa. "Why don't you have a cup of coffee?"

"Where's the bathroom?" said the girl.

"Will you show her the bathroom, Irene?"

"Yes, ma'am."

"Just tell me where it is, don't come with me," said the girl.

"Through that door, which leads to the bedroom. And the bathroom you can find," said Theresa.

"The eggs Florentine," said the girl. "Eggs anything." She left the room quickly.

"I hope she makes it," said Irene.

"Yes," said Theresa. "I think you'd better move this table out in the hall. Leave the coffee. I'll have some myself, now, and you might make some fresh, Irene."

"You're not gonna eat *any* lunch?"

"No."

"Nine dollars, right down the drain."

"I know, but I'm not hungry, so don't force me."

Theresa had two cups of coffee and several cigarettes. "I think I ought to go in and see how she is," she said.

"You want me to?" said Irene.

"No, I will," said Theresa.

She went to the bedroom, and the girl was lying on the bed, clad in her slip, staring at the ceiling. "Do you want anything, Evelyn?"

"Yes," said the girl.

"What?"

"Can I stay here a while?"

"Child, you can stay here as long as you like," said Theresa Livingston.

1964

The Hardware Man

Lou Mauser had not always had money, and yet it would be hard to imagine him without it. He had owned the store—with, of course, some help from the bank—since he was in his middle twenties, and that was twenty years ago as of 1928. Twenty years is a pretty long time for a man to go without a notable financial failure, but Lou Mauser had done it, and when it has been that long, a man's worst enemies cannot say that it was all luck. They said it about Lou, but they said it in such a way as to make it sound disparaging to him while not making themselves appear foolish. It would have been very foolish to deny that Lou had worked hard or that he had been a clever business man. "You can't say it was all luck," said Tom Esterly, who was a competitor of Lou's. "You might just as well say he sold his soul to the devil. Not that he wouldn't have, mind you. But he didn't have to. Lou always seemed to be there with the cash at the right moment, and that's one of the great secrets of success. Be there with the cash when the right proposition comes along."

Lou had the cash, or got hold of it—which is the same thing—when Ada Bowler wanted to sell her late husband's hardware store. Lou was in his middle twenties then, and he had already been working in the store at least ten years, starting as a stock boy at five dollars a week. By the time he was eighteen he was a walking inventory of Bowler's stock; he knew where everything was, everything, and he knew how much everything was worth; wholesale, retail, special prices to certain contractors, the different mark-ups for different customers. A farmer came in to buy a harness snap, charge him a dime; but if another farmer, one who bought his barn paint at Bowler's wanted a harness snap, you let him have it for a nickel. You didn't have to tell Sam Bowler what you were doing. Sam Bowler relied on your good sense to do things like that. If a boy was buying a catcher's mitt, you threw in a nickel Rocket, and sure as hell when that boy was ready to buy an Iver Johnson bicycle he would come to Bowler's instead of sending away to a mail-order house. And Lou

Mauser at eighteen had discovered something that had never occurred to Sam Bowler: the rich people who lived on Lantenengo Street were even more appreciative when you gave them a little something for nothing—an oil can for a kid's bike, an ice pick for the kitchen—than people who had to think twice about spending a quarter. Well, maybe they weren't *more* appreciative, but they had the money to show their appreciation. Give a Lantenengo Street boy a nickel Rocket, and his father or his uncle would buy him a dollar-and-a-quarter ball. Give a rich woman an ice pick and you'd sell her fifty foot of garden hose and a sprinkler and a lawn mower. It was all a question of knowing which ones to give things to, and Lou knew so well that when he needed the cash to buy out Sam Bowler's widow, he actually had two banks to choose from instead of just having to accept one bank's terms.

Practically overnight he became the employer of men twice his age, and he knew which ones to keep and which to fire. As soon as the papers were signed that made him the owner, he went to the store and summoned Dora Minzer, the bookkeeper, and Arthur Davis, the warehouse man. He closed his office door so that no one outside could hear what he had to say, although the other employees could see through the glass partitions.

"Give me your keys, Arthur," said Lou.

"My keys? Sure," said Arthur.

"Dora, you give me your keys, too," said Lou.

"They're in my desk drawer," said Dora Minzer.

"Get them."

Dora left the office.

"I don't understand this, Lou," said Arthur.

"If you don't, you will, as soon as Dora's back."

Dora returned and laid her keys on Lou's desk. "There," she said.

"Arthur says he doesn't understand why I want your keys. You do, don't you, Dora?"

"Well—maybe I do, maybe I don't." She shrugged.

"You two are the only ones that I'm asking for their keys," said Lou.

Arthur took a quick look at Dora Minzer, who did not look at him. "Yeah, what's the meaning of it, Lou?"

"The meaning of it is, you both put on your coat and hat and get out."

"Fired?" said Arthur.

"Fired is right," said Lou.

"No notice? I been here twenty-two years. Dora was here pretty near that long."

"Uh-huh. And I been here ten. Five of those ten the two of you been robbing Sam Bowler that I know of. That I know of. I'm pretty sure you didn't only start robbing him five years ago."

"I'll sue you for slander," said Arthur.

"Go ahead," said Lou.

"Oh, shut up, Arthur," said Dora. "He knows. I told you he was too smart."

"He'd have a hard time proving anything," said Arthur.

"Yeah, but when I did you know where you'd be. You and Dora, and two purchasing agents, and two building contractors. All in it together. Maybe there's more than them, but those I could prove. The contractors, I'm licked. The purchasing agents, I want their companies' business, so all I'm doing there is get them fired. What are you gonna tell them in Sunday School next Sunday, Arthur?"

"*She* thought of it," said Arthur Davis, looking at Dora Minzer.

"That I don't doubt. It took brains to fool Sam Bowler all those years. What'd you do with your share, Dora?"

"My nephew. I educated him and started him up in business. He owns a drug store in Elmira, New York."

"Then he ought to take care of you. Where did yours go, Arthur?"

"Huh. With five kids on my salary, putting them through High, clothes and doctor bills, the wife and her doctor bills. Music lessons. A piano. Jesus Christ, I wonder Sam didn't catch on. How did *you* catch on?"

"You just answered that yourself. I used to see all those kids of yours, going to Sunday School, all dolled up."

"Well, they're all married or got jobs," said Arthur Davis. "I guess I'll find something. Who are you gonna tell about this? If I say I quit."

"What the hell do you expect me to do? You're a couple of thieves, both of you. Sam Bowler treated everybody right. There's eight other people working here that raised families and didn't steal. I don't feel any pity for you. As soon as you get caught you try to blame it all on Dora. And don't forget this, Arthur." He leaned forward. "*You were gonna steal from me.* The two of you. This morning a shipment came in. Two hundred rolls of tarpaper. An hour later, fifty rolls went out on the wagon, but show me where we got any record of that sale of fifty rolls. That was this morning, Arthur. You didn't even wait one day, you or Dora."

"That was him, did that," said Dora. "I told him to wait. Stupid."

"They're all looking at us, out on the floor," said Arthur.

"Yes, and probably guessing," said Lou. "I got no more to say to either one of you. Just get out."

They rose, and Dora went to the outer office and put on her coat and hat and walked to the street door without speaking to anyone. Arthur went to the back stairs that led to the warehouse. There he unpacked a crate of brand-new Smith & Wesson revolvers and broke open a case of ammunition. He then put a bullet through his skull, and Lou Mauser entered a new phase of his business career.

He had a rather slow first year. People thought of him as a cold-blooded young man who had driven a Sunday School superintendent to suicide.

But as the scandal was absorbed into local history, the unfavorable judgment was gradually amended until it more closely conformed with the early opinion of the business men, which was sympathetic to Lou. Dora Minzer, after all, had gone away, presumably to Elmira, New York; and though there were rumors about the purchasing agents of two independent mining companies, Lou did not publicly implicate them. The adjusted public opinion of Lou Mauser had it that he had behaved very well indeed, and that he had proven himself to be a better business man than Sam Bowler. Only a few people chose to keep alive the story of the Arthur Davis suicide, and those few probably would have found some other reason to be critical of Lou if Arthur had lived.

Lou, of course, did not blame himself, and during the first year of his ownership of the store, while he was under attack, he allowed his resentment to harden him until he became in fact the ruthless creature they said he was. He engaged in price-cutting against the other hardware stores, and one of the newer stores was driven out of business because of its inability to compete with Lou Mauser and Tom Esterly.

"All right, Mr. Esterly," said Lou. "There's one less of us. Do you want to call it quits?"

"You started it, young fellow," said Tom Esterly. "And I can last as long as you can and maybe a *little* bit longer. If you want to start making a profit again, that's up to you. But I don't intend to enter into any agreement with you, now or any other time."

"You cut your prices when I did," said Lou.

"You bet I did."

"Then you're just as much to blame as I am, for what happened to McDonald. You helped put him out of business, and you'll get your share of what's left."

"Yes, and maybe I'll get your share, too," said Tom Esterly. "The Esterlys were in business before the Civil War."

"I know that. I would have bought your store if I could have. Maybe I will yet."

"Don't bank on it, young fellow. Don't bank on it. Let's see how good your credit is when you need it. Let's see how long the jobbers and the manufacturers will carry you. I *know* how far they'll carry Esterly Brothers. We gave some of those manufacturers their first orders, thirty, forty years ago. My father was dealing with some of them when Sam Bowler was in diapers. Mauser, you have a lot to learn."

"Esterly and Mauser. That's the sign I'd like to put up some day."

"It'll be over my dead body. I'd go out of business first. Put up the shutters."

"Oh, I didn't want you as a partner. I'd just continue the name."

"Will you please get out of my store?"

Tom Esterly was a gentleman, a graduate of Gibbsville High and Gettysburg College, prominent in Masonic circles, and on the boards of the older charities. The word upstart was not in his working vocabulary and he had no epithet for Lou Mauser, but he disliked the fellow so thoroughly that he issued one of his rare executive orders to his clerks: hereafter, when Esterly Brothers were out of an article, whether it was a five-cent article or a fifty-dollar one, the clerks were not to suggest that the customer try Bowler's. For Tom Esterly this was a serious change of policy, and represented an attitude that refused to admit the existence of Mauser's competition. On the street he inclined his head when Mauser spoke to him, but he did not actually speak to Mauser.

Lou Mauser's next offense was to advertise. Sam Bowler had never advertised, and Esterly Brothers' advertising consisted solely of complimentary cards in the high school annual and the program of the yearly concert of the Lutheran church choir. These cards read, "Esterly Bros., Est. 1859, 211 N. Main St.," and that was all. No mention of the hardware business. Tom Esterly was shocked and repelled to see a full-page ad in each of the town newspapers, announcing a giant spring sale at Bowler's Hardware Store, Lou Mauser, Owner & Proprietor. It was the first hardware store ad in Gibbsville history and, worse, it was the first time Mauser had put his name on Sam Bowler's store. Tom Esterly went and had a look, and, yes, Mauser not only had put his name in the ad; he had his name painted on the store windows in lettering almost as large as Bowler's. The sale was, of course, a revival of Mauser's price-cutting tactic, even though it was advertised to last only three days. And Mauser offered legitimate bargains; some items, Tom knew, were going at cost. While the sale was on there were almost no customers in Esterly Brothers. "They're all down at Mauser's," said Jake Potts, Tom's head clerk.

"You mean Bowler's," said Tom.

"Well, yes, but I bet you he takes Sam's name off inside of another year," said Jake.

"Where is he getting the money, Jake?"

"Volume. What they call volume. He got two fellows with horse and buggy calling on the farmers."

"Salesmen?"

"Two of them. They talk Pennsylvania Dutch and they go around to the farms. Give the woman a little present the first time, and they drive their buggies right up in the field and talk to the farmers. Give the farmers a pack of chewing tobacco and maybe a tie-strap for the team. My brother-in-law down the Valley told me. They don't try to sell nothing the first visit, but the farmer remembers that chewing tobacco. Next time the farmer comes to market, if he needs anything he goes to Bowler's."

"Well, farmers are slow pay. We never catered much to farmers."

"All the same, Tom, it takes a lot of paint to cover a barn, and they're buying their paint off of Mauser. My brother-in-law told me Mauser's allowing credit all over the place. Any farmer with a cow and a mule can get credit."

"There'll be a day of reckoning, with that kind of foolishness. And it's wrong, *wrong*, to get those farmers in debt. You know how they are, some of them. They come in here to buy one thing, and before they know it they run up a bill for things they don't need."

"Yes, I know it. So does Mauser. But he's getting the volume, Tom. Small profit, big volume."

"Wait till he has to send a bill collector around to the farmers. His chewing tobacco won't do him any good then," said Tom Esterly.

"No, I guess not," said Jake Potts.

"The cash. I still don't see where he gets his cash. You say volume, but volume on credit sales won't supply him with cash."

"Well, I guess if you show the bank a lot of accounts receivable. And he has a lot of them, Tom. A lot. You get everybody owing you money, most of them are going to pay you some day. Most people around here pay their bills."

"You criticizing our policy, Jake?"

"Well, times change, Tom, and you gotta fight fire with fire."

"Would you want to work for a man like Mauser?"

"No, and I told him so," said Jake Potts.

"He wanted to hire you away from me?"

"A couple of months ago, but I said no. I been here too long, and I might as well stay till I retire. But look down there, Tom. Down there between the counters. One lady customer. All the others are at Mauser's sale."

"He tried to steal you away from me. That's going too far," said Tom Esterly. "Would you mind telling me what he offered you?"

"Thirty a week and a percentage on new business."

"Thinking you'd get our customers to follow you there. Well, I guess I have to raise you to thirty. But the way it looks now, I can't offer you a percentage on new business. It's all going in the opposite direction."

"I didn't ask for no raise, Tom."

"You get it anyway, starting this week. If you quit, I'd just about have to go out of business. I don't have anybody to take your place. And I keep putting off the decision, who'll be head clerk when you retire. Paul Schlitzer's next in line, but he's getting forgetful. I guess it'll be Norman Johnson. Younger."

"Don't count on Norm, Tom."

"Mauser been making him offers?"

"I don't know for sure, but that's my guess. When a fellow starts acting independent, he has some good reason behind it. Norm's been getting in late in the morning and when ha' past five comes he don't wait for me to tell him to pull down the shades."

"Have you said anything to him?"

"Not so far. But we better start looking for somebody else. It don't have to be a hardware man. Any bright young fellow with experience working behind a counter. I can show him the ropes, before I retire."

"All right, I'll leave that up to you," said Tom Esterly. On his next encounter with Lou Mauser he stopped him.

"Like to talk to you a minute," said Tom Esterly.

"Fine and dandy," said Mauser. "Let's move over to the curb, out of people's way."

"I don't have much to say," said Tom Esterly. "I just want to tell you you're going too far, trying to hire my people away from me."

"It's a free country, Mr. Esterly. If a man wants to better himself. And I guess Jake Potts bettered himself. Did you meet my offer?"

"Jake Potts wouldn't have worked for you, offer or no offer."

"But he's better off now than he was before. He ought to be thankful to me. Mister, I'll make an offer to anybody I want to hire, in your store or anybody else's. I don't have to ask your permission. Any more than I asked your permission to run a big sale. I had new customers in my store that I never saw before, even when Sam Bowler was the owner. I made *you* an offer, so why shouldn't I make an offer to fellows that work for you?"

"Good day, sir," said Tom Esterly.

"Good day to you," said Lou Mauser.

Tom Esterly was prepared for the loss of Norman Johnson, but when Johnson revealed a hidden talent for window decorating, he felt cheated. The window that attracted so much attention that it was written up in both newspapers was an autumnal camping scene that occupied all the space in Mauser's window. Two dummies, dressed in gunning costume, were seated at a campfire outside a tent. An incandescent lamp simulated the glow of the fire, and real pine and spruce branches and fake grass were used to provide a woodland effect. Every kind of weapon, from shotgun to automatic pistol, was on display, leaning against logs or lying on the fake grass. There were hunting knives and compasses, Marble match cases and canteens, cots and blankets, shell boxes of canvas and leather, fireless cookers, fishing tackle, carbide and kerosene lamps, an Old Towne canoe, gun cases and revolver holsters, duck calls and decoys and flasks and first-aid kits. Wherever there was space between the merchandise items, Norman Johnson had put stuffed chipmunk and quail, and peering out from the pine and spruce were the mounted heads of a cinnamon bear, a moose, an elk, a deer, and high above it all was a stuffed wildcat, permanently snarling.

All day long men would stop and stare, and after school small boys would shout and point and argue and wish. There had never been anything like it in Bowler's or Esterly Brothers' windows, and when the display was removed at Thanksgiving time there were expressions of regret. The small boys had to find some place else to go. But Norman Johnson's hunting-camp window became an annual event, a highly profitable one for Lou Mauser.

"Maybe we should never of let Norm go," said Jake Potts.

"He's right where he belongs," said Tom Esterly. "Right exactly where he belongs. That's the way those medicine shows do business. Honest value, good merchandise, that's what we were founded on and no tricks."

"We only sold two shotguns and not any rifles this season, Tom. The next thing we know we'll lose the rifle franchise."

"Well, we never did sell many rifles. This is mostly shotgun country."

"I don't know," said Jake. "We used to do a nice business in .22's. We must of sold pretty close to three hundred of the .22 pump gun, and there's a nice steady profit in the cartridges."

"I'll grant you we used to sell the .22 rifle, other years. But they're talking about a law prohibiting them in the borough limits. Ever since the Leeds boy put the Kerry boy's eye out."

"Tom, you won't face facts," said Jake. "We're losing business to this fellow, and it ain't only in the sporting goods line or any one line. It's every which way. Kitchen utensils. Household tools. Paints and varnishes. There's never the people in the store there used to be. When you's first in charge, after your Pa passed on, just about the only thing we didn't sell was something to eat. If you can eat it, we don't sell it, was our motto."

"That was never our motto. That was just a funny saying," said Tom Esterly.

"Well, yes. But we used to have funny sayings like that. My clerks used to all have their regular customers. Man'd come in and buy everything from the same clerk. Had to be waited on by the same clerk no matter what they come in to buy. Why, I can remember old Mrs. Stokes one day she come in to borrow my umbrella, and I was off that day and she wouldn't take anybody else's umbrella. That's the kind of customers we used to have. But where are those people today? They're down at Lou Mauser's. Why? Because for instance when school opened in September every boy and girl in the public and the Catholic school got a foot-rule from Lou Mauser. They maybe cost him a half a cent apiece, and say there's a thousand children in school. Five dollars."

"Jake, you're always telling me those kind of things. You make me wonder if you wouldn't rather be working for Mauser."

"I'll tell you anything if it's for your own good. You don't have your Pa or your Uncle Ed to tell you no more. It's for my own good too, I'll admit. I retire next year, and I won't get my fifty a month if you have to close down."

"Close down? You mean run out of business by Mauser?"

"Unless you do something to meet the competition. Once before you said Mauser would have trouble with the jobbers and the manufacturers. Instead of which the shoe is on the other foot now. Don't fool yourself, Tom. Those manufacturers go by the orders we send in, and some articles we're overstocked from last year."

"I'll tell you this. I'd sooner go out of business than do things his way. Don't worry. You'll get your pension. I have other sources of income besides the store."

"If you have to close the store I'll go without my pension. I won't take charity. I'll get other work."

"With Mauser."

"No, I won't work for Mauser. That's one thing I never will do. He as good as put the gun to Arthur Davis's head, and Arthur was a friend of mine, crook or no crook. I don't know what Mauser said to Arthur that day, but whatever it was, Arthur didn't see no other way out. That kind of a man I wouldn't work for. He has blood on his hands, to my way of thinking. When I meet Arthur Davis in the after life I don't want him looking at me and saying I wasn't a true friend."

"Arthur would never say that about you, Jake."

"He might. You didn't know Arthur Davis as good as I did. There was a man that was all worries. I used to walk home from work with him sometimes. First it was worr'ing because Minnie wasn't sure she was gonna marry him. Then all them children, and Minnie sick half the time, but the children had to look just so. Music lessons. A little money to get them started when they got married. They say it was Dora Minzer showed him how they could knock down off of Sam Bowler, and I believe that. But I didn't believe what they said about something going on between him and Dora. No. Them two, they both had a weakness for money and that was all there was between them. How much they stole off of Sam Bowler we'll never know, but Arthur's share was put to good use, and Sam never missed it. Neither did Ada Bowler. Arthur wouldn't of stole that money if Sam and Ada had children."

"Now you're going too far. You don't know that, and I don't believe it. Arthur did what Dora told him to. And what about the disgrace? Wouldn't Arthur's children rather be brought up poor than have their father die a thief?"

"I don't know," said Jake. "Some of it was honest money. Nobody knows how much was stolen money. The children didn't know any of it was stolen money till the end. By that time they all had a good bringing-up. All a credit to their parents and their church and the town. A nicer family you couldn't hope to see. And they were brought up honest. Decent respectable youngsters, all of them. You can't blame them if they didn't ask their father where the money was coming from. Sam Bowler didn't get suspicious, did he? The only one got suspicious was Lou Mauser. And they say he kept his mouth shut for six or seven years, so he was kind of in on it. If I ever saw one of our fellows look like he was knocking down off of you, I'd report it. But Lou Mauser never let a peep out of him till he was the owner. I sometimes wonder maybe he was hoping they'd steal so much they'd bankrupt Sam, and then he could buy the store cheaper."

"Well, now that's interesting," said Tom Esterly. "I wouldn't put it past him for a minute."

"I don't say it's true, but it'd be like him," said Jake. "No, I'd never go to work for that fellow. Even at my age I'd rather dig ditches."

"You'll never have to dig ditches as long as I'm alive, and don't say you won't take charity. You'll take your pension from Esterly Brothers regardless of whether we're still in business or not. So don't let me hear any more of that kind of talk. In fact, go on back to work. There's a customer down there."

"Wants the loan of my umbrella, most likely," said Jake. "Raining, out."

Esterly Brothers lasted longer than Jake Potts expected, and longer than Jake Potts himself. There were some bad years, easy to explain, but there were years in which the store showed a profit, and it was difficult to explain that. Lou Mauser expanded; he bought the store property adjoining his. He opened branch stores in two other towns in the county. He dropped the Bowler name completely. Esterly Brothers stayed put and as is, the middle of the store as dark as usual, so that the electric lights had to burn all day. The heavy hardware store fragrance—something between the pungency of a blacksmith's shop and the sweetness of the apothecary's—was missing from Lou Mauser's well-ventilated buildings, and he staffed his business with young go-getters. But some of the old Esterly Brothers customers returned after temporarily defecting to Mauser's, and at Esterly's they found two or three of the aging clerks whom they had last seen at Mauser's, veterans of the Bowler days. Although he kept it to himself, Tom Esterly had obviously decided to meet the go-getter's competition with an atmosphere that was twenty years behind the times. Cash customers had to wait while their money was sent to the back of the store on an overhead trolley, change made, and the change returned in the wooden cup that was screwed to the trolley wire. Tom never did put in an electric cash register, and the only special sale he held was when he offered a fifty percent reduction on his entire stock on the occasion of his going out of business. Three successive bad years, the only time it had happened since the founding of the store, were unarguable, and he put an ad in both papers to announce his decision. His announcement was simple:

50% Off
Entire Stock
Going Out of Business
Sale Commences Aug. 1, 1922
ESTERLY BROTHERS
Est. 1859
Open 8 A.M.—9 P.M. During Sale
All Sales Cash Only—All Sales Final

On the morning after the advertisements appeared, Tom Esterly went to his office and found, not to his surprise, Lou Mauser awaiting his appearance.

"Well, what can I do for *you*?" said Tom.

"I saw your ad. I didn't know it was that bad," said Lou. "I'm honestly sorry."

"I don't see why," said Tom. "It's what you've been aiming at. Why did you come here? If you want to buy anything, my clerks will wait on you."

"I'll buy your entire stock, twenty cents on the dollar."

"I think I'll do better this way, selling to the public."

"There'll be a lot left over."

"I'll give that away," said Tom Esterly.

"Twenty cents on the dollar, Mr. Esterly, and you won't have to give none of it away."

"You'd want me to throw in the good will and fixtures," said Esterly.

"Well, yes."

"I might be tempted to sell to you. The stock and the fixtures. But the good will would have to be separate."

"How much for the good will?" said Lou Mauser.

"A million dollars cash. Oh, I know it isn't worth it, Mauser, but I wouldn't sell it to you for any less. In other words, it isn't for sale to you. A week from Saturday night at nine o'clock, this store goes out of business forever. But no part of it belongs to you."

"The last couple years you been running this store like a hobby. You lost money hand over fist."

"I had it to lose, and those three years gave me more pleasure than all the rest put together. When this store closes a lot of people are going to miss it. Not because it was a store. *You* have a *store*. But we had something better. We never had to give away foot-rules to schoolchildren, or undercut our competitors. We never did any of those things, and before we *would* do them we decided to close up shop. But first we gave some of the people something to remember. Our kind of store, not yours, Mauser."

"Are you one of those that held it against me because of Arthur Davis?"

"No."

"Then what did you hold against me?"

"Sam Bowler gave you your first job, promoted you regularly, gave you raises, encouraged you. How did you repay him? By looking the other way all the time that you knew Arthur Davis and Dora Minzer were robbing him. Some say you did it because you hoped Sam would go bankrupt and you could buy the business cheap. Maybe yes, maybe no. That part isn't what I hold against you. It was you looking the other way, never telling Sam what they were doing to him. *That* was when you killed Arthur Davis, Mauser. Sam Bowler was the kind of man that if you'd told him about Arthur and Dora, he would have kept it quiet and given them both another chance. You never gave them another chance. You didn't even give them the chance to make restitution. I don't know about Dora Minzer, but Arthur Davis had a conscience, and a man that has a conscience is entitled to put it to work. Arthur Davis would have spent the rest of his life trying to pay Sam back, and he'd be alive today, still paying Ada Bowler, no doubt. Having a hard time, no doubt. But alive and with his conscience satisfied. You didn't kill Arthur by firing him that day. You killed him a long time before that by looking the other way. And I'm sure you don't understand a word I'm saying."

"No wonder you're going out of business. You should of been a preacher."

"I thought about it," said Tom Esterly. "But I didn't have the call."

1964

The Pig

Lawrence W. Candler, age fifty-five, said goodnight to his secretary, to the receptionist, to the elevator man, and to two young men who had recently come to work for the firm. He had interviewed them while they were still in law school, and they seemed to know that his reports on them had been extremely favorable. They were always expectantly respectful, always interrupted their conversations and waited for him to greet them in the elevator, in the corridors. They were at that stage of their careers where they believed that he could perform some miracle that would get them partnerships at thirty-two instead of thirty-five. They were eager, hard-working, well-educated, and young, and at the moment he could not think of their names.

He could not for the life of him think of their names, and he did not try very hard. He hoped that they were not headed for the Biltmore Bar, but even if they were he was not going to invite them to have a drink with him. And they would have sense enough to keep their distance.

"The usual, Mr. Candler?" said the barman.

"No, today I'm going to change, thanks. Give me a double Scotch and water in a highball glass, please."

The barman's impassive acceptance of the order was almost as telling as a wisecrack would have been. Usually this barman began preparing a weak Scotch on the rocks as soon as he spotted Candler in the doorway. He made this drink strong, and quickly waited on the next customer. Not a word to Candler until Candler finished his drink, paid for it, and left a fifty-cent tip. "Thank you, Mr. Candler. Goodnight, sir," said the barman.

"Goodnight," said Candler, unable to remember the barman's name.

He stopped and bought a paper on his way to his train, folded the paper and tucked it under his arm, and took a seat in one of the coaches. In a few minutes the train was under way, and the trainman said, "No bridge game, Mr. Candler?"

"No, not today."

"The others were waiting for you," said the trainman.

"I may move up there later."

The trainman moved on. Lawrence Candler had never known *his* name. The conductor, yes; he had known the conductor's name and the names of several other trainmen through the years. As a rule he was good on names. Once, years ago, he had won a bet that he could come within ten names of reciting the roster of his college class. There was no special trick to it; it was just something he could do. One of his friends made a small joke about it. The friend said it was a knack that would come in handy when he went to work for Miles, Coudray, Witherspoon, Chartress and Ulrich, which was now Miles, Coudray, Ulrich, Candler and Beckwith. Occasionally in the past he had surprised himself by rattling off the names of the first ten players in the U.S.L.T.A. rankings, which he had not intentionally memorized. And he was never given full credit for his ability to recite the names of all the Supreme Court justices since 1900. As a lawyer he was expected to know that but he was the only lawyer among his friends who could do the complete list in ten minutes. They all left out Lurton, of Tennessee, probably because he had served only about four years.

Their names were Alfred Charles Stephano and Wilton No-Middle-Name Snodgrass, the young men who had come down in the elevator with him. Stephano was a graduate of Roxbury Latin, Dartmouth, and the Harvard Law School. Snodgrass had gone to Exeter, Yale, and the Yale Law School. Both young men had done their military service in the army, and Snodgrass was married to a niece of Channing Chartress. If you relaxed a little it all came back to you. The barman's name was Bart. It was important to relax. It was important not to panic, to do things like forgetting names and ordering an unusually large drink. It was equally important to adhere to his regular habits—and with that thought he rose and went forward to the club car.

"Where the hell were *you*?" said George Adams. "Look who I have to play with. This guy just made a little slam and we only bid four. I showed the son of a bitch my aces, but he stopped at four."

This guy, Harold Liggett, said, "Hello, Lawrence. You can have my place, if you like. It's yours anyway. And let me point out to you, Mr. Adams, if Mike had returned John's heart lead we'd have been set four tricks. Which, doubled and vulnerable, would have cost us plenty. Mike had the ace of hearts by itself."

"Keep your seat," said Lawrence Candler. "Hello, Mike. John."

"I phoned you at your office this morning," said Mike Post.

"I was out all day," said Lawrence Candler. "I got your message just before five o'clock, and I thought I might be seeing you on the train."

"We can talk about it later," said Mike Post. "You can come to my house or I'll go to yours. Is Ruth meeting you?"

"No. You can take me home and we'll talk about it on the way. I gather you heard from the Fidelity?"

"Yes. It's all set. I'll tell you about it later," said Mike. "Whose deal?"

"The blue cards, it's your deal," said George Adams.

"Sure you don't want to play, Lawrence?" said Harold Liggett.

"No, I want to read the paper," said Lawrence Candler. "But thanks."

It had been a mistake to avoid the club car. Among his friends, in the familiar atmosphere, he immediately got a feeling of security that would soon vanish, but that was good to have even for a few minutes. He realized now that his memory for names had returned to him simultaneously with his decision to go forward to the club car. The decision released him, temporarily, from terror and removed the memory block. He loved these men. George Adams, loud and profane, was the gentlest man of them all, but you had to see him with his semi-paralyzed daughter to discover that. Harold Liggett, thin almost to emaciation, had been given the Silver Star as a marine lieutenant on Guadalcanal. John Reese was a Phi Beta Kappa at Brown, who was in the advertising business instead of on the archeological expeditions where he belonged. And Mike Post, Lawrence Candler's closest friend, and a man to whom only big things seemed to have happened—big popularity, big unpopularity, big financial successes and losses, a big love affair that ended in a big scandal, a big airplane accident in which thirty-eight men and women were killed and Mike emerged a big hero. These were the men whom Lawrence Candler saw most often; twice or once a day, five days a week, ten months of the year counting vacations. He would miss them—or, more realistically, they would miss him. And he knew they would miss him. This was no time for spurious abnegation, for a rejection of the proven warmth that was in these men. When George Adams heard Lawrence Candler's news he would weep; Harold Liggett would smash something; John Reese would get drunk. In a few minutes now he would know without conjecture what Mike Post would do, because Mike Post was the only man he was going to tell.

John Reese, dummy, looked out the window and at his wrist-watch. "Make it fast, gentlemen. Four minutes to finish the hand," he said.

"Okay," said Mike Post. "I can't eat your king of clubs, George. I'll get over there with the spade, those diamonds are good, but I have to give you the club trick."

"Do you want to play it out?" said Harold Liggett. "My partner may not know his king of clubs is good." The others laughed; it was small revenge for George Adams's relentless criticism.

"I make it six-forty apiece," said John Reese. "Anybody want to carry it over till Monday?"

"Unbreakable rule," said Mike Post. "All accounts must be squared on Friday."

"All right, all right," said John Reese. "On the week, you're the big winner, Mike. Then comes Lawrence. Here are the figures. Next week you have to have a new accountant. I'm going to be in Detroit Monday, Tuesday, and Wednesday."

They all stood up, and money changed hands. "Where's your car, Mike?" said Lawrence Candler.

"Across the street at the garage. Left it there for a wash and polish. I trust you don't mind walking that far," said Mike.

"I'll make it," said Lawrence Candler. The train stopped, he said good-night to the others, and he and Mike left the station platform together.

"We're all set with the Fidelity," said Mike. "Hunter called me this morning, just after I got in. They had their lawyers go through the whole thing all over again, from top to bottom. They found everything in good order."

"I should hope so," said Lawrence Candler. "We've been working on those contracts since last October."

"I got the feeling that if you fellows wanted to lure Fidelity away, you wouldn't have much trouble getting their legal business."

"Well, thanks for the tip, but we're not looking for any new business right now. We have just about all we can handle and do a halfway decent job," said Lawrence Candler. "Also—we're losing one of our senior partners."

"Oh, really? Who?"

"Me," said Lawrence Candler. "I'll tell you about it in the car."

Mike looked at him. "I knew there was something on your mind. I didn't say anything to the others, but I caught a glimpse of you sitting back in one of the day coaches. There, the boy's bringing my car."

The largest convertible in the Chrysler line jumped to a halt in front of them.

"Testing the brakes, son?" said Mike.

"Huh?" said the young man.

"It's a good thing those brakes work."

"You're always kiddin', always putting me on," said the young man.

Mike Post and Lawrence got in the car. "Gentle irony doesn't work with that type. But if I said what I think he'd put a little hole in the gas tank, or drop a bit of sand in the oil spout."

"Then why say anything?" said Lawrence.

"Because I've never learned to keep my mouth shut."

"You kept your mouth shut about seeing me in the day coach," said Lawrence.

"That was different," said Mike. "I can keep quiet when someone else is involved."

"Yes, I know you can," said Lawrence. "Let's go to your house and have a drink."

"Fine. We won't be disturbed there. Madge won't be home much before eight. She's at some cocktail party."

"Ruth's at the same party, but I'd rather talk at your house," said Lawrence.

"Start spilling whenever you feel like it," said Mike.

"Well, the hard news—hard in more ways than one—will only take one sentence," said Lawrence. "I have about six months to live. Maybe seven. Maybe eight."

"Christ. I'm sorry," said Mike. "It's foolish to ask this, but I have to ask it. *You're sure?*"

"I have cancer of the pancreas. You know Sidney Devlin."

"Sure. He operated on one of my sisters. Is he your doctor?"

"No, but he was called in, and I've known him since we were in college. He was a fraternity brother of mine, back in the days when we took those things a little more seriously than they do now. I made him tell me the truth, more as a friend than as a doctor. I told him that I had to have the truth now, because depending on what he told me, I was about to make certain financial commitments. Tying up money in a way that would be all right if I could count on five more years, but would be very awkward for Ruth and the children if I was going to be around less than that."

"Yes, I think I know what you're talking about. The thing George is so sold on."

"That's the one," said Lawrence. "I've never said yes or no to George, and he won't have any trouble raising the money without my share. He spoke to you about it, too."

"Oh, yes. But I like faster action with my money. The thing can't miss if you can afford to be patient, but it'd be at least five years and maybe more before you begin getting anything back. I understand your position perfectly. You have your income from your law business, but I suppose that stops when you die. In other words, they don't keep on giving Ruth your full share?"

"They certainly don't. And they shouldn't. We're not set up that way."

"I didn't think so. Knowing nothing about law firms, but just as a guess," said Mike. "And that's how you wormed it out of Sidney Devlin? Some doctors wouldn't be so candid."

"Well, with cancer of the pancreas, as soon as I knew that, the rest was more or less a matter of how long."

They were at Mike's house. They left the car in the driveway and went to Mike's study. "I'm going to have a drink," said Mike. "What about you?"

"No, I had a big one before I caught the train."

"I suppose you shouldn't, although I wouldn't tell you not to," said

Mike. He poured a large whiskey on the rocks and sat down. He had a couple of swallows of the drink. "What is there I can do, Lawrence? You have a very orderly mind, so you must know how I could be useful."

"Well, of course you're being very useful now," said Lawrence. "I haven't told anyone at the office, or anywhere else."

"When did you find out?"

"Today. I spent most of the afternoon with Sid. Well, actually I was only with him a little over an hour. Then I went back to my office and held myself incommunicado. It wasn't difficult. I sat at my desk and an hour passed, but when I looked at my clock it was only ten minutes. Then ten minutes later I looked again and an hour had passed. That was how I spent the afternoon."

"Are you in pain?"

"Some, but I've gotten more or less used to it. That comes later. Which leads me to one of the things I wanted to discuss with you."

"Good," said Mike.

"When shall I tell Ruth?"

"I knew that was coming," said Mike. "I knew it, and God damn it, I'm not ready for it. As far as making up your mind for you, Lawrence, I'll never be ready for it, and you don't expect me to be. What you want to do is just talk it out with me, right?"

"Yes, but with complete frankness," said Lawrence. "You see, Mike, I have a theory that when you know with the certainty that I have that you're going to die, you ought not to put it off too long."

"You mean suicide?"

"Yes, but let's don't get into suicide for the moment. I watched my father die, or rather I watched my mother watching my father die. I could have been watching myself, too. We knew he wasn't going to last long. He had Bright's disease, as they called it then, and he was in the final stages of it. But he hung on and hung on. He'd have a bad night, then a good night, and that lasted for weeks. I was just out of college, living in Waterbury and getting ready to go to law school. But as I say, my father hung on, and I began to notice what it was doing to my mother. I wasn't bright enough or possibly honest enough to notice what it was doing to me, but as the days went by and he stayed alive, my mother got tired of him. That's putting it very coldly, but I think it's an accurate statement of what was happening to her without her knowing it. Almost but not quite saying, 'Good God, if you're going to die, die.' "

"And she didn't want to see him suffer," said Mike.

"That's what she told herself, and that's what she always believed. But I don't believe that. She simply exhausted her emotional resources—or he did, by hanging on. And now I'll tell you something else. When my mother was dying, about seven or eight years ago, *she* hung on. She had heart trouble and she was condemned. There was no chance that she would ever come downstairs again. And that was when I began to understand what she'd felt about my father. Because I was secretly saying, 'Mother, if you're going to die, die.' "

"Oh, I understand that, Lawrence. Someone that's been active, and reasonably healthy, we can't bear to see them any other way. It isn't anything to be ashamed of, unless you're going to profit by the person's death."

"Most of us do profit financially by a parent's death, or by the death of a husband or wife. Ruth will profit by mine, at least to the extent that she'll have more than she has now, and be able to spend it as she pleases. However that's a matter of almost no interest to me since I had my talk with Sid Devlin. On the contrary, I care so little about money for myself that all I want is a few dimes for phone calls and newspapers."

Mike smiled. "Rather gruesome joke, but you *have* changed."

"I have. If we didn't have to use money—dimes and quarters—I wouldn't touch it again. I'm practically light-headed about it. But that leads me to another problem. You know, I'm not a normal human being any more. I'm not one of *you*. I have different standards now, different from what I started the day with. And yet I'm a creature of habit and very conventional habits at that, as you well know. I would like to go around giving away money, but for instance if I had obeyed the impulse to empty my pockets for that nasty kid that brought you your car, I would have infuriated you and I wouldn't like to do that. In my present state of mind, as a lawyer I could have myself certified, declared incompetent and have a guardian appointed. I wonder how many people who saw me on the train would believe that they were looking at a totally irresponsible man. Do you believe it?"

"I believe that you believe it, momentarily. That you're temporarily in a state of shock. But that your conventional habits will prevail. That raises a question, though. Which is, if *I* had anything to say about it, would I want you to go the one way, or the other? Back to conventional habits, or on to complete light-headedness?"

"Thanks, Mike. That is understanding."

"Well, don't forget, I've always been somewhat unconventional. Done things more or less my own way."

"Yes, and there was nothing you ever did that I hadn't at some time or other restrained myself from doing. In my heart I thoroughly approved of your affair with Maude. You rather disappointed me when you went back to Madge."

"If you had told me that then—if anyone had said anything the least bit encouraging, I never would have gone back to Madge. But now I'm glad I did. I wouldn't want to have Maude around when I get *my* bad news, the kind of bad news you got today."

"Why not?"

"Because there wouldn't be any doubt about what she was thinking. Your father never knew that your mother was wishing he'd die—and anyway that's only a theory of yours, Lawrence. You could be wrong about that. But I know that when I get my stroke, or the doctor says I have this or that, I can count on Madge just as much as you can count on Ruth."

"Count on them for what, Mike?"

"Well, for one thing, to *be* there. Maude would run from a thing like that, but Madge won't run, and neither will Ruth. You *could* tell Ruth this afternoon, if you wanted to. I don't say that's the answer to your original question. There may be reasons for not telling her right away, but I feel sure you could tell her and she'd—adjust."

"The only real reason for not telling her right away is that I'd like to give her a few more weeks of not knowing about it. It's not a secret I'll be able to keep very long. I'm going to have to resign from the firm. I'm going to start having more pain. An operation. Et cetera. Ruth has all the time in the world, but I haven't, and I want to give her some of my time, so to speak. When I die, I want you to tell her about this conversation. I want her to know that I made her a present of these few weeks."

"All right," said Mike. "I'll tell her."

"And be sure and tell her that the most important part of the present was in postponing the time when she'd start to wish I would die. I think she'll understand that, even if you don't."

"I can understand it. I just don't happen to believe it," said Mike. He freshened his drink. "What about that other thing? If you seriously contemplate that, you're not going to tell Ruth, I hope."

"I seriously contemplate it. If I decide to do it, no, I won't mention it to Ruth. I'll just make my plans, and then go ahead and do it. It'll be clean and orderly, unmistakably what it's intended to be. No shooting or anything like that. Ruth had a cousin, married to a guy I never met. They lived in Pennsylvania somewhere. But he had the right idea. You close the garage door and turn on the car engine."

"I'm not going to try to talk you out of that, any more than I'd tell you not to take a drink," said Mike. "By the way, will you change your mind and have a drink?"

"Yes, I believe I will. A weak Scotch and water. On the rocks."

"How weak?"

"Oh, not too weak," said Lawrence. "I don't have to be quite so careful any more. I gave up cigarettes a year ago, but I think I'll start smoking again. Or maybe I won't. Ruth stopped when I did, and if I started again she wouldn't be able to resist them. God, those first two or three weeks were just about the worst period in our entire married life. I'd never want to go through *that* again." He looked at his friend, who was handing him a drink and laughing.

"I'm sorry, Lawrence, but I can't help it," said Mike. "You have no idea how funny that sounds. Maybe I have a twisted sense of humor."

"You have, and thank God for it," said Lawrence.

"As you know, I was in the infantry, and a guy in the infantry develops a peculiar sense of humor. Either that, or he goes animal. Sometimes both. I didn't have much of a sense of humor before I went in the army, but I think I began to develop one soon afterward. There I was, in my late thirties, and back in prep school. Bed checks. Discipline. Being told where I could smoke and couldn't. Having to be at a certain place at a certain time. And trying to study. Just like prep school, except that I had a seat on the Stock Exchange, married twice and actually had a son who *was* in prep school, and in some respects had more freedom than I did. It just struck me so funny, the whole thing. I didn't go around laughing about it all the time, but I couldn't fail to see the irony of it. Then when I went overseas I got a field promotion to captain the second week in combat. Why? Because my captain got his head blown off and I didn't. When we went into action we really went into it. We learned all about war in two days. I honestly didn't know much more about it after two years than I did after two days, but I came to rely on my sense of humor, and I became a pretty good officer. What my sense of humor did for me was to teach me to be fatalistic, not to count on support, or replacements, or the accuracy of our artillery, or supplies, or anything. Even on being killed. A couple of times, in Italy and in Germany, things got so bad that I thought the only thing left was to get killed, and guys that got too animal or had too much of a sense of humor did get killed. The sense-of-humor guys would get careless, and the animal guys got too brave. I probably was somewhere in between. But when I got out of the army I retained this sense of humor, which was part fatalistic and part cruel. I laugh at things I never used to laugh at before the war. And when you just said you'd never want to go through a couple of weeks of giving up smoking, I had to laugh. Here you are, a guy facing death, and you say a thing like that."

"Yes, in the circumstances it was a funny thing to say," said Lawrence.

"I was probably animalized, too, if there is such a word. For a long time after the war I couldn't force myself to feel any real sadness when anyone died, even anyone close to me. Now I do, but not as much as I ought to. At first all I cared about was the competition in business, especially when it involved knocking off another guy in a deal. And women. Till I finally met my match in Maude. She was in competition with every woman in the world, and every man. And most of all she was in competition with me. It took me about four years to fully understand that I was attractive to her because I was as tough as she was, and she kind of gave me a look at myself. And I didn't think I was a bit attractive. That was really why I went back to Madge. She was the opposite of Maude, and the opposite of me. It's only since I've been back with Madge that I've been able to think of myself as as nice a guy as I was before the war. But I'll never be quite as nice a guy. I'm not as helpful to you as I'd like to be. But if there's anything you want me to do, I'll do it."

"I never heard a shot fired in anger," said Lawrence. "They yanked me out of the infantry and put me to work reading contracts. I was in the army for four years, and just before I got out, an old-timer, a warrant officer, told me I didn't even know how to salute. He was right. I still don't know how to salute. I could tell you how much it cost the government to build several big camps, but that's about all. You got something out of the army. I didn't. Not that I was terribly anxious to get the Purple Heart, but if I'd been shipped overseas I might be better able to get through the next six months. For weeks at a time I was commuting, just as I am now, and I used to be embarrassed to wear the uniform. I'd get on the train and see those kids on their way to New London, to the submarine base, carrying their duffle bags and covered with ribbons, and I'd want to give them my seat. But of course a major doesn't give his seat to a j.g. Rank has its privileges."

Mike smiled. "R.H.I.P.," he said. "I'd forgotten that old expression. But I don't know if you'd be any better off if you'd seen action. Dr. Devlin has told you what to expect, and it seems to me you're facing up to it very well. My instinct would be to get drunk and stay drunk. Your instinct is the opposite. You won't even smoke a cigarette for fear that Ruth would start smoking again. Lawrence, while I've been prattling away about the army I've been thinking about you and Ruth."

"It wasn't prattling away, Mike."

"Well, anyway, what I've been thinking—I think you have to tell Ruth, and tell her right away. Don't, in other words, make her a present of those few weeks of silence. Make her a present of those extra weeks of closeness. Later on she's not going to want to think back and remember that when you needed her most, she was going to cocktail parties and playing golf, oblivious of what was happening to you. She has a right to know now, and not be kept in the dark even for a few weeks."

"What made you change your mind? You were inclined to agree with me about giving her those weeks."

"A little, because you'd mentioned suicide. But I don't think you are going to commit suicide. I think you're going to stay alive as long as you can, and if you're going to do that, you want all the help you can get from Ruth. I'm going back again to the army. I had a young guy named Pignelli, from some town outside Chicago. Pig, they used to call him. Before we were shipped overseas he was hopeless. Always out of uniform, buttons undone, hat on crooked, dirty equipment. But once we got over-seas—maybe being in Italy had something to do with it—but whatever it was, he became the most reliable soldier I had. We were the best outfit in the whole army. We were this, we were that. He did more for morale than a letter from home. Besides which, he was the perfect combination of sense of humor and animal. I made him a sergeant . . . Well, we got into a situation where the Germans had us completely cut off by mortar fire, pinned us in a kind of a gully, with behind us a hill too steep to climb and on both sides they were giving it to us with their mortars. There wasn't a man in the whole company that didn't know what had to be done, which was get to those mortars. Well, to make a long story short, Pig came to me and said, "Who's it going to be, Captain? Me and who else?' And I said, 'You, and any two others that will go with you.' He took off some religious medal he had around his neck and said it was for his mother. 'But if I ask you to give it back to me,' he said, 'I want another medal to go with it. A nice Catholic-looking medal, the D.S.C. Don't try to give me no Silver Star.' I regret to say that I put in for a posthumous D.S.C. for him but all they'd give him was the Silver Star. He didn't get close enough to put out the mortars, but the other two with him did. What has this got to do with Ruth?"

"Yes, I know you're not just prattling away," said Lawrence.

"Simply this. That people you count on *want* to be counted on. The Pig knew perfectly well that I was going to have to ask him to volunteer, and while I was figuring out how to say it, he saved me the trouble. The analogy isn't perfect, but it's good enough."

"So I must tell Ruth today?" said Lawrence.

"Tonight," said Mike. "She'll be pleased."

"Pleased?"

"The highest compliment you could ever pay her," said Mike. "That you need her, and need her so much that you had to tell her right away. That you need her every minute."

"Since you put it that way," said Lawrence. He reached for a cigarette, then dropped it back in the box. "This fellow, the Pig Pignelli. He sounds like quite a guy. Do you think you could accidentally, casually, tell Ruth about him?"

"Not casually," said Mike. "As far as I'm concerned, he won the war."

1964

Zero

It was so cold that no one was out. At the top of the hill, sitting in his car with the motor running, Dick Pfeister could see all of Main Street to the south, and in more than an hour not a soul had ventured forth on foot. Once in a while an automobile would come along, usually an out-of-town car on its way through. Once in a while it would be a truck, likewise on its way through and carrying five to ten tons of coal. Town people were staying in. The Orpheum had not even bothered to turn on its lights, and Richard Arlen and Carole Lombard, who were probably sitting in the sun in Southern California, or anyway had been doing so a few hours earlier, could not complain if their fans chose to stay home on such a night. The trolley from Gibbsville, due at eight-twenty, was reported two hours ago as stuck halfway up the mountain. The track was clear of snow, but something had gone wrong with the lubricating system and the trolley was just sitting there and the passengers had to wait until they could be transferred to a relief.

According to the information Dick Pfeister got from the traction company office, the trolley came to a halt and then the wheels would not turn. The motorman then had to walk down the track a couple of miles to the nearest emergency telephone. He was a brave and strong man, the motorman, to risk freezing to death. The thermometer outside the traction company office registered eight degrees below zero, and what it must have been like on the mountain was anybody's guess. The motorman was going to try to walk back to his car, which was at least better than sitting down and falling asleep. Meanwhile the passengers in the trolley had light and some heat, and help was on the way. They could have been a lot worse off.

The repair car, followed by the relief, had passed by about an hour ago on their way southward. The relief, with the passengers from the stalled trolley, should be along any minute now. Ordinarily the entire trip from Gibbsville took only fifty minutes, but this was not a night on which schedules were being observed. Tomorrow's papers would carry items giving the temperature in other Pennsylvania towns, like Snowshoe and Clarks Summit, and no doubt it *was* colder in those towns than in Mountain City; but it was cold enough to kill you here, and you died just as dead at Mountain City as at Snowshoe.

Down at the end of town a beam of light appeared, and Dick Pfeister watched it until the source of the beam, the relief car, came into view. He checked his fuel gauge; the tank was a little less than half full. He switched off his motor and got out of the car and went to the street corner where the trolley would stop. He stood in the doorway of Hutchinson's furniture store for protection from the cold wind. It was strange that no one else seemed to be meeting the trolley—and just then two automobiles came from different directions and stopped at the corner, apparently having heard at the last minute that the relief trolley was on its way.

The relief stopped at the corner, and three passengers got out. The first was a middle-aged woman with her arms full of bundles; the second was a man whom Dick Pfeister recognized: John J. Flaherty, the lawyer, who rode to and from the county seat five days a week. Flaherty was being met by his son; the woman by a man whom Dick Pfeister took to be her husband. The third passenger was Eva Novak. She was carrying a black imitation-leather hatbox and a heavy suitcase. She looked around, but Dick Pfeister did not come out of the doorway until the middle-aged woman and Flaherty had been taken away in their automobiles.

"Hey," he called to her.

She saw him, but she did not speak.

He went to her and picked up her luggage. "That's *my* car, across the street," he said.

"Okay," she said. "Where we going?"

"I'll take you to your sister's."

"I didn't have anything to eat. Is it all right if we get a sandwich or something? I didn't eat anything since I left Philly, only a milk shake in Gibbsville."

"Can't you get something at your sister's?" He opened the door of the car and she got in, and he put the luggage in the back.

"I'd sooner get something at the diner. I'll pay for it. I don't want to go to my sister's and the first thing I ask her for a meal. It's eleven o'clock at night, and she won't even be up at this hour."

"I'm not sure the diner's open," said Dick Pfeister.

"He's *always* open. You can see from here. Listen, if you don't want to come in with me, that's all right, but I gotta have a plate of soup or something. The last two hours all I could think of was a Yankee pot roast at Joe's diner."

"All right," said Dick Pfeister.

"You don't have to eat with me, if that's what you object to. You don't even have to let on you know me."

"It isn't that," he said.

"Yes it is. You don't want anybody to see me with you. Well, maybe I feel the same way, but first of all I'm hungry."

"Maybe there won't be anybody there."

"Don't be too sure of that. They're liable to come in. The best thing is you take me there and I go in alone, then you come in a couple minutes later. We don't have to leave together."

"It'll look fishy, you going in there alone on a night like this."

"Listen, Dick, I didn't ask you to meet me at the trolley. That was all your idea."

"What if I got a couple of hamburgers and a container of coffee? Would that satisfy you? I can't go in the diner with you, and that's all there is to it. And you can't go in there by yourself, not on this kind of night."

"For Christ's sake then, get me a couple hamburgers and some coffee. Just so I get something or I'll faint dead away. Then you'd have to take me to the doctor's. I'm still weak. I only been walking on my two feet since Monday. You have no idea."

They drove to the diner and Dick Pfeister got the hamburgers and coffee. He put them in her lap. "We'll drive out toward your sister's."

"Did he put sugar and cream in the coffee?" she said.

"Both."

"The container's hot. That's good," she said. She took the wax paper off one of the hamburgers and commenced to eat as they headed for the edge of town. She finished the first hamburger before they reached her sister's neighborhood of company houses. "Now I can have some coffee," she said. "It is hot. Do you want some?"

"I'll take a sip," he said.

"There's a quart of it, I don't want it all. You want a bite of hamburger?"

"No thanks," he said.

"So much the better," she said. "I shouldn't eat so fast. It isn't polite, but what do I give a darn about politeness? Do you have a cigarette? We smoked all ours on the trolley. Everybody ran out of cigarettes. I only had enough to last me to Mountain City, then I was gonna get another pack, but I shared mine with a fellow sitting next to me. First we smoked all his, then we smoked all mine. He just come from burying his uncle in Gibbsville.

"What was it like on the trolley? Were you scared?"

"I wasn't. What was there to be scared of? I was worried for the motorman. He walked a couple miles to phone the trolley company, to say we were stuck. If it wasn't for him we'd be there yet. He bundled up warm. Two pairs of gloves, two mufflers around his head. But they had to give him first aid. He passed out as soon as he got back in the trolley.

He was in terrible shape, the poor fellow. He was on the trolley I came in on. They were taking him to the doctor's. They said he had frostbite and might lose a couple toes. I don't know. That's what some person said. I know you *can* lose a foot if you get a bad frostbite. It happened to a buddy of my uncle's, worked at the Madeline Colliery. He got drunk and couldn't find his way home, a night like tonight. Stanley Bolitis. You probly noticed him, with the crutch."

"Yes, I know him," said Dick Pfeister. "What about you, Eva?"

"Oh, they told us we shouldn't worry. The electricity was connected up, so the lights were on and we got some heat."

"I didn't mean that."

"Oh." She took a long drag of her cigarette. "They said I wasn't supposed to take a job that I had to stand up all the time. I'll have to look for work that I can be sitting down. I thought of a telephone operator. They train you, and you don't have to have a high school diploma. They don't pay much to start, but they're all right to work for. I don't have any money left. I only had enough to get home."

"How much more do you need?"

"Well, that's up to you. Look in my purse, there's only a little over four dollars. I'll have to pay my sister board and room."

"How much did you tell her?"

"Oh, she guessed. She didn't tell her husband, or he wouldn't let me stay there. He'd put me out. He'd say be a girl in a house, but I can't even be that for a while. Not that I want to, but I couldn't if I wanted to."

"I don't have much money either. I brought fifty dollars with me you can have, but that's the last I can lay my hands on for I don't know how long."

"Well, I never said it was all your fault. It takes two. But this way is better than if I had the baby and I had to tell who the father was. That would sure be the end of you, Dick."

"I know that, for God's sake. You don't have to keep reminding me."

"No, but you don't have to act as if you were the one that was doing all the favors. *I* went to that crummy hospital, and I was the one that took a chance on dying. You pleaded and begged me, but since then you act as if you didn't have any responsibility. As soon as I can get work I don't care if I never see you again, the same as you feel about me. I'm going to save up till I have enough to go some place else, and then believe me, Dick, I'll get out of here so fast. I'm suppose to take it easy for two months, but I start looking for work tomorrow. Or anyway as soon as this cold spell lets up. I can't walk that far in this weather."

"Where do you expect me to get more money?"

"You work in a bank, you're suppose to know."

"Are you suggesting that I steal it?"

"That wouldn't do me any good, if you got caught stealing. I have enough to tell in confession without that on my conscience. No, don't start stealing on my account. But you have to get the money somewhere, till I find work."

"What if I can't get any more? Just can't?"

"Don't say you can't when you can. You can sell your car, borrow money on your house. Ask your father and mother."

"You might as well tell me to get it from my wife."

"Well, if she'd give it to you. You're doing everything to protect her, but what's she entitled to more than I am?"

He slapped her. It was not a hard slap, from his somewhat cramped position in the car, and it barely glanced off her face, but her left cheek received some of the blow. She put her hand to her cheek. "Wud you do that for? That was a lousy thing to do."

"I'm sorry I did it," he said.

"Yeah," she said.

"But you don't have to bring my wife into it."

"Bring her into it? She's in it whether she knows it or not. You can't keep her out of it. She's in it. Maybe she doesn't know it, but she is, and sooner or later she will know it. *Because you'll tell her.* I can keep quiet, I showed you that. But you'll tell her, if she don't find out for herself."

"Not me, I won't tell her."

"Yes, you. I got to thinking a lot about you, Dick, in that crummy hospital. I went in there and I signed my name Evelyn New. Evelyn New. As soon as I did that I was alone in the world, because if I died they didn't know my name. I couldn't have any visitors, I couldn't talk to anybody. They even said I couldn't have the priest if I was gonna die. All alone, see? So what I did was think, and I sure did think about you, Dick. All right, you were paying for it, but on account of yourself, not on account of me. I'm not surprised you slapped me."

"I apologize for that," he said.

"Apologize. That's just a word. If you thought you could get away with it, you'd murder me. Maybe you don't know that yet, but you would. That's why I wasn't surprised by you slapping me. You didn't only want to slap me. You wanted to murder me."

"That's what you figured out in the hospital?"

"Yes. When I thought you were in love with me I couldn't of figured that out, but down there I knew you weren't in love with me. That's all right. I wasn't in love with you any more, either."

"That sounds as if you wanted to murder me, too," he said.

"No, not murder you. I was doing enough killing for one person. Maybe the baby would have been another Paderewski, somebody famous like that."

"Paderewski? You mean the piano player? What made you think that?"

"Well, he'd of been only half Polish, so I guess not Paderewski. I don't know. Was there anybody famous in your family?"

"No."

"Well, maybe only a basketball player. That's when I got stuck on you, when you used to play basketball. You wouldn't even look at me then. I didn't know when I was better off."

"Oh, I looked at you, but you were too young."

"You only thought I was," she said. "Thank God for that, or we'd of been in worse trouble. Then my father was still alive, and speaking of murder he would of murdered you. If I had any brothers they would of murdered you. But instead of that you want to murder me."

"Ah, the hell with all this talk about murder. Nobody's going to murder anybody. That's all your imagination, because I gave you a slap in the face. I'm sorry for that, but I'm not going to keep on apologizing all night. I have to take you home or my alcohol will evaporate and the car'll boil over."

"All right. You said you had fifty dollars," she said.

"Here it is."

"Thanks. But don't forget, Dick, I'm gonna need some more."

"I'll try to get you another fifty next month, but I don't promise."

"How will you get it to me?"

"I'll mail it to you in cash."

"All right. Four weeks from tomorrow I'll be expecting it. Fifty cash. But don't put me off. Some of it has to go for medicine."

"I'll do the best I can, and whatever you do, don't you come in the bank. I don't want anybody to see me talking to you."

"It's no pleasure talking to you, either, Dick."

He moved the car closer to her sister's house. "Can you carry those bags all right?"

"Oh, sure. Those delicious hamburgers gave me my strength back."

He kept the motor idling until he saw the door open at her sister's house, then he drove home and put his car in the garage.

One lamp was burning in the kitchen in the otherwise darkened house, but he knew that Emily was still awake. As soon as he opened the kitchen door he knew she was awake. The house was still; she was not moving around upstairs; but from her to him came a hostile greeting. He put his overcoat and hat and arctics in the hall closet, making no sound. He went to the cellar and made sure that the furnace was all right for the night. When he returned to the kitchen she was sitting at the table in her blue flannel bathrobe and smoking a cigarette.

"I tried not to make any noise," he said.

"I was awake. I heard you come in."

"It's bitter out. Must be over ten below," he said.

"It's fourteen below outside the bathroom window," she said. "You want to tell me where you went to?"

"You mean after the meeting?"

"There was no meeting. Phil Irwin phoned to say it was called off."

"Yes, I found that out when I got there. There was a notice on the door of the gym. Alumni Association meeting postponed, account of severe weather. Phil didn't show up, but some of the others did, so we went over to the Elks and had a few beers. Jack Showers, Ed McGraney."

"Always Jack Showers and Ed McGraney," she said.

"They're on the athletic committee."

"And you never see them any other time. *I* never see them at all."

"Well, why should you? Got any pie or anything?"

"Pie on top of beer? You'll be yelling in your sleep all night. Why don't you have some pretzels?"

"Don't tell me what I'm hungry for, will you?"

"No, I won't tell you anything. You don't tell me anything but lies. You never went near the Elks tonight."

"I can prove it."

"Who by? Jack Showers and Ed McGraney all over again?"

"They were with me. Where do you think I was?"

"That's what I'm trying to find out. Listen to me, Dick. I know there's something funny going on, and I'm going to find out what it is. I'm not going to let you make a fool out of me. Whoever it is, it isn't one of my friends because I keep tabs on them. Norma. Elaine. Especially Norma. But it couldn't be her, because when I was checking up on you and her I found out she has another boy friend. But whoever it is, you might as well prepare yourself. I'm going to make trouble."

"Make trouble for yourself. That's what you're doing right now. And keep your voice down or you'll wake the kids."

"Oh, isn't that rich? You showing consideration for the kids. I like that, all right. It's all right to make a fool out of me and go whoring around, but we mustn't wake the kids. That's rich, that is. Go on up and wake them. Tell them where you were tonight, with some whore."

He slapped her. "Shut up," he said.

She drew away from him. "Don't you do *that* again, don't you *ever* do that again. I'll *kill* you first, Dick. I swear I will."

"Go ahead, you'd be doing me a favor," he said.

The strange, simple words shocked her. Whatever else he had said to her, these words she recognized as the truth; at this moment he wished to be dead and free, but not only free of her. More than to be free of her he wished to be free of the other woman. She could think of nothing to say, but she knew that no words of hers could threaten this man with trouble. She was looking at destruction, and she had had no part in it.

1963

Fatimas and Kisses

Around the corner from where I used to live there was a little store run by a family named Lintz. If you wanted ice cream, by the quart or by the cone, you could get it at Lintzie's; you could buy cigarettes and the less expensive cigars, a loaf of bread, canned goods, meats that did not require the services of a butcher, penny candy and boxed bon-bons, writing tablets and pencils, and literally hundreds of articles on display-cards that novelty salesmen had persuaded Lintzie to put on his shelves, and which he never seemed to reorder. I doubt if there are many stores like Lintzie's around any more, but his place was a great convenience for the people in the neighborhood. When a housewife ran short of something she would tell her child to go down to Lintzie's for the bottle of milk or the half pound of butter or the twenty cents' worth of sliced ham. And Lintzie would charge it. He well knew that the housewives in the neighborhood preferred to deal with the downtown meat markets and grocery stores, and that his trade was at least partly on a semi-emergency basis. That, and the fact that he allowed people to charge things, gave him the excuse to maintain a mark-up on most of his stock, and the housewives called him a highway robber. They called him that to his face. But they were careful how they said it. O'Donnell's meat market was the best, and Gottlieb had the best grocery store, but they were downtown and they would not open up for you if you needed a can of soup or a quart of milk at half past eight in the evening. Lintzie and his wife and two children lived upstairs over the store, and someone would always come down and open up for a customer.

Lintzie was a thin man with a Charlie Chaplin moustache and hollow cheeks that were made hollower still by his habit of leaving out his upper plate. He was young to have false teeth; in his late twenties. He had been in the Marine Corps, although he had not gone overseas, and all his worldliness, all his travels, were by benefit of his having been a Gott damn chyrene. He was a Pennsylvania Dutch farm boy, from somewhere east of Reading, and it wondered me, as the Dutch say, how he had ever heard of the marines. So, being in my teens and curious, I asked him. "How I heart abaht the Marine Corps? I didn't never hear about them till once I seen one of them there posters in the post office. I seen a picture of a marine, all dressed up in his plues, his rifle at right shoulder arms, his bayonet in a white scabbard. He looked handsome to me, so I went home and said to my old man I was going to enlist. I won't tell you what the old man said. He said to go ahead, only he said other things besides. Glad to get rid of me. Him and my brother could run the farm without me. My brother was glad to get rid of me too. That way the old man would leave him the farm and me nothing. So I went to where it said on the poster and signed the papers. By Jesus if I knew what it was like them first three months I would of never enlisted. Son of a bitch sergeant with a swagger stick. Drill. Bivouac. Snakes. By Jesus nights I was too tired to cut my throat. That's no joke. But I guess it all done me good. I come out stronger than I went in, but minus the most of my teeth."

"How did that happen?"

"Oh, I got in a fight with a sailor, me and another Gott damn chyrene we were on duty in the Lackawanna Railroad Station in Hoboken, New Chersey. We took him in custody, he was drunk. But then all of a sudden from all over come them sailors. I had a .45 in my holster but it done me no good. They must have been ten of them chumped us all at once, and one of them hit me across the mouth with my own billy club. That was all the fighting I ever done in the Gott damn chyrenes. The Lackawanna Railroad Station in Hoboken, New Chersey. I got a discharge in October 1918, two weeks before the armistice. But I used to raise a lot of hell in Philly and New York City and Boston, Mass. I could tell *you* some stories if you was older. I was a pretty good-looking fellow till them sailors chumped me. But the son of a bitch that started it, he got something like thirty years' hard labor."

"You identified him?"

"I sure did. I picked him out of twenty of the bastards. I hope he rots. I would of got corporal if it wasn't for him. Maybe I would of stayed in and got gunnery sergeant. But they let me go and now I can't even chew a steak, not with the teeth I got now."

Lintzie's wife was a placid, rather slovenly woman whose hair was never in place. She had an extraordinarily lovely complexion and white little teeth and large breasts that swayed unencumbered by a brassiere. When he addressed her by name, which was seldom, he called her Lonnie. She called him Donald or Lintzie; Lintzie, if she was shouting to him from the back of the store or upstairs, and Donald if she was standing near him. He hardly ever looked at her unless her back was turned. In front of people my age and younger he would say to her, "Go fix yourself up decent, for Christ's sake."

"Aah, shut up," she would say.

But when older people were present they hid their animosity by paying no attention to each other. One day when I went to buy cigarettes, which he was not supposed to sell to me, I waited for Lintzie or Lonnie to appear and wait on me, but neither came. I went back and reopened and closed the door so that the bell would ring again, and she came running downstairs. "Oh, it's you," she said.

"Will you give me a pack of Camels and a pack of Fatimas," I said.

"Charge or pay?"

"*Pay*," I said.

"Who are the Fatimas for? Some girl?"

"For my uncle," I said.

"Yeah, your uncle standing out there with the bicycle. You better watch out, Malloy. Her old lady catches her smoking cigarettes, they'll tell your old man and you'll get hail-Columbia. Give me thirty-five cents."

"Where's Lintzie?" I said.

"To Reading. Why?"

"Just wondered," I said.

"Why?"

"Just wondered," I said. I looked out toward the sidewalk and at the half-ton panel truck parked at the curb, driverless. She put two packs of Camels and two packs of Fatimas on the counter.

"I'll treat you to the butts," she said. "Okay?"

"Thanks," I said.

"The next time her old lady comes in, I won't say anything about you buying her kid Fatimas. Okay?"

"All right," I said.

They never knew—older people—at just what age you started to notice things like a driverless truck and a husband's absence and a delayed appearance, and put them all together. But now Lonnie knew that I had put them all together, and I knew that I had put them together accurately. My discovery was too momentous and mature to confide in the girl who was waiting with her bike. It was too much the kind of thing that I wanted to protect her from, and was indeed eager to protect her from all her life. Those were things I already knew too much about, along with the sight of death and the ugliness of things I had seen in my father's office and in ambulances, hospitals, the homes of the poor, when my father was still trying to make a doctor of me. I could barely endure to see those things myself, but I was a boy. She was a girl, and in ten years or maybe less she was going to be my wife. *Then* I might tell her some of those things, but now Fatimas and kisses were as much as she was ready for.

The bell tinkled as I opened Lintzie's door and tinkled again as I closed it. I guess it was the sound of the bell as much as the Fatimas I flashed that made her giggle. "You got them?" she said. It was a throaty whisper.

"Sure," I said. "Fat-Emmas for you, humps for me. Where do you want to go?"

"Have you got matches?"

"We don't need them. I have my magnifying glass." Matches in a boy's pockets were prima facie evidence of the cigarette habit, like nicotine stains on the fingers. A magnifying glass only created the suspicion that he had been seeing too much of Craig Kennedy, the scientific detective, in his struggles to outwit The Clutching Hand.

I went away to school around that time, and during vacations my hangout was a downtown drug store. Lintzie's was not that kind of place; the neighborhood kids congregated on the sidewalk, drawn to the store by the candy and ice cream, but Lintzie and Lonnie discouraged them from remaining inside. "Get your fingers off them Easter eggs," Lonnie would say. "Stop fooling around with them searchlights. Do you want to wear out the battery?" Lintzie and Lonnie would threaten to put items on the kids' family bills, and sometimes they made good on the threats. Sometimes they billed the wrong family; a fair amount of pilfering went on in spite of the Lintzes' vigilance, and you would see a kid who had just been driven out of the store furtively but proudly displaying a mechanical pencil or a put-and-take top or a carton of Fig Newtons that he had stolen. One of my younger brothers never came out of Lintzie's empty-handed, even if all he got was a cucumber. I did once see him steal a cucumber. The custom was known locally as the five-finger-grab, and it contributed to the Lintzies' pedophobia, which did not exclude their own messy children. "Go on up and wipe your nose," Lintzie would say. "Tell your mother to sew them buttons on." As a young buck who had danced with Constance Bennett and visited the Pre Cat, I stayed away from Lintzie's as much as possible during that period.

But then my father died and I had to get a job as cub reporter on one of the town papers. Temporarily—and I never considered it anything but temporary—my sphere of activity was limited to my own county. We had almost no income, and my mother kept us going by converting her bonds to cash, a desperation measure that obviously could not last forever. It did not make economic sense—nothing did—but very soon we were steady customers at Lintzie's instead of at the cash-and-carry a block away, where everything was much cheaper. My mother ceased to be a customer at O'Donnell's and Gottlieb's; lamb chops and asparagus seldom appeared on our dinner table. We bought a loaf of bread at a time, a jar of peanut butter, a half dozen eggs, a quarter pound of butter, a half-pint of cream, because at Lintzie's prices nothing must go to waste, to turn stale or sour. "On your way home, stop in at Lintzes' and get a can of tomato soup," my mother would say. She had never referred to it as Lintzie's and she was not going to start now. I had always been able to tell that she did not like Lintzie or his wife, and she liked them less when she owed them money twenty-nine days out of every month. They were not overly fond of her, either; she was a better bookkeeper than they, and never hesitated to prove it.

I had become, among other things, quite a drinker, although I was not yet twenty years old. How I managed to drink so much on no money is still somewhat of a mystery to me, but cheap booze was cheap, and politicians and "members of the sporting fraternity" were expected to buy drinks for newspaper men. "Why not?" an old-timer said to me. "It's small recompense for the dubious pleasure of their company." Lintzie was neither politician nor prizefight promoter, but one afternoon, when I stopped in for a last-minute purchase, he invited me to have a drink with him at Schmelinger's, a neighborhood saloon that had never bothered to pretend to be a speakeasy. "I'm broke," I said.

"I'll buy," said Lintzie.

"That's a different story," I said.

Schmelinger had been a patient of my father's and I therefore had never been a patron of Schmelinger's, but Lintzie was greeted with the gruff politeness of the barkeep toward the good customer. We sat at a table and had three or four whiskeys—straight, with water chasers—and spent a most enjoyable hour together. In that neighborhood nearly all the men were at work all day, and Lintzie had no men friends. I gathered that he would run over to Schmelinger's for a shot in the middle of the morning and along about three or four in the afternoon, before the housewives' and schoolkids' rush. That was on a Lincoln's birthday, a school holiday. I was rather sorry that I could not count on being fitted into Lintzie's schedule, but I need not have worried. He changed his schedule to fit mine.

At that stage of my life I took my charm for granted; I did not inquire into the possible reasons why a man who was ten years older than I would want to buy me four dollars' worth of expertly cut rye whiskey once or twice a week. But slowly I began to understand first that he had somehow become indifferent to the difference in our ages. From our conversation it appeared that during my time away at school I had somehow added ten, not four, years to my age. Secondly, like everyone else, he needed someone to talk to. And he talked. He had certain recollections of his Marine Corps days that he liked to dwell on repetitiously; practical jokes on comrades-in-arms, small revenges on young officers, standing two feet away from Woodrow Wilson, visits to a whorehouse on Race Street, Philadelphia. From his whorehouse reminiscences he would often proceed, with unconscious logic, to some revelations concerning Lonnie. Her people had intended her to be the wife of his brother, but when Lintzie came home on his first furlough he threw her on the ground and gave her what she'd been asking for. On his next furlough he married her despite the fact that his brother had meanwhile thrown her on the ground and given her what she'd been asking for. But Lintzie had been first, and the baby was almost surely his. Now that the kid was old enough to look like somebody, he did look more like Lintzie than like his brother, so Lintzie guessed he had not made any mistake in that respect. He was not so sure about the second kid, the daughter. She didn't look like anybody, like a Lintz *or* a Moyer (Lonnie having been a Moyer). But by the law of averages it was probably Lintzie's kid, and he had never been able to prove anything. Lonnie hardly ever went out of the house. Most of the time she waited on customers in her carpet slippers. When she had to go back home for her brother's funeral her shoes did not fit her, so she had to stop on the way to the station and buy a new pair. Two months later, when she was taking the kids to their first day at Sunday School, the new shoes were too small for her. It was hard to believe that she had ever been pretty, but when she was seventeen or eighteen she was as pretty as any girl in the Valley. Some girls didn't care what they looked like after they got married, and Lonnie was one of them. Well, which was worse: the ones who didn't care, or the ones who cared about nothing else and flirted with every son of a bitch with pants on? In another year or two you'd be able to leave her at a hose company picnic and she'd be as safe as if she stayed home. Lintzie had told her as much, and all she said was, "Aah, shut up." That was her answer for everything. Shut up. To Lintzie, to the kids, to her mother, but most of all to Lintzie, and she had said it so often that it sunk in, finally sunk in, and he *did* shut up.

After a while it sunk in on *her* that he had practically stopped talking to her, and she complained about it. He told her he was only doing what she had been telling him to do: she had been telling him for years to shut up, and that's what he did. If she didn't want to listen to anything he had to say, he would talk to her only when it was positively necessary. And her automatic reply to that statement was to tell him to shut up. He realized that she used the expression the way some people say "Go to hell" or "Aw, nuts," but "Aah, shut up" was actually what she said, and he took her at her word. To some extent it made life livable, not to have to talk to her. She was not very much of a talker, not what you'd call a chatterbox, a windbag, but half of what she said was complaints, bellyaching. If it wasn't about money, it was about her feet getting bigger, and if it wasn't about her feet it was why didn't he do more about raising the kids instead of sneaking off to Schmelinger's morning, noon, and night? The funny thing about her complaining was that it was never twice about the same thing. It was probably better than if she harped on the same thing all the time, which would soon drive a man crazy, but on the other hand, she would complain about something and if you paid enough at-

tention to go and do something about the complaint, you damn soon found
out that she didn't even remember complaining about it. Like the time
he went out and paid $185 for a new Stromberg-Carlson and she asked
what the hell did he want to have two radios for, entirely forgetting that
she had complained about the old radio and had specifically mentioned
the Stromberg-Carlson as the one she wanted next. One day, out of a
blue sky, she said to him, "Why didn't you stay in the marines? If you
stayed in the marines we'd be living in Hawaii instead of a dump like
this." It was such an infuriatingly unreasonable complaint that he hauled
off and gave her a kick in the behind. "What'd you kick me for?" she said.
Sometimes he thought she didn't have any brains in her head, but she
was no dumbbell. In some things she was pretty smart. He let her do the
ordering when some of the salesmen came around. She didn't know that
seven eights was fifty-six, but she never took the first price on anything,
and every time she ordered something, say a gross of pencils, she made
the salesman fork over something for nothing. Before she would even
begin talking about a sale she would demand free samples—candy, chewing gum, novelties—and use them later to reward kids who went on
errands for her.

In the strictest confidence and after more than the usual ration of rye
and water, Lintzie told me one day that Lonnie had discovered that most
housewives did not bother to keep tabs on what they bought. My mother
did not let her get away with it, he said, but other women in the neighborhood did not seem to notice when Lonnie added items to the monthly
bills. She was pretty good at it, too. It was hardly ever more than a dollar's
worth of stuff per account, but if you added a dollar to every bill it came
to around a hundred a month clear profit. At Christmas it was even more.
Anyway, it was well over a thousand dollars a year, which was Gott damn
good for a woman that couldn't multiply seven eights. Like picking it up
off the floor. Thereafter I did not mind taking Lintzie's free drinks. I was,
so to speak, the guest of the neighborhood housewives, among whom were
a few who had failed to settle accounts with my father's estate.

It also occurred to me that I was receiving a bribe from Lonnie that
supplemented the original four packs of cigarettes. It probably would have
done her no good to complain, but she could have protested when Lintzie
rang up a No Sale on the cash register and helped himself to the money
to pay for his hospitality to me. No doubt she was glad to get him out of
her sight. Nevertheless I became convinced that Lonnie was appreciative
of my early silence, if possibly a little apprehensive that I might break it
now that Lintzie and I were drinking companions. Ethically I was not
standing on firm ground, but my ethics and my morals and my conscience
were taking a continual beating in other areas as well. I was giving myself
trouble over girls and women and love and theology and national politics
and my uncontrollable temper. Not the easiest of my problems was my

willingness to spend as much time with a man whom I regarded as a moron. It was true that I was the victim of circumstances back beyond my control, but I was unable thereby to justify my association with this loquacious lout. Since I could not justify it, I gave up trying to.

Downtown, in back of a second-rate commercial hotel, was another saloon that was as wide open as Schmelinger's and served the same grade of whiskey. Unlike Schmelinger's it catered to a considerable transient trade, principally the traveling salesmen who stopped at the hotel. It was a busy joint, and often half filled with strangers. I went there one night, alone, and sat at a table to drink beer, eat pretzels, and read the out-of-town papers. At the next table were two strangers drinking rye and ginger ale. Salesmen, most likely, and getting drunk. They did not bother me, but I began to pick up some of their conversation. One was telling the other about a customer of his, nothing much for looks, but a positive, guaranteed lay. Nothing novel about that conversation between salesmen, but the speaker gave his companion directions on how to find the accommodating customer, and the address was Lintzie's store. "I got put on to her a couple years ago," he said. "Don't look for any great beauty. This is for a quick jazz when you don't have a date. No money. You give her a dozen samples or shave your prices a little. And you gotta watch out for the husband. He's in and out of the place all day. A boozer. My last time in this town, I was upstairs with the broad and the husband came back from the saloon. I had to hide in a closet till he went out again. All he had to do was open that closet door and I'm cooked, but I been taking off her for a couple years and that's the first time we ever had a close one. Don't tell her I sent you. The first time, you gotta make it on your own, but I want to tell you something, that—ain't—hard. And buddy, she likes it."

I could easily have struck up a conversation with the traveling man and learned more about Lonnie's behavior, but a friend of mine joined me and we were town people against strangers. The salesman had confirmed my suspicions about Lonnie, dormant suspicions because I had not realized that Lonnie was quite so adventurous or quite so careless. Oddly enough, my immediate impulse was to warn Lonnie to use some caution, and my second, contradictory to the first, was no more than a feeling of pity for Lintzie. The practical effect of what I had overheard was to give up my pleasant enough drinking sessions with Lintzie. There was going to be trouble there, I knew it, and I had a very positive wish to stay away from it. I did not want to be drinking with Lintzie while Lonnie was using his absence to entertain a gabby salesman.

In later years I came to believe that Lintzie's first suspicions of Lonnie dated from my withdrawal from our sessions at Schmelinger's. My excuse to him was flimsy, although based partly on fact: that the paper had promoted me to columnist, an extra job that had to be done on my own time. It was flimsy because Lintzie did not believe me. Whenever I saw him he gave me the special look of small dignity offended, the look of small people who do not feel entitled to anger. My subsequent theory about Lintzie's suspicions of Lonnie was that without me (or anyone else) to talk to, he was left entirely with his thoughts, and his world was very small. He had a wife, two kids who gave him no pleasure, and the clientele of his store for whom he had no respect. And of course he had the memories of his ten months as a private in the Marine Corps, patrolling railway stations and piers and being sneered at by sailors and petty officers; occasional visits to whorehouses along the Eastern Seaboard; the time he stood frozen at attention when the President of the whole Gott damn United States passed within two feet of him at the Union Depot in Washington. His brother had never been as far as New York, his father had never been as far as Philadelphia, his mother had never been to Reading before she was thirty. For a Berks County farm boy Lintzie had seen a lot of the world, but he had not been seeing much of it lately. Schmelinger ran a very sober saloon; the only decoration in the place was a pre-Prohibition framed brewery advertisement, depicting a goat in Bavarian costume raising a beer stein. Schmelinger himself was a strict Roman Catholic who had a daughter a nun and a son studying for priesthood. It was in these surroundings that Lintzie was spending a great deal of his time, probably as much of it as in his own store.

A full year and a little more passed during which I did not have a drink with Lintzie and actually did not set foot in his store. (My mother could send one of my brothers for those last-minute quarts of milk.) I was getting twenty dollars a week on the paper, and the owner, in his benevolence, allowed me to fill the tank of my four-cylinder Buick at the paper's expense. So I was coming up in the world, and I loved my column, which was one of the numerous imitations of F.P.A.'s Conning Tower. One afternoon, after the paper had gone to press and the other reporters had gone home, the phone rang on the city editor's desk and I went to answer it. "Malloy speaking," I said.

"Oh, it's you, Malloy. This is Christine Fultz."

"Hello, Chris, what have you got?" I said. She was a "correspondent" who picked up a few dollars a week for news tips and unreadable (and usually outdated) accounts of church suppers.

"Well, I'll tell you, there's something very funny going on out here."

"Is it funny enough to go in my column?"

"What column is that?" said Chris.

"Never mind. What have you got? Spill it."

"I want the credit for the tip, mind you."

"I'll see that you get the credit for the tip, but first you have to tell me what tip on what," I said.

"It's at Lintzie's. There's a whole crowd of people standing outside there."

"Maybe they're having a bargain sale."

"Be *serious*. Somebody said he shot her."

"Lintzie shot Lonnie?"

"That's what I said, didn't I? But I don't know if it's true or not. I couldn't get very near, there's such a crowd. There was another story circulating that he shot her and the two children, but I don't know that either."

"Are the police there?" I said.

"If they are, they're inside. I didn't see no police."

"When did this happen, do you know?"

"Well, it couldn't of happened very long ago, because I went past Lintzie's an hour ago and there was nobody there. But when I came back you should of seen the crowd. So it must of happened between the time I went past there an hour ago and when I was on my way home."

"Now you're using the old noodle, Chris. What else?"

"*Somebody* said he shot a *man*."

"Lintzie shot a man?"

"Don't go blaming me if that's just a rumor, but that's what one person told me. There's supposed to be a dead man in there, and Lonnie and the two kids."

"But Lintzie? Where is Lintzie?"

"I don't know. He's either inside or he got away. Or maybe he's dead too."

"That's the old noodle again, Chris. Well, thanks very much. You'll get credit for the tip."

"Are you coming out?"

"Try and stop me," I said.

In less than ten minutes I parked my car across the street from Lintzie's. It was my neighborhood, and everyone knew that I was working on the paper, so they made way for me. A cop, the newest on the force, got between me and the door. "No newspaper reporters," he said.

"Who said so? *You*, for Christ's sake? Get out of my way. If you'll turn your thick head around you'll see your boss waving to me to come in." Inside the store Joe Dorelli, a sergeant and detective—all detectives were sergeants—was signaling to me. "You see?" I said to the rookie cop. "I was covering murders when you were playing high school football." It was a lie, but rookie cops were our natural enemies. I went inside.

"What the hell is this, Joe?"

"Lintzie, the Dutch bastard. He come home and caught her in bed with a guy and he shot them. Then the kids come running in from the yard and he shot them too. You want to see the gun? Here's the gun." On the counter was a holster stamped USMC and in it was a Colt .45 automatic pistol.

"Where is Lintzie?" I said.

"Back in the kitchen, talking to the chief. You'd think he just got elected mayor, honest. He phoned in. Me and the chief come right out and the first thing he done was offer us a cigar. Then he took us upstairs and showed us the wife and the boy friend. Wait'll you see *them*. We're waiting for the fellow to come and take their pictures. Then Lintzie took us down in the cellar and showed us the two kids."

"He shot them down in the cellar?"

"No, on the stairway, between this floor and the bedroom. Then he carried them down in the cellar. I don't know why, and he doesn't either. I said to him why didn't he shoot himself while he was at it? That's what they often do. But he was surprised at such a question. Why should he shoot himself? He looked at me like I wasn't all there."

"Is he drunk?"

"You can smell it on him, but he don't act it. He asked were you here."

"He did?"

"By name," said Dorelli. "That's what I wanted to talk to you. Did you know this was gonna happen? Nobody knows who the guy is. Well, we know his name and he was some kind of a salesman. His wallet was in his pants pocket, hanging on the back of a chair. From Wilkes-Barre, he is, but working for a company over in Allentown. Sidney M. Pollock, thirty-two years of age. But did you know about him and the Lintz woman?"

"No, but I might recognize him."

"We'll get him identified all right."

"I'd like to take a look at him."

"From the front you would. You know what a .45 slug'll do. The right-hand cheekbone it went in. She got it in the heart. Two. He gave her one for good measure. The kids he gave one apiece. Five shots, four dead. But he was a marine, and they teach them to shoot in the marines. I took notice there was a picture of him in the bedroom. Marksman and expert rifleman. Well, do you want to take a look at them?"

I only wanted to see the dead man, and I did recognize him. He was the companion of the traveling salesman who had talked so seductively of Lonnie Lintz. Even after a year there was no mistaking that nose and that hairless skull. I could not have recognized the big-mouthed salesman; he had been sitting on my right; but Pollock had been facing him, and me. It was perhaps too much to say that if I had struck up a conversation with them that night, Pollock would not now be lying dead in his underwear on a messy bed in a strange town, in disgrace. I thought of Pollock's wife, if any, and his probably orthodox mother and father in Wilkes-Barre.

"Now you got another treat in store for you," said Dorelli. "Down in the cellar."

"No thanks," I said.

"Me either," said Dorelli. "I had to, but if I didn't have to I wouldn't have. Two kids, for Christ's sake, around the same age as two of mine. This guy is crazy, but don't you write that. That's what he'll claim—and maybe he had a right to kill her and the Jew, but not the kids. He can't pull that unwritten law on the kids. For that he deserves to fry."

"I didn't know you were such a family man, Joe."

"Listen, what you don't know about me would fill a book," he said. "You had enough, we'll go down and see if the chief'll let you talk to Lintz."

I waited in the store while Joe conferred with the chief. A cop named Lundy came in while I was there. "That's something you don't often hear in this town," he said.

"What's that?" I said.

"Them women out there, they want to lynch him."

"We've never had a lynching in this town," I said.

"We never will. It's just talk, but you don't often hear that kind of talk in Lantenengo County. Just talk, but all the same I'm gonna tell the chief to get him outa here."

"You mean you're thinking of *suggesting* to the chief," I said.

"Aah, smart guy," said Lundy. "I hear Lintz and you was great buddies."

"Doing some detective work at Schmelinger's, eh, Lundy? Do you think you'll solve this case?"

"I'll solve you one right in the puss, Malloy," said Lundy.

"Then you'll be right back on the garbage truck. We supported *this* mayor," I said.

Dorelli, at the rear of the store, beckoned to me.

"Any message you wish to convey to the chief, Lundy?" I said.

"No, you wouldn't get it right, just like that rag you work for," said Lundy. He laughed and I laughed. Lundy was a good cop and he knew I thought so.

"I'll put in a good word for you, then," I said.

"Jesus, don't do that. That'd be the ruination of me, a good word from you."

I joined Dorelli. "You can talk to him, but one of us has to be there."

"Oh, come on, Joe. There's no mystery about this case. Let me talk to him alone."

"We'll do it our way or not at all," said Dorelli.

"Then we'll do it your way," I said.

Dorelli led me to the kitchen. A uniformed cop was standing outside the kitchen door; the chief was sitting across the table from Lintzie, his chin on his chest, staring at him in silence. Obviously the chief had momentarily run out of questions to ask Lintzie. Lintzie turned when I entered. "Oh, there's my buddy. Hyuh, Malloy."

"Hello, Lintzie," I said.

"Say, Chief, let me send over to Schmelinger's for a pint," said Lintzie. "I'll pay for it."

"Pay for it? You got a lot to pay for, you son of a bitch," said the chief.

"I'll be down in the cellar," said Dorelli, and left.

"Well, I guess I went and done it," said Lintzie.

"How did you happen to pick today?" I said.

"I don't know," said Lintzie. "I was over at Schmelinger's and I guess I started to thinking to myself. There was a whole truckload of stuff piled up on the kitchen porch, waiting to be unpacked. I knowed Gott damn well Lonnie wouldn't start unpacking it. It had to be unpacked and put down in the cellar out of the way. So I said to myself if I got it all unpacked I could make the kids take it down in the cellar when they got home. It was a truckload of stuff from the wholesaler. Canned goods. Heavy. In wooden boxes. All I needed was my claw-hammer and I could unpack the stuff and the kids could take it down the cellar a couple cans at a time. Ten or fifteen minutes' work for me and I could be back at Schmelinger's. So I said to Gus I'd see him later and I come home."

"What time was that, Lintzie?" I said.

"Search me. I lost track of time," said Lintzie.

"About quarter of three," said the chief. "Between half past two and three, according to Schmelinger."

"I come in the store door, and I took notice to the salesman's car outside. But I went inside and no Lonnie, and no salesman. The chief don't believe me, but I caught her once before with a salesman, only it wasn't the same one."

"Why don't you believe him, Chief?"

"Because this was a deliberate murder. All this stuff about the packages on the back porch, that's the bunk."

"Look outside, the boxes are there right now in plain sight," said Lintzie.

"He pretended he was going to spend a couple hours at Schmelinger's, the way he usually did. But he only went there long enough to give his wife and the salesman time to go upstairs," said the chief. "He admitted himself he usually kept the .45 upstairs but today he had it hanging on a peg in the cellar stairway. This was a planned first-degree murder."

"How about that, Lintzie?" I said.

"The chief don't have to be right all the time."

"But why was the gun hanging in the stairway?"

"To get it out of the way of the kids. Lonnie said she caught the boy playing with it and I was to get it out of the way. So I took and hung it on a peg in the cellar stairway, where he couldn't reach it. That was two-three days ago. Lonnie could—I was just gonna say Lonnie could back me up on that, but I guess not now."

"No," I said. "So then what?"

"Yes, listen to this part, Malloy," said the chief.

"Then what? Then I went upstairs and caught them in bed."

"Wait a minute, Lintzie. You're skipping a lot. Did you get the gun and then go upstairs?" I said.

"Me? No. I went upstairs and caught them and then I got the gun."

"Did you, before you went upstairs, did you call Lonnie to see where she was? Upstairs or down-cellar?"

"Well, she could hear the bell when I come in the store."

"But you could have been a customer. You didn't call her, or did you?"

"He didn't call her, and he *didn't* come in the front door," said the chief. "He told Dorelli one story and me another, and now he's got an altogether different one. He told Dorelli he went around the back way and got his claw-hammer and started opening the boxes. There's no mark of a claw-hammer on any of the boxes, and anyway you make a certain amount of noise opening a wooden box with a claw-hammer. You know, you put the claws under the slats and you start using leverage and it makes a peculiar kind of a noise. But that would have warned the people upstairs. No, he came in the back door, where there is no bell, and he got the .45 and sneaked upstairs and took careful aim and killed the salesman. One shot. Then he let her have two slugs right in the heart. I had a look at the .45 and I'll tell you this much, Malloy. If all my men kept their guns in as good a condition I'd be satisfied. I know something about guns. If you leave a gun in a holster for any length of time, the oil gets gummy, but not this gun. This gun was cleaned and oiled I'd say in the last twenty-four, forty-eight hours."

"I always kept my gun in good condition," said Lintzie.

"Yes. For just such an occasion," said the chief.

"Tell me what you did, Lintzie," I said.

"I shot them, for Christ's sake. And then the Gott damn kids come yelling and screaming and I shot them, too. I ain't denying it. Go ahead and arrest me."

"Oh, we'll arrest you, Mr. Lintz," said the chief. "You *were* arrested, nearly an hour ago. Sergeant Dorelli placed you under arrest, but you don't have a very good memory."

"You shot the kids on the stairway, and then you told Dorelli that you carried them down to the cellar."

"That's what I done. Yeah."

"But I understand that a bullet from a .45 has a terrific impact, that it'll knock a grown man back several feet. So I was wondering, maybe when you shot the kids the impact knocked them down the stairs, and then you picked them up and carried them to the cellar. Is that about right, Lintzie?"

"No," he said.

"What did happen?"

"I held the kids, one at a time, and shot them," said Lintzie.

"Jesus," I said, and looked at the chief.

"They wouldn't hold still," he said.

"Jesus Christ," I said.

"Oh, this is quite a fellow," said the chief. "It takes a real man to grab hold of a kid with one hand and shoot him with the other. And do the same thing all over again with another kid."

"Which did you shoot first, Lintzie? The girl or the boy?"

"Her. Then he come at me. I don't remember holding him."

"The boy tried to defend his sister," said the chief.

"He didn't try to defend nobody, that kid. He was getting ready to shoot me. Him and Lonnie."

"But I thought Lonnie told you to hide the gun," I said.

"Till he got older, that's all. She was gonna wait a couple years till we had more money saved up."

"Oh, and then she was going to let him shoot you?" I said.

"You got the idea," said Lintzie. He grinned at me and sneered at the chief. "She thought I was dumb, but I wasn't so dumb."

"You said something about catching her with another man once before," I said. "You never told me about that."

"Yes, I did. Didn't I?"

"No, you never told me that. When did you catch her? Was it like today, you came home and found her with another man?"

"Night," he said.

"Oh, you came home one night and found her?"

"No! I was home. Upstairs. The night bell rang and she went down to see who it was."

"You thought it was a late customer," I said.

"I thought it was, but it was a foreigner. He had whiskers and he wore those funny clothes. You know. He had whiskers on his chin, all the girls were stuck on him."

"Oh, yes. Once I had a billygoat, he was old enough to vote. He had whiskers on his chin. I remember the song."

"This was *him*, though. Not a song."

"Oh, really? And he came in the store and made passes at Lonnie?"

"*She* made passes at *him*. She made passes at everybody except you. She didn't like you, or your mother, or any of you. Boy, oh, boy, the things she used to say about your old man."

"She never knew my old man, but what did she say about him?"

"How he used to operate on people when they didn't have nothing wrong with them. Any time your old lady wanted a new dress, your old man would operate on somebody."

"Oh, well that was true, of course," I said.

"Stop humoring him," said the chief.

"And that's why Lonnie never made passes at me, because she didn't like us. But what about this foreigner with the beard, Lintzie? Did you ever see him any place else? Did you ever see him at Schmelinger's?"

"He used to come in there but I never talked to him."

"He did come in there, though?"

"I seen him there," said Lintzie.

"He had whiskers. Did he wear a kind of a coat with little straps across the front?"

"Such a coat, yes," said Lintzie. "But I never seen him when you were there."

"No, but I think I knew the fellow you mean."

The chief looked at his gold hunting-case watch. "You had long enough, Malloy. I'm taking this fellow down to the squire's office."

"Charging him with first-degree murder?" I said.

"We sure are. An open-and-shut case, like this watch."

"I'll make you a small bet he never goes to Bellefonte," I said.

"I wouldn't take your money," said the chief.

"Bellefonte? Where the electric chair is?" said Lintzie. "Huh. Not me."

"See? He doesn't think so either," I said.

"Who did I used to guard during the war? Tell him, Malloy," said Lintzie.

"Woodrow Wilson, the President of the whole Gott damn United States," I said.

"Can I go upstairs a minute, Chief?" said Lintzie.

"No. You mean you want to go to the toilet?"

"No, I want to get something for Malloy."

"Call Lundy, tell him what it is and he'll get it," said the chief.

"My picture of me, upstairs on the bureau," said Lintzie.

"Oh, for Christ's sake. All right," said the chief.

Lundy went upstairs and brought down the photograph, which I had never seen before, of Private Donald Lintz, U.S.M.C., in his greens and the old-style cap that sat squarely on the top of his head, two badges for shooting pinned to the blouse.

"Put that in the paper, Malloy," said Lintzie.

"That I promise you," I said. "And how about pictures of Lonnie and the kids?"

"You want them too?" said Lintzie. "What do you want them for? I don't want them in the paper."

"Are there any more up there, Lundy?" I said.

"Sure," said Lundy. "Plenty. Her before she got fat, and the two kids."

"No, you can't have them," said Lintzie.

"Get them, Lundy," said the chief.

"You son of a bitch, Malloy," said Lintzie. "You want to make people feel sorry for them."

"Maybe he doesn't, but I do," said the chief. "Malloy, why do you think this fellow has a Chinaman's chance? You can tell me. The D.A. prosecutes, I don't."

"Can you spare five minutes?" I said.

"What for?"

"Will you come with me? It'll only take five minutes at the most," I said.

The chief called Dorelli, told him to keep an eye on Lintzie, and accompanied me to Schmelinger's. I pointed to the old-time beer ad on the wall. "There's Lonnie's other boy friend," I said. "Any fifty-dollar alienist will keep Lintzie out of the chair."

"Maybe you're right," said the chief.

"Something on the house, gentlemen?" said Schmelinger.

"Maybe you're right," said the chief.

"You, Malloy?"

"Not on the house," I said. "You've just lost your best cash customer."

"I won't miss him," said Schmelinger.

"He was good for fifty bucks a week and he never gave you any trouble," I said.

"I won't miss him," said Schmelinger. He ignored me and addressed the chief. "After this fellow stopped coming in with him he just sat there and stared at the Bock beer picture. And I bet you he don't even know it was there."

"Is that so? Well, thanks, Gus. Next time I'm out this way I'll have one with you," said the chief.

We walked in silence halfway to Lintzie's, then the chief spoke. "I thought a great deal of your father. What's a young fellow with your education throwing it all away when you could be doing some good in the world?"

"What education? I had four years of high school," I said.

"You were away to college," he said.

"Away, but not to college."

"Oh, then you're not much better than the rest of us," he said.

"I never said I was, Chief."

"You never said it, but you act it. Your father *was* better than most of us, but he didn't act it."

"No, he didn't have to," I said.

1966

Natica Jackson

One afternoon on her way home from the studio in her cream-yellow Packard 120 convertible coupe Natica Jackson took a wrong turn, deliberately. Every working day for the three years that she had been under contract at Metro she had followed the same route between Culver City and her house in Bel-Air: Motor Avenue, Pico Boulevard, Beverly Glen, Sunset Boulevard, Bel-Air. In the morning it was Bel-Air, Sunset Boulevard, Beverly Glen, Pico Boulevard, Motor Avenue, Culver City, the studio. She was fond of saying that she knew the way in her sleep, because many mornings she might as well have been asleep as the way she was. In the afternoons and early evenings, tired though she was, it was not quite the same. The reason it was not quite the same was that when she got through working it was like being let out of school. In those days she was still close enough to high school to have that feeling. It had not been so long since a Warner talent scout saw her in a school play in Santa Ana and wafted her the fifty thousand miles from Santa Ana to Hollywood. They gave her a seven-year contract beginning at $75 a week, and in six months she was released, just before they would have had to pay her $125 a week. Then she got an agent who helped someone at Metro discover that she could sing and dance; and pretty soon the public discovered that there was something in the spacing between her eyes and the width of her upper lip that made her stand out, made them want to know who she was. Among beautiful women and cute girls she was the one that the public liked. She became everybody's favorite niece, and she also looked extremely well in black opera-lengths. The studio teamed her up with Eddie Driscoll in two dreadful musicals, the second so dreadful that it was scrapped halfway through, but Jerry B. Lockman saw enough of it to want her for a straight, non-musical comedy he was doing, and she walked away with the picture. Walked away with it. In the executives' diningroom they could not agree that Natica Jackson had star quality, but no one could deny that she was ready for stardom. Not Garbo stardom, not Myrna Loy stardom, but sure as hell Joan Blondell stardom, and maybe, in the right pictures she would develop into another Jean Arthur. The God damn public liked her. She couldn't carry a picture by herself, but whenever she was in a picture the people would come out of the theater saying how wonderful she was.

She bought the house in Bel-Air with money she had not yet earned, but her agent knew what he was doing when he helped her finance it. "I don't want you rattling around some apartment on Franklin," he said. "I'm thinking of ten years from now, when you ought to be making easily a couple hundred thousand dollars a year. Move your mother in with you and stay out of the night spots."

"And have no fun," said Natica.

"Depends on what you mean by fun. You have Jerry Lockman."

"He can't take me out anywhere," she said.

"I'll take you anywhere you ought to go. Anywhere I can't take you, you shouldn't be there."

"Don't try to make me into something I'm not," said Natica.

"How do you know what you're not? You know Marie Dressler?"

"Tugboat Annie, you mean?"

"You know who she pals around with? Vanderbilts and Morgans, those kind of people. And you should make a year what she makes."

"Well, I hope she has more fun than I do."

"I hope you have as much fun when you're her age. Over sixty and making what she makes. Well loved throughout the entire civilized world. If all is not well with you and Jerry, get yourself a younger fellow. Only don't go for some trap drummer in a cheap night club. I'll look around and see if I find the right kind of fellow for you. I coulda told you a few things about Jerry, but you didn't take me into your confidence till it was too late. But we can get rid of Jerry. You *graduated* from his type pictures. I got great confidence in your future, Natica. Not just next week or the week after that. I'm talking about 1940, 1950, 1960!"

Natica had already been around Hollywood long enough to have respect for her agent, and she obeyed him in all things. Morris King was a rich man, an agent by choice, and not one of the artists' representatives who waited hopefully for a permanent connection with one of the studios. Morris had turned down offers of producer jobs. "I'll take L. B. Mayer's job, should they offer it to me, but not Eddie Mannix's or Benny Thau's," he would say. He had a big house in Beverly Hills, a 16-cylinder Cadillac limousine with a Negro chauffeur who wore breeches and puttees, and he had Ernestine, his wife, who according to other agents was the real brains of the Morris King Office. Ernestine would sit with Morris at the Beverly Derby, the Vine Street Derby, Al Levey's Tavern, the Vendome,

Lyman's downtown, with her fat forearms resting flat on the table and her hands clasped, her eyes sparkling as she followed the men's conversation. She would wait, she would always wait, until Morris or one of the other men asked her what *she* thought, and her opinions were always so clever or so completely destructive that the men would nod silently even when they did not agree. She had opinions on everything; who was going to be the boss at Universal, who was going to win the main event at the Legion Stadium, why was Natica Jackson worth Morris King's personal attention. "Ernestine thinks like a man," said one rival agent. "I was having a discussion with her and Morris the other night. We happen to be talking about something, and in the midst of it I pulled a couple cigars outa my pocket and accidentally I offered one to Ernestine. I didn't mean anything by it. It was just like I said, she thinks like a man, and I done it like you offer a coupla men a cigar. Did she get sore? No, she didn't get sore. You know what she said? She said, 'The supreme compliment.' I don't say she's *all* the brains, but when it comes to thinking I give her credit for fifty-one percent. I give her the edge. Incidentally, she *took* the cigar. She don't smoke, but she wanted the cigar for a souvenir, a memento."

The Kings had no children, and at forty-four Ernestine was as reconciled to childlessness as at twenty-two she had been fearful of pregnancy. They loved Morris's business, going out every night, and each other. But Morris thought he saw through Ernestine's interest in Natica Jackson. "She's a little like you, Teeny," he said. "If you had a daughter that's what she'd be like. She even resembles you facially."

"You think you're smart, don't you?" said Ernestine.

"Maybe not smart, but not dumb either," said Morris. "It's all right if you don't want to tell me. I got my own two eyes."

"I know you have, honey," she said. "But I was never as pretty as Natica Jackson. That I can't claim."

"I only said she resembles you facially. I didn't say she was the exact duplicate."

"What if she was the exact duplicate? Would you go for her?"

He rubbed his chin as though he were stroking a Vandyke. "You know what I think? I think you're trying to find out if I *do* go for her. Like I saw the facial resemblance back there two-three years ago, and said to myself here was a modern-day version of Ernestine Schluter. Well, if that's what you're thinking, you're all wrong. The first time I saw her I took notice she had a pair of legs like Ruby Keeler and a kind of a face on the order of Claudette Colbert, only not as pretty."

"Claudette has a pair of legs on her."

"I'm telling you what *I* thought, not what you're thinking now, if you'll let me continue," said Morris. "So I did a little selling job at Metro. Then *you* liked her and the public liked her, and you more or less took her under your wing. As to me going for her like Jerry Lockman went for her, you got no cause to be suspicious."

"I know, Morris, I know. I was just kind of putting you on the pan," said Ernestine.

"Sure. But you got something on your mind, whatever it is," he said.

"It isn't much. The way some of you men buy a prizefighter and have him for a hobby, that's my interest in Natica."

"You wanta buy her from me? I'll send you her contract and let you service her?"

"Not me. If there's anything I don't want to be it's a woman agent. But I'd like to have the say in her career, just for a hobby."

"All right."

"Starting with getting rid of Jerry Lockman."

"That's easy. She's fed up to here with Jerry."

"So am I, and she's been with him long enough. Everybody in town knows about Jerry and how he's peculiar, but if Natica keeps on being his girl they'll think the same of her. Get her a new fellow. An Englishman, or a writer, or I don't care if you get her an out-and-out pansy. But somebody that can be her escort."

"You want me to find a new girl for Jerry?"

"That shouldn't be hard. They're a dime a dozen in this town. The next new girl comes into your office, send her out to Jerry."

"Well, I guess I can do that," said Morris. "But you find a guy for Natica."

"All right," said Ernestine.

She found an Englishman who was also a writer and an out-and-out bisexual, who was more than willing to act as Natica's escort and lover. It was not the ideal arrangement for Natica, but they kept her busy at the studio, gave her bonuses for waiving vacations, and sent her home at night too tired to think. Alan Hildred, her English beau, sold the studio two original stories for Natica Jackson pictures, and one of them, *Uncles Are People*, was actually produced and did well. Twenty-five thousand dollars, less Morris King's ten percent, more than made up for the times when Natica did not wish to see him—or for the times when she did wish to see him. It became an understood thing that Alan Hildred was to make *some* money, as author of the original or collaborator on the screenplay, on every Natica Jackson picture. Natica's mother, who would have liked being a dress extra, was persuaded to take a job as saleslady in a florist's shop owned by Ernestine King. Natica's father, a brakeman on the Southern Pacific, went right on being a brakeman, but he had been separated from his wife for a good ten years. No one knew where Natica's brother was. Last heard from as a deckhand on one of the Dollar Line ships. But he was bound to turn up sometime and when he did he would have to be taken care of. Natica's maternal uncle, who had moved into the Jackson household when Natica's father left, was employed as a gardener at Warner Brothers. He had expected to move into the Bel-Air house, but there Natica put her foot down. "That dirty old son of a bitch can stay away from here," said Natica.

"That's no way to talk about your own flesh and blood," said her mother.

"Listen, Mom, there's no law says *you* have to live here either," said Natica. "You're making seventy-five a week."

"Yes, but for how long? My arthritis."

"Don't kid me, with your arthritis. If you have the arthritis I'll send you to the desert. Go see the doctor, and if he says you have the arthritis I'll get you a place to stay. But if Uncle Will think's he's moving in here, you just tell Uncle Will it was Mr. King got him the job at Warners', and the same Mr. King can get him kicked out on his big fat can."

"I don't see why Mr. King can't get me a job as a dress extra. Then I wouldn't have to be in and out of that refrigerator all day."

"Well, I'll tell you why," said Natica. "They don't want you on the lot is why. And another reason is because they give those jobs to people that can act. Professionals. The only acting you ever do is putting on this act with the arthritis. Don't you exhaust my patience, Mom. Just don't you exhaust my patience."

"Sometimes I wish we never left Santa Ana."

"Here's fifty bucks," said Natica. "Go on back."

"Yes, you'd like to get rid of me, wouldn't you?"

"Oh, cut it out. I'm tired," said Natica. "I get up at five o'clock in the morning and get pushed around all day, and when I get home evenings I have to listen to your bellyaching."

It was a day or two later that Natica Jackson, on her way home from the studio in her little Packard, deviated from her customary route. There was a point on Motor Avenue where the road bore to the right. At the left there was a street—she didn't know its name—that formed the other arm of a Y. She had wondered sometimes what would happen if she turned in at that street. Not that anything would happen except that she would be a little later getting home and she would have seen a Southern California real estate development that she had never seen before. But at least she would have gone home by a different way. And so she turned left into a street called Marshall Place.

She had to slow down. Marshall Place was a winding road, S-shaped and only three-car width and a tight squeeze at that. The houses were quite close together and English-looking, and Natica wondered if the street had been named after Herbert Marshall, the English actor. The cars that were parked in Marshall Place were cars that were suitable to the neighborhood: Buicks, Oldsmobiles, a Packard 120 like Natica's, a LaSalle coupe, an oldish foreign car with a name something like Delancey. It was a far superior neighborhood to the section of Santa Ana where Natica had lived, but she had so quickly become accustomed to Bel-Air that Marshall Place seemed almost dingy. She came to another turn in the road and now she could see Motor Avenue again, and she was not sorry to see it. Marshall Place was certainly nothing much, and whatever curiosity she had had about it was completely satisfied. Just another street where people who worked in offices lived. Fifty yards from Motor Avenue and farewell to Marshall Place—and then her car banged into a Pontiac.

The Pontiac was pulling out from the curb and she hit it almost broadside. It was a noisy collision in the quiet street. The driver of the Pontiac shouted, "What the hell?" and other things that she did not hear. She backed her car away and he reversed to the curbstone and got out. "What do you think you were doing?" he said. "Didn't you see my hand? I had my hand out, you know."

"I'm sorry," she said. "I didn't see your hand. It's kind of dark. I'm covered with every kind of insurance." She was wearing a silk scarf over her head and tied under her chin.

"Aren't you Natica Jackson, the actress?" he said.

"Yes," she said.

"I thought so," he said. "Well, my name is H. T. Graham, and I live in there, Number 8 Marshall Place. I suppose you have your driver's license and so forth? You'd better pull up to the curb or you'll be in the way of any cars that want to get through."

"Listen, Mr. Graham, don't start bossing me around like you were taking charge here. You say you had your hand out, but I don't have to take your word for it. The insurance company will pay for your damages, only don't start bossing me around. Here. Here's my driver's license and you can look on the steering if you want to copy down the registration."

"Don't pull any movie actress stuff on me," he said. "You were completely in the wrong and the condition of the two cars proves it. I didn't smack into you. You smacked into me." He took out a fountain pen and wrote down her name and address and various numbers in an appointment book. "Have you got a pencil?"

"No," she said.

"All right. Then I'll copy it all down for you." He did so, and tore a sheet out of his appointment book and handed it to her. "Some people would get a whole new car out of this, a crackup with a movie actress," he said. "But all I want is what I'm entitled to."

"Big-hearted Otis," she said.

"You movie people, you wonder why you're so unpopular with real people, but I'll tell you why. It's the way you're behaving now. Like a spoiled brat. You think a cheque from the insurance company is all that's necessary. This time you can drive your car home and tomorrow you can buy a new one. But the next time you may kill somebody. This is a narrow street, residential, small children. Luckily they're all home having their supper now, but a half an hour earlier this street would have been full of children. I read all about that drunken director that killed three people down in Santa Monica. He should have been put in the gas chamber."

"Listen, Mr. Graham, all I did was wrinkle your fender and put a few dents in your door."

"But if the window'd been up you could have blinded me with flying glass. Stop trying to make this seem like nothing."

"You stop trying to make it seem like a train wreck."

"Oh, go on home," he said. "And try and get home without killing anybody. Go on, beat it."

"I can't," she said.

"Naturally, your motor isn't running. Step on the starter."

"It isn't that," she said.

"Are you hurt?"

"No, not that either. I just don't want to drive. Would you mind going in your house and calling a taxi? Suddenly I lost my nerve or something. I don't know what it is."

"Are you sure you didn't bang your head on the windshield?" He looked at her closely.

"I'm not hurt. Please, will you just call me a taxi and I'll send somebody to pick up my car."

"No, no, I'll drive you home. You feeling faint or anything? Come on in and I'll get you a glass of water. Or maybe a brandy is what you need."

"Honestly, all I want is if you'll get me a taxi and I'll be all right. I'm doing a delayed take, I guess, but I positively couldn't drive home if you paid me."

He got in her car and drove it to Bel-Air. She spoke only to give him directions in the final stage of the ride. "Now I'll get *you* a taxi," she said, when they reached her house. "Can I offer you a drink?"

"No thanks," he said.

"I guess you expected me to have a big car with a chauffeur."

"It'd go with this house, all right," he said.

"It's too big for just my mother and I."

"Aren't you married?"

"No." She telephoned the taxi company. "There'll be a cab in five minutes," she said. "I'm sorry I was such a jerk back there."

"I was pretty rough on you."

"Oughtn't you to tell your wife where you are?"

"She's away. She and the kids are down at Newport."

"Oh, then I guess you were on your way out to dinner when I bumped into you."

"I was going over to Ralphs in Westwood. I usually go there when I'm batching it."

"How about a steak here? I have dinner by myself and go to bed around nine. My mother doesn't wait for me. She eats early and then goes to the show."

"So I'm all alone with a movie star. This is the first time that ever happened to me. I have a confession to make, though. I've never seen you on the screen. I recognized you from the ads, I guess. I don't go to the movies very much."

"Well, what do *you* do for a living? Maybe I don't buy what you sell, either."

"No, I don't guess you do. I'm a chemist with the Signal Oil Company."

"I buy oil," she said.

"Well, my job isn't the kind of oil you use. I'm supposed to be developing certain by-products."

"Whatever that means. Wouldn't you like to make a pass at me?"

"You mean it?" he said.

"Yes. If you don't, I'm liable to make a pass at you," she said. "Come on over and sit next to me."

"I don't get it," he said.

"Neither do I, but I don't care. I don't even care what you think of me. I'll never see you again, so it won't matter. But when the taxi comes, here, you give him this five-dollar bill and tell him you won't need him. That's him now. They're very prompt."

"You sure you want to go through with this?"

"Well, not if we start talking about it. Will you send the cab away?"

"Sure," he said. He went to the door and dismissed the taxi. "What about your mother?"

"My room's in a different part of the house. We can go back there now." She stood up and he embraced her, and they knew quite simply that they wanted each other. "See? You did want to make a pass at me."

"Sure I did, but I wouldn't have," he said.

"Well, I would have," she said. "Come on."

They went to her room and he stayed until eleven o'clock. "I wish you didn't have to go, but I have to be up at five o'clock. And I guess you'll probably want to phone your wife. Do you phone her every night?"

"Just about."

"Well, tell her you didn't phone her earlier because you were in bed with a movie star."

"Shall I say who?"

"No, maybe you better not. You're going to have to tell her about the accident, and that's the first thing she'll think of, is what happened after the accident. Do you realize something?"

"What?"

"You're never going to be able to mention my name again without her thinking you did go to bed with me. That's always going to be in the back of her mind."

"No."

"Yes. Believe me. That's what I'd think, and that's what she's going to think. That maybe, *maybe* that night you had the accident and didn't phone her, *maybe* you spent the night with Natica Jackson."

"I don't know but that you could be right," he said. "You have her figured out pretty well, for somebody that never saw her."

"That's because I think I know the kind of a girl you'd be married to. Did she ever know you were untrue to her?"

"Well, there was only one other time and that was in Houston, Texas."

"But I'll bet she watches you like a hawk."

"Yes, she's inclined to be jealous."

"And so are you."

"Yes, I guess I am," he said.

"Well, Hal Graham, I guess it's time you went home," she said. "I'll call you another cab." She did so.

"Where is your mother now?" he said.

"My mother? I guess she's in her room. Why?"

"I just wondered," he said. "You know, she'd think it was strange if she was sitting out there in the livingroom and I walked by."

"Well, she might," said Natica. "It doesn't happen all the time."

"That's what I meant."

"Don't get me wrong. It does happen. But not all the time," said Natica. "That is, I don't have a strange man here every night."

"I could tell that," he said.

"How?"

"Oh—it's hard to say. But you know these things. This house is so quiet, I got the impression that it's always quiet, and you're lonesome. Lonely, I guess is the better word. I get an altogether different impression than I had before."

"Of how a movie star lives?"

"Yes."

"Yes. Well, of course some of them are married. Most of them are," she said. "But I never got that lonely, that I wanted to marry the kind of guy that wanted to marry me. I wouldn't marry an actor, even if I was in love with him. But if I didn't marry an actor, who else would I marry? Regular people don't understand the way we have to live. The only person for me to marry is a director. Then I wouldn't be always wondering whether he married me because I was a movie star, because I made a lot of money. I'd be willing to marry a big director, but they all have somebody. A wife or a girl friend. Or both. Or they're queer."

"You wouldn't marry a queer," he said.

"No, I guess not. Of course some of them are double-gaited, and some of the double-gaited ones are just as masculine as anybody."

"Do you speak from experience? You sound it," he said.

"Don't start asking me about my experiences. By tomorrow morning you'll be one of my experiences. And I'll be one of yours."

"The big one. Practically the only one. I don't know whether I'll be able to take it so casually."

"Yes you will. You will because you have to. Maybe not casually, offhand. But don't look at the dark side. Look on the bright side. From now on you'll be able to say to yourself, these movie stars are just like anyone else."

"The only trouble with that argument is I didn't think of you as a movie star. I never would have made a play for a movie star."

"You didn't have to. The movie star made a play for you."

"I had other girls make a play for me."

"But you didn't go to bed with them."

"Before I was married I did, but not after I was married. Except for the girl in Houston, Texas."

"And she was a whore," said Natica.

"No. She was the wife of a friend of mine."

"Oh, I thought she was some girl you met at one of those conventions."

"It was a convention, but I knew her before. She and her husband live there in Houston. He's another chemist. I went to Cal with him, and she was there at the same time, a couple classes behind us."

"Was she your girl at Cal?"

"No. I didn't have a girl at Cal, till senior year. The girl I married."

"Oh, so the one in Houston—"

"Was never my girl. But when I showed up at the convention and we all had a lot of drinks, that's all it was. Her husband passed out completely, and she said we ought to make up for lost time."

"Was he your best friend?" said Natica.

"No, just a friend. A fraternity brother. He was never my best friend. I don't have a *best* friend. I have guys I like to go fishing with, and others I work with at the lab, and there's two or three of us that play tennis together. But for instance I don't have anybody that I could tell what happened tonight, even if I thought they'd believe me. You're the first person I ever told about the girl in Houston."

"Then maybe I'm your best friend," she said.

He smiled. "Well, at least temporarily," he said.

"Did you ever stop to think that maybe we're both kidding ourselves?"

"How so?"

"About never seeing each other again," she said.

"Well, we oughtn't to," he said.

"You're weakening," she said.

He stared at the empty fireplace. "Possibly," he said.

"I've weakened already," she said. "I go by your house every day, twice a day, only a half a block away. Today I just happened to feel like turning off Motor Avenue into Marshall Road."

"Place. Marshall Place. Yes, you told me," he said.

"Why?" she said.

"Because you were tired of taking the same route every day. You told me."

"But I didn't say why, because I don't *know* why," she said. "Why did I turn off today instead of last week, when your wife was home? Why did you happen to be starting your car at the same exact moment that I came along? Why did you feel like going to Ralphs at just that exact moment? If you stopped to tie your shoe or change your necktie, you wouldn't have been in your car when I hit it. It would have been sitting there at the curbstone, and I would have driven right by your house."

"The laws of probability."

"I don't know what that means," she said.

"Oh, I was just thinking of probability and chance, in mathematics. There wouldn't be any way to work it out mathematically, that I know of. So it comes down to luck, which is beyond our comprehension. Good luck or bad luck, or a little of both."

"Mathe-*matics*?"

"I use mathematics in my work, quite a lot."

"I thought you were a chemist, with test tubes full of oil."

"Actually I'm a chemical engineer, in research. It saves time to say I'm a chemist, since nobody knows or cares what kind of work I'm doing. Not even my wife. She was an English major, and if I told her what I did at the lab on any given day, she wouldn't understand it any more than you would. Plus the fact that it's a team operation, with five other men working on it."

"You have five men working under you?"

"As a matter of fact, I have," he said. "But how did you know I was in charge?"

"Just guessed," she said. "Then you must be pretty important."

"I'll be pretty important if I get the right results."

"And rich?"

"Rich? Well, no, not rich, but I'll be set for life. I probably am anyway. That is, I'll always make a pretty good living."

"What do they pay you now?"

He laughed. "Well, if you must know, eighteen thousand a year."

"I guess that's a lot in your business," she said.

"It's a lot in any business except yours, and I don't consider movies a business."

"Money is money," she said. "They don't look at a ten-dollar bill and say, 'Oh, this is Signal Oil Company money. That's worth twice as much as Metro money.' "

"No, they don't. But what will you be earning twenty years from now?"

"Two hundred thousand dollars a year," she said.

"What?"

"That's what Morris King says."

"Who the hell is Morris King?"

"My agent, and a multye-millionaire."

"Well, I hope he's right, for your sake," he said.

"He usually is. He advanced my career from seventy-five a week to seventy-five thousand a year, and next year I get more, and the year after that and the year after that."

"A young girl like you making that much money."

"Shirley Temple makes more, and she's a lot younger," said Natica. "But I'm getting started, according to Morris."

"Is that what you want most? Money?"

"I know God damn well I never want to be without it," she said.

"What about love? A home? Children?"

"Yeah, what *about* love? And a home and children. You picked a fine time to ask."

"Yes, I did, didn't I?"

"You have a home and children, and I suppose you love your wife, but you're still not satisfied."

"No, I guess I'm not," he said.

"Well? What do *you* want most?" she said. "Not money."

"No, not money for its own sake. I want to do certain things in my work, and I guess that's uppermost. And have a nice home and educate my children."

"And every once in a while somebody like me," said Natica.

"Yes."

"But not too often," she said. "You'd like to have your home and children and someone like me, off to one side, and your work uppermost. That's funny, me in the same category with your wife and kids. That would get a laugh in Culver City. But I guess that's the way most men would like to have it, and that's why I don't get married. I'm too independent, I guess."

"Maybe," he said.

"But I'm not independent," she said. "I have to get up at five o'clock in the morning and drive to Culver City. I'll toot my horn when I'm passing your house."

"You'd better have them check your alignment. You hit my car just hard enough to knock yours out of line."

"No, I think I'll just trade mine in on a new LaSalle. So the next time I run into you I'll have a new car. How early do you have to get up?"

"Oh, generally around seven," he said.

"You'll sleep soundly tonight," she said.

"I'll say I will."

"So will I," she said. "Be funny if all we got out of this experience was a good night's sleep for both of us. But don't count on it."

"I won't. What you started to say about if I stopped to tie my shoe, or put on a different necktie. We got sidetracked, but there's something in it."

She scribbled on a piece of paper. "Here. This is the number of my dressing-room. It's private, doesn't go through the Metro switchboard. If I don't answer it'll be my maid, but don't tell her anything. She gossips plenty about other girls she worked for, so she's sure to gossip about me. Tell her Mr. Marshall called, and I'll know who it was."

"I'll give you my number at the office," he said.

"No, I don't want to know it. You think it over, and if you want to see me again, call me up. But think it over first. You have the most to lose. Besides, *I* may not want to see *you*. But don't count on that, either."

"What's a good time to phone you?" he said.

"You have to keep trying. I never know when I'll be in my dressing-room or on the set." She looked at him, standing with his hand on the doorknob.

"What are you thinking?" he said.

"Wondering," she said. "But not really wondering. I know."

"So do I," he said.

"Left, and then straight down the hall," she said.

She heard the taxi pulling away. She reached out her hand to the table beside her bed and picked up a typescript, opened it to the next day's scene. "No," she said aloud and replaced the script and turned out the light.

At half past five the next morning she left her house, went down Sunset Boulevard, turned in at Beverly Glen and across to Pico and from Pico to Motor Avenue. She slowed down when she came to Marshall Place. She turned right and moved along in second gear. His car was at the curb. The left door and the running board had been given quite a banging. She looked up at the second-story windows. Two of them were wide open. His bedroom, without a doubt. He was sleeping there, and without a doubt he was sleeping heavily. If she tooted her horn she would wake up the whole neighborhood. She did not mind waking up the whole neighborhood, but it would be cruel mean to wake him. And so she kept going, through Marshall Place to the other end where it led into Motor Avenue, and ten minutes later she was on the Metro lot.

The early workers were already at their tasks and Natica Jackson was soon at hers, which began with the arrival of the young man from Makeup. "Somebody didn't get enough sleep last night," he said.

"You're so clever," said Natica.

"Oh, it's not bad," he said. "Not hopelessly bad. You're young. Not like some of these hags I have to bring to life again. Actually I love to work on you, Miss Jackson, especially around your eyes. But get your eight hours, always try to get your eight hours. And here's some of those drops for when you start shooting. Remember now, don't put them in your eyes till you're ready to shoot, and use them sparingly. They're very strong, and I don't want you to get used to them." He prattled on, and his prattling and professional ministrations returned her to her movie-actress world, and she stayed there all day. Lunch was brought to her in her dressing-room. She would read the gossip columns in the newspapers and the trade papers. She was visited by a man who owned a chain of theaters in New England, who was being given a tour of the studio. He wanted her *personal* autograph and not just one of those printed things that meant nothing. She asked him if he would care for a sandwich or something, but he thanked her and said he was having lunch with William Powell and Myrna Loy. She resumed eating her lunch and was interrupted by a girl from Publicity who wanted her to give an interview to the Hollywood correspondent of some paper in Madrid. "Don't do it if you don't feel like it," said the publicity girl. "But if you do, make sure you don't get alone with him. He's a knee-grabber." A stout man with a cigar tapped twice on her screendoor and pushed it open. "May I come in? Jason Margold, from New York City. I see you're eating gyour lunch," he said. "Would you rather I came back in ten-fifteen minutes?"

"Who did you say you were?"

"Jason Margold, from New York City. But I don' wanna disturb you while you're—I see you got a preference for cottage cheese. You know what's good with cottage cheese? Try a little Major Grey's chutney."

"What's this all about? Who are you?"

"My card," he said. "My business card."

She read it aloud. "Jason Margold, vice-president, Novelty Creations, New York, London, Paris. So what?"

He removed the day's newspapers from a folding chair, placed them on the floor, and seated himself. "You mind the cigah?"

"Quit stalling around, will you?" she said.

"I won't take but a minute of your time, Miss Jackson," he said. "It jus' happened I said to Jerry Lockman, I said who in his opinion was the real coming star on the Metro-Goldwyn lot."

"Oh, you know Jerry Lockman?"

"Jerry jus' happens to be my brother-in-law, once-removed. His sister, the former Sylvia Lockman, is still married to George Stern. George used to be married to my sister Evie till she passed away of heart trouble several years ago."

"And?"

"So I asked Jerry, who was the young star that they were banking on the most here at Metro-Goldwyn. And without a moment's hesitation he named you. Miss Natica Jackson. So I said right away I wanted to have this talk with you for the purpose of sounding you out on this excellent proposition whereby, whereby we could work this out to our mutual advantage and profit."

"Is this a tie-in?"

"Well, you might call it a tie-in, but tie-in usually means a product gets tied in to a certain motion picture and like they run your picture in the ads and the actress never gets a nickel out of it, only the publicity for the motion picture. We'd be willing to pay you a royalty on every item we sold bearing your name."

"What is the item? A pessary?"

"Huh?"

"You're so God damn mysterious, I thought you didn't want to come out and say what it was."

"Well, it isn't anything like what you mentioned, Miss Jackson. It's an item of hand luggage that we expect to sell up in the millions."

"If I got five cents on every pessary I'd make a lot of money, too. The Natica Jackson pessary."

"You got a sense of humor, I'll give you that," he said.

"I need it, in this business," said Natica. "Just a sec'." She dialed a number on the intra-studio telephone. "Me speak to Mr. Lockman. It's Natica Jackson."

"You checking on me?" said Margold.

"Hello, Jerry? This is my lunch-hour and I'm supposed to get some rest. What the hell do you mean sending some jerk relation of yours to my dressing-room? Come and get him out of here before I call the studio cops. That's *all*." She hung up daintily.

"Now*way*da minute. Why did you have to go and do that?" said Margold.

"Miss Garbo's dressing-room is down the way. Try *her*," said Natica Jackson.

"You din even listen to my proposition," said Margold.

"Screw, bum," she said. "Take a powder."

Margold left. It was fun to have Jerry Lockman in such an embarrassed position. She could imagine how he was stewing now, for fear that she would tell other executives about his brother-in-law once-removed. Let him stew. Let him roast in hell.

"The car's downstairs," said her maid.

It was an elderly Cadillac limousine, to take her to the back lot. "You ready to go? You got everything?" said Natica.

"I think I got everything," said the maid. "Two packs of Philip Morris, makeup box, your mules, two packs of Beech-Nut gum."

"Do you have the eye drops?"

"In the makeup box."

"We're off," said Natica. She was in a bathing suit and a bathrobe, ready for the scene on the back lot, in which she was to drive a motorboat a distance of forty feet. The scene had originally been written to take place in a diner, but it had been changed to give her an opportunity to wear the bathing suit. They had shot the scene five times that morning and it had never been right. They were afraid to expose her to the sun for more than a few minutes at a time. The last thing they wanted was for her to acquire a natural sunburn that would not match her body makeup. The shooting schedule called for a ballroom scene the next day, and two hundred extras had been hired for it, but if the fair skin of Natica Jackson was reddened by the sun in the motorboat scene, they would have to shoot around her. Moreover, the natural light changed at three o'clock in the afternoon, and if they didn't get the motorboat scene right before three they would have to come back and shoot it again sometime. The complications had nothing to do with the acting, but Natica was used to that. Acting was the last thing you did after everything else was ready, and you did that for two minutes at a time. Then they glued those two minuteses together until they had eighty minutes that made sense—and then they put you in another picture. She could not understand how people got an impression of you from this collection of two-minute, one-minute, thirty-second snatches, but they did, and if they liked you that was all that mattered. Of all the girls she had known in Santa Ana she was the only one who could say, "I'm going to get a new LaSalle," at eleven o'clock at night and be sure that it would be delivered to her the next afternoon. She was certainly the only Santa Ana girl who had been kissed by Robert Taylor, and Garbo had smiled at her. Life was funny.

They did the motorboat scene three times while the light was still right. The director rode back to Natica's dressing-room with her. "I think the second take'll be the one, but I won't know till I see the dailies," said the director. "Let me have a look at your nose."

"It feels all right," said Natica.

"Yeah, it looks all right," said the director. His name was Reggie Broderick and he had grown up in the business. He spoke the jargons of the camera and lighting crews, he knew or could improvise sight gags that were not in the script, and he loved to direct motion pictures. He was not quite an artist, but his pictures always displayed ironic touches that other directors admired. "You got a new fellow, Natica?" he said.

"Maybe," she said. "Why?"

"Maybe, meaning you're not sure he's going to be your fellow?" said Reggie Broderick.

"Something like that," she said.

"Well, that's all right," said Reggie. "But send him home early, in time to get your eight hours. It's a good thing we didn't have any close-ups today, or you'd have been a total loss."

"I'm sorry," she said.

"No harm done, but tonight go to bed early."

"Was it my eyes?" she said.

"It wasn't only your eyes. You went around all day with your buttons showing."

"My buttons? In a bathing suit?"

"Your nipples, dear," he said. "You were a woman fulfilled, today. You can hardly wait to get back to this guy, whoever he is. Which is all right, as long as you get your sleep."

"I never even thought about him, all day," she said.

"Subconsciously you never thought of anything else," he said.

"Well, maybe you have something there," she said.

"We only have twelve more days on this picture, kid. As a favor to me will you postpone any emotional crisis? Only twelve more days."

"You know what I said to him last night?" she said.

"No, I can't even *guess* what you said to him last night."

"We were talking about marriage—he's married. And I said the only kind of a guy that I ought to marry is a director. I wouldn't think of marrying an actor, and the only person I could think of marrying was a director."

"Well, I tell you what you do. You finish this picture for me and I'll marry you. Unless you had some other director in mind."

"I didn't even have *you* in mind," she said.

"I must be losing my grip," he said.

"You never showed any interest, that way," she said.

"That's because this is our first picture together," he said. "The next time we do one, I'll see to it that we have a couple weeks on location. Where would you like to go? Don't say Catalina. That's too near. How about the High Sierras?"

"Why does it have to be on location?"

"Because I have to go home at night otherwise," he said.

"Oh, this wasn't going to be marriage," she said.

"I thought we got away from marriage," he said.

"I'm back to it," she said. "I think you ought to marry me and see that I get to bed early."

"Or vice versa. But meanwhile what about this guy that kept you up last night? What do we do about him?"

"That's going to be a problem," she said.

"Who is he? Can you tell me? I'm not butting in, but you went serious on me all of a sudden. How is he going to be a problem?"

"I guess I *was* thinking about him all day, subconsciously. I expected him to phone me, and he didn't," she said.

"He might have phoned while there was nobody here," he said.

She shook her head. "I expected him to keep trying. I was here all during the lunch break, and my phone never rang. And we've been sitting here over half an hour."

"And there's some reason why you can't phone him," he said.

"I told him I wouldn't. That he had to phone me. I don't even know his number. I know where to reach him, but I told him I wasn't going to try, that it was up to him."

"Are you going to sit here all evening in case he does phone? I don't think that's such a good idea."

"No, if he hasn't phoned me by this time, he isn't going to," she said.

"How would you like to come home and take pot-luck with the Brodericks? Mona's a great fan of yours. If you don't mind eating dinner with two small boys, aged seven and ten."

"I can't figure you, Reggie," she said. "Are you a family man, or aren't you?"

"I'm a family man," he said.

"And a Catholic, I guess, with that name."

"A family man and a Catholic," he said. "But I've had some things to tell in confession. And not just eating meat on Friday."

"Then why didn't you go for me?"

"I don't always go for the girls in my pictures. Not even most of the time. Very seldom, in fact. It interferes with the work, and this is my job."

"But you like me. I can tell that. You've been nicer to me than any director I ever worked with," she said.

"Yes, I like you. I asked to do this picture, you know. They had me down for something else, but I wanted to work with you."

"Who was in the other picture?" she said.

"A prima donna. Somebody I never worked with, but I heard all about her from another director. And *she* wanted *me*. The studio got a little tough when I said I wanted to do this picture and not hers. They would have put me on suspension if they hadn't been afraid of the bad publicity. Not the bad publicity for me. They didn't give a damn about that. But it would have got out that I preferred working with you, and that would have given her a black eye. So they told her I was off on one of my benders and wouldn't be in shape by the starting date of her picture."

"Were you off on a bender?"

"No, but I'd have gone on one," he said.

"Why did you want to work with me?"

"Because so far all they've done is photograph you. I looked at every picture you ever made, including one dog you made at Warner's."

"And was that ever a dog!" she said.

"Then I saw you in a dumb musical they made here, and a comedy Jerry Lockman produced. You used to be his girl."

"Yes."

"I can understand why you gave him the air. They've never known what to do with you around here. This picture we're doing now. It isn't the greatest thing in the world for you, but I've made a good try with it. It's a common-ordinary program picture that'll make some money, but the pleasure I get out of it is what it'll do for you, and therefore for me. You're going to be surprised when you see this picture. How much have you seen?"

"Most of the footage that I'm in, but that's all," she said.

"Well, there's a lot more to the picture than that. By this time I can pretty well visualize the whole thing, the final cut. From now on you can figure to be in pictures the rest of your life. You have a career."

"I thought I *had* a career," she said.

"Two years? Three years? You'd be surprised how many women had two or three years at a big studio, and then disappeared. I don't mean disappeared to Republic. I mean disappeared entirely. And you never quite know why. They brought a girl out from New York. She was beautiful, she could act. She'd been a hit in two big plays on Broadway, and they signed her to a contract that was something fantastic. Five thousand a week. They gave her a deal that was absolutely unheard of for somebody that'd never been before a camera, but they wanted her. Do you know where she is now? She's back in New York, living in a hotel and waiting for Hollywood to come to their senses. She was in exactly two pictures. The first was one of the most expensive pictures they ever made here. The story costs alone amounted to over two hundred thousand dollars. A top director. An expensive cast. The works. And it wasn't bad. It really wasn't a bad picture. But nobody went to see it. The people didn't care whether this girl had a Broadway reputation, or how many writers worked on the picture. They couldn't knock her looks. She photographed beautifully, and she had a good voice. *I* couldn't figure out why the picture laid such an egg. Then I happened to be in New York about a year ago and I was having lunch at the Algonquin and this girl came in. I never knew her when she was in pictures, and I asked the guy I was having lunch with what she was doing. The guy was a playwright, knew all the Broadway crowd, and when I asked him about this dame he said— as if I was supposed to know—he said she had a new girl friend. She was a Lez. I'd never known that, and I don't think most people in Hollywood knew it. But do you know who did know it? Those people that pay to go to see movies. Most of them have never heard of the word Lesbian. Wouldn't know what I was talking about if I said some actress was a Lez. But they knew something was wrong, something was missing. Some warmth that wasn't there. As soon as I got back to the Coast I ran that picture, and there it was. But only after I'd been told. I called up the director, a friend of mine, and asked him about this dame. I put it to him straight. Did he know she was a Lez when he was working with her? He said no, never suspected it for one minute. He knew there was something lacking, but he blamed himself. He never knew about her till after she washed up in pictures, and then some New York actress told him."

"You should have asked me," said Natica.

"You know who I'm talking about?"

"Sure. Elysia Tisbury."

"Now how did you know? A high school kid from Santa Ana?"

"My feminine instinct," said Natica.

"No, I won't buy that. No."

"Well, I was given a hint," said Natica. "She used to go out with Alan Hildred."

"Oh, your English boy friend. So she did. So she did."

"But that doesn't mean I'm that way," said Natica.

"You know, if I ever found out that you were, I think I'd start wondering about myself," he said. "You're about the last person in the world I'd ever think that about."

"Ooh, but when I get to be a big star," she said.

"You're planning to turn Lez?"

"I'm thinking of it," she said. "Alan says I'm terribly unsophisticated."

"Well, he's not."

"I know. He tries to sophisticate me."

"A guy like that could sophisticate you right out of pictures. Or would, if you didn't have so much common sense."

"Well, I'll say this for Alan. He's fun to be with. Not all the time. But I never knew anybody like him in Santa Ana. There isn't anybody like him in Santa Ana."

"There aren't very many like him in Hollywood," he said.

"You don't like him, but you're not a woman. If I was just one of those girls I went to high school with, I never would have understood a person like Alan. All they ever wanted was to marry a boy that had a father that owned a bank or something. That wasn't what I wanted. I wasn't even sure what I did want till I got this offer from Hollywood. Then I knew what I wanted, all right."

"What?"

"To have every big star know who I was," she said. "Not for me to know every big star. But every big star to know me."

"Well, they just about do," he said.

"G.G. spoke to me one day. Not exactly spoke to me, but nodded her head and smiled. I think she knows me now."

"All right. What's next?"

"To have my name in lights on the Statue of Liberty."

"That seems reasonable enough," he said. "Then what?"

"After that? Well, maybe a statue of me there."

"That'll probably happen. The Goddess of Liberty doesn't look very American, and you do. After that, what?"

"You know Joan of Arc?"

"Not personally."

"I'd like to be something like her," she said.

"You don't want to be barbecued."

"No, I guess I wouldn't go for that part. Who were some of the other famous women?"

"Cleopatra, but she got a snake to bite her right on the teat."

"No. Who else? Queen Elizabeth."

"Too late. She was known as the virgin queen."

"Do you think she really was? How old was she?"

"You can forget her. She wasn't very pretty. Mata Hari, but she got shot."

"It'd be fun to be a spy, but if I was famous I couldn't be a very good spy. They all seem to get in some jam. Martha Washington, but they only know about her through George."

"And Lincoln's wife went off her rocker," he said.

"My trouble is, I'm not very glamorous. You can be famous without being glamorous. I'm pretty famous now, I guess, but people think they know all about me. America's niece, is what Alan calls me."

"You'll be more than that when we finish this picture."

"But not glamorous."

"No, but not all sweetness and light, for a change. The sexiest shot of you, you're wearing that housedress. I hope it gets by."

"I know which one that is. That was what you had the windmachine for. Where I'm standing on the roof."

"That's the one. Better than a skin-tight bathing suit. You should have heard them in the projection room when they saw that shot."

"What did they say?"

"They said, 'Wow!' And they meant every word of it," he said. "Tomorrow they'll see you in a bathing suit and it won't mean a thing. But in that housedress, with the wind against you, you might as well have been soaking wet. But at the Hays Office they watch out for dames in soaking-wet dresses. This way I may sneak it by them."

"Was Jerry Lockman at the rushes?"

"Jerry Lockman? Jerry Lockman, the way he stands now, couldn't get in a projection room if he paid admission. You don't keep up with your old boy friends. I hear they offered him the job of producing travelogs, and if he's smart he'll take it. They've gone sour on him."

"Oh dear. Why?"

"You never know the real reason."

"Maybe the public found out that he's a Lez," she said.

"You may be kidding, but the things that turn the big shots against a man make just about as much sense. You and I, what they call the talent people, we tend to overlook the fact that our jealousies are nothing compared to what goes on among the big shots. Now Jerry Lockman, for instance. He more or less discovered you, with a little help from Morris King. So Jerry was instrumental in helping your career. Fine. But there are fifteen other supervisors on the lot that *didn't* discover you. Every single one of them thinks that's a black mark against *him*. So there are fifteen supervisors, or associate producers, or whatever they want to call themselves, that automatically hate Jerry. One of them happens to be Joe Gelber, the man that's producing our picture. He particularly hates Jerry because you were Jerry's discovery, so Joe has to go after Jerry hammer and tongs. Joe absolutely has to see to it that Jerry gets none of the credit if our picture turns out well. Which it will, don't worry about that. It'll make nice money. But Jerry Lockman musn't be able to claim that he had even a tiny pinch of the credit for you. For the last six months, ever since Joe Gelber was assigned to this picture, he's had to put the knock on Jerry Lockman. Not only where you're concerned, but in every direction you can think of. I've heard him. He'll make fun of his clothes. Drops little jokes about his sex life. I heard him say it was very odd, very strange that Jerry went abroad on the *Europa* a couple years ago."

"What's wrong with that? I remember that," said Natica.

"The *Europa*? That's one of Hitler's boats. In case you're thinking of taking a trip abroad, young lady, don't book passage on the *Europa* or the *Bremen*. Not while you're under contract here. Hitler isn't very popular in Hollywood."

"Oh, *Hitler*. He's against the Jews," said Natica.

"Hitler's against the Jews, that's right."

"But Jerry's a Jew," she said.

"Sure he is. But what kind of a Jew will travel in a boat owned by Hitler? Every opportunity Joe gets, he puts the rap on Jerry. And when a guy like Joe Gelber goes to work on somebody, he never loses his temper or says things that aren't true. He'll point out a hundred little faults that nobody ever noticed before, or that never bothered anybody. Jerry Lockman's neckties are no worse than L. B. Mayer's. But if you keep hammering away, calling attention to any man's shortcomings, you can finally get somewhere. And Joe Gelber has finally done a job on Jerry Lockman."

"Isn't it childish?"

"Yes. Childish and vicious. And it's exactly what Jerry would have done to Joe Gelber if he'd had the chance."

"You bet he would," said Natica. "A phony intellectual is what Jerry used to call him."

"If there's anything intellectual about Joe Gelber, it sure is phony."

"I wouldn't know," she said. "He has all those books in his office. I wondered when he got time to read them, but I didn't say anything."

"Well, he's on my side now. And yours. By the way, why did you ask me if Jerry was at the rushes?"

"I was wondering what he'd say when they all said 'Wow.' He would have been the only one that knew what was underneath that dress."

"Would you care what he said?"

She hesitated. "I guess I wouldn't," she said. "Not any more. A few years ago I would have. But you know I discovered something. When a man and a woman have something peculiar about their sex life, people always laugh at the man. They make fun of the man, but not of the woman. Have you ever noticed?"

"I never thought of it before, but you may be right."

"Do you know why that is?" she said.

"No. I'd have to think about it."

"It's because men aren't supposed to be that much interested in sex. They should be more busy with their work and stuff. Sex is all right for women, but men ought to have it and forget about it."

"To rise supremely above it?" he said.

"I'm serious! A man that thinks about sex all the time, like Jerry, or Alan Hildred, I think he ought to have something else to think about."

"You're just restating an old poetic theory. 'Man's love is of his life a thing apart, 'tis woman's whole existance.' "

"Yes, we had that in high school," she said. "But look at the way a woman is constructed. She's built for sex. And a man—well, a man only partly. You never saw anybody put a brazeer on a man. Except at a drag. And even a drag! What do they do at a drag? They dress up like women."

"Do you really like sex, Natica?"

"I love it, but I'm a woman. I don't think men ought to like it so much. And yet every man I ever slept with does. Except that son of a bitch that didn't call me all day. Never gave me a jingle. And I know why. I was the one that made the first pass."

"Make a pass at *me*, dear heart, and *I'll* phone you tomorrow," he said.

"You know, I almost would. If we were at my house I would, but not here. Even in Jerry's office, when he'd lock the door and shut off the phone, I never felt right about it." She looked around her dressingroom, and shook her head. "Just a lousy chaise-lounge."

"For purity," he said. "Well, how about coming home and having dinner with us?"

"I just remembered. I'm supposed to have a brand-new LaSalle waiting for me." She dialed a studio number. "This is Miss Jackson. Natica Jackson. Do you have a car there for me? You have? How does it look? Does it have white-walls? Fine. Thank you. Okey-doke." She hung up.

"It's there?" he said.

"It's been there since early this afternoon. I'm glad. I loved my Packard, but I'm glad I don't have to see it again. Once I make up my mind to get rid of a thing, I don't care to see it any more. I wish I could be the same way about people."

"Who says you're not?" he said.

"It's not as easy with people," she said. "I'll give you the first ride in my new car."

"And have dinner with us?"

"I'd love to," she said.

"Let me call Transportation and I'll have somebody drive my car home, and maybe I ought to tell Mona you're coming. She won't want to have her hair up in curlers when you arrive."

"I won't mind."

"A figure of speech. I've never seen her hair up in curlers."

On the walk to the parking lot she was always half a step ahead of him. They admired the new car from all sides, and the parking attendant showed her the starting and lighting controls.

"Well, off we go," she said. Darkness had come.

She was a good driver and was taking pleasure in her new car. "Your new pony cart," he said.

"I never had one," she said.

"Hey! Straight ahead," he said. "Pico is straight ahead."

"This is Marshall Place, where I had my accident yesterday," she said. She had slowed down.

"Oh."

"He lives at Number 88. There, on the right. And there's his car. See the door, where I hit him? House all lit up. Maybe his wife came home unexpectedly. And maybe I'm just making excuses for him." She blew her horn, held her hand on the button, and drove away. "Well, so long to you, Mr. Hal Graham."

"He isn't one of our people," said Reggie Broderick. "Don't lose any sleep over him."

"Oh, you just don't want me to lose any sleep," she said.

They went to Broderick's house in Beverly Hills, and she was affable. The Broderick sons were delighted with her, the Broderick wife—after one hard look—was friendly. Natica gave the boys a ride in her new car (they chose to sit in the rumble seat), and when she brought them home again she did not get out of the car. She said goodnight to all the Brodericks and went home to Bel-Air. She lay in her warm, perfumed bath and wondered what the hell.

They finished the picture a day ahead of schedule, and Natica went away with Alan Hildred, to a borrowed cottage at a place called San Juan Capistrano. The water was too cold for her to swim in but Alan went in three or four times a day. They observed silences. He would take a pipe and book and be self-sufficient until mealtime, sitting in the sand close enough to hear if she called him. She slept late every morning, had breakfast of orange juice, toast and coffee; read the newspapers until lunchtime. After lunch she would read magazines and detective stories until sleep overtook her. She would nap for an hour, have coffee, and do some telephoning and letter-writing, and then it would be time for cocktails. He would have five, she would have two Martinis, and then dinner. The owners of the house, California friends of Alan's, had left behind an assortment of phonograph records as heterogeneous as the books on the shelves. Some good, some bad, and some cracked. At eleven o'clock, never later, she would go to bed and Alan would come in and make love to her, and for her it was a combination of sensation and detached remote observation. So it went for four days, as pleasant a stretch of time as she had ever known. On the fifth afternoon she went out and lay, belly-down, on the sand beside him. "Do you want to go home?" she said.

He took the pipe out of his mouth. "I suppose it's time we were thinking about it. Are you getting restless?"

"I could stay here forever, just like this," she said.

"Oh, really? I know *I* couldn't. I've got to think about making some money. So have you, for that matter. Don't they expect you for fittings next week?"

"Tuesday," she said. "Oh, I'm not kidding myself. I'm not rich enough to stop working, and I wouldn't want to anyhow. But I've been so relaxed, Alan. That was you. I never knew anybody that was so relaxing. You can just sit and read, and smoke your pipe, off by yourself, and be perfectly content."

"You didn't know that side of me," he said.

"How would I? I guess I never knew you till now," she said. "Were you ever married, Alan?"

"Oh, yes."

"You never mentioned your wife. I just took for granted you were always a bachelor."

"Oh, no, I had a wife. Would you like to hear about it?"

"I'm dying to," she said.

"Well, it isn't much of a story, actually," he said. He sat cross-legged, tailor-fashion, and ran sand through his hands. "I'm older than you think."

"I was sure you were older than you look."

"Mm, thanks. I'm thirty-seven."

"You had to be, to've been to all the places you've been to," she said.

"Well, in some of them I didn't stop very long." He laughed. "In one place they wouldn't even let me land. Apparently my reputation had preceded me."

"What were you then? Were you a writer then, too?"

"Not, uh, recognized as such. I'd written a very bad novel, but I believe it stopped selling at two hundred copies. It was reviewed in a Yorkshire paper, and a pal of mine mentioned it in *Sketch*. No, I wasn't a writer. Various other things, but not a writer. Odd jobs, some of them very odd indeed."

"How did you meet your wife?"

"That was just after the war. I'd been in it, and I was still wearing His Majesty's uniform. I had a week or two to go before I was required to get back into cits, and I took every advantage of that situation. There were a great many parties in London, and crashing them wasn't at all difficult. I was, let me see, twenty-two. Been to a *fairly* good public school. Had two pips on my shoulder straps, and I'd acquired the M.C., the Military Cross. By purchase. It made all the difference, you know. No one asked how I got it, but they'd look at the ribbon and nod approvingly and *compel* me to drink some more champagne. It was too good to last, and I was only too well aware of that fact. Consequently, when I was introduced to Miss Nellie Ridgeway, the soubrette, who'd just been divorced from one of our more solvent bookmakers, I confessed to an undying devotion to her. There was some truth to that. I'd seen her in one or two shows, and I remembered one of her best songs. 'You and I in Love,' it was called. She was forty. Or she may have been forty-two. Perhaps a trifle thick through the middle, and not too firm up above, but the legs were good. Well, she consented to be my bride. Her money was unfortunately tied up in real estate holdings, not easily converted to cash, and I had one hell of a time getting my hands on any of it. She gave me ten quid a week, pocket money, but out of that I had to pay her cab fares and odds and ends, and she was extremely disagreeable because she didn't have a show that season and was having to spend her non-theatrical income. Actually, she was quite a chiseler, as so many actresses are apt to be. Always economizing on food and drink unless it was for show. A great one for professional discounts, too, and my tailor didn't give professional discounts."

"Was she good in the hay?"

"In a word, no. But insatiable. Stingy women are apt to be, I've found."

"So you divorced her."

"I left her. I took a few things. Her best gewgaws were locked up in a safe to which I didn't have the combination, but I realized about a thousand pounds on cigarette cases and vanities and that sort of thing, and off I went. I left a note, saying I was going to Scotland to try to think things out and do some writing, and she'd hear from me soon. That gave me time to board a rusty old tub that was bound for South Africa. Very astute of me. Naturally she didn't quite believe the Scotland story, but expected me to head straight for the French Riviera. I wasn't the tramp steamer type, and certainly not the South Africa type. I was one of the Mayfair boys, or so she thought. I'd never given her any reason to think otherwise."

"How long were you married?"

"How long did we live together? Less than a year. We were never divorced. She died while I was on tour with the Miller Brothers-101 Ranch Circus. I read about it in the newspapers."

"What were you doing with the circus?"

"I was a Cossack."

"Could you ride?"

"Of course I could ride. I could do all those things. My father was a very keen sportsman, and as I was the only son amongst five daughters, I had a vigorous boyhood. Riding. Boxing. Shooting. Fishing. Not to mention the defense of my chastity against the onslaughts of the elder sisters. A nasty pair, they were. The English public school has a lot to answer for, but the upper middle-class English home such as mine, with five daughters and one rather pretty son—between the two I'll take the public school. It's possible to buy off an older boy with money or sweets, but two predatory older sisters are unbribable."

"Oh, well that's not just England. There was a girl on our street that had her little brother a nervous wreck, and her parents never caught on. Did you ever get married again?"

"No. The other side of me, that you've seen these past few days, has kept me from marriage or any similar involvement. I must have my privacy."

"Is that the way you pronounce it? You make it sound like an outdoor toilet. A Chic Sales. I say pry-vacy."

"Very well."

"What would you think of marrying me?" she said.

"Is that a proposal of marriage? I'd like you to state it more unequivocally."

"You mean lay it on the line? All right. Would you marry me?"

"Thank you very much, but no," he said. "I only wanted you to say it so it could go in my memoirs. October the somethingth, 1934. Received proposal of marriage from lovely young movie star. Why would you want to marry me, Natica? You know I've pimped and buggered my way around the world all these years. I know you're a lonesome kid, dissatisfied. But don't for heaven's sake get yourself into anything like that."

"If I didn't like it, I could get out of it," she said.

He lit a cigarette. "May I offer two bits' worth of advice?"

"Sure," she said.

"Don't marry before you're fifty," he said.

"Fifty?"

"Take lovers, and make a lot of money, but don't marry. It'll only complicate your life, and it isn't as if you had to prove something by getting a husband. That presents no problem."

"You're wrong. No one ever asked me to marry him."

"Well, that's a quibble, isn't it? You could have a husband if you liked. These few days down here have been pleasant for both of us. But they're only a holiday, and you can take a holiday when you feel like. Not always in such charming company, it's true, but the charming company can also be very difficult." He looked away. "I might bring a friend home with me. And he might be hard to get rid of. That *has* happened, you know."

"Oh."

"I can't help it, Natica," he said. "I seem to have a limited capacity for feminine companionship, and then I turn to someone of my own sex. Isn't that putting it delicately?"

"You get tired of girls, and then you go for the boys," she said.

"I was afraid you might put it more crudely, but I should have known better," he said. "You don't seem to mind."

"I never said I didn't mind, but it was sort of none of my business."

"Well, of course it wasn't, was it?" he said. "The Kings, or at least Ernestine King, made it worth my while to officiate as your gentleman-in-waiting. Unhappily, as I made more money, I spent more. Old friends turned up that I hadn't seen in years. One of them came to stay, or so he thought."

"How did you get rid of him? How do you get rid of people like that?"

"In this case, I took him for a ride. A modification of the Chicago gangster method. We drove up beyond Oxnard and I stopped the car on the roadside. It was late evening, and I daresay I'd given him the impression that I had romantic notions. But I got out of the car and pulled him out, and my old boxing lessons stood me in stood stead."

"You beat him?"

"Unmercifully," he said. "A boy for whom I'd once had a feeling of real tenderness. I couldn't stop punishing him. When he could no longer stand up, I gave him my boot. I left him there. What ugliness."

"Well, I guess he asked for it," she said.

"Oh, yes," he said. "He was no rose."

"That's another side of you I never saw," she said.

"And I hope you never do." He got to his feet and peeled off his sweatshirt. He was a slender man, with overdeveloped biceps and forearms that seemed to have been attached to the wrong torso. He walked slowly to the water and stood at knee depth, and when he was good and ready he dived in and swam out a long distance. She had seen him do that before, and the first time she was frightened, but when he returned, and she told him he had scared her, he had only smiled and said, "That's one thing I *can* do, my dear." Now she could see him, doing the dead man's float, and she was not worried about his ability to get back. But she knew with sudden clarity that one day—and it could be soon—he would not want to come back. He was—what was he? Thirty-seven—and ageless. He got older, because we all get older by the day, but he already spoke of his life, the events of his life, as though they had no relation to the present. An end had been put to his life, and the thing that had put an end to it was not an occurrence, a nasty event or a tragic occurrence, but simply the exhaustion of his will to live. She had never known anyone who caused her to think such thoughts. Everyone else spoke of things to come, for them, for her. But for Alan Hildred she had always been dimly aware that it was all over, and that she had forced or demanded the continuation of his existence. She had often put him aside, but she had always picked up with him again, and during this stretch of peace she had reached a state that she wanted to prolong by a marriage that could only be prolonged under precisely the conditions of these five days. If, this minute, he came out of the water and said he would marry her, she would go through with it. But the man floating in the troughs of the waves was going to stay there. He had tried to tell her that he was empty of desire for her, and it did not really matter now where he went next. She would let him go, and she would not ask him to come back.

She rose from the sand and returned to the house and took a bath. She put on a suit of lounging pajamas and went to the sitting-room, and presently he appeared, dressed in his blue blazer and slacks and rope-soled espadrilles. He had a scarf at his neck.

"Martini time?" he said.

"Sure," she said.

"It's a bit early, but the gin may warm me up," he said. "Besides, I have a rather important announcement to make."

"What's that?" she said.

"I'm leaving Hollywood," he said. He stirred the drinks and poured them.

"For good?"

"If you mean permanently, yes." He sipped his drink and obviously he was in a good mood. "I arrived here, in Hollywood, with something under two hundred dollars. I'm leaving with just under twenty thousand. I call that a successful sojourn, especially as the money was paid me for services rendered. Nothing illegal about it. They gave me twenty-five thousand apiece for the stories they bought for you, and they paid me to work on the scenarios. But it isn't going to last forever, is it? I imagine I could find someone a great deal less attractive than you to squire about, but you've spoiled me for the Nellie Ridgeway types. And I'm afraid the time has come when you're ready to give me my walking papers."

"What made you think that?"

"Your proposal of marriage, oddly enough. As I was lying out there in the deep blue sea, I asked myself what was behind your proposal. The good time we've had this week, obviously. But you've got to be back in town Tuesday next, and this relationship will never again seem as pleasant to you as it's been here. You had a premonition of that, too. I'm very happy to've made you at all happy, Natica, and in these four or five days I have given you some happiness, if that's not too big a word."

"Yes, you have," she said.

"Then forgive me if I desert you before you give me the air," he said.

"All right," she said. "You're under no obligations to me."

"Sensible girl," he said. "Extraordinarily sensible girl."

"Where will you go?"

"Sensible girl, asks the sensible question, too. I'm going home to England. I've been naughty, but my peccadillos have been committed in far-off lands. There's no one back home who's apt to turn me in for stealing Miss Ridgeway's gold lighters and ivory cigarette holders."

"And what will you do there?"

"Oh, we have a film industry in England, too, you know. And I have several imposing credits on Natica Jackson pictures. I shouldn't have too much trouble finding gainful, legitimate employment. And it's fifteen years since I've been home."

"Have you missed it?"

"Not in the beginning. But I don't want to die out here."

"Are you planing to die in England?" she said.

"Yes," he said. "And planning to is the word. My father cut me off when I married Miss Ridgeway, and all I'll have is the money I take back with me. I can live on that reasonably comfortably for four years without working in the films, without doing a tap. But I'm not going home to scrounge around or work as a dustman. I shall live at a certain scale, and when my money runs out, I'll shoot myself. Nothing terribly dramatic about that. Life isn't very dear to me anyhow. Look at mine. Look at me. Look what it's always been, and now I'm thirty-seven. Life has had its chance to be attractive to me, and I say it's failed dismally."

"I don't know whether you're joking or not," she said.

"I believe you know I'm *not* joking," he said. "I wish I could make love to you now, Natica, and have it mean much more than it ever has. But unfortunately all passion's spent. Will you accept that rather tired bouquet?"

"I accept it," she said.

"Will you also forgive me if I nip off first thing in the morning?"

"In whose car? You can't have mine."

"I'll hire one."

"I guess I might as well go too," she said. "I wouldn't want to stay here by myself."

"Splendid. Then let's get an early start, shall we?"

"Okay by me," she said.

They had dinner, and he drank more than usual. He finished the batch of Martinis, had sherry with his soup, and a Mexican red wine with his steak. He put a bottle of cognac at his side while he had coffee, and she saw that he was determined to get drunk. "I'm going to bed if we're getting up early," she said. "Did you tell Manuel we were leaving in the morning?"

"He's heartbroken," said Alan. "Rita's heartbroken, too, but not as much so as Manuel. He hopes we will come back many times and stay longer."

"Will you tip them in the morning?"

"Whatever you wish, my dear. I suggest twenty dollars, ten apiece."

"I'll give it to you in the morning," she said. "Goodnight."

In the morning her car was gone. Alan was gone, but his clothes had not been packed. She telephoned Morris King and had him send a Tanner Cadillac for her. When she arrived at Bel-Air her brand-new LaSalle was parked in her driveway, without a scratch on it. She never knew what Alan did with her car in the meanwhile. She never heard another word from him, ever, and neither did anyone else in picture business.

"I could fix it so he'd never get work at Gaumont-British," said Morris King.

"Why would you want to do that?" said Natica.

"I thought maybe you'd want me to," said Morris.

"What did he do to me? I wouldn't want to keep anyone out of a job."

"Well, he sort of humiliated you," said Morris.

"I think you got that idea from Ernestine," said Natica. "He sort of humiliated her, because he didn't turn out right. But I have nothing against him."

"Then okay, we'll forget him," said Morris. "You go in Tuesday for fittings, right?"

"Right," she said.

"I worked them for a $5000 bonus," said Morris.

"You did? Good for you, Morris."

"And it's all yours. No commission. That make you feel better?"

"Five hundred dollars better," she said.

"Buy yourself something nice with it, with my compliments. You can consider it my bonus for being a good girl. However, Natica, you gotta be ready to go on suspension after the next picture."

"I do? Why?"

"Because when this one's in the can, then I'm going after a new ticket. Tear up the present contract and write a new one for you. This they will not do without some cries of anguish, including they'll put you on suspension. They gotta do that, Natica. The suspension gimmick is something a studio gotta do to keep people in line. Not you, so much as other people. They'll make it look like it's costing you a lot of money to turn down your next picture, but you'll get the money back in the long grun.

That'll be taken care of. But I'm just forewarning gyou now, that this picture you work as hard as you ever worked in your whole life. Give them no cause for complaint, you see what I mean. Then they come around with a picture to follow this one and down we turn it. Flat. They turn around and say you don't work anywhere else, and so forth. Well, *we* know that. You're under contract to Metro, and you'll still owe them a couple more pictures under that contract. You can't work anywheres else. We know that. But in this business you strike while the iron is hot. I'm not waiting till they offer you a new contract, two pictures from now. I'm hitting them as soon as you finish this next one. They moan and wail, and they hit you with a suspension. But when they get done crying and threatening, I go in and talk to them and say who's the loser? And they know who's the loser. They are. You lose a few thousand dollars' salary on suspension, but it's big money if your suspension holds up a picture, and that's when New York starts calling gup. Straighten out that Jackson contract and quit futzing around, New York says."

"Well, I hope you're right," she said.

"Natalie, you're on the verge of—"

"Natica."

"Yeah, Natica. A slip of the tongue, when I get all enthused. Anyway, dear, we're gonna get you a contract that frankly you're not entitled to yet. Frankly, you're not. But we're only getting you what you'll be entitled to two or three years from now. I'm gonna fight to get you the kind of money they pay bigger stars than you are, but I'm doing it for a reason. You want to know what that reason is?"

"Sure."

"That reason is because your whole life is gonna be in pictures. Don't ever come to me and say get you out of a contract so you can do a Broadway play. If you do, you're gonna have to look for representation elsewhere. To me you are motion pictures and no place else. I don't want you to as much as walk on a Broadway stage. I don't want you monking around with Broadway."

"I'm not a stage actress. I know that," she said.

"You know it now, but these Broadway managers come out here and put the con on picture people. Art. The Theater. And all they do is stir up trouble. I got clients I *want* to go back and do a Broadway play every once in a while. *Let* them go back and take fifteen hundred a week or less. But that's for the actors and actresses that started on Broadway. I got all the confidence in the world in you, Natica, but I never want to see some Broadway critic take a crack at you because you're a movie star. You know why? Because I'll tell you why. Because I been going through the reviews of all your pictures since you were at Metro, and I never came across one single review that was a rap. Here and there they rap the picture, but never you. Everybody likes you. You. But some hundred-a-week guy on a New York paper is just liable to rap you because he don't like picture people."

"Well, that wouldn't kill me."

"Kill you, no. But out here they never saw a bad notice for you. They never *saw* one. And I don't want them to ever see one. But if some hundred-and-a-quarter critic on a New York paper raps you, the spell is broken, Natica. And we got a fortune at stake. Human nature is human nature, and once somebody takes a rap at you, others will follow suit. It's human nature, and I won't allow it. I got actors on my list that go back to Broadway, and if they get one good notice in some New York paper, it keeps them alive for a year. They come back here and work in pictures, make some money, and they start itching for Broadway again. So all right. They're not picture stars. They're Broadway people. You are a film star, and you stay that way."

"Morris?"

"What?"

"Is somebody trying to get me for Broadway?"

"Huh? What makes you ask that question at this particular time?"

"Are they?"

"Hell, there's always some manager wishing to capitalize on a picture reputation."

"What is it? A musical comedy, or a play without music?"

"You know, for a young girl that was never outside of the State of California, I have to hand it to you," he said. "Ernestine often said to me, she said one of these days you'd surprise me with how sharp you were."

"I learned it all from you, and Ernestine. You still haven't said what the offer was."

"A musical comedy," he said. "I told them to get lost. They wanted to pay you a thousand a week and no guarantee of any kind whatsoever. They wouldn't even guarantee me they'd open in New York. You could spend all that time in rehearsal, anywheres from three weeks to a couple months out of town, and they could close the show in Baltimore. I told them to get lost. Imagine you coming back here after closing a show on the road, and I go into L. B. Mayer's office and start telling him why you ought to have a new contract. It makes me positively sick to think of it."

"What did Ernestine say?"

"She was positively nauseous, the gall they have coming out here and making an offer like that. The guy said it was a chance to prove what you could really do. And Ernestine said to him right to his face, 'Fifty million people go to the movies every week, and they're all that much farther ahead of you, Mister.'"

"Mr. What?" said Natica.

"You want to know his name? It's a fellow named Jay Chase. If that name don't appeal to you he used to have another one when I knew him in the old days. But what the hell, I had a different name then myself, and Natica Jackson used to be Anna Jacobs if I'm not mistaken."

"Getting me off the subject of Jay Chase, Morris," she said.

"Yeah, I was. But I'll get you back on the subject I wanted to talk about. You and pictures. Natica, I see you—do you know what I see you as? I see you as like Garbo. Gable. Lionel Barrymore. Crawford. I see you as much a part of the Metro organization as Mr. Schenck. L. B. Mayer. The lion. Wally Beery. Them. Some of my clients I can never hope for such an arrangement, whereby they got a home lot and it's a regular second home to them. You think of Metro and automatically you think of Natica Jackson. You think of Natica Jackson and automatically you think of Metro. That's the way I want it to be, because that way you're set for life. I want that for you before you start getting married and maybe you marry a fellow that gets you all discontented. But if you got a permanent home lot, that much of your life is all taken care of."

"You want me to marry Metro."

"Exactly. Or Metro to marry you. I don't care how you put it."

"Some people say a star is better off independent," she said.

"Yeah, that's what they say. You hear that all the time, from actors that it don't look so good for their next option. You hear it from actors that the studio only wants them for one picture. You heat it from agents that can't land a contract for more than one picture. Yeah, a star is better off independent, once he got about two million stashed away and don't care if he never works. But that won't be you for another ten years or so. You're a working girl, Natica."

"That's the only thing you said so far that makes any sense to me. I'm a working girl," she said. "Morris, you and Ernestine stop filling me up with big talk. All of a sudden I'm not a kid any more. I was eighteen and got into pictures, and almost got out. Then you and Jerry Lockman and Joe Gelber and a half a dozen pictures, and this guy and that guy. And my folks sponging off of me, and I get overcharged in the stores. And nearly all the girls I went to high school with are married and started a family. And I'm nearly twenty-four years old. A woman. Not a girl any more. Sixty million girls would like to trade places with me, and I'd be one of them if I wasn't Natica Jackson. I'm lucky, and I know it. But one of these days don't be surprised if I blow my lid."

"You're entitled," he said.

"Just don't be surprised, that's all," she said.

"What are you thinking of doing?"

"I've been thinking of going after something *I* wanted, for a change."

"A fellow?"

"What else? I can buy nearly anything else," she said. "This one I couldn't buy."

"Oh, you got him picked out. Well, you talk to Ernestine and next week we'll take him to the fights. Is he—"

"Oh, no, Morris. You and Ernestine have to stay out of this."

"Who is the fellow? How did you conceal him from us?"

"You put your finger right on it," she said. "You and Ernestine and the studio have to know everything I do. But this was one time I got away with something. Imagine. I slept with a fellow, and you and Ernestine didn't know about it."

"When did you have time to?" he said.

"I get a kick out of this," she said. "I got you puzzled."

"Just don't get yourself into any trouble."

"I know. A fortune's at stake."

"And you want to be sure he's worth it. Don't do nothing you'll be sorry for."

"I sure will," she said. "I am already, but I didn't know how good that can feel. The only thing I *have* felt, these last couple of years."

"Married, this fellow?"

"The works. Married. A good job. Respectable."

"What does he get out of it? What good's it gonna do him?"

"Him? It may not do him any good at all," she said.

The new picture went into production and Natica Jackson was a dream to work with. Everybody said she was a dream to work with: the director, the other actors and actresses, the producer, the unit man from the publicity department, the script girl, the assistant director, the little people from Wardrobe and Makeup, the little people from Central Casting, the little people from Transportation. She had always been easy to work with, but now she was a dream. She was cooperative, tractable, patient, and cheerful; and she was punctual and always knew her lines. She was also good. There is in Hollywood a legendary tribute to a scene well played. It is that moment when a performer finishes a scene and the grips and the juicers burst out in spontaneous applause. It is a phony. It does not happen. But there is the real thing, which happens no more than once or twice in a dozen pictures. It is that moment when a performer has finished playing a scene, and for perhaps a count of three seconds no one on the set speaks. There is complete silence on the part of everyone who has been watching the scene. The silence is usually broken by the director, who says—and does not need to say—"We'll print that." Then all the people on the set go about their business once again, the better for having witnessed a minute-and-a-half of unrecapturable artistry. Natica had two such moments in the picture. One was during the scene in which she hears shots that she knows will kill her brother. The other was in a church pew, kneeling beside the gangster who she knows has killed him. In the one she blinks her eyes as though she were receiving the shots in her own body. In the other she is full of fear and loathing of her brother's murderer. Both were routine bits of screen writing, but they were redeemed by her potentially explosive underplaying. "This girl can go," said the director. "She can really go."

"Oh, she can go, all right," said Joe Gelber.

"Reggie Broderick told me she could go," said the director. "But you know how it is, Joe. One director can get it out of an actor, and the next director can't."

"You're getting it out of her, Andy," said Gelber.

"I know I am, but it had to be there in the first place," said Andrew Shipman. "What was she doing with that English fag?"

Gelber shrugged his shoulders. "What was she doing with Jerry Lockman?"

"That's true," said Shipman. "And who else did she have?"

"I don't know. Reggie Broderick, maybe."

"No, he said no," said Shipman. "He said she'll talk about it, but that's about as far as it gets."

"Well, you have over a month to find out."

"She may be what I call a cucumber," said Shipman. "Show business is full of cucumbers, but particularly in our business. They look good as hell, the answer to all your wildest dreams. But you get in bed with them and that's when you discover the cucumber. No steam. No blood. It's all an accident of how they photograph. Either that, or they save it for their acting. This girl may be a cucumber, but I hate to think so."

"She may be. Jerry Lockman, and the English fag. That's all we got to go on."

"Pending further investigation," said Shipman. "You're sure you never looked into the matter, Joe?"

"Listen, I'd tell you in a minute," said Gelber.

"Yes, I guess you would," said Shipman.

"I'd tell you quicker than you'd tell me. You held out on me before this."

"Only temporarily," said Shipman.

"Well, you want to know the truth, Andy," said Gelber. "I like them prettier than her. Either they gotta be prettier or so God damn perverted I don't want to be seen in public with them."

"You're as bad as Jerry Lockman," said Shipman.

"Maybe worse, but everybody found out about Jerry. I operate different. One big-mouthed dame spread it around about Jerry, because she was a star. Who would of listened to her if she wasn't a star? My motto is—well, I don't know. I guess I don't have any motto."

"I have. My motto is, if at first you don't succeed, you're wasting your time. I'll give you a report on Miss Jackson later on. But meanwhile, the kind of report the studio's interested in is all good. She can really go."

Every shooting day the girl who could really go drove her LaSalle past the Marshall Place intersections of Motor Avenue and was pleased with herself. Now the temptation to reenter Marshall Place and Hal Graham's life was completely controlled. Her mind was made up, she would call the shots. Early in the morning, on her way to the studio, as she came to the Marshall Place entrance she would call out, "Sleep well, get your beauty sleep, Mr. Graham. I'll be with you in a little while." First she must finish this picture, working hard and well and cheerfully. Then Morris King would make his demands, suspension would follow, and her time would be free. Homeward bound in the evenings, she would call out, as she came to Marshall Place, "Another day, another dollar, Mr. Graham. See you soon, Mr. Graham." She was happy. They were wonderful to her at the studio, they let her know they were pleased with her, and Morris King confided to her that he was planning to adjust his demands upward, so that her suspension might be longer than his original guesses of four to six weeks.

"The things I been hearing about your performance," said Morris. "If they were just a little smarter, the studio, they'd come to me and they'd offer to voluntarily tear up your contract. Imagine how good that would make them look? But the studio mind ain't constituted that way, so what'll happen is naturally I'll go in some day and they'll be able to tell by the look on my face that I didn't come in for any social call. But wouldn't they be so much smarter if they anticipated me?"

"And you say to them, you have all your other clients that will never work for Metro unless they give me a new contract," said Natica.

"You *think* it, and you get the thought across so *they* think it. But with Metro you don't threaten. RKO you can threaten. Universal you can threaten. Republic you don't even answer your phone. But Metro, the lion is the king of beasts, you know. You threaten without saying ganything. Jack Warner you can threaten, Harry Warner you don't. Harry Cohn threatens you first, and bars you from the lot. Sam Goldwyn don't use enough people, so when he wants somebody you let him come to you. He'll scream at your price, irregardless of what it is, but when he wants somebody he wants them, so you wait till he calms down and you knock off a few dollars and you got a deal. Agenting is a great business as long as they can't bully you. Nobody can bully me any more, and even Metro knows it, but all the same I'm careful who I threaten. None of these guys are using their own money, and I am."

"You're using my money if I get put on suspension," she said. "I'm the one that's not getting paid."

"You'll get it all back in the long grun. Just don't lose your confidence in yourself. And don't lose your confidence in me."

"I'm kidding," she said. "I've never been so confident in my whole life."

"Yeah, and it makes me wonder," said Morris. "Also it worries Ernestine. If you got one real friend in this business, it's Ernestine. So don't go antagonizing her too far. Everybody has to have one real friend in this business."

"Morris, you handle the studio, and let me ruin my own life," she said.

"I'll let you run your own life, but it sounded as if you said *ruin* your own life, by accident."

"Ruin is what I said," she said.

"All right, have it your own way," he said.

She invented, and rejected, a dozen ruses which would bring about her next encounter with Hal Graham. Some of them were neat and logical, and some relied on sloppy coincidence. They were all pleasant time-killers, anticipating the actual event, which she was willing to postpone because the postponement was in her hands. She was on the final week of the picture and beginning seriously to consider her plans for Graham and herself, and one afternoon Andrew Shipman told her she might as well go home early, that there was nothing more for her to do that day. "I'll need you in the morning," said the director. "Made up and on the set at eight-thirty."

"Eight-thirty? That's practically the afternoon," she said.

"Well, this won't take long. It's a retake of the long shots in front of the church. You might as well get used to loafing again."

"Thanks," she said. She did not point out to him that it would be close to five-thirty by the time she left the studio. Five-thirty was still better than seven-thirty.

She took off her makeup and changed into her slack suit and left the studio. It was still daylight as she drove up Motor Avenue, and as she proceeded she noticed that a pest was following her in a black Buick convertible. She was familiar with the type. They hung around the studio parking lots until they saw an actress leaving by herself. Sometimes they were impossible to shake until she got to the gate at Bel-Air, but once there she could stop and ask the watchman to intervene.

This one was the playful type. He began blowing his horn, and made no pretense whatever of not following her. She stepped on the gas, hoping to lose him, but he kept the same distance, and at Pico he even drove through the stop signal to keep up with her. Instead of turning at Beverly Glen she kept on to Westwood Boulevard, hoping that the added distance would enable her to lose him in the Pico traffic. The strategy did not work. She was driving through the university campus, with Sunset Boulevard in sight, when he drew up beside her and maintained her speed.

"Do you want me to call a cop?" she shouted at him.

"No," he said.

Then she recognized him. He was grinning. "How do you like my new car?" he called to her.

She pulled over and stopped the car, and he did likewise. He got out and came to her car. "So it was you," she said. "I thought it was some high school goon."

He put one foot on her running board and his elbows on the righthand door. "How've you been?" he said.

"Oh, eating my heart out because you never called," she said. "You know, I've forgotten your name."

"Hal Graham," he said. "I've been reading a lot of compliments about you."

"You have? I thought you didn't like picture people."

"I don't, but you're the one I knew," he said. "This is *your* new car, eh?"

"Not so new. I got it the day after you ran into me."

"I ran into you," he said. "Well, we'll skip that. How do you like my chariot? I just took delivery on it last week. I almost got a LaSalle, but the resale value is better on a Buick. Of course you don't have to worry about that angle."

"Do you want to get in and sit down, or would you rather follow me home?"

"Whatever you want me to do."

"If we stay here the autograph hounds will start collecting," she said.

"Yeah, these kids are UCLA. Up at Cal we have more sense."

"If you're going to be unpleasant—"

"No, just joking." He went back to his car, and when she pulled away his followed her to her house.

"Is your mother home?" he said.

"Why?"

"I don't know. I just asked," he said.

"No. She's down at Santa Ana at some funeral. Would you like a drink?"

"Are you having one?"

"No."

"Then I won't."

"The last time you were here, your wife was down in Balboa or some place. Did she ever get back?"

"The next day. One of the kids took sick and she came home."

"And that's why you decided not to call me?" she said.

"Partly. Not entirely," he said.

"You were ashamed of yourself."

"Yes, I guess so. There was no percentage for you or me."

"Then why did you follow me today, blowing your horn like a God damn idiot kid? Going through that light at Pico. All those people from the Fox lot. You could have killed a dozen."

"I just wanted to see you, that's all. To talk to you," he said.

"What about, for God's sake?"

"Listen, don't be so stupid. In the first place, you're not that stupid. As soon as I saw you I would have followed you to Santa Barbara."

"Why not make it San Francisco? Santa Barbara isn't very far. Well, what shall we talk about, Mr. Graham?"

"Nothing, if you're not more friendly."

"Don't expect me to be as friendly as the last time. I learned *my* lesson. You should have learned yours, too."

"Well, I didn't. I thought I did, but I didn't," he said.

"I guess not. Not if you were willing to follow me all the way to Santa Barbara. That must be a hundred miles. You *are* romantic."

"No, it isn't a hundred miles," he said. "It's closer to sixty."

"I have no sense of distance," she said.

"You're sore at me because I didn't phone you that time. I'll make it worse. The kid didn't get sick. I made that up. The fact of the matter is, if I would have seen you the next day I never would have stopped seeing you."

"Is that so?"

"Well, as far as I was concerned."

"So you went back and worked on your invention," she said. "You had some kind of an invention you were working on. How did it come out?"

"It's coming along. It isn't an invention. It's a process."

"Tell me all about it, but some other time. So you went back to your process, and the wife and kiddies. Have you had any more kiddies?"

He hesitated.

"Don't *tell* me," she said.

"There's one on the way," he said. "I got a raise, and my wife decided we could afford another child."

"Oh, it wasn't that you were so ashamed of yourself that you had a guilty conscience, and became attentive to her?" she said.

"I wonder."

"You're stupid, aren't you?" she said.

"In some things, I guess I am," he said. "I don't pretend to be very good about people. I remember telling you I didn't have any close friends. My wife says I'm too wrapped up in my work, but why shouldn't I be? I know I'm good and I'm headed somewhere. They gave me a raise, and next year the company's doubled my appropriation. My work is showing results two years ahead of time."

"Why, it's just like bringing a picture in ahead of schedule," she said. "You're stupid enough to be an actor, and you're almost good-looking enough to rate a screen test. You know you're good-looking, don't you?"

"So I've been told."

"Well, you are."

"Looks don't mean anything in my job. I never think about my looks, one way or the other. And it sure as hell wasn't my looks that you went for. You're with those movie actors all day."

"I want to ask you something. Is your wife pretty?"

"Oh, yes."

"Has she got a good shape?"

"Terrific. Beginning to get big now, with the kid on the way, but she has a great figure."

"Then why don't you get in your new Buick and dash home and jump right in the hay with her?"

"Because I don't feel like it."

"And why don't you feel like it?"

"Because I never got over you," he said.

"Oh, nuts," she said.

"That's true. And you never got over me. I told you, maybe you forgot, but I remember telling you I had plenty of girls before I was married."

"And then you quit, except for one girl in Dallas."

"Well, it was Houston, but I see you remember," he said. "I remember everything, too. I can tell you every word you said to me. I could draw you a sketch of the headboard on your bed. I am stupid about some things, because I don't care. But I remember everything about you."

"Well, do you want to refresh your memory?"

"If I do, Natica, this time we're starting something that may be hard to finish. I'm not going to just think about you all the time. So send me home now if you don't believe me."

"I believe you," she said.

"My wife's going to catch on, and she's going to make trouble."

"I know that. She would."

"Bad trouble, for you *and* me."

"Oh, stop talking about it. *Bad* trouble. What other kind is there?"

"Well, if I didn't love you it wouldn't be so bad. But I do."

"Do you? I never even thought about that," she said. "Well, maybe I did. Maybe I never thought about anything else."

"Why are you smiling?"

"Something a director said. It was about my buttons," she said. "I'll tell you later."

"Order me the hamburger and baked potato," said Morris King. "I want to go over and talk to Leo McCarey a minute."

"It'll get cold," said Ernestine.

"Well, order me one anyway and tell the girl to save it for me," he said.

"All right," said Ernestine. She turned to Natica. "What do you feel like having, Natica?"

"I think I'll have the avocado with the Russian dressing, to start with. Then I'll have the hamburger too."

Ernestine shook her head. "Where does it all go to? If I had the avocado—well, I'll have it anyhow." She waved the menu to summon the
waitress.

"Good evening, Mrs. King. You decided?"

"Hello, Maxine. Yes, there'll be two avocados with the Russian dressing,
and two hamburgers with the baked potato. Then also I want you to hold
a hamburger and baked potato for my husband. He's over with Mr.
McCarey."

"And coffee with?" said Maxine.

"Yes, I'll have coffee," said Natica. "How are you, Maxine?"

"I'm fine, thanks. I was home last Tuesday. They were all asking me
did I ever see you. I said you come in once in a while."

"I didn't know you two knew one another," said Ernestine.

"We went to high school together," said Natica.

"Yeah, but what a difference," said Maxine. "I end up in a balloon skirt
and look where she is today. Well, we're all proud of her. Nobody be-
grudges her success."

"Thank you," said Natica.

Maxine left. "She's cute," said Ernestine.

"Yes. She took a fellow away from me or maybe I would have married
him."

"How could she take a fellow away from *you?*"

"By being cute. She married him, too, but I guess it only lasted a little
while. Joe Boalsby. As dumb as they come, but awful pretty. Blond curly
hair and built like a Greek god."

Ernestine put her elbows on the table, and looked at Natica. "I had a
visit from your mother, Natica. She's fit to be tied."

"Well, get a rope and tie her."

"Is it true what she said? She said you put her out of the house."

"It's true," said Natica. "I got her an apartment on Spaulding. Eighty-
five a month, furnished, and a colored woman to come in five days a
week."

"Yes, well, Morris and I are kind of worried about that. You remember
when we helped you with the house in Bel-Air, it was the understanding
that your mother was to live there."

"I know," said Natica. "And I owe money on the house. But if my
mother stays, I go. I'll take the apartment on Spaulding."

"She's in the way. Is that it?"

"That's part of it. I don't care where I live, but it's got to be alone. No
member of my family is going to live with me. I can be out of the Bel-
Air house tomorrow. Morris can sell it, and give me what I put into it."

"You're too big a star now to have a dingy little apartment on Spaulding."

"It isn't a dingy little apartment. It's a duplex with plenty of room, and
the furniture is better than what my mother bought for the Bel-Air house.

Listen, Ernestine. Let's quit beating about the bush. I have a new fellow. He's married, and has a job and all like that. He has no intention of marrying me, and I have no intention of marrying him. So far his wife hasn't gotten wise to it, but she will sooner or later, and then I don't know what'll happen. But the way I feel now, I'll trade places with Maxine if necessary. You can take Metro-Goldwyn-Mayer and stick it. I'm crazy mad for this fellow, and I never was that way for anybody. You have Morris, that you were married to for twenty years, but all I ever had was Joe Boalsby, that ditched me for Maxine, and Jerry Lockman, and Alan Hildred, and this one and that one in between. Do you want me to shock you? Or maybe it won't. Maybe it won't shock you at all. But to show you how hard up you can get, I asked Alan Hildred to marry me. I think that's what frightened him off, the poor bastard."

"Yes, it would," said Ernestine. "Not because he's a fag. But because he's a snob. You knew he married that English actress, older than he was."

"He finally told me, but I had to ask him," said Natica.

"He was ashamed of it. He's ashamed of his whole life, because he's a snob. Everything about his life he's ashamed of. You know who seduced him, don't you? His older sisters. And he turned fairy when he went away to prep school."

"You had the same conversation with him I had."

"Uh-huh."

"You're not trying to tell me he was *your* boy friend," said Natica.

"The only one," said Ernestine.

"Why? Did Morris cheat on you?"

"Not that I know of. Maybe he did. But that wasn't my excuse. I didn't have any excuse, except that I wanted to have a lover, and Alan showed up at the right time. Maybe I would have gone for him no matter when he showed up. I know for a while there I had Alan Hildred on the brain. Brain, nothing. I was like any silly middle-aged dame that gets stuck on a younger man."

"How did you get to know him?" said Natica.

"Oh, he came in the office one day, trying to get Morris to handle him. About four years ago, this was. He had a copy of some book he wrote, and he gave it to Morris and said he didn't think there was a picture sale in it, but he understood the movies were looking for new writers. Morris never reads anything, so he took the book and said he'd have someone in the office look at it. Meaning me, of course, only he didn't say so. Well, you know how Alan could be, when he wasn't having one of his homo spells. Charming. And I was having a hard time keeping from making passes at elevator boys. So we walked out of the office together and we went to a speakeasy, and he began sizing me up, and the first thing I knew I was lending him a hundred dollars. Me! I never lend anybody a nickel, without a promissory note, but here I was giving this total stranger a hundred dollars that I knew I'd never get back. But it wasn't only the hundred dollars. Morris and I were worth well over a million and I could afford it. But that Alan, he knew my psychology. 'Wouldn't you like to see where I live? It's only a few steps from here,' he said. And I went. One room in a little bungalow just off Vine. So I had my lover. He never asked for too much. I told Morris to get him a job polishing English dialog. They were doing a lot of English plays that they got American writers to adapt, but the dialog was too American. So that's how Alan got in pictures. Two hundred a week. Three hundred. Never any screen credit, but a living, and learning a little about writing for pictures."

"And then you palmed him off on me," said Natica.

"Well, later. I got a little afraid that he'd tell one of his boy friends about Mrs. Morris King. I wasn't afraid of Alan. I always trusted him. He was a gentleman. But some of his boy friends were real scum. Male whores. And I was afraid I might get a disease, and give it to Morris. That frightened me as much as blackmail, so I gave him up."

"I could have got a disease," said Natica.

"You were old enough to look out for yourself," said Ernestine.

"Then *let* me look out for myself," said Natica. "If I was old enough then, I'm that much older now."

"You're right, you are," said Ernestine. "Well, I had to talk to you, though. Morris wanted me to, and I'll always do what he says. Tomorrow's the day he goes to Metro and hits them for a new contract, and he wanted me to talk to you."

"And you did," said Natica.

"And I didn't get you to change your mind."

"You didn't want me to, did you?"

"I'd like to been able to tell Morris I got you to change your mind. But in a thing like this, one woman trying to change another woman's mind is only wasting her breath. I just hope you come out of this no worse off than I did with Alan Hildred. I could of got myself into a lot of bad trouble, but instead of that I only made a fool of myself in my own eyes."

"Bad trouble. That's what he says we have to be ready for," said Natica.

"Well, if he knows that maybe he'll have some sense, or at least be a little more careful," said Ernestine. She patted the back of Natica's hand. "I'm with you, if you need anybody."

"Thanks, Ernestine. I guess all you can do is pacify my mother. Keep her out of my way."

"If it was all as easy as that," said Ernestine. "Three days' work as a dress extra and she'll be glad to go back to the flower shop. Your mother is one of the dumbest dumbbells I ever knew."

"And one of the meanest."

"Yes, I'll bet she is," said Ernestine. "There's Bing Crosby sitting down at McCarey's table. I better get Morris away from there or he won't have sense enough to leave them alone. *Maxine, will you tell my husband we want him back?*"

They sneak-previewed the new picture in Long Beach and Van Nuys and the comments were so good that the studio was in an awkward position, torn between the urgency to spread the word in the industry and the wisdom of postponing the happy news until Natica's contract was renegotiated. "They're playing it very smart," said Morris. "They can't suspend you till you turn down the next picture, so they don't seem like they're gonna show you a script. So you're still on salary. They may keep you on salary a long time without sending you a script. They can afford that. But on the other hand they want to be able to announce you in a new picture for next season. Sometimes they're smarter than I give them credit for."

"Well, what do you want me to do?"

"Keep out of trouble," he said. He was firmer, closer to anger, than she had ever seen him. "Get yourself in a scandal and all my work goes for nought. This fellow you're sleeping with, he's just about the perfect example of what a movie actress should lay off of. A young professional man, with a wife and kids and an excellent reputation. The All-American ideal husband, with the All-American ideal home. Broken up by a movie actress."

"Oh, you found out who he is," she said.

"You wouldn't tell me yourself, so I got someone else to find out for me. Yeah, a detective. The license number of his car, parked in your driveway. I got his credit rating, how much he earns, what he's working on. I guess you knew his father-in-law is a Presbyterian minister in Oakland."

"No, I didn't know that," she said.

"His uncle that he's named after, the same identical name, is the superintendent of schools in Whittier. Oh, I got it all, believe me. Your boy friend Graham, as far as I've been able to find out, there isn't a member of his family on either side that got so much as a parking ticket."

"Well, you don't want me getting mixed up with some saxophone player."

"You can lay off the sarcasm, too," said Morris. "You ever meet his wife?"

"No."

"Well, I got pictures of her when they were married and a trip they took the year before last. You know what type woman she is? The Irene Dunne type. In other words, he don't have the excuse of being married to some homely broad. This is a good-looking woman, and to cap the climax, she's having another kid. Oh, you picked good this time. What ever made you give up that English fag?"

"Graham."

"Well, what'll make you give up Graham?"

"Nothing. Nothing except Graham," she said.

"I wonder what'd make him give you up?"

"Right now, nothing. I don't say it's going to last, but we want it to."

"You just won't listen to anybody, will you?"

"I'll listen. I'm listening now," she said.

"This guy has a clean record, Natica. I spent over two thousand dollars checking, and outside of some college-boy dates, the only woman he ever got mixed up with was his wife."

"That may be," she said.

"You can count on it. Also, her record is even cleaner. She was a studious type and didn't have dates till she started going out with him. She wrote poems. She got some prize for writing a poem. People like that, you know, they're not like people in our business. They take things big. I'm trying to warn you."

"I've been warned. By Graham. I'll take the consequences."

"Big talk. What consequences? How much sleep are you gonna lose if you break up a home with three children?"

"Don't try that argument, Morris. I had to grow up without both my parents. I'm in love with this guy, and I don't want to think about anything else."

"All right. I give up."

"That's good. Don't try any fast ones," she said.

"When the roof falls in, I'll get you a good lawyer. That's all I can do now."

Beryl Graham's poetry prize was a certificate, eight inches by ten, made of a simulated parchment stock, and matted and framed. It rested, rather out of sight, on top of the built-in bookshelves of the den at 88 Marshall Place. The text of the document stated that the eighth annual first prize for poetry of the San Luis Obispo County Poetry Society was awarded to Miss Beryl Judson Yawkey for her sonnet, "If I at Dawning." The certificate shared space atop the bookshelves with Beryl's Bachelor of Arts degree, Hal Graham's Bachelor of Science degree, his commission as second lieutenant in the Army Reserve, and the Grahams' high school diplomas.

It should have been a comfortable room. The chairs were chosen for comfort; well cushioned and with pillows. An effort had been made, too, to create a comfortable relaxed atmosphere, with a sampler that said "God Bless Our Home," and the coats of arms of the Sigma Nu fraternity and the Pi Beta Phi sorority on the walls; a portable phonograph, a small radio, a portable typewriter, a magazine rack filled with recent copies of *Time* and *The Saturday Evening Post*, three silver-plated tennis trophies, half a dozen framed photographs of the Graham family. But everything in the room had been given its carefully selected place, and once given its place had never been put anywhere else. The room had acquired a stiffness that was the opposite of the intended effect. It was just like all the other rooms in the house, from kitchen to bedroom. The nubbly counterpanes had to be where they belonged at ten o'clock every morning, and at one P.M. the Venetian blinds on the west windows were closed against the strong afternoon sun.

Beryl Graham could not have lived any other way, no more than she could have permitted herself the fifteenth line of a sonnet. Sometime in the first year of her marriage she had arrived at a personal ritual of love-making, with limits beyond which she would not go, and the ritual remained constant throughout the succeeding years. She did not wish to hear of other women's and other men's variations. She accepted Hal's admiration of her body as a proper compliment not only to herself but to all womankind, and she would speak generously of another woman's "lovely" figure without going into detail that might cause her husband to dwell upon the individual woman as an individual. Beryl made herself the guardian of all women's mysteries. Being a woman was something that no man could ever understand, and he must be prevented from violating women's secrets. It was quite enough for him to be a partner to her climax. He must be satisfied with that intimacy, and he must then go to sleep, gratefully.

She was happiest in the company of other women. It was always a clouding conclusion to a pleasant afternoon when a husband would appear to call for his wife after a bridge game. It was a male intrusion into a feminine world, an end for that day to the pleasing gentleness of women's voices and the pretty sight of feminine things. Beryl loved her kitchen and her bathroom, the tapestries in her hall, the chinaware in her din-ingroom, and the husband and children that so admirably completed her establishment, *her* establishment among the establishments of other women. She had a son as well as a daughter, but a son was a boy and a boy was a child that was not a girl and children belonged to the mother, a woman. A boy was not a man, and even when he became a man he would become the husband of a woman. It would be nice if her boy went into the ministry. There was still time to direct his steps. He worshiped her, even if he did understand the terms of his father's profession. Howard in a pulpit was an inspiring dream. The Reverend Howard Yawkey Graham. She could see his name in white letters under glass on the sign on a church lawn up North. Sacramento. Fresno. Oakland. San Francisco. The Reverend Howard Yawkey Graham will preach on "Woman's Role Today."

Jean, of course, was already so much like her mother that Hal sometimes would jokingly refer to her as little Beryl. He could just as well have referred to Beryl as big Jean, for with the exception of the overt sexual relationship there was little difference in his treatment of the one and the other. Correspondingly, their treatment of him was tolerantly maternal. The daughter had learned fast.

Howard was nine years old, Jean was seven, and they had been told to expect a new little brother or sister. The age gap between Jean and the unborn child worried Beryl not at all. She fully expected the older children to assume a proper responsibility toward the child that she had tentatively named Emily, after Emily Dickinson. The difference in ages between Emily and the older children was perfectly calculated, she felt. One of the women in her group (whom she did not like very much) had introduced her to the term, sibling jealousy, which turned out to be a name for the hitherto nameless concern that Beryl had disposed of before undertaking her third pregnancy. She disposed of it by deciding firmly that Howard and Jean must learn to love "Emily" before she was born. In this she was succeeding nicely, and for a little while she had no unnecessary worries. In spite of the obstetrician's reassurances Beryl discontinued conventional lovemaking with Hal and they went back to the "heavy necking" that was as much as she would allow in the weeks before the formal announcement of their engagement and the wedding ceremony. Hal's protests were mild, and then he told her that he had decided to stay away from her until after the baby was born. He would sleep in the guest room.

It was such a sensible idea that she playfully accused Hal of suddenly acquiring the ability to read her mind. No man on earth could read her mind, she was certain, but she had so strongly wished that Hal would come to just that decision that she wondered if she did not possess some extra-sensory powers that could be as effective as the spoken word. In many marriages the husband and wife often found themselves thinking the same thought simultaneously, and Hal's decision might only be an extension of this common coincidence. The power of her wish had been undeniable, and if it had not been such an intimate matter, she would have mentioned it to her father as bearing a close relation to the power of prayer. It was too bad, in a way, that she had never discussed those things with her father. But then she had never discussed them with her mother either. She had never really discussed them with anyone, not excepting Hal. She was much too proud of being a woman to relax her own reserve. The same pride had often served her well when Hal made love to her; it was unthinkable that she would ever let him know that *he* could leave *her* unsatisfied. No woman should be that dependent on a man.

But nearly seven years had intervened since Hal had slept in the guest room, and in all those years not a single week had gone by without his getting in bed with her. It was healthy for him. Five years ago, when she had her appendix out, he had slept alone for five or six weeks, but that did not count. She remembered it, though, because he had been so nervous and irritable in spite of himself and his good intentions; and there had been a remarkable demonstration of men's dependence on sex when the doctor said it was completely safe for her to allow Hal to make love to her again. Overnight he became cheerful and relaxed and his old sweet self. Now that he had once again betaken himself to the guest room she began to look for indications of a return of his nervous irritability. At the end of the second week of his celibacy—a fair test—she could see no bad effects, physically or spritually. He was neither constipated nor petulant. She kept track of his bowel movements and she watched his manner with herself and the children. He was normal. And then she knew, for a fact beyond the suspicion stage, that Hal Graham was having sexual relations with another woman.

She did not need proof. She did not want proof, in the usual sense of the word. Hal Graham was all the proof she needed. She knew him like a book, a man who did complicated equations in a laboratory and could speak for an hour on problems so abstruse that not a hundred men in the entire State of California could follow him for five minutes. That was all there was to him, really, all that set him apart from the race of men. Otherwise he was a vapid, uninspiring person who drove a certain kind of car, played certain games, wore certain clothes, said certain things, and was now indulging certain animal instincts with a certain inferior type of female. Beryl Graham's contempt for her husband had never had occasion to be expressed. The feminine woman, to avoid being a freak, required a husband, a male to fertilize her and to signify his responsibility to her by giving her his name. The inconveniences attendant upon this convention were bearable so long as the relationship was not cheapened by disrespect. But sexual infidelity was disrespect of the most grievous kind. It placed the wife on equal terms of messy intimacy with the husband's mistress. The unfaithful husband sought in his mistress the thrilling shudder that was the proud woman's weakest moment. The cheap and traitorous woman gave him what he sought, and while she was a pitiable and contemptible person, she must be punished for her disloyalty to her sex.

The punishment, however, must be carefully thought out. It need not be visited directly upon the traitorous woman. It should unquestionably be administered indirectly through the offending, disrespectful man. And under no circumstances should it be of a character that would further lower the dignity of the offended wife. Beryl Graham almost automatically discarded the notion of divorce. There was no dignity in becoming the self-proclaimed victim of Hal Graham's disrespect. She next ruled out financial punishment. She could impose upon him a financial burden that he would carry all his life, but two factors decided her against that: fundamentally he cared very little about money, and, secondly, he was so indispensable to his company that they would make some arrangement to help him. It was quite possible, too, that the woman, whoever she was, had money of her own. She was certainly not costing Hal any money now. Beryl knew where every penny went.

No, the usual forms of punishment and revenge were not acceptable to Beryl Graham. They were insufficient, inadequate to the offense, and they were *unsubtle, unfeminine*. They were the thinking of men, the thinking of lawyers, and most lawyers were men.

In her present condition Beryl had plenty of opportunity for calm reflection. Her pregnancy gave her an excuse to give up tennis with the women of Marshall Place, and now that she was convinced of Hal's disrespect to her she used her pregnancy as an excuse to give up the enjoyment of her afternoon bridge games. After she sent the children off to school in the mornings she did her housework and was left with the entire day in which to be alone with her thoughts. When Marshall Place neighbors dropped in she would let them stay only a little while, and she soon discouraged their casual visits. It was not long before she had almost the whole day to herself, and she went through her household duties mechanically while occupying her mind with the problem of dealing with Hal and his unknown woman. It was not a problem that could be solved as he would solve one of his chemical formulae, if he solved chemical formulae. It was not a mathematical thing or a test tube thing; it was not a materialistic matter. It was a problem for a poet.

"How are you getting along?" he said to her one night, when the dishes were put away and the children had been put to bed.

"Me? Fine, thanks. Why?" said Beryl.

"I just wondered," he said. "You have any trouble with little Emily?"

"Not a bit," said Beryl.

"Do you feel life?"

"Of course I feel life," she said. "Men don't understand those things."

"I guess not," he said. "Well, I guess I'll say goodnight."

"Goodnight," she said. She gave him her cheek to kiss.

"Are you sure everything's all right?" he said.

"Why shouldn't it be?"

"I don't know," he said.

"If there's something bothering you, for heaven's sake tell me."

"Well, something is," he said.

"Oh? What?"

"The children. Well, not both children. But Howard said he hoped you'd have the baby soon."

"Why?" said Beryl.

"Because you're acting strangely. He didn't say that, but he thinks it."

"What *did* he say?"

"He said you talk to the baby as if it was alive."

"Well, it is alive."

"I know, but he doesn't understand that."

"And what did you tell him?"

"Well, I tried to explain that the baby's alive, and that it had to grow a little more before it was ready to be born."

"He knows that. I've told them that."

"But he doesn't understand why you'd talk to it now."

"Well, do *you?*"

"I do, because you used to talk to *him* before he was born, and Jean, too."

"I suppose I did," said Beryl. "I believe mothers *should* talk to their babies."

"They don't usually, before they're born," he said.

"Don't they? How would you know? There we are again, you see. A man is so different from a woman that it's just hopeless for him to try to understand us."

"All the same, Beryl, you have to admit it's kind of confusing to a young boy Howard's age, to overhear his mother talking to someone and you can't even see who she's talking to."

"I don't admit anything of the kind. It may be confusing to Howard, because he's a boy. But I'm sure it isn't confusing to Jean."

"I don't know," he said. "She hasn't mentioned it, but she wouldn't anyway. She doesn't confide in me, and never has."

"Naturally. If she had anything to say, she'd say it to me."

"I guess so," he said.

"Oh, I know so," said Beryl. "And there's nothing else on your mind?"

"No."

"Nothing out of the ordinary at the lab?"

"Not a thing," he said. "The usual slow progress. We try one thing, and if it doesn't work, we start all over again and try something else. But we know we're in the right direction."

"That must be such a great satisfaction, knowing you're at least in the right direction," she said. "But what if you found out some day that you were going in the wrong direction?"

"What do you mean by that?"

"Just what I say. Suppose you discovered that these last five years' work was all wasted? That you were completely wrong?"

He smiled. "That would be impossible, now. This scientific work, you know. Every step is experimental, yes, but when we've proved something by one experiment, that's scientific fact. Then we take up the next experiment. Step by step, experiment by experiment, we accumulate our scientific facts. Those are things you can't deny. Certain elements behave certain ways under certain conditions. Those aren't laws that man made. Man only discovers them."

"But what if something new comes along and proves you were wrong?" she said.

"Nothing new comes along. It was always there, but we hadn't discovered it. Where we can go wrong is through ignorance. But the things we've proved, scientifically, are never wrong."

"You're all so conceited. So sure you're right."

"Not for one minute," he said. "We're sure that the laws are right. The laws of physics, I mean. But the man that's sure *he's* right, disregarding those laws, doesn't belong in the lab. He *is* conceited, and we don't want him around."

"How interesting," she said.

"You're getting bored. I'll let you go to bed," he said. "Goodnight."

"Goodnight," she said.

He closed the door of her bedroom and she sat with the pillows propped up behind her and a limp-leather volume of Wordsworth's poems lying open at her side. She had a feeling that she was getting closer to the solution of her problem. Whatever it was, it would certainly involve his destruction. This blindly conceited man, with his prattle about laws, must be rendered harmless. There must be a castration of his egotism, so that he could never again take that superior tone. How he had gloated over her and her unconscious, innocent habit of talking to the child in her womb! Did *he*—*he*—presume to judge her strange?

On the morning of the second Friday after the preceding conversation Beryl waited until Hal had left the house and then announced to the children that she had a surprise for them. They were not to go to school that day, but instead she was taking them to Newport a day early. Daddy, she said, would join them the next day.

She drove them to their cottage, had them get into their bathing suits, and informed them that as a special treat she was taking them for a ride in a motorboat. They went to Red Barry's pier, where the Grahams customarily hired boats, and Red gave them a new Chris-Craft because he trusted Beryl's ability to handle it.

They took off into the San Pedro Channel, which was calm, and when they were about five miles from shore, Beryl stopped the boat and told Howard he could go for a swim. The boy dived in, and Beryl then told Jean that she could go in too. The girl was somewhat reluctant, but she lowered herself into the water. Beryl then started the motor and pulled away. She made a wide circle until she saw first the boy and then the girl disappear beneath the surface. She circled again several times before turning back to shore.

In the words of Red Barry: "She brought the boat in all right, and tied it up herself. And then I thought to myself. 'Hey, wait a minute,' and I asked her. I said where were the two kids? And she looked at me like I was asking some kind of a dumb question, and said, 'They're out there somewhere.' And I said to her what did she mean by out there somewhere, and did she mean she had some kind of an accident? You know, I thought she was out of her mind from shock. But she was just as calm as if nothing happened, and I took notice her dress wasn't wet. Her hair was dry. In other words, she hadn't been in the water. And I thought, Jesus Christ, what *is* this? So I right away went to my shack and phoned the police. I didn't know what the hell else to do. Now there's a woman I been dealing with, her and Graham, five or six years at least. I would of trusted her with my own kids. And it isn't as if she wasn't a great swimmer. Pregnant, yes, but maybe that's the cause of it. You know, when a woman's expecting, and it's six or seven years since she had a child, it's hard to say. In fact, if you ask me, it's hard to tell about them anyway. Like I thought, well the first thing I better do is repaint that boat a different color, but I'm a son of a bitch if there wasn't a party of four wanted to take it out the following Sunday. They asked specially for it. I couldn't let them have it, though. The police impounded it. And how would you like to be Graham the rest of your life? He wasn't even here, but how do you live that down? Because right away people began saying he must of had something to do with it. A guy is married to a crazy woman, a real monster, but they try to shift the blame on him. Well, I guess if I didn't know him I'd probably think the same thing."

Morris and Ernestine King came out of the Beverly Derby, the one-legged newsboy handed Morris the folded morning papers and was handed a fifty-cent piece. "You want to go to the Troc for a little while?" said Morris.

"I don't know. For a little while," said Ernestine.

"Yeah, we might as well go for a little while. It's early."

Their car was crossing from the parking lot.

"What's the headline? There's a big headline," said Ernestine.

"There's always a big headline," said Morris. "Mother Held in Tots' Drowning.' Now that's nice. To practically accuse a mother of drowning her kids."

"Let me see it," said Ernestine.

He handed her the *Examiner*, and she read the big story. "If I live to be a hundred, I'll never get used to Newport being in California. To me, Newport—wait a minute. Oh, *wait a minute*. Morris. What's the name of Natica's boy friend?"

"The name of Natica Jackson's boy friend? Some name like Hamilton. One of those names. Why?"

"Hamilton," said Ernestine. "You're sure it isn't Graham?"

"Graham is what it is," said Morris King.

"Harold T. Graham?"

"Yeah, why?" said Morris.

"Get in the car," said Ernestine. She spoke to the chauffeur. "Eddie, take us out to Miss Jackson's house."

"Natica Jackson, in Bel-Air?" said the chauffeur.

"Yes, and I'm sorry, Eddie, but don't figure on getting home at a decent hour tonight," she said.

"That's all right, ma'am, as long as I can have tomorrow off," said Eddie.

"Don't even count on that," she said.

Morris was reading the newspaper under the dome light of the town car as they proceeded out Wilshire Boulevard. He finished the *Examiner* and read the *Times*. Before they had got as far as Beverly Glen he refolded both papers and put out the light. "You got any ideas?" he said.

"First we have to find Natica," said Ernestine.

"Yeah, first we find her, then what?"

"What's the use of ideas till we had a chance to talk to her?"

"I guess so," said Morris. "I was thinking we ought to secrete her someplace. I hope we can secrete her before she finds out about this."

"We don't know anything, where she is or what she knows. Have a cigar to steady your nerves."

"A good stiff hooker of brandy is what my soul cries out for at this particular moment," said Morris.

"You're behaving admirably, Morris," said Ernestine. "Considering what's going on inside. When the chips are down, I have to hand it to you."

"And a hell of a lot of chips are down right now. A matter of two hundred thousand dollars, our end. A million-eight for Miss Natica Jackson. And from the studio's point of view, *you* guess. Now when we get there, I'm gonna let you handle the situation. One woman to another, till we find out where we are. But I want to be in the room all the time."

"If she's there," said Ernestine.

"If she ain't there, I want to go somewhere and get pissy-assed drunk."

"No, you don't want to do that," said Ernestine.

"There you're wrong. I won't do it, but I'll want to. I want to now. If I wasn't afraid of you thinking I was a kyoodle, I'd quit the business tonight."

"Never would I think that, Morris," she said.

The car halted at Natica's door and they got out. Morris pushed the doorbell button, and after a pause the door was swung open by Natica, who closed it quickly behind them. "I had to be sure who it was," she said. "I apologize for making you wait."

"You got a peephole?" said Morris.

"Yes. It isn't in the door. It's off to one side so it won't show the light. It's in the lavatory."

"Oh, good idea," said Morris. "You had any other visitors?"

"No," said Natica. "I phoned you, but they said you were out for the evening."

"We came out of the Beverly Derby and Ernestine happen to take a glance at the morning papers."

"Oh, you found out that way," said Natica. "Can I get you both a drink?"

"You wouldn't have any celery tonic?" said Morris.

"What's that?" said Natica.

"If you have a Coke or some ginger ale," said Ernestine. "Morris'll get it. Dearie, bring me a ginger ale with maybe a little twist of lemon peel."

"What do you want, Natica?" said Morris.

"A big slug of brandy, but I guess I better stick to Coke," said Natica. "Thanks, both of you, for showing up like this."

"Yeah. Well, you two talk while I get the drinks," said Morris.

Natica sat down and lit a cigarette. They were in a small room which contained a portable bar, and ordinary conversational tones sufficed. "He was supposed to come here around five," she said.

"This is Graham, you're talking about?" said Morris.

"Uh-huh. I had a hair appointment for three o'clock, but I decided the hell with it and lucky I did or I wouldn't of been here when he phoned. He was phoning from some gas station on the way to Newport. The police down there notified him what happened and told him he better get there right away. That was after he got back from lunch. He usually has lunch with some fellows on LaCienega every Friday, and then he goes back to the lab. The laboratory. So the police finally got in touch with him around ha' past two. He told me what they told him. That the two children met with an accident and his wife was at the police station. He asked them to put her on, but they said she was in custody. The poor guy, he asked them what they meant by that and all they'd say was he better get down there as soon as he could. They wouldn't even tell him if the kids were alive or dead. They said they didn't know for sure. And he started to tell them he thought his wife and the kids were still home. They weren't supposed to leave till tomorrow. But the cop said he didn't want to talk any more on the phone, and for Hal to get there as soon as possible. The rest I got by listening to the radio."

"We have the morning papers," said Ernestine. Morris served the drinks and took a chair. "And naturally you haven't heard any more from Graham?" said Ernestine.

"No. And he said for me not to try and get in touch with him. He said it looked very bad, and he didn't want me to get mixed up in it. God, I don't want to get mixed up in it either, but I'd like to help him."

"And the only way to help him is to stay the hell out of it," said Morris. "The only way."

"Oh, sure. I know that," said Natica. "There isn't any doubt about it, is there? I mean, she did drown the two kids?"

"Wait till you read the papers and you'll be convinced of that," said Morris. "They're holding her on an open charge, but the whole thing is there for anybody to read. They got him quoted saying he didn't know why she'd do it. The grief-stricken husband and father, it says. The pregnant mother showed no signs of remorse or even awareness of the tragedy. The father went out on a Coast Guard boat to join in the search, which already attracted more than fifty small craft containing volunteers and curiosity-seekers. The *Times* has an aerial photograph of the boats, and there's a statement here from a veteran fishing captain who says it may be days before the children's bodies are found. A man named Barry rented her the boat and he's the one that reported it to the police. He refused to talk to reporters, but it was learned that he observed her return to his pier and questioned her as to the whereabouts of the children, and she is alleged to have told Barry that he would find the children 'out there.' He then telephoned the police. Mrs. Graham was taken into custody while returning on foot to the attractive cottage which the family had rented annually for the past five years. And so forth. I'd say the woman was what they call criminally insane."

"She talked to herself," said Natica.

"She did?" said Ernestine.

"And not to herself, really. She talked to the baby in her womb. She worried the poor kids, according to Hal. But he wasn't as worried as they were, because he remembered she did the same thing when she was carrying the boy *and* the girl."

"She'll get off," said Morris.

"They'll put her away somewhere," said Ernestine. "It's too bad they didn't a long time ago."

"Yes, you're right," said Morris. "But now let's talk about you, Natica. First, who knows you were sleeping with Graham?"

"Well, you two do. She didn't. That I know for a fact. She never accused Hal of sleeping with anybody. Not once, and she wasn't the kind that would let him get away with it."

"She wasn't the kind that would murder her two children, either. That's how well Graham knew her," said Morris. "So we don't know what she knew. Who else?"

"Nobody, unless Hal told some friend of his, and he said he didn't."

"It'd be pretty hard for a guy like that to not brag about getting in the hay with Natica Jackson," said Morris.

"He wasn't the bragging kind," said Natica.

"And he had something to lose," said Ernestine. "How about you? Who did *you* tell?"

"A long time ago, Reggie Broderick, but I never told him who the guy was," said Natica.

"What about your servants? Your mother?" said Ernestine.

"My mother doesn't know a damn thing about him. The cook and the maid, if he gets his picture in the paper—"

"Which you can be damn sure he will, tomorrow," said Morris.

"Let me finish. The cook never saw him. The maid could have, if she hid somewhere and watched him leave, a long time ago. Lately he never came in the front door, or left by it. I have a door in my bedroom that opens out into the garden and then through the back gate. I'm not worried about the maid. And if he had to phone me he used the name of Mr. Marshall. There's one person that does know, Morris."

"Who's that?"

"Your detective," said Natica.

"God damn it, that's the thing that's been plaguing me. I knew there was somebody. I knew it, God damn it."

"He has his name. License number. Address. Every damn thing about him and his wife," said Natica. "So, it's up to you, I guess."

"It's absolutely up to me," said Morris.

"Who was it? Rosoff?" said Ernestine.

"Yeah."

"Well, how much can you trust him? He never popped off before."

"No, but he never had anything as big as this," said Morris.

"How much do you think he'd settle for?" said Ernestine.

Morris shook his head. "Who knows? A pension, the rest of his life."

"Well, he wouldn't be the first in this town to get that kind of a pension," said Ernestine. "Do you have his number?"

"Yes, I guess so. You mean with me? Yes. Why?"

"I have an idea," said Ernestine. "Get him on the phone, tonight. Right away. Tell him you have a big job for him, but don't say right away what it is. Find out if he connects up this Graham with the one he investigated."

"He will."

"All right, suppose he does. I have to think a minute," said Ernestine. They were all three silent, until Ernestine tapped her kneecap. "This is what you do. The minute he thinks you're buying him off, you're in for it. He'll bleed you, he'll bleed Natica. I wouldn't even be surprised if he tried to take the studio."

"That he better not try, if he wants to walk around on two legs," said Morris. "Me and Natica he can take, but the studio won't fool around with a small-time operator like Rosoff."

"So you don't want him thinking you're buying him off. Instead of that, you want him thinking you want him to do a little dirty work. You're in it together. You pretend you're taking him into your confidence. 'Rosie,' you say—now let me think." She paused. "I got it. You tell him you're worried about Natica getting mixed up in this thing. Be frank, like. And you say you got a tip that Mrs. Graham, Beryl, went to Europe several years ago and had a child by somebody that wasn't her husband. You aren't sure whether it was Paris, London, or Monte Carlo. But you want him to go abroad right away, as quick as he can, and check the hospital records of all the private hospitals in Paris and London. You'll pay all expenses and fifty dollars a day, or whatever he charges. But he has to do it right away or you'll have to get someone else."

"It won't work," said Morris.

"I guarantee you it will, Morris. Fifty dollars a day and all expenses? I know Rosie well enough to know he won't pass up a chance like that. That's, uh, for two months that's three thousand dollars plus his living, plus a little larceny on the expense account. And a nice deluxe trip to Europe."

"You're spending my money, Teeny, but what for? What do I get out of it?"

"Jesus Christ! The one thing you want right now. Time. *Time.* You get this goniff out of the way for the next five, six, seven weeks. He won't find anything, but he won't be around here making trouble. By the time he gets back to L.A., Mrs. Graham will be put away somewhere. And by that time there'll be five other scandals for the newspapers to occupy their attention. If Rosie wants to blackmail us then, we laugh in his face. But I wouldn't laugh in his face tonight, or next week. Tonight I'm afraid of him. Tomorrow I'm afraid of him. I'm afraid of him till he gets on board The Chief and I'm still afraid of him till he gets on board the *Ile de France*. Then I begin to rest easy."

"It'll work," said Morris. "It'll positively work. Natica, where's your phone?"

"Right there where you're sitting," said Natica.

Within an hour Morris had tracked down Rosoff at a gambling house on the Sunset Strip. "Rosie? You winning, or losing? Well, can you meet me at the Vine Street Derby in three-quarters of an hour? I need your very urgent help in a matter, and it won't keep till tomorrow. Right, Rosie. If you get there first you tell Chilios I'm on my way, and if I'm there first I'll wait there. But be a good boy now, Rosie, and don't you keep me waiting." Morris hung up. "He says he's winning. I say he's losing or he wouldn't answer the phone. You couldn't get him away from that blackjack game if he was winning. I seen him on two or three occasions blow a couple months' pay inside of an hour. So did you, Teeny."

"Yes I did," said Ernestine. "He's a chump from the word go. You want me to come with you?"

"This time, no. If you were there, he'd smell a rat. No offense, sweetheart. But you know. He'd be looking for an angle. With just me there, he don't get suspicious. You ladies wish to sit and talk, keep one another company till I phone you?"

"If Natica wants my company," said Ernestine.

"Of course I do, you silly," said Natica.

"All right. Then get going, Morris. And good luck," said Ernestine.

"Too bad Natica's not a hunchback. I could rub it for luck. Why wouldn't it be just as lucky to give you a little rub in front?" said Morris. "Wuddia say, Natica?"

"Get out of here," said Ernestine.

"Ah, she knows I'm only kidding."

"Yeah, but do *you* know it?" said Ernestine.

He left.

"There goes a nice little fellow," said Ernestine. "Tough. Shrewd. He'll murder you in a business deal. He'll have the gold out of your teeth before you open your mouth. But if he likes you, once he gets to liking you, you never saw such real, genuine loyalty. And he likes you, Natica."

"I'm positive of that," said Natica.

"How do you feel?" said Ernestine.

"I feel all right. I felt panicky till you and Morris got here. I couldn't think who to turn to. The only person I could think of was Reggie Broderick. All the people I know in Hollywood, and the only ones I had to turn to were you and Morris and Reggie. I would of phoned Alan Hildred if I knew where he was."

"Yes, in a spot like this you could count on Alan. A no-good English fag, but you could count on him in this kind of situation. Well, that's four people. That's not so bad."

"I ought to feel worse about those two little children, but I don't. He was crazy about them, Hal. But the mother never let him get very close to them."

"What do you know about her?" said Ernestine.

"Hardly anything, it turns out. I thought I knew a lot, mostly from knowing him. But he didn't know much about her either. Married all that time and that's as well as they ever got to know each other. You'd think a married couple would know each other better, but they didn't. I know one thing about her he told me."

"What?"

"She never wanted to look at his private parts. He could look at her, but she wouldn't look at him. She wasn't modest about herself, but he always had to keep covered up till they turned out the lights. She wasn't a Lez, but she hated men."

"She was a Lez," said Ernestine.

"That's what I said, but he said no. She liked to be laid, but she didn't care what happened to him. It was all for her. I don't know, Ernestine. I often felt the same way with Alan. Maybe I'm like her."

"I doubt that," said Ernestine.

"I was with Alan."

"But not with Graham," said Ernestine.

"No, not with Graham."

"Well, you see I was just the opposite with Alan," said Ernestine. "If he told me to—one time he did tell me to do something terrible in front of one of his boy friends, and I did. That was the last time I had anything to do with him, but he had that power over me. That was why I had to stop seeing him. But he had no power over you, and Graham did."

"I would have done anything Graham wanted me to, anywhere, any time. And I would now."

"Well, with me it was Alan. Starting with the first time I ever met him, when I lent him a hundred dollars."

"How did you have the strength to break it off?" said Natica.

"I don't know. Fear, I guess. Not strength. If he could make me do that in front of his boy friend, what next? Those kind of people, people like Alan, that have that much power over a person, maybe the good Lord only gives them so much power. If they had a little more power—but they don't. And that's how the good Lord protects us. You see what I mean?"

"Yes, but how do we protect ourselves from ourselves?"

"Search me. I guess we don't, till we get frightened."

"You think I'm gonna get frightened?"

"Yes, I do," said Ernestine.

"You're right. I am frightened. I'm frightened of that crazy woman with the child in her womb."

"Of what she'll do, or what she'll say?"

"Neither one. I don't think she can do anything, locked up in an institution. And nobody'll pay much attention to what she says."

"Then what are you frightened of?" said Ernestine.

"Her. I never even saw her, and I probably never will. But I'll be afraid of her for the rest of my life, like she was some kind of a ghost. Her and those two children, but mostly her. I want to talk to Reggie Broderick."

"What the hell for, Natica?"

"He's a Catholic."

"I'm Jewish. You can talk to me."

"No, I remember those Catholic girls I grew up with. They'd get into trouble—not just knocked up, but other kinds of trouble—and they weren't as afraid as the rest of us."

"It only seemed that way. They were just as afraid, if not more so. And anyway, is Reggie Broderick going to get rid of your ghost? I doubt that, Natica. Him *or* his religion. Think it over before you start spilling everything to Reggie."

"Well, maybe you're right," said Natica. "Right now I don't know my ass from first base. I wish to hell I could get drunk. I wish Hal Graham would walk in this room. Only I don't. A terrible thing is I don't want to see him and maybe I never will want to again, with that damn crazy murderess looking over his shoulder at me. That's my ghost, Ernestine."

"Yes, I see what you mean," said Ernestine.

"What happens to her baby when it's born?"

"I don't know what the law says about that."

"I wasn't thinking about the law. I was wondering about the child's future."

"I imagine the father will be given custody, and I suppose he'll move away. Maybe change his name. Get a new job and so forth."

"Do you know something, Ernestine? As sure as we're sitting here, he's never going to see me again. He'll want to, maybe, but the kind of man he is, he'll have a ghost, too. Not only his wife locked up in an institution, but a child to raise. And he'll never try to see me. And all of a sudden I'm beginning to realize that that crazy woman knew what she was doing."

"What?"

"Just as if she called me on the phone and told me. Maybe she doesn't know my name, even, but I get it inside me, Ernestine. She's telling me."

"Telling you what, dear?" said Ernestine.

"She's saying, 'This is what you have to live with. Ann Jacobs or Natica Jackson, or whatever you call yourself, this is what you have to look forward to.' "

"I wish I didn't believe that," said Ernestine.

"But you do," said Natica.

"I won't lie to you. It's the only thing to believe that makes any sense," said Ernestine.

They were silent for a moment, then Natica spoke. "I told him once, if he hadn't stopped to put on a necktie I never would have smacked into his car."

"I don't get it," said Ernestine.

"Oh, I'll tell you sometime, but not now," said Natica.

"We ought to be hearing from Morris," said Ernestine.

"No hurry. I can wait," said Natica. "I have complete confidence in Morris."

1966

We'll Have Fun

It was often said of Tony Costello that there was nothing he did not know about horses. No matter whom he happened to be working for—as coachman, as hostler, as blacksmith—he would stop whatever he was doing and have a look at an ailing horse and give advice to the owner who had brought the horse to Tony. His various employers did not object; they had probably sometime in the past gotten Tony's advice when he was working for someone else, and they would do so again sometime in the future. A year was a long time for Tony to stay at a job; he would quit or he would get the sack, find something else to do, and stay at that job until it was time to move on. He had worked for some employees three or four times. They would rehire him in spite of their experience with his habits, and if they did not happen to have a job open for him, they would at least let him bed down in their haylofts. He did not always ask their permission for this privilege, but since he knew his way around just about every stable in town—private and livery—he never had any trouble finding a place to sleep. He smoked a pipe, but everybody knew he was careful about matches and emptying the pipe and the kerosene heaters that were in most stables. And even when he was not actually in the service of the owner of a stable, he more than earned his sleeping privilege. An owner would go out to the stable in the morning and find that the chores had been done. "Oh, hello, Tony," the owner would say. "Since when have you been back?"

"I come in last night."

"I don't have a job for you," the owner would say.

"That's all right. Just a roof over me head temporarily. You're giving that animal too much oats again. Don't give him no oats at night, I told you."

"Oh, all right. Go in the kitchen and the missus will give you some breakfast. That is, if you want any breakfast. You smell like a saloon."

"Yes, this was a bad one, a real bad one. All I want's a cup of coffee, if that's all right?"

"One of these nights you'll walk in front of a yard engine."

"If I do I hope I'll have the common sense to get out of the way. And if I don't it'll be over pretty quick."

"Uh-huh. Well, do whatever needs to be done and I'll pay you two dollars when I get back this evening."

The owner could be sure that by the end of the day Tony would have done a good cleaning job throughout the stable, and would be waiting in patient agony for the money that would buy the whiskey that cured the rams. "I got the rams so bad I come near taking a swig of kerosene," he would say. He would take the two dollars and half-walk, half-run to the nearest saloon, but he would be back in time to feed and bed down the owner's horse.

It would take a couple of days for him to get back to good enough shape to go looking for a steady job. If he had the right kind of luck, the best of luck, he would hear about a job as coachman. The work was not hard, and the pay was all his, not to be spent on room and board. The hardest work, though good pay, was in a blacksmith's shop. He was not young any more, and it took longer for his muscles to get reaccustomed to the work. Worst of all, as the newest blacksmith he was always given the job of shoeing mules, which were as treacherous as a rattlesnake and as frightening. He hated to shoe a mule or a Shetland pony. There were two shops in town where a mule could be tied up in the stocks, the apparatus that held the animal so securely that it could not kick; but a newly shod mule, released from the stocks, was likely to go crazy and kill a man. If he was going to die that way, Tony wanted his executioner to be a horse, not a God damn mule. And if he was going to lose a finger or a chunk of his backside, let it be a horse that bit him and not a nasty little bastard ten hands high. Blacksmithing paid the best and was the job he cared the least for, and on his fiftieth birthday Tony renounced it forever. "Not for fifty dollars a week will I take another job in a blacksmith's," he swore.

"You're getting pretty choosy, if you ask me," said his friend Murphy. "Soon there won't be no jobs for you of any kind, shape or form. The ottomobile is putting an end to the horse. Did you ever hear tell of the Squadron A in New York City?"

"For the love of Jesus, did I ever hear tell of it? Is that what you're asking me? Well, if I was in New York City I could lead you to it blindfolded, Ninety-something-or-other and Madison Avenue, it is, on the right-hand side going up. And before I come to this miserable town the man I worked for's son belonged to it. Did I ever hear tell of the Squadron A!"

"All right. What is it now?" said Murphy.

"It's the same as it always was—a massive brick building on the right-hand side—"

"The organ-i-zation, I'm speaking of," said Murphy.

"Well, the last I seen in the papers, yesterday or the day before, this country was engaged in mortal combat with Kaiser Wilhelm the Second. I therefore hazard the guess that the organ-i-zation is fighting on our side against the man with the withered arm."

"Fighting how?"

"Bravely, I'm sure."

"With what for weapons?"

"For weapons? Well, being a cavalry regiment I hazard the guess that they're equipped with sabre and pistol."

"There, you see? You're not keeping up to date with current happenings. Your Squadron A that you know so much about don't have a horse to their name. They're a machine-gun outfit."

"Well, that of course is a God damn lie, Murphy."

"A lie, is it? Well how much would you care to bet me—in cash?"

"Let me take a look and see how much I have on me?" said Tony. He placed his money on the bar. "Eighteen dollars and ninety-four cents. Is this even money, or do I have to give you odds?"

Murphy placed nineteen dollars on the bar. "Even money'll be good enough for me, bein's it's like taking the money off a blind man."

"And how are we to settle who's right?" said Tony.

"We'll call up the newspaper on the telephone."

"What newspaper? There's no newspaper here open after six P.M."

"We'll call up the New York *World*," said Murphy.

"By long distance, you mean? Who's to pay for the call?"

"The winner of the bet," said Murphy.

"The winner of the bet? Oh, all right. I'll be magnanimous. How do you go about it? You can't put that many nickels in the slot."

"We'll go over to the hotel and get the operator at the switchboard, Mary McFadden. She's used to these long-distance calls."

"Will she be on duty at this hour?"

"Are you trying to back out? It's only a little after eight," said Murphy.

"Me back out? I wished I could get the loan of a hundred dollars and I'd show you who's backing out," said Tony.

In silence they marched to the hotel, and explained their purpose to Mary McFadden. Within fifteen minutes they were connected with the office of *The World*, then to the newspaper library. "Good evening, sir," said Murphy. "This is a long-distance call from Gibbsville, Pennsylvania. I wish to request the information as to whether the Squadron A is in the cavalry or a machine-gun organ-i-zation." He repeated the question and waited. "He says to hold the line a minute."

"Costing us a fortune," said Tony.

"Hello? Yes, I'm still here. Yes? Uh-huh. Would you kindly repeat that information?" Murphy quickly handed the receiver to Tony Costello, who listened, nodded, said "Thank you," and hung up.

"How much do we owe you for the call, Mary?" said Murphy.

"Just a minute," said the operator. "That'll be nine dollars and fifty-five cents."

"Jesus," said Tony. "Well, one consolation. It's out of your profit, Murphy."

"But the profit is out of your pocket," said Murphy. "Come on, we'll go back and I'll treat you. Generous in victory, that's me. Like Ulysses S. Grant. He give all them Confederates their horses back, did you ever know that, Costello?"

"I did not, and what's more I don't believe it."

"Well, maybe you'd care to bet on that, too? Not this evening, however, bein's you're out of cash. But now will you believe that the ottomobile is putting an end to the horse?"

"Where does the ottomobile come into it? The machine gun is no ottomobile."

"No, and I didn't say it was, but if they have no use for the cavalry in a war, they'll soon have no use for them anywhere."

"If you weren't such a pinch of snuff I'd give you a puck in the mouth. But don't try my patience too far, Mr. Murphy. I'll take just so much of your impudence and no more. With me one hand tied behind me I could put you in hospital."

"You're kind of a hard loser, Tony. You oughtn't to be that way. There's more ottomobiles in town now than horses. The fire companies are all motorizing. The breweries. And the rich, you don't see them buying a new pair of cobs no more. It's the Pierce-Arrow now. Flannagan the undertaker is getting rid of his blacks, he told me so himself. Ordered a Cunningham 8."

"We'll see where Flannagan and his Cunningham 8 ends up next winter, the first time he has to bring a dead one down from the top of Fairview Street. Or go up it, for that matter. There's hills in this town no Cunningham 8 will negotiate, but Flannagan's team of blacks never had the least trouble. Flannagan'll be out of business the first winter, and it'll serve him right."

"And here I thought he was a friend of yours. Many's the time you used his stable for a boudoir, not to mention the funerals you drove for him. Two or three dollars for a half a day's work."

"There never was no friendship between him and I. You never saw me stand up to a bar and have a drink with him. You never saw me set foot inside his house, nor even his kitchen for a cup of coffee. The rare occasions that I slept in his barn, he was never the loser let me tell you. Those blacks that he's getting rid of, I mind the time I saved the off one's life from the colic. Too tight-fisted to send for Doc McNary, the vet, and he'd have lost the animal for sure if I wasn't there. Do you know what he give me for saving the horse? Guess what he give me."

"Search me," said Murphy.

"A pair of gloves. A pair of gauntlets so old that the lining was all wore away. Supposed to be fleece-lined, but the fleece was long since gone. 'Here, you take these, Tony,' said Mr. Generous Flannagan. I wanted to say 'Take them and do what with them?' But I was so dead tired from being up all night with the black, all I wanted to do was go up in his hayloft and lie down exhausted. Which I did for a couple of hours, and when I come down again there was the black, standing on his four feet and give me a whinny. A horse don't have much brains, but they could teach Flannagan gratitude."

After the war the abandonment of horses became so general that even Tony Costello was compelled to give in to it. The small merchants of the town, who had kept a single horse and delivery wagon (and a carriage for Sunday), were won over to Ford and Dodge trucks. The three-horse hitches of the breweries disappeared and in their place were big Macks and Garfords. The fire companies bought American LaFrances and Whites. The physicians bought Franklins and Fords, Buicks and Dodges. (The Franklin was air-cooled; the Buick was supposed to be a great hill-climber.) And private citizens who had never felt they could afford a horse and buggy, now went into debt to purchase flivvers. Of the three leading harness shops in the town, two became luggage shops and one went out of business entirely. Only two of the seven blacksmith shops remained. Gone were the Fleischmann's Yeast and Grand Union Tea Company wagons, the sorrels and greys of the big express companies. The smooth-surface paving caused a high mortality rate among horses, who slipped and broke legs and had to be shot and carried away to the fertilizer plant. The horse was retained only by the rich and the poor; saddle horse for the rich, and swaybacked old nags for the junk men and fruit peddlers. For Tony Costello it was not so easy as it once had been to find a place to sleep. The last livery stable closed in 1922, was converted into a public garage, and neither the rats nor Tony Costello had a home to go to, he said. "No decent, self-respecting rat will live in a garridge," he said. "It's an inhuman smell, them gazzoline fumes. And the rats don't have any more to eat there than I do meself."

The odd jobs that he lived on made no demands on his skill with horses, but all his life he had known how to take proper care of the varnish and the brightwork of a Brewster brougham, the leather and the bits and buckles of all kinds of tack. He therefore made himself useful at washing cars and polishing shoes. Nobody wanted to give him a steady job, but it was more sensible to pay Tony a few dollars than to waste a good mechanic on a car wash. He had a flexible arrangement with the cooks at two Greek restaurants who, on their own and without consulting the owners, would give him a meal in exchange for his washing dishes. "There ain't a man in the town has hands any cleaner than mine. Me hands are in soapy water morning, noon, and night," he said.

"It's too bad the rest of you don't get in with your hands," said Murphy. "How long since you had a real bath, Tony?"

"Oh, I don't know."

"As the fellow says, you take a bath once a year whether you need it or not," said Murphy. "And yet I've never seen you need a shave, barring the times you were on a three-day toot."

"Even then I don't often let her grow more'n a couple of days. As long as I can hold me hand steady enough so's I don't cut me throat. That's a temptation, too, I'll tell you. There's days I just as soon take the razor in me hand and let nature take its course."

"What stops you?" said Murphy.

"That I wonder. Mind you, I don't wonder too much or the logical conclusion would be you-know-what. My mother wasn't sure who my father was. She didn't keep count. She put me on the streets when I was eight or nine years of age. 'You can read and write,' she said, which was more than she could do. With my fine education I was able to tell one paper from another, so I sold them."

"You mean she put you out with no place to sleep?"

"Oh, no. She let me sleep there, providing she didn't have a customer. If I come home and she had a customer I had to wait outside."

"I remember you telling me one time your father worked for a man that had a son belonged to the Squadron A. That time we had the bet."

"That was a prevarication. A harmless prevarication that I thought up on the spur of the moment. I ought to know better by this time. Every time I prevaricate I get punished for it. That time I lost the bet. I should have said I knew about the Squadron A and let it go at that, but I had to embellish it. I always knew about the Squadron A. From selling papers in the Tenderloin I got a job walking hots at the race track, and I was a jock till I got too big. I couldn't make the weight any more, my bones were too heavy regardless of how much I starved myself and dried out. That done something to me, those times I tried to make a hundred and fifteen pounds and my bones weighed more than that. As soon as I quit trying to be a jock my weight jumped up to a hundred and fifty, and that's about what I am now."

"What do you mean it done something to you?" said Murphy.

"Be hard for you to understand, Murphy. It's a medical fact."

"Oh, go ahead, Doctor Costello."

"Well, if you don't get enough to eat, the blood thins out and the brain don't get fed properly. That changes your whole outlook on life, and if the brain goes too long without nourishment, you get so's you don't care any more."

"Where did you get that piece of information?"

"I trained for a doctor that owned a couple trotters over near Lancaster. Him and I had many's the conversation on the subject."

"I never know whether to believe you or call you a liar. Did you get so's you didn't care any more?"

"That's what I'm trying to get through your thick skull, Murphy. That's why I never amounted to anything. That's why poor people stay poor. The brain don't get enough nourishment from the blood. Fortunately I know that, you see. I don't waste my strength trying to be something I ain't."

"Do you know what I think, Tony? I think you were just looking for an excuse to be a bum."

"Naturally! I wasn't looking for an excuse, but I was looking for some reason why a fellow as smart as I am never amounted to anything. If I cared more what happened to me, I'd have cut my throat years ago. Jesus! The most I ever had in my life was eight hundred dollars one time a long shot came in, but I don't care. You know, I'm fifty-five or -six years of age, one or the other. I had my first woman when I was fifteen, and I guess a couple hundred since then. But I never saw one yet that I'd lose any sleep over. Not a single one, out of maybe a couple hundred. One is just like the other, to me. Get what you want out of them, and so long. So long till you want another. And I used to be a pretty handsome fellow when I was young. Not all whores, either. Once when I was wintering down in Latonia—well, what the hell. It don't bother me as much as it used to do. I couldn't go a week without it, but these days I just as soon spend the money on the grog. I'll be just as content when I can do without them altogether."

. . . One day Tony was washing a brand-new Chrysler, which was itself a recent make of car. He was standing off, hose in hand, contemplating the design and colors of the car, when a young woman got out of a plain black Ford coupe. She was wearing black and white saddle shoes, bruised and spotted, and not liable to be seriously damaged by puddles of dirty water on the garage floor, but Tony cautioned her. "Mind where you're walking, young lady," he said.

"Oh, it won't hurt these shoes," she said. "I'm looking for Tony Costello. I was told he worked here."

"Feast your eyes, Miss. You're looking right at him," he said.

"You're Tony Costello? I somehow pictured an older man," she said.

"Well, maybe I'm older than I look. What is there I can do for you?"

She was a sturdily built young woman, past the middle twenties, handsome if she had been a man, but it was no man inside the grey pullover.

"I was told that you were the best man in town to take care of a sick horse," she said.

"You were told right," said Tony Costello. "And I take it you have a sick horse? What's the matter with him, if it's a him, or her if it's a her?"

"It's a mare named Daisy. By the way, my name is Esther Wayman."

"Wayman? You're new here in town," said Tony.

"Just this year. My father is the manager of the bus company."

"I see. And your mare Daisy, how old?"

"Five, I think, or maybe six," said Esther Wayman.

"And sick in what way? What are the symptoms?"

"She's all swollen up around the mouth. I thought I had the curb chain on too tight, but that wasn't it. I kept her in the stable for several days, with a halter on, and instead of going away the swelling got worse."

"Mm. The swelling, is it accompanied by, uh, a great deal of saliva?"

"Yes, it is."

"You say the animal is six years old. How long did you own her, Miss Wayman?"

"Only about a month. I bought her from a place in Philadelphia."

"Mm-hmm. Out Market Street, one of them horse bazaars?"

"Yes."

"Is this your first horse? In other words, you're not familiar with horses?"

"No, we've always lived in the city—Philadelphia, Cleveland Ohio, Denver Colorado. I learned to ride in college, but I never owned a horse before we came here."

"You wouldn't know a case of glanders if you saw it, would you?"

"No. Is that a disease?" she said.

"Unless I'm very much mistaken, it's the disease that ails your mare Daisy. I'll be done washing this car in two shakes, and then you can take me out to see your mare. Where do you stable her?"

"We have our own stable. My father bought the Henderson house."

"Oh, to be sure, and I know it well. Slept in that stable many's the night."

"I don't want to take you away from your work," she said.

"Young woman, you're taking me *to* work. You're not taking me away from anything."

He finished with the Chrysler, got out of his gum boots, and put on his shoes. He called to the garage foreman, "Back sometime in the morning," and did not wait for an answer. None came.

On the way out to the Wayman-Henderson house he let the young woman do all the talking. She had the flat accent of the Middle West and she spoke from deep inside her mouth. She told him how she had got interested in riding at cawlidge, and was so pleased to find that the house her father bought included a garage that was not really a garage but a real stable. Her father permitted her to have a horse on condition that she took complete care of it herself. She had seen the ad in a Philadelphia paper, gone to one of the weekly sales, and paid $300 for Daisy. She had not even looked at any other horse. The bidding for Daisy had started at $100; Esther raised it to $150; someone else went to $200; Esther jumped it to $300 and the mare was hers.

"Uh-huh," said Tony. "Well, maybe you got a bargain, and maybe not."

"You seem doubtful," she said.

"We learn by experience, and you got the animal you wanted. You'll be buying other horses as you get older. This is only your first one."

They left the car at the stable door. "I guess she's lying down," said Esther.

Tony opened the door of the box stall. "She is that, and I'm sorry to tell you, she's never getting up."

"She's dead? How could she be? I only saw her a few hours ago."

"Let me go in and have a look at her. You stay where you are," he said. He had taken command and she obeyed him. In a few minutes, three or four, he came out of the stall and closed the door behind him.

"Glanders, it was. Glanders and old age. Daisy was more like eleven than five or six."

"But how could it happen so quickly?"

"It didn't, exactly. I'm not saying the animal had glanders when you bought her. I do say they falsified her age, which they all do. Maybe they'll give you your money back, maybe they won't. In any case, Miss Wayman, you're not to go in there. Glanders is contagious to man and animal. If you want me to, I'll see to the removal of the animal. A telephone call to the fertilizer plant, and they know me there. Then I'll burn the bedding for you and fumigate the stable. You might as well leave the halter on. It wouldn't be fair to put it on a well horse."

The young woman took out a pack of cigarettes and offered him one. He took it, lit hers and his. "I'm glad to see you take it so calmly. I seen women go into hysterics under these circumstances," he said.

"I don't get hysterics," she said. "But that's not to say I'm not in a turmoil. If I'd had her a little while longer I *might* have gotten hysterical."

"Then be thankful that you didn't have her that much longer. To tell you the truth, you didn't get a bargain. There was other things wrong with her that we needn't go into. I wouldn't be surprised if she was blind, but that's not what I was thinking of. No, you didn't get a bargain this time, but keep trying. Only, next time take somebody with you that had some experience with horses and horse-dealers."

"I'll take you, if you'll come," she said. "Meanwhile, will you do those other things you said you would?"

"I will indeed."

"And how much do I owe you?" she said.

He smiled. "I don't have a regular fee for telling people that a dead horse is dead," he said. "A couple dollars for my time."

"How about ten dollars?"

"Whatever you feel is right, I'll take," he said. "The state of my finances is on the wrong side of affluence."

"Is the garage where I can always reach you?" she said.

"I don't work there steady."

"At home, then? Can you give me your telephone number?" she said.

"I move around from place to place."

"Oh. Well, would you like to have a steady job? I could introduce you to my father."

"I couldn't drive a bus, if that's what you had in mind. I don't have a license, for one thing, and even if I did they have to maintain a schedule. That I've never done, not that strict kind of a schedule. But thanks for the offer."

"He might have a job for you washing buses. I don't know how well it would pay, but I think they wash and clean those buses every night, so it would be steady work. Unless you're not interested in steady work. Is that it?"

"Steady pay without the steady work, that's about the size of it," he said.

She shook her head. "Then I don't think you and my father would get along. He lives by the clock."

"Well, I guess he'd have to, running a bus line," said Tony. He looked about him. "The Hendersons used to hang their cutters up there. They had two cutters and a bob. They were great ones for sleighing parties. Two-three times a winter they'd load up the bob and the two cutters and take friends down to their farm for a chicken-and-waffle supper. They had four horses then. A pair of sorrels, Prince and Duke. Trixie, a bay mare, broke to saddle. And a black gelding named Satan, Mr. Henderson drove himself to work in. They were pretty near the last to give up horses, Mr. and Mrs. Henderson."

"Did you work for them?"

"Twice I worked for them. Sacked both times. But he knew I used to come here and sleep. They had four big buffalo robes, two for the bob and one each for the cutters. That was the lap of luxury for me. Sleep on two and cover up with one. Then he died and she moved away, and the son Jasper only had cars. There wasn't a horse stabled in here since Mrs. moved away, and Jasper wouldn't let me sleep here. He put in that gazzoline pump and he said it wasn't safe to let me stop here for the night. It wasn't me he was worried about. It was them ottomobiles. Well, this isn't getting to the telephone."

During the night he fumigated the stable. The truck from the fertilizer plant arrived at nine o'clock and he helped the two men load the dead mare, after which he lit the fumigating tablets in the stalls and closed the doors and windows. Esther Wayman came up from the house at ten o'clock or so, just as he was closing the doors of the carriage house. "They took her away?" she said.

"About an hour ago. Then I lit candles for her," he said.

"You what?"

"That's my little joke, not in the best of taste perhaps. I don't know that this fumigating does any good, but on the other hand it can't do much harm. It's a precaution you take, glanders being contagious and all that. You have to think of the next animal that'll be occupying that stall, so you take every precaution—as much for your own peace of mind as anything else, I guess."

"Where did you get the fumigating stuff?"

"I went down to the drug store, Schlicter's Pharmacy, Sixteenth and Market. I told them to charge it to your father. They know me there."

"They know you everywhere in this town, don't they?"

"Yes, I guess they do, now that I stop to think of it."

"Can I take you home in my car?"

"Oh, I guess I can walk it."

"Why should you when I have my car? Where do you live?"

"I got a room on Canal Street. That's not much of a neighborhood for you to be driving around in after dark."

"I'm sure I've been in worse, or just as bad," she said.

"That would surprise me," he said.

"I'm not a sheltered hothouse plant," she said. "I can take care of myself. Let's go. I'd like to see that part of town."

When they got to Canal Street she said, "It isn't eleven o'clock yet. Is there a place where we can go for a drink?"

"Oh, there's places aplenty. But I doubt if your Dad would approve of them for you."

"Nobody will know me," she said. "I hardly know anybody in this town. I don't get to know people very easily. Where shall we go?"

"Well, there's a pretty decent place that goes by the name of the Bucket of Blood. Don't let the name frighten you. It's just a common ordinary saloon. I'm not saying you'll encounter the Ladies Aid Society there, but if it didn't have that name attached to it—well, you'll see the kind of place it is."

It was a quiet night in the saloon. They sat at a table in the back room. A man and woman were at another table, drinking whiskey by the shot and washing it down with beer chasers. They were a solemn couple, both about fifty, with no need to converse and seemingly no concern beyond the immediate appreciation of the alcohol. Presently the man stood up and headed for the street door, followed by the woman. As she went out she slapped Tony Costello lightly on the shoulder. "Goodnight, Tony," she said.

"Goodnight, Marie," said Tony Costello.

When they were gone Esther Wayman said, "She knew you, but all she said was goodnight. She never said hello."

"Him and I don't speak to one another," said Tony. "We had some kind of a dispute there a long while back."

"Are they husband and wife?"

"No, but they been going together ever since I can remember."

"She's a prostitute, isn't she?"

"That's correct," said Tony.

"And what does he do? Live off her?"

"Oh, no. No, he's a trackwalker for the Pennsy. One of the few around that ain't an I-talian. But she's an I-talian."

"Are you an Italian? You're not, are you?"

"Good Lord, no. I'm as Irish as they come."

"You have an Italian name though."

"It may sound I-talian to you, but my mother was straight from County Cork. My father could be anybody, but most likely he was an Irishman, the neighborhood I come from. I'm pretty certain he wasn't John Jacob Astor or J. Pierpont Morgan. My old lady was engaged in the same occupation as Marie that just went out."

"Doesn't your church—I mean, in France and Italy I suppose the prostitutes must be Catholic, but I never thought of Irish prostitutes."

"There's prostitutes wherever a woman needs a dollar and doesn't have to care too much how she gets it. It don't even have to be a dollar. If they're young enough they'll do it for a stick of candy, and the dollar comes later. This is an elevating conversation for a young woman like yourself."

"You don't know anything about myself, Mr. Costello," she said.

"I do, and I don't," he said. "But what I don't know I'm learning. I'll make a guess that you were disappointed in love."

She laughed. "Very."

"What happened? The young man give you the go-by?"

"There was no young man," she said. "I have never been interested in young men or they in me."

"I see," he said.

"Do you?"

"Well, to be honest with you, no. I don't. I'd of thought you'd have yourself a husband by this time. You're not at all bad-looking, you know, and you always knew where your next meal was coming from."

"This conversation *is* beginning to embarrass me a little," she said.

"Sometime I may tell you all about myself. In fact, I have a feeling I will. But not now, not tonight."

"Anytime you say," said Tony. "And one of these days we'll go looking for a horse for you."

"We'll have fun," she said.

1968

About the Editor

FRANK MACSHANE is the author of *The Life of John O'Hara* and of several other literary biographies. He teaches at Columbia University and lives in New York.